MORE PLUMS IN ONE

MORE PLUMS IN ONE

Janet Evanovich

ST. MARTIN'S PRESS ❧ NEW YORK

This is a work of fiction. All of the characters, organizations, and events portrayed in these novels are either products of the author's imagination or are used fictitiously.

FOUR TO SCORE. Copyright © 1998 by Evanovich, Inc. HIGH FIVE. Copyright © 1999 by Evanovich, Inc. HOT SIX. Copyright © 2000 by Evanovich, Inc. All rights reserved. Printed in the United States of America. No part of this book may be used or reproduced in any matter whatsoever without written permission except in the case of brief quotations embodied in critical articles or reviews. For information address St. Martin's Press, 175 Fifth Avenue, New York, N.Y. 10010.

www.stmartins.com

ISBN-13: 978-0-312-36296-6
ISBN-10: 0-312-36296-X

First Edition: April 2007

10   9   8   7   6   5   4   3   2   1

FOUR
TO
SCORE

Thanks to Shannon Hendrix for suggesting the title for this book.

ONE

LIVING IN TRENTON in July is like living inside a big pizza oven. Hot, airless, aromatic.

Because I didn't want to miss any of the summer experience I had the sunroof open on my Honda CRX. My brown hair was pulled up into a wind-snarled, curls-gone-to-frizz ponytail. The sun baked the top of my head, and sweat trickled under my black spandex sports bra. I was wearing matching spandex shorts and a sleeveless oversized Trenton Thunders baseball jersey. It was an excellent outfit except it gave me no place to stick my .38. Which meant I was going to have to borrow a gun to shoot my cousin Vinnie.

I parked the CRX in front of Vinnie's storefront bail bonds office, lunged out of the car, stalked across the sidewalk, and yanked the office door open. "Where is he? Where is that miserable little excuse for a human being?"

"Uh oh," Lula said from behind the file cabinet. "Rhino alert."

Lula is a retired hooker who helps clean up the filing and sometimes rides shotgun for me when I do my fugitive apprehension thing. If people were cars, Lula would be a big, black '53 Packard with a high-gloss chrome grille, oversized headlights, and a growl like a junkyard dog. Lots of muscle. Never fit in a compact space.

Connie Rosolli, the office manager, pushed back at her desk when I entered. Connie's domain was this one front room where friends and relatives of miscreants came to beg money. And to the rear, in an inner office, my cousin Vinnie slapped Mr. Johnson around and conversed with his bookie.

"Hey," Connie said, "I know what you're bummed about, and this wasn't my decision. Personally, if I were you, I'd kick your cousin's pervert ass around the block."

I pushed a clump of hair that had strayed from the ponytail back from my face. "Kicking isn't good enough. I think I'll shoot him."

"Go for it!" Lula said.

"Yeah," Connie agreed. "Shoot him."

Lula checked out my clothes. "You need a gun? I don't see no gun bulges in that spandex." She hiked up her T-shirt and pulled a Chief's Special out of her cut-off denim shorts. "You could use mine. Just be careful; it sights high."

"You don't want a little peashooter like that," Connie said, opening her desk drawer. "I've got a forty-five. You can make a nice big hole with a forty-five."

Lula went for her purse. "Hold on here. If that's what you want, let me give you the big stud. I've got a forty-four magnum loaded up with hydroshocks. This baby'll do *real* damage, you see what I'm saying? You could drive a Volkswagen through the hole this sweetheart makes."

"I was sort of kidding about shooting him," I told them.

"Too bad," Connie said.

Lula shoved her gun back in her shorts. "Yeah, that's damn disappointing."

"So where is he? Is he in?"

"Hey, Vinnie!" Connie yelled. "Stephanie's here to see you!"

The door to the inner office opened and Vinnie poked his head out. "What?"

Vinnie was 5'7", looked like a weasel, thought like a weasel, smelled like a French whore and was once in love with a duck.

"You know what!" I said, hands fisted on hips. "Joyce Barn-hardt, that's what. My grandma was at the beauty parlor and heard you hired Joyce to do skip tracing."

"So what's the big deal? I hired Joyce Barnhardt."

"Joyce Barnhardt does makeovers at Macy's."

"And you used to sell ladies' panties."

"That was entirely different. I blackmailed you into giving me this job."

"Exactly," Vinnie said. "So what's your point?"

"Fine!" I shouted. "Just keep her out of my way! I *hate* Joyce Barnhardt!"

And everybody knew why. At the tender age of twenty-four, af-ter less than a year of marriage, I'd caught Joyce bare-assed on my dining room table, playing hide-the-salami with my husband. It was the only time she'd ever done me a favor. We'd gone through school together, where she'd spread rumors, told fibs, ruined friendships and peeked under the stall doors in the girls' bathroom to see people's underpants.

She'd been a fat kid with a terrible overbite. The overbite had been minimalized by braces, and by the time Joyce was fifteen she'd trimmed down to look like Barbie on steroids. She had chemically enhanced red hair done up in big teased curls. Her nails were long and painted, her lips were high gloss, her eyes were rimmed in navy liquid liner, her lashes gunked up with blue-black mascara. She was an inch shorter than me, five pounds heavier and had me beat by two cup sizes. She had three ex-husbands and no children. It was rumored she had sex with large dogs.

Joyce and Vinnie were a match made in heaven. Too bad Vin-nie was already married to a perfectly nice woman whose father happened to be Harry the Hammer. Harry's job description read "expediter," and Harry spent a lot of his time in the presence of men who wore fedoras and long black overcoats.

"Just do your job," Vinnie said. "Be a professional." He waved his hand at Connie. "Give her something. Give her that new skip we just got in."

Connie took a manila folder from her desktop. "Maxine Nowicki. Charged with stealing her former boyfriend's car. Posted bond with us and failed to show for her court appearance."

By securing a cash bond Nowicki had been free to leave the lockup behind and return to society at large while awaiting trial. Now she'd failed to appear. Or in bounty-hunter speak, she was FTA. This lapse of judicial etiquette changed Nowicki's status to felon and had my cousin Vinnie worrying that the court might see fit to keep his bond money.

As a bond enforcement officer I was expected to find Nowicki and bring her back into the system. For performing this service in a timely manner I'd get ten percent of her bond amount. Pretty good money since this sounded like a domestic dispute, and I didn't think Maxine Nowicki would be interested in blowing the back of my head off with a .45 hollow tip.

I riffled through the paperwork, which consisted of Nowicki's bond agreement, a photo, and a copy of the police report.

"Know what I'd do?" Lula said. "I'd talk to the boyfriend. Anybody pissed off enough to get his girlfriend arrested for stealing his car is pissed off enough to snitch on her. Probably he's just waiting to tell someone where to go find her."

It was my thought too. I read aloud from Nowicki's charge sheet. "Edward Kuntz. Single white male. Age twenty-seven. Residing at Seventeen Muffet Street. Says here he's a cook."

I PARKED in front of Kuntz's house and wondered about the man inside. The house was white clapboard with aqua trim around the windows and tangerine paint on the door. It was half of a well-cared-for duplex with a minuscule front yard. A three-foot-tall statue of the Virgin Mary dressed in pale blue and white had been planted on the perfectly clipped patch of lawn. A carved wood heart with red lettering and little white daisies had been hung on the neighboring door, proclaiming that the Glicks lived there. The Kuntz side was free of ornamentation.

I followed the sidewalk to the porch, which had been carpeted in green indoor-outdoor carpet, and rang the Kuntz doorbell. The door opened and a sweaty, muscle-bulging, half-naked man looked out at me. "What?"

"Eddie Kuntz?"

"Yeah?"

I passed him my business card. "Stephanie Plum. I'm a bond enforcement officer, and I'm looking for Maxine Nowicki. I was hoping you could help me."

"You bet I can help you. She took my car. Can you believe it?" He jerked his stubbled chin toward the curb. "That's it right there. Lucky for her she didn't scratch it up. The cops picked her up driving through town in it, and they brought the car back to me."

I glanced back at the car. A white Chevy Blazer. Freshly washed. I almost was tempted to steal it myself.

"You were living together?"

"Well, yeah, for a while. About four months. And then we had this disagreement, and next thing I know, she's gone with my car. It wasn't that I wanted her arrested . . . it was just that I wanted my car back. That was why I called the police. I wanted my car."

"Do you have any idea where she might be now?"

"No. I tried to get in touch with her to sort of patch things up, but I couldn't find her. She quit her job at the diner and nobody's seen her. I stopped around her apartment a couple times, and there was never anybody home. I tried calling her mother. I called a couple of her girlfriends. No one seems to know anything. I guess they could have been lying to me, but I don't think so." He winked at me. "Women don't lie to me, you know what I mean?"

"No," I said. "I don't know what you mean."

"Well, I don't like to brag, but I have a way with women."

"Uh huh." It must have been the pungent aroma they found so attractive. Or maybe the overdeveloped, steroid-pumped muscles that made him look like he needed a bra. Or maybe it was the way he couldn't conduct a conversation without scratching his balls.

"So what can I do for you?" Kuntz asked.

Half an hour later I left with a list of Maxine's friends and relatives. I knew where Maxine banked, bought her booze, shopped for groceries, dry-cleaned her clothes and had her hair done. Kuntz promised to call me if he heard from Maxine, and I'd promised to reciprocate in kind if I turned up anything interesting. Of course, I'd had my fingers crossed when I'd made the promise. I suspected Eddie Kuntz's way with women was to make them run screaming in the opposite direction.

He stood on the porch and watched me angle into my car.

"Cute," he called. "I like when a chick drives a sporty little car."

I sent him a smile that felt a lot like a grimace and peeled away from the curb. I'd gotten the CRX in February, sucked in by a shiny new paint job and an odometer that read 12,000 miles. Cherry condition, the owner had said. Hardly ever driven. And that was partly true. It was hardly ever driven with the odometer cable connected. Not that it mattered. The price had been right, and I looked good in the driver's seat. I'd recently developed a dime-sized lesion on my exhaust pipe, but if I played Metallica loud enough I could hardly hear the muffler noise. I might have thought twice about buying the car if I'd known Eddie Kuntz thought it was cute.

My first stop was the Silver Dollar Diner. Maxine had worked there for seven years and had listed no other source of income. The Silver Dollar was open twenty-four hours. It served good food in generous portions and was always packed with overweight people and penny-pinching seniors. The families of fatties cleaned their plates, and the seniors took leftovers home in doggy bags . . . butter pats, baskets of rolls, packets of sugar, half-eaten pieces of deep-fried haddock, coleslaw, fruit cup, grease-logged french fries. A senior could eat for three days off one meal at the Silver Dollar.

The Silver Dollar was in Hamilton Township on a stretch of road that was clogged with discount stores and small strip malls. It was almost noon, and diner patrons were scarfing down burgers and BLTs. I introduced myself to the woman behind the register and asked about Maxine.

"I can't believe she's in all this trouble," the woman said. "Maxine was responsible. Real dependable." She straightened a stack of menus. "And that business about the car!" She did some eye rolling. "Maxine drove it to work lots of times. He gave her the keys. And then all of a sudden she's arrested for stealing." She gave a grunt of disgust. "Men!"

I stepped back to allow a couple to pay their bill. When they'd pocketed their complimentary mints, matchbooks and toothpicks and exited the diner I turned back to the cashier. "Maxine failed to show for her court appearance. Did she give any indication that she might be leaving town?"

"She said she was going on vacation, and we all thought she was due. Been working here for seven years and never once took a vacation."

"Has anyone heard from her since she's left?"

"Not that I know of. Maybe Margie. Maxine and Margie always worked the same shift. Four to ten. If you want to talk to Margie you should come back around eight. We get real busy with the early-bird specials at four, but then around eight it starts to slack off."

I thanked the woman and went back to my CRX. My next stop would be Nowicki's apartment. According to Kuntz, Nowicki had lived with him for four months but had never gotten around to moving out of her place. The apartment was a quarter mile from the diner, and Nowicki had stated on her bond agreement that she'd resided there for six years. All previous addresses were local. Maxine Nowicki was Trenton clear to the roots of her bleached blond hair.

The apartment was in a complex of two-story, blocky, red-brick buildings anchored in islands of parched grass, arranged around macadam parking lots. Nowicki was on the second floor with a first-floor entrance. Inside private stairwell. Not good for window snooping. All second-floor apartments had small balconies on the back side, but I'd need a ladder to get to the balcony. Probably a woman climbing up a ladder would look suspicious.

I decided to go with the obvious and knock on the door. If no one answered I'd ask the super to let me in. Many times the super was cooperative in this way, especially if he was confused as to the authenticity of my fake badge.

There were two front doors side by side. One was for upstairs and one was for downstairs. The name under the upstairs doorbell read Nowicki. The name under the downstairs doorbell read Pease.

I rang the upstairs doorbell and the downstairs door opened and an elderly woman looked out at me.

"She isn't home."

"Are you Mrs. Pease?" I asked.

"Yes."

"Are you sure Maxine isn't home?"

"Well, I guess I'd know. You can hear everything in this cheapskate apartment. If she was home I'd hear her TV. I'd hear her walking around. And besides, she'd stop in to tell me she was home and collect her mail."

Ah hah! The woman was collecting Maxine's mail. Maybe she also had Maxine's key.

"Yes, but suppose she came home late one night and didn't want to wake you?" I said. "And then suppose she had a stroke?"

"I never thought of that."

"She could be upstairs right now, gasping her last breath of air."

The woman rolled her eyes upward, as if she could see through walls. "Hmmm."

"Do you have a key?"

"Well, yes . . ."

"And what about her plants? Have you been watering her plants?"

"She didn't ask me to water her plants."

"Maybe we should go take a look. Make sure everything is okay."

"Are you a friend of Maxine's?"

I held up two fingers side by side. "Like this."

"I suppose it wouldn't hurt to check. I'll be right back with the key. I've got it in the kitchen."

Okay, so I fibbed a little. But it wasn't such a bad fib because it was for a good cause. And besides, she *could* be dead in her bed. And her plants *could* be dying of thirst.

"Here it is," Mrs. Pease said, brandishing the key.

She turned the key in the lock and pushed the door open.

"Hell-*oo*-o," she called in her warbling old lady's voice. "Anybody home?"

No one answered, so we crept up the stairs. We stood in the little entrance area and looked into the living room–dining room.

"Not much of a housekeeper," Mrs. Pease said.

Housekeeping had nothing to do with it. The apartment had been trashed. It wasn't a fight because nothing was smashed. And it wasn't clutter from a last-minute scurry to leave. Cushions were pulled off the couch and flung onto the floor. Cupboard doors were open. Drawers were pulled from the hutch and turned upside down, contents spilled out. I did a quick walk-through and saw more of the same in the bedroom and bath. Someone had been looking for something. Money? Drugs? If it was robbery it had been very specific, because the TV and VCR were untouched.

"Someone has ransacked this apartment," I said to Mrs. Pease. "I'm surprised you didn't hear the drawers being flung around."

"If I was home I would have heard it. It must have been when I was out to bingo. I go to bingo every Wednesday and Friday. I don't get home until eleven. Do you think we should report this to the police?"

"It wouldn't serve much purpose right now." Except to notify the police that I'd been in Maxine's apartment sort of illegally. "We don't know if anything's been taken. Probably we should wait for Maxine to come home and let her call the police."

We didn't see any plants to water, so we tippytoed back down the stairs and locked the door.

I gave Mrs. Pease my card and asked her to call me if she should see or hear anything suspicious.

9

She studied the card. "A bounty hunter," she said, her voice showing surprise.

"A woman's got to do what a woman's got to do," I said.

She looked up and nodded in agreement. "I suppose that's true."

I squinted into the lot. "According to my information Maxine owns an '84 Fairlane. I don't see it here."

"She took off in it," Mrs. Pease said. "Wasn't much of a car. Always something or other broken on it, but she loaded it up with her suitcase and took off."

"Did she say where she was going?"

"On vacation."

"That was it?"

"Yep," Mrs. Pease said, "that was it. Usually Maxine's real talkative, but she wasn't saying anything this time. She was in a hurry, and she wasn't saying anything."

NOWICKI'S MOTHER lived on Howser Street. She'd posted the bond and had put up her house as collateral. At first glance this seemed like a safe investment for my cousin Vinnie. Truth was, getting a person kicked out of his or her house was a chore and did nothing to endear a bail bondsman to the community.

I got out my street map and found Howser. It was in north Trenton, so I retraced my route and discovered that Mrs. Nowicki lived two blocks from Eddie Kuntz. Same neighborhood of well-kept houses. Except for the Nowicki house. The Nowicki house was single-family, and it was a wreck. Peeling paint, crumbling roof shingles, saggy front porch, front yard more dirt than grass.

I picked my way over rotting porch steps and knocked on the door. The woman who answered was faded glory in a bathrobe. It was getting to be mid-afternoon, but Mrs. Nowicki looked like she'd just rolled out of bed. She was a sixty-year-old woman wearing the ravages of booze and disenchantment with life. Her doughy face showed traces of makeup not removed before calling it a night. Her voice had the rasp of two packs a day, and her breath was hundred proof.

"Mrs. Nowicki?"

"Yeah," she said.

"I'm looking for Maxine."

"You a friend of Maxy's?"

I gave her my card. "I'm with the Plum Agency. Maxine missed her court date. I'm trying to find her so we can get her rescheduled."

Mrs. Nowicki raised a crayoned brown eyebrow. "I wasn't born yesterday, honey. You're a bounty hunter, and you're out to get my little girl."

"Do you know where she is?"

"Wouldn't tell you if I did. She'll get found when she wants to."

"You put your house up as security against the bond. If Maxine doesn't come forward you could lose your house."

"Oh yeah, that'd be a tragedy," she said, rummaging in the pocket of her chenille robe, coming up with a pack of Kools. "*Architectural Digest* keeps wanting to do a spread, but I can't find the time." She stuck a cigarette in her mouth and lit up. She sucked hard and squinted at me through the smoke haze. "I owe five years' back taxes. You want this house you're gonna hafta take a number and get in line."

Sometimes bail jumpers are simply at home, trying to pretend their life isn't in the toilet, hoping the whole mess will go away if they ignore the order to appear in court. I'd originally thought Maxine would be one of these people. She wasn't a career criminal, and the charges weren't serious. She really had no reason to skip out.

Now I wasn't so sure. I was getting an uncomfortable feeling about Maxine. Her apartment had been trashed, and her mother had me thinking maybe Maxine didn't want to be found right now. I slunk back to my car and decided my deductive reasoning would be vastly improved if I ate a doughnut. So I cut across town to Hamilton and parked in front of Tasty Pastry Bakery.

I'd worked part-time at Tasty Pastry when I was in high school. It hadn't changed much since then. Same green-and-white linoleum floor. Same sparkling clean display cases filled with Italian cookies, chocolate chip cannoli, biscotti, napoleons, fresh bread and coffee cakes. Same happy smell of fried sweet dough and cinnamon.

Lennie Smulenski and Anthony Zuck bake the goodies in the back room in big steel ovens and troughs of hot oil. Clouds of flour and sugar sift onto table surfaces and slip under foot. And lard is transferred daily from commercial-sized vats directly to local butts.

I choose two Boston cremes and pocketed some napkins. When I came out I found Joe Morelli lounging against my car. I'd known Morelli all of my life. First when he was a lecherous little kid, then as a dangerous teen. And finally as the guy who at age eighteen, sweet-talked me out of my underwear, laid me down on the floor behind the eclair case one day after work and relieved me of my virginity. Morelli was a cop now, and the only way he'd get back into my pants would be at gunpoint. He worked Vice, and he looked like he knew a lot about it firsthand. He was wearing washed-out Levi's and a navy T-shirt. His hair needed cutting, and his body was perfect. Lean and hard-muscled with the best ass in Trenton . . . maybe the world. Buns you wanted to sink your teeth into.

Not that I intended to nibble on Morelli. He had an annoying habit of periodically popping up in my life, frustrating the hell out of me and then walking off into the sunset. I couldn't do much about the popping up or the walking off. I *could* do something about the frustrating. From here on out, Morelli was erotica non grata. Look but Don't Touch, that was my motto. And he could keep his tongue to himself, thank you.

Morelli grinned by way of hello. "You're not going to eat both those doughnuts all by yourself, are you?"

"That was the plan. What are you doing here?"

"Drove by. Saw your car. Thought you'd need some help with those Boston cremes."

"How do you know they're Boston cremes?"

"You always get Boston cremes."

Last time I saw Morelli was back in February. One minute we were in a clinch on my couch with his hand halfway up my thigh, and then next thing I knew, his pager went off and he was gone. Not to be seen for five months. And now here he was . . . sniffing at my doughnuts.

"Long time, no see," I said.

"I've been undercover."

Yeah, right.

"Okay," he said. "I could have called."

"I thought maybe you were dead."

The smile tightened. "Wishful thinking?"

"You're scum, Morelli."

He blew out a sigh. "You're not going to share those doughnuts, are you?"

I got into my car, slammed the door, squealed out of the lot and headed for home. By the time I got to my apartment I'd eaten both the doughnuts, and I was feeling much better. And I was thinking about Nowicki. She was five years older than Kuntz. High school graduate. Twice married. No children. Her file photo showed me a blowzy blonde with big Jersey hair, lots of makeup and a slim frame. She was squinting into the sun and smiling, wearing four-inch heels, tight black stretch pants and a loose flowing sweater with sleeves pushed up to her elbows and a V neck deep enough to show cleavage. I half expected to find writing on the back of the picture . . . "If you want a good time, call Maxine Nowicki."

Probably she'd done exactly what she'd said. Probably she'd stressed out and gone on vacation. Probably I shouldn't exert myself because she'd come home any day now.

And what about her apartment? The apartment was bothersome. The apartment told me Maxine had bigger problems than a simple auto theft charge. Best not to think about the apartment. The apartment only muddied the waters and had nothing to do with my job. My job was simple. Find Maxine. Bring her in.

I locked the CRX and crossed the lot. Mr. Landowsky stepped out the building's back door as I approached. Mr. Landowsky was eighty-two and somehow his chest had shrunk over the years, and now he was forced to hike his pants up under his armpits.

"Oi," he said. "This heat! I can't breathe. Somebody should do something."

I assumed he was talking about God.

"That weatherman on the morning news. He should be shot. How can I go out in weather like this? And then when it gets so hot they keep the supermarkets too cold. Hot, cold. Hot, cold. It gives me the runs."

I was glad I owned a gun, because when I got as old as Mr. Landowsky I was going to eat a bullet. The first time I got the runs in the supermarket, that was it. BANG! It would all be over.

I took the elevator to the second floor and let myself into my apartment. One bedroom, one bath, living room–dining room, uninspired but adequate kitchen, small foyer with a strip of pegs for hanging coats and hats and gun belts.

My hamster, Rex, was running on his wheel when I came in. I told him about my day and apologized for not saving him some doughnut. He looked disappointed at the doughnut part so I rooted around in my refrigerator and came up with a few grapes. Rex took the grapes and disappeared into his soup can. Life is pretty simple when you're a hamster.

I moseyed back into the kitchen and checked my phone messages.

"Stephanie, this is your mother. Don't forget about dinner. I have a nice roast chicken."

Saturday night and I was having chicken dinner with my parents. And it wasn't the first time. It was a weekly occurrence. I had no life.

I dragged myself into the bedroom, flopped onto the bed and watched the minute hand creep around the dial on my wristwatch until it was time to go to my parents'. My parents eat dinner at six o'clock. Not a minute sooner or later. That's the way it is. Dinner at six or your life is ruined.

MY PARENTS live in a narrow duplex on a narrow lot on a narrow street in a residential part of Trenton called the Burg. When I arrived my mother was waiting at the door.

"What is this outfit you're wearing?" she asked. "You have no clothes on. How is this to dress?"

"This is a Thunders baseball jersey," I told her. "I'm supporting local sports."

My Grandma Mazur peeked from behind my mother. Grandma Mazur moved in with my parents shortly after my grandfather went heavenward to dine with Elvis. Grandma figures she's of an age to be beyond convention. My father thinks she's of an age to be beyond life.

"I need one of those jerseys," Grandma said. "Bet I'd have men following me down the block if I was dressed up like that."

"Stiva, the undertaker," my father murmured from the living room, head buried in the paper. "With his tape measure."

Grandma linked her arm in mine. "I've got a treat for you today. Just wait till you see what I've cooked up."

In the living room the paper was lowered, and my father's eyebrows raised.

My mother made the sign of the cross.

"Maybe you should tell me," I said to Grandma.

"I was gonna keep it as a surprise, but I suppose I could let you in on it. Being that he'll be here any minute now."

There was dead silence in the house.

"I invited your boyfriend over for dinner," Grandma said.

"I don't have a boyfriend!"

"Well, you do now. I arranged everything."

I spun on my heel and headed for the door. "I'm leaving."

"You can't do that!" Grandma yelled. "He'll be real disappointed. We had a nice long talk. And he said he didn't mind that you shoot people for a living."

"I don't shoot people for a living. I *almost never* shoot people." I thunked my head against the wall. "I hate fix-ups. Fix-ups are always awful."

"Can't be any more awful than that bozo you married," Grandma said. "Only one way to go after that fiasco."

She was right. My short-lived marriage had been a fiasco.

There was a knock on the door, and we swiveled our heads to look down the hall.

"Eddie Kuntz!" I gasped.

"Yep," Grandma said. "That's his name. He called up here looking for you, and so I invited him to dinner."

"Hey," Eddie said through the screen.

He was wearing a gray short-sleeved shirt open halfway down his chest, pleated slacks and Gucci loafers, no socks. He had a bottle of red wine in his hand.

"Hello," we said in unison.

"Can I come in?"

"Sure you can come in," Grandma said. "I guess we don't leave handsome men standing at the door."

He handed the wine to Grandma and winked. "Here you go, cutie."

Grandma giggled. "Aren't you the one."

"I almost never shoot people," I said. "*Almost* never."

"Me too," he said. "I hate unnecessary violence."

I took a step backward. "Excuse me. I need to help in the kitchen."

My mother hurried after me. "Don't even think about it!"
"What?"

"You know what. You were going to sneak out the back door."
"He's not my type."

My mother started filling serving dishes with food from the stove. Mashed potatoes, green beans, red cabbage. "What's wrong with him?"

"He's got too many buttons open on his shirt."

"He could turn out to be a nice person," my mother said. "You should give him a chance. What would it take? And what about supper? I have this nice chicken that will go to waste. What will you eat for supper if you don't eat here?"

"He called Grandma *cutie*!"

My mother had been slicing up the chicken. She took a drumstick and dropped it on the floor. She kicked it around a little, picked it up and put it on the edge of the plate. "There," she said, "we'll give him this drumstick."

"Deal."

"And I have banana cream pie for dessert," she added to seal the bargain. "So you want to make sure you stay to the end."

Be still my heart.

TWO

I TOOK MY PLACE at the table, next to Eddie Kuntz. "You were trying to get in touch with me?"

"Yeah. I lost your card. I put it down somewhere and couldn't find it. So I looked you up in the phone book . . . only I got your parents. Good thing, too. Granny told me you're hard up for a man, and it turns out I'm between women right now, and I don't mind older chicks. So I guess this is your lucky day."

The chick made a valiant effort not to stab her fork into Eddie Kuntz's eyeball. "What did you want to talk to me about?"

"I got a call from Maxine. She said she had a message for me and it was coming by airmail tomorrow. I said tomorrow was Sunday, and there was no airmail on Sunday, so why doesn't she just tell me the message. Then she called me some names." He gave me a face like Maxine had hurt his feelings for no good reason. "Real abusive," he said.

"Was that it?"

"That was it. Except she said she was going to make me squirm. And then she hung up."

BY THE TIME we got to the banana cream pie I was feeling antsy. Nowicki had called Kuntz, so Nowicki was alive, and that was good. Unfortunately, she was sending him airmail. Airmail meant distance. And distance was bad. Even more bothersome was the fact that Eddie Kuntz's napkin was moving on his lap without benefit of hands. My first inclination was to shout "Snake!" and shoot, but probably that wouldn't hold up in court. Besides, as much as I disliked Eddie Kuntz, I could sort of identify with a man who got a stiffie over banana cream pie.

I scarfed down a piece of pie and cracked my knuckles. I glanced at my watch. "Gee, look at the time!"

My mother gave me her resigned mother look. The one that said, So go . . . at least I got you to stay through dessert and now I know you had one good meal this week. And why can't you be more like your sister, Valerie, who's married and has two kids and knows how to cook a chicken.

"Sorry, I have to run," I said, pushing back from the table.

Kuntz paused with his fork midway to his mouth. "What? We leaving?"

I retrieved my shoulder bag from the kitchen. "*I'm* leaving."

"He's leaving too," my father said, head bent over his pie.

"Well, this was nice," Grandma said. "This didn't go so bad."

KUNTZ DANCED behind me when I opened my car door. Up on the balls of his feet. Lots of energy. Tony Testosterone. "How about we go somewhere for a drink?"

"Can't. I've got work to do. I need to finish up a lead."

"Is this about Maxine? I could go with you."

I slid behind the wheel and cranked the engine over. "Not a good idea. But I'll give you a call if anything turns up."

Look out world. Bounty hunter in action.

The diner was less than half filled when I arrived. Most of the people were lingering over coffee. In another hour a younger crowd would straggle in for dessert or fries after the movies let out.

The shift had changed, and I didn't recognize the woman working the register. I introduced myself and asked for Margie.

"Sorry," the woman said. "Margie didn't come in today. Called in sick. Said she might not be here tomorrow, either."

I retreated to my car and rummaged through my bag, searching for the list of family and friends I'd gotten from Kuntz. I ran down the list in the fading light. There was one Margie. No last name, no phone, and for address Kuntz had written "yellow house on Barnet Street." He'd also added that Margie drove a red Isuzu.

The sun was a thin scarlet smudge on the horizon when I got to Barnet, but I was able to spot the yellow bungalow and red car. A woman with a heavily bandaged hand stepped out of the yellow house to fetch her cat just as I crept to a stop at the curb. She grabbed the gray cat when she saw me and disappeared behind her door. Even from the curb I could hear the bolt being thrown.

At least she was home. My secret fear had been that she'd disappeared and was sharing rent with Maxine in Cancún.

I hitched my bag onto my shoulder, plastered a friendly smile on my face, marched up the short cement walk and knocked on her door.

The door opened with the security chain in place. "Yes?"

I passed my card through to her. "Stephanie Plum. I'd like to talk to you about Maxine Nowicki."

"Sorry," she said. "I have nothing to say about Maxine. And I'm not feeling good."

I peeked through the crack in the door and saw she held her bandaged hand to her chest. "What happened?"

She looked at me slack faced and dead eyed, obviously medicated. "It was an accident. A kitchen accident."

"It looks pretty bad."

She blinked. "I lost a finger. Well, I didn't actually lose it. It was on the kitchen counter. I took it to the hospital and got it sewed back on."

I had an instant vision of her finger lying on the kitchen counter. Little black dots danced in front of my eyes, and I felt sweat pop out on my upper lip. "I'm sorry!"

"It was an accident," she said. "An accident."

"Which finger was it?"

"The middle finger."

"Oh man, that's my favorite finger."

"Listen," she said. "I gotta go."

"Wait! Just one minute more. I really need to know about Maxine."

"There's nothing to know. She's gone. There's nothing more I can tell you."

I SAT in my car and took a deep breath. From now on, I was going to be more careful in the kitchen. No more fishing around the garbage disposal looking for bottle caps. No more flamboyant whacking away at salad greens.

It was too late to hit any more people on the list, so I headed home. The temperature had dropped a few degrees, and the air getting sucked through the sunroof was pleasant. I cruised across town, parked behind my apartment building and swung through the rear entrance.

Rex stopped running on his wheel when I walked into the living room. He looked at me, whiskers twitching.

"Don't ask," I said. "You don't want to know." Rex was squeamish about things like chopped-off fingers.

My mother had given me some chicken and some pie to take home. I broke off a chunk of the pie and gave it to Rex. He shoved the crust into his cheek pouch, and his shiny black eyes almost popped out of his head.

Probably I'd looked like that earlier today when Morelli had asked for a doughnut.

I ALWAYS KNOW it's Sunday because I wake up feeling apologetic. That's one of the cool things about being a Catholic . . . it's a multifaceted experience. If you lose the faith, chances are you'll keep the guilt, so it isn't as if you've been skunked altogether. I rolled my head and looked at the digital readout on my clock. Eight. Still time to make late mass. I really should go. My eyes grew heavy at the thought.

Next time I opened my eyes it was eleven. Gosh. Too late to go to church. I heaved myself out of bed and padded to the bathroom, telling myself it was okay because God was willing to forgive little things like skimpy church attendance. Over the years I'd evolved my religion and constructed the Benevolent God. The Benevolent God also didn't care about such trifles as cussing and fibbing. The Benevolent God looked into a person's heart and knew if she'd been naughty or nice in the grand scheme of things. In my world, God and Santa Claus did not micromanage lives. Of course, that meant you couldn't count on them to help you lose weight, either.

I stepped out of the shower and shook my head by way of styling my hair. I dressed in my usual uniform of spandex shorts and halter-style sports bra and topped it off with a Rangers hockey jersey. I took another look at my hair and decided it needed some help, so I did the gel, blow-dry, hair spray routine. When I was done I was several inches taller. I stood in front of the mirror and did the Wonder Woman thing, feet spread, fists on hips. "Eat dirt, scumbag," I said to the mirror. Then I did the Scarlett thing, hand to my heart, coy smile. "Rhett, you handsome devil, how you do go on."

Neither of those felt exactly right for the day, so I took myself into the kitchen to see if I could find my identity in the refrigerator. I was plowing through a Sara Lee frozen cheesecake when the phone rang.

"Hey," Eddie Kuntz said.

"Hey," I answered.

"I got the letter from Maxine. I thought you might want to take a look."

I CRUISED over to Muffet Street and found Eddie Kuntz standing on his minuscule front lawn, hands dangling loose at his sides, staring at his front window. The window was smash city. Big hole square in the middle. Lots of fracture lines.

I slammed the door when I got out of the car, but Kuntz didn't turn at the sound, nor at my approach. We stood there for a moment, side by side, studying the window disaster.

"Nice job," I said.

He nodded. "Square in the middle. Maxine was on the softball team in high school."

"She do this last night?"

Another nod. "I was going to bed. I turned the light off and CRASH . . . a brick came sailing through my front window."

"Airmail," I said.

"Yeah, goddamn airmail. My aunt is apeshit. She's my landlady. Her and Uncle Leo live in the other half of this piece of crap. The only reason she isn't out here wringing her hands is on account of she's at church."

"I didn't realize you were renting."

"What, you think I'd pick out these paint colors? Do I look like one of those poofie guys?"

Hell no. Poofie guys don't think a rip in an undershirt represents a fashion statement.

He handed me a piece of white paper. "This was tied around the brick."

The letter was handwritten and addressed to Kuntz. The message was simple. It told him he'd been a jerk, and if he wanted his property back, he was going to have to go on a treasure hunt. It said his first clue was "in the big one." And then a bunch of mixed-up letters followed.

"What does this mean?" I asked him.

"If I knew I wouldn't be calling you, would I? I'd be out on a goddamn treasure hunt." He threw his hands into the air. "She's wacko. I should have known she was wacko from the beginning. She had a thing about spies. Was always watching those stupid Bond movies. I'd be banging her from behind, and she'd be watching James Bond on the television. Can you believe it?"

Oh yeah.

"You snoop around, right?" he said. "You know all about being a spy? You know about cracking codes?"

"I don't know anything about being a spy," I told him. "And I don't know what this says."

In fact, not only didn't I know anything about being a spy, I didn't even know much about being a bounty hunter. I was just bumbling along, trying to pay my rent, praying I'd win the lottery.

"So now what?" Kuntz asked.

I reread the note. "What is this property she's talking about?"

He gave me a minute-long, blank look. "Love letters," he finally said. "I wrote her some love letters, and I want them back. I don't want them floating around now that we're broken up. There's some embarrassing things in them."

Eddie Kuntz didn't seem like the type to write love letters, but what do I know? He *did* seem like the type to trash an apartment. "Did you go to her apartment looking for the letters?"

"Yeah, but the apartment was all locked up."

"You didn't break in? You didn't have a key?"

"Break in? You mean like bash down the door?"

"I walked through Maxine's apartment yesterday. Someone has torn it apart."

Again, the blank look. "I don't know anything about it."

"I think someone was looking for something. Could Maxine have been keeping drugs?"

He shrugged. "Who knows with Maxine. Like I said, she's screwy."

It was nice to know Maxine was in the area, but aside from that I couldn't get too excited about a note I couldn't read. And I definitely didn't want to hear more about Kuntz's sex life.

24

He draped an arm around my shoulders and leaned close. "I'm gonna level with you, sweetie-pie. I want to get those letters back. It might even be worth something to me. You know what I mean? Just because you're working for this bail bonds guy doesn't mean you can't work for me, too, right? I'd pay good money. All you have to do is let me talk to Maxie before you turn her over to the cops."

"Some people might consider that to be double-dipping."

"A thousand dollars," Kuntz said. "That's my final offer. Take it or leave it."

I stuck out my hand. "Deal."

Okay, so I can be bought. At least I don't come cheap. And besides, it was for a good cause. I didn't especially like Eddie Kuntz, but I could understand about embarrassing love letters since I'd written a few myself. They'd gone to my slimy ex-husband, and I'd consider a thousand dollars well spent if I could get them back.

"I'll need the letter," I said to him.

He handed it over and gave me a punch in the shoulder. "Go for it."

THE NOTE said the first clue was "in the big one." I looked at the jumble of letters that followed, and I saw no pattern. Not such a surprise, since I was missing the puzzle chromosome and couldn't do puzzles designed for nine-year-olds. Fortunately, I lived in a building filled with seniors who sat around all day doing crosswords. And this was sort of like a crossword, right?

My first choice was Mr. Kleinschmidt in 315.

"Ho," Mr. Kleinschmidt said when he answered the door. "It's the fearless bounty hunter. Catch any criminals today?"

"Not yet, but I'm working on it." I handed him the airmail message. "Can you unscramble this?"

Mr. Kleinschmidt shook his head. "I do crosswords. This is a jumble. You have to go ask Lorraine Klausner on the first floor. Lorraine does jumbles."

"Everyone's a specialist today."

"If Mickey Mouse could fly he'd be Donald Duck."

I wasn't sure what that meant, but I thanked Mr. Kleinschmidt and I tramped two flights down and had my finger poised to ring Lorraine's bell when her door opened.

"Sol Kleinschmidt just called and told me all about the jumbled-up message," Lorraine said. "Come in. I have cookies set out."

I took a chair across from Lorraine at her kitchen table and watched her work her way through the puzzle.

"This isn't exactly a jumble," she said, concentrating on the note. "I don't know how to do this. I only do jumbles." She tapped her finger on the table. "I do know someone who might be able to help you, but . . ."

"But?"

"My nephew, Salvatore, has a knack for this sort of thing. Ever since he was little he's been able to solve all kinds of puzzles. One of those freak gifts."

I looked at her expectantly.

"It's just that he can be odd sometimes. I think he's going through one of those conformity things."

I hoped he didn't have a tongue stud. I had to struggle not to make guttural animal sounds when I talked to people wearing tongue studs. "Where does he live?"

She wrote an address on the back of the note. "He's a musician, and he mostly works nights, so he should be home now, but maybe it would be best if I call first."

SALVATORE SWEET lived in a high-rise condo overlooking the river. The building was sandblasted cement and black glass. The landscaping was minimal but well maintained. The lobby was newly painted and carpeted in tones of mauve and gray. Hardly a nonconformist's paradise. And not low-rent, either.

I took the elevator to the ninth floor and rang Sweet's doorbell.

A moment later the door opened and I found myself face-to-face with either a very ugly woman or a very gay guy.

"You must be Stephanie."

I nodded my head.

"I'm Sally Sweet. Aunt Lorraine called and said you had a problem."

He was dressed in tight black leather pants held together at the sides with leather lacing that left a strip of pale white flesh from ankle to waist, and a black leather vest that molded around cone-shaped, eat-your-heart-out-Madonna breasts. He was close to seven feet tall in his black platform pumps. He had a large hook nose, red roses tattooed on his biceps and—thank you, Lord—he didn't have a tongue stud. He was wearing a blond Farrah Fawcett wig, fake eyelashes and glossy maroon lipstick. His nails had been painted to match his lips.

"Maybe this isn't a good time . . ." I said.

"As good as any."

I had no idea what to say or where to look. The truth is, he was fascinating. Sort of like staring at a car crash.

He looked down at himself. "You're probably wondering about the outfit."

"It's very nice."

"Yeah, I had the vest made special. I'm lead guitar for the Lovelies. And let me tell you, it's fucking impossible to keep a good manicure through the weekend as a lead guitarist. If I'd known how things would turn out for me, I'd have taken up the fucking drums."

"Looks like you're doing okay."

"Success is my middle name. Two years ago I was straight as an arrow, playing for Howling Dogs. You ever hear of Howling Dogs?"

I shook my head. "No."

"Nobody fucking heard of Howling Dogs. I was fucking living in a fucking packing crate in the alley behind Romanos Pizza. I've been punk, funk, grunge and R&B. I've been with the Funky Butts, the Pitts, Beggar Boys, and Howling Dogs. I was with Howling Dogs the longest. It was a fucking depressing experience. I couldn't stand fucking singing all those fucking songs about fucking hearts fucking breaking and fucking goldfish fucking going to heaven. And then I had to fucking look like some western dude. I mean, how can you have any self-respect when you have to go on stage in a cowboy hat?"

I was pretty good at cussing, but I didn't think I could keep up with Sally. On my best day, I couldn't squeeze all those "f" words into a sentence. "Boy, you can really curse," I said.

"You can't be a fucking musician without fucking cursing."

I knew that was true, because sometimes I watched rockumentaries on MTV. My eyes strayed to his hair. "But now you're wearing a Farrah Fawcett wig. Isn't that kind of like a cowboy hat?"

"Yeah, only this is a fucking statement. This is fucking politically correct. See, this is the ultimate sensitive man. This is taking my female shit out of the closet. And like I'm saying, here it is, you know?"

"Un huh."

"And besides, I'm making a shitload of money. I caught the wave on this one. This is the year of the drag queen. We're like a freaking fucking invasion." He took the note from my hand and studied it. "Not only am I booked solid for every weekend for two years . . . I get money stuffed in my goddamn pants. I got money I don't know what to do with."

"So I guess you feel lucky to be gay."

"Well, just between you and me, I'm not actually gay."

"You're a cross-dresser."

"Yeah. Something like that. I mean, I wouldn't mind being sort of gay. Like, I guess I could dance with a guy, but I'm not doing any of that butt stuff."

I nodded. I felt like that about men, too.

He got a pen from a hall table and made some marks on the note. "Lorraine said you're a bounty hunter."

"I almost never shoot anybody," I said.

"If I was a bounty hunter I'd fucking shoot *lots* of people." He finished scribbling on the paper and gave it back to me.

"You're probably gonna find this hard to believe, but I was sort of weird when I was a kid."

"No!"

"Yeah. I was like . . . out there. So I used to spend a lot of time talking to Spock. And Spock and me, we'd send messages to each other in code."

"You mean Spock from *Star Trek*?"

"Yeah, that's the dude. Boy, Spock and I were tight. We did this code thing every day for years. Only our codes were hard. This code is too easy. This code is just a bunch of run-together letters with some extra shit thrown in. 'Red and green and blue. At Cluck in a Bucket the clue waits for you.' "

"I know Cluck in a Bucket," I said. "It's just down from the bonds office."

The trash containers in the Cluck in a Bucket parking lot are colored red, green and blue. The green and the blue are for recycling paper and aluminum. The big red one is for garbage. I'd bet my apprehension fee the next clue was in the garbage.

A second man came to the door. He was neatly dressed in Dockers and a perfectly pressed button-down shirt. He was shorter than Sweet. Maybe 5'9". He was slender and totally hairless, like a bald Chihuahua, with soft brown eyes hidden behind thick glasses, and a mouth that seemed too wide, too sensuous for his small pinched face and little button nose.

"What's going on?" he asked.

"This is Stephanie Plum," Sally said. "The one Lorraine called about."

The man extended his hand. "Gregory Stern. Everyone calls me Sugar."

"Sugar and I are roommates," Sally said. "We're in the band together."

"I'm the band tart," Sugar said. "And sometimes I sing."

"I always wanted to sing with a band," I said. "Only, I can't sing."

"I bet you could," Sugar said. "I bet you'd be wonderful."

"You'd better go get dressed," Sally said to Sugar. "You're going to be late again."

"We have a gig this afternoon," Sugar explained. "Wedding reception."

Yeeesh.

CLUCK IN A BUCKET is on Hamilton. It's housed in a cement cube with windows on three sides. And it's best known not for its outstanding food but for the giant rotating chicken impaled on a thirty-foot flagpole anchored in the parking lot.

I cruised into the lot and stopped short of the red Dumpster. The temperature had to be a hundred in the shade with a hundred percent humidity. My sunroof was open, and when I parked the car I felt the weight of the heat settling around me. Maybe when I found Nowicki I'd have my air-conditioning fixed, or maybe I'd spend a few days at the beach . . . or maybe I'd pay my rent and avoid eviction.

I walked to the Dumpster, thinking about ordering lunch. Two pieces of chicken plus a biscuit and slaw and an extra large soda sounded about right.

I peeked over the edge of the Dumpster, gave an involuntary gasp and staggered back a few feet. Most of the garbage was in bags, but some of the bags had split and had spewed out guts like bloated roadkill. The stench of vegetable rot and gangrenous chicken boiled over the Dumpster and had me reassessing my lunch plans. It also had me reassessing my job. There was no way I was scrounging in this mess for the stupid clue.

I returned to my car and called Eddie Kuntz on my cell phone. "I've deciphered the note," I told him. "I'm at Cluck in a Bucket, and there's another clue here. I think you'd better come see for yourself."

Half an hour later, Kuntz pulled into the lot. I was sitting in my car, slurping down my third giant-sized Diet Coke, and I was sweating like a pig. Kuntz looked nice and cool in his new sport utility vehicle and factory-installed air. He'd changed his clothes from the sweat-stained boxers he'd worn this morning to a black fishnet undershirt, black spandex shorts that didn't do much to hide Mr. Lumpy, two gold chains around his neck, and brand-new Air Jordans that looked to be about a size 42.

"All dressed up," I said to him.

"Gotta maintain the image. Don't like to disappoint the chicks."

I handed him the decoded note. "The next clue is in the red Dumpster."

He walked to the Dumpster, stuck his head over the edge and recoiled.

"Pretty ripe," I said. "Maybe you want to put on some old clothes before you go in there."

"What, are you nuts? I'm not wading through that shit."

"It's your note."

"Yeah, but I've hired *you*," Eddie said.

"You didn't hire me to go Dumpster surfing."

"I hired you to find her. That's all I want. I just want you to find her."

He had two pagers clipped onto his spandex shorts. One of them beeped and displayed a message. He read the message and sighed. "Chicks," he said. "They never stop."

Right. It was probably from his mother.

He went to his car and made a couple of calls on his car phone. He finished the calls and came back to me. "Okay," he said, "it's all taken care of. All you have to do is stay here and wait for Carlos. I'd stay, but I got other things to do."

I watched him leave, then I turned and squinted beyond the lot. "Hey Maxine," I yelled. "You out there?" If it had been me I'd have wanted to see Kuntz slopping around in the garbage. "Listen," I said, "it was a good idea, but it didn't work out. How about you let me buy you a couple pieces of chicken?"

Maxine didn't come forward, so I sat in my car and waited for Carlos. After about twenty minutes a flatbed truck pulled into the lot and unloaded a backhoe. The flatbed driver fired up the backhoe, rolled it to the Dumpster and put the bucket under the bin's bottom edge. The Dumpster tipped in slow motion and then crashed to the pavement and lay there like a big dead dinosaur. Garbage bags hit the ground and burst, and a glass jar clinked onto the blacktop, rolled between the bags and came to rest a few feet from where I was standing. Someone had used a Magic Marker to write "clue" on the outside of the jar.

The backhoe driver looked over at me. "You Stephanie?"

I was staring, transfixed, at the Dumpster and the mess in front of me, and my heart was beating with a sickening thud. "Unh huh."

"You want me to spread this garbage around some more?"

"No!"

People were standing in the doorways and staring through the windows of Cluck in a Bucket. Two high school kids dressed in yellow-and-red Cluck uniforms ran across the lot to the backhoe.

"What are you doing? What are you doing?" one of the kids yelled.

"Hey, don't get your undies in a bunch," the driver said to the kid. "Life's too short." He motored the backhoe onto the flatbed, got behind the wheel, gave us a military salute and drove off.

We all stood there, momentarily speechless.

The kid turned to me. "Do you know him?"

"Nope," I said. "Never saw him before in my life."

I WAS less than a mile from my apartment, so I grabbed the jar, jumped into my car and headed for home. All the way, I kept looking over my shoulder, half expecting to be tracked down like a dog by the garbage police.

I unlocked my door and called to Rex. "Another one of those days."

Rex was asleep in his soup can and made no response, so I

went into the kitchen and made myself a peanut butter and olive sandwich. I cracked open a beer and studied the new encrypted message while I ate. I looked for run-together words and extra letters, but it was all a big glob of nothing to me. Finally I gave up and called Sally. His phone rang three times and his machine kicked in. "Sally and Sugar aren't home, but they'd just *loooooove* to talk to you, so leave a message."

I left my name and number and went back to staring at the note. By three o'clock my eyes felt fried and there was no word from Sally, so I decided to go door-to-door to the seniors again. Mr. Kleinschmidt told me it wasn't a crossword. Lorraine told me it wasn't a jumble. Mr. Markowitz told me he was watching TV and didn't have time for such nonsense.

The light was blinking on my phone machine when I returned to my kitchen.

The first message was from Eddie Kuntz. "So where is she?" That was it. That was the whole message.

"What a moolack," I said to the answering machine.

The second message was from Ranger. "Call me."

Ranger is a man of few words. He's Cuban-American, former Special Forces, he makes a much better friend than an enemy, and he's Vinnie's numero uno bounty hunter. I dialed Ranger's number and waited to hear breathing. Sometimes that was all you got.

"Yo," Ranger said.

"Yo yourself."

"I need you to help me take down a skip."

This meant Ranger either needed a good laugh or else he needed a white female to use as a decoy. If Ranger needed serious muscle he wouldn't call me. Ranger knew people who would take on the Terminator for a pack of Camels and the promise of a fun time.

"I need to get an FTA out of a building, and I haven't got what it takes," Ranger said.

"And just exactly what is it that you're lacking?"

"Smooth white skin barely hidden behind a short skirt and tight sweater. Two days ago Sammy the Gimp bought the farm. He's laid out at Leoni's, and my man, Kenny Martin, is in there paying his respects."

"So why don't you just wait until he comes out?"

"He's in there with his mother and his sister and his Uncle Vito. My guess is they'll leave together, and I don't want to wade through the whole Grizolli family to get at this guy."

No kidding. The landfill was littered with the remains of people who tried to wade through Vito Grizolli.

"Actually, I had plans for tonight," I said. "They include living a little longer."

"I just want you to get my man out the back door. I'll take it from there."

I heard the disconnect, but I shouted into the phone anyway. *"What are you freaking nuts?"*

FIFTEEN MINUTES LATER I was dressed in four-inch FMPs (short for "fuck-me pumps," because when you walked around in them you looked like Whorehouse Wonder Bitch). I shimmied into a low-cut black knit dress that was bought with the intent of losing five pounds, gunked up my eyes with a lot of black mascara and beefed up my cleavage by stuffing Nerf balls into my bra.

Ranger was parked on Roebling, half a block from the funeral home. He didn't turn when I pulled to the curb, but I saw his eyes on me in the rearview mirror.

He was smiling when I slid in beside him. "Nice dress you're almost wearing. You ever think about changing professions?"

"Constantly. I'm thinking about it now."

Ranger handed me a photo. "Kenny Martin. Age twenty-two. Minor league loser. Charged with armed robbery." He glanced at the black leather bag I had draped on my shoulder. "You carrying?"

"Yes."

"Is it loaded?"

I stuck my hand in the bag and rooted around. "I'm not sure, but I think I've got a few bullets in here somewhere. . . ."

"Cuffs?"

"I definitely have cuffs."

"Defense spray?"

"Yep. Got defense spray."

"Go get 'em, tiger."

I sashayed across the street and up the steps to Leoni's. A small knot of old Italian men stood smoking on the front porch. Conversation stopped when I approached, and the group parted to let me pass. There were more people in the vestibule. None of them was Kenny Martin. I went to room one, where Sammy the Gimp was on display, resting nicely in an ornate mahogany casket. There were lots of flowers and lots of old Italian women. No one seemed to be too upset about Sammy's demise. No heavily sedated widow. No wailing mother. No Kenny.

I said good-bye to Sammy and tottered down the hall in my heels. There was a small foyer at the end of the hall. The foyer opened to the back door, and Kenny Martin was standing in front of the door, sneaking a smoke. Beyond the door was a covered driveway, and somewhere beyond the driveway was Ranger.

I leaned against the wall across from Kenny and smiled. "Hi."

His eyes fixed onto my Nerf balls. "Are you here to see Sammy?"

I shook my head no. "Mrs. Kowalski in room two."

"You don't look all broke up."

I shrugged.

"If you was all broke up I could comfort you. I got lots of ways to comfort a woman."

I raised an eyebrow. "Hmm?"

He was 5'10" and a solid 190 pounds. He was dressed in a dark blue suit and white shirt with the top button popped open.

"What's your pleasure, dollie?" he asked.

I looked him up and down and smiled as if I liked what I saw. "What's your name?"

"Kenny. Kenny 'the Man' Martin."

Kenny the Man. Unh! Mental head slap. I extended my hand. "Stephanie."

In lieu of a handshake he laced his fingers into mine and stepped closer. "Pretty name."

"I was going outside for some fresh air. Want to join me?"

"Yeah, sure. Nothing in here but dead people. Even the people who are alive are dead, you know what I mean?"

A little girl ran down the hall to us. "Kenny, Mama says we have to go now."

"Tell her I'll be there in a minute."

"She said I'm supposed to bring you *now*!"

Kenny did palms-up. A gesture of the futility of arguing. Everyone knows you never win against an Italian mother. "Maybe I could call you sometime?" Kenny said to me. "Maybe we could get together later."

Never underestimate the power of a Nerf ball. "Sure. Why don't we go outside, and I'll write down my number. I really need some air."

"Now!" the kid yelled.

Kenny made a lunge at the kid, and she whirled and ran back to Mama, shrieking at the top of her lungs.

"I gotta go," Kenny said.

"One second. I'll give you my business card." I had my head in my bag, scrounging for my defense spray. If I couldn't get him to walk through the door, I'd give him a shot of spray and drag him out.

I heard more footsteps on the carpet and looked up to find a woman striding toward us. She was slim and pretty with short blond hair. She was wearing a gray suit and heels, and her expression turned serious when she saw me with Kenny.

"Now I see the problem," she said to Kenny. "Your mother sent me to fetch you, but it looks like you've got a complication here."

"No complication," Kenny said. "Just tell her to keep her shirt on."

"Oh yeah," the woman said. "I'm going to tell your mother to keep her shirt on. That's like a death wish." She looked to me, and then she looked to Kenny, and then she smiled. "You don't know, do you?" she asked Kenny.

I was still searching for the spray. Hair brush, flashlight, travel pack of tampons. Damn it, where was the spray?

"Know what?" Kenny said. "What are you talking about?"

"Don't you ever read the paper? This is Stephanie Plum. She blew up the funeral home last year. She's a bounty hunter."

"You're shitting me!"

Oh boy.

THREE

KENNY GAVE ME a shot to the shoulder that knocked me back a couple of feet. "Is that true, what Terry said? Are you a bounty hunter?"

"Hey!" I said. "Keep your hands off me."

He gave me another whack that had me against the wall. "Maybe you need to be taught a lesson not to mess with Kenny."

"Maybe you need to be taught a lesson not to jump bail." I had my hand in my bag, and I couldn't find the lousy defense spray, so I hauled out a can of extra-hold hair spray and let him have it square in the face.

"Yeow," Kenny yelped, jumping back, hands to his face. "You bitch, I'll get you for this. I'll . . ." He took his hands away. "Hey, wait a minute. What is this shit?"

Terry's smile widened. "You've been hair-sprayed, Kenny."

The little girl and an older woman hustled down the hall.

"What's going on?" the woman wanted to know.

An old man appeared. Vito Grizolli, looking like he'd walked off the set of *The Godfather*.

"Kenny's been hair-sprayed," Terry told everyone. "He put up a pretty good fight, but he just didn't have the muscle to stand up to extra hold."

The mother turned on me. "You did this to my boy?"

I tried not to sigh, but one escaped anyway. Some days it doesn't pay to get out of bed. "I'm a bond enforcement officer," I told her. "I work for Vincent Plum. Your son failed to appear in court, and now I need to bring him in to reschedule and have his case reviewed."

Mrs. Martin sucked in air and faced-off at Kenny. "You did that? You didn't go to court? What's the matter with you? Don't you know anything?"

"It's all bullshit," Kenny said.

Mrs. Martin smacked him on the side of the head. "You watch your language!"

"And how is this to dress?" she said to me. "If you were my daughter I wouldn't let you out of the house."

I scrambled away before she could smack me, too.

"Kids," Vito Grizolli said. "What's happening to this world?"

From a man who had people killed on a regular basis.

He shook his finger at Kenny. "You should have kept your court date. You do this like a man. You go with her now, and you let the lawyers do their job."

"I got hair spray in my eye," Kenny said. "It's watering. I need a doctor."

I held the back door open for him. "Don't be such a big baby," I said. "I get hair spray in my eyes all the time."

Ranger was waiting under the canopy. He was dressed in a black T-shirt and black assault pants tucked into black boots. He had a body like Schwarzenegger, dark hair slicked back off his face and a two-hundred-watt smile. He was drop-dead sexy, he was as sane as Batman, and he was a primo bounty hunter.

He gave me all two hundred watts. "Nice touch with the hair spray."

"Don't start."

MONDAY MORNING I woke up feeling restless. I wanted to move on Maxine Nowicki, but I was stalled on the clue. I looked at the note again and felt frustration gnawing at me. Sally Sweet hadn't returned my call. I was itching to call him again, but it was eight o'clock, and I thought it was possible drag queens weren't early risers.

I was on my second cup of coffee when the phone rang.

"It's me," Sally said.

I read the note over the phone, letter by letter.

Silence.

"Sally?"

"I'm thinking. I'm thinking. I've been up all night, looking sexy, shaking my ass. It isn't easy, you know."

I could hear yelling in the background. "What's going on?"

"It's Sugar. He's got breakfast all made."

"Sugar makes your breakfast?"

"I'm on the phone with Stephanie," Sally yelled back.

"Boy, I don't have anyone make breakfast for me."

"What you have to do is live with a gay guy," Sally said. "They're into this cooking shit."

Something to think about.

"I don't want to rush your breakfast," I said. "I'll be home for another hour, then I'm going to the office. When you figure it out you can call me at the office, or you can leave a message on my machine."

"Ten four, kemosabe."

I took a shower and dressed for another scorcher day. I gave Rex fresh water and some hamster food, which he didn't deem worthy to so much as sniff at.

I slung my black leather tote over my shoulder, locked up and took the stairs to the lobby. Outside, the blacktop was steaming, and the sun was beginning to throb in a murky sky. I played Savage Garden all the way to the office and arrived psyched because I'd had good traffic karma, sailing through the lights.

Connie was bent over a file when I walked in. Her black hair was teased high around her face like a movie set that was all facade. Everything up front and nothing in the back. Killer hair as long as she didn't turn around.

"If you want to talk to the man, he isn't in," she said.

Lula popped up from behind a bank of file cabinets. "He's doin' a nooner with a goat today. I saw it on his calendar."

"So how's it going?" Connie asked. "Any action on the Nowicki thing?"

I passed a copy of the note to Connie and Lula. "I have a message from her that's written in some kind of code."

"Lost me," Lula said. "Code isn't one of my specialties."

Connie sunk two teeth into a heavily lipsticked lower lip. "Maybe the numbers are really letters."

"I thought of that, but I couldn't get it to work."

We all stared at the note for a while.

"Might not mean anything," Lula finally said. "Might be a joke."

I nodded. Joke note was a possibility.

"I helped Ranger with an apprehension yesterday," I said. "Kenny Martin."

Connie gave a low laugh. "Vito Grizolli's nephew? Bet that was fun."

"There was a woman with him that I can't place. I know I've seen her before, but it keeps slipping away from me."

"What'd she look like?"

"Slim, pretty, short blond hair. He called her Terry."

"Terry Gilman," Connie said. "Used to be Terry Grizolli. Was married to Billy Gilman for about six hours and kept his name."

"Terry Grizolli! That was Terry Grizolli?" Terry Grizolli was two years older than me and had been linked with Joe Morelli all through high school. She'd been voted prom queen and had created a school scandal by choosing Joe as her escort. After graduation, she'd gone on to become a professional cheerleader for the New York Giants. "I haven't seen her in years," I said. "What's she doing now? Is she still a cheerleader?"

"Rumor has it she's working for Vito. She has a lot of money and no discernible job."

"You telling me she's like a wise guy?"

"Affirmative action," Connie said.

The front door opened, and we all turned to look. Lula was the first to find her voice. "Killer earring."

It was a parrot swinging on a gold hoop that was looped through one of Sally's ears.

"Got it at the shore," he said. "You buy a pair of thong briefs and they throw in the earring." He made a grab at his ass and hiked himself up. "Christ, I don't know how they wear these thong things. They're giving me hemorrhoids."

He was minus the Farrah wig, and his own hair was a mess of dark brown corkscrew strands. Sort of Rasta without the dreds. He was wearing cut-off denims, a white T-shirt, red clogs and was freshly manicured with silver polish.

"This is Sally Sweet," I told Connie and Lula.

"I bet," Lula said.

Sally handed me the translation of the coded message and looked around. "I thought there'd be wanted posters on the walls and gun racks filled with shotguns."

"This isn't Dodge City," Lula said. "We got some class here. We keep the guns in the back room with the pervert."

I read the note. "'One-thirty-two Howser Street. Under the bench.' That's Maxine's mother's address."

Sally slouched onto the couch. "When I was a kid I watched reruns of Steve McQueen. Now *he* was a bounty hunter."

"Damn skippy," Lula said. "He was the shit."

"So now what?" Sally wanted to know. "We going to Howser Street?"

Foreboding sliced into my stomach. We?

Lula slammed her file drawer shut. "Hold on. You're not going off without me! Suppose something goes wrong? Suppose you need a big full-figure woman like me to help straighten things out?"

I like Lula a lot, but last time we worked together I gained seven pounds and almost got arrested for shooting a guy who was already dead.

"*I'm* going to Howser Street," I said. "Only me. One person. Steve McQueen worked alone."

"I don't mean to be insulting," Lula said, "but you ain't no Steve McQueen. And something happens you'll be happy I'm around. Besides, this'll be fun . . . the two of us working on a case together again."

"Three of us," Sally said. "I'm going, too."

"Oh boy," Lula said. "The three muffkateers."

LULA GAVE THE NOWICKI HOUSE the once-over. "Don't appear like Maxine's mama spends much time spiffing up the old homestead."

We were in Lula's Firebird with Sally in the backseat doing air guitar to Lula's rap music. Lula cut the engine, the music stopped, and Sally snapped to attention.

"Looks kind of spooky," Sally said. "You guys have guns, right?"

"Wrong," I said. "We don't need guns to retrieve a clue."

"Well, this is fucking disappointing. I figured you'd kick the door down and blast yourselves into the house. You know, rough up some people."

"You want to cut down on the breakfast drugs," Lula said to Sally. "You keep going like this all your nose hairs are gonna fall out."

I unbuckled my seat belt. "There's a little wooden bench on the front porch. With any luck, we won't have to go in the house."

We crossed the patchy lawn, and Lula tested the bottom porch step, pausing when it groaned under her weight. She moved to the next step and picked her way around floorboards that were obviously rotted.

Sally tiptoed behind her. *Clonk, clonk, clonk* with his clogs. Not exactly the stealth transvestite.

They each took an end of the bench and flipped it over.

No note stuck to the bottom.

"Maybe it blew away," Lula said.

There wasn't a stray breath of air in all of Jersey, but we checked the surroundings anyway, the three of us fanning out, covering the yard.

No note.

"Hunh," Lula said. "We been given the runaround."

There was a crawl space under the porch, enclosed with wooden lattice. I dropped to hands and knees and squinted through the lattice. "The note said 'under the bench.' It could have meant under the porch, under the bench." I jogged to the car and retrieved a flashlight from the glove compartment. I returned to the porch, scrunched low and flashed the beam around the dirt floor. Sure enough, there was a glass jar directly under the part of the porch that supported the bench.

Two yellow eyes caught in the light, held for a second, and skittered away.

"Do you see it?" Lula wanted to know.

"Yep."

"Well?"

"There are eyes under there. Little beady yellow ones. And spiders. Lots of spiders."

Lula gave an involuntary shiver.

Sally made another adjustment on his thong.

"I'd go get it, but a big woman like me wouldn't fit," Lula said. "Sure is a shame it isn't just a little roomier."

"I think you'd fit."

"Nope, unh ah, I know I wouldn't fit."

I considered the spiders. "I might not fit, either."

"I'd fit," Sally said, "but I'm not doing it. I paid twenty bucks for this manicure, and I'm not fucking it up crawling under some rat-infested porch."

I hunkered down for another look. "Maybe we can stick a rake in there and pull the jar out."

"Nuh ah," Lula said. "A rake isn't gonna be big enough. You gotta go in from the end here, and it's too far away. Where you gonna get a rake anyway?"

"We can ask Mrs. Nowicki."

"Oh yeah," Lula said. "From the looks of this lawn she does lots of gardening." Lula stood on tiptoes and looked in a window on the side of the house. "Probably not even home. Seems like she'd be out by now what with us up on her porch and all." Lula moved to another window and pressed her nose to the glass. "Uh oh."

"What uh oh?" I hated uh oh.

"You'd better look at this."

Sally and I trotted over and pressed our noses to the glass.

Mrs. Nowicki was stretched out on the kitchen floor. She had a bloody towel wrapped around the top of her head, and an empty bottle of Jim Beam was on the floor beside her. She was wearing a cotton nightgown, and her bare feet were splayed toes out.

"Looks to me like dead city," Lula said. "You want a rake, you better get it yourself."

I knocked on the window. "Mrs. Nowicki!"

Mrs. Nowicki didn't move a muscle.

"Think this must have just happened," Lula said. "If she'd laid there for any amount of time in this heat she'd be swelled up big as a beach ball. She'd have burst apart. There'd be guts and maggots all over the place."

"I hate to miss seeing the guts and maggots," Sally said. "Maybe we should come back in a couple hours."

I turned from the window and headed for the car. "We need to call the police."

Lula was on my heels. "Hold the phone on the *we* part. Those police people give me the hives."

"You're not a hooker anymore. You don't have to worry about the police."

"One of them traumatic emotional things," Lula said.

Ten minutes later, two blue-and-whites angled to the curb behind me. Carl Costanza emerged from the first car, looked at me and shook his head. I'd known Carl since grade school. He was always the skinny kid with the bad haircut and wise mouth. He'd bulked up some in the last few years, and he'd found a good barber. He still had the wise mouth, but under it all, he was a decent person and a pretty good cop.

"Another dead body?" Carl asked. "What are you going for, a

45

record? Most bodies found by an individual in the city of Trenton?"

"She's on the kitchen floor. We haven't been in the house. The door is locked."

"How do you know she's on the floor if the door is locked?"

"I was sort of looking in the window, and . . ."

Carl held up his hand. "Don't tell me. I don't want to hear this. Sorry I asked."

The cop in the second car had gone to the side window and was standing there, hands on gun belt. "She's on the floor all right," he said, peering in. He rapped on the window. "Hey, lady!" He turned to us and narrowed his eyes against the sun. "Looks dead to me."

Carl went to the front door and knocked. "Mrs. Nowicki? It's the police." He knocked louder. "Mrs. Nowicki, we're coming in." He gave the door a good shot with his fist, the rotted molding splintered off, and the door swung open.

I followed Carl into the kitchen and watched while he stooped over Mrs. Nowicki, feeling for a pulse, looking for a sign of life.

There were more bloody towels in the sink and a bloody paring knife on the counter. My first thought had been gunshot, but there were no guns in sight and no sign of struggle.

"You better call this in for the ME," Carl said to the second cop. "I don't know exactly what we've got here."

Sally and Lula had taken positions against the wall.

"What do you think?" Lula asked Carl.

Carl shrugged. "Nothing much. She looks pretty dead."

Lula nodded. "That what I thought, too. Soon as I saw her I said to myself, Hell, that woman's dead."

The second cop disappeared to make the call, and Lula inched closer to Mrs. Nowicki. "What do you think happened to her? I bet she fell and hit her head, and then she wrapped her head in a towel and croaked."

That sounded reasonable to me . . . except for the paring knife with blood and pieces of hair stuck to it.

Lula bent at the waist and examined the towel, wrapped turban style. "Must have been a good clonk she took. Lots of blood."

Usually when people die their bodies evacuate and the smell gets bad fast. Mrs. Nowicki didn't smell dead. Mrs. Nowicki smelled like Jim Beam.

Carl and I were both registering this oddity, looking at each other sideways when Mrs. Nowicki opened one eye and fixed it on Lula.

"YOW!" Lula yelled, jumping back a foot, knocking into Sally. "Her eye popped open!"

"The better to see you with," Mrs. Nowicki rasped out, alto voiced, one pack short of lung cancer.

Carl stepped into Mrs. Nowicki's line of sight. "We thought you were dead."

"Not yet, honey," Mrs. Nowicki said. "But I'll tell you, I have one hell of a headache." She raised a shaky hand and felt the towel. "Oh, yeah, now I remember."

"What happened?"

"It was an accident. I was trying to cut my hair, and my hand slipped, and I gave myself a little nick. It was bleeding some, so I wrapped my head in a towel and took a few medicinal hits from the bottle." She struggled to sit. "Don't exactly know what happened after that."

Lula had her hand on her hip. "Looks to me like you drained the bottle and passed out. Think you took one too many of them medicinal hits."

"Looks to me like she didn't take enough," Sally murmured. "I liked her better dead."

"I need a cigarette," Mrs. Nowicki said. "Anybody got a cigarette?"

I could hear cars pulling up outside and footsteps in the front room. The second uniform came in, followed by a suit.

"She isn't dead," Carl explained.

"Maybe she used to be," Lula said. "Maybe she's one of them *living* dead."

"Maybe you're one of them *nut cases*," Mrs. Nowicki said.

47

Lights from an EMS truck flashed outside, and two paramedics wandered into the kitchen.

I eased my way out the door, to the porch and onto the lawn. I didn't especially want to be there when they unwound the towel.

"I don't know about you," Lula said, "but I'm ready to leave this party."

I didn't have a problem with that. Carl knew where to find me if there were questions. Didn't look like there was anything criminal here, anyway. Drunken lush slices scalp with a paring knife and passes out. Probably happens all the time.

We piled into the Firebird and hauled ass back to the office. I said good-bye to Lula and Sally, slid behind the wheel of my CRX and motored home. When things calmed down I'd go back with some sort of long-handled mechanism for retrieving the bottle. I didn't want to explain to the cops about the clues.

In the meantime, there were a few phone calls I could make. I'd only gotten partially through Eddie Kuntz's list. It wouldn't hurt to run through the rest of the names.

Mrs. Williams, one of my neighbors, was in the lobby when I swung through the doors. "I've got a terrible ringing in my ears," she said. "And I'm having a dizzy spell."

Another neighbor, Mrs. Balog, was standing next to Mrs. Williams, checking her mailbox. "It's the hardening of the arteries. Evelyn Krutchka on the third floor has it something awful. I heard her arteries are just about turned to stone."

Most of the people in my building were seniors. There were a couple of single mothers with babies, Ernie Wall and his girlfriend, May, and one other woman my age, who only spoke Spanish. We were the segment of society on fixed incomes or incomes of dubious reliability. We weren't interested in tennis or sitting at poolside. For the most part we were a quiet, peaceful group, armed to the teeth for no good reason, violent only when a premium parking slot was at stake.

I took the stairs to the second floor, hoping they'd have some effect on the pie I'd had for breakfast. I let myself into my apartment and made an instant left turn into the kitchen. I stuck my head in the refrigerator and pushed things around some, searching for the perfect lunch. After a few minutes of this I decided on a hard-boiled egg and a banana.

I sat at my dining room table, which is actually in a little alcove off my living room, and I ate my egg and started on the list of names and businesses Kuntz had given me. I dialed Maxine's cleaner first. No, they hadn't seen her lately. No, she didn't have any clothes to pick up. I called my cousin Marion, who worked at Maxine's bank, and asked about recent transactions. No new postings, Marion said. The most recent transaction was two weeks ago when she withdrew three hundred dollars from the outside ATM.

Last name on the list was a 7-Eleven in north Trenton, a quarter mile from Eddie Kuntz and Mama Nowicki. The night manager had just come on when I called. She said a woman meeting Maxine's description had been in the night before. She remembered the woman because she was a regular. It had been late at night and store traffic had been slow. The woman had been chatty and had relieved the tedium.

I stuffed Maxine's photo into my shoulder bag and took off for the 7-Eleven to confirm the identification. I parked nose-in to the curb at the front of the store and stared beyond the plate glass windows to the register. There were four men in line. Three still in suits, looking rumpled from the heat and the workday. By the time I made my way through the door, there were two men left. I waited for them to complete their business before introducing myself to the woman behind the counter.

She extended her hand. "Helen Badijian. I'm the night manager. We spoke on the phone."

Her brown hair was plaited in a single braid that reached to her shoulder blades, and her face was devoid of makeup with the exception of eyes lined in smudgy black liner. "I didn't get it straight on the phone," Helen said. "Are you with the police?"

I usually try to avoid answering that question directly. "Bond enforcement," I said, leaving Helen to believe whatever. Not that I

49

would *lie* about police affiliation. Imitating a police officer isn't smart. Still, if someone misunderstood because they weren't paying attention . . . that wasn't my problem.

Helen looked at Maxine's photo and nodded her head. "Yep, that's her. Only she's a lot more tan now."

So I knew two things. Maxine was alive, and she had time to sit in the sun.

"She bought a couple packs of cigarettes," Helen said. "Menthol. And a large Coke. Said she had a long drive ahead of her. I asked her if she was going to buy a lottery ticket because that's what she always did . . . bought a ticket every week. She said no. Said she didn't need to win the lottery anymore."

"Anything else?"

"That was it."

"You notice the car she was driving?"

"Sorry. I didn't notice."

I left my card and asked Helen to call if Maxine returned. I expected the card would go in the trash the moment I pulled out of the lot, but I left one anyway. For the most part, people would talk to me when confronted face-to-face but were unwilling to take a more aggressive step like initiating a phone call. Initiating a phone call felt like snitching, and snitching wasn't cool.

I rolled out of the lot and drove past the hot spots . . . Margie's house, Maxine's apartment, Kuntz's house, Mama Nowicki's house and the diner. Nothing seemed suspicious. I was itching to get the next clue, but there were people out on Howser Street. Mrs. Nowicki's neighbor was watering his lawn. A couple of kids were doing curb jumps on skateboards. Better to wait until dark, I thought. Two more hours and the sun would go down and everyone would move inside. Then I could skulk around in the shadows and, I hoped, not have to answer any questions.

I returned to my apartment and found Joe Morelli sitting on the floor in my hall, back to the wall, long legs stretched in front of him, crossed at the ankles. He had a brown paper bag next to him, and the entire hall smelled like meatballs and marinara.

I gave him the silent question look.

"Stopped by to say hello," Morelli said, getting to his feet.

My gaze dropped to the bag.

Morelli grinned. "Dinner."

"Smells good."

"Meatball subs from Pino's. They're still hot. I just got here."

Ordinarily I wouldn't let Morelli into my apartment, but it would be a sin against everything holy to turn away Pino's meatballs.

I unlocked the door, and Morelli followed me in. I dumped my shoulder bag on the small hall table and swung into the kitchen. I took two plates from the wall cabinet and set them on the counter. "I'm having a hard time believing this is entirely social."

"Maybe not entirely," Morelli said, close enough for me to feel his breath on the back of my neck. "I thought you might want a medical update on Maxine Nowicki's mother."

I put the subs on plates and divided up the tub of coleslaw. "Is it going to ruin my appetite?"

Morelli moved off to the fridge in search of beer. "She was scalped. Like in the old cowboy and Indian movies. Only in this case, not enough was removed to kill her."

"That's sick! Who would do such a thing?"

"Good question. Nowicki isn't saying."

I took the plates to the table. "What about prints on the knife?"

"None."

"Not even Mrs. Nowicki's?"

"Correct. Not even Mrs. Nowicki's."

I ate my sub and thought about this latest turn of events. Scalped. Yuk.

"You're looking for her daughter," Morelli said. Statement, not question.

"Yep."

"Think there could be a tie-in?"

"Two days ago I interviewed one of Maxine's friends from the diner. She had a big bandage on her hand. Said she'd whacked her finger off in a kitchen accident."

"What's this friend's name?"

"Margie something. Lives on Barnet. Works the dinner shift at the Silver Dollar."

"Any other mutilations I should know about?"

I tried some of the coleslaw. "Nope. That's it. It's been a slow week."

Morelli watched me. "You're holding something back."

"What makes you say that?"

"I can tell."

"You can tell nothing."

"You're still mad at me for not calling."

"I am *not mad!*" I slammed my fist down on the table, making my beer bottle jump in place.

"I *meant* to call," Morelli said.

I stood and gathered the empty plates and the silverware. *CRASH, clang, clang!* "You are a dysfunctional human being."

"Oh yeah? Well, you're fucking frightening."

"Are you saying you're afraid of me?"

"Any man in his right mind would be afraid of you. You know that scarlet letter thing? You should have a tattoo on your forehead that says 'Dangerous Woman. Stand Back!' "

I stormed into the kitchen and slapped the dishes onto the countertop. "I happen to be a very nice person." I turned on him and narrowed my eyes. "What's so dangerous about me?"

"Lots of things. You have that look. Like you want to pick out kitchen curtains."

"I do *not* have that look!" I shouted. "And if I did it would *not* be for *your* kitchen curtains!"

Morelli backed me into the refrigerator. "And then there's the way you make my heart beat fast when you get excited like this." He leaned into me and kissed the curve of my ear. "And your hair . . . I love your hair." He kissed me again. "Dangerous hair, babe."

Oh boy.

His hands were at my waist and his knee slid between mine.

"Dangerous body." His lips skimmed my mouth. "Dangerous lips."

This wasn't supposed to be happening. I had decided against this. "Listen, Morelli, I appreciate the meatball sub and all, but . . ."

"Shut-up, Stephanie."

And then he kissed me. His tongue touched mine, and I thought, Well, what the hell, maybe I am dangerous. Maybe this isn't such a bad idea. After all, there was a time when I'd wanted nothing more than a Morelli-induced orgasm. Well, here was my chance. It wasn't as if we were strangers. It wasn't as if I didn't *deserve* it.

"Maybe we should go into the bedroom," I said. Get away from sharp knives in case something goes wrong and I'm tempted to stab him.

Morelli was wearing jeans with a navy T-shirt. Under the drape of the T-shirt he was wearing a pager and a .38. He unclipped his pager and put it in the refrigerator. He threw the bolt on the front door and kicked his shoes off in the hall.

"What about the gun?" I asked.

"The gun stays. Nothing's stopping me this time. You change your mind, and I'll shoot you."

"Um, there's the issue of safety."

He had his hand on his zipper. "Okay, I'll leave it on the night-stand."

"I wasn't talking about the gun."

Morelli stopped the progress of the zipper. "You're not on the pill?"

"No." I didn't think sex once a millennium warranted it.

"What about . . ."

"I haven't got any of them, either."

"Shit," Morelli said.

"Nothing in your wallet?"

"You're going to find this hard to believe, but cops aren't required to carry emergency condoms."

"Yes, but . . ."

"I'm not eighteen years old. I no longer score with nine out of ten women I meet."

That was encouraging. "I don't suppose you'd want to tell me the current ratio?"

"Right now, it's zero for zero."

"We could try a plastic sandwich bag."

Morelli grinned. "You want me bad."

"Temporary insanity."

The grin widened. "I don't think so. You've wanted me for years. You've never gotten over having me touch you when you were six."

I felt my mouth drop open and instantly closed it with a snap, leaning forward, hands fisted to keep from strangling him. "You are such a jerk!"

"I know," Morelli said. "It's genetic. Good thing I'm so cute."

Morelli was many things. Cute wasn't one of them. Cocker spaniels were cute. Baby shoes were cute. Morelli wasn't cute. Morelli could look at water and make it boil. Cute was much too mild an adjective to describe Morelli.

He reached out and tugged at my hair. "I'd run to the store, but I'm guessing your door would be locked when I got back."

"It's a good possibility."

"Well, then I guess there's only one thing to do."

I braced myself.

FOUR

MORELLI PADDED into the living room and picked up the channel changer. "We can watch the ball game. The Yankees are playing. You got any ice cream?"

It took me a full sixty seconds to find my voice. "Raspberry Popsicles."

"Perfect."

I'd been replaced by a raspberry Popsicle, and Morelli didn't look all that unhappy. I, on the other hand, wanted to smash something. Morelli was right . . . I wanted him bad. He might have been right about the curtains too, but I didn't want to dwell on the curtains. Lust I could manage, but the very thought of wanting a relationship with Morelli made my blood run cold.

I handed him his Popsicle and sat in the overstuffed armchair, not trusting myself to share the couch, half afraid I'd go after his leg like a dog in heat.

Around nine-thirty I started looking at my watch. I was thinking about the clue under Mrs. Nowicki's porch, and I was wondering how I was going to get it. I could borrow a rake from my parents. Then I could extend the handle with something. I'd probably have to use a flashlight, and I'd have to work fast because people were bound to see the light. If I waited until two in the morning the chances of someone being up to see me were greatly reduced. On the other hand, a flashlight beam at two in the morning was much more suspicious than a flashlight beam at ten at night.

"Okay," Morelli said, "what's going on? Why do you keep looking at your watch?"

I yawned and stretched. "Getting late."

"It's nine-thirty."

"I go to bed early."

Morelli made tsk, tsk, tsk sounds. "You shouldn't fib to a cop."

"I have things to do."

"What sort of things?"

"Nothing special. Just . . . things."

There was a knock at the door, and we both glanced in the direction of the sound.

Morelli looked at me speculatively. "You expecting someone?"

"It's probably old Mrs. Bestler from the third floor. Sometimes she forgets where she lives." I put my eye to the security peephole. "Nope. Not Mrs. Bestler." Mrs. Bestler didn't have big red hair like Little Orphan Annie. Mrs. Bestler didn't wear skin-tight black leather. Mrs. Bestler's breasts weren't in the shape of ice-cream cones.

I turned back to Morelli. "I don't suppose I could get you to wait in the bedroom for a moment or two . . ."

"Not on your life," Morelli said. "I wouldn't miss this for anything."

I threw the bolt and opened the door.

"I don't know why I'm doing this," Sally said. "I'm like sucked into this bounty hunter trip."

"The excitement of the chase," I said.

"Yeah. That's it. It's the fucking chase." He held a jar out to me. "I went back and got the clue. Borrowed one of those long-handled duster things. I decoded the note, but I don't know what it means."

"Weren't there people around, wondering what you were doing?"

"When you look like this nobody asks. They're all happy as shit I'm not close-dancing on their front lawn with Uncle Fred." He lifted his chin a fraction of an inch and gave Joe the once-over. "Who's this?"

"This is Joe Morelli. He was just leaving."

"No I wasn't," Morelli said.

Sally stepped forward. "If she says you're leaving then I think you're leaving."

Morelli rocked back on his heels and grinned. "You gonna make me?"

"You think I can't?"

"I think somebody should help you pick out a bra. This year the rounded look is in."

Sally looked down at his ice-cream cones. "They're my trade-mark. I'm making a fucking fortune off these babies." He looked up and sucker-punched Morelli in the gut.

"Oof," Morelli said. Then he narrowed his eyes and lunged at Sally.

"No!" I yelped, jumping between them.

There was some close-in scuffling. I got clipped on the chin and went down like a sack of sand. Both men stooped to pick me up.

"Back off," I yelled, slapping them away. "Don't either of you touch me. I don't need help from you two infantile morons."

"He insulted my breasts," Sally said.

"That's what happens when you have breasts," I shouted. "People insult them. Get used to it."

Joe glared at Sally. "Who are you? And what's with this jar?"

Sally extended his hand. "Sally Sweet."

Joe took the offered hand. "Joe Morelli."

They stood like that for a moment or two, and I saw a red flush begin to creep into Sally's cheeks. The cords in Morelli's neck grew prominent. Their hands remained clasped and their bodies jerked in rigid struggle. The morons were arm wrestling.

"That does it," I said. "I'm getting my gun. And I'm going to shoot the winner."

Eyes slid in my direction.

"Actually, I've gotta run," Sally said. "I've got a gig at the shore tonight, and Sugar's waiting in the car."

"He's a musician," I told Morelli.

Morelli took a step backward. "It's always a treat to meet Stephanie's friends."

"Yeah," Sally said, "my fucking pleasure."

Morelli was grinning when I closed and locked the door. "You never disappoint me," he said.

"What was that wrestling match about?"

"We were playing." He glanced down at the jar. "Tell me about this."

"Maxine Nowicki has been leaving clues for Eddie Kuntz. Sort of a revenge-driven scavenger hunt. The clues are always in code. That's where Sally comes in. He's good at cracking codes." I opened the jar, removed the paper and read the message. "'Our spot. Wednesday at three.'"

"They have a spot," Morelli said. "Makes me feel all romantic again. Maybe I should make a fast run to the drugstore."

"Suppose you went to the drugstore. How many would you buy? Would you buy one? Would you buy a month's worth? Would you buy a whole case?"

"Oh boy," Morelli said. "This is about curtains, isn't it?"

"Just want to get the rules straight."

"How about we live one day at a time."

"One day at a time is okay," I said. I suppose.

"So if I go to the drugstore you'll let me back in?"

"No. I'm not in the mood." In fact, I was suddenly feeling damn cranky. And for some unknown reason the image of Terry Gilman kept popping up in my mind.

Morelli ran a playful finger along my jawbone. "Bet I could change your mood."

I crossed my arms over my chest and looked at him slitty eyed. "I don't think so."

"Hmmm," Morelli said, "maybe not." He stretched, and then he sauntered into the kitchen and retrieved his pager from the refrigerator. "You're in a bad mood because I wouldn't commit to a case."

"Am not! I absolutely would *not* want a case commitment!"

"You're cute when you lie."

I pointed stiff-armed to the door. "Out!"

THE FOLLOWING MORNING, I could have called Eddie Kuntz and told him the newest message, but I wanted to talk to him face-to-face. Maxine Nowicki's apartment had been ransacked, and two people connected to her had been mutilated. I was thinking maybe someone wanted to find her for something other than love letters. And maybe that someone was Eddie Kuntz.

Kuntz was washing his car when I drove up. He had a boom box on the curb, and he was listening to shock jock radio. He stopped when he saw me and shut the radio off.

"You find her?"

I gave him the note with the translation. "I found another message."

He read the message and made a disgusted sound. "'Our spot,'" he said. "What's that supposed to mean?"

"You didn't know you had a spot?"

"We had lots of spots. How am I supposed to know which spot she's talking about?"

"Think about it."

Eddie Kuntz stared at me, and I thought I caught a hint of rubber burning.

"She's probably talking about the bench," he said. "The first time we met was in the park, and she was sitting on a bench, looking at the water. She was always talking about that bench like it was some kind of shrine or something."

"Go figure."

Kuntz gave me a hands-up. "Women."

A Lincoln Town Car eased to the curb. Navy exterior, tinted windows, half a block long.

"Aunt Betty and Uncle Leo," Eddie said.

"Big car."

"Yeah. I borrow it sometimes to pick up a few extra bucks."

I wasn't sure if he meant driving people around or running people over. "I have your occupation listed as cook, but you seem to be home a lot."

"That's because I'm between jobs."

"When was your last job as a cook?"

"I dunno. This morning. I toasted a waffle. What's it to you?"

"Curious."

"Try being curious about Maxine."

Aunt Betty and Uncle Leo walked up to us.

"Hello," Aunt Betty said. "Are you Eddie's new girlfriend?"

"Acquaintance," I told her.

"Well, I hope you turn into a girlfriend. You're Italian, right?"

"Half Italian. Half Hungarian."

"Well, nobody's perfect," she said. "Come in and have some cake. I got a nice pound cake at the bakery."

"Gonna be another scorcher today," Uncle Leo said. "Good thing we got air."

"You got air," Kuntz said. "My half doesn't have air. My half's hotter'n hell."

"I gotta get in," Uncle Leo said. "This heat is murder."

"Don't forget about the cake," Betty said, following Leo up the steps. "There's cake any time you want it."

"So you're doing other stuff to find Maxine, right?" Kuntz asked. "I mean, you're not just waiting for these clues, are you?"

"I've been going through the list of names and businesses you gave me. The manager of the Seven-Eleven said Maxine stopped by Sunday night. So far, no one else has seen her."

"Christ, she's here all the time leaving these stupid clues. Why doesn't someone see her? What is she, the freaking Phantom?"

"The manager of the Seven-Eleven said something that stuck in my mind. She said Maxine always used to buy a lottery ticket, but this time she said she didn't need to win the lottery anymore."

The line of Kuntz's mouth tightened. "Maxine's a lunatic. Who knows what she's thinking."

I suspected Eddie Kuntz knew exactly what Maxine was thinking.

"You need to be on that bench tomorrow at three," I told Kuntz. "I'll call you in the morning and make the final arrangements."

"I don't know if I like this. She pitched a rock into my window. There's no telling what she might do. Suppose she wants to snuff me?"

"Throwing a rock through a window doesn't equate with killing someone." I stared at him for a moment. "Does she have a reason for wanting to kill you?"

"I pressed charges against her. Is that a reason?"

"It wouldn't be for me." This loser wasn't worth doing time for. "Hard to say about Maxine."

I LEFT KUNTZ fiddling with his boom box. I'm not sure why I'd felt compelled to see him in person. I suppose I wanted to look him in the eye and learn if he'd scalped Maxine's mother. Unfortunately, in my experience, eyes are vastly overrated as pathways to the soul. The only thing I saw in Eddie Kuntz's eyes was last night's booze tally, which I could sum up as being too much.

I looped past Mrs. Nowicki's house and saw no sign of life. Her windows were closed shut. Shades were drawn. I parked the car and went to the door. No one answered my knock. "Mrs. Nowicki," I called out. "It's Stephanie Plum." I knocked again and was about to leave when the door opened a crack.

"Now what?" Mrs. Nowicki said.

"I'd like to talk."

"Lucky me."

"Can I come in?"

"No."

The entire top of her head was bandaged. She was without makeup and cigarette, and she looked old beyond her years.

"How's your head?" I asked.

"Been worse."

"I mean from the cut."

She rolled her eyes up. "Oh, that . . ."

"I need to know who did it."

"I did it."

"I saw the blood. And I saw the knife. And I know you didn't do this to yourself. Someone came looking for Maxine. And you ended up getting hurt."

"You want my statement? Go read it from the cops."

"Did you know someone visited Maxine's friend, Marjorie, and chopped off her finger?"

"And you think the same guy did both of us."

"It seems reasonable. And I think it would be better for Maxine if I found her before he does."

"Life is a bitch," Mrs. Nowicki said. "Poor Maxie. I don't know what she did. And I don't know where she is. What I know is that she's in a lot of trouble."

"And the man?"

"He said if I talked he'd come back and kill me. And I believe him."

"This is all in confidence."

"It don't matter. There's nothing I can tell you. There were two of them. I turned around and there they were in my kitchen. Average height. Average build. Wearing coveralls and stocking masks. Even had on those disposable rubber gloves like they wear in the hospital."

"How about their voices?"

"Only one spoke, and there wasn't anything to remember about it. Not old. Not young."

"Would you recognize the voice if you heard it again?"

"I don't know. Like I said, there wasn't anything to remember."

"And you don't know where Maxine is staying?"

"Sorry. I just don't know."

"Let's try it from another direction. If Maxine wasn't living in her apartment and didn't have to go to work every day . . . where would she go?"

"That's easy. She'd go to the shore. She'd go to get some ocean air and play the games on the boardwalk."

"Seaside or Point Pleasant?"

"Point Pleasant. She always goes to Point Pleasant."

This made sense. It accounted for the tan and the fact that she wasn't conducting business in Trenton.

I gave Mrs. Nowicki my card. "Call me if you hear from Maxine or think of anything that might be helpful. Keep your doors locked and don't talk to strangers."

"Actually, I've been thinking of going to stay with my sister in Virginia."

"That sounds like a good idea."

I TURNED LEFT onto Olden and caught a glimpse of a black Jeep Cherokee in my rearview mirror. Black Cherokees are popular in Jersey. They're not a car I'd ordinarily notice, but from somewhere in the recesses of my subconscious a mental abacus clicked in and told me I'd seen this car one time too many. I took Olden to Hamilton and Hamilton to St. James. I parked in my lot and looked around for the Cherokee, but it had disappeared. Coincidence, I said. Overactive imagination.

I ran up to my apartment, checked my answering machine, changed into my swimsuit, stuffed a towel, a T-shirt and some sunscreen into a canvas tote, pulled on a pair of shorts and took off for the shore.

The hole in my muffler was getting bigger, so I punched up the volume on Metallica. I reached Point Pleasant in less than an hour, then spent twenty minutes looking for cheap parking on the street.

I finally found a space two blocks back from the boardwalk, locked up and hooked the tote bag over my shoulder.

When you live in Jersey a beach isn't enough. People have energy in Jersey. They need things to do. They need a beach with a boardwalk. And the boardwalk has to be filled with rides and games and crappy food. Add some miniature golf. Throw in a bunch of stores selling T-shirts with offensive pictures. Life doesn't get much better than this.

And the best part is the smell. I've been told there are places where the ocean smells wild and briny. In Jersey the ocean smells of coconut-scented suntan lotion and Italian sausage smothered in fried onions and peppers. It smells like deep-fried zeppoles and chili hot dogs. The scent is intoxicating and exotic as it expands in the heat rising from crowds of sun-baked bodies strolling the boardwalk.

Surf surges onto the beach and the sound is mingled with the rhythmic *tick, tick, tick* of the spinning game wheels and the high-pitched *Eeeeeeee* of thrill seekers being hurtled down the log flume.

Rock stars, pickpockets, homies, pimps, pushers, pregnant women in bikinis, future astronauts, politicians, geeks, ghouls, and droves of families who buy American and eat Italian all come to the Jersey shore.

When I was a little girl, my sister and I rode the carousel and the whip and ate cotton candy and frozen custard. I had a stomach like iron, but Valerie always got sick on the way home and threw up in the car. When I was older, the shore was a place to meet boys. And now I find myself here on a manhunt. Who would have thought?

I stopped at a frozen custard stand and flashed Maxine's photo. "Have you seen her?"

No one could say for sure.

I worked my way down the boardwalk, showing the picture, distributing my cards. I ate some french fries, a piece of pizza, two chunks of fudge, a glass of lemonade and a vanilla-and-orangeswirl ice-cream cone. Halfway down the boardwalk I felt the pull of the white sand beach and gave up the manhunt in favor of perfecting my tan.

You have to love a job that lets you lie on the beach for the better part of the afternoon.

THE LIGHT was frantically blinking on my answering machine when I got home. If I had more than three messages my machine always went hyper. Blink, blink, blink, blink—faster than Rex could twitch his whiskers.

I accessed the messages and all were blank. "No big deal," I said to Rex. "If it's important, they'll call back."

Rex stopped running on his wheel and looked at me. Rex went nuts over blank messages. Rex had no patience to wait for people to call back. Rex had a problem with curiosity.

The phone rang, and I snatched it up. "Hello."

"Is this Stephanie?"

"Yes."

"This is Sugar. I don't suppose Sally is with you."

"No. I haven't seen Sally all day."

"He's late for dinner. He told me he'd be home, but he isn't here. I thought maybe he was off doing some bounty hunter thing since that's all he talks about anymore."

"Nope. I worked alone today."

I OPENED the curtains in my bedroom and looked out across the parking lot. It was mid-morning and already the heat was shimmering on the blacktop. A dog barked on Stiller Street, behind the lot. A screen door banged open and closed. I squinted in the direction of the barking dog and spotted a black Jeep Cherokee parked two houses down on Stiller.

No big deal, I said to myself, lots of people drive black Jeep Cherokees. Still, I'd never seen a Cherokee there before. And it really did remind me of the car that had been tailing me. Best to check it out.

I was wearing cut-off jeans and a green Big Dog T-shirt. I stuck my .38 into the waistband of the jeans and pulled the shirt over the gun. I walked around like this for a few minutes, trying to get used to the idea of carrying, but I felt like an idiot. So I took the gun out and returned it to its place in the brown bear cookie jar.

I rode the elevator to the small lobby, exited from the front entrance and walked one block down St. James. I hung a left at the corner, continued on for two blocks, turned and came up behind the Cherokee. The windows were tinted, but I could see a shadowy form at the wheel. I crept closer and knocked on the driver's-side window. The window rolled down and Joyce Barnhardt smiled out at me.

"Ciao," Joyce said.

"What the hell do you think you're doing?"

"I'm staking you out. What does it look like I'm doing?"

"I suppose there's a reason?"

Joyce shrugged. "We're both after the same person. I thought it wouldn't hurt to see what pathetic attempts you've made to find her . . . before I take over and get the job done."

"We aren't after the same person. That simply isn't done. Vinnie would never give the same case to two different agents."

"A lot you know."

I narrowed my eyes.

"Vinnie didn't think you were making any progress, so he gave Maxine Nowicki to me."

"I don't believe you."

Joyce held her contract up for me to see. "Authorized by the Vincent Plum Agency to apprehend Maxine Nowicki . . .," she read.

"We'll see about this!"

Joyce made a pouty kissy face.

"And stop following me!"

"It's a free country," Joyce said. "I can follow you if I want to."

I huffed off, back to my building. I stomped upstairs, got my keys and my shoulder bag, stomped back downstairs and gunned the CRX out of the lot . . . with Joyce close on my back bumper.

I didn't bother to lose her. I turned onto Hamilton and in less than five minutes was at the office. Joyce parked half a block back and stayed in her car while I stormed through the front door.

"Where is he? Where is that miserable little worm?"

"Uh oh," Lula said. "Been there, done that."

"Now what?" Connie said.

"Joyce Barnhardt, that's what. She showed me a contract authorizing her to bring in Maxine Nowicki."

"That's impossible," Connie said. "I issue all the contracts, and I don't know anything about it. And besides, Vinnie never gives out an FTA to two different agents."

"Yeah, but remember that Joyce person came in real early on Tuesday morning," Lula said. "And she and Vinnie were locked in his office together for almost an hour, and they were making those weird barnyard sounds."

"I forgot my gun again," I said.

"I got a gun," Connie said, "but it isn't going to do you any good. Vinnie went to North Carolina yesterday to pick up a jumper. He should be back the end of the week."

"I can't work like this," I said. "She's in my way. She's following me around."

"I can fix that," Lula said. "Where is she? I'll go talk to her."

"She's in the black Cherokee, but I don't think that's a good idea."

"Don't worry about nothing," Lula said, swinging through the door. "I'll be real diplomatic. You wait here."

Lula, diplomatic?

"Lula," I yelled, "come back here. I'll take care of Joyce Barnhardt."

Lula reached the car and was standing by the curbside rear quarter panel. "This the one?" she called to me.

"Yes, but . . ."

Lula pulled a gun out from under her T-shirt and—BANG!

She blew a cantaloupe-sized hole in Joyce's back tire. She had the gun back under the shirt by the time Joyce got out of the car.

Joyce saw the tire and her mouth dropped open.

"Did you see that?" Lula asked Joyce. "A guy came by here and shot up your tire. And then fast as anything, he ran away. I don't know what this world is coming to."

Joyce looked from Lula to the tire and from Lula to the tire, all the while her mouth still open but no words coming out.

"Well, I gotta get back to work," Lula said, turning her back on Joyce, walking back to the office.

"I can't believe you did that!" I said to Lula. "You can't just go around shooting out people's tires!"

"Look again," Lula said.

Connie was at her desk. "Anybody want to go to Mannie's for lunch today? I'm in a pasta mood."

"I have to follow up on a lead," I told her.

"What kind of lead?" Lula wanted to know. "There gonna be action? If there is, I want to go along, because I'm in an action mood now."

Truth is, I could use another person to keep an eye out for Maxine. I'd have preferred Ranger, but that was going to be awkward with Lula standing in front of me, hankering after action.

"No action," I said. "This is a boring lead. Very boring."

"It's about Maxine, isn't it? Oh boy, this is gonna be great. That body we found last time was almost dead. Maybe this time we'll hit the jackpot."

"We'll need to take your car," I said to Lula. "If there's a takedown we can't all fit in my CRX."

"Fine by me," Lula said, retrieving her purse from a file drawer. "I got air in my car. And another advantage, my car's parked out back, so we don't have to put on our sympathy face to Joyce, being that she's got a flat tire and we don't. Where we going anyway?"

"Muffet Street. North Trenton."

"I STILL DON'T LIKE THIS," Kuntz said. "Maxine is crazy. Who knows what she'll do. I'm gonna feel like a sitting duck out there."

Lula was standing behind me on Kuntz's porch. "Probably just another dumb-ass note taped to the bottom of the bench. Think you should stop your whining," she said to Kuntz, "on account of it makes you look like a wiener. And with a name like Kuntz you gotta be careful what you look like."

Eddie cut his eyes to Lula. "Who's this?"

"I'm her partner," Lula said. "Just like Starsky and Hutch, Cagney and Lacey, the Lone Ranger and What's-his-name."

Truth is, we were more like Laurel and Hardy, but I didn't want to share that information with Kuntz.

"We'll be in place ahead of time," I said. "Don't worry if you don't see us. We'll be there. All you have to do is show up and go sit on the bench and wait."

"What if there's trouble?"

"Wave your arms if you need help. We won't be that far away."

"You know which bench, right?"

"The bench next to the flagpole."

"Yeah. That's the one."

Betty stuck her head out next door. "Hello, dear. Isn't it a lovely day? Are you young people planning some sort of activity? If I was your age I'd go on a picnic today."

"We're working today," Lula said. "We got a big lead to follow up on."

"Betty," Leo yelled from deep in the house, "where's my coffee cake? I thought you were bringing me a piece of coffee cake."

Betty pulled her head in and closed the door, shutting off the flow of cold air.

"Nosy old bag," Kuntz said. "You can't do nothing around here without her knowing it."

"Why do you stay if you dislike it so much?"

"Cheap rent. I get a break because I'm family. Betty's my mother's sister."

"YOU KNOW what we need?" Lula said, sliding behind the wheel, buckling herself in. "We need some disguises. I bet Maxine knows what you look like by now. And the way I remember that part of the park, there aren't a lot of places to hide. We're gonna have to hide out in the open. We're gonna need some disguises."

I'd been thinking similar thoughts. Not that we needed disguises but that we were going to have a hard time making ourselves invisible.

"I know just the place to get a good disguise, too," Lula said. "I know where we can get wigs and everything."

Twenty minutes later we were standing outside the door to Sally's condo.

"This feels a little weird," I said.

"You know someone else who's got wigs?"

"I don't need a wig. I can stuff my hair up under a ball cap."

Lula rolled her eyes. "Oh yeah, that's gonna fool a lot of people."

The door opened and Sally looked out at us. His eyes were bloodshot, and his hair was standing on end.

"Yikes," Lula said.

"What's the matter? This the first time you've seen a hungover transvestite?"

"Not me," Lula said. "I've seen lots of 'em."

Lula and I followed him into the living room. "We have a strange sort of favor to ask," I said. "We need to go on a stakeout this afternoon, and I'm worried about being recognized. I thought you could help me with a disguise."

"Who do you want to be . . . Barbarella, Batgirl, the fucking slut next door?"

FIVE

"MAYBE I COULD just borrow a wig," I said to Sally.

He ambled off to the bedroom. "What do you want? Farrah? Orphan Annie? Elvira?"

"Something that won't attract attention."

He returned with a blond wig and held it out for approval. "This is from my Marilyn collection. Very popular with older men who like to be spanked."

I was thinking *Yuk,* but Lula looked like she was filing it away in case she decided to return to her former profession.

Sally pinned my hair back and tugged the wig on. "Needs something."

"Needs Marilyn lips," Lula said. "Can't have Marilyn hair without Marilyn lips."

"I don't know how to do lips," Sally said. "Sugar always does my lips. And Sugar isn't here. We sort of had a fight, and he went off in a snit."

"You two fight a lot?" Lula asked.

"Nope. Never. Sugar's real easy to live with. He's just a little nerdy, you know. Like, he thinks I shouldn't be hanging out with you because it's too dangerous. That's what we had the fight about."

"Jeez," I said. "I don't want to come between you and your roommate."

"No problem, man. Sugar's cool. He's just one of those worry-wart motherfuckers." Sally opened a professional-size makeup case. "Here's lots of shit if you know how to use it."

I choose candy-apple-pink lipstick and made big, glossy, pouty lips.

Sally and Lula stood back and did the take-a-look thing.

"Gotta lose the shoes," Lula said. "Never gonna get away with those lips and that hair and those shoes."

Sally agreed. "The shoes aren't Marilyn."

"I saw these great shoes at Macy's," Lula said. "They'd be perfect."

"No! I'm not going to Macy's. I want to get to the park early, so we can hang out and watch for Maxine."

"Only take a minute," Lula said. "You'd go bonkers over these shoes."

"No. And that's final."

"Just let me put some lip gloss on and I'll be ready to go," Sally said.

Lula and I sent each other a look that said, Uh oh.

Sally paused with lip gloss in hand. "You didn't think you were going to leave me here, did you?"

"Well, yeah," I said.

"This is bounty hunter shit," Lula said. "And you don't know any bounty hunter shit."

"I know other kinds of shit. And beside, I don't think you know a big fucking bunch of bounty hunter shit, either."

I was staring at the wall, and I was thinking it might feel good to run full tilt and bash my head against it. "Stop! We'll *all* go. We'll *all* pretend to be bounty hunters."

Sally turned to the hall mirror and smeared lip gloss on his lips. "Sugar gave me this cool cherry-tasting shit to use on my lips. He says I've got to keep my lips from getting chapped so my lipstick goes on nice and smooth. I'm telling you, this woman stuff is complicated."

He was wearing leather sandals, cut-offs that were so short he had cheek showing, a sleeveless T-shirt and a two-day beard.

"Not sure you totally got the hang of this woman stuff," Lula said. "Think maybe you'd do better shaving your ass than worrying about lip shit."

IT WAS a little after one when we got to the park.

"Those shoes make all the difference," Lula said, staring down at my new shoes. "Didn't I tell you those shoes were the shit?"

"Slut shoes," Sally said. "Retro fucking slut."

Great. Just what I needed, another pair of retro slut shoes— and an extra $74 on my Macy's charge card.

We were sitting in the parking lot, and directly in front of us was a large man-made lake. A jogging path circled the lake, sometimes snaking through patches of trees. A snack bar and rest rooms were in a cinder-block building to our right. To the left was an open field with swing sets and wooden structures for climbing. Benches had been placed at the water's edge but were empty at this time of day. The park saw more use in early evening when the temperature dropped. Seniors came to watch the sunset and families came to feed the ducks and play children's games.

"Kuntz will be sitting on the bench by the flagpole," I said. "Instructions were that he should be there at three."

"I bet she pops him," Sally said. "Why else would you set someone up like that?"

I didn't think there was much chance that Maxine would pop him. The bench was too exposed. And there were no good escape routes. I didn't suppose Maxine was a rocket scientist, but I didn't think she was entirely stupid, either. It looked to me like Maxine was playing with Eddie Kuntz. And it looked to me like she was the only one who thought the game was funny.

I passed the photo of Maxine around. "This is what she looks like," I said. "If you see her, grab her and bring her to me. I'll be covering the area between the snack bar and the car. Lula, you take the playground. Sally, I want you to sit on the bench by the boat ramp. Keep your eye out for snipers." I did a mental eye roll on this one. "And watch that no one rushes Kuntz after he sits down."

Not only had Sally and Lula talked me into buying platform sandals with strappy tie things halfway up my calf, they'd also managed to get me to trade my shorts for a black stretch miniskirt. It was an excellent disguise except for the fact that I couldn't run, sit or bend.

At two o'clock a couple of women arrived and took off jogging. Not Maxine. I walked down to the snack bar and bought a bag of popcorn to feed to the ducks. Two older men did the same. A few more joggers showed up. Men, this time. I fed the ducks and waited. Still no sign of Maxine. Lula was sitting on a swing, filing her nails. Sally had stretched out on the ground behind his bench and appeared to be sleeping. Do I have a team, or what?

For as long as I'd been there, no one had approached the bench by the pole. I'd inspected it from top to bottom when I'd first arrived and found nothing unusual. One of the joggers had returned from his run and sat two benches down, unlacing his shoes and drinking from a water bottle.

Kuntz arrived at 2:55 and went straight to the bench.

Lula looked up from her filing, but Sally didn't move a muscle. Kuntz stood at the bench for a moment. He paced away from it. Nervous. Didn't want to sit down. He looked around, spotted me at the snack bar and silently mouthed something that looked like "Holy shit."

I had a short panic attack, fearing he'd come over to me, but then he turned and slouched onto the bench.

A black Jeep Cherokee rolled into the lot and parked next to Kuntz's Blazer. I didn't need a crystal ball to figure this one out. Joyce had followed Kuntz. Not much I could do about that now. I watched the car for a while but there was no action. Joyce was sitting tight.

Ten minutes ticked by. Fifteen minutes. Twenty. Nothing was happening. The park population had increased, but no one was approaching Kuntz, and I didn't see Maxine. Two guys carrying a cooler chest walked toward the water. They stopped and spoke to the jogger who was still sitting on the bench near Kuntz. I saw the jogger shake his head no. The two guys exchanged glances. There was a brief discussion between them. Then one of the guys opened the chest, took out a pie and smushed it into the jogger's face.

The jogger jumped to his feet. "Jesus Christ!" he shrieked. "What are you nuts?"

Lula was off the swing and moving in. Joyce ran down from the parking lot. Kuntz edged off his bench. Even Sally was on his feet.

Everyone converged on the jogger, who had one of the pie guys by the shirt. People were yelling "Break it up" and "Stop" and trying to untangle the two men.

"I was only doing my job!" the pie guy was saying. "Some lady told me to get the guy sitting on the bench by the fountain."

I glared at Eddie Kuntz. "You dunce! You were on the wrong bench!"

"The fountain, the flagpole . . . how am I supposed to keep track of these things?"

The aluminum pie plate and globs of chocolate cream pie were lying ignored on the ground. I fingered through the remains and found the scrap of paper, tucked into a plastic bag. I stuffed the bag, chocolate globs and all, into my purse.

"What's that?" Joyce said. "What did you just put in your purse?"

"Pie crust. I'm taking it home for my hamster."

She grabbed at my shoulder strap. "I want to see it."

"Let go of that strap!"

"Not until I see what you put in your purse!"

"What's going on here?" Lula asked.

"Stay out of this, fatso," Joyce said.

"Fatso," Lula said, eyes narrowed. "Who you calling fatso?"

"I'm calling *you* fatso, you big tub of lard."

Lula reached out to Joyce, Joyce made a squeak, her eyes went blank, and she crashed to the ground.

Everyone turned to Joyce.

"Must have fainted," Lula said to the crowd. "Guess she's one of those women can't stand to see men fighting."

"I saw that!" I said to Lula, keeping my voice low. "You zapped her with your stun gun!"

"Who me?"

"You can't do that! You can't zap someone just because they call you fatso!"

"Oh, excuse me," Lula said. "Guess I didn't understand that."

Joyce was coming around, making feeble movements in her arms and legs. "What happened?" she murmured. "Was I struck by lightning?"

Kuntz sidled up to me. "Like your disguise. Want to go out for a drink later?"

"No!"

"Try *me*," Sally said to Kuntz. "It's *my* wig. And I wouldn't look bad in that skirt, either."

"Jesus," Kuntz said to me. "Is he with you?"

"Damn right, I'm with her," Sally said. "I'm the fucking cryptographer. I'm part of the team."

"Some team," Kuntz said. "A fruit and a fatso."

Lula leaned forward. "First off, let me tell you something. I'm not a fatso. I happen to be a big woman." She reached into her purse and came out with the stun gun. "Second, how'd you like to have your brain scrambled, you dumb, overdeveloped gorrilla?"

"No!" I said. "No more brain scrambling."

"He called us names," Lula said. "He called Sally a fruit."

"Well, okay," I said. "Just this once, but then no more scrambling."

Lula looked at her stun gun. "Damn. I used all my juice. I got a low battery here."

Kuntz made a hands-in-the-air, I-give-up, I-hired-a-loser gesture and walked away. Several bystanders helped Joyce to her feet. And Lula and Sally and I retreated to the car.

"So what was it you and Joyce were squabbling about?" Lula wanted to know.

"I got another clue. As soon as I saw the pie I knew it was supposed to be for Eddie Kuntz, and I figured there was a clue in it. Joyce saw me pick the clue up off the ground." I pulled the plastic bag from my purse. "Ta dah!" I sang.

"Hot dang!" Lula said. "You are *so* good."

"We're like the A-team," Sally said.

"Yeah, only the A-team didn't have no drag queen," Lula said.

"Mr. T liked jewelry," Sally said. "I could be Mr. T."

"Nuh uh. I want to be Mr. T on account of he was big and black like me."

Sally had taken the note out of the bag and was reading it. "This is interesting. She keeps changing the code. This is much more sophisticated than the others."

"Can you read it?"

"Hey, I'm the fucking code master. Just give me some time."

I PARKED in the lot to my apartment building and took the stairs to the second floor. Mrs. Delgado, Mr. Weinstein, Mrs. Karwatt and Leanne Kokoska were standing, staring at my door.

"Now what?" I asked.

"Someone left you a message," Mrs. Karwatt said. "I was going out with the garbage when I noticed it."

"It's a pip, too," Mrs. Delgado said. "Must be from one of them hoodlums you're out to get."

I stepped up and looked at the door. The message was scribbled in black marker: "I hate you! And I'll get even!"

"Who do you suppose did this?" Leanne asked. "Are you on a real dangerous case? You after a murderer or something?"

Truth is, I had no idea anymore who I was after.

"Permanent marker," Mr. Weinstein said. "Gonna be the devil to get off. Probably gonna have to paint over it."

"I'll call Dillon," I told them, shoving the key in the lock. "Dillon will fix it for me."

Dillon Ruddick was the super, and Dillon would fix anything for a smile and a beer.

I let myself into my apartment, and my neighbors went off looking for a new adventure. I slipped the safety chain into place, bolted my door and headed for the kitchen. The light was blinking on my answering machine. One message.

I punched Replay. "This is Helen Badijian, the manager at the Seven-Eleven." There was a pause and some fumbling. "You left your card here and said I should call if I had information about Miss Nowicki."

I dialed the 7-Eleven and Helen answered.

"I'm very busy now," she said. "If you could drop by later, maybe around ten, I think I might have something for you."

This was turning into a halfway decent day. Sally was working on the clue, and the 7-Eleven woman had a potential lead.

"We need to celebrate," I told Rex, trying to overlook the fact that I was actually very creeped out by the message on my door. "Pop-Tarts for everyone."

I looked in my cupboard, but there were no Pop-Tarts. No cookies, no cereal, no cans of spaghetti, no soup, no extra jars of peanut butter. A piece of paper was taped to the cupboard door. It was a shopping list. It said, "buy everything."

I took the note down and shoved it into my bag so I wouldn't forget what I needed and slung the bag over my shoulder. I had my hand on the doorknob when the phone rang.

It was Kuntz. "So, about that drink?"

"No. No drink."

"Your loss," he said. "I saw you fingering the pie on the ground. You find another note?"

"Yes."

"And?"

"And I'm working on it."

"Looks to me like we're not making much progress with the note crappola. All we ever get are more notes."

"There might be more. The manager at the Seven-Eleven called and said she had something for me. I'm going to stop around later tonight."

"Why later? Why don't you go now? Cripes, can't you move faster on this? I need those letters."

"Maybe you should tell me what this is really about. I'm having a hard time believing you're in this much of a sweat about a couple of love letters."

"I told you they could be embarrassing."

"Yeah, right."

I LOOKED in my shopping cart and wondered if I had everything. Ritz crackers and peanut butter for when I felt fancy and wanted to make hors d'oeuvres, Entenmann's coffee cake for PMS mornings, Pop-Tarts for Rex, salsa so I could tell my mother I was eating vegetables, frosted flakes in case I had to go on a stakeout, corn chips for the salsa.

I was in the middle of my inventory when a cart crashed nose to nose into mine. I looked up and found Grandma Mazur driving and my mother one step behind.

My mother closed her eyes. "Why me?" she said.

"Dang," Grandma Mazur said.

I was still in the wig and the little skirt. "I can explain."

"Where did I go wrong?" my mother wanted to know.

"I'm in disguise."

Mrs. Crandle rattled her cart down the aisle. "Hello, Stephanie, dear. How are you today?"

"I'm fine, Mrs. Crandle."

"Some disguise," my mother said. "Everybody knows you. And why do you have to be disguised as a tramp? Why can't you ever be disguised as a normal person?" She looked into my cart.

79

"Jars of spaghetti sauce. The checkout clerk will think you don't cook."

My left eye had started to twitch. "I have to go now."

"I bet this is a good getup for meeting men," Grandma said. "You look just like Marilyn Monroe. Is that a wig? Maybe I could borrow it sometime. I wouldn't mind meeting some men."

"You loan her that wig and anything happens, I'm holding you responsible," my mother said.

I UNPACKED my groceries, replaced the wig with a Rangers hat, traded the skirt in for a pair of shorts and resigned the retro slut shoes to a back corner of my closet. I shared a Pop-Tart with Rex and cracked a beer open for myself. I called Dillon to tell him about my door, and then I went out the bedroom window to my fire escape to think. The air was still and sultry, the horizon dusky. The parking lot was filled with cars. The seniors were all home at this time of day. If they went out to eat it was for the early bird special at the diner, and even if they went to the park to sit for a half hour they were home by six. If they were eating in it was at five o'clock so as not to interfere with *Wheel of Fortune* and *Jeopardy!*

Most cases I get from Vinnie are routine. Usually I go to the people who put up the bond and explain to them that they'll lose their house if the skip isn't found. Ninety percent of the time they know where the skip is and help me catch him. Ninety percent of the time I have a handle on the sort of person I'm dealing with. This case didn't fall into the ninety percent. And even worse, this case was weird. A friend had lost a finger, and a mother had been scalped. Maxine's treasure hunt seemed playful by comparison. And then there was the message on my door. "I hate you." Who would do such a thing? The list was long.

A pickup pulled away from the curb half a block away, exposing a black Jeep Cherokee which had been parked behind the pickup. Joyce.

I allowed myself the luxury of a sigh and drained the beer bottle. You had to respect Joyce's tenacity, if nothing else. I raised my bottle in a salute to her, but there was no response.

The problem with being a bounty hunter is it's all on-the-job training. Ranger is helpful, but Ranger isn't always around. So most of the time when something new comes up I end up doing it wrong before I figure out how to do it right. Joyce, for instance. Clearly, I don't know how to get rid of Joyce.

I crawled back through the window, got another bottle of beer and another Pop-Tart, stuffed the portable phone under my arm and went back to the fire escape. I ate the Pop-Tart and washed it down with beer and all the while I watched the black Cherokee. When I finished the second bottle of beer I called Ranger.

"Talk," Ranger said.

"I have a problem."

"So what's your point?"

I explained the situation to Ranger, including the tire and the park episode. There was a silence where I sensed he was smiling, and finally he said, "Sit tight, and I'll see what I can do."

Half an hour later, Ranger's $98,000 BMW rolled to a stop in my parking lot. Ranger got out of the car and stood for a moment staring at me on my fire escape. He was wearing an olive-drab T-shirt that looked like it had been painted on him, GI Joe camouflage pants and shades. Just a normal Jersey guy.

I gave him a thumbs-up.

Ranger smiled and turned and walked across the lot and across the street to the black Cherokee. He walked to the passenger-side door, opened the door and got in the car. Just like that. If it had been me in the car, the door would have been locked, and no one looking like Ranger would get in. But this is me, and that was Joyce.

Five minutes later, Ranger exited the car and returned to my lot. I dove through my window, rushed out the door, down the stairs and skidded to a stop in front of Ranger.

"Well?"

"How bad do you want to get rid of her? You want me to shoot her? Break a bone?"

"No!"

Ranger shrugged. "Then she's gonna stick."

There was the sound of a car engine catching and headlights flashed on across the street. We both turned to watch Joyce pull away and disappear around the corner.

"She'll be back," Ranger said. "But not tonight."

"How'd you get her to leave?"

"Told her I was gonna spend the next twelve hours ruining you for all other men, and so she might as well go home."

I could feel the heat rush to my face.

Ranger gave me the wolf smile. "I lied about it being tonight," he said.

AT LEAST Joyce was gone for a while, and I didn't have to worry about her following me to the 7-Eleven. I trudged upstairs to my apartment, made myself a peanut butter and Marshmallow Fluff sandwich on worthless white bread and channel surfed until it was time to go see Helen Badijian.

Most of the time I enjoyed my aloneness, relishing the selfish luxury of unshared space and ritual. Only *my* hand held the television remote, and there was no compromise on toilet paper brand or climate control. And even more, there was a tentative, hopeful feeling that I might be an adult. And that the worst of childhood was safely behind me. You see, I said to the world, I have my own apartment. That's good, right?

Tonight my satisfaction with the solitary life was tempered by a bizarre message still scrawled on my door. Tonight my aloneness felt lonely, and maybe even a little frightening. Tonight I made sure my windows were closed and locked when I left my apartment.

En route to Olden I did a two-block detour, checking my mirror for headlights. There'd been no sign of Joyce, but better to be safe than sorry. I had a feeling this was a good lead, and I didn't want to pass it on to the enemy.

I reached the 7-Eleven a few minutes before ten. I sat in my car a while to see if Joyce would miraculously appear. At 10:05 there was no Joyce, but from what I could see through the store's plate glass windows there was also no Helen Badijian. A young guy was behind the register, talking to an older man. The older man was waving his arms, looking royally pissed off. The young guy was shaking his head, yes, yes, yes.

I entered the store and caught the end of the conversation.

"Irresponsible," the older man was saying. "No excuse for it."

I wandered to the back and looked around. Sure enough. Helen wasn't here.

"Excuse me," I said to the clerk. "I thought Helen Badijian would be working tonight."

The clerk nervously looked from me to the man. "She had to leave early."

"It's important that I speak to her. Do you know where she can be reached?"

"Girlie, that's the hundred-dollar question," the older man said.

I extended my hand. "Stephanie Plum."

"Arnold Kyle. I own this place. I got a call about an hour ago from the cops telling me my store was unattended. Your friend Helen just walked out of here. No notice. No nothing. Didn't even have the decency to lock up. Some guy came in to buy cigarettes and called the cops when he figured out there was no one here."

I had a real bad feeling in my stomach. "Was Helen unhappy with her job?"

"Never said anything to me," Arnold said.

"Maybe she got sick and didn't have time to leave a note."

"I called her house. Nobody's seen her. I called the hospital. She isn't there."

"Have you looked everywhere in the store? A storage room? The cellar? Bathroom?"

"Checked all that out."

"Does she drive to work? Is her car still here?"

Arnold looked to the young guy.

"It's still here," the young guy said. "I parked next to it when I came in. It's a blue Nova."

"Must have gone off with one of her friends," Arnold said. "You can't trust anyone these days. No sense of responsibility. A good time comes along, and they kiss you good-bye."

I turned my attention to the clerk. "Any money missing?"

He shook his head no.

"Any sign of struggle? Anything knocked over?"

"I got here first," Arnold said. "And there wasn't anything. It looked like she just waltzed out of here."

I gave them my card and explained my relationship with Helen. We did a brief behind-the-counter search for a possible note, but nothing turned up. I thanked Arnold and the clerk and asked them to call if they heard from Helen. I had my hands on the counter, and I looked down and saw it. A book of matches from the Parrot Bar in Point Pleasant.

"Are these yours?" I asked the clerk.

"Nope," he said. "I don't smoke."

I looked at Arnold. "Not mine," he said.

"Do you mind if I snitch them?"

"Knock yourself out," Arnold said.

At the risk of seeming paranoid I checked my rearview mirror about sixty times on the way home. Not so much for Joyce, but for the guys who might have spooked or snatched Helen Badijian. A week ago, I'd have drawn the same conclusion as Arnold . . . that Helen took off. Now that I knew about chopped-off fingers and scalpings I took a more extreme view of events.

I parked in my lot, did a fast look around, inhaled a deep breath and bolted from my car. Across the lot, through the rear entrance, up the stairs to my apartment. The hate message was still on my door. I was breathing hard, and my hand was shaking so that it took concentration to get the key in the lock.

This is stupid, I told myself. Get a grip! But I didn't have a grip, so I locked myself in and checked under the bed, in the closets and behind the shower curtain. When I was convinced I was safe I ate the Entenmann's coffee cake to calm myself down.

When I was done with the cake I called Morelli and told him about Helen and asked him to check on her.

"Just exactly what did you have in mind?"

"I don't know. Maybe you could see if she's in the morgue. Or in the hospital, getting some missing body part sewed back on. Maybe you could ask some of your friends to keep an eye out for her."

"Probably Arnold's right," Morelli said. "Probably she's at a bar with a couple friends."

"You really think so?"

"No," Morelli said. "I was just saying that to get you off the phone. I'm watching a ball game."

"There's something that really bothers me here that I didn't tell you."

"Oh boy."

"Eddie Kuntz was the only one who knew I was going to see Helen Badijian."

"And you think he got to her first."

"It's crossed my mind."

"You know there was a time when I'd say to myself . . . How does she do it? How does she get mixed up with these weirdos? But now I don't even question it. In fact, I've come to expect such things of you."

"So are you going to help me, or what?"

SIX

I DIDN'T LIKE the idea that I might be responsible for Helen's disappearance. Morelli had agreed to make a few phone calls, but I still felt unsatisfied. I pulled the Parrot Bar matches out of my pocket and examined them. No hastily scribbled messages on the inside flap. For that matter, nothing to identify them as Maxine's. Nevertheless, first thing in the morning, I'd be on my way to Point Pleasant.

I went to the phone book and looked up Badijian. Three of them. No Helen. Two were in Hamilton Township. One was in Trenton. I called the Trenton number. A woman answered and told me Helen wasn't home from work yet. Easy. But not the right answer. I wanted Helen to be home.

Okay, I thought, maybe what I needed to do was go see for myself. Take a look in Kuntz's windows and see if he had Helen tied to a kitchen chair. I strapped on my black web utility belt and filled the pockets. Pepper spray, stun gun, handcuffs, flashlight, .38 Special. I thought about loading the .38 and decided against it. Guns creeped me out.

I shrugged into a navy windbreaker and scooped my hair up under my hat.

Mrs. Zuppa was coming in from bingo just as I was leaving the building. "Looks like you're going to work," she said, leaning heavily on her cane. "What are you packin'?"

"A thirty-eight."

"I like a nine-millimeter myself."

"A nine's good."

"Easier to use a semiautomatic after you've had hip replacement and you walk with a cane," she said.

One of those useful pieces of information to file away and resurrect when I turn eighty-three.

Traffic was light at this time of night. A few cars on Olden. No cars on Muffet. I parked around the corner on Cherry Street, a block down from Kuntz, and walked to his house. Downstairs lights were on in both halves. Shades were up. I stood on the sidewalk and snooped. Leo and Betty were feet up in side-by-side recliners watching Bruce Willis bleed on TV.

Next door, Eddie was talking on the phone. It was a portable, and I could see him pacing in his kitchen in the back of the house.

Neighboring houses were dark. Lights were on across the street, but there was no activity. I slipped between the houses, avoiding the squares of light thrown onto the grass from open windows, and crept in shadow to the back of Kuntz's house. Snatches of conversation drifted out to me. Yes, he loved her, Kuntz said. And yes, he thought she was sexy. I stood in deep shade and looked through the window. His back was to me. He was alone, and there were no whacked-off body parts lying on his kitchen table. No Helen chained to the stove. No unearthly screams coming from his cellar. The whole thing was damn disappointing.

Of course, Jeffrey Dahmer kept his trophies in his refrigerator. Maybe what I should do is go around front, knock on the door, tell Kuntz I was in the neighborhood and thought I'd stop in for that drink. Then I could look in his refrigerator when he went for ice.

I was debating this plan when a hand clamped over my mouth and I was dragged backward and pressed hard into the side of the house. I kicked out with my feet, and my heart was pounding in my chest. I got a hand loose and went for the pepper spray, and I heard a familiar voice whisper in my ear.

"If you're looking to grab something, I can do better than pepper spray."

"Morelli!"

"What the hell do you think you're doing?"

"I'm investigating. What does it look like I'm doing?"

"It looks like you're invading Eddie Kuntz's privacy." He pushed my jacket aside and stared down at my gun belt. "No grenades?"

"Very funny."

"You need to get out of here."

"I'm not done."

"Yes, you are," Morelli said. "You're done. I found Helen."

"Tell me."

"Not here." He took my hand and tugged me forward, toward the street.

The light over Eddie's back stoop went on, and the back screen door creaked open. "Somebody out here?"

Morelli and I froze against the side of the house.

A second door opened. "What is it?" Leo said. "What's going on?"

"Somebody's creeping around the house. I heard voices."

"Betty," Leo yelled, "bring the flashlight. Turn on the porch light."

Morelli gave me a shove. "Go for your car."

Keeping to the shadows, I ran around the neighboring duplex, cut back through the driveway and scuttled across yards, heading for Cherry. I scrambled over a four-foot-high chain-link fence, caught my foot on the cross section and sprawled facedown on the grass.

Morelli hoisted me up by my gun belt and set me in motion.

His pickup was directly behind my CRX. We both jumped in our cars and sped away. I didn't stop until I was safely in my own parking lot.

I slid from behind the wheel, locked my car and assumed what I hoped was a casual pose, leaning against the CRX, ignoring the fact that my knees were scraped and I had grass stains the entire length of my body.

Morelli sauntered over and stood back on his heels, hands in his pockets. "People like you give cops nightmares," he said.

"What about Helen?"

"Dead."

My breath caught in my chest. "That's terrible!"

"She was found in an alley four blocks from the Seven-Eleven. I don't know much except it looks like there was a struggle."

"How was she killed?"

"Won't know for sure until they do the autopsy, but there were bruises on her neck."

"Someone choked her to death?"

"That's what it sounds like." Morelli paused. "There's something else. And this is not public information. I'm telling you this so you'll be careful. Someone chopped her finger off."

Nausea rolled through my stomach, and I tried to pull in some oxygen. There was a monster out there . . . someone with a sick, twisted mind. And I'd unleashed him on Helen Badijian by involving her in my case.

"I hate this job," I said to Morelli. "I hate the bad people, and the ugly crimes, and the human suffering they cause. And I hate the fear. In the beginning, I was too stupid to be afraid. Now it seems like I'm always afraid. And if all that isn't bad enough, I've killed Helen Badijian."

"You didn't kill Helen Badijian," Morelli said. "You can't hold yourself responsible for that."

"How do you get through it? How do you go to work every day, dealing with all the bottom feeders?"

"Most people are good. I keep that in front of me so I don't lose perspective. It's like having a basket of peaches. Somewhere in the middle of the basket is a rotten peach. You find it and remove it. And you think to yourself, Well, that's just the way it is with

JANET EVANOVICH

peaches . . . good thing I was around to stop the rot from spreading."

"What about the fear?"

"Concentrate on doing the job, not on the fear."

Easy to say, hard to do, I thought. "I assume you came to Kuntz's house looking for me?"

"I called to give you the news," Morelli said, "and you weren't home. I asked myself if you'd be dumb enough to go after Kuntz, and the answer was yes."

"You think Kuntz killed Helen?"

"Hard to say. He's clean. Has no record. The fact that he knew you were seeing Helen might have no bearing on this at all. There could be someone out there working entirely independently, turning up the same leads you're turning up."

"Whoever they are, they're ahead of me now. They got to Helen."

"Helen might not have known much."

That was possible. Maybe all she had were the matches.

Morelli locked eyes with me. "You aren't going back after Kuntz, are you?"

"Not tonight."

SALLY CALLED while I was waiting for my morning coffee to finish dripping.

"The code was fun, but the message is boring," Sally said. " 'The next clue is in a box marked with a big red X.' "

"That's it? No directions to find the box?"

"Just what I read. You want the paper? It's sort of a mess. Sugar tidied the kitchen this morning and accidentally tossed the clue in the trash masher. I was lucky to find it."

"Is he still mad?"

"No. He's on one of his cleaning, cooking, interior decorating benders. He got up this morning and made scratch waffles, sausage patties, fresh squeezed orange juice, a mushroom omelet,

90

put a coffee cake in the oven, scoured the kitchen to within an inch of its life and took off to buy new throw cushions for the couch."

"Dang. I was afraid he might be upset because I borrowed the wig."

"Nope. He was all Mr. Congeniality this morning. Said you could borrow the wig anytime you wanted."

"What a guy."

"Yeah, and he makes a bitchin' waffle. I have rehearsal at ten in Hamilton Township. I can stop on my way and give you the clue."

I poured a mug of coffee and called Eddie Kuntz.

"She was here," he said. "The bitch was spying on me last night. I was on the phone, and I heard someone talking outside, so I ran out to look, but she got away. There were two of them. Maxine and someone else. Probably one of her wacky girlfriends."

"You sure it was Maxine?"

"Who else would it be?"

Me, that's who, you big dumb jerk. "I got the pie clue worked out. The next clue is coming in a box with a big red X on it. You have any boxes like that sitting on your lawn?"

"No. I'm looking out my front window, and I don't see any boxes."

"How about in back?"

"This is stupid. Clues and boxes and . . . Shit, I found the box. It's on my back stoop. What should I do?"

"Open the box."

"No way. I'm not opening this box. There could be a bomb in it."

"There's no bomb."

"How do you know?"

"It's not Maxine's style."

"Let me tell you about Maxine. Maxine has no style. Maxine's a nut case. You feel so confident about this box, you come over and open it."

"Fine. I'll come over and open it. Just leave it where it is, and I'll be there as soon as I can."

I finished my coffee and gave Rex some Cheerios for breakfast.

"Plan for the day," I said to Rex. "Wait for Sally to drop off the note. Next thing I drive over to Kuntz's house to open the box. Then I spend the rest of the day in Point Pleasant looking for Maxine. Is that a plan, or what?"

Rex rushed out of his soup can, stuffed all the Cheerios into his cheeks and rushed back into the soup can. So much for Rex.

I was debating if a second cup of coffee would give me heart palpitations when someone knocked on my door. I answered the knock and stared out at a flower delivery person, just about hidden behind a huge flower spray.

"Stephanie Plum?"

"Yes!"

"For you."

Wow. Flowers. I love getting flowers. I took the flowers and stepped back. And the flower person stepped forward into my apartment and leveled a gun at me. It was Maxine.

"Tsk, tsk, tsk," she said. "Fell for the old flower delivery routine. What'd you just get off the banana boat?"

"I knew it was you. I just wanted to talk to you, so I didn't let on."

"Yeah, right." She kicked the door closed and looked around. "Put the flowers on the kitchen counter and then stand facing the refrigerator, hands on the refrigerator door."

I did as she said, and she cuffed me to the fridge door handle.

"Now we're going to talk," she said. "This is the deal. Stop being such a pain in the ass and I'll let you live."

"Would you really shoot me?"

"In a heartbeat."

"I don't think so."

"Miss Know-it-all."

"What's with these clues?"

"The clues are for the jerk. I wanted to make him jump like he made me jump. But you had to come along, and now you do all his dirty work for him. What is it with this guy and women? How does he manage?"

"Well, I can't speak for anyone else, but I'm doing it for the money."

"I'm so stupid," she said. "I did it for free."

"There's something else going on here," I said. "Something serious. Do you know about your apartment being ransacked? Do you know about Margie and your mother?"

"I don't want to get into that. There's nothing I can do now. But I can tell you one thing. I'm going to get what's coming to me from that son of a bitch Eddie Kuntz. He's going to pay for everything he did."

"You mean like scalping your mother?"

"I mean like breaking my nose. I mean like all the times he got drunk and smacked me around. All the times he cheated on me. All the times he took my paycheck. And the lies about getting married. That's what he's going to pay for."

"He said you took some love letters that belong to him."

Maxine tipped her head back and laughed. It was a nice honest throaty laugh that would have been contagious if I hadn't been chained to my refrigerator. "That's what he told you? Boy, that's good. Eddie Kuntz writing love letters. You probably own stock in the Brooklyn Bridge, too."

"Listen, I'm just trying to do a job."

"Yeah, and I'm trying to have a life. This is my advice to you. Forget about trying to find me because it isn't going to happen. I'm only hanging around to have some fun with the jerk and then I'm out of here. Soon as I'm done yanking Kuntz's chain I'm gone."

"You have money to make you disappear?"

"More than God has apples. Now I'm going to tell you something about that box. It's filled with dog doody. I spent all day in the park, filling a plastic bag. The clue is in the doody in the plastic bag. I want the jerk to paw through that doody. And trust me, he wants to find me bad enough to do it. So back off and don't help him out."

I felt my lip involuntarily curl back. Dog doody. Ugh.

"That's all I have to say to you," Maxine said. "Go look for somebody else and stop helping the jerk."

"Are you the one who wrote on my door?"

She turned to leave. "No, but it's a pretty cool message."

"You're going to leave the key to the cuffs, aren't you?"

She looked at me and winked and waltzed away, closing the door behind her.

Damn! "I'm not the only one after you!" I yelled. "Watch out for that bitch Joyce Barnhardt!" Shit. She was getting away. I yanked at the cuffs, but they were secure. No knives or helpful kitchen utensils within reach. Phone too far away. I could yell until doomsday and Mr. Wolensky, across the hall, wouldn't hear me over his TV. Think, Stephanie. Think! "Help!" I yelled. "Help!"

No one came to help. After about five minutes of yelling and fuming I started to feel a headache coming on. So I stopped yelling, and I looked in the refrigerator for something that would stop a headache. Banana cream pie. There was some left from Saturday. I ate the pie and washed it down with milk. I was still hungry, so I ate some peanut butter and a bag of baby carrots. I was finishing up with the carrots when there was another knock at my door.

I went back to the yelling "Help!" routine.

The door swung open and Sally stuck his head in. "Fucking kinky," he said. "Who cuffed you to the fridge?"

"I had a little scuffle with Maxine."

"Looks like you lost."

"Don't suppose you saw her hanging out in the parking lot."

"Nope."

My biggest fear was that she'd gotten away, never to be found. My second biggest fear was that Joyce had nabbed her. "Go down to the basement and get Dillon, the super, and ask him to come up with his hacksaw."

Twenty minutes later I was still wearing a bracelet, but at least I was free of the refrigerator. Sally had left for rehearsal. Dillon was on his way downstairs with a six-pack under his arm. And I was late for an appointment with a box full of dog shit.

I barreled down the stairs and out the door. I started toward my car but pulled up short when Joyce rolled into the parking lot.

"Joyce," I said, "long time, no see." I peeked into her car, looking for Maxine. "You still following me?"

"Hell no. I have better things to do than to sit around all day waiting for someone to get hit with a pie. I came by to tell you good-bye."

"Giving up?"

"Getting smart. I don't need you to find Maxine."

"Oh yeah? Why is that?"

"I know where she's hiding. I have a contact who knows all about Maxine's transactions. Too bad you were never in retail like me. I made a lot of connections."

The driver's-side window rolled up, and Joyce roared out of the lot, down the street.

Great. Joyce has connections.

I crossed to the CRX and noticed that someone had left a note under my windshield wiper.

I said I'd get even and I meant it. I've been watching you and I know he was here. This is your last warning. Leave my boyfriend alone! Next time I soak something with gasoline I'll strike a match to it.

This was about somebody's boyfriend. And only one person came to mind. Morelli. Ugh! To think I almost went to bed with him. I squeezed my eyes shut. I fell for all that talk about no condoms and no sex. What was I thinking? I should have known better than to believe anything Morelli told me. And it wasn't hard to guess the girlfriend's name. Terry Gilman. This threat had mob written all over it. And Connie had said Terry was connected.

I sniffed at my car. Gasoline. I put my finger to the hood. It was still wet. Morelli's unhinged girlfriend must have just been here. Probably did this while I was chained to the refrigerator. No big deal, I thought. I'd run the CRX through a car wash.

I stuck the key in the door lock more out of force of habit than actual thought. The key didn't go through the usual turn, which meant the door wasn't locked. I looked closer and saw the scratches made next to the window. Someone had used a jimmy bar to pop the lock.

I had a premonition of bad news.

I did a fast peek in the window. Nothing seemed stolen. The radio looked intact. I opened the driver's side door and the gasoline smell almost knocked me to my knees. I put my hand to the seat. It was soaked. The floor mats were soaked. The dash was soaked. Gasoline pooled in nooks and crannies.

Shit! Goddamn Morelli. I was more angry at him than I was at Terry. I looked around the lot. No one there but me.

I whipped out my cell phone and started dialing. No answer at Morelli's house. No answer at his office number. No answer on his car phone. I kicked a tire and did some inventive swearing.

I was parked in a back corner of the lot with no cars in the immediate vicinity. It seemed to me the safest thing to do right now was to leave the car parked and let some of the gas evaporate away. I opened the windows wide, went back to the apartment building and called Lula at the office.

"I need a ride," I told Lula. "Car problems."

"OKAY, so tell me again about this box," Lula said, lining the Firebird up with the curb in front of Kuntz's house.

"Maxine says it's filled with dog doody, so we shouldn't touch it."

"You believe Maxine? Suppose it's a bomb?"

"I don't think it's a bomb."

"Yeah, but are you sure?"

"Well, no."

"I tell you what. I'm staying on the front porch while you open that box. I don't want to be anywhere near that box."

I walked around to the back of the house, and sure enough, there was the box, sitting on the stoop. The box was about a foot square. It was heavy cardboard, sealed up with tape, marked with a red X.

Kuntz was at the screen door. "Took you long enough."

"You're lucky we came at all," Lula said. "And if you don't change your attitude we're gonna leave. So what do you think of that?"

I crouched down and examined the box. Nothing ticking. Didn't smell like dog shit. No warning labels that said Dangerous Explosives. Truth is, anything could be in the box. Anything. Could be cooties left over from Desert Storm. "Looks okay to me," I said to Kuntz. "Go ahead and open it."

"You're sure it's safe?"

"Hey," Lula said, "we're trained professionals. We know about these things. Right, Stephanie?"

"Right."

Kuntz stared at the box. He cracked his knuckles and pulled his lips tight against his teeth. "Damn that Maxine." He took a Swiss army knife out of his pocket and bent to the box.

Lula and I discreetly stepped away from the stoop.

"You're sure?" he asked again, knife poised.

"Oh yeah." Another step backward.

Kuntz slit the tape, parted the flaps and peeked into the box. Nothing exploded, but Lula and I kept our distance all the same.

"What the hell?" Kuntz said, looking more closely. "What is this? Looks like a plastic bag sealed with one of those twisty tie things and filled with chocolate pudding."

Lula and I exchanged glances.

"I suppose the clue's in the bag," Kuntz said. He poked at the bag, his face contorted, and he uttered something that sound like "Ulk."

"Something wrong?" Lula asked.

"This isn't pudding."

"Well, look on the bright side," Lula said. "It didn't explode, did it?"

"Gosh, look at the time," I said, tapping my watch. "I'm going to have to run."

"Yeah, me too," Lula said. "I got things to do."

The color had drained from Kuntz's face. "What about the clue?"

"You can call me later, or you can leave it on the machine. Just read the letters off to me."

"But . . ."

Lula and I were gone. Around the side of the house. Into the Firebird. Down the street.

"Now what?" Lula said. "Gonna be hard to top that for excitement. Not every day I get to see a box full of poop."

"I need to look for Maxine. I'm not the only one to figure out she's in Point Pleasant. Unfortunately, I've got a vandalized car sitting in my parking lot, and I'm going to have to take care of that first."

I tried Morelli on the cell phone again, and got him in his car.

"Your girlfriend visited me," I said.

"I don't have a girlfriend."

"Bull*shit*!"

I read him the note and told him about my door and my car.

"Why do you think it's my girlfriend?" Morelli wanted to know.

"I can't think of anyone else who would make a woman so totally deranged."

"I appreciate the compliment," Morelli said. "But I'm not involved with anyone. I haven't been for a long time."

"What about Terry Gilman?"

"Terry Gilman wouldn't pour gasoline on your car. Terry Gilman would politely knock on your door, and when you answered she'd gouge your eyes out."

"When was the last time you saw Terry?"

"About a week ago. I ran into her in Fiorello's Deli. She was wearing a little denim skirt, and she looked very fine, but she's not the woman in my life right now."

I narrowed my eyes. "So who *is* the woman in your life now?"

"You."

"Oh. Then what is this boyfriend stuff all about?"

"Maybe it's Maxine. You said it happened after she chained you to the refrigerator."

"And she's talking about Kuntz? I don't know. It doesn't feel right."

LULA PARKED next to the CRX, and we got out to assess the damage.

"I don't know how you get rid of this much gasoline," Lula said. "It's everywhere. It's even spilled on the outside. You got gas puddles here."

I needed to call the police and get a report on file, and then I needed to call my insurance company. The car needed to be professionally cleaned. I probably had a deductible, but I couldn't remember the amount. Not that it mattered. I couldn't drive the car like this.

"I'm going inside to make a couple phone calls," I told Lula. "If I hustle I might be done with this in time to go to Point Pleasant and look for Maxine."

"You know what I love about Point Pleasant? I love those half-orange and half-vanilla swirly frozen custard cones. Maybe I'll have to go with you. Maybe you could use a bodyguard."

A blue Fairlane swung into the lot and skidded to a stop behind us.

"Holy cats," Lula said. "It's old lady Nowicki, driving half in the bag."

Mrs. Nowicki lurched out of the car and swayed over. "I heard that, and I'm not half in the bag. If I was half in the bag I'd be a lot happier."

She was dressed in poison-green spandex. She'd troweled on full face makeup, a cigarette was stuck in the corner of her mouth and wisps of orange frizz framed a poison-green turban . . . which I knew hid a freshly scalped head.

She looked at my car and gave a bark of laughter. "This yours?"

"Yeah."

"Didn't anybody tell you the gasoline's supposed to go in the tank?"

"Something you want to see me about?"

"I'm leaving town," Mrs. Nowicki said. "And I have some news for you. Maxine would be real mad if she knew I told you this, but I think you were right about it being better you found her than . . . you know."

"You've heard from her?"

"She brought her car around for me. Said she didn't need it anymore."

"Where is she?"

"Well, she used to be in Point Pleasant, like I thought. But she said people got wind of that so she's moved to Atlantic City. She wouldn't give me an address, but I know she likes to play at Bally's Park Place. Thinks the odds are better there."

"You're sure?"

"Well, pretty sure." She took a deep drag on the cigarette which just about wore it down to the filter. Blue smoke filtered out her nose, and she flicked the butt away. It hit the pavement, rolled under my car and . . . *phunff!* The car ignited.

"YIKES!" Lula and I yelped, jumping back.

The car was engulfed in a big yellow fireball.

"FIRE! FIRE!" Lula and I hollered.

Mrs. Nowicki turned to look. "What?"

KABOOM! There was an explosion, Mrs. Nowicki got knocked on her ass, and a second fireball erupted. Lula's Firebird!

"My car! My baby!" Lula yelled. "Do something! Do something!"

People were pouring out of the building, and sirens wailed in the distance. Lula and I stooped over Mrs. Nowicki, who was stretched out on the pavement, face up, eyes wide.

"Uh oh," Lula said. "You aren't gonna be dead again, are you?"

"I need a cigarette," Mrs. Nowicki said. "Light me up."

A squad car slid into the lot, lights flashing. Carl Costanza got out of the car and walked over to me. "Pretty good," he said. "Looks like you blew up two cars this time."

"One was Lula's."

"We gonna have to look for body parts? Last time you blew up a car we found body parts a block away."

"You only found one single foot a block away. Most of the parts were right here in the lot. Personally, I think Mrs. Burlew's dog carried the foot there."

"So what about this time? We gotta go looking for feet?"

"Both cars were unoccupied. Mrs. Nowicki got shook up, but I think she's okay."

"She's so okay, she left," Lula said. "She could do that on account of her piece-of-junk car didn't get cooked."

"She left?" My voice sounded like Minnie Mouse's. I couldn't believe she left after causing the accident.

"Just this second," Lula said. "Saw her just leave the lot."

I looked out to St. James, and an unsettling thought flashed into my head. "You don't suppose she did this on purpose, do you?"

"Blew up both our cars so we couldn't go off looking for her daughter? You think she's smart enough to think of something like that?"

THE FIRE TRUCKS left first, then the police, then the tow trucks. And now all that was left was a charred, sanded spot on the blacktop.

"Oh well," Lula said. "Easy come, easy go."

"You don't seem very upset. I thought you loved that car."

"Well the radio wasn't working right, and it got a ding on the side of the door at the supermarket. I can go out and get a new one now. Soon as I get the paperwork done I'm going car shopping. Nothing I like better than car shopping."

Nothing I *hated* more than car shopping. I'd rather have a mammogram than go car shopping. I never had enough money to get a car I really liked. And then there were the car salesmen . . .

second only to dentists in their ability to inflict pain. Ick. An involuntary shiver gripped my spine.

"See, I'm one of those positive type people," Lula went on. "My glass isn't half empty. Nuh uh. My glass is always half full. That's why I'm making something of myself. And anyway, there's people lots worse off than me. I didn't spend *my* afternoon looking for a note in a box full of dog poop."

"Do you think Mrs. Nowicki was telling the truth about Atlantic City? She could have been trying to throw us off the trail."

"Only one way to find out."

"We need wheels."

We looked at each other and did a double grimace. We both knew where there was an available car. My father had a powder-blue-and-white '53 Buick sitting in his garage. From time to time I'd been desperate enough to borrow the beast.

"No, no, no," Lula said. "I'm not going down to Atlantic City in that big blue pimpmobile."

"Where's your positive attitude? What about all that cup-is-half-full stuff?"

"Fuck the cup is half full. I can't be cool in that car. And I don't ride in no uncool car. I got a reputation at stake. You see a big black woman sliding across the seat in that car, and you think one thing. Twenty-five dollars for a blow job. I'm telling you, if you aren't Jay Leno you got no business being in that car."

"Okay, let me get this straight. If I decide to go to Atlantic City, and the only car I can come up with is Big Blue . . . you don't want to go with me."

"Well, since you put it that way . . ."

I called Lula a cab, and then I trudged up the stairs to my apartment. I let myself in and went straight to the refrigerator for a beer. "I have to tell you," I said to Rex. "I'm getting discouraged."

I checked my answering machine and received a terse message from Eddie Kuntz. "I got it."

Kuntz didn't sound any happier when I called him back. He

read the letters out to me. Fifty-three in all. And he hung up. No inquiring as to my health. No suggestion to have a nice day.

I dialed Sally and transferred the burden onto him. "By the way," I said. "What kind of car do you have?"

"Porsche."

Figures. "Two seater?"

"Is there any other kind?"

Room for me. No room for Lula. She'd understand. After all, this was business, right? And the fact that her car just got blown up, that was business too, right? "It wasn't my fault," I said. "I wasn't the one who tossed the cigarette."

"I must have been beamed up for a minute there," Sally said. "I think I just got a couple sentences from the other side."

I explained about the cars' catching fire and about the lead from Mrs. Nowicki.

"Sounds like we need to go to Atlantic City," Sally said.

"You think we could squash Lula into the Porsche with us?"

"Not even if we greased her."

I gave an internal sigh of regret and told Sally we'd go in my car and I'd pick him up at seven. No way was I going to be able to cut Lula out of this caper.

SEVEN

"OTHER MOTHERS have daughters who get married and have children," my mother said. "I have a daughter who blows up cars. How did this happen? This doesn't come from *my* side of the family."

We were at the table, eating dinner, and my father had his head bent over his plate, and his shoulders were shaking.

"What?" my mother said to him.

"I don't know. It just struck me funny. Some men could go a lifetime and never have their kid blow up a car, but I have a daughter who's knocked off three cars and burned down a funeral home. Maybe that's some kind of record."

Everyone sat in shocked silence because that was the longest speech my father had made in fifteen years.

"Your Uncle Lou used to blow up cars," my father said to me. "You don't know that, but it's true. When Louie was young he worked for Joey the Squid. Joey owned car lots back then, and he was in a war with the Grinaldi brothers, who also owned car lots. And Joey would pay Louie to blow up Grinaldi cars. Louie got paid by the car. Fifty dollars a car. That was big money in those days."

"You've been to the lodge, drinking," my mother said to my father. "I thought you were supposed to be out with the cab?"

104

My father forked in some potatoes. "Nobody wanted to take a cab. Slow day."

"Did Uncle Lou ever get caught?"

"Never. Lou was good. The Grinaldi brothers never suspected Lou. They thought Joey was sending out Willy Fuchs. One day they clipped Willy, and then Lou stopped blowing up Grinaldi cars."

"Ommigod."

"Worked out okay," my father said. "Lou went into the wholesale fruit business after that and did pretty good."

"Funky bracelet you got on your arm," Grandma said. "Is it new?"

"Actually, it's half of a pair of cuffs. I accidentally locked myself into them and then couldn't find the key. So I had to hacksaw one of them off. I need to go to a locksmith to get this half opened, but I haven't had the time."

"Muriel Slickowsky's son is a locksmith," my mother said. "I could call Muriel."

"Maybe tomorrow. I have to go to Atlantic City tonight. I'm checking out a lead on Maxine."

"I should go along," Grandma said, jumping out of her chair, heading for the stairs. "I could help. I blend right in there. Atlantic City's full of old babes like me. Let me change my dress. I'll be ready in a jiffy!"

"Wait! I don't think . . ."

"Wasn't nothing good on TV tonight anyway," Grandma called from the second floor. "And don't worry, I'll come prepared."

That brought me out of my seat. "No guns!" I looked over at my mother. "She doesn't still have that forty-five, does she?"

"I looked all over in her room, and I couldn't find it."

"I want her strip-searched before she gets in my car."

"Not enough money in the universe," my father said. "Not under threat of death would I look at that woman naked."

105

LULA, Grandma Mazur and I stood in the hall, waiting for Sally to answer his doorbell. I was wearing a short denim skirt, white T-shirt and sandals. Grandma was wearing a red-and-blue print dress with white sneakers. Lula was wearing a low-cut red knit dress that hiked up about three inches below her ass, red-tinted hose and red satin sling-back heels.

And Sally opened the door in full drag. Black bitch queen wig, skin-tight silver-sequined sheath that stopped three inches below *his* ass, and strappy silver platform heels that put him at a startling 6'8" without the hair.

Sally gave me the once-over. "I thought we were supposed to be in disguise."

"I'm disguised as a fox," Lula said.

"Yeah, and I'm disguised as an old lady," Grandma said.

"My mother wouldn't let me go if I was disguised as somebody," I said.

Sally tugged at his dress. "I'm disguised as Sheba."

"Girlfriend," Lula said to him, "you are the shit."

"Sally's a drag queen," I explained to Grandma.

"No kidding," Grandma said. "I always wanted to meet a drag queen. I always wanted to know what you do with your dingdong when you wear girl's clothes."

"You're supposed to wear special underpants that tuck you under."

We all looked down at the crotch-level bulge in the front of Sally's dress.

"So sue me," Sally said. "They give me a rash."

Lula tipped her nose in the air. "What's that smell? Mmm-mmm, I smell something baking."

Sally rolled his eyes. "It's Sugar. He's in a fucking frenzy. He must have gone through ten pounds of flour in the last two hours."

Lula muscled past Sally into the kitchen. "Lord," she said, "will you look at this . . . cakes as far as the eye could see."

Sugar was at the counter, kneading bread dough. He looked up when we came in and gave us an embarrassed smile. "You probably think I'm weird to be doing all this baking."

"Honey, I think you're cute as a button," Lula said. "You ever want a new roommate you give me a call."

"I like the way it smells when you have something in the oven," Sugar said. "Like home."

"We're going to Atlantic City," I said to Sugar. "Would you like to join us?"

"Thanks, but I have a pie ready to go in, and this dough has to rise, and then I have some ironing . . ."

"Damn," Lula said, "you sound like Cinderella."

Sugar poked at his dough. "I'm not much of a gambler."

We each took a cookie from a plate on the counter and herded ourselves out of the kitchen, down the hall and into the elevator.

"What a sad little guy," Lula said. "He don't look like he has much fun."

"He's a lot more fun when he's in a dress," Sally said. "You put him in a dress and his whole personality changes."

"Then why don't he always wear a dress?" Lula wanted to know.

Sally shrugged. "I don't know. Guess that doesn't feel right, either."

We crossed the sleek marble lobby and walked the flower-bordered path to the lot.

"Over here," I said to Sally. "The blue-and-white Buick."

Sally's mascared lashes snapped open. "The Buick? Holy shit, is this *your* car? It's got portholes. Fucking portholes! What's under the hood."

"A V-eight."

"Yow! A V-eight! A fucking V-eight!"

"Good thing he don't have them tuck underpants on," Lula said. "He'd rupture himself."

The Buick was a man thing. Women hated it. Men loved it. I thought it must have something to do with the size of the tires. Or maybe it was the bulbous, egglike shape . . . sort of like a Porsche on steroids.

"We'd better get going," I said to Sally.

He took the keys out of my hand and slid behind the wheel.

"Excuse me," I said. "This is *my* car. I get to drive."

"You need someone with balls to drive this car," Sally said.

Lula stood hip stuck out, hand on hip. "Hah! And you think we don't have balls? Look again, Tiny Tim."

Sally held tight to the wheel. "Okay, what'll it take? I'll give you fifty bucks if you let me drive."

"I don't want money," I said. "If you want to drive the car, all you have to do is ask."

"Yeah, you just don't go pulling this macho shit on us," Lula said. "We don't stand for none of that. We don't take that bus."

"This is gonna be great," Sally said. "I always wanted to drive one of these."

Grandma and Lula piled in back, and I got in front.

Sally pulled a slip of paper from his purse. "Before I forget, here's the latest clue."

I read it aloud. "'Last clue. Last chance. Blue Moon Bar. Saturday at nine.'"

Maxine was getting ready to bolt. She was setting Eddie up one last time. And what about me? I thought she might be setting me up one last time, too, by sending me on a wild-goose chase to Atlantic City.

THE FIRST THING I always notice about Atlantic City is that it's not Las Vegas. Vegas is all splash from the outside to the inside. Atlantic City is not so much about neon lights as about good parking. The casinos are built on the boardwalk, but truth is, nobody gives a damn about the boardwalk. A.C. is not about ocean. A.C. is about letting it ride. And if you're a senior citizen, so much the better. This is the Last Chance Saloon.

The city's slums sit butt-flush with the casinos' back doors.

Since Jersey is not about perfection this isn't a problem. For me, Jersey is about finding the brass ring and grabbing hold, and if you have to go through some slums to get to the slots . . . fuck it. Crank up your car window, lock your door and roll past the pushers and pimps to valet parking.

It's all very exhilarating.

And while it's not Vegas, it's also not Monte Carlo. You don't see a lot of Versace gowns in Atlantic City. There are always some guys at the craps table with slicked-back hair and pinkie rings. And there are always some women dressed up like bar singers standing next to the oily, pinkie ring guys. But mostly what you see in Atlantic City is sixty-five-year-old women wearing polyester warm-up suits, toting buckets of quarters, heading for the poker machines.

I could go to New York or Vegas with Lula and Sally and never be noticed. In Atlantic City it was like trying to blend in with Sigfried and Roy and five of their tigers.

We came onto the floor, four abreast, letting the noise wash over us, taking it all in . . . the mirrored ceiling, the 3-D carpet, the flashing lights, and hustling, swirling crowds of people. We moved through the room and old men walked into walls, pit bosses turned silent, waitresses stopped in their tracks, chips were dropped on the floor and women stared with the sort of openmouthed curiosity usually reserved for train wrecks. As if they'd never seen a seven-foot transvestite and a two-hundred-pound black woman with blond baloney curls all dressed up like Cher on a bad day.

Do I know how to conduct an undercover operation, or what?

"Good thing I got my Social Security check yesterday," Grandma said, eyeing the slots. "I feel lucky."

"Pick your poison," Lula said to Sally.

"Blackjack!"

And off they all went.

"Keep your eyes open for Maxine," I said to their departing backs.

I walked the room for an hour, lost $40 shooting craps, but got a free beer for a $5 tip. I hadn't run across Maxine, but then that wasn't a surprise. I found a sectional with good visibility and settled in to watch the people.

At eleven-thirty Grandma appeared and sank down next to me. "Won twenty bucks on my first machine, and then it turned on me," she said. "Bad luck all night after that."

"Got any money left?"

"None. Still, it wasn't all wasted. I met a real looker. He picked me up at the two-dollar poker machines, so you know he's no cheapskate."

I raised my eyebrows.

"You should have stayed with me. I could have gotten you fixed up, too."

Oh boy.

A small white-haired man approached us. "Here's your Manhattan," he said to Grandma, handing her a drink. "And who's this?" he asked, turning to me. "This must be your granddaughter."

"This here's Harry Meaker," Grandma said to me. "Harry's from Mercerville, and he had bum luck tonight, too."

"I always got bum luck," Harry said. "Had bum luck all my life. Been married two times, and both wives died. Had a double bypass last year, and now I'm clogging up again. I can feel it. And look at this. See this red scaly patch on my nose? Skin cancer. Gonna have it cut out next week."

"Harry came down on the bus," Grandma said.

"Prostate problems," Harry said. "Need a bus with a toilet on it." He looked at his watch. "I gotta go. Bus leaves in a half hour. Don't want to miss it."

Grandma watched him walk away. "What do you think? He's a live one, huh? For a while, anyway."

Lula and Sally trudged over and plopped down on the couch next to me.

"Didn't hear no gunfire, so I guess no one saw Maxine," Lula said.

"Maxine was the smart one," Sally said. "She stayed home."

I looked at him. "Not a good night?"

"Cleaned me out. I'm going to have to do my own nails this week."

"I could do them for you," Lula said. "I'm real good at nails. See those little palm trees on my nails? I put them on myself."

"Hold it," I said, getting to my feet. "Look at that woman in the turquoise slacks by the craps table. The one with all the yellow hair . . ."

The woman had her back to me, but she'd turned a moment ago, giving me a good look at her face. And she looked a lot like Maxine.

I started walking toward her when she turned again and stared directly at me. Recognition registered simultaneously for both of us. She pivoted on her heel and disappeared into a crush of people at the far side of the table.

"I see her!" Lula said, one step behind me. "Don't lose sight!"

But I had lost sight. The room was crowded, and Maxine wasn't dressed in red spangles like Lula. Maxine blended right in.

"I got my eye on her," Grandma yelled. "She's going for the boardwalk."

Grandma had climbed onto a blackjack table and was standing, sneakered feet planted wide. The dealer made a grab for her, and Grandma hit him on the head with her purse. "Don't be rude," she said to the dealer. "I just come up here to get a good look on account of the osteoporosis shrunk me and now I'm too short."

I took off at a run for the boardwalk entrance, weaving between clusters of gamblers, trying not to mow anyone over. In two heartbeats I was out of the game room, into the wide hallway leading to the door. I caught a glimpse of big straw hair in front of me, saw it bob through the double glass door. I was pushing people away and yelling "Excuse me" and I was breathing heavy. Too many doughnuts, not enough exercise.

I swung through the door and saw Maxine ahead of me, running for all she was worth. I kicked it up a notch, and I heard Lula and Sally clattering and swearing half a block back.

Maxine made a sharp turn off the boardwalk, down a side

street. I made the same turn just as a car door slammed and an engine caught. I ran to the car, reached it just as its wheels spun. And then the car was gone. And since Maxine was nowhere to be seen, I supposed Maxine was gone, too.

Sally slid to a stop and bent at the waist to catch his breath. "That's it for me, man. From now on fuck the heels."

Lula crashed into him. "Heart attack. Heart attack."

We were all walking around, gasping for breath, and Grandma trotted up. "What happened? What'd I miss? Where is she?"

"Got away," I said.

"Dang!"

Three guys came out of the shadows at us. They looked to be late teens, wearing baggy homey pants and unlaced court shoes.

"Hey, momma," one said. "What's happening?"

"Give me a break," Sally said.

"Whoa," the kid said. "Big bitch!"

Sally straightened his wig. "Thanks."

The kid pulled a Buck knife out of his pants pocket. "How about giving me your purse, bitch?"

Sally hiked up his skirt, reached into his briefs and pulled out a Glock. "How about using that knife to slice off your balls?"

Lula whipped a gun out of her red satin purse and Grandma hauled out her .45 long-barrel.

"Day my make, punk," Grandma said.

"Hey, I don't want any trouble," the kid said. "We were just having some fun."

"I want to shoot him," Sally said. "Nobody'll tell, right?"

"No fair," Lula said. "I want to shoot him."

"Okay," Grandma said. "On the count of three, we'll all shoot him."

"No shooting!" I said.

"Then how about if I kick the shit out of him?" Sally said.

"You're all nuts," the kid said, backing away. "What kind of women are you?" His friends took off, and he ran after them.

Sally put his gun back in his pants. "Guess I flunked the estro-gen test."

We all stared at his crotch, and Grandma said what Lula and I were thinking.

"I thought that bulge was your dingdong," Grandma said.

"Jesus," Sally said, "who do you think I am, Thunder the Won-der Horse? My gun wouldn't fit in my purse."

"You need to get a smaller gun," Lula said. "Ruins your lines with that big old Glock in your drawers."

GRANDMA, Lula and Sally were asleep fifteen minutes out of At-lantic City. I drove the big car in the dark and the quiet, thinking about Maxine. I still wasn't convinced this was anything other than a wild-goose chase. True, I'd seen Maxine, just as her mother had said, but she'd gotten away a little too easily. And she hadn't looked all that surprised to see me. Her car had been parked on a dark side street. Not the sort of thing a lone woman would do. It was safer and more convenient to park in the parking garage. She'd taken off in a black Acura. And while I didn't actually see her get in the car, I suspected she wasn't driving. It had all been too fast. The motor had caught the instant I heard the car door slam shut.

So I was thinking maybe she wanted to throw me off. Maybe she was still in Point Pleasant. Maybe she'd paid her rent for the month and didn't want to move. So when she discovered her mother had informed on her, she concocted this scenario to keep me away from Point Pleasant. Or maybe this was another game. Maybe Eddie Kuntz had been right about Maxine's fascination with James Bond.

I dropped Sally off first, then Lula, and Grandma last.

"Mom thinks you've gotten rid of that gun," I said to Grandma.

"Hunh," Grandma said. "Imagine that."

My mother was at the front door, standing arms crossed, look-ing out at us. If I was a good daughter I'd go in and have some cookies. But I wasn't that good a daughter. I loved my mother, but love only goes so far when you're trying to explain how your grandmother ended up standing on a blackjack table in a packed casino.

I waited for Grandma to successfully negotiate the steps, then I waved good-bye and drove away in the big blue car. I made every light on Hamilton, turned at St. James and felt a nervous flutter in my stomach at the sight of emergency vehicles at the corner. Cop cars, fire trucks, EMTs. The parking lot to my building was filled with them. Lights were blazing, and the squawk of loudspeakers carried back to me. Sooty water ran in the gutter, and people dressed in bathrobes and hastily put together outfits milled about on the sidewalks. Whatever it was, it seemed to be over. Firefighters were packing up. Some of the curious were dispersing.

Fear arrowed into me. *Next time I'll strike a match.*

The street was blocked, so I parked where I was and ran across the small patch of grass that bordered the lot. I shielded my eyes from the glare of the lights and squinted through a haze of smoke and diesel fumes, counting windows to locate the fire. Second floor, two apartments over. The fire was in my apartment. The window glass was broken and the surrounding brick was blackened. No other apartment showed any damage.

My only coherent thought was of Rex. Rex was trapped in a glass aquarium in the middle of all that ruin. I stumbled to the building's back door, begging for a miracle, not sure if I was screaming or crying, focused only on Rex. I was dragging in air that felt thick and unbreathable. Like swimming through Jell-O. Vision and sound distorted. Hands pulling at me as I struggled to cross the crowded lobby. I heard my name being called.

"Here!" Mr. Kleinschmidt shouted. "Over here!"

He was with Mrs. Karwatt, and Mrs. Karwatt had both arms wrapped around Rex's glass aquarium.

I shoved my way through to them, barely able to believe Rex had been saved. "Is he okay? Is Rex okay?" I asked, raising the lid to see for myself, tilting the soup can to look at a startled Rex.

Probably it's silly to feel so much affection for a hamster, but

Rex is my roommate. Rex keeps my apartment from feeling empty. And besides that, he likes me. I'm almost sure of it.

"He's fine," Mrs. Karwatt said. "We got him out right away. Thank goodness you gave me a key to your apartment. I heard the explosion and went right in. Lucky the fire started in your bedroom."

"Was anyone hurt?"

"No one was hurt. It was all in your apartment. Mrs. Stinkowski below you has some water damage, and we all smell smoky, but that's it."

"This must be a doozy of a case you're on," Mr. Kleinschmidt said. "Someone blew up your car and your apartment all in one day."

Kenny Zale clomped over to me. I went to grade school with Kenny, and for a while in high school dated his older brother, Mickey. Kenny was a fireman now. He was dressed in boots and black bunker pants, and his face was grimy with sweat and soot.

"Looks like you visited my apartment," I said to Kenny.

"Maybe you should think about getting a different job."

"How bad is it?"

"The bedroom's gone. That's where it started. Looks to me like someone pitched a firebomb through your window. The bathroom is salvageable. The living room is pretty much trashed. The kitchen will probably be okay when it gets cleaned up. You'll need new flooring. Probably have to paint. There's a lot of water damage."

"Can I get in?"

"Yeah. This would be a good time. The fire marshal's up there now. He'll probably walk you through to let you get what you can, and then he'll seal it until the investigation's over and he's sure it's safe."

"John Petrucci still the fire marshal?"

"Yeah. You're probably on intimate terms."

"We've spent some time together. I wouldn't say we were intimate."

He grinned and ruffled my hair. "I'm glad you weren't in bed when this happened. You'd be toast."

I left Rex with Mrs. Karwatt, ran the stairs and worked my way through the crush of people in the hall. The area around my apartment was water soaked and sooty. The air was acrid. I looked through the door and my heart contracted. The destruction was numbing. The walls were black, the windows broken, the furniture unrecognizable as anything other than drenched, charred rubble.

I'm a firm believer in denial. My reasoning is why deal with unpleasantness today when you could get hit by a bus tomorrow. And if you procrastinate long enough, maybe the issue will go away. Unfortunately, this issue wasn't going away. This issue was beyond denial. This issue was fucking depressing.

"Shit!" I shrieked. "Shit, shit, shit, shit!"

Everyone on the floor stopped what they were doing and stared at me.

"Okay," I said. "I feel better now." It was a lie, of course, but it felt good to say.

Petrucci walked over. "You got any idea who did this?"

"No. Do you?" Another lie. I had a few ideas.

"Somebody with a pretty good arm."

That could be Maxine. The softball star. But it still felt wrong. It felt more like mob . . . like Joe's pal, Terry.

I gingerly stepped into the kitchen. The brown bear cookie jar was untouched. The phone looked okay. The soot and water were pervasive and depressing. I bit down hard on my lip. I wasn't going to cry. Rex was safe. Everything else was replaceable, I told myself.

We went room by room, and not much was salvageable. A few cosmetics that had been in the bathroom and a hair dryer. I put them in a bag from the kitchen.

"Well, this isn't so bad," I said to Petrucci. "I've been wanting to redecorate. I just wish the bathroom had gone."

"What, you don't like orange and brown?"

"Do you think it's too late to burn the bathroom?"

Petrucci looked pained. Like I'd asked him to fart in public. "You have insurance for all your stuff?"

"Yes." Maybe.

Mrs. Karwatt was waiting in the hall with Rex. "Are you okay? Do you have some place to stay? You could sleep on my couch tonight."

I took the cage from her. "That's nice of you to offer, but I'll probably go home to my parents. They have a spare bedroom."

Old Mrs. Bestler was in the elevator. "Going down," she said, leaning on her walker. "First floor, ladies' handbags."

The doors opened to the lobby, and the first person I saw was Dillon in his superintendent coveralls.

"I was just going up to take a look," he said. "Guess I'll have to get the paintbrush out."

"Gonna take a lot of paint." My lip was trembling again.

"Hey, don't worry about it. Remember when Mrs. Baumgarten set fire to her Christmas tree? The whole apartment was burned to a crisp. Nothing left but ashes. And now look . . . good as new."

"It's worth a case of Guinness for you to take a sledgehammer to the bathroom."

"What, you don't like orange and brown?"

I WAS GLAD I'd parked the Buick on the street, out of sight of the fire-blackened building. Out of sight, out of mind. Sort of. The Buick was quiet and womblike. Nice and insulating against the outside world. The doors were locked, and the activity was all in front of me, half a block away.

Rex and I sat in the car and tried to collect our thoughts. After a while Rex started running on his wheel, and I assumed his thoughts were all collected. My thoughts were taking longer to come together. My thoughts were running in frightening directions. Someone wanted me scared and maybe dead. There was a remote possibility it was the same someone who was chopping off fingers and whacking off scalps, and I didn't like the idea that this was in my future.

I rested my head on the steering wheel. I was exhausted, and I was on the brink of tears. And I was afraid if I started crying I wouldn't stop for a long, long time.

I looked at my watch. It was two A.M. I needed to get some sleep. Where? The most obvious solution was to go home to my parents, but I didn't want to put their lives in jeopardy. I didn't want the next target for a firebomb to be their house on High Street. So where could I go? A hotel? There are no hotels in Trenton. There are some in Princeton, but they were forty minutes away, and I was reluctant to spend the money. I could call Ranger, but no one knows where Ranger lives. If Ranger took me in for the night, he'd probably have to kill me in the morning to make sure his secret was safe. Lula? That was sort of a scary idea. Better to face the scalper than sleep with Lula. There was my best friend, Mary Lou, and there was my sister, Valerie, but I didn't want to endanger them, either. I needed someone who was expendable. Someone I didn't have to worry about. Someone who had extra room.

"Oh boy," I said to Rex. "Are you thinking what I'm thinking?"

I sat for another five minutes, but I couldn't come up with a better solution to my problem, so I turned the key in the ignition and slowly drove past the lone fire truck at the end of the street. I tried not to look at my apartment, but I caught a glance of the fire escape from the corner of my eye. My chest gave a painful constriction. My poor apartment.

I took a deep breath. I didn't want to die. And I didn't want someone to hate me. And I absolutely did *not* want to cry.

"Don't worry about a thing," I said to Rex. "This will all work out. We've had bad times before, right?"

I took Hamilton to Chambers and followed Chambers to Slater. Two blocks down Slater I found the house I was looking for. It was a modest brown-shingled row house. All lights were off. I closed my eyes. I was dog tired, and I didn't want to do this.

"Maybe we should sleep in the car tonight," I said to Rex. "Then tomorrow we can get something more permanent."

Rex was doing a four-minute mile on the wheel. He blinked at me once, and that was it. The mental message was, You're on your own, kid.

Truth is, I didn't want to stay in my car. The crazy person could come and get me while I slept. He could jimmy the window, and he could cut off all my fingers. I looked at the house again. This was the one place I could feel safe and not be completely freaked out if the house was destroyed. This house belonged to Joe Morelli.

I hauled my cell phone out of my bag and dialed.

The phone rang six times before Joe answered with a mumbled hello.

"Joe?" I said. "It's Stephanie."

"Does this involve death?"

"Not yet."

"Does it involve sex?"

"Not yet."

"I can't imagine why else you'd be calling me."

"Someone firebombed my apartment tonight, and I need a place to stay."

"Where are you?"

"In front of your house."

An upstairs curtain was pulled aside.

"I'll be right down," Joe said. "Don't get out of your car until I open my door."

EIGHT

I HAULED Rex's cage off the front seat. "Now remember," I said, "no sniveling over the fact that our life is sucky. And no getting all mushy because Morelli is so hot. And no crying. We don't want Morelli thinking we're losers."

Morelli was on his small cement front porch. The door was open behind him, and I could see light from the upstairs hall. He was barefoot, dressed in cut-offs that rode his hips. His hair was tousled from sleep, and he had a gun in his hand, hanging loose at his side. "You talking to someone?"

"Rex. He's a little nervous about all this."

Morelli took the cage from me, kicked his door shut and carried Rex into the kitchen. He put the cage on the counter and flipped the overhead light on. It was an old-fashioned kitchen with dated appliances and Formica counters. Cupboards had been recently painted with cream enamel, and there was new linoleum on the floor. A pot sat soaking in the sink. Looked like Morelli'd had spaghetti for supper.

Morelli put a quart of cold milk and a bag of Oreos on the small wood table that pressed against one kitchen wall. He took two glasses from the dish drain, sat down at the table and poured out two glasses of milk.

"So," he said, "you want to talk about it?"

"I was in Atlantic City looking for Maxine tonight, and while I was gone someone pitched a firebomb through my bedroom window. The whole apartment went up. Fortunately, Mrs. Karwatt had a key and managed to rescue Rex."

Morelli stared at me for a beat with his unreadable cop face. "Remember those purple shoes you bought last year?"

"Reduced to ashes."

"Damn. I had plans for those shoes. I've spent a few sleepless nights thinking about you wearing those shoes and nothing else."

I helped myself to a cookie. "You need a life."

"Tell me about it. I spent last weekend laying linoleum." He took a second cookie. "I notice you're driving the Buick. What happened to the CRX?"

"Remember I told you about how someone soaked it with gasoline? Well, it sort of exploded."

"It exploded?"

"Actually, it caught fire first. Then it exploded."

"Hmm," Morelli said, eating the top half of the Oreo.

A tear slid down my cheek.

Morelli stopped eating. "Wait a minute. Is this for real? You aren't making this up?"

"Of course this is for real. Why else do you think I'm here?"

"Well, I thought . . ."

I jumped up, and my chair crashed to the floor. "You thought I made this up so I could come over here in the middle of the night and crawl into your bed!"

The line to Morelli's mouth tightened. "Let me get this straight. Yesterday, someone actually blew up your car and your apartment. And now you want to move in with me? What, do you hate me? You're a walking disaster! You're Calamity Jane in fucking spandex!"

"I am *not* a walking disaster!" But he was right. I was a walking disaster. I was an accident waiting to happen. And I was going to cry. My chest ached and my throat felt like I'd swallowed a baseball and tears gushed out of my eyes. "Shit," I said, swiping the tears away.

Morelli grimaced and reached out to me. "Listen, I'm sorry. I didn't mean—"

"Don't touch me!" I shrieked. "You're right. I'm a disaster. Look at me. I'm homeless. I'm carless. And I'm hysterical. What kind of a bounty hunter gets hysterical? A loser bounty hunter, that's what kind. A l-l-loser."

"Maybe milk wasn't the right choice here," Morelli said. "Maybe you could use some brandy."

"And there's more," I sobbed. "I lost forty bucks on craps, and I was the only one who didn't have a gun tonight!"

Morelli pulled me into his arms and held me close to him. "That's okay, Steph. Forty dollars isn't so much. And lots of people don't have guns."

"Not in New Jersey. Not bounty hunters."

"There are some people in Jersey who don't have a gun."

"Oh yeah? Name one."

He held me at arm's length and grinned. "I think we should get you up to bed. You'll feel better in the morning."

"About the bed . . ."

He pushed me toward the stairs. "I have a spare bedroom made up."

"Thanks."

"And I'll leave my door open in case you get lonely."

And I'd lock my door in case I got weak.

I AWOKE DISORIENTED, staring at a ceiling that wasn't mine. The walls were covered with faded green paper patterned with barely discernible viney flowers. Comforting in an old-fashioned way. Morelli had inherited this house from his Aunt Rose and hadn't changed much. My guess was the simple white curtains that hung on the windows had been chosen by Rose. It was a small room with a queen-size bed and a single chest of drawers. The floors were wood, and Morelli had placed a rag throw rug beside the bed. It was a sunny room and much quieter than my own bedroom, which faced out to the parking lot. I was sleeping in one of Morelli's T-shirts, and I was now faced with grim reality. I had no clothes. No clean underwear, no shorts, no shoes, no nothing. First thing would be a trip to Macy's for an emergency wardrobe.

There was a clock radio on the chest of drawers. It was nine o'clock. The day had started without me. I opened my door and peeked into the hall. All was silent. No sign of Morelli. A piece of paper had been taped to my door. It said Morelli had gone off to work and I should make myself at home. It said there was an extra key for me on the kitchen table and towels laid out in the bathroom.

I showered and dressed and went downstairs in search of breakfast. I poured myself a glass of orange juice and looked in at Rex.

"No doubt about it, I made an idiot out of myself last night," I said.

Rex was sleeping in his soup can and didn't show a lot of concern. Rex had seen me in my idiot state before.

I ate a bowl of cereal and took a look at the house. It was clean and orderly. The food in the cupboard was basic. the pots were second generation. Six glasses. Six dishes. Six bowls. Shelf paper left from Aunt Rose. He had a coffeemaker, but he hadn't made coffee, nor had he made breakfast. No dirty dishes. No new dishes in the dish drain. Morelli would stop on the way to work for coffee and whatever. Cops weren't known for their excellent diets.

I remembered Morelli's living room furniture from his apartment. Utilitarian. Comfort without style. It seemed off in the row house. The row house needed to be overstuffed with magazines on the coffee table and pictures on the walls.

Rooms were shotgunned. Living room, dining room, kitchen. Because Morelli lived in the middle of the block, there were no windows in the dining room. Not that it mattered. I couldn't see Morelli using the dining room. In the beginning, when Morelli had first moved here, I couldn't see him in the house at all. Now it suited him. Not that Morelli had turned domestic. It was more that the house had assumed independence. As if Morelli and the house had reached an agreement to coexist and leave it at that.

I called my mother and told her there'd been a fire and I was staying with Morelli.

"What do you mean, you're staying with Morelli? Ommigod, you're married!"

"It's not like that. Morelli has an extra bedroom. I'm going to pay him rent."

"We have an extra bedroom. You could stay here."

"I've tried that before, and it doesn't work. Too many people using one bathroom." Too many homicidal maniacs wanting to kill me.

"Angie Morelli is gonna have a fit."

Angie Morelli is Joe's mother. A woman both revered and feared in the Burg.

"Angie Morelli's a good Catholic woman, and she's not as open-minded as I am," my mother said.

The Morelli women were good Catholics. The men broke every commandment. The men played Monday night poker with the Antichrist.

"I have to go," I said. "I just wanted you to know I was okay."

"Why don't you and Joe come over for dinner tonight? I'm making meat loaf."

"We're not a couple! And I have things to do."

"What things?"

"Things."

My next phone call was to the office. "My apartment got fire-bombed," I told Connie. "I'm staying with Morelli for a while."

"Good move," Connie said. "You on the pill?"

I straightened the kitchen, pocketed the key and took off for the mall. Two hours later I had a week's worth of clothes and a maxed-out charge card.

It was noon when I got to the office. Connie and Lula were at Connie's desk eating Chinese.

"Help yourself," Lula said, nudging a cardboard carton. "We

got lots. We got fried rice, shrimp clumps and Kung Fu something."

I picked at a shrimp clump. "Heard from Vinnie yet?"

"Not a word," Connie said.

"How about Joyce? Heard from her?"

"Nope. And she hasn't brought Maxine in, either."

"I been thinking about Maxine," Lula said. "I think she's in Point Pleasant. And I wouldn't be surprised if her mama was there, too. That Atlantic City thing was a big phony wild-goose chase to keep us away from Point Pleasant. Her getaway don't feel right. That car was sitting there waiting for her to come out and take off. I think her mama set us up."

I tried some of the Kung Fu stuff. "I've been thinking the same thing."

LULA AND I stood in the middle of the boardwalk, across from the Parrot Bar, and clipped our pagers onto our shorts. I was wearing Day-Glo orange running shorts that had been on sale at Foot Locker, and Lula was wearing yellow-and-black tiger-striped spandex. She'd had her yellow ringlets beaded so that all over her head were four-inch strands of fluorescent pink, poison-green and bright yellow beads. It was ninety-six in the shade, the ocean was millpond calm, the sky was a cloudless azure, and you could fry an egg on the sand. We were here to find Maxine, but already I could see Lula getting distracted by the frozen custard stand.

"This is the plan," I said to Lula. "You're going to hang out here and keep your eye on the Parrot Bar, and I'm going to canvass the beach and the boardwalk. Page me if you see Maxine or anyone associated with her."

"Don't worry, nobody'll get by me. I'd just like to see that bony-ass mother. I'll grab her by what little hair she's got left, and I'll—"

"No! No grabbing, no shooting, no gassing, no stun-gunning! If you spot someone just stick with them until I get to you."

"Suppose it's self-defense?"

"There will be no self-defense. Don't let anyone see you. Try to blend in."

"I need an ice cream to blend in," Lula said, her hair beads jumping around, clacking every time she moved her head. "You give me an ice cream and I'll look like everybody else here."

Well hell, Tallulah, then go get an ice cream.

I walked north first. I'd brought a pair of mini-binoculars that I trained on the beach since Maxine seemed like the sunbather type. I went slowly and methodically, wandering through the arcades and bars. I walked beyond the amusement area to where the boardwalk was plain old boardwalk. After an hour of this I turned and headed back to Lula.

"Haven't seen anybody I know," Lula said when I reached her. "No Maxine. No Maxine's mama. No Joyce. No Travolta."

I stared into the bar across the way, and I didn't see any of those people, either. I took a brush and an elastic scrunchy out of my bag and pulled my hair back, off my neck, into a ponytail. I had a real desire to jump in the ocean, but I decided to settle for a lemonade. I was down to the wire with Maxine. I didn't have time to waste on such frivolity as lowering my body temperature.

I left Lula on the bench, got a lemonade and continued to walk and to scan the south end of the beach. I walked past a series of spin-the-wheel games and came to an arcade. I stepped into the cool shade and moseyed past the claw machines and the skillo ramps. I looked over at the wall where the prizes were displayed and stopped in my tracks. A woman stood at the wall, surveying the prizes. Five pieces of Farberware for 40,000 points. Wooden lighthouse for 9,450. Looney Tunes watch, 8,450. Dirt Devil, 40,100. Boom box, 98,450 points. The woman seemed to be counting the tickets she held in her hand. One hand held the tickets. And the other hand was heavily bandaged. She had brown hair, slim body.

I stepped farther back in the room and waited to see her face. She stood there for a moment longer, turned and walked to the redemption desk. It was Margie. I scooted past the desk, behind Margie's back, out to the boardwalk and paged Lula. She was just a short distance away. She looked up when the pager went off. I caught her eye and gave her a "come here" wave.

Margie was still at the desk when Lula trotted up.

"What's going on?" Lula asked.

"You remember I told you about Maxine's friend, Margie?"

"The one had her finger chopped off."

"Yes. That's her at the redemption desk."

"Point Pleasant sure is a popular place."

Margie took a large box from an arcade employee and moved to the side door that opened to the street. She passed through the door and turned right, away from the boardwalk. Lula and I watched her walk to the end of the block and cross the street. We followed after her, Lula a little less than a block away and me behind Lula. Margie crossed another street, continued on and went into a house in the middle of the next block.

We held our positions and watched for a while, but Margie didn't come out. The house was a single-story bungalow with a small front porch. Surrounding houses were similar. Lots were small. Cars were parked on both sides of the street.

We weren't in a good position to conduct any kind of surveillance. We'd driven to Point Pleasant in a car that drew attention. My only consolation was that even if we had a more generic car, there were no parking places open.

"So I take it you think this Margie is with Maxine. And maybe Maxine's mama is there, too," Lula said.

"Yeah. Problem is, I don't know if Maxine's in the house right now."

"I could be the Avon lady," Lula said. "Ding dong, Avon calling."

"If Maxine's mother is in there she'll recognize you."

"Think maybe we be recognized standing on the street like this, too," Lula said.

Very true. "Okay, this is what we'll do. We'll go see if Maxine's in the house. If she isn't at home, we'll sit down with Margie and watch some TV until Maxine shows up."

"Sounds like a plan to me. You want the back door or the front door?"

"Front door."

"And you probably don't want me to shoot anybody."

"Shooting isn't my favorite thing."

Lula walked along the side of the house to the back, and I went to the front door. I knocked twice and Margie answered.

Her eyes opened wide in surprise. "Oh!"

"Hi," I said. "I'm looking for Maxine."

"Maxine isn't here."

"You wouldn't mind if I came in and looked for myself?"

Maxine's mother swayed into view. "Who is it?" She took a long drag on her cigarette and let the smoke curl from her nose, dragon style. "Christ, it's you. You know, you're getting to be a real pain in the ass."

Lula came in from the kitchen. "Hope nobody minds my coming in. The back door wasn't locked."

"Oh God," Mrs. Nowicki said. "Tweedledum."

There was an empty box in the middle of the floor with a lamp sitting beside it.

"You win this lamp at the arcade?" Lula asked Margie.

"It's for my bedroom," Margie said. "Twenty-seven thousand points. Yesterday, Maxine won a deep fat fryer."

"Hell, we won just about everything in this house," Mrs. Nowicki said.

"Where's Maxine now?" I asked.

"She had some errands to run."

Lula sat down on the couch and picked up the channel changer for the TV. "Guess we'll be waiting then. You don't mind if I watch TV, do you?"

"You can't do this," Mrs. Nowicki said. "You can't just waltz in here and make yourself at home."

"'Course we can," Lula said. "We're bounty hunters. We can do anything we want. We're protected by a dumb-ass law made back in 1869 when people didn't know any better."

"Is that true?" Mrs. Nowicki wanted to know.

"Well, actually the law doesn't cover control of the channel changer," I said. "But it does give us a lot of rights when it comes to the pursuit and capture of a felon."

There was the sound of gravel crunching in the driveway between houses, and Margie and Mrs. Nowicki exchanged glances.

"That's Maxine, isn't it?" I asked.

"You're going to ruin everything for us," Mrs. Nowicki said. "We had this all planned out, and now you're screwing it up."

"I'm screwing it up? Look at you two. You've been scalped and had your finger chopped off. Back in Trenton there's a dead store clerk. And you're still playing this stupid treasure hunt game."

"It isn't that simple," Margie said. "We can't leave yet. They have to pay the price."

A car door slammed and Mrs. Nowicki gave a start. "Maxie!" she yelled.

Lula gave Mrs. Nowicki a bump with her hip. Mrs. Nowicki lost her balance and flopped onto the couch, and Lula sat on her. "I know I'll get hollered at if I shoot you," Lula said. "So I'll just sit on you until you be quiet."

"I can't breathe," Mrs. Nowicki said. "You ever think about cutting back on the helpings?"

Margie had a trapped animal look, like she couldn't decide whether to shout a warning or bolt for the door herself.

"Sit," I told her, pulling an industrial-size can of pepper spray out of my bag, shaking the can to make sure it was active. "Don't go running around confusing things."

I was hidden by the door when Maxine came in, but Lula was in full view, sitting on Mrs. Nowicki.

"Lo," Lula said to Maxine.

"Shit," Maxine said. Then she did an about-face and lunged for the door.

I kicked the door closed and aimed the spray at her. "Stop! Don't make me use this."

Maxine took a step back and raised her hands.

"Now get off me, you big load of blubber," Mrs. Nowicki said to Lula.

I had a pair of cuffs stuck into the waistband of my shorts. I handed the cuffs to Lula and told her to secure Maxine.

"Sorry to have to do this," I said to Maxine. "The charges against you are minimal. If you cooperate you might not even get jail time."

"It's not jail time I'm worried about," Maxine said. "It's dead time."

Lula reached out to snap the cuffs, and without warning the front and back doors crashed open. Joyce Barnhardt, dressed in swat black with "bounty hunter" emblazoned on her T-shirt, charged into the room with guns drawn. There were three other women with her, all dressed like Joyce, all armed like Rambo on rampage, all yelling "Freeze" at the top of their lungs and doing those squatting cop stances you see in the movies.

Margie's new lamp got knocked over and crashed on the floor, and Margie and Mrs. Nowicki and Maxine started yelling and running around, trying to protect their stuff. They were yelling "Oh no!" and "Help!" and "Don't shoot!" Lula dove behind the couch and made herself as small as anyone weighing two hundred pounds could make herself. And I was yelling at everyone to stop yelling.

There was a lot of confusion and a lot of people in that one small room, and it suddenly occurred to me that Maxine wasn't one of them. I heard gravel fly against the house and looked out the window to see Maxine gun the car out of the driveway and take off down the road.

I didn't have a car, so there wasn't much point in my rushing out. And I sure as hell wasn't going to help Joyce catch Maxine, so I didn't say anything. I just backed off and sat down in a big, overstuffed chair and waited for things to calm down. What I really wanted to do was to wade in and beat Joyce to a bloody pulp, but I didn't want to set a bad example for Lula.

Joyce had recruited her cousin Karen Ruzinski and Marlene Cwik to help with the takedown. I didn't know the third woman.

Karen had two little kids, and I guess she was happy to get out of the house and do something different.

"Hey Karen," I said, "where are the kids? Day care?"

"They're with my mother. She's got a pool in her yard. One of those big ones with the deck around it." Karen set her gun down on the coffee table and pulled her wallet out of one of the pockets in her SWAT pants. "Look here," she said. "This is Susan Elizabeth. She starts school this year."

Mrs. Nowicki picked up Karen's gun, squeezed a shot off, and a chunk of plaster fell out of the ceiling onto the television set. Everyone stopped dead in their tracks and stared at Mrs. Nowicki.

Mrs. Nowicki leveled the gun at Joyce. "Party's over."

"You're in big trouble," Joyce said. "You're harboring a fugitive."

A humorless smile slashed Mrs. Nowicki's face. "Honey, I'm not harboring anything. Look around. You see a fugitive?"

Understanding registered in Joyce's eyes. "Where's Maxine?"

Now I was smiling with Mrs. Nowicki. "Maxine left," I said.

"You deliberately let her get away!"

"Not me," I said. "I wouldn't do such a thing. Lula, would I do such a thing?"

"Hell no," Lula said. "You're a professional. Although, I gotta say, you haven't got no cool bounty hunter shirt like they do."

"She can't have gone far," Joyce said. "Everybody out to the car."

Mrs. Nowicki searched through her pockets, found a cigarette and stuck it in her mouth. "Maxie's long gone. They'll never find her."

"Just out of morbid curiosity," I said. "What's this all about?"

"It's about money," Mrs. Nowicki said. Then she and Margie laughed. Like that was a good joke.

MORELLI WAS SLOUCHED in front of the television when I got back to the house. He was watching *Jeopardy!*, and there were three empty beer bottles alongside his chair.

"Bad day?" I asked.

"To begin with . . . you were telling the truth about your apartment. I checked. It's a big black cinder. Ditto for your car. Following along in the same vein, word has gotten out that we're living together, and my mother expects us for dinner tomorrow at six."

"No!"

"Yes."

"Anything else?"

"The case I've been working on for the last four months collapsed."

"I'm sorry."

Morelli made a disgusted gesture. "It happens."

"Have you had anything to eat?"

An eyebrow raised, and he looked at me sideways. "What did you have in mind?"

"Food."

"No. I haven't had any of that."

I went to the kitchen and said hello to Rex, who was sitting on a small mound of assorted dinner treats. Compliments of Morelli, Rex was feasting on a grape, a miniature marshmallow, a crouton, and a beer nut. I removed the marshmallow and ate it, so Rex wouldn't run the risk of requiring a filling in his fang.

"So what do you want?" I asked Morelli.

"Steak, mashed potatoes, green beans."

"How about a peanut butter sandwich?"

"That would be my second choice."

I made two peanut butter sandwiches and brought them into the living room.

Morelli looked at his sandwich. "What are these lumps?"

"Olives."

He opened the sandwich and looked inside. "Where's the jelly?"

"No jelly."

"I think I need another beer."

"Just eat it!" I yelled. "What do I look like, Betty Crocker? I didn't have a great day, either, you know. Not that anybody asked me about my day!"

Morelli grinned. "What about your day?"

I slumped onto the couch. "Found Maxine. Lost Maxine."

"Happens," Morelli said. "You'll find her again. You're the bounty hunter from hell."

"I'm afraid she's getting ready to bolt big time."

"Can't blame her. There are some scary guys out there."

"I asked her mother what this was all about, and she said it was about money. Then she laughed."

"You saw her mother?"

I filled Morelli in on the details, and he didn't look happy when I was done.

"Something has to be done about Barnhardt," he said.

"Any ideas?"

"Nothing that wouldn't get my shield taken away."

There was a moment of silence between us.

"So," I said, "how well do you know Joyce?"

The grin returned. "What do you mean?"

"You know what I mean."

"You want a full accounting of my sex life up to this moment?"

"That would probably take days."

Morelli slouched a little lower in his chair, his legs stretched in front of him, his lips curved into a smile, his eyes dark and dreamy. "I don't know Joyce as well as I know you."

The phone rang, and we both gave a start. Morelli had the cordless on the table beside him. He answered and mouthed "Your mother."

I was making no, no, no signals, but Morelli continued to smile and handed the phone over to me.

"I saw Ed Crandle this afternoon," my mother said. "He said don't worry, he'll take care of everything. He's going to drop the forms off here."

Ed Crandle lived across the street from my mother, and he sold insurance. I guessed this meant that I had some. Ordinarily I could look in my desk drawer to check. That wasn't possible now that my desk drawer and everything in it was smoke.

"And that nice superintendent, Dillon Ruddick, called and said your apartment was sealed for security right now, so you can't get in. But he said he was going to start work on it next week. Also, a woman named Sally would like you to call her back."

I thanked my mother and again declined dinner and the use of my room. I hung up and called Sally.

"Shit," Sally said, "I just heard about your apartment. Hey, I'm really sorry. Is there anything I can do? You need a place to crash?"

I told him I was staying with Morelli.

"I would have fucking wrestled him into the ground if I wasn't wearing heels," Sally said.

When I got off the phone Morelli had pulled the plug on *Jeopardy!* and was watching a ball game. I felt gritty from sweat, the back of my neck was scratchy with sunburn, and I could see my nose glowing. Should have used sunblock.

"I'm going to take a shower," I said to Morelli. "It's been a long day."

"Is this a sexual shower?"

"No. This is an I've-been-sweating-all-day-at-the-shore shower."

"Just checking," Morelli said.

The bathroom, like the rest of the house, was faded but clean. It was smaller than my apartment bathroom, and the fixtures were older. But the era of construction was more graceful. Morelli had stacked towels on a shelf above the toilet. His toothbrush, toothpaste and razor took up the left side of the sink vanity. I'd placed my toothbrush and toothpaste on the right. His and hers. I gave myself a mental shake. Get a grip, Stephanie . . . this isn't a romance novel. This is the result of a firebombing. There was an over-the-sink medicine cabinet, but I couldn't bring myself to open the door. It seemed like prying, and I was sort of afraid what I might find.

I showered and brushed my teeth and was toweling my hair dry when Morelli knocked on the door.

"Eddie Kuntz's on the phone," Morelli said. "You want him to call back?"

I wrapped the big bath towel around myself, cracked the door, and stuck my hand out. "I'll take it."

Morelli handed me the phone, and his eyes locked on my towel. "Shit," he whispered.

I tried to close the door, but he was still holding on to the phone. I was holding the towel with one hand, and the phone with the other, and I was nudging the door closed with my knee. I saw his eyes darken and soften, like liquid chocolate. I knew the look. I'd seen it before, and it had never turned out well for me.

"This isn't good," Morelli said, his gaze now wandering the length of the three-inch opening between door and jamb, from the towel to my legs and back to the towel.

"Hello?" Kuntz said at the other end of the line. "Stephanie?"

I tried to twist the phone out of Morelli's hand, but he was holding fast. My heart was going *ka-thunk, ka-thunk* in my chest, and I was starting to sweat in unusual places.

"Tell him you'll call him back," Morelli said.

NINE

I CLENCHED MY TEETH. "Let go of the phone!"

Morelli relinquished the phone but kept his foot in the doorway.

"What?" I said to Kuntz.

"I want a progress report."

"The report is that there's no progress."

"You'd tell me, right?"

"Yeah, sure. And by the way, someone soaked my car with gasoline and firebombed my apartment. You wouldn't happen to know who that someone was, would you?"

"Jeez. No. You think it was Maxine?"

"Why would Maxine firebomb my apartment?"

"I don't know. Because you're working for me?"

Morelli reached in and took the phone. "Later," he said to Kuntz. Then he disconnected and tossed the phone in the sink.

"This isn't a good idea," I said. But I was thinking, Why not? My legs were shaved. I didn't hardly have any clothes on so that awkward step was eliminated. And after everything I'd been through, I deserved an orgasm. I mean, it was the least I could do for myself.

Morelli moved in and nuzzled my bare shoulder. "I know," he said. "This is a terrible idea." His mouth brushed just below my earlobe. We locked eyes for a heartbeat, and Morelli kissed me. His mouth was gentle, and the kiss lingered. When I was in high school my best friend, Mary Lou, told me she heard Morelli had fast hands. Actually, just the opposite was true. Morelli knew how to go slow. Morelli knew how to drive a woman crazy.

He kissed me again, our tongues touched, and the kiss deepened. His hands were at my waist and then at my back pressing me into him, and either he had one hell of an erection or else his night stick was rammed into my stomach. I was pretty sure it was an erection, and I thought if I could just get that nice big, stiff, magical thing deep inside me all my worries would fade away.

"I've got some," Morelli said.

"Some what?"

"Some condoms. I've got a carton. Serious investment. Top of the line."

The way I was feeling I figured that carton wouldn't take us to Sunday.

And then his mouth was on me again, kissing my neck, my collarbone, the swell of my breast at the top of the towel. And then the towel was gone and Morelli took his mouth to my nipple and fire flashed through me. His hands were everywhere, exploring, caressing . . . teasing. His mouth dropped lower, trailing a string of kisses to my navel, my belly, my . . . OMMIGOD!

Mary Lou had also told me she'd heard Morelli had a tongue like a lizard, and now I knew firsthand the accuracy of that rumor. God bless the wild kingdom, I thought with a new appreciation for reptiles. I had my fingers tangled in his hair, and my bare ass pressed against the sink, and I was thinking, *Oh, yum!* I was on the brink. I could feel it coming . . . the delicious pressure, the heat and mind-emptying need for release.

And then he moved his mouth half an inch to the left.

"Go back!" I gasped. "Go back. GO BACK!"

Morelli kissed my inner thigh. "Not yet."

I was feeling frantic. I was so close! "What do you mean, not yet!"

"Too soon," Morelli said.

"Are you kidding me? It's not too soon! It's been years!"

Morelli stood, scooped me up, carried me into his bedroom and dropped me onto his bed. He stripped off his T-shirt and shorts, all the while watching me with dilated eyes, all black pupil beneath the black fringe of his lashes. His hands were steady, but his breathing was ragged. And then his briefs were gone and he was naked. And I wasn't sure anymore if this was going to work. It had been a long time, and he looked awfully big. Bigger than I'd remembered. Bigger than he'd felt through his clothes. He took a condom out of the box, and I scooted up to the headboard. "On second thought . . ." I said.

Morelli grabbed me by the ankles, pulled me down flat on my back and pushed my legs apart. "No second thoughts," he said, kissing me. And then he put his finger on me in precisely *that* spot. He moved the finger a little, and now I was thinking he was looking just right. Not really too big at all. Now I was thinking I had to find a way to get the damn thing inside me. It wasn't bad to look at, but it wasn't really doing all that much for me bobbing around on its own.

I grabbed hold and tried to direct it, but Morelli moved out of reach. "Not yet," he said.

What was with this not yet all the time! "I think I'm ready."

"Not nearly," Morelli said, dropping lower, doing some more of the terrific tongue torture.

Well okay, if this was what he really wanted to do it was fine by me because I actually liked this a lot. In fact, I was almost there. Another thirty seconds and I was going to fly off into the great beyond, shrieking like a banshee.

And then he moved a half inch to the left . . . again.

"Bastard," I said . . . in a loving sort of way. I reached out and stroked him, heard his breath catch at my touch. I drew my fingertip across the little slit at the top, and Morelli went very still. I had his attention. I dipped my head down and gave him a lick.

"Christ," Morelli gasped, "don't do that. I'm not Superman!"

Had me fooled. I went on a much more extensive tasting expedition, and suddenly Morelli was galvanized into action. In an instant, I was on my back and Morelli was poised over me.

"Not yet," I said. "It's not time."

He snapped the condom on.

"The hell it isn't."

Heh, heh, heh, I thought.

THE FOLLOWING MORNING I awoke in a tangle of damp sheets and warm Morelli. We'd made a respectable dent in the condom supply, and I was feeling very relaxed. Morelli stirred beside me, and I cuddled into him.

"Mmm," he said.

Two hours later there were a few less condoms in the box and Morelli and I were both lying facedown and slack limbed on the bed. I was thinking that sex was an excellent thing, but I probably didn't need any more now for ten or fifteen years. I eyeballed the distance between the bed and the bathroom and wondered if I could walk that far. The phone rang, and Morelli passed it over to me.

"I was wondering what I should wear tonight," Sally said. "Do you think I should be a man or a woman?"

"Doesn't matter to me," I said. "Lula and I are going to be women. You want to meet us there, or you want me to pick you up?"

"I'll meet you there."

"Okeydokey."

I turned to Morelli. "Are you working today?"

"Half day, maybe. I need to talk to a couple people."

"Me too." I dragged myself off the bed. "About dinner tonight . . ."

"Don't even think about standing me up," Morelli said. "I'll track you down and find you and make your life a living hell."

I did a mental grimace and managed to get myself into the bathroom without hardly grunting or whimpering. The sex god-

139

dess was a trifle sore this morning, feeling a little like a human wishbone.

I took a shower, dressed and ambled down to the kitchen. I'd never seen Morelli in the morning, and I'm not sure what I'd expected, but it wasn't the half-man, half-beast that was reading the paper and drinking coffee. Morelli was wearing a misshapen T-shirt and rumpled tan shorts. He was sixteen hours beyond a five o'clock shadow, and he hadn't combed his hair, which was multiple weeks beyond needing a haircut.

It had been sexy last night. This morning it was downright frightening. I poured out coffee and a bowl of cereal and sat across from him at the small table. The back door was open, and the morning air coming through it was cool. In another hour it would turn hot and steamy. Already the cicadas were singing. I thought about my own kitchen and sad charred apartment and my throat closed over. Remember what Morelli told you, I thought. Concentrate on the positive. The apartment will be okay. Brand-new carpet and paint. Better than before. And what had he said about the fear? Concentrate on doing the job, not on the fear. Okay, I thought, I can do that. Especially when I was sitting across from the man of my dreams.

Morelli drained his coffee cup and continued to read the paper.

I found myself wanting to refill the cup. And I didn't want to stop there. I wanted to make breakfast for Morelli. Hotcakes and bacon and fresh squeezed orange juice. Then I wanted to do his laundry and put fresh sheets on the bed. I looked around. The kitchen wasn't bad, but it could be cozier. Fresh flowers, maybe. A cookie jar.

"Uh oh," Morelli said.

"What uh oh?"

"You have that look . . . like you're redesigning my kitchen."

"You don't have a cookie jar."

Morelli looked at me like I was from Mars. "That's what you were thinking?"

"Well, yeah."

140

Morelli considered that for a moment. "I've never actually seen the purpose for a cookie jar," he finally said. "I open the box. I eat the cookies. I throw the box away."

"Yes, but a cookie jar makes a kitchen homey."

I got another one of those Mars looks.

"I keep my gun in my cookie jar," I said by way of further explanation.

"Honey, a man can't keep his gun in a cookie jar. It just isn't done."

"Rockford did it."

He got up and gave me a kiss on the top of my head. "I'm gonna take a shower. If you leave before I'm out, promise me you'll be home by five."

So much for the man of my dreams. I gave him one of my favorite Italian hand gestures, which he didn't see because he was already out of the room. "Fuck the cookie jar," I said to Rex. "And he can do his own goddamn laundry, too." I finished my cereal, rinsed the bowl and put it in the dishwasher. I slung my black leather tote over my shoulder and took off for the office.

"OMMIGOD," CONNIE SAID WHEN I walked into the office, "you did it!"

"Excuse me?"

"How was it? I want details."

Lula looked up from the stack of files she was sorting. "Yep," she said, "you did the deed all right."

I felt my eyes go wide. "How do you know?" I sniffed at myself. "Do I smell?"

"You just got that look like you've been totally fucked," Lula said. "Sort of relaxed."

"Yeah," Connie said. "Satisfied."

"It was the shower," I said. "I took a really long relaxing shower this morning."

"Wish I had a shower like that," Lula said.

141

"Is Vinnie in?"

"Yeah, he got back late last night. Hey, Vinnie," Connie yelled. "Stephanie's here!"

We heard him mumble "Oh Christ" from deep inside his office, and then his door opened. "What?"

"Joyce Barnhardt, that's what."

"So I gave her a job." Vinnie squinted at me. "Jesus, you just get laid?"

"I don't believe this," I said, hands in the air. "I took a shower. I did my hair. I put on makeup, new clothes. I had breakfast. I brushed my goddamn teeth. How does everyone know I got laid?"

"You look different," Vinnie said.

"Satisfied," Connie said.

"Relaxed," Lula added.

"I don't want to talk about it," I shouted. "I want to talk about Joyce Barnhardt. You gave her Maxine Nowicki. How could you do that? Nowicki is my case."

"You weren't having any luck with it, so I figured what the hell, let Joyce take a shot at it, too."

"I know how Joyce got that case," I said. "And I'm going to tell your wife."

"You tell my wife, and she'll tell her father, and I'll be dead. And then you know where you'll be? Unemployed."

"He got a point there," Lula said. "We all be unemployed."

"I want her off the case. Lula and I had Maxine in custody, and Joyce barged in with the slut troop and screwed everything up."

"Okay, okay," Vinnie said. "I'll talk to her."

"You're going to take Nowicki away from her."

"Yeah."

"Sally called and said he was going to the bar tonight," I told Lula. "Do you want to come, too?"

"Sure, I don't want to miss any of the fun."

"Need a ride?"

"Not me," Lula said. "I got a new car." Her eyes slid past me to the front door. "What I need now is a man to put in it. He got a name on him, too."

Connie and I swiveled to look. It was Ranger, dressed in black, hair slicked into a ponytail, small gold hoop earring shining like the sun.

"Yo," Ranger said. He stared at me for a moment and smiled. He raised his eyebrows. "Morelli?"

"Shit," I said. "This is embarrassing."

"Came by to get the papers on Thompson," Ranger said to Connie.

Connie handed him a folder. "Good luck."

"Who's Thompson?"

"Norvil Thompson," Ranger said. "Stuck up a liquor store. Took four hundred dollars and change and a quart of Wild Turkey. Started celebrating in the parking lot where he parked his car, passed out and was found by a parking attendant who called the police. Didn't show up for his court date."

"Like always," Connie said.

"He's done this before?"

"Twice."

Ranger signed his part of the contract, passed it back to Connie and looked over at me. "Want to help me round up this cowboy?"

"He isn't going to shoot at me, is he?"

"Ah," Ranger said, "if only it was that simple."

Ranger was driving a new black Range Rover. Ranger's cars were always black. They were always new. They were always expensive. And they were always of dubious origin. I never asked Ranger where he got his cars. And he never asked me my weight.

We cut through center city and turned right onto Stark Street. Ranger cruised past the auto body and the gym into a neighborhood of blighted row houses. It was midday, and welfare mothers and kids were on the stoops, looking for relief from the sweltering interiors of their airless rooms.

I leafed through the file to familiarize myself with Thompson.

Black male, 5'9", 175 pounds, age sixty-four. Respiratory problems. That meant we couldn't use pepper spray.

Ranger parked in front of a three-story brick building. Gang slogans were spray-painted on the stoop and under the two first-floor windows. Fast-food flotsam had banked against the curb and crumpled wrappers littered the sidewalk. The entire neighborhood smelled like a big bean burrito.

"This guy isn't as dangerous as he looks on the sheet," Ranger said. "Mostly he's a pain in the ass. He's always drunk, so it doesn't do any good to threaten him with a gun. He's got asthma, so we can't spray him. And he's old, so you look like a fool if you beat him to a pulp. What we want to do is cuff him and carry him out. That's why you're along. Takes two to carry him out."

Wonderful.

Two women were sitting two doors down. "You coming after old Norvil?" the one asked. "He run his bail again?"

Ranger raised his arm in acknowledgment. "Hey, Regina, how's it going?"

"Picking up now that you're here." She swiveled her head to the ground-level open window. "Yo, Deborah," she hollered. "Ranger's here. Gonna give us some entertainment."

Ranger moved into the building and started climbing the stairs. "Third floor," he said.

I was getting an uncomfortable feeling about this apprehension. "What did she mean . . . entertainment?"

Ranger was on the second-floor landing. "There are two tenants on the third floor. Thompson is on the left. One room and bath. Only one way out. He should be at home at this time of day. Regina would have told me if she'd seen him leave."

"I get the feeling there's something else I should know about this guy."

Ranger was halfway up the third flight of stairs. "Only that he's freaking nuts. And if he whips his dick out to take a leak, stand back. He tagged Hanson once, and Hanson swears he was fifteen feet away."

Hanson was another bounty hunter. Mostly worked for Gold Star Bail Bonds on First Street. Hanson had never struck me as someone who would fabricate war stories, so I turned around and started doing double-time down the stairs. "That's it for me. I'll call Lula to come pick me up."

My progress was halted by a hand grabbing the back of my shirt. "Guess again," Ranger said. "We're in this together."

"I don't want to get peed on."

"Just keep your eyes open. If he goes for his dick we'll both jump him."

"You know I could have lots of good jobs," I said. "I don't need to be doing this."

Ranger had his arm around me, encouraging me to walk up the stairs. "This isn't just a job. This is a service profession. We uphold the law, babe."

"Is that why you do this? Because you believe in the law?"

"No. I do this for the money. And because hunting people is what I do best."

We reached Thompson's door, and Ranger motioned me to one side while he knocked.

"Lousy fuckers," someone called from inside the room.

Ranger smiled. "Norvil's home." He gave another rap. "Open the door. I need to talk to you."

"I saw you out on the sidewalk," Norvil said, the door still closed, "and I'll open this door when hell freezes over."

"I'm going to count to three, and then I'm going to break in," Ranger said. "One, two . . ." He tried the doorknob, but the door was still locked. "Three." No response from inside. "Damn, stubborn old drunk," Ranger said. He stepped back and gave the door a solid kick just to the left of the doorknob. There was the sound of splintering wood, and the door crashed open.

"Lousy fuckers," Norvil yelled.

Ranger cautiously stepped into the doorway, gun in hand. "It's okay," he said to me. "He isn't armed."

I moved into the room and stood beside Ranger. Norvil was on the far side of the room with his back against the wall. To his right was a chipped Formica table and a single wooden chair. Half the table was taken over with a cardboard box filled with food. Ritz crackers, Count Chocula cereal, a bag of marshmallows, a bottle of ketchup. A dorm-sized refrigerator was on the floor by the table. Norvil was dressed in a faded T-shirt that said "Get Gas From Bud" and a pair of baggy, soiled khakis. And he was holding a carton of eggs.

"Lousy fuckers," he said. And before I realized what was happening . . . SPLAT. I got hit in the forehead with an egg. I jumped back, and the ketchup bottle sailed by my ear, smashed on the doorjamb and ketchup splattered everywhere. This was followed by the pickle jar and more eggs. Ranger caught an egg on his arm, and I got one square on my chest. I turned to dodge a jar of mayo and got hit in the back of the head with another egg. Norvil was in a frenzy, throwing whatever he laid hands on . . . crackers, croutons, corn chips, knives and spoons, cereal bowls and dinner plates. A bag of flour exploded in his hands, and flour flew in all directions. "Rotten pinko, commie bastards," he shouted, searching through the box for more ammo.

"Now!" Ranger said.

We both lunged for Thompson, going for his arms. Ranger locked a cuff on one wrist. We struggled to secure the other. Norvil took a swing at me, catching me in the shoulder. I lost my footing in the cracker crumbs and flour and went down hard to the floor. I heard the second cuff click closed and looked up at Ranger.

Ranger was smiling. "You okay?"

"Yeah. I'm just peachy."

"You have enough food on you to feed a family of four for a week."

Ranger had none. A small stain on one arm where he'd gotten hit by the egg.

"So why is it you're so clean and I'm such a mess?"

"For one thing, I didn't stand in the middle of the room, making a target of myself. For another thing, I didn't fall on the floor and roll in flour." He reached a hand out to me and helped me up. "First rule of combat. If someone throws something at you, step out of the way."

"Devil whore," Norvil shouted at me.

"Listen," I shouted back, "I was due. And it's none of your business anyway."

"He calls everyone a devil whore," Ranger said.

"Oh."

Norvil planted his feet wide. "I'm not going anywhere."

I looked at the stun gun on Ranger's utility belt. "How about we zap him?"

"You can't zap me," Norvil said. "I'm an old man. I got a pacemaker. You screw up my pacemaker and you'll be in big trouble. It could even kill me."

"Boy," I said, "that's tempting."

Ranger took a roll of duct tape off his gun belt and taped Norvil's legs together at the ankles.

"I'm gonna fall over," Norvil said. "I can't stand like this. I got a drinking problem, you know. I fall over sometimes."

Ranger got Norvil by the armpits and tipped him backward. "Grab his feet," he said. "Let's get him to the car."

"Help!" Norvil yelled. "I'm being kidnapped! Call the police. Call the Muslims!"

We got him to the second-floor landing, and he was still yelling and wriggling. I was working hard to hold him. Egg and flour were caked in my hair, I smelled like pickle brine, and I was sweating like a pig. We started down the second flight; I missed a step and slid the rest of the way on my back.

"No problem," I said, hoisting myself up, wondering how many vertebrae I'd cracked. "You can't keep Wonder Woman down."

"Wonder Woman looks a little beat," Ranger said.

Regina and Deborah were sitting on their stoop when we hauled Norvil out.

"Lord, girl," Regina said. "What happened to you? You look like a big corn dog. You've been all breaded up."

Ranger opened the Range Rover's rear door, and we tossed Norvil inside. I limped around to the passenger side and stared at the pristine leather seat.

"Don't worry about it," Ranger said. "You get it dirty I'll just get a new car."

I was pretty sure he was kidding.

I WAS on the small front porch, rooting around in my bag, looking for the key to Morelli's house when the door opened.

"I'm not even going to make a guess on this one," Morelli said.

I pushed past him. "You know Norvil Thompson?"

"Old guy. Robs stores. Goes nuts when he drinks . . . which is always."

"Yep. That's Norvil. I helped Ranger bring him in."

"I take it Norvil wasn't ready to go."

"Threw everything he had at us." I looked down at myself. "I need a shower."

"Poor baby. I could help."

"No! Don't come near me!"

"This isn't about the cookie jar, is it?"

I dragged myself up the stairs and into the bathroom. I stripped and stepped under the steaming water. I washed my hair twice and used a cream rinse, but my hair wouldn't come clean. I got out of the shower and took a look at my hair. It was the egg. It had hardened like cement, and little pieces of eggshell were stuck in the cement.

"Why me?" I said.

Morelli was on the other side of the bathroom door. "Are you all right? Are you talking to yourself?"

I wrenched the door open. "Look at this!" I said, pointing to my hair.

"Looks like eggshell."

"It won't come out."

Morelli leaned closer under the guise of examining my hair, but he was actually looking down my towel. "Hmm," he said.

"Listen, Morelli, I need help here."

"We haven't got much time."

"Help with my hair!"

"Honey, I don't know how to tell you this, but I think your hair is beyond my help. The best I could do is take your mind off it."

I searched through the medicine chest and came up with some scissors. "Cut the egg out."

"Oh boy."

Five minutes later Morelli looked up from his job and met my eyes in the mirror. "That's all of it."

"How bad is it?"

"You remember when Mary Jo Krazinski had ringworm?"

My mouth dropped open.

"It's not that bad," Morelli said. "Mostly it's just shorter . . . in spots." His finger traced a line along my bare shoulder. "We could be a few minutes late."

"No! I'm not going to be late for your mother. Your mother scares the hell out of me." His mother scared the hell out of everyone but Joe. Morelli's mother could see around corners. His father had been a drunk and a philanderer. His mother was beyond reproach. She was a housewife of heroic proportions. She never missed mass. She sold Amway in her spare time. And she didn't take crap from anyone.

Morelli slid his hand under my towel and kissed the back of my neck. "This'll only take a minute, babe."

A burning sensation skittered through my stomach and my toes curled. "I have to get dressed," I said. But I was thinking, Ohhhh, this feels good. And I was remembering what he'd done the night before, and *that* had felt even better. His hands found my breasts, and his thumb rubbed across my nipple. He whispered a few things he wanted to do to me, and I felt a little dribble of drool escape from the corner of my mouth.

Half an hour later, I was rushing around my room, searching for clothes to wear. "I can't believe I let you talk me into that!" I said. "Look how late we are!"

Morelli was fully clothed and smiling. "This cohabiting thing isn't so bad," he said. "I don't know why I didn't try it out sooner."

I stepped into my underpants. "You didn't try it out sooner because you were afraid to make a commitment. And in fact, you still haven't made a commitment."

"I bought an entire carton of condoms."

"That's a commitment to sex, not to a relationship."

"It's a start," Morelli said.

I glanced over at him. "Maybe." I pulled a little cotton sundress out of the closet. It was the color of sun-bleached straw and buttoned in the front like a shirt. I dropped the dress over my head and smoothed over a few wrinkles with my hand.

"Shit," Morelli said. "You look great in that dress."

I checked out his Levi's. He was hard again. "How did that happen?"

"You want to learn a new game?" Morelli asked. "It's called Mr. and Mrs. Rover."

"News flash," I said. "I don't iron. I don't eat raw fish. And I don't do dog stuff. You lay a hand on me, and I swear, I'm going for my gun."

MRS. MORELLI opened the door to us and smacked Joe on the side of the head. "Sex fiend. Just like your father, God rest his rotten soul."

Morelli grinned down at his mother. "It's a curse."

"It wasn't my fault," I said. "Honestly."

"Your Grandma Bella and your Aunt Mary Elizabeth are here," Mrs. Morelli said. "Watch your language."

Grandma Bella! My mouth went dry and black dots danced in front of my eyes. Grandma Bella put the curse on Diane Fripp, and Diane had her period nonstop for three months! I rechecked the buttons on the front of my dress and subtly felt to make sure I'd gotten my underwear back on.

Grandma Bella and Aunt Mary Elizabeth were in the living room, sitting side by side on the couch. Grandma Bella is a small white-haired lady dressed in traditional Italian black. She'd come to this country as a young woman, but back then the Burg was more Italian than Sicily, so she'd kept her old-country ways. Mary Elizabeth is Bella's younger sister and is a retired nun. They both had highball glasses in their hands and cigarettes hanging out of their mouths.

"So," Grandma Bella said, "the bounty hunter."

I sat on the edge of the seat of a wing-back chair and pressed my knees together. "Nice to see you, Grandma Bella."

"I hear you're living with my grandson."

"I'm . . . renting a room in his house."

"*Hah!*" she shouted. "Don't make up fibs to me or I'll put the eye on you."

I was doomed. I was fucking doomed. Even as I sat there I could feel my period coming on.

TEN

"THERE'S NO SUCH THING as the eye," Joe said. "Don't try to scare Stephanie."

"You don't believe in anything," Bella said. "And I never see you in church." She shook her finger at him. "Good thing I pray for you."

"Dinner's ready," Mrs. Morelli said. "Joseph, help your Grandma Bella into the dining room."

This was the first time I'd been in Mrs. Morelli's house. I'd been in the garage and the backyard. And of course I'd passed by countless times, always speaking in hushed whispers and never dillydallying for fear Mrs. Morelli would come get me by the ear and accuse me of wearing day-old underwear or not brushing my teeth. Her husband was known for not sparing the belt on his sons. Mrs. Morelli needed none of that. Mrs. Morelli could nail you to the wall with a single word. "Well," she would say, and the hapless victim would confess to anything. Everyone but Joe. As a kid Joe had run wild and unchecked.

The house was more comfortable than I'd expected. It felt like a family house, used to the noise and confusion of children. First Joe and his siblings, and now there were grandchildren. The furniture was slipcovered and clean. The carpet freshly vacuumed. The tabletops polished. There was a small wooden toy chest under one of the front windows and a child's rocker beside the chest.

The dining room was more formal. The table was set with a lace cloth. The hutch displayed worn heirloom china. Two bottles of wine sat uncorked and breathing at the head of the table. There were white lace curtains on the windows and a traditional, burgundy Oriental rug under the table.

We all took our seats; and Mary Elizabeth said grace while I eyed the antipasto.

After grace, Grandma Bella raised her wineglass. "To Stephanie and Joseph. Long life and many bambinos."

I glanced over at Joe. "You want to field this one?"

Joe took some ravioli and sprinkled them with grated cheese. "Only two bambinos. I can't afford a big family on a cop's salary."

I cleared my throat and glared at Morelli.

"Okay, okay," Morelli said. "*No* bambinos. Stephanie moved in with me because she needs a place to live while her apartment gets repaired. That's all there is to it."

"What do you think, I'm a fool?" Grandma Bella said. "I see what goes on. I know what you do."

Morelli helped himself to chicken. "Stephanie and I are just good friends."

I went rigid with my fork halfway to my mouth. He'd used those words to describe his relationship with Terry Gilman. Wonderful. Now what was I supposed to believe? That I was on equal footing with Terry? Well, you pushed him into it, stupid. You forced him to tell Bella this wasn't a serious relationship. Well, yeah, I thought, but he could have made me sound a *little* more important than Terry Gilman!

Bella's head rolled back, and she put her hands palms down on the table. "Silence!"

Mary Elizabeth made the sign of the cross.

Mrs. Morelli and Joe exchanged long-suffering glances.

"Now what?" I whispered.

"Grandma Bella's having a vision," Joe said. "It goes with having the eye."

Bella's head snapped up, and she pointed two fingers at Joe and me. "I see your wedding. I see you dancing. And I see after that you will have three sons, and the line will continue."

I leaned toward Joe. "Those things you bought . . . they were good quality, right?"

"The best money can buy."

"I gotta go lay down now," Bella said. "I always gotta rest after I have a vision."

We waited while she left the table and climbed the stairs. The bedroom door clicked closed, and Joe's mother gave an audible sigh of relief.

"Sometimes she gives me the willies," Mary Elizabeth said.

And then we all dug into the meal, avoiding talk about marriage and babies and crazy old Italian women.

I sipped my coffee and scarfed down a plateful of homemade cookies, keeping one eye on the time. Eddie Kuntz wouldn't show at the bar until nine, but I wanted to be in place earlier than that. My plan was to plant Lula and Sally inside the bar while I did surveillance on the street.

"It was very nice of you to invite me for dinner," I told Mrs. Morelli. "Unfortunately, I have to leave early. I have to go to work tonight."

"Is this bounty hunter work?" Mary Elizabeth wanted to know. "Are you hunting down a fugitive?"

"Sort of."

"It sounds exciting."

"It sounds like a sin against nature," Grandma Bella said from the hallway, freshly risen from the guest bed. "No kind of work for someone expecting."

"Grandma Bella," I said. "I'm really not expecting."

"A lot you know," she said. "I've been to the other side. I see these things. I got the eye."

"OKAY," I said to Morelli when we were half a block from the house, "just how accurate is this eye thing?"

"I don't know. I never paid much attention to it." He turned onto Roebling and pulled over to the curb. "Where are we going?"

"I'm going to the Blue Moon Bar. It's the next point of pickup in Maxine's treasure hunt. Take me back to the house, and I'll get my car."

Morelli swung out into traffic. "I'll go with you. Wouldn't want anything to happen to my unborn child."

"That's not funny!"

"All right. The truth is there's only crap on television tonight, so I might as well come along."

The Blue Moon Bar was down by the State Complex. There was a public parking lot on the next block, and there was on-street parking in front of the bar. There were small businesses on either side of the bar, but the businesses were closed at this time of the night. The bar had been a disco in the seventies, a sports bar in the eighties, and a year before it had been transformed into a fake micro-brewery. It was basically one large room with a copper vat in the corner, a bar running the entire length of one side and tables in the middle of the room. Besides serving booze, the Blue Moon Bar sold snack food. French fries, onion rings, nachos and fried mozzarella. On Saturday nights it was packed.

It was still early for the bar crowd, and Morelli was able to get a spot on the street, two cars down from the door. "Now what?" Morelli asked.

"Kuntz's supposed to show up at nine. Then we see what happens."

"What usually happens?"

"Nothing."

"Gosh, I can't wait."

By eight-thirty Lula and Sally were in the building. Kuntz arrived fifteen minutes later. I left Morelli in the truck with a photo of Maxine, and I went in to be with Kuntz.

"You look different," Kuntz said.

"I had some hair problems."

"No, that's not it."

"New dress."

"No. It's something else. I can't put my finger on it."

Thank goodness for that.

Lula and Sally came over and stood with us at the bar.

"What's doin'," Sally said.

"We're wasting more time, that's what's doin'," Kuntz said. "I hate these dumb treasure hunt things." His eyes held mine for a moment and then fixed on a point over my shoulder. I turned to see what had caught his attention.

It was Joyce Barnhardt in a very short, very tight black leather skirt and an orange knit tank top.

"Hello, Stephanie," Joyce said.

"Hello, Joyce."

She flashed a smile on Kuntz. "Hello, handsome."

I turned to Lula, and we made the finger-down-the-throat, tongue-stuck-out gag gesture to each other.

"If I had those breasts I could clean up," Sally whispered to me. "I could make enough money in a year to fucking retire. I wouldn't ever have to put on another pair of heels."

"What are you doing here, Joyce? I thought Vinnie was going to talk to you."

"It's a free country," Joyce said. "I can go where I want. Do what I want. And right now what I want is to get Maxine."

"Why?"

"Just for the fun of it," Joyce said.

"Bitch."

"Slut."

"Whore."

"Cunt."

I kicked Joyce in the shin. I draw the line at *cunt*. And besides, ever since that day I caught her bare-assed on my dining room table with my husband, I've been wanting to kick her.

Joyce responded by grabbing my hair.

"Yow!" I said. "Let go!"

She wouldn't let go, so I gave her a good pinch in the arm.

"Hold on here," Lula said. "I can tell you don't know nothing about fighting. This woman got you by the hair, and all you can do is give her a pinch?"

"Yeah, but it'll leave a bruise," I said.

Joyce yanked harder at my hair. Then suddenly she gave a squeak, and she was on her back, on the floor.

I glared over at Lula.

"Well, I just wanted to see if the new batteries were working," Lula said.

"So how much do you think breasts like that would cost?" Sally asked. "Do you think they'd look good on me?"

"Sally, those are real breasts."

Sally bent down and took a closer look. "Damn."

"Uh oh," Lula said. "I don't know how to break this to you, but we're missing someone."

I looked around. Kuntz was gone. "Sally, you check the men's room. Lula, you search the room here. I'll see if he's outside."

"What about Joyce?" Lula said. "Maybe we should shove her over in the corner where people won't trip on her."

Joyce's eyes were glazed, and her mouth was open. Her breathing seemed normal enough, considering she'd just taken a few volts.

"Joyce?" I said. "You okay?"

One of her arms flailed out.

A small crowd had accumulated.

"Dizzy spell," I told everyone.

"I read in the manual sometimes people wet themselves when they have one of these dizzy spells," Lula said. "Wouldn't that be fun?"

Joyce's legs started flopping around, and her eyes came into focus.

Lula hoisted her up and sat her in a chair. "You should see a doctor about these spells," Lula said.

Joyce nodded. "Yeah. Thanks."

We got Joyce a cold beer and went off to find Kuntz.

I went outside to Morelli. "You see Eddie Kuntz leave?"

"What's he look like?"

"Five-eleven. Bodybuilder. He was wearing black pleated slacks and a black short-sleeve shirt."

"Yeah, I saw him. He left about five minutes ago. Drove off in a Chevy Blazer."

"He alone?"

"Yep."

"Nobody followed him?"

"Not that I noticed."

I returned to the bar and stood at the entrance looking for Sally and Lula. The room was crowded, and the noise level had risen considerably. I was jostled forward and then sharply yanked back, face-to-face with an angry woman I didn't recognize.

"I knew it was you!" she said. "You *bitch*."

I knocked her hands off me. "What's your problem?"

"You're my problem. Everything was fine before you came along."

"What are you talking about?"

"You know what I'm talking about. And if you have any sense in that big bimbo head of yours you'll get out of town. You'll go far away. Because if you don't I'm gonna find you and turn you into a pile of ashes . . . just like your apartment."

"You set fire to my apartment!"

"Hell no, not me. Do I look crazy enough to do something like that?"

"Yes."

She laughed very softly, but her eyes were small and hard with emotions that had nothing to do with joy. "Believe what you want. Just stay away from my boyfriend." She gave me a rough shove backward and stalked off toward the door, disappearing in the crowd.

I started after her, but the guy next to me moved in. "So," he said, "you want a boyfriend all your own?"

"Jesus," I said. "Get a life."

"Hey," he said, "just asking. No reason to get all huffy."

I shoved my way around him, but the woman was gone. I worked through the room to the door. I looked outside. I went back inside and looked some more. No luck.

I found Sally and Lula at the bar.

"This is impossible," Lula said. "There's wall-to-wall people here. You can't hardly even get a drink, much less find someone."

I told them Morelli saw Kuntz take off in the Blazer, but I didn't tell them about the angry woman. The angry woman was a separate issue. Probably.

"If there's not gonna be any more action here, Sally and me are taking off for this place he knows has good music," Lula said. "You want to come with?"

"No thanks, I'm calling it a night."

Sally and Lula gave each other the elbows.

"SO WHAT HAPPENED?" Morelli asked when I got back to the truck.

"Nothing."

"Just like always?"

"Yeah, except this was more nothing than usual." I rummaged through my shoulder bag, found my cell phone and dialed Kuntz. No answer. "This is too weird. Why would he leave the bar like that?"

"Were you with him the whole time? Maybe someone gave him another clue, and he went off on his own."

We were still parked at the curb, and I was thinking I should go back to the bar and ask some questions. "Wait here," I told Morelli.

"Again?"

"This will only take a few minutes."

I went to the bartender who'd been tending bar near us when Joyce went down.

"Do you remember the dark-haired guy I was with?" I asked. "The one dressed in black."

"Yeah. Eddie Kuntz."

"You know him?"

"No. Some woman came in around seven, right after I came on. She gave me a picture of Kuntz and ten dollars to pass him a note."

"Do you know what the note said?"

"Nope. It was in a sealed envelope. Must have been good, though. He left as soon as he read it."

Well, duh.

I returned to Morelli, slouched down in the seat and closed my eyes. "Stick a fork in me, I'm done."

Morelli turned the key in the ignition. "You sound bummed."

"Bummed at myself. I was stupid tonight. I let myself get distracted." Even more embarrassing, I hadn't immediately thought to question the bartender. And that wasn't all that had me bummed. Morelli had me bummed. He didn't understand about cookie jars. He gave his mother the wrong answer at the table. And I hated to admit it, but that eye thing had me worried. My God, what if Bella was right and I was pregnant?

I looked over at Morelli. His features were softened by shadow, but even in the dark I could see the paper-thin scar that sliced through his right eyebrow. A few years ago, Morelli had walked into a knife. And he'd probably walk into another. Maybe a bullet. Not a comforting thought. Nor was his love life comforting. In the past, Morelli'd had a short attention span when it came to romance. From time to time, he'd shown flashes of protective tenderness for me, but I wasn't always a priority. I was a friend, like Terry Gilman and the pissed-off woman, whoever the hell she was.

So I was thinking maybe Morelli wasn't prime husband material. Not even counting the fact that he didn't *want* to get married. Okay, now for the big one. Was I in love with Morelli? Hell, yes. I'd been in love with him since I was six years old.

I smacked myself in the forehead with the heel of my hand. "Unh."

Morelli gave me a sideways glance.

"Just thinking," I said.

"Must have been some thought. You almost knocked yourself out."

The thing is, while I was in love with Morelli for all these years, I'd always known it was best if nothing came of it. Loving Morelli was like loving cheesecake. Hours of misery on the StairMaster, working off ugly fat, in return for a moment of blissful consumption.

All right, maybe it wasn't as bad as all that. Morelli had matured. How *much* he'd matured I couldn't nail down. Truth is, I didn't know a lot about Morelli. What I knew was that I had a hard time trusting him. Past experience led me to believe blind faith in Morelli might not be a smart thing.

In fact, now that I thought about it, maybe *love* wasn't the right word. Maybe *enamored* was better. I was *definitely* enamored.

We rode in silence for most of the way home. Morelli had the golden oldies station on, and I was sitting on my hands so I wouldn't rip the knob off the radio.

"You look worried," Morelli said.

"I was thinking about the note the bartender gave to Eddie Kuntz. He said Kuntz read it and took off."

"And?"

"The other notes were all in code. Kuntz couldn't figure them out. That's why Sally was brought into it. Sally was always the only one who could read the notes."

Morelli cruised down his street and parked in front of his house. "I don't suppose you'd consider turning all this over to the police?"

And cut myself out of a recovery fee and leave the possibility open for Joyce to bring Maxine in? Fat chance. "Nope. I wouldn't consider it."

Lights were blinking off in the downstairs windows in Joe's neighborhood. Early to bed, early to rise meant you had a job that allowed you to make the mortgage payment every month. Blocks away cars hummed on Chambers, but there was no traffic on Joe's street.

"I had something else sort of odd happen tonight," I said. "I had a run-in with a woman at the bar."

Morelli unlocked his front door and flipped the light switch. "And?"

I gave Morelli the details of the conversation. "So what do you think?" I asked.

"I don't know what to think. Obviously it wasn't Terry."

"No. It wasn't Terry. There was something familiar about her, though. Like maybe I'd seen her someplace before. You know, like a nameless face in the supermarket."

"You think she firebombed your apartment?"

"I wouldn't write her off the list. You recognize any women going in or out?"

"No. Sorry."

Our eyes locked, and we both knew the doubt was there.

He tossed his keys on a sideboard, shrugged out of his jacket and tossed it across the lone wooden chair. He moved to the kitchen, where he checked his answering machine, unclipped his gun and his pager and laid them on the counter. "You need to pass that information about the woman on to the arson squad."

"Should I call tonight?"

Morelli closed the distance between us and took me in his arms. "Monday will be soon enough."

"Hmm," I said, in a less than encouraging voice.

"What hmm?"

"I'm not sure this is a good idea."

He kissed me lightly on the mouth. "This was never a good idea."

"Exactly. You see, this is exactly what I mean."

"Oh shit," Morelli said. "You're not going to make this all complicated, are you?"

My voice rose an octave. "Damn right I'm going to make this complicated. What do you think this is here anyway?"

"This is . . . satisfying mutual needs."

"A good fuck."

"Well, yeah."

I shoved him away. "Don't you ever need more than a good fuck?"

"Not right now! And what about you? You going to tell me you don't need it?"

"I have control over my needs."

"Yeah, right."

"I do!"

"That's why your nipples are hard."

I looked down at my dress. You could see the shape of my nipples behind the cotton fabric. "They've been like that all day. There's something wrong with them."

A smile twitched at the corners of Morelli's mouth. "You want me bad."

Damn skippy I wanted him. And that made me even more furious. Where were my principles? I wasn't sure I believed his answer about the woman who confronted me at the bar. I sensed a continuing relationship of some sort between him and Terry Gilman. And here I was with hard nipples! Ugh.

"I can do without you just fine," I said. "Don't call me. I'll call you."

"You won't last through the night."

Egotistical jerk. "Fifty bucks says I will."

"You want to bet on this?" He sounded incredulous.

"The first one to crack pays up."

Morelli's brows lowered and his eyes narrowed. "Fine. It won't be me, sweetheart."

"Hah!"

"Hah!"

I whirled around and stomped up the stairs. I brushed my teeth, got into my nightshirt and crawled into bed. I laid there for a half hour in the dark, feeling cranky and lonely, wishing Rex wasn't in the kitchen, wondering what ever possessed me to make that stupid bet. Fear, I thought. That's what possessed me. Fear of being dumped again. Fear of getting screwed over. Fear of defective condoms. Finally I got out of bed and stomped back down the stairs.

Morelli was in the living room, slouched in his favorite chair, watching television. He gave me a long, considering look.

"I came to get Rex," I said, swishing past him.

Morelli was still watching me when I returned carrying the hamster cage. The look was speculative and quietly unnerving.

"What?" I said.

"Nice nightshirt."

SUNDAY MORNING I opened my eyes and thought about Maxine Nowicki. I'd been on the case for a week. It felt like three. I dressed in shorts and T-shirt, and without even bothering to comb my hair, carted Rex to the kitchen.

Morelli glanced up from the paper when I padded in. He took in my hair and smiled. "Trying to help me win the bet?"

I poured out a mug of coffee and looked at the white bakery bag on the table. "Doughnuts?"

"Yeah. I was going to go to church, but I decided to get doughnuts instead."

I sat across from him and selected a Boston creme. "I've been on this Nowicki case for a week, and I don't think I'm making any progress."

"Imagine how the merry mutilator-murderer feels. He's hacking people up and making no progress."

"There's that." I reached behind me for the portable phone and dialed Kuntz. "No answer."

Morelli gave a chunk of doughnut to Rex and topped his cup. "Maybe we should take a ride over there this morning."

This caught my attention. "You have one of those cop feelings, don't you?"

"Feels funky."

I agreed. It felt funky. I ate two doughnuts, read the funnies and went upstairs to take a shower. I left the door unlocked, but Morelli didn't traipse inside. Good, I told myself. This was much better. Yeah, right.

Morelli was waiting for me when I came down the stairs. "Ready," I said.

Morelli looked at the big black leather tote bag draped over my shoulder. "You have a gun in there, don't you?"

"Christ, Morelli, I'm a bounty hunter."

"You have a permit to carry concealed?"

"You know I don't."

"Then get rid of the gun."

"You're wearing a gun!"

"I'm a cop."

I screwed up my mouth. "Big deal."

"Listen," Morelli said, "this is just the way it is. I'm a cop, and I can't go out with you when I know you're carrying concealed illegally. Besides, the thought of you with a gun in your hand scares the crap out of me."

As well it should. "Fine," I said, taking the gun out of my bag. "Just don't come running to me for help." I looked around. "So where do I put this?"

Morelli rolled his eyes and put the gun in a drawer in the sideboard. "You only had one, right?"

"What do I look like, Hopalong Cassidy?"

THE FIRST THING Morelli and I noticed was that Eddie Kuntz's car was nowhere to be seen. The second was that no one was answering the door. Morelli and I looked in the front window. No lights burning. No bodies on the floor. No sign of struggle. No Kuntz.

We were standing there with our noses pressed to the glass when the Lincoln Town Car pulled up.

"What's going on?" Leo wanted to know.

"I'm looking for Eddie," I said. "Have you seen him?"

Betty joined us on the porch. "Is something wrong?"

"They're looking for Eddie," Leo said. "When did we see him last? Yesterday?"

"Last night," Betty said. "He went out a little after eight. I remember because I was watering my flowers."

"Was his car here this morning?"

"Now that you mention it, I don't remember seeing it," Betty said.

"Saturday night," Leo said. "You know how it is with a young man."

Morelli and I looked at each other.

"Could be," Morelli said.

I gave them my card with my phone and pager numbers. "Just in case," I said.

"Sure," Leo said, "but don't worry. He's just partying."

They disappeared into their cool, dark house and the door clicked closed. No cake invitation.

Morelli and I went back to the truck.

"So?" I said.

"It would make sense that the note was personal and not from Maxine. It would explain the fact that it wasn't in code."

"You really believe that?"

Morelli shrugged. "It's possible."

I stared into the Glick front window. "They're watching us. I can see them standing a few feet back from the window."

Morelli rolled the engine over. "You have plans?"

"I thought I might visit Mrs. Nowicki."

"Isn't that a coincidence? I woke up this morning thinking it would be a good day to go to the shore."

The temperature was in the eighties. The sky was the color of putty. And the humidity was so high I could feel the air lying on my face. It wasn't a good day to go anywhere . . . unless it was out of Jersey.

"You aren't going to play Buddy Holly all the way to Point Pleasant, are you?"

"What's wrong with Buddy Holly?"

I grimaced. He probably liked the Three Stooges, too.

IT STARTED RAINING when we hit Point Pleasant. A nice steady soaker that chased everyone off the beach. It was the sort of rain farmers liked. Except there weren't any farmers in Point Pleasant—only bummed-out vacationers.

I directed Morelli to the Nowicki house, and we sat outside for a while, watching. There were no cars in the driveway. No lights on inside. No sign of activity.

"Looks a lot like Eddie Kuntz's house," I said.

"Yeah," Morelli said. "Let's go take a look."

We ran for the shelter of the porch and rang the bell. Neither of us expected an answer. When we didn't get one, we snooped in the windows.

"We missed the party," Morelli said.

The front room was a mess. Lamps knocked over, tables on end, chair cushions askew. Not from Joyce, either. This was a different mess.

I tried the door, but it was locked. We ran around back and crowded onto the small stoop. No luck with that door, either.

"Damn," I said. "I bet there are clues inside. Maybe even bodies."

"One way to find out." Morelli smashed the door window with his gun butt.

I jumped back. "Shit! I don't believe you did that. Didn't you watch the O. J. trial? Cops can't just bust into places."

Morelli had his arm through the hole in the glass. "It was an accident. And I'm not a cop today. It's my day off."

"You should team up with Lula. You'd make a great pair."

ELEVEN

Morelli opened the door, and we carefully picked our way around the broken glass. He looked under the sink, found a pair of rubber gloves, put them on and wiped his prints off the doorknob. "You don't need to worry about prints," he said. "You were here legitimately two days ago."

We did a fast walk-through just to make sure there were no bodies, dead or alive. Then we methodically worked our way through the rooms. Closets, drawers, hidden places, garbage bags.

All of their clothes were gone, and as far as I could tell, so were the prizes they'd won. They'd been in a hurry. Beds were unmade. Food had been left in the fridge. There'd been a struggle in the living room, and no one had bothered to make repairs. We didn't find anything that might hint at a new address. No sign of drugs. No bullets embedded in woodwork. No bloodstains.

My only conclusion was that they weren't great housekeepers and were probably going to end up with diverticulitis. They ate a lot of bologna and white bread, smoked a lot of cigarettes, drank a lot of beer and didn't recycle.

"Gone," Morelli said, snapping the gloves off, returning them to the sink.

"Any ideas?"

"Yeah. Let's get out of here."

We ran to the truck, and Morelli drove to the boardwalk. "There's a pay phone at the top of the ramp," he said. "Call the police and tell them you're a neighbor, and you noticed a back window was broken in the house next door. I don't want to leave that house open for vandalism or robbery."

I took stock of myself and decided I couldn't get much wetter, so I sloshed through the rain to the phone, made the call and sloshed back.

"Everything go okay?" he asked.

"They didn't like that I wouldn't tell them my name."

"You're supposed to make something up. Cops expect it."

"Cops are weird," I said to Morelli.

"Yeah," he said, "cops scare the hell out of me."

I took my shoes off and buckled myself in. "You want to hazard a guess on what happened in the living room back there?"

"Someone came after Maxine, chased her around the living room and got hit from behind by a blunt instrument. When he woke up the three women were gone."

"Maybe that someone was Eddie Kuntz."

"Maybe. But that doesn't explain why he's still missing."

THE RAIN STOPPED halfway home, and Trenton showed no sign of relief from the heat. The hydrocarbon level was high enough to etch glass, and the highways hummed with road rage. Air conditioners were failing, dogs had diarrhea, laundry mildewed in hampers, and sinus cavities felt filled with cement. If the barometric pressure dropped any lower everyone's guts would be sucked through the soles of their feet into the bowels of the earth.

Morelli and I barely noticed any of this, of course, because we were born and raised in Jersey. Life is about survival of the fittest, and Jersey is producing the master race.

We stood dripping in Morelli's foyer, and I couldn't decide what I wanted to do first. I was starving, I was soaked, and I wanted to call and see if Eddie Kuntz had turned up. Morelli prioritized my actions by stripping in the hall.

"What are you doing?" I asked.

He'd removed his shoes and socks and shirt and had his thumbs stuck in his shorts. "I don't want to track water all through the house." A smile tugged at his mouth. "You have a problem with this?"

"No problem at all," I said. "I'm taking a shower. Does that give you any problems?"

"Only if you use all the hot water."

He was on the phone when I came downstairs. I was clean, but I couldn't get dry. Morelli didn't have air, and at this time of the day it was possible to work up a sweat doing nothing. I prowled through the refrigerator and decided on a ham-and-cheese sandwich. I slapped it together and ate standing at the counter. Morelli was writing on a pad. He looked up at me, and I decided this was cop business.

When he got off the phone he picked at the deli ham I'd left out. "That case I was working on has just been reopened. Something new turned up. I'm going to take a fast shower, and then I'm going to have to go out. I'm not sure when I'll be back."

"Today? Tomorrow?"

"Today. I just don't know when."

I finished my sandwich and straightened the kitchen. Rex had crawled out of his soup can and was looking neglected, so I gave him a small chunk of cheese and a crust of bread. "We're not doing too good here," I told him. "I keep losing people. Now I can't find the guy I'm working for."

I tried calling Eddie Kuntz. No answer. I looked up Glick in the phone book and called Betty.

"Have you seen Eddie yet?" I asked.

"No."

I hung up and did some pacing. Someone knocked on the front door.

It was a little Italian lady.

"I'm Joe's godmother, Tina Ragusto," she said. "You must be Stephanie. How are you, dear? I just heard. I think it's wonderful."

I didn't know what she was talking about, and I suspected it was better that way. I made a vague gesture toward the stairs. "Joe's in the shower."

"I can't stay. I'm on my way to a jewelry party." She handed me a white shirt box. "I just wanted to drop this off." She lifted the lid and spread the tissue paper, so I could see what lay beneath. Her round face smoothed with her smile. "You see?" she said. "Joseph's christening outfit."

Ulk.

She gave me a pat on the cheek. "You're a good Italian girl."

"Half Italian."

"And a good Catholic."

"Umm . . ."

I watched her walk to her car and drive away. She thought I was pregnant. She thought I was marrying Joe Morelli, the man voted "least trustworthy male to date my daughter" by mothers statewide. And she thought I was a good Catholic. How had this happened?

I was standing in the foyer, holding the box, when Joe came down. "Was someone here?"

"Your godmother. She brought me your christening outfit."

Morelli picked it out of the box and looked at it. "Good grief, it's a dress."

"What do you want me to do with it?"

"Put it in a closet somewhere, and I'd appreciate it if you kept the dress part quiet."

I waited until Morelli was out of sight, and then I looked down at my stomach. "No way," I said. I looked at the christening dress. It was kind of pretty. Old-fashioned. Very Italian. Damn, I was getting all choked up over Morelli's dress. I ran upstairs with the dress, put it on Morelli's bed, ran out of the room and slammed the door closed.

I went to the kitchen and called my best friend, Mary Lou, who had two kids and knew about pregnancy.

"Where are you?" Mary Lou wanted to know.

"I'm at Morelli's."

"Ommigod! It's true! You're living with Morelli! And you didn't tell me! I'm your best friend. How could you do this to me?"

"I've only been here for three days. And it's no big deal. My apartment burned up, and Morelli had an extra room."

"You did it with him! I can hear it in your voice! How was it? I want details!"

"I need a favor."

"Anything!"

"I need one of those pregnancy test things."

"Ommigod! You're pregnant! Ommigod. Ommigod!"

"Calm down. I'm not pregnant. I just want to make sure. You know, peace of mind. And I don't want to buy one myself, because if anybody sees me it'll be all over."

"I'll be right there. Don't move."

Mary Lou lived about a half mile away. Her husband, Lennie, was okay but he had to be careful not to drag his knuckles when he walked. Mary Lou never cared much about intelligence in a man. Mary Lou was more into packaging and stamina.

Mary Lou and I have been friends since the day we were born. I was always the flake, and Mary Lou was always the under-achiever. Maybe *underachiever* isn't the right word. It was more that Mary Lou had simple goals. She wanted to get married and have a family. If she could marry the captain of the football team, even better. And that's exactly what she did. She married Lennie Stankovic, who was captain of the football team, graduated high school and went to work for his father. Stankovic and Sons Plumbing and Heating.

I wanted to marry Aladdin so I'd get to fly on his magic carpet. So you can see that we were coming from different places.

Ten minutes later Mary Lou was at the front door. Mary Lou is four inches shorter than me and five pounds heavier. None of her weight is fat. Mary Lou's solid. Mary Lou's built like a brick shit-house. If I ever do tag team wrestling, Mary Lou's going to be my partner.

"I've got it!" she said, barreling into the foyer, brandishing the test kit. She stopped short and looked around. "So this is Morelli's house!"

This was said in hushed tones of awe usually reserved for Catholic miracles like weeping statues of the Virgin.

"Oh man," she said. "I always wanted to see the inside of Morelli's house. He isn't home, right?" She took off up the stairs. "I want to see his bedroom!"

"It's the one to the left."

"This is it!" she shrieked, opening the door. "Ommigod! Did you do it on this bed?"

"Yeah." And on my bed. And on the couch, the hall floor, the kitchen table, in the shower . . .

"Holy shit," Mary Lou said, "he's got a carton of condoms. What is he . . . a fucking rabbit?"

I took the little brown bag from her hand and peeked inside. "So this is it?"

"It's simple. All you have to do is pee on the plastic strip and wait for it to change color. Good thing it's summer and you're wearing a T-shirt, because the hard part is not getting your sleeve wet."

"Darn," I said. "I don't have to go right now."

"You need beer," Mary Lou said. "Beer always works."

We went to the kitchen, and we each had two beers.

"You know what's missing in this kitchen?" Mary Lou said. "A cookie jar."

"Yeah, well, you know how it is with men."

"They don't know anything," Mary Lou said.

I opened the box and removed the foil packet. "I can't get this open. I'm too nervous."

Mary Lou took it from me. Mary Lou had nails like razor wire. "We gotta time this. And don't tip the plastic strip. You have to collect the pee in that little indentation."

"Ick."

We went upstairs, and Mary Lou waited outside the door while I did the test. Friendship among women does not include viewing each other's urine.

"What's happening?" Mary Lou yelled through the door. "Do you see a plus sign or a negative sign?"

My hand was shaking so badly I was lucky I didn't drop the whole thing in the toilet. "I don't see anything yet."

"I'm timing," Mary Lou said. "It takes three minutes max."

"Three minutes," Mary Lou yelled again, and she opened the door. "Well?"

Little black dots were dancing in front of my eyes and my lips felt numb. "I'm going to faint." I sat down hard on the floor and put my head between my knees.

Mary Lou took the test strip. "Negative. Yes!"

"God, that was close. I was really worried. We used condoms every single time, but Bella said—"

"Joe's Grandma Bella?" Mary Lou gasped. "Oh shit! Bella didn't give you the eye, did she? Remember when she put it on Raymond Cone and all his hair fell out?"

"Worse than that, she told me I was pregnant."

"Then that's it," Mary Lou said. "The test is wrong."

"What do you mean the test is wrong? The test isn't wrong. Johnson and Johnson doesn't make mistakes."

"Bella knows these things."

I got up off the floor and splashed water on my face. "Bella's a crackpot." Even as I said it I was mentally doing the sign of the cross.

"How far overdue are you?"

"I'm not actually overdue yet."

"Wait a minute. You can't take this test if you aren't overdue. I thought you knew that."

"What?"

"It takes time to develop the hormone. When's your period?"

"I don't know. In about a week, I guess. Are you telling me this test isn't valid?"

"That's what I'm telling you."

"Fuck!"

"I gotta go," Mary Lou said. "I told Lennie I'd bring pizza home for supper. You want to eat with us?"

"No. Thanks anyway."

After Mary Lou left I slouched in the chair in the living room and stared at the blank television screen. Taking the pregnancy test had exhausted me.

I heard a car pull up and footsteps on the pavement outside the house. It was another little Italian lady.

"I'm Joseph's Aunt Loretta," she said, handing me a foil-topped casserole. "I just heard. And don't worry, dear, these things happen. We don't talk about it, but Joseph's mother had sort of a hurry-up wedding, too, if you know what I mean."

"It's not what it seems."

"The important thing is that you eat good food. You aren't throwing up, are you?"

"Not yet."

"Don't worry about getting the dish back to me. You can give it to me at the shower."

My voice rose an octave. "The shower?"

"I gotta go," she said. "I gotta visit my neighbor in the hospital." She leaned forward and lowered her voice. "Cancer," she whispered. "Terrible. Terrible. She's rotting away. Her insides are rotted, and now she's got sores all over her body. I had a cousin once who rotted like that. She turned black and just before she died her fingers fell off."

"Eeeee*euw*."

"Well," she said, "you enjoy the casserole."

I waved good-bye and carted the warm casserole off to the kitchen. I set it on the counter and banged my head against the cabinet door a couple of times. "Argh."

I lifted a corner of the foil and peeked inside. Lasagna. Smelled good. I cut a square for myself and scooped it onto a plate. I was thinking about seconds when Morelli came home.

He looked at the lasagna and sighed. "Aunt Loretta."

"Yep."

"This is out of control," he said. "This has to stop."

"I think they're planning a shower."

"Shit."

I got up and rinsed my plate, so I wouldn't be tempted to cut another wedge of lasagna. "How'd things go today?"

"Not that good."

"Want to talk about it?"

"Can't. I'm working with the Feds. It's not supposed to go public."

"You don't trust me."

He cut a slab of lasagna and joined me at the table. "Of course I trust you. It's Mary Lou I don't trust."

"I don't tell Mary Lou everything!"

"Look, it's not your fault. You're a woman, so you blab."

"That's disgusting! That's so sexist!"

He took a bite of lasagna. "I have sisters. I know women."

"You don't know *all* women."

Morelli considered me. "I know you."

I could feel my face get warm. "Yeah, well, we should talk about that."

He pushed back in his chair. "It's your nickel."

"I don't think I'm cut out for irresponsible sex."

He thought about that for a beat and gave an almost imperceptible nod. "We have a problem then, because I don't think I'm cut out for marriage. At least not now."

Wow. Big surprise. "I wasn't proposing marriage."

"What were you proposing?"

"I wasn't proposing anything. I guess I was just setting boundaries."

"You know, you're one of those women who drive men nuts.

176

Men drive off bridges and drink too much because of women like you. And it was your fault in the bakery, too."

I narrowed my eyes. "You want to explain that to me?"

Morelli smiled. "You smelled like a jelly doughnut."

"You jerk! That's what you wrote on the bathroom wall in Mario's Sub Shop. You said I was warm and sweet and good to eat. And then you went on to describe how you did it! It got back to my parents, and I was grounded for three months. You have no scruples!"

His eyes darkened. "Don't confuse me with that eighteen-year-old kid."

We glared at each other for a couple of beats, and the silence was shattered by the sound of something smashing through Morelli's living room window.

Morelli bolted from his chair and ran for the front room. I was close behind, almost slamming into him when he stopped short.

A bottle lay in the middle of his living room floor, and there was a fire-blackened rag stuck into the mouth of the bottle. A Molotov cocktail that had burned itself out because the bottle hadn't broken on impact.

Morelli skirted the bottle, rushed into the hall and out the door.

I got to the door in time to see Morelli aim and fire at a retreating car. Only the gun didn't fire. It went *click, click, click.* Morelli looked at the gun in disbelief.

"What's wrong?" I asked.

"This is your gun. I got it out of the sideboard when I ran through the hall. It hasn't got any bullets in it!"

"Bullets are creepy."

Morelli looked dazed. "What good is a gun without bullets?"

"It's good for scaring people. Or you can hit people with it. Or you can use it to break windows . . . or crack walnuts."

"You recognize that car?"

"No. You get a look at the driver?"

Morelli shook his head. "No." He stalked through the house, took his gun and pager off the kitchen counter and clipped them to his belt. He called the dispatcher and gave him the car description. Then he called someone else with the plate number. He took an extra clip out of a kitchen drawer and put it in his pocket while he waited on the plate.

I was standing behind him, and I was trying hard to stay calm, but I was shaking inside, and I was having flashbacks of my ruined apartment. If I'd been home, in bed, when the bottle had exploded, I'd have been killed, charred beyond recognition. As it was I'd lost just about everything I owned. Not that it was much . . . but it was all I had. And now it had almost happened again.

"That was for me," I said, relieved that my voice didn't tremble and give me away.

"Probably," Morelli said. He murmured something into the phone and hung up. "The car was reported stolen a couple hours ago."

He gingerly picked up the bottle with a kitchen towel and put it in a paper bag. Then he set the bag on the kitchen counter. "Fortunately, this guy didn't choose his bottle wisely, and when he threw it, it landed on carpet."

The phone rang, and Morelli snatched at it.

"It's for you," he said. "It's Sally."

"I need help," Sally said. "I have a gig tonight, and I can't figure out this makeup shit."

"Where's Sugar?"

"We had another fight, and he took off."

"Okay," I said, reacting more than thinking, still feeling numbed by the second attempt to end my life. "I'll be right over."

"Now what?" Morelli asked.

"I need to help Sally with his makeup."

"I'll go with you."

"Not necessary."

"I think it is."

"I don't need a bodyguard." What I really meant was *I don't want to get you killed, too.*

"Then consider this to be a date."

178

WE KNOCKED twice, and Sally just about ripped the door off its hinges when he yanked it open. "Shit," he said, "it's you."

"Who'd you think it would be?"

"I guess I was hoping it was Sugar. Look at me. I'm a wreck. I don't know how to do any of this shit. Sugar always gets me dressed. Christ, I haven't got the right hormones for this fucking shit, you know what I mean?"

"Where'd Sugar go?"

"I don't know. We had another fight. I don't even know how it started. Something about me not appreciating his coffee cake."

I looked around. The house was beyond immaculate. Not a speck of dust anywhere. Nothing out of place. Through the kitchen door I could see the kitchen counters neatly lined with cakes, pies, loaves of bread, glass jars filled with cookies and homemade fudge.

"I didn't even realize he was all that upset," Sally said. "He got dressed and left when I was in my bubble bath."

Morelli arched an eyebrow. "Bubble bath?"

"Hey, give me a break here. RuPaul says you're supposed to take a goddamn bubble bath, so that's what I do. Gets you in touch with your fuckin' female side."

Morelli grinned.

Sally was wearing black bikini Calvins and panty hose, and he was holding a contraption that looked like a corset with breasts. "You gotta help me," he said. "I can't get into this by myself."

Morelli held up a hand. "You're on your own."

Sally looked over at him. "What, are you homophobic?"

"Nope," Morelli said. "I'm Italian. There's a difference."

"Okay," I said. "What do I have to do?"

Sally wiggled into the corset and got it in place. "Tighten this fucker up," he said. "I need to get a waist."

I pulled at the strings, but I couldn't get them to go together. "I can't do this. I haven't got enough hand strength."

We both looked at Morelli.

179

Morelli gave a disgusted sigh. "Shit," he said, heaving himself off the couch. He took hold of the strings, put his foot to Sally's butt and yanked.

"Oof," Sally said. He looked over his shoulder at Morelli. "You've done this before."

"Dolan used to wear one of these when he went undercover."

"I don't suppose you did Dolan's makeup?"

"Sorry," Morelli said, "makeup's way out of my league."

Sally looked to me.

"No sweat," I said. "I'm from the Burg. I was putting makeup on Barbie before I could walk."

Half an hour later I had him appropriately slutted up. We tugged on his wig and did some last-minute combing. Sally zipped himself into a short black leather skirt and a black leather top that looked like Madonna meets the Hell's Angels. He slipped his size-fourteen feet into a pair of platform heels, and he was ready to go.

"How are you doing on time?" I asked.

He grabbed his guitar case. "I'm cool. So how do I look? Am I pretty?"

"Well, uh . . . yeah." If you like almost-seven-feet-tall, slightly bow-legged, hook-nosed guys with hairy chests and arms dressed up like the bride of the Valkyries.

"You should come with me," Sally said. "I'll introduce you to the rest of the band, and you could stay and watch the show."

"Do I know how to take a girl on a date, or what?" Morelli said.

We took the elevator with Sally and followed him out of the lot. He looped around down by the river and got on Route 1 north.

"That was nice of you to help him with his corset," I said.

"Yeah," Morelli said. "I'm Mr. Sensitivity."

Sally went about fifteen miles and put his blinker on, so we'd know he was turning. The club was on the right side of the high-way, all lit up in red and pink neon lights. Already there were a lot of cars in the lot. The sign on the rooftop advertised an all-girl re-vue. I guessed that was Sally.

Sally crawled out of the Porsche and straightened his skirt. "We've played here for four weeks now," he said. "We're like fucking regulars."

Regular what I didn't know.

Morelli looked around the lot. "Where's Sugar's car?"

"The black Mercedes."

"Sugar does okay."

Sally grinned. "You ever see him in drag?"

We both shook our heads no.

"When you see him you'll understand."

We followed Sally in through the kitchen entrance.

"If I go through the front I'll get fucking mobbed," he said. "These people are animals."

We went down a dreary narrow hall to a back room. The room was filled with smoke and noise and the Lovelies. All five of them. All dressed in various forms of leather . . . with the exception of Sugar. Sugar was wearing a blood-red satin dress that fit him like his own skin. It was short and tight and so smooth in front I thought he must have been surgically altered. His makeup was flawless. His lips were full and pouty, painted in high gloss to match the dress. He wore the Marilyn wig, and on my best day I never looked that good. I slid a sideways glance at Morelli, and he obviously was caught in the same dumbstruck fascination that I was experiencing. I shifted my attention back to Sugar and realization suddenly hit me.

"The woman in the bar was Sugar," I whispered to Morelli. "It was a different blond wig, but I'm sure it was Sugar."

"Are you kidding me? He was right in front of you, and you didn't recognize him?"

"It happened so fast, and the room was dark and crowded. And besides, look at him! He's beautiful!"

Sugar saw the three of us come into the room, and he was on his feet, calling Sally an ungrateful slut.

"Christ," Sally said, "what's he talking about? Don't you have to be a chick to be a slut?"

"You *are* a chick, you dumb shit," one of the other drag queens said.

Sally grabbed his package and gave it a hike up.

"I'd like to talk to you in private," Morelli said to Sugar.

"You don't belong here, and I'm not talking to you," Sugar said. "This is the band's dressing room. Now get the hell out."

Morelli crossed the room in three strides, backing Sugar into a corner. They stood talking like that for a few minutes, and then Morelli eased off. "Nice meeting you," he said to the other band members, who were shuffling foot to foot in awkward silence. "Talk to you later," he said to Sally.

When we left Sugar was still in the corner, his eyes small and glittery, not a part of his baby doll face.

"Jeez," I said. "What did you say to him?"

"I asked him if he was involved in the firebombings."

"And what did he tell you?"

"Not much."

"He sure makes a beautiful woman."

Morelli gave his head a small shake of amazement. "Christ, for a minute there I didn't know whether I wanted to punch him in the face or ask him for a date."

"We going to stay to watch the band?"

"No," Morelli said. "We're going out to the lot to check out the Mercedes, and then we're going to run a check on Sugar."

THE MERCEDES was clean, and so was Sugar. No priors for Gregory Stern. When we got back to Morelli's house there were two cop cars parked in front and several people milling around on the sidewalk. Morelli parked the truck and got out and walked over to the nearest uniform, who happened to be Carl Costanza.

"Been waiting for you," Carl said. "Didn't know if you wanted us to board your window."

"No. It'll be okay for tonight, and tomorrow I'll get a glass guy over here."

"You coming in, or you gonna do the report in the morning?" Carl asked.

"I'll do it in the morning."

"Congratulations," Costanza said to me. "I hear you're preggers."

"I'm *not* preggers!"

Costanza draped an arm around me and leaned close. "Would you like to be?"

I rolled my eyes.

"Okay, but remember me in case you change your mind," Carl said.

An old man in a bathrobe came up to Morelli and gave him the elbow. "Just like old times, huh? I can remember when Ziggy Kozak's house got machine-gunned into Swiss cheese. Boy, I tell you, those were the days."

Morelli went into the house, got the firebomb and gave it to Carl. "Have this checked for prints and put it in the lockup. Anybody canvass the neighborhood for a witness?"

"No witnesses. We did every house."

"How about the car?"

"Hasn't turned up yet."

The cops got into their cars and drove off. The people dispersed. I followed Morelli into the living room, where we both stood looking at the glass shards scattered over the floor.

"I'm really sorry," I said. "This is my fault. I shouldn't have come here."

"Don't worry about it," Morelli said. "Life was getting dull."

"I could move out."

Morelli grabbed me by the front of my shirt and pulled me to him. "You're just afraid you're going to cave and have to pay me fifty dollars."

I felt a smile come on. "Thanks."

Morelli leaned in and kissed me. He had his knee between my legs and his tongue in my mouth, and I got a hot rush that dropped my stomach about six inches.

He backed off and grinned at me. "Good night."

I blinked. "G'nite."

The grin widened. "Gotcha."

I grit my teeth. "I'm going to bed."

"I'll be down here if you get lonely. I'm going to sleep on the couch tonight just to make sure no one crawls through my window and walks off with my television."

TWELVE

I WAS UP early, but Joe was up earlier. He'd cleaned the glass away and was eating lasagna for breakfast when I trooped into the kitchen.

I poured coffee and gave the lasagna a wistful glance.

"Go for it," Morelli said.

If I ate the lasagna I'd have to do something physical, like jog a couple of miles. Not my favorite activity. I preferred to get my exercise by walking through a shopping mall. Okay, what the hell, I should probably go out for a run anyway. Keep in shape, and all that crap.

I sat across from him and dug in. "You back on the mystery case today."

"Surveillance."

I hated surveillance. Surveillance meant you sat in a car all by yourself until your ass fell asleep. And if you left to go to the bathroom all hell broke loose and you missed it.

Morelli pushed his empty plate away. "What are your plans?"

"Find Maxine."

"And?"

"And that's it. I have no ideas. I'm out of leads. Everyone's disappeared. Eddie Kuntz's probably dead. For all I know Mrs. Now-icki, Margie and Maxine are dead. Dead and buried."

"Boy, it's nice to see you so positive this morning."

"I like to start out right."

Morelli got up and rinsed his plate. "I have to go to work. If you were an ordinary person I'd tell you to be careful. Since you are who you are, I'll just wish you good luck. Oh, yeah, and someone's supposed to show up at nine to fix the window. Can you hang around until he's done?"

"No problem."

He kissed me on the top of the head and left.

I looked at Rex. "This feels a little strange," I said. "I'm not used to being a housewife."

Rex sat on his haunches and stared at me. At first glance you might think he was contemplating what I'd just said. More likely he wanted a grape.

For lack of something better to do I called Eddie Kuntz. No answer. "Dead," I said to Rex. I wanted to drive over and have another chat with Betty, but I had to wait for the glass to get fixed. I had a second cup of coffee. And then I had a second piece of lasagna. At nine o'clock the glazier arrived, and he was followed by yet another Italian lady bearing food. A chocolate cake this time. I ate half while I waited for the windows.

I DIDN'T HAVE TO KNOCK on the door to know Eddie Kuntz wasn't home. No car out front. No lights anywhere. Windows and doors closed up tight. The only thing missing was black crepe.

I knocked on Betty's door instead.

"What can I tell you?" Betty said. "He's not home. Like I told you before, last I saw him was Saturday."

She didn't look worried or confused. What she looked was pissed. Like I was bothering her.

"Does he do this a lot? Do you think we should notify the police?"

"He's on a bender," Leo said from his chair in front of the TV. "He picked up one of his trashy girlfriends, and they're shacked up somewhere. That's the end of it. He'll be home when he's home."

"You're probably right," I said. "Still, it might not hurt to do a little investigating. Maybe it would be a good idea if we checked out his apartment. You have a key?"

Leo was more adamant this time. "He's on a bender, I'm telling you. And you don't go snooping around in a man's home just because he goes on a bender. Anyway, why are you so interested in finding Eddie? I thought you were looking for Maxine Nowicki."

"Eddie's disappearance might be related."

"For the last time, I'm telling you it's not a disappearance."

Sounded like denial to me, but what do I know? I went back to the Buick and drove to Mrs. Nowicki's house. It looked even worse than it had the first time I saw it. No one was cutting the grass, and a dog had done number two right in the middle of the sidewalk. Just for the hell of it I walked around the house and looked in the windows. No sign of life.

I got back in the car and headed for Margie's house. I took New York to Olden, turned onto Olden and spotted the beat-up Fairlane Morelli uses for surveillance. He was parked across the street from the 7-Eleven where Helen Badijian had worked before her death. Morelli was working with the Feds, so I assumed it was drugs, but really it could be anything from running guns to black-market babies. Or maybe he'd stopped there to have lunch and take a nap.

Margie's house looked better kept than Nowicki's, but empty all the same. I looked in the windows, and I wondered what Margie had done with her cat.

The next-door neighbor stuck her head out her front door and caught me peeking in Margie's window.

"I'm looking for Margie," I said. "I work with her at the diner, and I haven't seen her for a couple days, so I got worried. She doesn't seem to be home."

"She went on vacation. She said it was too hard to work with her finger cut like that, so she took some time off. I think she went to the shore. I'm surprised you didn't know."

"I knew she wasn't working. I didn't know she went to the shore." I looked around. "Where's her cat? She take it with her?"

"No. They don't allow cats in the house she rented. I'm feeding the cat. It's no bother."

I was half a block away when it hit me. The finger! She'd have to have it looked at. She'd have to get her stitches removed. And Maxine's mother probably needed medical attention, too. She'd still had her head all wrapped up when I saw her in Point Pleasant.

I hustled to the office so I could use the by-street directory. Connie was doing her nails, and Lula had her ears plugged in to a Walkman. Lula's back was to me, and her beads were clicking around her head, and her ass was going side to side in some jive step. She caught me in her peripheral vision and turned the Walkman down.

"Uh oh," she said. "You're not getting any."

"How do you know that?" I yelled. I threw my hands into the air. "I don't believe this!"

Vinnie poked his head around the corner. "What's all the racket about?"

"Stephanie's here," Connie said.

Vinnie had a cigar in his mouth that I'm willing to bet was twice the size of his dick. "Where's Maxine? I forfeit my money in five days, for crissake. I should never have taken Barnhardt off."

"I'm closing in."

"Right," Vinnie said. "Closing in on my liver." He ducked into his office and slammed the door.

I traced Margie's address in the directory and came up with her last name. There are three hospitals in the Trenton area. Helene Fuld is a short distance from Nowicki's neighborhood. Margie's address is equal distance between Helene Fuld and St. Francis.

I went home to Joe's house, helped myself to another wedge of chocolate cake and called my cousin Evelyn, who works at Helene Fuld. I gave her the two names and asked her to nose around. Neither Margie nor Mama Nowicki was wanted by the police, so (assuming they were alive) they had no reason not to return to their doctors. Their only concern was keeping me from following them back to Maxine.

IT WAS three o'clock, and I was sort of hoping another Italian lady would stop around with something new for dinner. I kept looking out the window, but I didn't see any big black cars bearing food. This posed a problem because the idea of being in Morelli's kitchen, making him dinner, felt like a Doris Day movie.

Evelyn called and told me it was my lucky day. Both women had been treated at Fuld. Both women would go to their own doctors for follow-up. She gave me the names of the attending physicians and also the names listed for primary care through their medical plans. I told her I owed her. She said a detailed description of Morelli in bed would do the trick.

I called the doctors and lied my ass off to their receptionists, telling them I'd forgotten my appointment time. Both women had Wednesday appointments. Shit, I was good.

Morelli dragged in with a sweat stain the length of his gray T-shirt. He went to the refrigerator and stuck his head in the freezer. "I've gotta get air in this house."

I thought the weather was pretty good compared to yesterday. Today you could sort of see a yellow glow where the sun was behind the layer of funk air.

He pulled his head out of the freezer, tossed his gun on the counter and got a beer.

"Bad day?"

"Average."

"I saw you in north Trenton."

"You made me?"

"I recognized the car. I figured you were watching the Seven-Eleven."

"And watching, and watching, and watching."

"Drugs?"

"Funny money."

"I thought you weren't supposed to tell me."

"Fuck it. Treasury has this case so screwed up it doesn't matter. There've been bogus twenties coming out of Trenton for five years that we know of . . . probably more. Treasury has everything in place. They go in to get the guy. No plates where the plates are supposed to be. No paper. No nothing. Including no funny money traffic. We can't even make an arrest. We look like a bunch of fucking amateurs. Then all of a sudden, yesterday, a couple of the twenties get passed at the convenience store on Olden. So we start all over, looking to see who goes in that store."

"The clerk didn't know who passed them?"

"They were discovered at the bank when the teller was counting them out for deposit."

"What do you think?"

"I think we had the right guy the first time. Some fluky thing happened and the stuff wasn't there."

"I just had a weird thought. We attributed Helen Badijian's death to her connection with Maxine. Maybe it didn't have anything to do with Maxine. Maybe it had to do with the funny money."

"I thought of that, too, but the MO ties it to Maxine. Cause of death to Badijian was a blow to the head, but she also had one of her fingers chopped off."

I had an even weirder thought, but I didn't want to say it out loud and sound like a dunce.

The phone rang, and Morelli answered. "Yes, Mrs. Plum," he said.

I jumped out of my chair and started to run for the front door. I was halfway through the dining room when Morelli snagged me by the back of my shirt and stopped my progress with a sharp yank that had me pressed against his chest.

"Your mother," he said, handing me the phone.

"Stephanie," my mother said. "What is this I hear about your being pregnant?"

"I'm not pregnant. This is a living arrangement, not a marriage."

FOUR TO SCORE

"Everybody's talking. Everybody thinks you're pregnant. What should I tell Mrs. Crandle?"

"Tell her I'm not pregnant."

"Your father wants to talk to you."

I could hear the phone being transferred and then some breathing.

"Dad?"

"Yeah," he said. "How's the Buick running? You gotta give it high test, you know."

"Don't worry. I always give it high test." I *never* gave it high test. It didn't deserve high test. It was ugly.

He gave the phone back to my mother, and I could hear my mother rolling her eyes at him.

"I have a nice pot roast on the stove," she said. "With peas and mashed potatoes."

"Okay," I said. "I'll come for dinner."

"And Joseph."

"No. He can't make it."

"Yes, I can," Joe said.

I gave a big sigh. "He'll come, too."

I disconnected and gave him the phone. "You'll be sorry."

"NOTHING LIKE BEING PREGNANT to give a woman a glow," Grandma said.

"I may be glowing, but I'm not pregnant."

Grandma looked down at my stomach. "You look pregnant."

It was all that damn Italian food. "It's cake," I said.

"You might want to get rid of that cake before the wedding," Grandma said. "Or you're going to have to buy one of them empire gowns that don't have a waist."

"I'm not getting married," I said. "There's no wedding."

Grandma sat up straighter. "What about the hall?"

"What hall?"

"We figured you'd hold your reception at the Polish National

191

Hall. It's the best place for it, and Edna Majewski said they had a cancellation, but you'd have to act fast."

"You didn't hire a hall!"

"Well, we didn't put down no deposit," Grandma said. "We weren't sure of the date."

I looked to Joe. "You explain it."

"Stephanie's apartment got damaged in the fire, and she's renting a room from me until her apartment's repaired."

"How about sex?" Grandma asked. "Are you having sex?"

"No." Not since Saturday.

"If it was me, I'd have sex," Grandma said.

"Christ," my father said, at the head of the table.

My mother passed me the potatoes. "I have forms for you to fill out for the insurance. Ed was over at your apartment and said there was nothing left of it. He said the only thing that was left was the cookie jar. He said the cookie jar was fine."

I silently dared Morelli to say something about the cookie jar, but Morelli was busy cutting his meat. The phone rang and Grandma went to the kitchen to answer it.

"It's for you, Stephanie," Grandma yelled.

"I been calling all over, trying to track you down," Lula said. "I got some news. Joyce Barnhardt called Vinnie just before we were getting ready to leave, and Connie listened in. Joyce told Vinnie she'd make him bark like a dog if he put her back on the case and guess what?"

"I can guess."

"Yeah, so then she goes on to tell Vinnie how she's getting her leads on Maxine. And now we know the name of the little jack-off that's helping Joyce."

"*Yes!*"

"So I figure maybe you and me should pay him a visit."

"Now?"

"You got something better to do?"

"No. Now will be fine."

"I'll pick you up then on account of I'm not riding in that Buick."

Everyone stopped eating when I returned to the table.

"Well?" Grandma said.

"It was Lula. I'm going to have to eat and run. We have a lead on a case."

"I could go, too," Grandma said. "Like last time."

"Thanks, but I'd rather you stayed home and entertained Joe."

Grandma winked at Morelli, and Morelli looked like a snake that just swallowed a cow and got it stuck in his throat.

Ten minutes later, I heard a car pull to the curb outside. Rap music thumped through the house, the music cut off and in moments Lula was at the door.

"We got a lot of pot roast," Grandma said to Lula. "You want some?"

My mother was on her feet, setting an extra plate.

"Pot roast," Lula said. "Boy, I like pot roast." She pulled a chair up and shook out her napkin.

"I always wanted to eat with a Negro," Grandma said.

"Yeah, well, I always wanted to eat with a boney-assed old white woman," Lula said. "So I guess this works out good."

Grandma and Lula did some complicated handshake thing.

"Bitchin'," Grandma said.

IT WAS the first time I'd ridden in the new Firebird, and I was feeling envious.

"How can you afford a car like this working as a file clerk? And how come your insurance came through, and I'm still waiting?"

"First off, I got low overhead where I'm living. And second, I just keep leasing these suckers. You barbecue a car and they give you a new one. No sweat."

"Maybe I should look into that."

"Just don't tell them about how your cars keep getting blown up. They might think you're a risk, you know what I'm saying?" Lula had taken High to Hamilton. "This guy, Bernie, works at the supermarket on Route Thirty-three. When he's not stacking oranges he's selling wacky tobaccy, which is the common link between Barnhardt and Mama Nowicki. Nowicki talks to Bernie, then Bernie talks to Barnhardt."

"Joyce said it was a retail connection."

"Ain't that the truth."

"From what Connie got on the phone it seems he's also visually challenged."

"Blind?"

"Ugly."

She turned into the supermarket lot and rolled to a stop in a front slot. Not many people were shopping at this time of the night.

"Joyce said he was a horny little troll, so if you don't want to buy dope maybe you can promise him favors."

"As in sexual favors?"

"You don't have to deliver," Lula said. "All you gotta do is promise. I'd do it, but I think he's more your type."

"What type is that?"

"White."

"How do I find him?"

"Name's Bernie. Works in Produce. Looks like a horny little troll."

I pulled the visor mirror down, fluffed my hair and applied fresh lip gloss. "Do I look okay?"

"From what I hear, this guy won't care if you bark and chase cars."

I didn't have trouble finding him. He was stickering grapefruits with his back to me. He had a lot of curly black hair on the back and sides of his head and none on the top. The top of his head looked like a big pink egg. He was just under five feet, and built like a fireplug.

I put a sack of potatoes in my cart, and I cruised over to him. "Excuse me," I said.

He turned, tilted his head back and looked at me. His fat fish lips parted slightly, but no words came out.

"Nice apples," I said.

He made a gurgling sound, and his eyes slid down to my chest.

"So," I said, "you have any dope?"

"What are you kidding me? What do I look like?"

"A friend of mine said I could get some dope from you."

"Oh yeah? Who's your friend?"

"Joyce Barnhardt."

This got his eyes to light up in a way that told me Joyce probably hadn't paid cold cash for her marijuana.

"I know Joyce," he said. "But I'm not saying I sold her any dope."

"We have another mutual friend."

"Who's that?"

"Her name's Nowicki."

"I don't know anybody named Nowicki."

I gave him a description.

"That must be Francine," he said. "She's a pip. I just never knew her last name."

"Good customer?"

"Yeah. She buys lots of fruit."

"See her lately?"

His voice got crafty. "What's it worth to you?"

I didn't like the sound of this. "What do you want?"

Bernie made a smoochy sound.

"Gross!"

"It's because I'm short, isn't it?"

"No. Of course not. I like short men. They, um, try harder."

"Then it's the hair, right? You want a guy with hair."

"Hair doesn't matter. I could care less about hair. And besides, you have plenty of hair. It's just not on the top of your head."

"Then what?"

"You don't just go around making smoochy sounds at women! It's . . . cheap."

"I thought you said you were friends with Joyce."

"Oh yeah. I see your point."

"So how about it?"

"The truth is, I'm not actually attracted to you."

"I knew it. I could tell all along. It's my height."

Jeez, the poor schnook really had a thing about his height. I mean, it wasn't as if he could help being born short or having a head like a bowling ball. I didn't want to compound his problem, but I didn't know what to say. And then I thought of Sally! "It's not your height," I said. "It's me. I'm a lesbian."

"You're shitting me!"

"No. Really."

He looked me up and down. "Are you sure? Christ, what a waste! You don't look like a lesbian."

I guess he thought lesbians had a big *L* burned into their foreheads, or something. Although, since I don't know any lesbians I'm not exactly an authority.

"You have a girlfriend?" he asked.

"Yeah, sure. She's . . . waiting in the car."

"I want to see her."

"Why?"

"Because I don't believe you. I think you're just trying to be nice to me."

"Look, Bernie, I want some information on Nowicki."

"Not until I see your girlfriend."

This was ridiculous. "She's shy."

"Okay, I'll go out there."

"No! I'll go get her." Jesus!

I jogged out to the parking lot and leaned in the window at Lula. "I'm in kind of a bind here. I need you to help me out. I need a lesbian girlfriend."

"You want me to find you one? Or you want me to be one?"

I explained the situation to her, and we hoofed it back to Bernie, who was rearranging his grapefruits.

"Hey, little dude," Lula said. "What's the word?"

Bernie looked up from the grapefruits and almost jumped out of his shoes. "Whoa!"

Guess Bernie hadn't expect my girlfriend to be a two-hundred-pound black woman wearing pink spandex.

"Jeez!" Bernie said. "Jeez!"

"So Stephanie tells me you know old lady Nowicki."

Bernie vigorously nodded his head. "Yeah."

"You see her lately?"

Bernie just stared at Lula.

"Earth to Bernie," Lula said.

"Unh?"

"You see old lady Nowicki lately?"

"Yesterday. She came in to get some, you know, fruit."

"How often does she like to buy fruit?"

Bernie chewed on his lower lip. "Hard to say. She's not regular."

Lula draped an arm around Bernie and almost smothered him in her right breast. "See, the thing is, Bern, we'd like to talk to Nowicki, but we're having a hard time finding her on account of she's not staying in her house. Now if you could help us out here, we'd be grateful. *Real* grateful."

A bead of sweat rolled down the side of Bernie's face, from his bald dome to in front of his ear. "Oh crap," he said. And I could tell from the way he said it that he wanted to help us out.

Lula gave him another squeeze. "Well?"

"I dunno. I dunno. She never says much."

"She always come in alone?"

"Yeah."

I gave him my card. "If you remember something, or if you see Nowicki, you give me a call right away."

"Sure. Don't worry."

We got to the car, and I had another one of those weird thoughts. "Wait here," I said to Lula. "I'll be right back."

Bernie had been standing in the front of the store, watching us through the glass. "Now what?" he said. "You forget something?"

"When Nowicki bought her fruit from you, did she pay you with a twenty?"

He sounded surprised at the question. "Yeah."

"You still have it?"

He stared at me blank-faced for a minute. "I guess . . ." He took his wallet from his back pocket and looked inside. "Here it is. It's the only twenty I got. It must be it."

I rooted around in my shoulder bag and found some money. I counted out two tens. "I'll trade you."

"Is that it?" he asked.

I gave him a sly smile. "For now."

"You know, I wouldn't mind just watching."

I patted him on the top of his head. "Hold that thought."

"We didn't find out much," Lula said when I got into the car.

"We know she was in Trenton yesterday."

"Not many places three women can stay in Trenton," Lula said. "Not like down the shore where there's lots of motels and lots of houses to rent. Hell, the only hotels we got charge by the hour."

That was true. It was the state capital, and it didn't actually have a hotel. This might leave people to think no one wanted to stay in Trenton, but I was sure this was a wrong assumption. Trenton is cool. Trenton has everything . . . except a hotel.

Of course, just because Nowicki was doing business with Bernie didn't mean she had to be in Trenton proper.

We took one last spin past Eddie Kuntz's house, the Nowicki house and Margie's house. All were dark and deserted.

Lula dropped me off in front of Morelli's house and shook her head. "That Morelli got one fine ass, but I don't know if I'd want to live with a cop."

My sentiments exactly.

The windows were open to bring air into the house, and Morelli's television carried out to the street. He was watching a ball game. I felt the truck hood. Warm. He'd just gotten home. His front door was open like the windows, but the screen door was locked.

"Hey!" I yelled. "Anybody home?"

Morelli padded out barefoot. "That was fast."

"Didn't seem all that fast to me."

He relocked the screen and went back to the television.

I don't mind going out to the ballpark. You could sit in the sun and drink beer and eat hot dogs, and the whole thing was an event. Baseball on television put me into a coma. I dug into my pocket, found the twenty and passed it over to Morelli. "I stopped for a soda in north Trenton and got this in change. I thought it'd be fun to check its authenticity."

Morelli looked up from the game. "Let me get this straight. You bought a soda, and you got a twenty in change. What'd you give her, a fifty?"

"Okay, so I don't want to tell you where I got it right now."

Morelli examined the bill. "Goddamn," he said. He turned it over and held it to the light. Then he patted the couch cushion next to him. "We need to talk."

I sat down with reservation. "It's phony, isn't it?"

"Yep."

"I had a hunch. Is it easy to tell?"

"Only if you know what to look for. There's a small line in the upper right corner where the plate is scratched. They tell me the paper isn't exactly right, either, but I can't see it. I only know by the scratch mark."

"Was the guy you tried to bust from north Trenton?"

"No. And I was pretty sure he was working alone. Counterfeiting like this is usually a mom-and-pop deal. Very small." He draped his arm over the back of the couch and stroked the nape of my neck with a single finger. "Now, about the twenty . . ."

THIRTEEN

IT WAS HOPELESS. Morelli was going to worm this out of me.

"The twenty came from Francine Nowicki, Maxine's mother," I said. "She passed it to a dope dealer yesterday."

I told him the rest of the story, and when I was done he had a strange expression on his face.

"How do you walk into these things? It's . . . spooky."

"Maybe I have the eye."

As soon as I said it I regretted it. The eye was like the monster under the bed. Not something to tempt out of hiding.

"I really thought it was a one-man operation," Morelli said. "The guy we were watching fit the profile. We watched him for five months. And we never pegged anyone as being an accomplice."

"It would explain a lot about Maxine."

"Yeah, but I still don't get it. During that five-month period this guy never made physical contact with Kuntz or Maxine."

"Did you actually see him passing the money?"

"No. That was part of the problem. Everything we had on him was circumstantial and coincidence."

"Then why did you move?"

"It was the Feds' call. There were events that led us to believe he was printing."

"But he wasn't."

"No. Not money, anyway." Morelli looked at the twenty again. "It's very possible there are just a bunch of these twenties floating around, and Nowicki's mother inadvertently passed one on."

There was a knock on the door, and Morelli went to get it.

It was Sally.

"He's bananas!" Sally said. "He tried to kill me! The poor dumb sonnovabitch tried to fucking kill me."

Sally looked like an overgrown, demented, testosterone-gone-berserk schoolgirl. Plaid pleated skirt, crisp white blouse, grungy sweat socks and beat-up Reeboks. No makeup, no wig, two-day beard, hairy chest peeking out the top of the blouse.

"Who's trying to kill you?" I asked. I assumed it was his roomie, but with the way Sally was dressed it could be most anyone.

"Sugar. He's freaked out. Stormed out of the club after the gig on Sunday night and didn't come home until about an hour ago. Walked in the door with a gallon of gasoline and a Bic lighter and said he was going to torch the place, claiming he was in love with me. Can you believe it?"

"Go figure."

"He was ranting on about how everything was fine until you showed up, and then I stopped paying attention to him."

"Doesn't he know you're not gay?"

"He said if you hadn't interfered I would have developed an attraction for him." Sally ran his hand through his Wild Man of Borneo hair. "My luck, someone goes fucking gonzo over me, and it's a guy."

"Could have something to do with the way you dress."

Sally looked down at his skirt. "I was trying this on when he barged in. I'm thinking of changing my image to wholesome."

Morelli and I both bit into our lower lips.

"So what happened?" Morelli asked. "Did he set fire to the apartment?"

"No. I wrestled the gas can out of his hands and threw it out the window. He tried to set fire to the rug with his Bic, but the rug

201

wouldn't burn. All he did was make big black melt spots and stink the place up. Synthetic fibers, you know. Finally he gave up and ran away to get more gas. I decided I wasn't going to wait around to get turned into a briquette, so I stuffed a bunch of clothes into a couple of garbage bags and took off."

Morelli had a grim expression on his face. "And you came here."

"Yeah. I thought with the way you handled him in the club, and with you being a cop and all, this was a safe place to stay." He held up his hands. "Just for a couple days! I don't want to impose."

"Shit," Morelli said. "What does this look like, a halfway house for potential victims of homicidal maniacs?"

"It might not be such a bad idea," I said. "If Sally let it be known he was living here, we might draw Sugar in."

Truth is, I was enormously relieved to know the identity of the firebomber. And I was sort of relieved to find it was Sugar. Better than the mob. And better than the guy who cuts off fingers.

"Two things wrong with that," Morelli said. "Number one, I can't get excited about my house being turned into an inferno. Number two, grabbing Sugar won't do much good if we can't convict him of a crime."

"No problem there," Sally said. "He told me about how he firebombed Stephanie's apartment and how he tried to burn down this house, too."

"You willing to testify to that?"

"I can do better than testify. I've got his diary out in the car. It's filled with juicy details."

Morelli leaned against the counter, arms crossed over his chest. "The only way I'll agree to this is if neither of you actually stays here. You put the word out that you're living with me, and twice a day you go in and out the front door, so it looks real. Then I put you in a safe house for the night."

"Put Sally in a safe house," I said. "I'll help with surveillance."

"No way," Sally said. "I'm not being left out on all the fun."

"Neither of you does surveillance," Morelli said. "And it's not open to debate. It's my way or it's no way."

"What safe house did you have in mind?"

Morelli thought about it a minute. "I could probably put you with one of my relatives."

"Oh no! Your grandmother would find me and give me the eye."

"What's the eye?" Sally wanted to know.

"It's a curse," I said. "It's one of those Italian things."

Sally shivered. "I don't like that curse stuff. One time I was down in the islands, and I accidentally ran over this voodoo person's chicken, and the voodoo person said she was gonna make my dick fall off."

"Well?" Morelli asked. "Did it fall off?"

"Not yet, but I think it might be getting smaller."

Morelli grimaced. "I don't want to hear this."

"I'll go home to my parents," I said. "And Sally can come with me."

We both looked at Sally in the skirt.

"You have any jeans in the car?" I asked.

"I don't know what I have. I was in a real rush. I didn't want to be there when Sugar got back with more gasoline."

Morelli put in a call to have Sugar picked up, and then we dragged Sally's clothes in from his car. We left the Porsche parked at the curb, behind the Buick, and we pulled the shades on the front downstairs windows. Then Morelli called his cousin, Mooch, to come get Sally and me at nine in the alley behind his house.

Thirty minutes later Morelli got a call from Dispatch. Two uniforms had gone over to check on Sally's apartment and had found it on fire. The building had been evacuated without injury. And Dispatch said the fire was under control.

"He must have come back right away," Sally said. "I didn't think he'd set fire to everything if I was gone. It must have just about killed him to torch all of those cakes and pies."

"I'm really sorry," I said. "Do you want me to go over there with you? Do you want to see it?"

"I'm not going anywhere near that place until Sugar's strapped to a bed in the loony bin. Besides, it wasn't even my place. I was renting from Sugar. All the furniture was his."

"YOU SEE, this is much better," my mother said, opening the door for me. "I have your bedroom all ready. As soon as you called we put on new sheets."

"That's nice," I said. "If it's okay with you, I'll let Sally sleep in my room, and I'll bunk with Grandma Mazur. It'll only be for a day or two."

"Sally?"

"He's just behind me. He had to get his bags out of the car."

My mother looked over my shoulder and froze as Sally ambled into the foyer.

"Yo, dudes," Sally said.

"What's happening?" Grandma chimed back.

"Jesus H. Christ," my father said, from his chair in the living room.

I carted Rex off to the kitchen and set his cage on the counter. "No one's supposed to know Sally and I are living here."

My mother looked pale. "I won't tell a soul. And I'll kill anyone who does."

My father was on his feet. "What kind of getup is that?" he asked, pointing at Sally. "Is that a kilt? Are you a Scot?"

"Heck no," Grandma said. "He's no Scot. He's a transvestite . . . only he doesn't strap down his dingdong on account of it gives him a rash."

My father looked at Sally. "You mean you're one of them Tinkerbell boys?"

Sally stood up a little taller. "You got a problem with that?"

"What kind of car you drive?"

"Porsche."

My father threw his hands in the air. "You see? A Porsche. Not even an American car. That's what's wrong with you weirdos. You don't want to do nothing like you're supposed to. There wasn't anything wrong with this country when everybody was buying American cars. Now everywhere you look it's some Japanese piece of caca and look at the trouble we're in."

"Porsche is German."

My father rolled his eyes. "German! Now there's a country. They can't even win a war. You think they're gonna help me get what I got coming to me from Social Security?"

I grabbed one of the garbage bags. "Let me help you get this upstairs."

Sally followed after me. "You sure this is okay?"

I had the bag halfway to the second floor. "Yeah. My father likes you. I could tell."

"No, I don't," my father said. "I think he's a fruitcake. And any man who looks that bad in a skirt has a patriotic duty to stay in the closet where no one can see him."

I pushed the bedroom door open, set the bag inside, and gave Sally fresh towels.

Sally was standing in front of the mirror I had on the back of my door.

"You think I look bad in this skirt?" Sally asked.

I studied the skirt. I didn't want to hurt his feelings, but he looked like a mutant from Planet of the Apes. He was probably the hairiest transvestite ever to wear a garter belt. "It's not terrible, but I think you're more of a straight skirt kind of guy. And leather is good on you."

"Dolores Dominatrix."

More like Wanda the Werewolf. "You could go with the wholesome look," I said, "but it would require a lot of shaving."

"Fuck that," Sally said. "I hate shaving."

"You could try a body waxing."

"Man, I did that once. Shit, it hurt like hell."

Good thing he didn't have ovaries.

"Now what?" Sally said. "I can't go to bed this early. I'm a night person."

"We don't have a car so we're sort of limited, but Morelli's only about a half mile from here. We could walk over and see if any-thing's happening. Look through your stuff and see if you have something dark."

Five minutes later Sally came downstairs in black jeans and a faded black T-shirt.

"We're going for a walk," I said. "Don't feel like you have to wait up. I have a key."

Grandma sidled up to me. "Do you want the 'big boy'?" she whispered.

"No, but thanks for offering."

SALLY AND I strained our eyes and ears all the way to Morelli's neighborhood. Unlike Lula, who never admitted to being scared, Sally and I were perfectly comfortable with the knowledge that Sugar had us ready to jump out of our skin.

We stopped at the corner of Morelli's block and looked things over. There were cars on either side of the street. No vans. Morelli's truck was parked, so I guessed Morelli was home. Shades were still drawn, and the lights were on. I assumed there was someone watching the outside of the house, but I couldn't pick him out.

This was a nice neighborhood. Similar to my parents'. Not as prosperous. Houses were mostly occupied by seniors who'd lived there all their adult lives or by young couples just starting out. The seniors were on fixed incomes, clipping coupons, buying tennis shoes on sale at Kmart, doing only the most essential house main-tenance, thankful their mortgages were paid and they could stay in their homes for taxes. The young couples painted and papered and filled their houses with furniture from Sears. And they marked time while they built equity and hoped their properties would ap-preciate, so they could buy bigger tract houses in Hamilton Town-ship.

I turned to Sally. "Do you think Sugar will come here looking for you?"

"If he doesn't come for me, he'll come for you. He was fucking flipped out."

We walked to the middle of the block and stared across the street at Morelli's house. A shoe scuffed on the stoop behind us, and a figure slid from deep shadow. Morelli.

"Out for a stroll?" he asked.

I looked beyond him at the bike parked on the small yard. "Is that a Ducati?"

"Yeah. I don't get to ride it much."

I moved closer. It was the 916 Superbike. Red. The motorcycle to die for. Smart choice for tailing someone who'd just firebombed your house. Faster and better maneuverability than a car. I found myself liking Morelli more now that I knew he owned a Duc.

"You out here alone?" I asked.

"For now. Roice is coming on at two."

"I guess they weren't able to pick Sugar up."

"We're looking for the car, but so far it's a big zero."

Headlights appeared at the end of the street, and we all shrank back against the house. The car rolled past us and turned two blocks down. We eased forward, out of hiding.

"Sugar have friends outside of the band?" Morelli asked Sally.

"Lots of casual friends. Not many close ones. When I first joined the band, Sugar had a lover."

"Would Sugar go to him for help?"

"Not likely. It wasn't a happy parting."

"How about the band? You have anything scheduled?"

"Rehearsal on Friday. Club date on Saturday."

That seemed like a millennium away. And Sugar would have to be a fool to show up. It had been stupid of him to attack Morelli. Cops get touchy when someone drops a firebomb in a fellow officer's house.

"Get in touch with the other band members," Morelli said to Sally. "Let them know you're staying with Stephanie and me. Ask if they've seen Sugar."

I looked over at Morelli. "You'll call me if anything happens?"

"Sure."

"You have my pager number?"

"Committed to memory."

I'd done this drill before. He wouldn't call me. Not until it was all over.

Sally and I crossed the street, entered Morelli's house, walked the length of it and exited the back door. I stood for a moment in the yard and thought about Morelli, lost in shadow again, his street appearing deserted. It gave me a creepy feeling. If Morelli could disappear, so could Sugar.

ONCE A WEEK Grandma Mazur went to the beauty parlor and had her hair shampooed and set. Sometimes Dolly would use a rinse and Grandma would have hair the color of an anemic apricot, but mostly Grandma lived with her natural color of steel gray. Grandma kept her hair short and permed with orderly rows of curls marching across her shiny pink scalp. The curls stayed miraculously tidy until the end of the week, when they'd begin to flatten and blend together.

I'd always wondered how Grandma had managed this feat. And now I knew. Grandma rolled her pillow under her neck so barely any skull touched the bed. And Grandma slept like the dead. Arms crossed over her chest, body straight as a board, mouth open. Grandma never moved a muscle, and she snored like a drunken lumberjack.

I crawled out of bed at six A.M. bleary-eyed and rattled from my night's experience. I'd had maybe thirty minutes of sleep, and that had been accumulated time. I grabbed some clothes and dressed in the bathroom. Then I crept downstairs and made coffee.

An hour later I heard movement overhead and recognized my mother's footsteps on the stairs.

"You look terrible," she said. "You feel okay?"

"You ever try to sleep with Grandma?"

"She sleeps like the dead."

"You got it."

Doors opened and slammed shut upstairs, and my grand-mother yelled for my father to get out of the bathroom.

"I'm an old lady," she yelled. "I can't wait all day. What are you doing in there anyway?"

More doors slamming, and my father clomped into the kitchen and took his place at the breakfast table. "I gotta go out with the cab this morning," he said. "Jones is in Atlantic City, and I said I'd cover his shift."

My parents owned their house free and clear, and my father got a decent pension from the post office. He didn't need the money from hacking. What he needed was to get out of the house, away from my mother and my grandmother.

The stairs creaked, and an instant later Sally's frame filled the doorway. His hair stood out from his head in snarls, his eyes were half closed and he stood stoop shouldered and barefoot, hairy arms dangling from my too-small, fuzzy pink robe.

"Man," he said, "this house is frantic. I mean, like, what time is it, dude?"

"Oh jeez," my father said, grim-faced, "he's wearing ladies' clothes again."

"It was in the closet," Sally said. "Guess the clothes fairy left it for me."

My father opened his mouth to say something, my mother gave him a sharp look, and my father snapped his mouth shut.

"What's that you're eating?" Sally asked.

"Cereal."

"Far out."

"Would you like some?"

He shuffled to the coffeemaker. "Just coffee."

Grandma Mazur hustled in. "What's going on? I didn't miss anything, did I?"

I was sitting at the table, and I could feel her breath on the back of my head. "Something wrong?"

"Just looking at this new-style hairdo you got. Never seen anything like it, what with these big chunks cut outta the back."

I closed my eyes. The egg. "How bad is it?" I asked my mother. As if I didn't already know.

"If you have some free time you might want to go to the beauty parlor."

"I thought it was some punk thing," Sally said. "It'd be rad if it was purple. Maybe spiked out."

AFTER BREAKFAST, Sally and I took another walk over to Morelli's house. We stood in the alley behind the house, and I dialed Morelli on my cell phone.

"I'm in your yard," I told him. "I didn't want to walk through your back door and get blown away."

"No problem."

Morelli was at the sink, rinsing out his coffee mug. "I was just getting ready to take off," he said. "They found Kuntz's car parked in the farmers' market lot by the tracks."

"And?"

"That's it."

"Blood? Bullet holes?"

"Nope," Morelli said. "A-one condition. At first glance doesn't look like anything was stolen. No vandalism. No sign of struggle."

"Was it locked?"

"Yep. My guess is it was left there sometime early this morning. Any sooner than that and it would have been stripped clean."

"Anything happen here last night?"

"Nothing. Very quiet. What are you up to today?"

I picked at my hair. "Beauty parlor."

A grin tugged at the corners of Morelli's mouth. "Going to ruin my handiwork?"

"You didn't take any more hair off than you absolutely had to, right?"

"Right," Morelli said, the grin still in place.

Usually, I got my hair done by Mr. Alexander at the mall. Unfortunately, Mr. Alexander couldn't work me into his busy schedule today, so I opted for Grandma's salon, the Clip and Curl on Hamilton. I had a nine-thirty appointment. Not that it mattered. My gossip rating was so high I could walk into Clip and Curl any time of the day or night, no waiting necessary.

We left through the front door, and I noticed the van parked across the street.

"Grossman," Morelli said.

"He have a Duc in that van?"

"No. He's got a two-way radio, a crossword puzzle book, and a jelly jar."

I had my eye on the Porsche and the butter-soft leather seats. And I knew I'd look very cool in the Porsche.

"Forget it," Morelli said. "Take the Buick. If you get into trouble the Buick is built like a tank."

"I'm going to the beauty parlor," I said. "I'm not going to get into trouble."

"Cupcake, your middle name is trouble."

Sally was standing between the Porsche and the Buick. "So, like, what's it gonna be?" he asked.

"The Porsche," I said. "Definitely the Porsche."

Sally buckled himself in. "This car does zero to a hundred in a fucking second." He cranked the engine over and catapulted us off the curb.

"Yow!" I said. "This is a family neighborhood. Slow down!"

Sally looked at me from behind reflector shades. "I like speed, man. Speed is good."

I had my hands braced on the dashboard. "Stop street! *Stop street!*"

"Stops on a dime," Sally said, stomping on the brake.

I jerked against the shoulder harness. "Ulk."

Sally lay an affectionate hand on the steering wheel. "This car is like a total engineering experience."

"Are you on drugs?"

"No way. Not this early in the day," Sally said. "What do I look like, a bum?"

He turned onto Hamilton and lead-footed it to Clip and Curl. He parked and looked at the shop over the tops of his glasses. "Retro."

Dolly had converted the downstairs part of her two-story house into a beauty parlor. I'd come here as a little girl to get my bangs cut, and nothing had changed since then. If it was midday or Saturday, the place would be packed. Since it was early morning only two women were under dryers. Myrna Olsen and Doris Zayle.

"Ommigod," Myrna said, shouting over the noise of the dryer. "I just heard the news about you marrying Joseph Morelli. Congratulations."

"I always knew you two would get married," Doris said, pushing the dryer off her head. "You were made for each other."

"Hey, I didn't know you dudes were married," Sally said. "Way to go."

Everyone gaped at Sally. Men didn't come into the Clip and Curl. And Sally pretty much looked like a man today . . . with the possible exceptions of his lip gloss and two-inch dangly rhinestone earrings.

"This is Sally," I told them.

"Chill," Sally said, giving them a rapper fist kind of greeting. "Thought maybe I'd get a manicure. My nails are like trashed."

They looked confused.

"Sally's a drag queen," I said.

"Isn't that something," Myrna said. "Imagine."

Doris leaned forward. "Do you wear dresses?"

"Mostly skirts," Sally said. "I'm too long-waisted for dresses. I don't think they're flattering. Of course, I have a couple gowns. Gowns are different. *Everyone* looks good in a gown."

"Being a drag queen must be so glamorous," Myrna said.

"Yeah, well, it's okay until they start to throw beer bottles at you," Sally said. "Getting hit with beer bottles is a fucking bummer."

Dolly examined my hair. "What on earth happened to you? It looks like someone cut big chunks out of your hair."

"I got egg stuck in it, and it got hard, and it had to get cut out."

Myrna and Doris rolled their eyes at each other and went back under the dryers.

An hour later Sally and I slid back into the Porsche. Sally had cherry-red nails, and I looked like Grandma Mazur. I looked at myself in the visor mirror and felt tears pooling behind my eyes. My naturally curly hair was cut short, and perfect Tootsie Roll curls covered my head.

"Massive," Sally said. "They look like fucking dog turds."

"You should have told me she was doing this!"

"I couldn't see. I was drying my nails. Excellent manicure."

"Take me to Joe's house. I'm going to get my gun and kill myself."

"It just needs to be a little mussed," Sally said. He reached over. "Let me fix it up for you. I'm good at this."

I looked in the mirror when he was done. *"Eeeeek!"* I looked like Sally.

"See," he said. "I know just how to do it. I have naturally curly hair, too."

I took another look. I guessed it was better than the dog turds.

"Maybe we should cruise over to north Trenton," I said. "Check out Eddie Kuntz. Make sure he isn't sitting in his kitchen having lunch."

Sally stepped on the gas, and my head snapped back.

"Jackrabbit start," he said.

"How long have you had this car?"

"Three weeks."

My radar was tingling. "You have a license?"

"Used to."

Oh boy.

———

THE LINCOLN TOWN CAR was in front of the Glick half of the house. Of course, Kuntz's half was without car.

"This doesn't feel good," I said to Sally.

"Like maybe ol' Eddie Kuntz is fish food."

I imagined, now that Eddie's car had been found abandoned, his aunt and uncle would be wringing their hands. Maybe they'd be distraught enough to let me into Eddie's apartment to snoop around.

Leo Glick opened his front door before I had a chance to knock.

"Saw you drive up," he said. "What kind of cockamammy car is that anyway? Looks like a big silver egg."

"It's a Porsche," Sally said.

Leo squinted at him. "What's with the earrings?"

"I felt like being pretty today, man," Sally said, shaking his head to give Leo the full effect. "See how they sparkle in the sun? Fucking awesome, huh?"

Leo backed up a step, as if Sally might be dangerous. "What do you want?" he asked me.

"I don't suppose you've heard from Eddie?"

"Don't suppose I have. And I gotta tell you I'm getting sick of people asking about him. First the cops come this morning to tell us about his car. Big deal. He left his car somewhere. Then some bimbo comes around asking about him. And now here you are on my doorstep with Miss America."

"What kind of bimbo? Do you remember her name?"

"Joyce."

Great. Just what I need. More Joyce.

"Who is it?" Betty called from inside the house. She looked around Leo's shoulder. "Oh, it's you. Why do you keep bothering us? Why don't you just mind your own business?"

"I'm surprised you aren't more worried about your nephew. What about his parents? Aren't his parents worried?"

"His parents are in Michigan. Visiting. We got relatives there," Leo said. "And we aren't worried, because Eddie's a bum. He does this all the time. The only reason we put up with him is because he's blood. We give him cheap rent, but that don't mean we have to baby-sit him."

"You mind if I look around?"

"Damn right I mind," Leo said. "I don't want no one creeping around my house."

"As it is, I've had the phone ringing ever since the police were here. Everyone wanting to know what's going on," Betty said.

"Next thing you know there'll be TV trucks pulling up, and I'll be on the evening news because *her* nephew's a bum."

"He's your nephew, too," Betty said.

"Only by marriage, and that don't hardly count."

"He's not so bad," Betty said.

"He's a bum. *A bum!*"

FOURTEEN

SALLY AND I stood at the curb by the Porsche and watched the Glicks making shooing motions at us.

"They're like . . . lame people," Sally said.

"When I first met them I had the feeling they liked Kuntz. At least Betty. In the beginning she was inviting me in for pound cake. And she was warm. Sort of motherly."

"Maybe they're the ones who offed ol' Eddie. Maybe he didn't pay his rent. Maybe he insulted Betty's pound cake."

I didn't think they offed Eddie Kuntz, but I did think they were acting odd. If I had to pin down emotions I'd say they were scared and angry. They definitely didn't want me sticking my nose into their business. Which meant either they had something to hide or else they didn't like me. Since I couldn't imagine anyone not liking me, I was going to assume they had something to hide. And the most obvious thing they would have to hide would be knowledge of Eddie Kuntz. Like maybe whoever snatched him had gotten in touch with Uncle Leo and Aunt Betty and had scared the beejeebers out of them.

Or here's another thought. Maybe Kuntz's mixed up with the counterfeit stuff and has gone underground. Maybe the note passed through the bartender was to warn him. And maybe Kuntz

216

told Uncle Leo that he's okay and that Leo should keep his mouth shut and not let anybody come snooping . . . or else. Jesus, maybe his closets are filled with stacks of twenties!

Betty was still making the shooing sounds, but now she was mouthing the word *go*.

"How about I drive," I said to Sally. "I've always wanted to drive a Porsche." Also, I've always wanted to live.

My pager went off, and I looked at the number. It wasn't familiar. I hauled my cell phone out of my shoulder bag and dialed.

The voice at the other end was excited. "Jeez, that was fast!"

I squinted at the phone. Like squinting would help me to think better. "Who is this?"

"Bernie! You know, the vegetable guy. And I got news for you. Francine Nowicki just came in. She wanted some special produce, if you get my drift."

Yes! "Is she there now?"

"Yeah. I was real smart. I told her I couldn't get anything for her until I went on my break, and then I called you right away. I figured your friend said she'd be grateful and all."

"I'm on my way. Make sure Mrs. Nowicki stays there until I arrive."

"Your friend's with you, right?"

I disconnected and jumped into the car. "We just got a break!" I said, buckling myself in, plugging the key into the ignition. "Mama Nowicki's shopping for fruit."

"Far out," Sally said. "Fruit is cosmic."

I didn't want to tell him what sort of fruit Bernie was selling. I was afraid he'd clean Bernie out and there wouldn't be any left for Maxine's mother.

I took off from the curb with my foot to the floor.

"*Wow!* Warp speed, Mr. Sulu," Sally said. "Excellent."

Ten minutes later, give or take a few seconds, I cruised into the supermarket lot and parked. I wrote a note to Bernie telling him to give Francine Nowicki enough "produce" for only one day, and instructed him to tell her she'd have to come back tomorrow for

217

the rest. Just in case I lost her today. I signed it "Love and kisses, your new friend, Stephanie." And then I added that Lula sent her love, too.

"There's a little guy in the produce department who looks like R2D2," I told Sally. "Give him this note and take off. If you see Maxine's mother, don't go near her. Just give Bernie the note and come back here, so we can follow her when she leaves."

Sally loped across the lot on his long legs, earring glittering in the sunlight, rat's nest hair bobbing as he walked. He swung through the big glass doors and turned toward Produce. I lost sight of him for a moment and then he was back in my line of vision, heading out.

"She was there," he said, folding himself into the little car. "I saw her standing by the apples. You can't miss her with that big bandage on her head. She's got it covered with a scarf, but you can still see it's a bandage underneath."

I'd chosen a spot off to the side, next to a van so we'd be less visible. We fell into silence, watching the door.

"There!" Sally yelped. "She's coming!"

We scrunched down in our seats, but it wasn't necessary. Mrs. Nowicki was parked in the front on the other side of the lot. And she wasn't being careful. Just another day in the life of a housewife. Out to do the marketing, scoring some dope from Businessman Bernie.

She was driving an old, beat-up Escort. If she was flush with funny money, she sure wasn't spending it on transportation. I let her get some space on me, and then I crept out of the lot after her. After a half mile I had a depressing feeling about her destination. After another half mile I was sure. She was going home. Maxine wasn't Albert Einstein, but I also didn't think she was dumb enough to hide out at her mother's house.

Mrs. Nowicki parked in front of her house and shuffled inside. If I thought Maxine was on the premises I had the right as a bounty hunter to break down the door and go in guns drawn. I wasn't going to do this because, first off, I didn't have a gun with me. And secondly, I'd feel like an idiot.

"Guess it wouldn't hurt to talk to her," I said.

Sally and I knocked on the door and Mrs. Nowicki stepped into view. "Look what the cat drug in," she said.

"How's your head?" This was my friendly approach, designed to throw drunken, pothead Mrs. Nowicki off guard.

She drew on her cigarette. "My head's peachy. How's your car?"

So much for friendly. "The insurance company felt sorry for me, so they gave me this Porsche."

"Yeah, up your ass," she said. "The Porsche belongs to the freak."

"Seen Maxine lately?"

"Not since she took off at the beach."

"You left the house early."

"Got tired of sand," Maxine said. "What's it to you?"

I moved past her, into her living room. "You don't mind if I look around?"

"You got a search warrant?"

"Don't need one."

Her eyes followed me as I moved through the house. "This is harassment."

It was a small bungalow. All on one floor. Easy to see Maxine wasn't there. "Looks like you're packing."

"Yeah, I'm cleaning out my Dior stuff. I decided I was only wearing Versace from now on."

"If you see Maxine . . ."

"Right. I'm gonna call you."

There was an end table and chair by the door. A .38 had been placed on the end table.

"You think you need that?" I asked.

Mrs. Nowicki stubbed her cigarette out in the ashtray by the gun. "Doesn't hurt to be careful."

We got back in the car and my pager beeped, displaying my mother's number.

Grandma answered my callback. "We just wanted to know if you'll be home for dinner," Grandma said.

"Probably."

"And what about Sally?"

"Sally, too."

"I saw he was wearing rhinestones when he went out today. You think I should get dressed up for supper?"

"Not necessary."

I took off and drove back to the supermarket. I had one last detail to check out with Bernie.

Sally and I staggered through the heat into the air-conditioned store. Bernie was ripping leaves off heads of lettuce when he saw us. His eyes got round, and by the time we got up to him, he was jiggling around, unable to stand still.

"Oh man," Bernie said, "you're back! Holy cow!" He was beaming at Sally, and he was wringing his hands. "I thought I recognized you, but I wasn't sure. And then when I saw you just now I knew! You're Sally Sweet! Jeez, I'm a big fan. A *big* fan! I go to the club all the time. I love that all-girl revue. Boy, you guys are great. And that Sugar. She's the best. I could really go for her. She's the most beautiful woman I've ever seen."

"Sugar's a guy," I said.

"Get out!"

"Hey," I said. "I know about these things."

"Oh yeah. I forgot. You look so normal."

"Did Francine Nowicki pay you with another twenty?"

"Yep. I got it right here." He took it out of his shirt pocket. "And I did what you said. I only gave her a couple pieces of fruit. Too bad, too, because I could have made a real killing. She had a lot of money on her. She took out a roll of twenties big enough to choke a horse."

I took the twenty from him and looked at it. It had the scratch mark in the corner.

Bernie was on tiptoe, trying to see the bill. "What's with the interest in the twenty. It marked or something?"

"No. Just checking to see if it's real."

"Well? Is it?"

"Yep." Real counterfeit.

"We need to go now," I said. "Thanks for calling me."

"My pleasure." He was gaping at Sally again. "It's been a real treat to meet you," he said. "I don't suppose I could have your autograph."

Sally took the black marking pen out of Bernie's shirt pocket and wrote "Best wishes from Sally Sweet" on Bernie's bald dome.

"There you go, dude," Sally said.

"Oh man," Bernie said, looking like he'd burst with happiness. "Oh man! This is so great."

"You do that a lot?" I asked Sally.

"Yeah, but usually when I do head writing I have to write a lot smaller."

"Hmm."

I wandered over to the cookie aisle to pick out some lunch, and I wondered if Morelli was still watching the 7-Eleven. I could save him a lot of trouble. I was pretty sure Maxine's mother had been the one to pass the phony twenties. It was her neighborhood store. And she didn't seem shy about floating the bad bills. The upside to telling Morelli about Francine Nowicki passing another bogus twenty dollars was that he'd probably abandon the store and watch Francine for me. The flip side was that if anything went down I couldn't trust him to include me. And if he brought Maxine in, and I wasn't along for the ride, neither Vinnie nor I would get our money.

Sally and I settled on a box of Fig Newtons and a couple of sodas. We went through checkout and ate in the car.

"So, lay this marriage gig on me," Sally said. "I always thought Morelli was just nailing you."

"We're not married. And he's not *nailing* me."

"Yeah, right."

"Okay, so he used to be nailing me. Well, actually, he only nailed me for a very short time. And it wasn't nailing. Nailing sounds like body piercing. What we had was . . . uh, consensual sex."

"Consensual sex is excellent."

I nodded in agreement and popped another Fig Newton into my mouth.

"I guess you got a thing going for Morelli though, huh?"

"I don't know. There's something there. I just can't figure out what it is."

We chewed Fig Newtons and thought about that for a while.

"You know what I don't get?" Sally said. "I don't understand why everyone was working so hard to throw us off the trail five days ago, and now old lady Nowicki is back in her house. We walked right up to her, and she didn't care."

He was right. Obviously something had changed. And my fear was that Maxine was good-bye. If Maxine was safely on her way to a new life, Mrs. Nowicki could afford to take more chances. And so could Margie. I hadn't stopped at Margie's house, but I was sure she was there, packing her valuables, explaining to her cat why Mommy was going to be gone for a long, long time. Probably paying the cat-sitting neighbor off in bad twenties.

But of course she wasn't ready to leave yet. She had a doctor's appointment. And so did Francine. Good thing for me, because I'd be hard-pressed to do surveillance. I wasn't exactly the FBI. I didn't have any of their cool surveillance equipment. For that matter, I didn't even have a car. A silver Porsche, a '53 Buick, and a red Firebird weren't gonna cut it as primo stealth vehicles. I was going to have to find a car that would go unnoticed, so I could sit in front of the Nowicki house tomorrow.

"No!" Morelli said. "You can't borrow my pickup. You're death on cars."

"I am *not* death on cars!"

"Last time you used my car it got blown up! Remember that?"

"Well, if you're going to hold that against me . . ."

"And what about your pickup? And your CRX? Blown up!"

"Technically, the CRX caught fire."

Morelli scrunched his eyes closed and smacked the heel of his hand against his forehead. "Unh!"

It was a little after four. Sally was watching television in the living room, and Morelli and I were in the kitchen. Morelli'd just gotten in, and he looked like he'd had another one of those days. Probably I should have waited for a better time to ask him about the truck, but I had to be at my mother's in an hour for dinner. Maybe I should try a different approach. I ran my fingertip across his sweat-soaked T-shirt and leaned *very* close. "You look . . . hot."

"Honey, I'm about as hot as a man can get."

"I might be able to do something about that."

His eyes narrowed. "Let me get this straight. Are you offering sex for the use of my truck?"

"Well, no, not exactly."

"Then what *are* you offering?"

I didn't know what I was offering. I'd intended this to be sort of playful, but Morelli wasn't playing.

"I need a beer," Morelli said. "I've had a really long day, and it's going to be even longer. I have to relieve Grossman in an hour."

"Anything new turn up on Kuntz's car?"

"Nothing."

"Anything happen at the Seven-Eleven?"

"Nothing." He pulled on his beer. "How was your day?"

"Slow. Not a lot going on."

"Who you want to watch?"

"Mrs. Nowicki. She moved back into her house. I went in to talk to her, and she was packing."

"Doesn't mean she's going to take you to Maxine," Morelli said.

I shrugged. "It's all I've got."

"No, it's not," Morelli said. "You're sitting on something."

I raised an eyebrow. It said, Oh yeah?

Morelli chucked the empty beer bottle into the recycling bin. "This better not have to do with the counterfeiting case I'm on. I'd hate to think you were withholding evidence."

"Who me?"

He took a step closer and pinned me to the counter. "So, how bad do you want my truck?"

"Pretty bad."

His gaze dropped to my mouth. "*How* bad?"

"Not that bad."

Morelli gave a disgusted sigh and backed off. "Women."

Sally was watching MTV, singing along with the groups, doing his head-banger thing.

"Jesus," Morelli said, looking into the living room, "it's a wonder he doesn't shake something loose."

"I CAN'T loan you my car," my father said. "It's gotta go in to get serviced tomorrow. I got an appointment. What's wrong with the Buick you're driving?"

"The Buick is no good for surveillance," I said. "People stare at it."

We were at the table, and my mother was serving out stuffed cabbage. *Plop*, onto my plate, four cabbage rolls. I opened the button on my shorts and reached for my fork.

"I need a new car," I said. "Where's my insurance money?"

"You need a steady job," my mother said. "Something that pays benefits. You're not getting any younger, you know. How long can you go chasing hoodlums all over Trenton? If you had a steady job you could finance a car."

"Most of the time my job is steady. I just got stuck with a lemon of a case here."

"You live from hand to mouth."

What could I say; she was right.

"I could get you a job driving a school bus," my father said, digging into his dinner. "I know the guy does the hiring. You make good money driving a school bus."

"One of them daytime shows did a thing on school bus drivers,"

Grandma said. "And two of the drivers got bleeding hemorrhoids on account of the seats weren't any good."

My eye had started to twitch again. I put my finger to it to make it stop.

"What's wrong with your eye?" my mother asked. "Do you have that twitch back?"

"Oh, I almost forgot," Grandma said. "One of your friends came looking for you today. I said you were out working, and she gave me a note for you."

"Mary Lou?"

"No, not Mary Lou. Someone I didn't know. Real pretty. Must have been one of those makeup ladies at the mall, because she was wearing a ton of makeup."

"Not Joyce!"

"No. I'm telling you it was someone I didn't know. The note's in the kitchen. I left it on the counter by the phone."

I pushed away from the table and went to get the note. It was in a small, sealed envelope. "STEPHANIE" had been printed in neat block letters on the face of the envelope. It looked like an invitation to a shower or a birthday party. I opened the envelope and put a hand to the counter to steady myself. The message was simple. "DIE BITCH." And in smaller script it said when I least suspected it he'd make his move. It was written on a recipe card.

What was even more disturbing than the message in the note was the fact that Sugar had waltzed right into my parents' house and handed the envelope to Grandma.

I returned to the table and wolfed down three cabbage rolls. I didn't know how to handle this. I needed to warn my family, but I didn't want to scare them half to death.

"Well?" Grandma said. "What's in the note? Looked like an invitation."

"That was someone I know from work," I said. "Actually, she's not a nice person, so if you ever see her again, don't let her in the house. In fact, don't even open the door to her."

"Ommigod," my mother said. "Another lunatic. Tell me she doesn't want to shoot you."

"Actually . . ."

My mother made the sign of the cross. "Holy Mary, mother of God."

"Don't get going with the Holy Mary stuff," I said to my mother. "It's not that bad."

"So what should I do if I see her again?" Grandma asked. "You want me to put a hole in her?"

"No! I just don't want you to invite her in for tea!"

My father helped himself to more cabbage rolls. "Next time put in less rice," he said.

"Frank," my mother said, "are you listening to this?"

My father picked up his head. "What?"

My mother smacked herself on the forehead.

Sally had been bent over his plate, shoveling in cabbage rolls like there was no tomorrow. He paused and looked at me, and I could hear the gears grinding in his brain. Pretty girl. Lots of makeup. Note. Bad person. "Uh oh," Sally said.

"I'm going to have to eat and run," I said to my mother. "I have to work tonight."

"There's chocolate chip cookies for desert."

I laid my napkin on the table. "I'll put them in a bag."

My mother jumped to her feet. "I'll do it."

We had labor laws in the Burg. Mothers do brown bags. That's it. No exceptions. All over the country people were looking for ways to get out of work. In the Burg, housewives militantly guarded their responsibilities. Even working mothers refused to relinquish the assembling of lunch or leftovers. And while other family members might from time to time be recruited to mop the kitchen floor, do the laundry, polish the furniture, no one performed the task to housewife standards.

I took the cookie bag and ushered Sally out of the house. It was early, and we really didn't need to leave, but I didn't think I'd hold up to the grilling. There was no good way to tell my mother I was being stalked by a homicidal drag queen.

My mother and grandmother were at the door, watching us get in the car. They stood backs straight, hands clasped. Lips pressed tight together. Good Hungarian women. My mother wondering where she went wrong, wondering why I was riding around with a man wearing rhinestone earrings. My grandmother wishing she was with us.

"I have a key," I called to them. "So, it probably would be a good idea to lock up."

"Yeah," Sally added, "and don't stand in front of any open windows."

My mother did another sign of the cross.

I started the car. "We need to end this," I told Sally. "I'm fed up with being scared, worrying that Sugar's going to jump out at me and set my hair on fire."

"I talked to all the guys in the band, and no one's heard from him."

I drove toward Chambers. Truth is, I'd abdicated dealing with Sugar. "Tell me about Sugar," I said. "Tell me the stuff you told the police."

"We were roommates for about six months, but I don't know a whole lot about him. His family's in Ohio. They couldn't deal with the gay thing, so Sugar split. I've been with the band for about a year, but in the beginning I mostly hung with the guys from Howling Dog.

"About six months ago Sugar had this knock-down, drag-out fight with his boyfriend, John. John moved out, and I moved in. Only I wasn't like John, you know. I was like just a roommate."

"Sugar didn't think so."

"Guess not. Man, this is a real piece of shit, on account of we were like the perfect roommates. Sugar's a neat freak. Always cleaning, cleaning, cleaning. And I'm like, not into that, so it was cool. I mean, man, we didn't fight over who got to do the fucking vacuuming. And he's real good with the girl shit. He knows all about foundation and blush and the best hair spray. You should have seen me before I moved in with him. I was like a fucking barbarian. I mean, I've like lived with a couple chicks, but I never paid any attention to how they got the fucking eyeliner on. This girl shit is complicated.

"Sugar knew all about it. He even helped me pick out clothes. That was the one thing we did together. Shop. He was a fucking shopping fool. Sometimes he'd bring clothes home for me. Like I wouldn't even have to go with him."

So now I understood the shorts with the ass hanging out.

"He was in drag when he gave the note to Grandma," I said. "It takes special equipment to look like a woman, and it's unlikely Sugar had time to take anything out of the apartment. So either he has a second apartment or else he bought new."

"Probably bought new," Sally said. "Sugar makes lots of money. Five times what I'm making. Some of the things you need to get in New York, but that's not a real problem."

"Too bad he torched the apartment. We might have been able to find something there."

"And the police have the diary."

Common sense told me to give this over to Joe, but when I ran through the benefits they didn't add up. The department was already motivated to find Sugar. They were probably already putting out the maximum effort. What we needed here was talent from a different direction. What we needed was Ranger.

I called his private number, his pager, and finally connected on his car phone.

"Help," I said.

"No kidding."

I filled him in on recent harrowing events.

"Bummer," Ranger said.

"Yeah, so what do you think I should do?"

"Increase his discomfort. Invade his space and do whatever makes him crazy."

"In other words, set myself up as a target."

"Unless you know where he lives. Then we go there and take him down. But I figure you don't know where he lives."

I looked in my rearview mirror and saw Ranger's black BMW slide to the curb behind me about half a block away.

"How did you find me?" I asked.

"I was in the neighborhood. Saw you turn onto Chambers. Is that guy wearing rhinestones?"

"Yep."

"Nice touch."

"Okay, we'll go to Sugar's favorite hangouts. See what we can stir up."

"I'm in the wind, babe."

Whatever the hell that meant.

"I HAVE IT ALL mapped out," Sally said, pulling into a small parking lot next to a downtown restaurant. "This is the first stop."

I looked at the sign on the side of the building. DANTE'S IN-FERNO. Like, oh boy.

"Don't worry about the name," Sally said. "It's just a restaurant. Serves spicy food. Sugar likes spicy food."

The restaurant was basically one large room. Walls were decorated with faux frescoes depicting various scenes where satyrs and minotaurs frolicked in hell and other hot places. No Sugar.

Two men waved to Sally, and Sally waved back.

"Hey, dudes," Sally said, moving through the room to their table. "I'm looking for Sugar. Don't suppose you've seen him to-night?"

"Sorry," they said. "Haven't seen Sugar all week."

After Dante's we did a full circuit of bars and restaurants with no luck.

"I know we're out here doing this looking for Sugar thing," Sally finally said, "but the truth is I'd crap in my pants if he all of a sudden popped up. I mean, he's crazy. He could, like, fucking Bic me."

I was trying not to think about it. I was telling myself Ranger was out there. . . . somewhere. And I was trying to be careful, staying alert and on guard, always looking, ready to react. I thought if Sugar wanted to get in my face and slash me to ribbons, I'd stand a chance. If he just wanted to get rid of me, he could probably do it. Hard to avoid a bullet from a man who thinks he has nothing left to lose.

The sun had set and dusk had settled around us, not doing much for my nervous stomach. Too many shadows now. Sally had known someone in almost every place we'd visited. No one had admitted to having seen Sugar, but that didn't mean it was true. The gay community was protective of its own, and Sugar was well liked. My hope was that someone had been lying and a phone call had been made that would send Sugar out prowling.

"We have many places left to try?" I asked Sally.

"A couple clubs. We'll save the Ballroom for last."

"Would Sugar go out in drag?"

"Hard to say. Depends on his mood. He'd probably feel safer in drag. I know I always do. You put that makeup on, and it's *watch out world!*"

I could relate to that. My makeup always increases with my insecurity. In fact, at that very moment I had an overwhelming desire to crayon my lids with bright blue eye shadow.

We stopped in at the Strip, Mama Gouches, and Curly's. Only one place left. The Liberty Ballroom. Appropriately named. If you didn't have balls, you didn't want to go there. I figured I had balls when I needed them, so there was no problem.

I drove past the State Complex, which always felt weirdly deserted at night. Acres of unoccupied parking spaces, eerily lit by halogen light. Empty buildings with black glass windows, looking like the death star.

The Ballroom was on the next block, next to the high-rise seniors' housing known to one and all as the Warehouse.

All night long Sally had been telling people we'd end up at the Ballroom. And now that we were here my skin was crawling and all my little hairs were standing on end. It was fear and dread premonition, plain and simple. I knew Sugar was in there. I knew he was waiting for us. I parked and looked around for Ranger. No Ranger in sight. That's because he's in the wind, I told myself. You can't see the wind. Or maybe the wind went home to watch Tuesday night fights.

Sally was cracking his knuckles next to me. He felt it, too. We looked at each other and grimaced.

"Let's do it," I said.

FIFTEEN

SALLY AND I stood inside the door and looked around. Bar and cocktail tables in the front. Small dance floor to the rear. Very dark. Very crowded. Very noisy. My understanding was that the Ballroom was a gay place, but clearly not everyone here was gay.

"What are all these ungay people doing here?" I asked Sally.

"Tourists. The guy who owns this place was going bust. It was a gay bar, but there weren't enough gay men in Trenton to make a go of it. So Wally got this great idea . . . he hired some guys to come in and dance and get all smoochy with each other, so the place would look *really* gay. Word got out, and the place started filling up. Like you could come here to see homos and be fucking politically correct." Sally smiled. "Now it's trendy."

"Like you."

"Yeah. I'm fucking trendy."

Sally waved to someone. "See that guy in the red shirt? That's Wally, the owner. He's a genius. The other thing he does is give the first drink free to day-trippers."

"Day-trippers?"

"Yuppies who want to be gay-for-a-day. Like suppose you're a guy, and you think it'd be a kick to get dressed up in your wife's clothes and go out to a bar. This is the place! You get a free drink.

And on top of that, you're trendy, so it's all okay. You can even bring your wife, and she can try out being dyke-for-a-day."

The woman standing next to me was dressed in a black leather vest and black leather hot pants. She had an expensive perm that gave her perfect red curls all over her head, and she was wearing brown lipstick.

"Hi!" she said to me, all cheery and chirpy. "Want to dance?"

"No thanks," I said. "I'm just a tourist."

"Me too!" she squealed. "Isn't this place too much? I'm here with my husband, Gene. He wants to see me slow dance with a woman!"

Gene looked very preppy in Dockers and a plaid sport shirt with a little horse stitched onto the pocket. He was swilling a drink. "Rum Coke," he said to me, leaning across his wife. "Want one?"

I shook my head no. "I have a gun in my shoulder bag," I said. "A big one."

Gene and his wife moved away and disappeared in the crowd.

Sally had an advantage at 6'4". He was swiveling his head, looking the crowd over.

"See him?" I asked.

"No."

I didn't like being stuck in the Liberty Ballroom. It was too crowded, too dark. People were jostling me. It would be easy for Sugar to come up on me here . . . like Jack Ruby shooting Lee Harvey Oswald. That could be me. One shot to the gut and I'd be history.

Sally put his hand to my back to steer me forward, and I jumped and shrieked. "Yikes!"

"What? *What?*" Sally yelled, looking around panic-stricken.

I had my hand to my heart. "I might be a tad nervous."

"My stomach's a mess," Sally said. "I need a drink."

Sounded like a good idea to me, so I trailed behind him to the bar. Every time he'd push through people they'd turn and look and go, "Hey, it's Sally Sweet! I'm a real fan." And Sally would go, "Shit, man, that's cool."

"What do you want?" Sally asked.

"Beer in a bottle." I figured if Sugar attacked me, I could brain him with my beer bottle. "I didn't realize you were so famous," I said to Sally. "All these people know you."

"Yeah," Sally said, "probably half the people in this room have slipped a five under my garter belt. I'm like regional."

"Sugar's here somewhere," the bartender said, passing drinks to Sally. "He wanted me to give you this note."

The note was in the same tidy little invitation-sized envelope Sugar had given Grandma. Sally opened the envelope and read the note card.

" 'Traitor.' "

"That's it?" I asked.

"That's all it says. 'Traitor.' " He shook his head. "He's wigged, man. Beyond Looney Tunes. Looney Tunes is funny. This isn't funny."

I belted back some beer and told myself to stay calm. Okay, so Sugar was a little over the edge. It could be worse. Suppose the guy who was going around chopping off fingers was after me? That would be worrisome. *He'd* already killed someone. We didn't know for sure if Sugar was a killer. Arson didn't necessarily mean he was a killer type. I mean, arson was remote, right? So no point to getting all freaked out ahead of time.

Ranger moved next to me. "Yo," Ranger said.

"Yo yourself."

"Is the man here?"

"Apparently. We haven't spotted him yet."

"You armed?"

"Beer bottle."

He gave me a wide smile. "Good to know you're on top of things."

"No grass growing here," I said.

I introduced Ranger and Sally to each other.

"Shit," Sally said, gaping at Ranger. "Jesus shit."

"Tell me what I'm looking for," Ranger said.

We didn't exactly know.

"Blond Marilyn wig, red dress with short skirt," the bartender said.

Same outfit he had been wearing onstage at the club.

"Okay," Ranger said. "We're going to walk through the room and look for this guy. Pretend I'm not here."

"You going to be the wind again?" I asked.

Ranger grinned. "Wiseass."

Women spilled drinks and walked into walls at the sight of Ranger grinning. Good thing he didn't want to be the wind. The wind would have had a hard time with this group.

We cautiously elbowed our way to the back, where people were dancing. Women were dancing with women. Men were dancing with men. And a man and a woman in their seventies, who must have been from a different planet and had accidentally landed on Earth, were dancing together.

Two men stopped Sally to tell him Sugar was looking for him.

"Thanks," Sally said, ashen faced.

Ten minutes later, we'd circled the room and had come up empty.

"I need another drink," Sally said. "I need drugs."

The mention of drugs made me think of Mrs. Nowicki. No one was watching her. I just hoped to God she was hanging around for her doctor's appointment. Priorities, I told myself. The apprehension money wouldn't do me much good if I was dead.

Sally went off to the bar, and I went off to the ladies' room. I pushed through the door labeled Rest Rooms and walked the length of a short hall. Men's room on one side. Ladies' room on the other. Another door at the end of the hall. The door closed behind me, locking out the noise.

The ladies' room was cool and even more quiet. I had a moment of apprehension when I saw it was empty. I looked under the three stall doors. No size-ten red shoes. That was stupid, I thought. Sugar wouldn't go to the ladies' room. He was a man, after all. I went into a stall and locked the door. I was sitting there enjoying the solitude when the outer door opened and another woman came into the room.

After a moment I realized I wasn't hearing any of the usual sounds. The footsteps had stopped in the middle of the room. No purse being opened. No running water. No opening and closing of another stall door. Someone was silently standing in the middle of the small room. Great. Caught on the toilet with my pants down. A woman's worst nightmare.

Probably my overactive imagination. I took a deep breath and tried to steady my heartbeat, but my heartbeat wouldn't steady, and my chest felt like it was on fire. I did a mental inventory of my shoulder bag and realized the only genuine weapon was a small canister of pepper spray.

There was the scrape of high heels on the tile floor, and a pair of shoes moved into view. Red.

Shit! I clapped a hand over my mouth to keep from whimpering. I was on my feet now. And I was dressed. And I felt sick to my stomach.

"Time to come out," Sugar said.

I reached for my bag, hanging on the hook on the back of the door, but before I could grab it the bolt popped off and the door was wrenched open, taking my bag with it.

"I did everything for him," Sugar said, tears streaming down his cheeks. "I kept the apartment clean, and I made all his favorite food. And it was working—until you showed up. He liked me. I know he did. You ruined everything. Now all he thinks about is this bounty hunter business. I can't sleep at night. I worry all the time that he's going to get hurt or killed. He has no business being a bounty hunter."

He held a gun in one hand, and he swiped at his tears with the other. Both hands were shaking, and he was scaring the hell out of me. I had my doubts that he was a killer, but an accidental gunshot wound is just as deadly as an intentional one.

"You've got this all wrong," I said. "Sally just decodes messages for me. He doesn't do anything dangerous. And besides, he really does like you. He thinks you're terrific. He's outside. He's been looking for you all night."

"I've made up my mind," Sugar said. "This is the way it's going to be. I'm going to get rid of you. It's the only way I can protect Sally. It's the only way I can get him back." He motioned to the door with the gun. "We need to go outside now."

This was good, I thought. Going outside was a break. When we walked through the Ballroom, Ranger would kill him. I carefully inched my way to the door and stepped out into the hall, moving slowly, not wanting to spook Sugar.

"No, no," Sugar said. "You're going the wrong way." He pointed to the door at the other end of the hall. "*That* way."

Damn.

"Don't think about trying something dumb. I'll shoot you dead," he said. "I could do it, too. I could do anything for Sally."

"You're in enough trouble. You don't want to add murder to the list."

"Ah, but I do," he said. "I've gone too far. Every cop in Trenton is looking for me. And do you know what will happen to me when I'm locked up? No one will be gentle. I'm better off on death row. You get your own room on death row. I hear they let you have a television."

"Yes, but eventually they *kill* you!"

More tears streaked down his cheek, but his eyeliner didn't smudge. The man knew makeup.

"No more talking," he said, pulling the hammer back on the revolver. "Outside. Now. Or I'll shoot you here. I swear I will."

I opened the door and looked out. There was a small employee parking lot to the right and two Dumpsters to the left. A single overhead bulb lit the area. Beyond the Dumpsters was a black-topped driveway. Then a grassy lawn and the seniors' building. It was a really good place for him to shoot me. It was private and sound wouldn't carry. And he had several exits. He could even choose to go back into the building.

My heart was going ka-*thunk*, ka-*thunk*, and my head felt

spongy. "Wait a minute," I said. "I need to go back inside. I forgot my shoulder bag."

He closed the door behind him. "You don't need your shoulder bag where you're going."

"Where's that?"

"Well, I don't know exactly. Wherever you go when you're dead. Climb into the Dumpster so I can shoot you."

"What are you nuts? I'm not climbing into the Dumpster. That thing is disgusting."

"Okay, fine, then I'll just shoot you here." He pulled the trigger and *click*.

No bullet in the chamber. Standard safety procedure.

"Darn," he said. "I can't do anything right."

"You ever shoot a gun before?"

"No. But it didn't seem like it'd be all that complicated." He looked at the gun. "Ah, I see the problem. The guy I borrowed the gun from left one of the bullets out."

He sighted the gun at me, and before he had time to pull the trigger, I jumped behind one of the Dumpsters. *Bang, zing.* A bullet hit the Dumpster. *Bang, zing* again. We were both so panicked we were acting unreasonably. I was running between Dumpsters like a tin duck in a shooting gallery, and Sugar was firing at shadows.

He got off five rounds, and then there was the telltale *click* again. He was out of bullets. I peeked out from my hiding place.

"Shit," he said. "I'm such a loser I can't even shoot somebody. Damn." He plunged his hand into his red purse and came out with a knife.

He was between me and the back door. My only real option was to run like hell around the building or across the grass to the seniors' building. He looked more athletic than me, but he was in heels and a skirt, and I was wearing shorts and sneakers.

"I'm not giving up," he said. "I'll do it with my bare hands if I have to. I'll rip your heart out!"

I didn't like the sound of that, so I took off across the grass for all I was worth, running full out for the seniors' building. I'd been in the building before. There was always a guard at the door at this time of the night. The front of the building was well lit. There were two double glass doors, and then the guard. Beyond the guard was a lobby where the old folks sat.

I could hear Sugar laboring behind me, breathing heavily and shrieking for me to stop so he could kill me.

I barreled through the doors and hollered for the guard, but no guard came running. I looked over my shoulder and saw the knife arc down at me. I spun to the side, and the knife blade sliced through the sleeve of my Rangers jersey.

The lobby couches were filled with seniors.

"Help!" I yelled. "Call the police! Get the guard!"

"No guard," one woman explained. "Budget cuts."

Sugar lunged again.

I jumped away, grabbed a cane from an old geezer and started slashing at Sugar.

I'm one of those people who imagine themselves acting heroically at disasters. Saving children from school buses dangling precipitously from bridges. Performing first aid at car wrecks. Rescuing people from burning buildings. The truth is, I totally lose my cool in an emergency, and if things turn out okay, it's through no effort of mine.

I was blindly slashing at Sugar. My nose was running and I was making animal sounds, and by sheer accident I connected with the knife and sent it sailing through the air.

"You bitch!" Sugar shrieked. "I hate you! I hate you!" He hurled himself at me, and we went down to the ground.

"In my day, you'd never see two women fighting like that," one of the seniors said. "It's all of that violence on television. That's what does it."

I was rolling around with Sugar, and I was shouting "Call the police, call the police." Sugar grabbed me by my hair and yanked, and when I jerked back I caught him with my knee and pushed his gonads a good six inches into his body. He rolled off me into a fetal position and threw up.

I flopped over onto my back and look up at Ranger.

Ranger was grinning again. "Need any help?"

"Did I wet my pants?"

"No sign of it."

"Thank God."

RANGER, SALLY AND I stood on the sidewalk in front of the se-niors' building and watched the police drive off with Sugar. I'd pretty much stopped shaking, and my skinned knees had stopped bleeding.

"Now what am I going to do?" Sally said. "I'm never going to be able to get into that corset all by myself. And what about makeup?"

"It's not easy being a drag queen," I said to Ranger.

"Fuckin' A," Ranger said.

We walked back to the club parking lot and found our cars. The night was humid and starless. The air-conditioning system droned from the club roof, and canned music and muffled conversation spilled out the open front door into the lot.

Sally was unconsciously bobbing his head in time to the music. I loaded him into the Porsche and thanked Ranger.

"Always enjoy seeing you in action," Ranger said.

I drove out of the lot and headed for Hamilton. I noticed my knuckles were white on the wheel and made another effort to relax.

"Man, I'm really stoked," Sally said. "I think we should do more clubs. I know this great place in Princeton."

I'd just almost been shot, slashed, and choked to death. I wasn't feeling all that stoked. I wanted to sit someplace quiet and nonthreatening and eat my mother's cookies.

"I need to talk to Morelli," I said. "I'm going to pass on the clubs, but you can go on your own. You don't have to worry about Sugar now."

"Poor little guy," Sally said. "He isn't really a bad person."

I supposed that was true, but I was having a hard time finding a lot of sympathy for him. He'd destroyed my car and my apart-

ment and had tried to kill me. And if that wasn't enough, he'd ruined my Gretzky Rangers jersey. Maybe I'd feel more generous tomorrow, when I'd regained my good humor. Right now, I was
tending toward grouchy.

I turned at Chambers and wound my way to Morelli's. The van
was no longer on his street, and I didn't see the Duc. Lights were
on in the downstairs part of Morelli's house. I assumed he'd been
told about Sugar and had ended the stakeout. I took my cookies
and angled out of the Porsche.

Sally slid over to the driver's seat. "Later, dude," he said, taking
off with his foot to the floor.

"Later," I said, but the street was already empty.

I knocked on the screen door. "Yo!" I hollered above the TV.

Morelli padded out and opened the door for me. "Were you
really rolling around on the floor at the senior citizens' home?"

"You heard."

"My mother called. She said Thelma Klapp phoned her and
told her you just beat the crap out of some pretty blond woman.
Thelma said that since you were pregnant and all she thought you
shouldn't be rolling around like that."

"The pretty blond woman wasn't a woman."

"What's in the bag?" Morelli wanted to know.

Morelli could sniff out a cookie a mile away. I took one and
handed the bag over to him. "I have to talk to you."

Morelli flopped onto the couch. "I'm listening."

"About Francine Nowicki, Maxine's mother . . ."

Morelli went still. "Now I'm *really* listening. What about
Francine Nowicki?"

"She passed another phony twenty. And my informant tells me
Francine had a roll of them."

"That's why you were so hot to put her under surveillance. You
think she's mixed up in this counterfeiting thing and she's going to
take off . . . along with Maxine."

"I think Maxine might already be gone."

"Why are you still interested if you think Maxine's gone?"

JANET EVANOVICH

I took another cookie. "I don't know for sure that she's gone. And maybe she's not so gone that I can't find her."

"Especially if her mother or her friend rats on her."

I nodded. "There's always that possibility. So what do you say, can I use your truck?"

"If she's still there in the morning I'll put a van in place."

"Her doctor appointment's at three."

"Why did you decide to tell me?"

I slouched lower on the couch. "I need help. I don't have the right equipment to do any kind of decent surveillance. And I'm tired. I hardly slept last night, and I've had a nightmare day. This guy emptied a revolver at me tonight, and then he chased me with a knife in his hand. I hate when people do that!" I was trying to eat a cookie, but my hand was shaking so bad I could hardly get it to my mouth. "Look at me. I'm a wreck!"

"Adrenaline surplus," Morelli said. "As soon as it wears off you'll sleep like the dead."

"Don't say that!"

"You'll feel better in the morning."

"Maybe. Right now I'm happy for whatever assistance you can give me."

Morelli got up and shook out cookie crumbs. "I'm going to get a glass of milk. Want one?"

"Sure."

I stretched out the length of the couch. He was right about the adrenaline. I'd stopped shaking and now I was exhausted.

I HAD a moment of disorientation when I opened my eyes. And then I realized I'd fallen asleep on Morelli's couch. And now it was morning. Sunlight was streaming through the front windows, and I could smell coffee brewing in the kitchen. Morelli had removed my shoes and covered me with a summer quilt. I did a quick check to make sure the rest of my clothes were intact before feeling too grateful.

I shuffled into the kitchen and poured out some coffee.

Morelli was buckling his gun onto his belt. "I've gotta run," he said. "I called your mother last night and told her you were here. I figured she'd worry."

"Thanks. That was nice of you."

"Help yourself to whatever. If anything comes up today, you can get me on my pager."

"Are you watching Nowicki?"

Morelli paused. "She's gone. I had someone check last night. The house is empty."

"Damn!"

"We might still get her. There's an alert out for her. The Treasury has resources."

"The doctor—"

"Nowicki canceled her appointment yesterday."

He gulped the rest of his coffee, put the mug in the sink and took off. He got to the middle of the dining room, stopped and stared down at his shoe for a minute. Thinking. I saw him give his head a single shake. He turned, strode back into the kitchen, pulled me to him and kissed me. Lots of tongue. Hungry hands.

"Jesus," he said, backing off. "I'm in really bad shape."

And he was gone.

MY MOTHER looked up expectantly when I came into the kitchen. Well? the look said. Did you sleep with him?

My grandmother was at the table with a cup of tea. My father was nowhere to be seen. And Sally was at the head of the table, eating chocolate chip cookies, once again wearing my bathrobe.

"Hey, dude," Sally said to me.

"Sally was telling us all about last night," Grandma said. "Boy, I sure wish I'd been there. Sally said you were the bomb."

"Of all places," my mother said, "the senior citizens' home. What were you thinking? You know how they talk!"

"We've had three phone calls so far this morning," Grandma

said. "This is the first chance I've had to sit down with my tea. It's just like we're movie stars!"

"So what's new?" I asked Sally. "You have plans for the day?"

"I'm moving. Got a new place to live. Ran into some friends last night who were looking to replace a roommate. They've got a house in Yardley."

"Dang," Grandma said. "I'm going to miss seeing you sitting there in that pink bathrobe."

I puttered around until Sally was out of the house. Then I took a shower and straightened my room. I didn't like that I'd lost Mrs. Nowicki. All because I hadn't told Morelli the whole story soon enough. *"Damn!"* I yelled out. Now all I needed was for Joyce Barnhardt to haul Maxine in. *"Shit!"*

My mother knocked on my bedroom door. "Are you all right in there?"

I opened the door. "No, I'm not all right. I'm bummed! I've screwed this case up, and now I have to worry about Joyce Barnhardt making my apprehension."

My mother gave a sharp inhale. "Joyce Barnhardt! Joyce Barnhardt couldn't carry your water pail! You're better than Joyce Barnhardt!"

"You think so?"

"Just go fix whatever it is you botched. I'm sure it isn't that bad. This woman you're after has to be out there somewhere. People don't just disappear."

"It isn't that easy. I've lost all my leads." With the exception of Bernie the horny drug dealer, who I wasn't crazy about seeing again.

"Do you know that for sure?"

Actually, no.

"You're right," I said. "It wouldn't hurt to check a few things out." I grabbed my shoulder bag and headed for the stairs.

"Will you be home for supper?" my mother asked. "We're having fried chicken and biscuits and strawberry shortcake."

"I'll be home."

My enthusiasm did another dip when I saw the Buick waiting for me. It was hard to be Wonder Woman in the Buick. It would be much easier to be Wonder Woman on a Duc, for instance.

I crawled onto the big bench seat and peered over the steering wheel at the powder-blue hood stretching endlessly in front of me. I turned the key and accelerated. *Bzzzzzzzup,* the car sucked gas and rolled up the street.

Morelli had covered Mrs. Nowicki's house, but he hadn't gone to see Margie. There was a slim chance that Mrs. Nowicki might be with Margie.

I didn't feel encouraged when I pulled up at Margie's house. Her car wasn't there, and neither was Mrs. Nowicki's. I went to the door and found it locked. No one answered my knock. I tiptoed around and looked in windows and saw no sign of life. No breakfast dishes left on the kitchen counter. No socks left lying on the floor. No cat curled in an armchair. The neighbor didn't pop out. Maybe she was used to me snooping.

I crossed the lawn and rapped on the neighbor's door.

She looked puzzled at first, then she placed me. "You're Margie's friend!" she said.

"Yes, and I'm still looking for Margie."

"You just missed her. She was home for a day, and now she's gone again."

"Do you know where she went?"

"I didn't ask. I just assumed it was back to the shore."

"Well, thanks," I said. "I'll catch up with her one of these times."

I went back to the car and sat there berating myself for a few minutes. "Stupid, stupid, *stupid!*" I said.

I was on the road, so I thought, What the hell, I'll make a last-ditch effort and double-check on Maxine's mother. No stone unturned.

I didn't see a car in front of her house, either, but I parked and went to her door. I knocked, and the door swung open. "Hello?" I called. No answer. I went room to room and was relieved not to find anyone dead, or scalped, or hacked into little pieces.

Maxine's mother hadn't lived well. The double bed mattress sagged miserably in the middle. The sheets were threadbare. A faded chenille spread served as blanket and bedspread. Both were littered with burns from cigarettes. The furniture was old and scarred, beyond polish. Rugs were soiled. Sinks were stained and chipped. The kitchen wastebasket was filled with booze bottles. And the house reeked from stale smoke and mildew.

There were no scribbled notes indicating travel plans. No magazine pages dog-eared to cruise advertisements. No fake twenties carelessly discarded. Mrs. Nowicki was gone and didn't expect to be back. I thought the open door was a blatant message. Let the wipe-ass scavengers pick this shit over, the door said. I'm movin' on.

I went back to the Buick and tried to piece things together, but I didn't have nearly enough information. What I knew was that Margie, Maxine's mother and Maxine were sticking together. I knew that Francine Nowicki had a bunch of bad twenties. I suspected that Eddie Kuntz wanted Maxine for more than love letters. And I knew someone wanted information on Maxine bad enough to kill for it.

I thought the most confusing element in all of this was the disappearance of Eddie Kuntz. He'd been missing for four days. I thought he'd have floated in on the tide by now.

I've checked on Margie and Maxine, I thought. I should check on Eddie Kuntz, too. Trouble was, I hated to tangle with Betty and Leo again. It was getting unpleasant. Of course, I could just ride by. Stopping could be optional.

I put the Buick in gear and cruised over to Muffet Street, pausing in front of the Glicks' house. Didn't look like anybody was home in either side. No Lincoln Town Car parked at the curb. I could feel my fingers getting twitchy, wanting to see if Eddie's front door would swing open like Francine's. Maybe since no one was around I could even *help* it swing open.

My heart did a little tap dance. Stephanie, Stephanie, Stephanie, don't even think what you're thinking! What if you get caught inside! Okay, I have to admit, getting caught inside would be a downer. I needed a lookout. I needed Lula. The office was about ten minutes away.

I hauled out my cell phone and dialed the office.

"Yeah, sure," Lula said. "I'm good at lookout shit. I'll be right there."

"I'm going to try to get inside," I told her. "I'll take my cell phone with me. You sit across the street and be cool and call me if Betty or Leo comes home. Then I'll go out the back door."

"You can count on me," Lula said.

I drove to the end of the block, turned the corner and parked. Then I walked back to the Glicks' house and marched up the stairs to the porch. Just to be sure I knocked on the Glicks' door. No answer. I looked in the window. No one walking around. I did the same on the Kuntz side. I tried the door. Locked. I ran around to the back. No luck there, either. I should have called Ranger instead of Lula. Ranger had a way with locks. I used to carry a set of lock picks, but I could never get them to work, so I threw them away.

I glanced over at Eddie's back window, next to the door. It was cracked open! No air-conditioning in the Kuntz side. You could probably bake bread on the kitchen floor. I slunk off the porch and gave the window a nudge. Stuck. I looked around. There was no activity in the neighborhood. No dogs barking. No neighbors watering grass. No kids playing. Too hot. Everyone was inside, running their air conditioners, watching television. Good for me.

I discreetly dragged a garbage can over to the window and climbed on. I balanced on my knees, gave the window a good hard shot and ZZZING! The window sailed open. I didn't hear anybody yelling "Hey, you! What are you doing?" so I figured everything was cool. I mean, it wasn't like I was breaking and entering, because I hadn't actually broken anything.

I slid the window back down and ran to the front of the house to make sure the Glicks hadn't come home. When I didn't see the Lincoln I felt a little more comfortable, so that my heart slowed down to almost normal. I did the upstairs first, methodically going room by room. When I got to the downstairs I looked out the window and saw the red Firebird parked two houses down. I searched the kitchen last. Milk in the refrigerator. And upstairs in his bedroom there'd been dirty clothes on the floor. Things that would lead me to believe he hadn't intended to go on a trip.

I found two key rings in the junk drawer by the sink. One key ring held several keys. Car key, house key, a locker key. The other key ring only held one key. My mother lived in a duplex like this, and her junk drawer held two key rings, too. One was an extra set of keys. The other was the key to next door.

SIXTEEN

I LOOKED AT MY WATCH. I'd been in the house for a half hour. Probably I shouldn't push my luck, but I really wanted to take a quick tour of the Glick half. It'd be helpful to find a ransom note left lying on the Glicks' kitchen counter. The key was in the drawer calling to me. *Use me. Use me.* Okay, what was the worst that could happen? The Glicks would catch me, and I'd be embarrassed. But that wouldn't happen because Lula was watching.

I pocketed the key, closed the window to within an inch of the sill, slipped out the door and stuck the key in the Glicks' lock. Bingo. The door clicked open.

The first thing I noticed was the wash of cool air. It had to be forty degrees in Betty Glick's kitchen. It was like walking into a re-frigerator. The no-wax linoleum floor was spotless. The appliances were new. The countertops were Formica butcher block. The theme was country kitchen. Wooden hearts painted barn red and Newport blue, inscribed with homey messages, were hung on the walls. A small pine turned-leg table had been positioned under the back window. The toaster snuggled under a crafts fair toaster cover. Pot holders and dish towels sported rooster designs, and in a color-ful, hand-painted bowl was the essential orange-scented potpourri.

Only problem was that the potpourri did nothing to disguise

the fact that Betty Glick's kitchen smelled bad. Betty needed some baking soda down her sink drain. Or maybe Betty needed to empty the garbage. I did a quick look through the cupboards and drawers. Nothing unusual there. Also no dead rats or rotting chicken carcasses. The waste container was scrubbed clean and lined with a plastic bag. So *what* was that smell? There was a kitchen telephone, but no answering machine to snoop on. The sticky pad beside the telephone was blank, waiting for an important message. I looked in the refrigerator and the broom closet, which had been converted into a small pantry.

The smell was stronger on the broom closet side of the room, and suddenly I knew what I was smelling. Uh oh, I thought, take me out of here, feet! But my feet weren't listening. My feet were creeping closer to the source of the smell. My feet were heading for the cellar door next to the broom closet.

My cell phone was in my shoulder bag, and my shoulder bag was hung on my shoulder. I looked inside the bag to make sure the LED was lit. Yep. The phone was working.

I opened the cellar door and flipped the light switch. "Hel-*lo*-o," I called. If I'd have gotten an answer, I'd have fainted.

I crept halfway down the stairs and saw the body. I'd expected it would be Eddie or maybe Maxine. This body was neither. It was a man in a suit. Late fifties, early sixties, maybe. Very dead. He'd been placed on a tarp. No blood anywhere. I wasn't a forensics expert, but from the way this guy's eyes were bulging and his tongue was sticking out I'd say he hadn't died of natural causes.

So what the hell did this mean? Why would Betty have a corpse in her basement? I know it sounds crazy, but it struck me as especially odd since Betty was such a tidy housekeeper. The basement had been finished off with tile flooring and an acoustical ceiling. Laundry area to one side. Storage to the other, including some large equipment under another tarp. An average basement . . . except for the dead guy.

I stumbled back up the stairs and popped into the kitchen just as Betty and Leo came through the front door.

"What the hell?" Leo said. "What the hell is this?"

I didn't know what was going on, but it didn't feel healthy to hang around in Betty's kitchen. So I bolted for the back door.

BANG! A bullet sailed past my ear and embedded itself in the doorjamb.

"Stop!" Leo shouted. "Stop right where you are."

He'd dropped the box he'd been carrying, and he was aiming a semiautomatic at me. And he was looking much more professional with a gun in his hand than Sugar had looked.

"You touch that back door, and I'll shoot you," Leo said. "And before you die I'll chop your fingers off."

I stared at him bug-eyed and open-mouthed.

Betty rolled her eyes. "You and those fingers," she said to Leo.

"Hey, it's my trademark, okay?"

"I think it's silly. And beside, they did it in that movie about that short person. Everyone will think you're a copycat."

"Well, they're wrong. I did it first. I was clipping fingers years ago in Detroit."

Betty retrieved the box Leo had dropped, carted it into the kitchen and set it on the counter. I read the printing on the side. It was a new chain saw. Black and Decker, 120 horsepower, portable.

Eek.

"You're not going to believe this," I said, "but there's a dead guy in your cellar. Probably you should call the police."

"You know when things start to go wrong, it all turns to crap-ola," Leo said. "You ever notice that?"

"Who is he?" I asked. "The man down there."

"Nathan Russo. Not that it matters to you. He was my partner, and he got nervous. I had to settle his nerves."

My phone rang inside my shoulder bag.

"Christ," Leo said, "what is that? One of those cellular phones?"

"Yeah. I should probably answer it. It might be my mother."

"Put your bag on the counter."

I put it on the counter. Leo rummaged through it with his free hand, found the phone and shut it off.

"This is a real pain in the ass now," Leo said. "Bad enough I have to get rid of *one* body. Now I have to get rid of *two*."

"I told you not to do it in the cellar," Betty said. "I *told* you."

"I was busy," Leo said. "I didn't have a lot of time. I didn't notice you helping any to get the money together. You think it's easy to get all that money?"

"I know this is a sort of dumb question," I said. "But what happened to Eddie?"

"Eddie!" Leo threw his hands in the air. "None of this would have happened if it wasn't for that bum!"

"He's just young," Betty said. "He's not a bad person."

"Young? He ruined me! My life's work . . . pooof! If he was here I'd kill him, too."

"I don't want to hear that kind of talk," Betty said. "He's blood."

"*Hah*. Wait until you're out on the street because your no-good nephew blew our pension plan. Wait until you need to get into a nursing home. You think they're gonna let you into assisted living on your good looks? No sirree."

Betty put her grocery bag on the small kitchen table and started to unpack. Orange juice, bread, bran flakes, a box of three-ply jumbo-sized trash bags. "We should have gotten two boxes of these trash bags," she said.

This made me swallow hard. I had a pretty good idea what they were going to do with the trash bags and chain saw.

"So go back to the store," Leo said. "I'll start downstairs, and you can go get more bags. We forgot to get steak sauce anyway. I was gonna grill steaks tonight."

"My God," I said. "How can you think of grilling steaks when you've got a dead man in your basement?"

"You gotta eat," Leo said.

Betty and Leo were standing with their backs to the side window. I looked over Leo's shoulder and saw Lula bob up and look in the window at us, her hair beads flopping around.

"Do you hear funny clicking sounds?" Leo asked Betty.

"No."

They both stood listening.

Lula bobbed up a second time.

"There it is again!"

Leo turned, but Lula was gone from the window.

"You're hearing things," Betty said. "It's all this stress. We should take a vacation. We should go to someplace fun like Disney World."

"I know what I heard," Leo said. "And I heard something."

"Well, I wish you'd hurry up and kill her," Betty said. "I don't like standing here like this. What if one of the neighbors comes over? How will it look?"

"Downstairs," Leo said to me.

"And don't make a mess," Betty said. "I just cleaned down there. Choke her like you did Nathan. That worked out good."

It was the second time in twenty-four hours someone had pointed a gun at me, and I was beyond scared. I was vacillating between cold, stark terror and being truly pissed. My stomach was hollow from fear, and the rest of my body was spastic with the need to grab Leo by his shirtfront and rap his head against the wall until his fillings fell out of his teeth.

I imagined Lula was scrambling to help, calling the police. And I knew what I needed was to stall for time, but it was hard to think coherently. I was sweating in Betty's forty-degree kitchen. It was the cold sweat of someone facing death badly. Not ready to go.

"I don't g-g-get it," I said to Leo. "Why are you doing all this killing?"

"I only kill when I have to," Leo said. "It's not like it's indiscriminate. I wouldn't have killed that sales clerk, but she pulled Betty's ski mask off."

"She seemed like such a nice girl, too," Betty said. "But what could we do?"

"I'm a n-n-nice girl," I said.

"We didn't even get any information from her," Leo said. "I cut off her finger to show I was serious, and she still wouldn't talk. What kind of a person is that? All she said was that Maxine was in

Point Pleasant. Big deal. Point Pleasant. Maxine and twenty thousand other people."

"Maybe that was all she knew."

Leo shrugged.

I did a panicked search for another question. "You know what else I don't get? I don't get why you scalped Mrs. Nowicki. Everybody else had their finger cut off."

"I forgot my clippers," Leo said. "And all she had in the house was this dinky paring knife. You can't do real good work with a paring knife. Not unless it's supersharp."

"I keep telling you, you should take ginko," Betty said. "You don't remember anything anymore."

"I'm not taking any damn ginko. I don't even know what ginko is."

"It's an herb," Betty said. "Everybody takes it."

Leo rolled his eyes. "Everybody. Unh."

Lula bobbed up at the window again. And this time she had a gun in her hand. She squinted and sighted and BAM! The window shattered, and a rooster pot holder hanging from a hook on the opposite wall jumped in place.

"Jesus H. Christ," Leo said, dodging aside, whirling around to face the window.

"Drop your gun, you punk-ass old coot," Lula yelled. "You don't drop your gun, I'm gonna bust a cap up your ass!"

Leo shot at the window. Lula returned fire, taking out the microwave. And Betty and I dove under the table.

Sirens whooped in the distance.

Leo ran for the front door, where there was more gunfire and a lot of cussing from both Leo and Lula. Police strobes flashed through the front windows, and there was more shouting.

"I hate this part," Betty said.

"You've done this before?"

"Well, not exactly like this. It was much more orderly last time."

Betty and I were still under the table when Morelli came in.

"Excuse me," Morelli said to Betty. "I'd like to speak to Ms. Plum in private."

Betty crawled out and stood and looked like she didn't know where to go.

I crawled out, too. "You might want to detain her," I said to Morelli.

Morelli passed her off to a uniform and glared at me. "What the hell's going on here? I answer my page and it's Lula screaming how someone's shooting you."

"Well, he didn't actually get around to shooting me."

Morelli sniffed. "What's that smell?"

"Dead guy in the basement. Leo's partner."

Morelli wheeled around and went downstairs. A minute later he came up smiling. "That's Nathan Russo."

"And?"

"He's our friendly neighborhood funny money distributor. He's the guy we've been watching."

"Small world."

"There's a press down there, too. Under a tarp."

I felt my face crumple and my eyes fill with tears. "He wanted to kill me."

"I know the feeling," Morelli said. He put an arm around me and kissed the top of my head.

"I hate to cry," I said. "I get all blotchy, and it makes my nose run."

"Well, you're not blotchy right now," Morelli said. "Right now you're white. The guy downstairs has more color than you." He guided me through the house to the porch, where Lula was pacing, looking like she'd break out in hives any minute. Morelli sat me down on the step and told me to put my head between my legs.

After a minute the clanging stopped in my head, and I didn't feel like throwing up anymore. "I'm okay," I said. "I feel better."

Lula sat next to me. "First time I ever saw a white person who really was white."

"Don't go anywhere," Morelli said. "I need to talk to both of you."

"Yessir, boss," Lula said.

Morelli squatted next to me and lowered his voice. "You weren't in this house illegally, were you?"

"No." I shook my head for emphasis. "The door was open. I was invited in. The wind blew the door . . ."

Morelli narrowed his eyes. "You want to pick one?"

"Which one do you like?"

"Christ," Morelli said.

He went back into the house, which was now filled with cops. An EMS truck had arrived. No need for that. No one had been hurt, and the body in the basement would go home with the coroner in his body snatcher truck. Neighbors had collected on the sidewalk by the EMS truck. Others stood on porches across the street. Betty and Leo were sitting in two separate blue-and-whites. They'd be kept apart from now on and questioned independently.

"Thanks for coming to my rescue," I said to Lula. "Boy, you really nailed that pot holder."

"Yeah, only I was aiming for Leo. Sorry I didn't call you in time. I kept getting interference. Lucky I got through to Morelli right away."

At the end of the block a black Jeep screeched to a halt and a naked man jumped out.

"Goddamn!" Lula said. "I know that naked motherfucker."

I was on my feet and running. The naked motherfucker was Eddie Kuntz! Eddie saw the crowd in front of his house and immediately scurried behind some shrubbery. I skidded to a stop directly in front of the shrub and stared. Kuntz was tattooed head to toe with colorful messages like "pencil dick" and "woman beater" and "I like to be butt-fucked."

"Ommigod," I said, trying hard not to be obvious about comparing messages with equipment displayed.

Kuntz was rabid. "They've been holding me hostage. They tattooed my entire body!"

Lula was next to me. "Think they been generous with the pencil dick," she said. "Think you're more a stubby eraser."

"I'm going to kill her," Kuntz said. "I'm going to find her and kill her."

"Maxine?"

"And don't think you're getting your thousand dollars, either."

"About the car you just got out of . . ."

"It was that other bounty hunter. The one with the knockers. Said she'd picked up a police call on her scanner and was heading over here. She picked me up on Olden. That's where Maxine dumped me off. Olden! In front of the Seven-Eleven!"

"Do you know where Maxine was going?"

"The airport. All three of them. They're in a blue Honda Civic. And I take that back about the thousand. You bring that cunt to me, and I'll make you goddamn rich."

I whirled around and ran for the Firebird.

Lula was pounding pavement behind me. "I'm on it," she was saying. "I'm on it!"

We both jumped in the car, and Lula rocketed away before I even had my door closed.

"They'll take Route One," she said. "That's why they dropped him off on Olden. They were heading for One." She cornered Olden with two wheels touching pavement, took the turnoff and hit Route 1 north.

I'd been so excited I'd forgotten to ask which airport. Like Lula, I'd just assumed it was Newark. I looked over at the speedometer and saw it hovering at ninety. Lula put her foot to the floor, and I braced myself and turned my face away.

"They got that little prick good," Lula said. "I almost hate to pick Maxine up. You gotta admire her style."

"Creative," I said.

"Damn skippy."

Actually, I thought the tattooing might be a little excessive. I didn't like Eddie Kuntz but I had to wince at the thought of Maxine needling him head to foot.

I was looking for the blue Honda, and I was also looking for Joyce. Wouldn't you know, Joyce would happen on Eddie Kuntz. If there was a naked man anywhere near Joyce, she'd find him.

"There they are!" I yelled. "On the side of the road."

"I see 'em," Lula said. "Looks like Maxine got stopped by the cops."

Not the cops. They got stopped by Joyce Barnhardt, who'd stuck a portable red flasher on the roof of her Jeep. We pulled in behind Joyce and ran to see what was happening.

Joyce was standing on the shoulder of the road, holding a gun on Maxine, Mrs. Nowicki and Margie. The three women were spread-eagled on the ground by Joyce with their hands cuffed behind their backs.

Joyce smiled when she saw me. "You're a little late, sweetie-pie. I've already made the apprehension. Too bad you're such a loser."

"Hunh," Lula said, slitty eyed.

"You've got three people cuffed, Joyce, and only one of them is a felon. You have no right to manhandle the other two women."

"I can manhandle whoever I want," Joyce said. "You're just pissy because I got your collar."

"I'm pissy because you're being an unprofessional jerk."

"Careful what you say to me," Joyce said. "You get me annoyed and you and lard butt might find yourselves on the ground with these three. I've got a couple more cuffs left."

"Excuse me," Lula said. "Lard butt?"

Joyce trained her gun on Lula and me. "You've got thirty seconds to get your fat asses out of here. And you should both look for new jobs, because it's clear I'm the primo bounty hunter now."

"Yeah," Lula said. "We don't deserve to have a cool job like bounty hunter. I've been thinking maybe I'd get a job at that new place just opened, Lickin' Chicken. They tell me you work there

258

you get to eat whatever you want. You even get them biscuits when they're fresh out of the oven. Here, let me help you get these women into your car."

Lula hoisted Maxine to her feet, and when she handed her over to Joyce, Joyce made a sound like "Ulk" and crumpled to the ground.

"Oops," Lula said. "Another one of them dizzy spells."

Helped along by a few volts from Lula's stun gun.

There was a medium-sized duffel bag on the backseat in Joyce's car. I searched through the bag and found the keys to the cuffs. I unlocked Mrs. Nowicki's cuffs and then Margie's cuffs. I stepped away. "You're on your own," I told them. "I'm not authorized to arrest you, but Treasury is looking for you, and you'd be smart to turn yourselves in."

"Yeah, sure," Mrs. Nowicki said. "I'm gonna do that."

Lula got Maxine to her feet and dusted her off, while Mrs. Nowicki and Margie shuffled uncomfortably on the side of the road.

"What about Maxie?" Margie asked. "Can't you let Maxie go, too?"

"Sorry. Maxine has to report back to the court."

"Don't worry about it," Maxine said to her mother and Margie. "It'll work out okay."

"Don't feel right to leave you like this," Mrs. Nowicki said.

"It's no big deal," Maxine said. "I'll meet up with you after I get this straightened out."

Mrs. Nowicki and Margie got into the blue Honda and drove away.

Joyce was still lying on the ground, but she'd started to twitch a little, and one of her eyes was open. I didn't want Joyce to get accosted while she was coming around, so Lula and I picked Joyce up and stuffed her into the Jeep. Then we took the Jeep keys and locked Joyce in, nice and snug and safe. The little red light was still flashing on the roof of her car, so chances were good that a cop would stop to investigate. Since the little red light was illegal, it was possible that Joyce might get arrested. But then, maybe not. Joyce was good at talking cops out of tickets.

MAXINE WASN'T FEELING TALKATIVE on the way to the station, and I suspected she was composing her story. She looked younger than she had in her photo. Less trampy. Maybe that's what happens when you tattoo out anger. Like breathing life back into a drown victim. In goes the good air, out comes the bad air. Or maybe it was the hundred-dollar haircut and color, and the seventy-five-dollar DKNY T-shirt. Maxine didn't look like she was hurting for money.

The Trenton Police Station is on North Clinton. The building is red brick and utilitarian. The parking lot is Brooklyn south . . . about an acre of second-rate blacktop surrounded by ten-foot-high chain-link fencing. The hope is that the fencing will prevent the theft of police cars, but there's no guarantee.

We pulled into the police lot and saw there were two cruisers backed up to the drop-off behind the building. Leo Glick was helped from one of the cars. He looked our way. His gaze was piercing and angry.

"No sense making a big scene," I said to Lula. "We'll take Maxine in through the front so she doesn't have to deal with Leo."

Sometimes, if court was in session, I could take my apprehension directly to the judge, but court was adjourned for the day, so I walked Maxine back to the docket lieutenant. I gave him my paperwork and handed Maxine over.

"I have a message for you," he said. "Morelli called in about five minutes ago and left this number. Wants you to call him back. You can use the phone in the squad room."

I made the call and waited for Morelli to come on the line.

"Since you're at the station I assume you brought Maxine in," Morelli said.

"I always get my man."

"That's a scary thought."

"I was speaking professionally."

"I need a rundown on what happened at the house here."

I skipped over the part about using Kuntz's key to get into the house and told him the rest.

"How did you get to me so fast today?" I asked.

"I was back on surveillance at the Seven-Eleven." There was a moment of silence between us when I could hear people talking in the background. "Kuntz is being cooperative," Morelli said. "He's so pissed off he's willing to tell us anything we want to know. He said Maxine was on her way to the airport."

"Yeah. I got her on Route One."

"She alone?"

"Nope."

"I'm waiting," Morelli said.

"Margie and Mrs. Nowicki were with her."

"And?"

"And I let them go. I wasn't authorized to arrest them." And I didn't especially want to see them caught. I had a hard time believing they were involved in the counterfeiting. For that matter, I hadn't especially wanted to bring Maxine in, either. What I suspected was that they'd extorted money from Leo and were on their way to the good life. This was really terrible, but something inside me wanted them to succeed.

"You should have told me right away. You knew I wanted to talk to Maxine's mother."

Morelli was mad. He was using his cop voice.

"Anything else?" I asked.

"That's it for now."

I stuck out my tongue at the phone and hung up. I was feeling very mature.

MY FATHER was slouched in his chair, watching baseball on television. My grandmother was asleep sitting up, head back on the couch, and my mother was next to her, crocheting. This was a nightly pattern, and there was comfort in the ritual. Even the house itself seemed to fall into a satisfied stupor when the dishes were done and the only sound was the drone of the ball game.

I was outside, on my parents' steps, doing nothing. I could have been doing something deep, like thinking about my life, or Mother Teresa's life, or life in general, but I couldn't get turned on by that. What turned me on right now was the luxury of doing nothing.

After I'd handed Maxine over, I'd gone to see my apartment and had been surprised to find repairs were already underway. I'd visited with Mrs. Karwatt and Mrs. Delgado, and then I'd gone back to Morelli's house and packed up my few possessions. The threat of danger was gone, and staying with Morelli now would have smacked of relationship. What was wrong was that there was no relationship. There was great sex and some genuine affection, but the future was too far in the future to feel comfortable. And on top of that, Morelli made me nuts. Morelli pushed all my buttons without even trying. Not to mention Grandma Bella. Not to mention all those Morelli sperms swimming upstream, trying to bash their way through the end of the condom. My eye started to twitch, and I put my finger to it. You see? That's what Morelli does to me . . . gives me an eye twitch.

Better to live with my parents than Morelli. If I could just make it through a few weeks with my parents, I could move back into my own apartment, and then my life will get back to normal. And then my eye will stop twitching.

It was almost ten, and there was no activity on the street. The air was still and dense. The temperature had dropped. There were a few stars overhead, struggling to shine through Trenton's light pollution, not having much luck with it.

Someone was bouncing a basketball blocks away. Air conditioners hummed, and a lone cricket chirped in the side yard.

I heard the whine of a motorcycle, and I thought there was a slim chance I knew the biker. The sound was mesmerizing. Not the thunder of a hog. This was the sound of a crotch rocket. The bike drew closer, and finally I saw the outline under the streetlight at the end of the block. It was a Ducati. All speed and agility and Italian sexiness. The perfect bike for Morelli.

He eased the Duc to the curb and removed his helmet. He was wearing jeans and boots and a black T-shirt, and he looked like the sort of man a woman had to worry about. He kicked the stand out and strolled over to me.

"Nice night to be sitting out," he said.

I was reminded of the time I went to Girl Scout camp and sat too close to the fire and my boots started smoking.

"Thought you'd want to know how the interrogation went."

I leaned forward, greedy with curiosity. Of course I wanted to know!

"It was a total bitchfest," Morelli said. "I've never seen so many people so eager to incriminate themselves. It turns out that Leo Glick has a record a mile long. He grew up in Detroit, working for the Angio family. Was an enforcer. Twenty years ago he decided he was getting too old to do muscle work, so he apprenticed himself to a printer he met in prison. The printer, Joe Costa, had a set of really good plates. Leo spent three years with Costa, learning the business, and then one day Costa got dead. Leo doesn't know how this happened."

I rolled my eyes.

"Yeah," Morelli said. "That's what I think, too. Anyway, Leo and Betty left Detroit and moved to Trenton, and after a couple years they set up shop.

"Leo knew Nathan Russo from Detroit. Nathan was a bag man for the Angios. Leo got Nathan to relocate and launder for him. It was all pretty clever. Nathan runs a dry-cleaning business. Betty was the go-between, and she made all the exchanges in bundles of laundry. Very sanitary."

"That's terrible."

Morelli grinned.

"What about Maxine?" I asked.

"Maxine was in love with Kuntz, but Kuntz is a real asshole. Slaps women around. Maxine isn't the first. Abuses them in other ways, too. Kept telling Maxine she was stupid.

"So one day they have a real bad fight and Maxine takes off with Kuntz's car. Kuntz figures he'll show her, so he presses charges and has her arrested. Maxine gets out on bail and is berserk. She goes back to Kuntz and pretends to be lovey, but what she really wants is to get even. Kuntz has been bragging about what a big gangster he is and how he has this counterfeit operation going. Maxine goads him into showing her the plates, and Eddie, with his very small brain, goes next door when Leo and Betty are at the supermarket and gets the plates and the account book and a duffel bag of twenties. Then Maxine screws his brains out, sends him into the shower to get ready for round two, and takes off with everything."

"Maxine is the shit."

"Yes," Morelli said. "Maxine is definitely the shit. In the beginning it was just supposed to be a revenge game. You know, make Kuntz sweat. Send him on a treasure hunt from hell. But Leo finds out about it and sets off to find Maxine, Detroit style. He interrogates Marge and Maxine's mother, and they don't know anything about anything."

"Even after he encourages them to talk by slicing off a body part."

"Yeah. Leo's not too good at character analyses. He doesn't know he can't get blood from a stone. Anyway, when Maxine finds out about the finger and the scalping, she's outraged, and she decides to cut her mother and Marge in and go for the gold.

"She's gone through the account books by now, so she knows she's dealing with Leo. She calls him up and gives him the terms. A million in real money for the plates and the account book."

"Did Leo have that kind of money?"

"Apparently. Of course, Maxine's denying the extortion part of the story."

"Where's the million?"

Morelli looked like he really liked this part. "Nobody knows. I think it's out of the country. It's possible the only charges that'll stick against anyone is the original auto theft and the failure to appear against Maxine. There isn't actually any proof of extortion."

"What about kidnapping Eddie Kuntz?"

"No charges pressed. If you had 'pencil dick' tattooed all over your ass would you want to go public? Besides, most of those tattoos weren't permanent. The first night Eddie was kidnapped Maxine locked him in a room with a bottle of gin. He got stinking drunk and passed out and when he woke up he was Mr. Tattoo."

I was looking at the Duc, and I was thinking that it was very cool and that if I had a Duc I'd *really* be the shit.

Morelli nudged my knee with his. "Want to go for a ride?"

Of course I wanted to go for a ride. I was dying to get my legs around those 109 horses and feel them wind out.

"Do I get to drive?" I asked.

"No."

"Why not?"

"It's *my* bike."

"If I had a Ducati, I'd let *you* drive."

"If you had a Ducati you probably wouldn't talk to a lowlife like me."

"Remember when I was six and you were eight, and you conned me into playing choo-choo in your father's garage?"

Morelli's eyes narrowed. "We aren't going to go through this again, are we?"

"I never got to be the train. *You* were always the train. *I* always had to be the tunnel."

"I had better train equipment."

"You owe me."

"I was eight years old!"

"What about when I was sixteen, and you seduced me behind the eclair case at the bakery?"

"What about it?"

"I never got the top. I was only the bottom."

"This is entirely different."

"This is no different! This is the same thing!"

"Jesus," Morelli said. "Just get on the damn bike."

"You're going to let me drive, right?"

"Yeah, you're going to drive."

I ran my hand over the bike. It was sleek and smooth and red.

Morelli had a second helmet strapped to the backseat. He unhooked the cord and gave me the helmet. "Seems a shame to cover up all those pretty curls."

I buckled on the helmet. "Too late for flattery."

It had been a while since I'd driven a bike. I settled myself onto the Duc and looked things over.

Morelli took the seat behind me. "You know how to drive this, right?"

I revved the engine. "Right."

"And you have a license?"

"Got a bike license when I was married to Dickie. I've kept it current."

He held me at the waist. "This is going to even the score."

"Not nearly."

"Entirely," he said. "In fact, this ride's going to be so good you're going to owe *me* when it's done."

Oh boy.

HIGH
FIVE

ACKNOWLEDGMENTS

Thanks to Mary Anne Day, Joy Gianolio, Nancy Hunt, Merry Law, Lisa Medvedev, Catherine Mudrak, Fran Rak, Hope Sass, Karen Swee, Elaine Vliet, Joan Walsh, and Vicki Wiesner, The Women Mystery Writers Reading Group, for suggesting the title for this book.

ONE

WHEN I WAS a little girl I used to dress Barbie up without underpants. On the outside, she'd look like the perfect lady. Tasteful plastic heels, tailored suit. But underneath, she was naked. I'm a bail enforcement agent now—also known as a fugitive apprehension agent, also known as a bounty hunter. I bring 'em back dead or alive. At least I try. And being a bail enforcement agent is sort of like being bare-bottom Barbie. It's about having a secret. And it's about wearing a lot of bravado on the outside when you're really operating without underpants. Okay, maybe it's not like that for all enforcement agents, but I frequently feel like my privates are alfresco. Figuratively speaking, of course.

At the moment I wasn't feeling nearly so vulnerable. What I was feeling at the moment was desperate. My rent was due, and Trenton had run out of scofflaws. I had my hands palms down on Connie Rosolli's desk, my feet planted wide, and hard as I tried, I couldn't keep my voice from sounding like it was coming out of Minnie Mouse. "What do you mean, there are no FTAs? There are always FTAs."

"Sorry," Connie said. "We've got lots of bonds posted, but nobody's jumping. Must have something to do with the moon."

FTA is short for failure to appear for a court date. Going FTA is a definite no-no in the criminal justice system, but that doesn't usually stop people from doing it.

Connie slid a manila folder over to me. "This is the only FTA I've got, and it's not worth much."

Connie is the office manager for Vincent Plum Bail Bonds. She's a couple of years older than me, which puts her in her early thirties. She wears her hair teased high. She takes grief from no one. And if breasts were money, Connie'd be Bill Gates.

"Vinnie's overjoyed," Connie said. "He's making money by the fistful. No bounty hunters to pay. No forfeited bonds. Last time I saw Vinnie in a mood like this was when Madame Zaretsky was arrested for pandering and sodomy and put her trained dog up as collateral for her bond."

I cringed at the mental image this produced because not only is Vincent Plum my employer, he's also my cousin. I blackmailed him into taking me on as an apprehension agent at a low moment in my life and have come to sort of like the job . . . most of the time. That doesn't mean I have any illusions about Vinnie. For the most part, Vinnie is an okay bondsman. But privately, Vinnie is a boil on the backside of my family tree.

As a bail bondsman Vinnie gives the court a cash bond as a securement that the accused will return for trial. If the accused takes a hike, Vinnie forfeits his money. Since this isn't an appealing prospect to Vinnie, he sends me out to find the accused and drag him back into the system. My fee is 10 percent of the bond, and I only collect it if I'm successful.

I flipped the folder open and read the bond agreement. "Randy Briggs. Arrested for carrying concealed. Failed to appear at his court hearing." The bond amount was seven hundred dollars. That meant I'd get seventy. Not a lot of money for risking my life by going after someone who was known to carry.

"I don't know," I said to Connie, "this guy carries a knife."

Connie looked at her copy of Briggs' arrest sheet. "It says here it was a small knife, and it wasn't sharp."

"How small?"

"Eight inches."

"That isn't small!"

"Nobody else will take this," Connie said. "Ranger doesn't take anything under ten grand."

Ranger is my mentor and a world-class tracker. Ranger also never seems to be in dire need of rent money. Ranger has other sources of income.

I looked at the photo attached to Briggs' file. Briggs didn't look so bad. In his forties, narrow-faced and balding, Caucasian. Job description was listed as self-employed computer programmer.

I gave a sigh of resignation and stuffed the folder into my shoulder bag. "I'll go talk to him."

"Probably he just forgot," Connie said. "Probably this is a piece of cake."

I gave her my *yeah, right* look and left. It was Monday morning and traffic was humming past Vinnie's storefront office. The October sky was as blue as sky gets in New Jersey, and the air felt crisp and lacking in hydrocarbons. It was nice for a change, but it kind of took all the sport out of breathing.

A new red Firebird slid to curbside behind my '53 Buick. Lula got out of the car and stood hands on hips, shaking her head. "Girl, you still driving that pimpmobile?"

Lula did filing for Vinnie and knew all about pimpmobiles first-hand since in a former life she'd been a 'ho. She's what is gently referred to as a big woman, weighing in at a little over two hundred pounds, standing five-foot-five, looking like most of her weight's muscle. This week her hair was dyed orange and came off very autumn with her dark brown skin.

"This is a classic car," I told Lula. Like we both knew I really gave a fig about classic cars. I was driving The Beast because my Honda had caught fire and burned to a cinder, and I didn't have any money to replace it. So here I was, borrowing my uncle Sandor's gas-guzzling behemoth . . . again.

"Problem is, you aren't living up to your earning potential," Lula said. "We only got chickenshit cases these days. What you need is to have a serial killer or a homicidal rapist jump bail. Those boys are worth something."

"Yeah, I'd sure like to get a case like that." Big fib. If Vinnie ever gave me a homicidal rapist to chase down I'd quit and get a job selling shoes.

Lula marched into the office, and I slid behind the wheel and reread the Briggs file. Randy Briggs had given the same address for home and work. Cloverleaf Apartments on Grand Avenue. It wasn't far from the office. Maybe a mile. I pulled into traffic, made an illegal U-turn at the intersection, and followed Hamilton to Grand.

The Cloverleaf Apartments building was two blocks down Grand. It was redbrick-faced and strictly utilitarian. Three stories. A front and a back entrance. Small lot to the rear. No ornamentation. Aluminum-framed windows that were popular in the fifties and looked cheesy now.

I parked in the lot and walked into the small lobby. There was an elevator to one side and stairs to the other. The elevator looked claustrophobic and unreliable, so I took the stairs to the second floor. Briggs was 2B. I stood outside his door for a moment, listening. Nothing drifted out. No television. No talking. I pressed the doorbell and stood to the side, so I wasn't visible through the security peephole.

Randy Briggs opened his door and stuck his head out. "Yeah?"

He looked exactly like his photo, with sandy blond hair that was neatly combed, cut short. He was unbearded, unblemished. Dressed in clean khakis and a button-down shirt. Just like I'd expected from his file . . . except he was only three feet tall. Randy Briggs was vertically challenged.

"Oh, shit," I said, looking down at him.

"What's the matter?" he said. "You never see a short person before?"

"Only on television."

"Guess this is your lucky day."

I handed him my business card. "I represent Vincent Plum Bail

Bonds. You've missed your court date, and we'd appreciate it if you'd reschedule."

"No," Briggs said.

"Excuse me?"

"No. I'm not going to reschedule. No. I'm not going to court. It was a bogus arrest."

"The way our system works is that you're supposed to tell that to the judge."

"Fine. Go get the judge."

"The judge doesn't do house calls."

"Listen, I got a lot of work to do," Briggs said, closing his door. "I gotta go."

"Hold it!" I said. "You can't just ignore an order to appear in court."

"Watch me."

"You don't understand. I'm appointed by the court and Vincent Plum to bring you in."

"Oh, yeah? How do you expect to do that? You going to shoot me? You can't shoot an unarmed man." He stuck his hands out. "You gonna cuff me? You think you can drag me out of my apartment and down the hall without looking like an idiot? Big bad bounty hunter picking on a little person. And that's what we're called, Toots. Not midget, not dwarf, not a freaking Munchkin. Little person. Get it?"

My pager went off at my waist. I looked down to check the read-out and *slam*. Briggs closed and locked his door.

"Loser," he called from inside.

Well, that didn't go as smoothly as I'd hoped. I had a choice now. I could break down his door and beat the bejeezus out of him, or I could answer my mother's page. Neither was especially appealing, but I decided on my mother.

My parents live in a residential pocket of Trenton nicknamed the Burg. No one ever really leaves the Burg. You can relocate in Antarctica, but if you were born and raised in the Burg you're a Burger for life. Houses are small and obsessively neat. Televisions are large and loud. Lots are narrow. Families are extended. There are no pooper-scooper laws in the Burg. If your dog does his business on someone else's lawn, the next morning the doo-doo will be on your front porch. Life is simple in the Burg.

I put the Buick into gear, rolled out of the apartment building lot, headed for Hamilton, and followed Hamilton to St. Francis Hospital. My parents live a couple blocks behind St. Francis on Roosevelt Street. Their house is a duplex built at a time when families needed only one bathroom and dishes were washed by hand.

My mother was at the door when I pulled to the curb. My grandmother Mazur stood elbow to elbow with my mother. They were short, slim women with facial features that suggested Mongol ancestors . . . probably in the form of crazed marauders.

"Thank goodness you're here," my mother said, eyeing me as I got out of the car and walked toward her. "What are those shoes? They look like work boots."

"Betty Szajak and Emma Getz and me went to that male dancer place last week," Grandma said, "and they had some men parading around, looking like construction workers, wearing boots just like those. Then next thing you knew they ripped their clothes off and all they had left was those boots and these little silky black baggie things that their ding-dongs jiggled around in."

My mother pressed her lips together and made the sign of the cross. "You didn't tell me about this," she said to my grandmother.

"Guess it slipped my mind. Betty and Emma and me were going to bingo at the church, but it turned out there wasn't any bingo on account of the Knights of Columbus was holding some to-do there. So we decided to check out the men at that new club downtown." Grandma gave me an elbow. "I put a fiver right in one of those baggies!"

"Jesus H. Christ," my father said, rattling his paper in the living room.

Grandma Mazur came to live with my parents several years ago when my grandpa Mazur went to the big poker game in the sky.

My mother accepts this as a daughter's obligation. My father has taken to reading *Guns & Ammo*.

"So what's up?" I asked. "Why did you page me?"

"We need a detective," Grandma said.

My mother rolled her eyes and ushered me into the kitchen. "Have a cookie," she said, setting the cookie jar on the small Formica-topped kitchen table. "Can I get you a glass of milk? Some lunch?"

I lifted the lid on the cookie jar and looked inside. Chocolate chip. My favorite.

"Tell her," Grandma said to my mother, giving her a poke in the side. "Wait until you hear this," she said to me. "This is a good one."

I raised my eyebrows at my mother.

"We have a family problem," my mother said. "Your uncle Fred is missing. He went out to the store and hasn't come home yet."

"When did he go out?"

"Friday."

I paused with a cookie halfway to my mouth. "It's Monday!"

"Isn't this a pip?" Grandma said. "I bet he was beamed up by aliens."

Uncle Fred is married to my grandma Mazur's first cousin Mabel. If I had to guess his age I'd have to say somewhere between seventy and infinity. Once people start to stoop and wrinkle they all look alike to me. Uncle Fred was someone I saw at weddings and funerals and once in a while at Giovichinni's Meat Market, ordering a quarter pound of olive loaf. Eddie Such, the butcher, would have the olive loaf on the scale and Uncle Fred would say, "You've got the olive loaf on a piece of waxed paper. How much does that piece of waxed paper weigh? You're not gonna charge me for that waxed paper, are you? I want some money off for the waxed paper."

I shoved the cookie into my mouth. "Have you filed a missing persons report with the police?"

"Mabel did that first thing," my mother said.

"And?"

"And they haven't found him."

I went to the refrigerator and poured out a glass of milk for myself. "What about the car? Did they find the car?"

"The car was in the Grand Union parking lot. It was all locked up nice and neat."

"He was never right after that stroke he had in ninety-five," Grandma said. "I don't think his elevator went all the way to the top anymore, if you know what I mean. He could have just wandered off like one of those Alzheimer's people. Anybody think to check the cereal aisle in the supermarket? Maybe he's just standing there 'cause he can't make up his mind."

My father mumbled something from the living room about my grandmother's elevator, and my mother slid my father a dirty look through the kitchen wall.

I thought it was too weird. Uncle Fred was missing. This sort of thing just didn't happen in our family. "Did anybody go out to look for him?"

"Ronald and Walter. They covered all the neighborhoods around the Grand Union, but nobody's seen him."

Ronald and Walter were Fred's sons. And probably they'd enlisted their kids to help, too.

"We figure you're just the person to take a crack at this," Grandma said, "on account of that's what you do . . . you find people."

"I find criminals."

"Your aunt Mabel would be grateful if you'd look for Fred," my mother said. "Maybe you could just go over and talk to her and see what you think."

"She needs a detective," I said. "I'm not a detective."

"Mabel asked for you. She said she didn't want this going out of the family."

My internal radar dish started to hum. "Is there something you're not telling me?"

"What's to tell?" my mother said. "A man wandered off from his car."

I drank my milk and rinsed the glass. "Okay, I'll go talk to Aunt Mabel. But I'm not promising anything."

UNCLE FRED AND Aunt Mabel live on Baker Street, on the fringe of the Burg, three blocks over from my parents. Their ten-year-old Pontiac station wagon was parked at the curb and just about spanned the length of their rowhouse. They've lived in the rowhouse for as long as I can remember, raising two children, en-tertaining five grandchildren, and annoying the hell out of each other for over fifty years.

Aunt Mabel answered my knock on her door. She was a rounder, softer version of Grandma Mazur. Her white hair was perfectly permed. She was dressed in yellow polyester slacks and a matching floral blouse. Her earrings were large clip-ons, her lip-stick was a bright red, and her eyebrows were brown crayon.

"Well, isn't this nice," Aunt Mabel said. "Come into the kitchen. I got a coffee cake from Giovichinni today. It's the good kind, with the almonds."

Certain proprieties were observed in the Burg. No matter that your husband was kidnapped by aliens, visitors were offered coffee cake.

I followed after Aunt Mabel and waited while she cut the cake. She poured out coffee and sat opposite me at the kitchen table.

"I suppose your mother told you about your uncle Fred," she said. "Fifty-two years of marriage, and *poof*, he's gone."

"Did Uncle Fred have any medical problems?"

"The man was healthy as a horse."

"How about his stroke?"

"Well, yes, but everybody has a stroke once in a while. And that stroke didn't slow him down any. Most of the time he remembered things no one else would remember. Like that business with the garbage. Who would remember a thing like that? Who would even care about it? Such a fuss over nothing."

I knew I was going to regret asking, but I felt compelled. "What about the garbage?"

Mabel helped herself to a piece of coffee cake. "Last month there was a new driver on the garbage truck, and he skipped over our house. It only happened once, but would my husband forget a thing like that? No. Fred never forgot anything. Especially if it had to do with money. So at the end of the month Fred wanted two dollars back on account of we pay quarterly, you see, and Fred had already paid for the missed day."

I nodded in understanding. This didn't surprise me at all. Some men played golf. Some men did crossword puzzles. Uncle Fred's hobby was being cheap.

"That was one of the things Fred was supposed to do on Friday," Mabel said. "The garbage company was making him crazy. He went there in the morning, but they wouldn't give him his money without proof that he'd paid. Something about the computer messing up some of the accounts. So Fred was going back in the afternoon."

For two dollars. I did a mental head slap. If I'd been the clerk Fred had talked to at the garbage company I'd have given Fred two dollars out of my own pocket just to get rid of him. "What garbage company is this?"

"RGC. The police said Fred never got there. Fred had a whole list of errands he was going to do. He was going to the cleaners, the bank, the supermarket, and RGC."

"And you haven't heard from him."

"Not a word. Nobody's heard anything."

I had a feeling there wasn't going to be a happy ending to this story.

"Do you have any idea where Fred might be?"

"Everyone thinks he just wandered away, like a big dummy."

"What do you think?"

Mabel did an up-and-down thing with her shoulders. Like she

didn't know what to think. Whenever I did that, it meant I didn't want to *say* what I was thinking.

"If I show you something, you have to promise not to tell anyone," Mabel said.

Oh boy.

She went to a kitchen drawer and took out a packet of pictures. "I found these in Fred's desk. I was looking for the checkbook this morning, and this is what I found."

I stared at the first picture for at least thirty seconds before I realized what I was seeing. The print was taken in shadow and looked underexposed. The perimeter was a black plastic trash bag, and in the center of the photo was a bloody hand severed at the wrist. I thumbed through the rest of the pack. More of the same. In some the bag was spread wider, revealing more body parts. What looked like a shinbone, part of a torso maybe, something that might have been the back of the head. Hard to tell if it was man or woman.

The shock of the pictures had me holding my breath, and I was getting a buzzing sensation in my head. I didn't want to ruin my bounty-hunter image and keel over onto the floor, so I concentrated on quietly resuming breathing.

"You have to give these to the police," I said.

Mabel gave her head a shake. "I don't know what Fred was doing with these pictures. Why would a person have pictures like this?"

No date on the front or the back. "Do you know when they were taken?

"No. This is the first I saw them."

"Do you mind if I look through Fred's desk?"

"It's in the cellar," Mabel said. "Fred spent a lot of time down there."

It was a battered government-issue desk. Probably bought at a Fort Dix yard sale. It was positioned against a wall opposite the washer and dryer. And it was set on a stained piece of wall-to-wall carpet that I assumed had been saved when new carpet was laid upstairs.

I pawed through the drawers, finding the usual junk. Pencils and pens. A drawer filled with instruction booklets and warranty cards for household appliances. Another drawer devoted to old issues of *National Geographic*. The magazines were dog-eared, and I could see Fred down here, escaping from Mabel, reading about the vanishing rain forests of Borneo.

A canceled RGC check had been carefully placed under a paperweight. Fred had probably made a copy to take with him and had left the original here.

There are parts of the country where people trust banks to keep their checks and to simply forward computer-generated statements each month. The Burg isn't one of those places. Residents of the Burg aren't that trusting of computers or banks. Residents of the Burg like paper. My relatives hoard canceled checks like Scrooge McDuck hoards quarters.

I didn't see any more photos of dead bodies. And I couldn't find any notes or sales receipts that might be connected to the pictures.

"You don't suppose Fred killed this person, do you?" Mabel asked.

I didn't know what I supposed. What I knew was that I was very creeped out. "Fred didn't seem like the sort of person to do something like this," I told Mabel. "Would you like me to pass these on to the police for you?"

"If you think that's the right thing to do."

Without a shadow of a doubt.

I had phone calls to make, and my parents' house was closer than my apartment and less expensive than using my cell phone, so I rumbled back to Roosevelt Street.

"How'd it go?" Grandma asked, rushing into the foyer to meet me.

"It went okay."

"You gonna take the case?"

"It's not a case. It's a missing person. Sort of."

"You're gonna have a devil of a time finding him if it was aliens," Grandma said.

I dialed the central dispatch number for the Trenton Police Department and asked for Eddie Gazarra. Gazarra and I grew up together, and now he was married to my cousin Shirley the Whiner. He was a good friend, a good cop, and a good source for police information.

"You need something," Gazarra said.

"Hello to you, too."

"Am I wrong?"

"No. I need some details on a recent investigation."

"I can't give you that kind of stuff."

"Of course you can," I said. "Anyway, this is about Uncle Fred."

"The missing Uncle Fred?"

"That's the one."

"What do you want to know?"

"Anything."

"Hold on."

He was back on the line a couple minutes later, and I could hear him leafing through papers. "It says here Fred was reported missing on Friday, which is technically too early for a missing person, but we always keep our eyes open anyway. Especially with old folks. Sometimes they're out there wandering around looking for the road to Oz."

"You think that's what Fred's doing? Looking for Oz?"

"Hard to say. Fred's car was found in the Grand Union parking lot. The car was locked up. No sign of forced entry. No sign of struggle. No sign of theft. There was dry cleaning laid out on the backseat."

"Anything else in the car? Groceries?"

"Nope. No groceries."

"So he got to the dry cleaner but not the supermarket."

"I have a chronology of events here," Gazarra said. "Fred left his house at one o'clock, right after he ate lunch. Next stop that we know of was the bank, First Trenton Trust. Their records show he withdrew two hundred dollars from the automatic teller in the lobby at two thirty-five. The cleaner, next to Grand Union in the same strip mall, said Fred picked his cleaning up around two forty-five. And that's all we have."

"There's an hour missing. It takes ten minutes to get from the Burg to Grand Union and First Trenton."

"Don't know," Gazarra said. "He was supposed to go to RGC Waste Haulers, but RGC says he never showed up."

"Thanks, Eddie."

"If you want to return the favor, I could use a baby-sitter Saturday night."

Gazarra could always use a baby-sitter. His kids were cute but death on baby-sitters.

"Gee, Eddie, I'd love to help you out, but Saturday's a bad day. I promised somebody I'd do something on Saturday."

"Yeah, right."

"Listen, Gazarra, last time I baby-sat for your kids they cut two inches off my hair."

"You shouldn't have fallen asleep. What were you doing sleeping on the job, anyway?"

"It was one in the morning!"

My next call was to Joe Morelli. Joe Morelli is a plainclothes cop who has skills not covered in the policeman's handbook. A couple months ago, I let him into my life and my bed. A couple weeks ago, I kicked him out. We'd seen each other several times since then on chance encounters and arranged dinner dates. The chance encounters were always warm. The dinner dates took the temperature up a notch and more often than not involved loud talking, which I called a discussion and Morelli called a fight.

None of these meetings had ended in the bedroom. When you grow up in the Burg there are several mantras little girls learn at an early age. One of them is that men don't buy goods they can get for free. Those words of wisdom hadn't stopped me from giving my goods away to Morelli, but they *did* stop me from *continuing* to give them away. That plus a false pregnancy scare. Although I have to admit, I had mixed feelings about not being pregnant. There was a smidgen of regret mixed with the relief. And probably it was the regret more than the relief that made me take a more serious look at my life and my relationship with Morelli. That and the realization that Morelli and I don't see eye-to-eye on a lot of things. Not that we'd entirely given up on the relationship. It was more that we were in a holding pattern with each of us staking out territory . . . not unlike the Arab-Israeli conflict.

I tried Morelli's home phone, office number, and car phone. No luck. I left messages everywhere and left my cell phone number on his pager.

"Well, what did you find out?" Grandma wanted to know when I hung up.

"Not much. Fred left the house at one, and a little over an hour later he was at the bank and the cleaner. He must have done something in that time, but I don't know what."

My mother and my grandmother looked at each other.

"What?" I asked. "What?"

"He was probably taking care of some personal business," my mother said. "You don't want to bother yourself with it."

"What's the big secret?"

Another exchange of looks between my mother and grandmother.

"There's two kinds of secrets," Grandma said. "One kind is where nobody knows the secret. And the other kind is where everybody knows the secret, but *pretends* not to know the secret. This is the second kind of secret."

"So?"

"It's about his honeys," Grandma said.

"His honeys?"

"Fred always has a honey on the side," Grandma said. "Should have been a politician."

"You mean Fred has affairs? He's in his seventies!"

"Midlife crisis," Grandma said.

"Seventy isn't midlife," I said. "Forty is midlife."

Grandma slid her uppers around some. "Guess it depends how long you intend to live."

I turned to my mother. "You knew about this?"

My mother took a couple deli bags of cold cuts out of the refrigerator and emptied them on a plate. "The man's been a philanderer all his life. I don't know how Mabel's put up with it."

"Booze," Grandma said.

I made myself a liverwurst sandwich and took it to the table. "Do you think Uncle Fred might have run off with one of his girlfriends?"

"More likely one of their husbands picked Fred up and drove him to the landfill," Grandma said. "I can't see cheapskate Fred paying for the cleaning if he was going to run off with one of his floozies."

"You have any idea who he was seeing?"

"Hard to keep track," Grandma said. She looked over at my mother. "What do you think, Ellen? You think he's still seeing Loretta Walenowski?"

"I heard that was over," my mother said.

My cell phone rang in my shoulder bag.

"Hey, Cupcake," Morelli said. "What's the disaster?"

"How do you know it's a disaster?"

"You left messages on three different phones plus my pager. It's either a disaster or you want me bad, and my luck hasn't been that good today."

"I need to talk to you."

"Now?"

"It'll only take a minute."

THE SKILLET IS a sandwich shop next to the hospital and could be better named the Grease Pit. Morelli got there ahead of me. He was standing, soda in hand, looking like the day was already too long.

He smiled when he saw me . . . and it was the nice smile that included his eyes. He draped an arm around my neck, pulled me to him, and kissed me. "Just so my day isn't a complete waste," he said.

"We have a family problem."

"Uncle Fred?"

"Boy, you know everything. You should be a cop."

"Wiseass," Morelli said. "What do you need?"

I handed him the packet of pictures. "Mabel found these in Fred's desk this morning."

He shuffled through them. "Christ. What is this shit?"

"Looks like body parts."

He tapped me on the head with the stack of pictures. "Comedian."

"You have any ideas here?"

"They need to go to Arnie Mott," Morelli said. "He's in charge of the investigation."

"Arnie Mott has the initiative of a squash."

"Yeah. But he's still in charge. I can pass them on for you."

"What does this mean?"

Joe shook his head, still studying the top photo. "I don't know, but this looks real."

I MADE AN illegal U-turn on Hamilton and parked just short of Vinnie's office, docking the Buick behind a black Mercedes S600V, which I suspected belonged to Ranger. Ranger changed cars like other men changed socks. The only common denominator with Ranger's cars was that they were always expensive and they were always black.

Connie looked over at me when I swung through the front door. "Was Briggs really only three feet tall?"

"Three feet tall and uncooperative. I should have read the physical description on his application for appearance bond before I knocked on his door. Don't suppose anything else came in?"

"Sorry," Connie said. "Nothing."

"This is turning into a real bummer of a day. My uncle Fred is missing. He went out to run errands on Friday, and that was the last anyone's seen him. They found his car in the Grand Union parking lot." No need to mention the butchered body.

"I had an uncle do that once," Lula said. "He walked all the way to Perth Amboy before someone found him. It was one of them senior moments."

The door to the inner office was closed, and Ranger was nowhere to be seen, so I guessed he was talking to Vinnie. I cut my eyes in that direction. "Ranger in there?"

"Yeah," Connie said. "He did some work for Vinnie."

"Work?"

"Don't ask," Connie said.

"Not bounty hunter stuff."

"Not nearly."

I left the office and waited outside. Ranger appeared five minutes later. Ranger's Cuban-American. His features are Anglo, his eyes are Latino, his skin is the color of a mocha latte, and his body is as good as a body can get. He had his black hair pulled back into a ponytail. He was wearing a black T-shirt that fit him like a tattoo and black SWAT pants tucked into black high-top boots.

"Yo," I said.

Ranger looked at me over the top of his shades. "Yo yourself."

I gazed longingly at his car. "Nice Mercedes."

"Transportation," Ranger said. "Nothing fancy."

Compared to what? The Batmobile? "Connie said you were talking to Vinnie."

"Transacting business, babe. I don't *talk* to Vinnie."

"That's sort of what I'd like to discuss with you . . . business. You know how you've kind of been my mentor with this bounty hunter stuff?"

"Eliza Doolittle and Henry Higgins Do Trenton."

"Yeah. Well, the truth is, the bounty huntering isn't going all that good."

"No one's jumping bail."

"That too."

Ranger leaned against his car and crossed his arms over his chest. "And?"

"And I've been thinking maybe I should diversify."

"And?"

"And I thought you might help me."

"You talking about building a portfolio? Investing money?"

"No. I'm talking about *making* money."

Ranger tipped his head back and laughed softly. "Babe, you don't want to do that kind of diversifying."

I narrowed my eyes.

"Okay," he said. "What did you have in mind?"

"Something legal."

"There's all kinds of legal."

"I want something entirely legal."

Ranger leaned closer and lowered his voice. "Let me explain my work ethic to you. I don't do things I feel are morally wrong. But sometimes my moral code strays from the norm. Sometimes my moral code is inconsistent with the law. Much of what I do is in that gray area just beyond entirely legal."

"All right then, how about steering me toward something mostly legal and definitely morally right."

"You sure about this?"

"Yes." No. Not at all.

Ranger's face was expressionless. "I'll think about it."

He slipped into his car, the engine caught, and Ranger rolled away.

I had a missing uncle who quite possibly had butchered a woman and stuffed her parts into a garbage bag, but I also was a month overdue on my rent. Somehow I was going to have to manage both problems.

TWO

I WENT BACK to Cloverleaf Apartments and parked in the lot. I got a black nylon web utility belt from the back of the Buick and strapped it on, arming it with a stun gun, pepper spray, and cuffs. Then I went in search of the building superintendent. Ten minutes later I had a key to Briggs' apartment and was at his door. I rapped twice and yelled, "Bail enforcement." No answer. I opened the door with the key and walked in. Briggs wasn't there.

Patience is a virtue bounty hunters need and I lack. I found a chair facing the door and sat down to wait. I told myself I'd stay for as long as it took, but I knew it was a lie. To begin with, being in his apartment like this was a little illegal. And then there was the fact that I was actually pretty scared. Okay, so he was only three feet tall . . . that didn't mean he couldn't shoot a gun. And it didn't mean he didn't have friends who were six-foot-four and nuts.

I'd been sitting for a little over an hour when there was a knock at the door, and I realized a piece of paper had been slipped under the doorjamb.

"Dear Loser, I know you're there," the message on the paper said, "and I'm not coming home until you leave."

Great.

MY APARTMENT BUILDING bears a striking resemblance to Cloverleaf. Same blocky brick structure, same minimalist attention to quality. Most of the tenants in my building are senior citizens with a few Hispanics thrown in to make things interesting. I'd come directly home after vacating Briggs' apartment. I'd gotten my mail when I'd passed through the lobby, and I didn't have to open the envelopes to know the contents. Bills, bills, bills. I unlocked my door, tossed the mail on the kitchen counter, and checked my answering machine for messages. None. My hamster, Rex, was asleep in his soup can in his cage.

"Hey, Rex," I said. "I'm home."

There was a slight rustling of pine shavings but that was it. Rex wasn't much for small talk. I went to the refrigerator to get him a grape and found a sticky note tacked to the door. "I'm bringing dinner. See you at six." The note wasn't signed, but I knew it was from Morelli by the way my nipples got hard.

I threw the note into the trash and dropped the grape into Rex's cage. There was a major upheaval of shavings. Rex appeared butt-first, stuffed the grape into his cheek pouch, blinked his shiny black eyes, twitched his whiskers at me, and scooted back into the can.

I took a shower, did the gel-and-blow-dry thing with my hair, dressed in jeans and a denim shirt, and flopped onto the bed face-down to think. My usual thinking position is on my back, but I didn't want to wreck my hair for Morelli.

The first thing I thought about was Randy Briggs and how it would feel good to drag him by his little feet down the stairs of his apartment building, with his stupid melon head going bump, bump, bump on the steps.

Then I thought about Uncle Fred, and I got a sharp pain in my left eyeball. "Why me?" I said, but there was no one around to answer.

Truth is, Fred wasn't exactly Indiana Jones, and I couldn't

imagine anything other than an Alzheimer's attack happening to Fred, in spite of the gory photographs. I searched my mind for memories of him, but found very little. When he smiled it was big and phony, and his false teeth made a clicking sound. And he walked with his toes pointed out . . . like a duck. That was it. Those were my memories of Uncle Fred.

I dozed off while walking down memory lane, and suddenly I awoke with a start, all senses alert. I heard the front door to my apartment click open, and my heart started knocking around in my chest. I'd locked the door when I'd gotten home. And now someone had opened it. And that someone was in my apartment. I held my breath. Please, God, let it be Morelli. I didn't much like the idea of Morelli sneaking into my apartment, but it was a lot more palatable than coming face-to-face with some ugly, droolly guy who wanted to squeeze my neck until my tongue turned purple.

I scrambled to my feet and searched for a weapon, settling for a stiletto-heeled pink-satin pump left over from a stint as bridesmaid for Charlotte Nagy. I crept out of my bedroom, through the living room, and peeked into the kitchen.

It was Ranger. And he was dumping the contents of a large plastic container into a bowl.

"Jesus," I said, "you scared the hell out of me. Why don't you try knocking next time."

"I left you a note. I thought you'd be expecting me."

"You didn't sign the note. How was I supposed to know it was you?"

He turned and looked at me. "Were there any other possibilities?"

"Morelli."

"You back with him?"

Good question. I glanced at the food. Salad. "Morelli would have brought sausage sandwiches."

"That stuff'll kill you, Babe."

We were bounty hunters. People shot at us. And Ranger was

worried about trans fats and nitrates. "I'm not sure our life expectancy is all that good anyway," I said.

My kitchen is small, and Ranger seemed to be taking up a lot of space, standing very close. He reached around me and snagged two salad bowls from the over-the-counter cabinet. "It's not length of life that's important," he said. "It's the quality. The goal is to have purity of mind and body."

"Do you have a pure mind and body?"

Ranger locked eyes with me. "Not right now."

Hmm.

He filled a bowl with salad and handed it to me. "You need money."

"Yes."

"There are lots of ways to make money."

I stared down into my salad, pushing greens around with my fork. "True."

Ranger waited for me to look up at him before he spoke. "You sure you want to do this?"

"No, I'm not sure. I don't even know what we're talking about. I don't actually know what it is that you *do*. I'm just searching for a second profession that'll supplement my income."

"Any restrictions or preferences?"

"No drugs or illegal gun sales."

"Do you think I'd deal drugs?"

"No. That was thoughtless."

He helped himself to salad. "What I have going now is a renovation job."

This sounded appealing. "You mean like interior decorating?"

"Yeah. Guess you could call it interior decorating."

I tried the salad. It was pretty good, but it needed something. Croutons fried in butter. Big chunks of fattening cheese. And beer. I looked in vain for another bag. I checked the refrigerator. No beer there either.

"This is the way it works," Ranger said. "I send a team in to renovate, and then I place one or two people in the building to take care of long-term maintenance." Ranger looked up from his food. "You're keeping in shape, right? You run?"

"Sure. I run all the time." I run *never*. My idea of exercise is to barrel through a shopping mall.

Ranger gave me a dark look. "You're lying."

"Well, I *think* about running."

He finished his food and put the bowl in the dishwasher. "I'll pick you up tomorrow at five A.M."

"Five A.M.! To start an interior decorating job?"

"It's the way I like to do it."

A warning message flashed through my brain. "Maybe I should know more—"

"It's routine. Nothing special." He checked his watch. "I have to go. Business meeting."

I didn't want to speculate on the nature of his business meeting.

I BUZZED THE television on, but couldn't find anything to watch. No hockey. No fun movies. I went to my shoulder bag and pulled out the large envelope from the copier. I'm not sure why, but I'd made color copies of the pictures before meeting Morelli. I'd been able to fit six photos to a page and had filled four pages. I spread the pages on my dining-room table.

Not nice stuff to look at.

When the photos were laid out side-by-side, certain things became evident. I was pretty sure there was only one body and that it wasn't the body of an old person. No gray hair. And the skin was firm. Difficult to tell if it was a woman or a young man. Some of the pictures had been taken quite close. Some were from further away. It didn't look like the parts were ever rearranged. But the bag was sometimes pulled down to reveal more.

Okay, Stephanie, put yourself in the photographer's shoes. Why are you taking these pictures? Trophy shots? I didn't think so, because none showed the face. And there were twenty-four pictures here, so the roll was intact. If I wanted a remembrance of this grisly act, I'd want a face shot. Ditto for proof that the job had been done. Proof of a kill required a face shot. What was left? A visual record by someone who didn't want to disturb the evidence. So maybe Uncle Fred happened on a bag of body parts and ran out and got himself a point-and-shoot. And then what? Then he put the pictures in his desk drawer and disappeared while running errands.

That was my best guess, as weak as it was. The truth is, the pictures could have been taken five years ago. Someone could have given them to Fred for safekeeping or as a macabre joke.

I stuffed the prints back into their envelope and grabbed my shoulder bag. I thought searching the neighborhood around Grand Union would be wasted effort, but I felt the need to do it anyway.

I drove to a residential area behind the strip mall and parked on the street. I grabbed my flashlight and set out on foot, walking streets and back alleys, looking behind bushes and trash cans, calling Fred's name. When I was a kid I had a cat named Katherine. She showed up on our doorstep one day and refused to leave. We started feeding her on the back porch, and then somehow she found her way into the kitchen. She went out at night to roam the neighborhood, and slept curled up in a ball on my bed during the day. One night Katherine went out and never came back. For days I walked the streets and alleys, looking behind bushes and trash cans, calling her name, just like I was doing now for Fred. My mother said cats sometimes wander off like that when it's their time to die. I thought it was a lot of hooey.

I STUMBLED OUT of bed at four-thirty, staggered into the bathroom and stood in the shower until my eyes opened. After a while my skin started to shrivel, and I figured I was done. I toweled off and shook my head by way of styling my hair. I didn't know what I was supposed to wear for interior decorating, so I wore what I always wore . . . jeans and a T-shirt. And then to dress it up, just in case this actually turned out to be interior decorating, I added a belt and a jacket.

Ranger was waiting in the parking lot when I swung out the back door. He was driving a shiny black Range Rover with tinted side windows. Ranger's cars were always new and their point of purchase was never easy to explain. Three men took up the back-seat. Two were black, one was of indeterminate origin. All three men had Marine buzz cuts. All were wearing black SWAT pants and black T-shirts. All were heavily muscled. Not an ounce of fat among them. None of them looked like interior decorators.

I buckled myself into the seat next to Ranger. "Is that the inte-rior decorating team in the backseat?"

Ranger smiled in the predawn darkness and cruised out of the lot.

"I'm dressed different from everybody else," I said.

Ranger stopped at the light on Hamilton. "I've got a jacket and a vest for you in the back."

"This isn't interior decorating, is it?"

"There's all kinds of interior decorating, Babe."

"About the vest—"

"Kevlar."

Kevlar was bulletproof. "Rats," I said. "I hate getting shot at. You know how I hate getting shot at."

"Just a precaution," Ranger said. "Probably no one will get shot." Probably?

We rode in silence through center city. Ranger was in his zone. Thinking private thoughts. The guys in back looking like they had no thoughts at all—ever. And me, debating jumping out of the car at the next light and running like hell back to my apartment. And at the same time, as ridiculous as it sounds, I was keeping an eye peeled for Fred. He was stuck in my brain. It was like that with my cat, Katherine, too. She'd been gone fifteen years, but I always looked twice when I caught a glimpse of a black cat. Unfinished business, I guess.

"Where are we going?" I finally asked.

"Apartment building on Sloane. Gonna do some house clean-ing."

Sloane Street runs parallel and two blocks over from Stark. Stark is the worst street in the city, filled with drugs and despair and feed-lot housing. The ghetto gentrifies as the blocks march south, and much of Sloane is the demarcation line between the lawless and the law-abiding. It's a constant struggle to hold the line and keep the pushers and hookers off Sloane. And word is that lately Sloane's been losing the battle.

Ranger drove three blocks up Sloane and parked. He nodded at the yellow-brick building across the street, two doors down. "That's our building. We're going to the third floor."

The building was four stories tall, and I guessed there were two or three small apartments on each floor. Ground-level brick was covered with gang graffiti. Windows were dark. No street traffic. Wind-blown trash banked against curbs and collected in doorways.

I glanced from the building to Ranger. "You sure this is legal?"

"Been hired by the landlord," Ranger said.

"Does this housecleaning involve people or is it just . . . things?"

Ranger looked at me.

"There's a legal process involved in getting people and their possessions out of an apartment," I said. "You need to present an eviction notice and—"

"The legal process is moving a little slow," Ranger said. "And in the meantime, the kids in this building are being harassed by the people who come to shoot up in 3C."

"Think of this as community service," one of the guys in the back said.

The other two nodded. "Yeah," they said. "Community service."

I cracked my knuckles and chewed on my lower lip.

Ranger angled from behind the wheel, walked to the rear of the Range Rover, and opened the door. He gave everyone a flak vest, and then he gave everyone a black windbreaker that had SE-CURITY printed in large white letters on the back.

I strapped my vest on and watched while everyone else buckled on black nylon web utility belts and holstered guns.

"Let me take a wild guess here," Ranger said, slinging an arm around my shoulder. "You forgot to bring your gun."

"Interior decorators don't use guns."

"They do in this neighborhood."

The men were lined up in front of me.

"Gentlemen," Ranger said, "this is Ms. Plum."

The indeterminate-origin guy put his hand out. "Lester Santos."

The next man in line did the same. "Bobby Brown."

The last man was Tank. It was easy to see how he'd come by the name.

"I better not get into trouble for this," I said to Ranger. "I'm going to be really bummed if I get arrested. I hate getting arrested."

Santos grinned. "Man, you don't like to get shot. You don't like to get arrested. You don't know how to have fun at all."

Ranger shrugged into his jacket and set off, crossing the street with the band of merry men closing ranks behind him.

We entered the building and climbed two flights of stairs. Ranger went to 3C and listened at the door. The rest of us flattened against the wall. No one spoke. Ranger and Santos stood, guns in hand. Brown and Tank held flashlights.

I braced myself, expecting Ranger to kick the door down, but instead, he took a key from his pocket and inserted it in the lock. The door started to open but caught on a security chain. Ranger took two steps back and threw himself at the door, catching the door at chain height with his shoulder. The door popped open, and Ranger was in first. Then everyone was in except me. Lights flashed on. Ranger shouted, "Security!" and everything was chaos. Half-naked people were scrambling off floor mattresses. Women were shrieking. Men were swearing.

Ranger's team went room by room, cuffing people, lining them up against the living room wall. Six people in all.

One of the men was berserk, waving his arms to avoid getting cuffed. "You can't do this, you fuckers," he was yelling. "This is my apartment. This is private property. Somebody call the fucking police." He pulled a knife from his pants pocket and flicked it open.

Tank grabbed the guy by the back of his shirt, lifted him off his feet, and threw him out the window.

Everyone went still, staring dumbstruck at the shattered glass. My mouth was open and my heart had gone dead in my chest.

Ranger didn't look all that disturbed. "Have to replace that window," he said.

I heard a groan and some scraping sounds. I crossed the room to the window and looked out. The guy with the knife was spread-eagle on the fire escape, making feeble attempts to right himself.

I clapped a hand to my heart, relieved to find it had started beating again. "He's on the fire escape! God, for a minute there I thought you dumped him three stories."

Tank looked out the window with me. "You're right. He's on the fire escape. Sonovagun."

It was a small apartment. One small bedroom, one small bath, small kitchen, small living room. Kitchen counters were littered with fast-food wrappers and bags, empty soda cans, food-encrusted plates, and cheap, dented pots. The Formica was scarred with burn marks from cigarettes and crack cookers. Used syringes, half-eaten bagels, filthy dish towels, and unidentifiable garbage clogged the sink. Two stained and torn mattresses had been pushed against the wall in the living room. No lamps, no tables, no chairs, no sign that civilized man occupied the apartment. Just filth and clutter. The same refuse that banked against gutters outside filled the rooms of 3C. The air was stale with the odors of urine and pot and unwashed bodies and something nastier.

Santos and Brown herded the bedraggled occupants into the hall and down the stairs.

"What happens to them now?" I asked Ranger.

"Bobby'll drive them over to the meth clinic and drop them off. They're on their own from there."

"No arrests?"

"We don't do arrests. Not unless someone's FTA."

Tank returned from the car with a cardboard box filled with interior decorating supplies, which in this case consisted of disposable gloves, trash bags, and a coffee can for syringes.

"This is the deal," Ranger said to me. "We strip the apartment of everything not nailed down. Tomorrow the landlord will bring someone in to clean and do repairs."

"What's to stop the tenant from returning?"

Ranger just stared at me.

"Right," I said. "Stupid question."

IT WAS MIDMORNING when we went through with the broom. Santos and Brown had positioned themselves on folding chairs in the small vestibule downstairs. They were to take the first security shift. Tank was on his way to the landfill with the mattresses and bags of garbage. Ranger and I were left to lock up the apartment.

Ranger angled the brim of a Navy SEALs ball cap to shade his eyes. "So," he said, "what do you think of security work? You want to be on the team? I can let you take the graveyard shift with Tank."

"He isn't going to throw any more people out windows, is he?"

"Hard to say, Babe."

"I don't know if I'm cut out for this."

Ranger took his SEALs hat off and put it on me, tucking my hair behind my ears, letting his hands linger a moment too long. "You have to believe in what you're doing."

That could be a problem. And Ranger could be a problem. I was feeling much too attracted to him. Ranger wasn't listed under *potential boyfriends* in my Rolodex. Ranger was listed under *crazed mercenaries*. An attraction to Ranger would be like chasing after the doomsday orgasm.

I took a steadying breath. "I guess I could try a shift," I said. "See how it goes."

———

I WAS STILL wearing the hat when Ranger dropped me off at my apartment. I removed the cap and held it out to him. "Don't forget your SEALs hat."

Ranger looked at me from behind dark glasses. His eyes hidden. His thoughts unreadable. His voice soft. "Keep it. Looks good on you."

"It's a righteous hat."

He smiled. "Live up to it, Babe."

I pushed through the double glass doors into the lobby. I was about to take the stairs when the elevator opened and Mrs. Bestler leaned out. "Going up," she said. "Step to the rear of the car."

Mrs. Bestler was eighty-three and had an apartment on the third floor. When things got boring she played elevator operator.

"Morning, Mrs. Bestler," I said. "Second floor."

She hit the two button and eyeballed me. "Looks like you've been working. Catch any bad guys today?"

"Helped a friend clean an apartment."

Mrs. Bestler smiled. "What a good girl." The elevator stopped and the doors opened. "Second floor," Mrs. Bestler sang out. "Better dresses. Designer suits. Ladies' lounge."

I let myself into my apartment and went straight to the phone machine and its blinking red light.

I had two messages. The first was from Morelli, and it was for dinner. Miss Popularity, that's me.

"Meet you at Pino's at six," Morelli said.

Morelli's invitations always produced mixed emotions. The initial reaction was a sexual rush at the sound of his voice, the rush was followed by a queasy stomach while I considered his motives, and the queasy stomach eventually gave way to curiosity and anticipation. Ever the optimist.

The second message was from Mabel. "A man just came asking

about Fred," Mabel said. "Something about a business deal, and he needed to find Fred right away. I explained how I couldn't help him, but I said you were on the job, so he shouldn't worry. I thought you might want to know."

I called Mabel back and asked who the man was and what he looked like.

"He was about my height," she said. "And he had brown hair."

"Caucasian?"

"Yes. And now that you mention it, he didn't give me his name."

"What kind of business deal was he talking about?"

"I don't know. He didn't say."

"Okay," I said. "Let me know if he bothers you again."

I checked in with the office to see if there were any new FTAs and was told no luck. I called my best friend, Mary Lou, but she couldn't talk because her youngest kid was sick with a cold, and the dog had eaten a sock and had just pooped it out on the living room rug.

I was contemplating Rex's soup can with new appreciation when the phone rang.

"I got it," Grandma said. "I got a name for you. I was at the beauty parlor this morning getting a set, and Harriet Schnable was there for a perm, and she said she heard at bingo that Fred's been paying calls on Winnie Black. Harriet isn't one of those to make something of nothing."

"Do you know Winnie Black?"

"Only through the seniors' club. She goes on the bus trip to Atlantic City sometimes. Her and her husband, Axel. I guess that's how Fred meets most of his honeys these days . . . at the seniors' meetings. A lot of those women are real hot to trot, if you know what I mean. I even got Winnie's address," Grandma said. "I called Ida Lukach. She's the club's membership chairman. She knows everything."

I took down the address and thanked Grandma.

"Personally, I'm hoping it was aliens," Grandma said. "But then I don't know what they'd want with an old fart like Fred."

I settled my new hat on my brown bear cookie jar and traded my jeans for a beige suit and heels. I didn't know Winnie Black, and I thought it wouldn't hurt to look professional. Sometimes people responded better to a suit than to jeans. I grabbed my shoulder bag, locked the apartment, and joined Mrs. Bestler in the elevator.

"Did he find you?" Mrs. Bestler wanted to know.

"Did who find me?"

"There was a man looking for you. Very polite. I let him off on your floor about ten minutes ago."

"He never knocked on my door. I would have heard him. I was in the kitchen almost the whole time."

"Isn't that odd." The elevator door opened to the lobby, and Mrs. Bestler smiled. "First floor. Ladies' handbags. Fine jewelry."

"What did the man look like?" I asked Mrs. Bestler.

"Oh, dear, he was big. Very big. And dark-skinned. African-American."

Not the man Mabel just called about. That guy was short and Caucasian.

"Did he have long hair? Maybe pulled back into a ponytail?"

"No. He almost didn't have any hair at all."

I did a fast check of the lobby. No big guy lurking in the corners. I exited the building and looked around the lot. Nobody there either. My visitor had disappeared. Too bad, I thought. I'd love an excuse not to visit Winnie Black. I'd talk to a census taker, a vacuum-cleaner salesman, a religious zealot. All preferable to Winnie Black. It was bad enough knowing cheapskate Uncle Fred had a girlfriend. I really didn't want to *see* her. I didn't want to confront Winnie Black and have to imagine her in the sack with duck-footed Fred.

WINNIE LIVED IN a little bungalow on Low Street. White clapboard with blue shutters and a red door. Very patriotic. I parked, marched up to her front door, and rang the bell. I hadn't any idea what I was going to say to this woman. Probably something like, Excuse me, are you going around the block with my uncle Fred?

I was about to ring a second time when the door opened and Winnie Black peered out at me.

She had a pleasant, round face and a pleasant, round body, and she didn't look like the sort to boff someone's uncle.

I introduced myself and gave her my card. "I'm looking for Fred Shutz," I said. "He's been missing since Friday, and I was hoping you might be able to give me some information."

The pleasant expression froze on her face. "I'd heard he was missing, but I don't know what I can tell you."

"When did you see him last?"

"The day he disappeared. He stopped by for some coffee and cake. He did that sometimes. It was right after lunch. And he stayed for about an hour. Axel, my husband, was out getting the tires rotated on the Chrysler."

Axel was getting his tires rotated. Unh! Mental head slap. "Did Fred seem sick or worried? Did he give any indication that he might be going off somewhere?"

"He was . . . distracted. He said he had something big going on."

"Did he say any more about it?"

"No. But I got the feeling it had to do with the garbage company. He was having a problem with his account. Something about the computer deleting his name from the customer list. And Fred said he had the goods on them, and he was going to make out in spades. Those were his exact words—'make out in spades.' I guess he never got to the garbage company."

"How do you know he never got to the garbage company?" I asked Winnie.

Winnie seemed surprised at the question. "Everyone knows."

No secrets in the Burg.

"One other thing," I said. "I found some photographs on Fred's desk. Did Fred ever mention any photographs to you?"

"No. Not that I can think of. Were these family photographs?"

"They were pictures of a garbage bag. And in some of the pictures you could see the bag's contents."

"No. I would have remembered something like that."

I looked over her shoulder into the interior of her neat little house. No husband in sight. "Is Axel around?"

"He's at the park with the dog."

I got back in the Buick and drove two blocks to the park. It was a patch of well-tended grass, two blocks long and a block wide. There were benches and flower beds and large trees, and there was a small kids' play area at one end.

It wasn't hard to spot Axel Black. He was sitting on a bench, lost in thought, with his dog at his side. The dog was a small mutt type, sitting there, eyes glazed, looking a lot like Axel. The difference was that Axel had glasses and the dog had hair.

I parked the car and approached the two. Neither moved, even when I was standing directly in front of them.

"Axel Black?" I asked.

He looked up at me. "Yes?"

I introduced myself and gave him my card. "I'm looking for Fred Shutz," I said. "And I've been talking to some of the seniors who might have known Fred."

"Bet they've been giving you an earful," Axel said. "Old Fred was a real character. Cheapest man who ever walked the earth. Argued over every nickel. Never contributed to anything. And he thought he was a Romeo, too. Always cozying up to some woman."

"Doesn't sound like you thought much of him."

"Had no use for the man," Axel said. "Don't wish him any harm, but don't like him much either. The truth is, he was shifty."

"You have any idea what happened to him?"

"Think he might have paid too much attention to the wrong woman."

I couldn't help thinking maybe he was talking about Winnie as being the wrong woman. And maybe he ran Fred over with his Chrysler, picked him up, shoved him in the trunk, and dumped him into the river.

That didn't explain the photographs, but maybe the photographs had nothing to do with Fred's disappearance.

"Well," I said, "if you think of anything, let me know."

"You bet," Axel said.

Fred's sons, Ronald and Walter, were next on my list. Ronald was the line foreman at the pork roll factory. Walter and his wife, Jean, owned a convenience store on Howard Street. I thought it wouldn't hurt to talk to Walter and Ronald. Mostly because when my mother asked me what I was doing to find Uncle Fred I needed to have something to say.

Walter and Jean had named their store the One-Stop. It was across the street from a twenty-four-hour supermarket and would have been driven out of business long ago were it not for the fact that in one stop customers could purchase a loaf of bread, play the numbers, and put down twenty dollars on some nag racing at Freehold.

Walter was behind the register reading the paper when I walked into the store. It was early afternoon, and the store was empty. Walter put the paper down and got to his feet. "Did you find him?"

"No. Sorry."

He took a deep breath. "Jesus. I thought you were coming to tell me he was dead."

"Do you think he's dead?"

"I don't know what I think. In the beginning I figured he just wandered off. Had another stroke or something. But now I can't figure it. None of it makes sense."

"Do you know anything about Fred having problems with his garbage company?"

"Dad had problems with everyone," Walter said.

I said good-bye to Walter, fired up the Buick, and drove across town to the pork roll factory. I parked in a visitor slot, went inside, and asked the woman at the front desk to pass a note through to Ronald.

Ronald came out a few minutes later. "I guess this is about Dad," he said. "Nice of you to help us look for him. I can't believe he hasn't turned up by now."

"Do you have any theories?"

"None I'd want to say out loud."

"The women in his life?"

Ronald shook his head. "He was a pip. Cheap as they come and could never keep his pecker in his pants. I don't know if he can still fire up the old engine, but he's still running around. Christ, he's seventy-two years old."

"Do you know anything about a disagreement with the garbage company?"

"No, but he's had a year-long feud with his insurance company."

THREE

I LEFT THE pork roll factory's parking lot and headed across town. It was almost five and government workers were clogging the roads. That was one of the many good things about Trenton. If you needed to practice Italian hand signals, there was no shortage of deserving bureaucrats.

I made a fast stop back at my apartment for some last-minute beautifying. I added an extra layer of mascara, fluffed my hair, and headed out.

Morelli was at the bar when I got to Pino's. He had his back to me, and he was lost in thought, elbows on the bar, head bent over his beer. He wore jeans and running shoes and a green plaid flannel shirt unbuttoned over a Gold's Gym T-shirt. A woman at the opposite end of the bar was watching him in the behind-the-bar mirror. Women did that now. They watched and wondered. When he was younger and his features were softer, women did more than watch. When he was younger, mothers statewide warned their daughters about Joe Morelli. And when he was younger, daughters statewide didn't give a darn what their mothers told them. Morelli's features were more angular these days. His eyes were less inviting to strangers. Women included. So women watched and wondered what it would be like to be with Morelli.

I knew, of course, what it was like to be with Morelli. Morelli was magic.

I took the stool next to him and waved a "beer, please" signal to the bartender.

Morelli gave me an appraising look, his eyes dilated black in the dim bar light. "Business suit and heels," he said. "That means you've either been to a wake, a job interview, or you tried to trick some nice old lady out of information she shouldn't be giving you."

"Door number three."

"Let me guess . . . this has to do with your uncle Fred."

"Bingo."

"Having any luck?"

"Hard to say. Did you know Fred fooled around? He had a girl-friend."

Morelli grinned. "Fred Shutz? Hell, that's encouraging."

I rolled my eyes.

He took our beer glasses off the bar and motioned to the area set aside for tables. "If I was Mabel I'd be happy Fred was going elsewhere," he said. "I don't think Fred looks like a lot of fun."

"Especially since he collects pictures of dismembered bodies."

"I gave the pictures to Arnie. He didn't look happy. I think he was hoping Fred would turn up hitching a ride down Klockner Boulevard."

"Is Arnie going to do anything on this?"

"He'll probably go back and talk to Mabel some more. Run the photos through the system to see what comes up."

"Did you already run them through?"

"Yeah. And I didn't get anything."

There was nothing fancy about Pino's. At certain times of the day the bar was filled with cops unwinding after their shift. And at other times of the day the tables set aside for diners were filled with hungry Burg families. In between those times, Pino's was home to a few regular drunks, and the kitchen was taken over by cockroaches as big as barn cats. I ate at Pino's in spite of the roach rumor because Anthony Pino made the best pizza in Trenton. Maybe in all of Jersey.

Morelli gave his order and tipped back in his chair. "How friendly are you feeling toward me?"

"What'd you have in mind?"

"A date."

"I thought *this* was a date."

"No. This is dinner, so I can ask you about the date."

I sipped at my beer. "Must be some date."

"It's a wedding."

I sat up straighter in my chair. "It isn't *my* wedding, is it?"

"Not unless there's something going on in your life that I don't know about."

I blew out a sigh of relief. "Wow. For a minute there I was worried."

Morelli looked annoyed. "You mean if I asked you to marry me, that's the reaction I'd get?"

"Well, yeah."

"I thought you wanted to get married. I thought that was why we stopped sleeping together . . . because you didn't want sex without marriage."

I leaned forward on the table and cocked a single eyebrow at him. "Do you want to get married?"

"No, I don't want to get married. We've been all through this."

"Then my reaction doesn't matter, does it?"

"Jesus," Morelli said. "I need another beer."

"So what's with the wedding?"

"My cousin Julie's getting married on Saturday, and I need a date."

"You're giving me four days' notice to go to a wedding? I can't be ready for a wedding in four days. I need a new dress and shoes. I need a beauty parlor appointment. How am I going to do all this with four days' notice?"

"Okay, fuck it, we won't go," Morelli said.

"I guess I could do without the beauty parlor, but I definitely need new shoes."

"Heels," Morelli said. "High and spiky."

I fiddled with my beer glass. "I wasn't your last choice, was I?"

"You're my only choice. If my mother hadn't called this morning I wouldn't have remembered the wedding at all. This case I'm on is getting to me."

"Want to talk about it?"

"That's the last thing I want to do."

"How about Uncle Fred, want to talk about him some more?"

"The playboy."

"Yeah. I don't understand how he could just disappear."

"People disappear all the time," Morelli said. "They get on a bus and start life over. Or they jump off a bridge and float out with the tide. Sometimes people help them disappear."

"This is a man in his seventies who was too cheap to buy a bus ticket and would have had to walk miles to find a bridge. He left his cleaning in the car. He disappeared in the middle of running errands."

We both momentarily fell silent while our pizza was placed on the table.

"He'd just come from the bank," Morelli said when we were alone. "He was an old man. An easy mark. Someone could have driven up to him and forced him into their car."

"There were no signs of struggle."

"That doesn't mean one didn't take place."

I chewed on that while I ate my pizza. I'd had the same thought, and I didn't like it.

I told Morelli about my conversation with Winnie Black.

"She know anything about the pictures?"

"No."

"One other thing," Morelli said. "I wanted to tell you about Benito Ramirez."

I looked up from the pizza. Benito Ramirez was a heavyweight professional boxer from Trenton. He liked to punish people and didn't limit the punishing to inside the ring. He liked to beat up on women. Liked to hear them beg while he inflicted his own brand of sick torture. And in fact, I knew some of that torture had ended in death, but there'd always been camp followers who'd gotten posthumous credit for the worst of Ramirez's crimes. He'd been involved in my very first case as a bounty hunter, and I'd been instrumental in putting him behind bars. His incarceration hadn't come soon enough for Lula. Ramirez had almost killed her. He'd raped her and beat her and cut her in terrible places. And then he'd left her naked, bloody body on my fire escape for me to find.

"What about Ramirez?" I asked Morelli.

"He's out."

"Out where?"

"Out of jail."

"*What?* What do you mean, he's out of jail? He almost killed Lula. And he was involved in a whole bunch of other murders." Not to mention that he'd stalked and terrorized *me*.

"He's released on parole, doing community service, and getting psychiatric counseling." Morelli paused to pull off another piece of pizza. "He had a real good lawyer."

Morelli had said this very matter of fact, but I knew he didn't feel matter of fact. He'd put on his cop face. The one that shut out emotion. The one with the hard eyes that gave nothing away.

I made a display of eating. Like I wasn't too bothered by this news either. When in fact, nausea was rolling through my stomach. "When did this happen?" I asked Morelli.

"Yesterday."

"And he's in town?"

"Just like always. Working out in the gym on Stark."

A big man, Mrs. Bestler had said. African-American. Polite. Prowling in my hall. Sweet Jesus, it might have been Ramirez.

"If you even *suspect* he's anywhere near you, I want to know," Morelli said.

I'd shoved another piece of pizza into my mouth, but I was having a hard time swallowing. "Sure."

We finished the pizza and dawdled over coffee.

"Maybe you should spend the night with me," Morelli said. "Just in case Ramirez decides to look you up."

I knew Morelli had other things in mind beyond my safety. And it was a tempting offer. But I'd already taken that bus, and it seemed like a ride that went nowhere. "Can't," I said. "I'm working tonight."

"I thought things were slow."

"This isn't for Vinnie. This is for Ranger."

Morelli did a little grimace. "I'm afraid to ask."

"It's nothing illegal. It's a security job."

"It always is," Morelli said. "Ranger does all kinds of security. Ranger keeps small Third World countries secure."

"This has nothing to do with gunrunning. This is legitimate. We're doing front-door security for an apartment building on Sloane."

"Sloane? Are you crazy? Sloane's at the edge of the war zone."

"That's why the building needs policing."

"Fine. Let Ranger get someone else. Trust me, you don't want to be out looking for a parking place on Sloane in the middle of the night."

"I won't have to look for a parking place. Tank's picking me up."

"You're working with a guy named Tank?"

"He's big."

"Jesus," Morelli said. "I had to fall in love with a woman who works with a guy named Tank."

"You love me?"

"Of course I love you. I just don't want to marry you."

I STEPPED OUT of the elevator and saw him sitting on the floor in the hall, next to my door. And I knew he was Mabel's visitor. I stuck my hand in my shoulder bag, searching for my pepper spray. Just in case. I rooted around in the bag for a minute or two, finding lipsticks and hair rollers and my stun gun, but no pepper spray.

"Either you're searching for your keys or your pepper spray," the guy said, getting to his feet. "So let me help you out, here." He reached into his pocket, pulled out a canister of pepper spray, and tossed it to me. "Be my guest," he said. And then he pushed my door open.

"How'd you do that? My door was locked."

"God-given talent," he said. "I thought it would save time if I searched your apartment before you got home."

I shook the spray to make sure it was live.

"Hey, don't get all bent out of shape," he said. "I didn't wreck anything. Although, I have to tell you, I did have fun in your panty drawer."

Instinct said he was playing with me. There was no doubt in my mind he'd gone through my apartment, but I doubted he lingered with my lingerie. Truth is, I didn't have a lot and what I had wasn't especially exotic. I felt violated all the same, and I would have sprayed him on the spot, but I didn't trust the spray in my hand. It was his, after all.

He rocked back on his heels. "Well, aren't you going to ask me in? Don't you want to know my name? Don't you want to know why I'm here?"

"Talk to me."

"Not here," he said. "I want to go in and sit down. I've had a long day."

"Forget it. Talk to me here."

"I don't think so. I want to go inside. It's more civilized. It would be like we were friends."

"We're not friends. And if you don't talk to me right now, I'm going to gas you."

He was about my height, five-foot-seven, and built like a fire-plug. It was hard to tell his age. Maybe late thirties. His brown hair was receding. His eyebrows looked like they'd been fed steroids. He was wearing ratty running shoes, black Levi's, and a dark gray sweatshirt.

He gave a big sigh and hauled a .38 out from under the sweatshirt. "Using the pepper spray wouldn't be a good idea," he said, "because then I'd have to shoot you."

My stomach dropped an inch and my heart started banging in my chest. I thought about the pictures and how someone had gotten themselves killed and mutilated. Fred had gotten involved somehow. And now I was involved, too. And there was a reasonable chance that I was being held at gunpoint by a guy who was on a first-name basis with the photographed garbage bag.

"If you shoot me in the hall, my neighbors will be all over you," I said.

"Fine. Then I'll shoot them, too."

I didn't like the idea of him shooting someone, especially me, so we both went into my apartment.

"This is much better," he said, heading for the kitchen, opening the refrigerator and getting a beer.

"Where'd that beer come from?"

"It came from me. Where do you think, the beer fairy? Lady, you need to go food shopping. It's unhealthy to live like this."

"Who *are* you?"

He shoved the gun under his waistband and stuck his hand out. "I'm Bunchy."

"What kind of a name is Bunchy?"

"When I was a kid I had this underwear problem."

Ugh. "You have a real name?"

"Yeah, but you don't need to know it. Everybody calls me Bunchy."

I was feeling better now that the gun wasn't pointed at me. Feeling good enough to be curious. "So what's this business deal with Fred?"

"Well, the truth is, Fred owes me some money."

"Uh-huh."

"And I want it."

"Good luck."

He chugged half a bottle of beer. "Now, see, that's not a good attitude."

"How did Fred come to owe you money?"

"Fred likes to play the ponies once in a while."

"Are you telling me you're Fred's bookie?"

"Yeah, that's what I'm telling you."

"I don't believe you. Fred didn't gamble."

"How do you know?"

"Besides, you don't look like a bookie," I said.

"How do bookies look?"

"Different." More respectable.

"I figure you're looking for Fred, and I'm looking for Fred, and maybe we can look for Fred together."

"Sure."

"See, that wasn't so difficult."

"Are you gonna go now?"

"Unless you want me to stay and watch television."

"No."

"I got a better television, anyway," he said.

AT 12:30 I was downstairs, waiting for Tank. I'd taken a nap, and I was feeling halfway alert. I was dressed in black jeans, black T-shirt, Ranger's SEALs hat, and the black SECURITY jacket. At Ranger's request, I had my gun clipped to my belt, and my shoulder bag held the other essentials—stun gun, pepper spray, flashlight, and cuffs.

The lot was eerie at this time of the night. The seniors' cars were fast asleep, their hoods and roofs reflecting light from the halogen floods. The macadam looked mercurial. The neighborhood of small single-family houses behind my building was dark and quiet. Occasionally there was the whir of traffic on St. James. Headlights flashed at the corner and a car turned into my lot. I had a moment of stomach-fluttering panic that this wasn't Tank, that this might be Benito Ramirez. I held my ground, thinking about the gun on my hip, telling myself I was cool, I was bad, I was a dangerous woman not to be messed with. Make my day, punk, I thought. Yeah, right. If it turned out to be Ramirez I'd wet my pants and run screaming back into the building.

The car was black and shiny. An SUV. It rolled to a stop in front of me, and the driver's side window slid down.

Tank looked out. "Ready to rock and roll?"

I took the seat beside him and buckled up. "Do you expect a lot of rockin' and rollin' tonight?"

"I expect none. Working this shift is like watching grass grow."

That was a relief. I had a lot to think about, and I didn't especially want to see Tank in action. Even more, I didn't want to see myself in action.

"I don't suppose you know a bookie named Bunchy, do you?"

"Bunchy? Nope. Never heard of him. He local?"

"Actually, I'm not sure."

The ride across town was quiet. One vehicle was parked at the curb in front of the Sloane Street apartment building. It was another new black SUV. Tank parked behind it. Beyond the building on either side and across the street, cars lined the curb.

"One of the things we like to enforce is a no-parking zone in front of the building," Tank said. "Keeps things clean. The tenants have parking behind the building. Only security vehicles are allowed here at the door."

"And if someone wants to park here?"

"We discourage it."

Master of understatement.

Two men were in the lobby. They were dressed in black, wearing the SECURITY jackets. One came forward when we approached and unlocked the door.

Tank stepped in and looked around. "Anything happening?"

"Nothing. Been quiet all night."

"When was the last time you walked?"

"Twelve."

Tank nodded.

The men gathered their belongings—a large Thermos, a book,

and a gym bag—and pushed through the lobby door. They stood for a moment on the street, taking it in, before climbing into their SUV and motoring off.

A small table and two folding chairs had been placed against the far lobby wall, enabling the security team to watch both the door and the stairs. There were two walkie-talkies on the table.

Tank locked the front door, took one of the walkie-talkies, and clipped it to his belt. "I'm going to do a walk-through. You stay here and keep your eye on things. Call me if anyone approaches the door."

I sent him a salute.

"Snappy," he said. "I like that."

I sat in the folding chair and watched the door. No one approached. I watched the stairs. Nothing going on there, either. I checked out my manicure. Not great. I looked at my watch. Two minutes had gone by—478 minutes more and I could go home.

Tank ambled down the stairs and took his seat. "Everything's cool."

"Now what?"

"Now we wait."

"For what?"

"For nothing."

Two hours later, Tank was comfortably slouched in his chair, arms crossed, eyes slitted but vigilant, watching the door. His metabolism had dropped to reptilian. No rise and fall of his chest. No shifting of position—250 pounds of security in suspended animation.

I, on the other hand, had given up trying to keep from falling off my chair and was stretched out on the floor where I could doze without killing myself.

I heard Tank's chair creak. Heard him lean forward. I opened an eye. "Time for another walk-through?"

Tank was on his feet. "Someone's at the door."

I sat up to see, and *BANG*! There was the loud discharge of a gun, and then the sound of glass shattering. Tank pitched back, hit the table, and crashed to the floor.

The gunman rushed into the lobby, gun still in hand. It was the man Tank had thrown through the window, the occupant of apartment 3C. His eyes were wild, his face pale. "Drop the gun," he yelled at me. "Drop the fucking gun."

I looked down, and sure enough, I was holding my gun. "You aren't going to shoot me, are you?" I asked, my voice sounding hollow in my head.

He was wearing a long raincoat. He ripped the coat open and held it wide to show a bunch of packets duct-taped to his body. "You see this? These are explosives. You don't do what I say, and I'll blow us up."

I heard a clunk and realized the gun had slipped from my fingers and fallen onto the floor.

"I need to get into my apartment," he said. "I need to get in now."

"It's locked."

"So get a key."

"I don't have a key."

"Jesus," he said, "so kick the damn door down."

"Me?"

"You see anyone else here?"

I looked down at Tank. He wasn't moving.

The raincoat guy waved his gun in the direction of the stairs. "Move."

I edged around him and took the stairs to the third floor. I stood in front of the door to 3C and tried the handle. Locked, all right.

"Kick it in," the raincoat guy said.

I gave it a kick.

"Christ! That's not a kick. Don't you know anything? Don't you watch television?"

I took a couple of steps back and hurled myself at the door. I hit sideways and bounced off. Nothing happened to the door. "That worked when Ranger did it," I said.

The raincoat guy was sweating, and the gun was shaking in his hand. He turned to the door, aimed the gun with two hands, and squeezed the trigger twice. Wood splintered, and there was the sound of metal on metal. He kicked the door at lock height, and the door crashed open. He jumped in, hit the light switch, and looked everywhere at once. "What happened to my stuff?"

"We cleaned the apartment."

He ran into the bedroom and bathroom and back to the living room. He opened all the cabinet doors in the kitchen. "You had no right," he screamed at me. "You had no right to take my stuff."

"There wasn't much."

"There was a lot! Do you know what I had here? I had good stuff. I had pure. Jesus, do you know how bad I need a hit?"

"Listen, how about if I drive you to the clinic. Get you some help."

"I don't want the clinic. I want my stash."

The occupant of apartment 3A opened her door. "What's going on?"

"Get back in your apartment and lock your door," I said. "We have a little problem here."

The door slammed shut and the lock clicked.

The raincoat guy was running around in his apartment again. "Jesus," he was saying. "Jesus. Jesus."

Another woman appeared in the hall. She was frail and stooped. Her age had to be upwards of a hundred. Her short white hair stuck up in tufts. She was dressed in a worn pink flannel nightgown and big fuzzy slippers. "I can't sleep with all this racket," she said. "I've lived in this building for forty-three years, and I've never seen such goings-on. This used to be a nice neighborhood."

The raincoated guy whipped around, pointed his gun at the woman, and fired. The bullet tore into the wall behind her.

"Bite me," the old lady said, pulling a nickel-plated 9mm from somewhere in the folds of her nightgown, aiming the gun two-handed.

"No!" I yelled. "Don't shoot. He's wired with—"

Too late. The old lady drilled the guy, the sound of my voice lost in the blast.

I WOKE UP strapped to a gurney. I was in the apartment-house lobby, and the lobby was filled with people, mostly cops. Morelli's face swam into focus. He was moving his mouth, but he wasn't saying anything.

"What?" I yelled. "Speak up."

He shook his head, waved his hands, and I saw him mouth, "Take her away." A paramedic rolled the gurney out of the lobby into the night air. We clattered over the sidewalk, and then I felt myself lifted into the ambulance, the flashing strobes blinding against the black sky.

"Hey, wait a minute," I said. "I'm fine. Let me up. Untie these straps."

IT WAS MIDMORNING when I was released from the hospital. I was dressed and pacing when Morelli strode into my room with my discharge papers.

"They're letting you go," he said. "If I had my way, I'd move you upstairs to psychiatric."

I stuck my tongue out at him because I was feeling exceptionally mature. I grabbed my bag, and we fled the room before the nurse arrived with the mandatory wheelchair.

"I have a lot of questions," I said to Morelli.

He steered me toward the elevator. "I have a few of my own. Like, what the hell happened?"

"Me first. I need to know about Tank. No one will tell me anything. Is he, um, you know—?"

"Dead? No. Unfortunately. He was wearing a flak vest. The impact of the bullet knocked him back and stunned him. He hit his head when he fell and was out for a while, but he's fine. And by the way, where were you when he was shot?"

"I was stretched out on the floor. It was past my bedtime."

Morelli grinned. "Let me get this straight. You didn't get shot because you fell asleep on the job?"

"Something like that. It sounded better the way I phrased it. What about the guy with the bomb?"

"So far they've found a shoe and a belt buckle in the vicinity of what's left of the apartment—which, by the way, isn't much—and some teeth on Stark Street."

The elevator door opened, and we both stepped in.

"You're kidding about the teeth, right?"

Morelli grimaced and pushed the button.

"Nobody else hurt?"

"No. The old lady got knocked on her ass just like you. Can you corroborate her story that it was self-defense?"

"Yeah. The drug guy got a round off before she blew him up. It should be embedded in the wall . . . if the wall's still there."

We exited the downstairs lobby and crossed the street to Morelli's truck.

"Now what?" Morelli asked. "Your place? Your mother's house? My place? You're welcome to stay with me if you're feeling shaky."

"Thanks, but I need to go home. I want to take a shower and change my clothes." Then I wanted to go look for Fred. I was antsy to retrace Fred's steps. I wanted to stand in the parking lot where he'd disappeared and get psychic vibes. Not that I'd ever gotten psychic vibes from anything before, but hey, there's always a first time. "By the way, do you know a bookie named Bunchy?"

"No. What's he look like?"

"Average short Italian guy. Forty, maybe."

"Doesn't do anything for me. How do you know him?"

"He visited Mabel, and then he visited me. He claims Fred owes him money."

"Fred?"

"If Fred wanted to play the horses, why wouldn't he place his bets with his son?"

"Because he doesn't want anyone to know he's gambling?"

"Oh, yeah. I didn't think of that." Duh.

"I talked to your doctor," Morelli said. "He told me you're supposed to stay quiet for a couple days. And he said the ringing in your ears should diminish over time."

"The ringing's already a lot better."

Morelli glanced at me sideways. "You're not going to stay quiet, are you?"

"Define 'quiet.'"

"At home, reading, watching television."

"I might do some of that."

Morelli pulled into my parking lot and rolled to a stop. "When you're up to it, you need to stop in at the station and make a formal report."

I jumped out. "Okay."

"Hold it," Morelli said, "I'll go up with you."

"Not necessary. Thanks anyway. I'm fine."

Morelli was grinning again. "Afraid you might lose control in the hall and beg me to come in and make love to you?"

"In your dreams, Morelli."

When I got up to my apartment the red light on my phone machine was blinking, blinking, blinking. And Bunchy was asleep on my couch.

"What are you doing here?" I yelled at him. "Get up! Get out! This isn't the Hotel Ritz. And do you realize what you're doing is breaking and entering?"

"Boy, don't get your panties in a bunch," he said, getting to his feet. "Where have you been? I got worried about you. You didn't come home last night."

"What are you, my mother?"

"Hey, I'm concerned, that's all. You should be happy to have a friend like me." He looked around. "Do you see my shoes?"

"You are *not* my friend. And your shoes are under the coffee table."

He retrieved the shoes and laced them up. "So where were you?"

"I had a job. I was moonlighting."

"Must have been some job. Your mother called and said she heard you blew someone up."

"You talked to my mother?"

"She left a message on your machine." He was looking around again. "Do you see my gun?"

I turned on my heel and went in to the kitchen to play my messages.

"Stephanie, it's your mother. What's this about an explosion? Edna Gluck heard from her son, Ritchie, that you blew someone up? Is this true? Hello? Hello?"

Bunchy was right. Damn that big-mouth Ritchie.

I played the second message. Breathing. As was message number three.

"What's with the breathing?" Bunchy wanted to know, standing in the middle of my kitchen floor, hands stuck in his pockets, his rumpled, beyond-faded, plaid flannel shirt hanging loose.

"Wrong number."

"You'd tell me if you had a problem, right? Because, you know, I have a way of solving problems like that."

No doubt in my mind. He didn't look like a bookie, but I had no trouble at all believing he could solve *that* kind of problem. "Why are you here?"

He prowled through my cabinets, looking for food, finding nothing that interested him. Guess he wasn't crazy about hamster pellets.

"I wanted to know if you found anything," he said. "Like, do you have clues or something?"

"No. No clues. Nothing."

"I thought you were supposed to be this hotshot detective."

"I'm not a detective at all. I'm a bail enforcement agent."

"Bounty hunter."

"Yeah. Bounty hunter."

"So, that's okay. You go out and find people. That's what we want to have happen here."

"How much money did Fred owe you?"

"Enough that I want it. Not enough to make a man feel like he had to disappear. I'm a pretty nice guy, you know. It isn't like I go around breaking people's knees 'cause they don't pay up. Well, okay, so sometimes I might break a knee, but it's not like it happens every day."

I rolled my eyes.

"You know what I think you should do?" Bunchy said. "I think you should go check at his bank. See if he's taken any money out. I can't do things like that on account of I look like I might break people's knees. But you're a pretty girl. You probably got a friend works in the bank. People would want to do a favor for you."

"I'll think about it. Now go away."

Bunchy ambled to the door. He took a beat-up brown leather jacket from one of the pegs on the wall and turned to look at me. His expression was serious. "Find him."

What hung unsaid in the air was . . . or else.

I slipped the bolt behind him. First chance I had I was going to have to get a new lock. Surely someone made a lock that actually kept people out.

I called my mother back and explained to her that I hadn't blown someone up. He'd sort of blown himself up with some help from an old lady in a pink nightgown.

"You could have a good job," my mother said. "You could take lessons from that place that advertises on television and teaches you to be a computer operator."

"I have to go now."

"How about dinner. I'm making a nice pot roast with potatoes and gravy."

"I don't think so."

"Pineapple upside-down cake for dessert."

"Okay. I'll be there at six."

I erased the breathing messages and told myself they were wrong numbers. But in my heart, I knew the breather.

I double-checked all the locks on my door, and I checked to make sure my windows were secure and no one was hiding in a closet or under the bed. I took a long, hot shower, wrapped myself in a towel, stepped out of the bathroom . . . and came face-to-face with Ranger.

FOUR

"*YIKES!*" I JUMPED back and clapped my hand to my chest, tightening my towel. "What are you doing here?" I yelled at Ranger.

His eyes dropped to the towel and then back to my face. "Returning your hat, Babe." He put the SEALs hat on my head and adjusted it over my damp hair. "You left it in the lobby."

"Oh. Thanks."

Ranger smiled.

"What?" I asked.

"Cute," Ranger said.

I narrowed my eyes. "Anything else?"

"You doing the shift with Tank tonight?"

"You're still policing that building?"

"It's got a big hole in it, Babe. Gotta keep the bad guys out."

"I'll pass on that one."

"No problem. I have other jobs you can try on."

"Oh, yeah? Like what?"

Ranger shrugged. "Things turn up." He reached behind him and came up with a gun. My gun. "Found this in the lobby, too." He tucked the gun under the top edge of my towel, wedging it between my breasts, his knuckles brushing against me.

My breath caught in my throat, and for a moment I thought my towel might catch fire.

Ranger smiled again. And I did more eye narrowing.

"I'll be in touch," Ranger said.

And then he was gone.

Dang. I carefully extracted the gun from the towel and put it in the cookie jar in the kitchen. Then I went back to my door to examine the locks. Worthless pieces of junk. I locked them anyway, including the bolt. I didn't know what more I could do.

I went into the bedroom, dropped the towel, and shimmied into a sports bra and Jockey bikinis. This wasn't going to be one of those silk and lace days. This was going to be a no-nonsense Jockey day all the way through.

Half an hour later, I was out the door, dressed in jeans and a denim shirt. I buckled myself into Big Blue and motored out of the lot. Two blocks later, I turned onto Hamilton and noticed a car close on my tail. I swiveled in my seat and looked at the driver. Bunchy. I pressed my lips together, getting a smile and a wave from him. This guy was unreal. He'd pulled a gun on me, and probably he had something to do with the body in the garbage bag, but I was having a hard time working up any real fear of him. In all honesty, he was sort of likeable . . . in an annoying kind of way.

I swerved to the curb, yanked the emergency brake up, got out, and stomped over. "What are you doing?" I shouted into his window.

"Following you."

"Why?"

"I don't want to miss anything. In case you get lucky and find Fred, I want to be there."

"I don't know how to break this to you, but between you and me, I think it's unlikely that Fred is going to be in any shape to repay your money if and when I find him."

"You think he's fish food?"

"It's a possibility."

He shrugged. "Call me crazy, but I'm an optimist."

"Fine. Go be an optimist someplace else. I don't like you following me around. It's creepy."

"I won't be any bother. You won't even know I'm here."

"You're driving six inches from my rear. How am I going to not know you're here?"

"Don't look in your mirror."

"And I don't think you're a bookie, either," I said. "Nobody knows you. I've been asking around."

He smiled, like this was pretty funny. "Oh, yeah? Who do you think I am?"

"I don't know."

"Let me know when you find out."

"Asshole."

"Sticks and stones," Bunchy said. "And I bet your mother wouldn't like you using that language."

I huffed off to the Buick, jammed myself behind the wheel, and drove to the office.

"You see that guy parked behind me?" I asked Lula.

"The one in the piece-of-shit brown Dodge?"

"His name's Bunchy, and he says he's a bookie."

"He don't look like no bookie to me," Lula said. "And I never heard of anyone named Bunchy."

Connie squinted out the window, too. "I don't recognize him, either," she said. "And if he's a bookie, he's not doing all that good."

"He says Fred owes him money, and he's following me in case I find Fred."

"Does that float your boat?" Lula wanted to know.

"No. I need to get rid of him."

"Permanently? 'Cause I got a friend—"

"No! Just for the rest of the day."

Lula took another look at Bunchy. "If I shoot out his tires, will he shoot back?"

"Probably."

"I don't like when they shoot back," Lula said.

"I thought maybe I could trade cars with you."

"Trade my Firebird for that whale you drive? I don't think so. Friendship don't go *that* far."

"Fine! Great! Forget I asked!"

"Hold on," Lula said. "Don't have to go getting all snippy. I'll have a talk with him. I can be real persuasive."

"You aren't going to threaten him, are you?"

"I don't threaten people. What kind of woman you think I am?"

Connie and I watched her sashay out the office over to the car. We knew what kind of woman she was.

Lula was wearing a canary-yellow spandex miniskirt and a stretchy top that was at least two sizes too small. Her hair was orange. Her lipstick was bright pink. And her eyelids were gold glitter.

We heard her say, "Hello, handsome," to Bunchy, and then she lowered her voice, and we couldn't hear any more.

"Maybe you should try to sneak away while Lula's got his attention," Connie said. "Maybe you could roll the Buick back nice and easy, and he won't notice."

I thought chances of Bunchy not noticing were pretty slim, but I was willing to try. I quickly walked to the car, snuck in on the curb side, and slid behind the wheel. I released the emergency brake, held my breath, and turned the key in the ignition. *Varoooom.* A V8 does *not* sneak.

Bunchy and Lula both turned to look at me. I saw Bunchy say something to Lula. And Lula grabbed Bunchy by the shirtfront and yelled "*Go!*" to me. "I got him," she said. "You can count on me!"

Bunchy slapped at her hand, and Lula squashed herself into the car window with her big yellow ass hanging out, looking from the outside like Pooh Bear stuck in the rabbit hole. She had Bunchy by the neck, and when I drove by I saw her plant a kiss square on his mouth.

MABEL WAS IN the kitchen making tea when I got there.

"Anything new in the investigation?" she asked.

"I talked to the man who was looking for Fred. He says he's Fred's bookie. Did you know Fred was gambling?"

"No." She paused with the tea bag in her hand. "Gambling," she said, testing the word. "I had no idea."

"He could be lying," I said.

"Why would he do that?"

Good question. If Bunchy wasn't a bookie, then what? What was his involvement?

"About those pictures," I said to Mabel. "Do you have any idea when they might have been taken?"

Mabel added water to her teapot. "I think it must have been recently because I never saw them before. I don't go into Fred's desk all the time, but every now and then I need something. And I never saw any pictures. Fred doesn't take pictures. Years ago, when the kids were little, we used to take pictures. Now Ronald and Walter bring us pictures of the grandchildren. We don't even own a camera anymore. Last year we had to take pictures of the roof for the insurance company, and we got one of those disposable cameras."

I left Mabel to her tea and got back behind the wheel. I looked up and down the street. So far, so good. No Bunchy.

My next stop was the strip mall where Fred did his shopping. I parked in the same area where Fred's car was found. It was about the same time of day. Weather was similar. Seventy and sunny. There were enough people moving around that a scuffle would be noticed. A man walking around dazed would probably be noticed too, but I didn't think that's what I was looking for.

First Trenton was located at the end of the strip mall. It was a branch office with a drive-through window outside and full-service banking inside. Leona Freeman was a teller at First Trenton. She was a second cousin on my mother's side, a couple years older than me, and she had a head start on the family thing, with four kids, two dogs, and a nice husband.

Business was slow when I walked in, and Leona waved at me from behind the counter. "Stephanie!"

"Hey, Leona, how's it going?"

"Pretty good. What's with you? You want some money? I gotta lot."

I grinned.

"Bank joke," Leona said.

"Did you hear about Fred going missing?"

"I heard. He was in here right before it happened."

"Did you see him?"

"Yeah, sure. He got money from the machine, and then he went in to see Shempsky."

Leona and I went to school with Allen Shempsky. He was an okay guy who'd worked his way up the ladder and was now a VP. And this was a new development. No one had said anything about Fred going to see Shempsky. "What'd Fred want with Allen?"

Leona shrugged. "Don't know. He was in there talking to Allen for about ten minutes. He didn't stop to say hello or anything when he came out. Fred was like that. Not the most sociable person."

Shempsky had a small private office tucked between two other small private offices. His door was open, so I stuck my head in.

"Knock, knock," I said.

Allen Shempsky looked at me blank-faced for a moment, and then I saw recognition kick in. "Sorry," he said, "my mind was someplace else. What can I do for you?"

"I'm looking for my uncle Fred. I understand he talked to you just before he disappeared."

"Yeah. He was thinking of taking out a loan."

"A loan? What kind of a loan?"

"Personal."

"He say what he needed the money for?"

"No. Wanted to know what interest rates were and how long would it take. That sort of thing. Preliminary stuff. No paperwork or anything. I think he was only in here for maybe five minutes. Ten tops."

"Did he seem upset?"

"Not that I remember. Well, not any more than usual. Fred was sort of a grumpy guy. The family ask you to look for Fred?"

"Yeah." I stood and gave Shempsky my card. "Let me know if you think of anything significant."

A loan. I couldn't help wondering if it was to pay off Bunchy. I didn't think Bunchy was a bookie, but I wouldn't be shocked to find he was a blackmailer.

The dry cleaner was in the middle of the strip of buildings, next to Grand Union. I knew the woman behind the counter by sight, but not by name. I brought my clothes here too, sometimes.

She remembered Fred, but not much else. He'd picked up his clothes and that was it. No conversation. They'd been busy at the time. She hadn't paid a lot of attention to Fred.

I went back to the Buick and stood there, looking around, trying to imagine what might have happened. Fred had parked in front of Grand Union, anticipating that he'd have groceries to carry. He'd laid the cleaning neatly on the backseat, then closed and locked the car. Then what? Then he'd disappeared. The mall opened to a four-lane highway on one side. Behind the mall was an apartment complex and the neighborhood of single-family houses where I'd searched for Fred.

The RGC office was down by the river, on the other side of Broad. It was an industrial area of warehouses and mom-and-pop factories. Not especially scenic. Perfect for a waste hauler.

I eased into traffic and pointed Big Blue's nose west. Ten minutes and seven lights later, I rolled down Water Street, squinting at the somber brick buildings, looking for numbers. The road was cracked and pocked with potholes. Parking lots associated with businesses were ringed by chain-link fences. Sidewalks were empty. Windows were dark and lifeless. I didn't need to see the numbers, RGC was easy to spot. Large sign. Lots of garbage trucks parked in the lot. There were five visitor slots next to the building. They were all empty. No surprise there. It didn't exactly smell like roses outside.

I parked in one of the slots and scurried inside. The office was small. Linoleum floor, death-pallor-green walls, and a counter cut the room in half. There were two desks and file cabinets in the back half of the room.

A woman got up from one of the desks and stood at the counter. A plaque on the counter read MARTHA DEETER, RECEP-TIONIST, and I assumed this was Martha.

"Can I help you?" Martha asked.

I introduced myself as Fred's niece and told her I was looking for Fred.

"I remember speaking to him," she said. "He went home to get his canceled check and never returned. It never occurred to me that something might have happened to him. I just assumed he'd given up. We get a lot of people in here trying to get something for nothing."

"Go figure."

"Exactly. That's why I sent him home for the check. The old ones are the worst. They're all on fixed incomes. They'll say any-thing to hang on to a dollar."

There was a man sitting at the second desk. He got up and moved next to Martha. "Perhaps I can be of assistance here. I'm the bookkeeper, and I'm afraid this is my problem. Truth is, this has happened before. It's the computer. We just can't get it to rec-ognize certain customers."

Martha tapped a finger on the counter. "It's *not* the computer. There are people out there who'll take advantage. People think it's okay to gyp big business."

The man gave me a tight smile and extended his hand. "Larry Lipinski. I'll make sure the account is set straight."

Martha didn't look happy. "We really should see the canceled check."

"For goodness' sakes," Lipinski said to Martha, "the man disap-peared in the middle of his errands. He probably had the check on him. How do you expect them to show you the check?"

"Supposedly the Shutzes have been customers for years. They must have canceled checks from previous quarters," she said.

"I don't believe this," Lipinski said. "Give it a rest. It's the computer. Remember last month? We had the same problem."

"It isn't the computer."

"It is."

"Isn't."

"Is."

I backed out of the office and slipped out the door. I didn't want to be around for the bitch-slapping and hair-pulling. If Fred was going to "make out in spades," it seemed unlikely he'd make his killing with these two.

Half an hour later I was back at Vinnie's. His door was shut and there were no bond seekers at Connie's desk. Lula and Connie were discussing meatloaf.

"That's disgusting," Lula said, eyeballing Connie's sandwich. "Whoever heard of mayonnaise on meatloaf? Everybody knows you gotta put ketchup on meatloaf. You can't put no dumb-ass mayonnaise on it. What is that, some Italian thing?"

Connie gave Lula a stiff middle finger. "*This* is an Italian thing," she said.

I snitched a corn chip from the bag on Connie's desk. "So what happened?" I asked Lula. "You and Bunchy going steady now?"

"He's not such a bad kisser," Lula said. "He had a hard time giving it his full attention at first, but after a while I think he was into it."

"I'm going after Briggs," I said. "You want to ride shotgun?"

"Sure," Lula said, pulling a sweatshirt over her head. "Better than sitting around here. It's damn boring in here today." She had keys in her hand. "And I'm driving. You have a pipsqueak sound system in that Buick, and I need Dolby. I need mood music. I gotta get myself ready to kick some butt."

"We're not kicking butt. We're finessing."

"I could do that, too," Lula said.

I followed Lula out the door to her car. We buckled ourselves in, the CD player clicked on, and the bass almost lifted us off the ground.

"So what's the plan?" Lula asked, pulling into Briggs' parking lot. "We need a plan."

"The plan is that we knock on his door and lie."

"I could get into that," Lula said. "I like to lie. I could lie your ass off."

We crossed the lot and took the stairs. The hall was empty, and there was no noise coming from Briggs' apartment.

I flattened against the wall, out of sight, and Lula knocked twice on Briggs' door.

"How's this?" she asked. "I look okay? This here's my nonthreatening look. This look says, Come on, motherfucker, open your door."

If I saw Lula on the other side of my apartment door, wearing her nonthreatening look, I'd hide under my bed. But hey, that's me.

The door opened with the security chain in place and Briggs peeked out at Lula.

"Howdy," Lula said. "I'm from downstairs, and I got a petition for you to sign on account of they're gonna raise our rent."

"I didn't hear anything about a rent raise," Briggs said. "I didn't get any notice."

"Well, they're gonna do it all the same," Lula said.

"Sons of bitches," Briggs said. "They're always doing something in this building. I don't know why I stay here."

"Cheap rent?" Lula asked.

The door closed, the chain slid off, and the door opened wide.

"Hey!" Briggs said when Lula and I pushed past him into the apartment. "You can't just barge in like this. You tricked me."

"Look again," Lula said. "We're bounty hunters. We can barge if we want to. We got rights."

"You have *no* rights," Briggs said. "It's a bogus charge. I was carrying a ceremonial knife. It was engraved."

"A ceremonial knife," Lula said. "Seems like a little dude like you should be able to carry a ceremonial knife."

"Exactly," Randy said. "I'm unjustly accused."

"'Course it don't matter," Lula said. "You still gotta go to the pokey with us."

"I'm in the middle of a big project. I don't have time."

"Hmmm," Lula said. "Let me explain to you how this works. Bottom line is, we don't give a doody."

Briggs pressed his lips together and folded his arms tight across his chest. "You can't make me go."

"Sure we can," Lula said. "You're just a little pipsqueak. We could make you sing 'Yankee Doodle' if we wanted. 'Course, we wouldn't do that on account of we're professionals."

I pulled a pair of cuffs out of my back pocket and clamped one of the bracelets on Briggs.

Briggs looked at the cuff like it was the flesh-eating virus. "What's this?"

"Nothing to be alarmed about," I said. "Standard procedure."

"Eeeeeeeee," Briggs shrieked. "Eeeeeeeee."

"Stop that!" Lula yelled. "You sound like a girl. You're creeping me out."

He was running around the room now, waving his arms and still shrieking. "Eeeeeeeee."

"Get a grip!" Lula said.

"Eeeeeeee."

I made a grab for the cuff but missed. "Stand still," I ordered.

Briggs bolted past Lula, who was dumbstruck, rooted to the floor, and then ran out the door.

"Get him," I yelled, rushing at Lula. "Don't let him get away!" I pushed her into the hall, and we thundered down the stairs after Briggs.

Briggs sprinted through the small lobby, through the front door, and into the parking lot.

"Well, damn," Lula said, "I can hear his little feet going, but I can't see him. He's lost in between all these cars."

We separated and walked into the lot, Lula going one way and me the other. We stopped and listened for footsteps when we got to the outer perimeter.

337

"I don't hear him anymore," Lula said. "He must be going tippytoe."

We started to walk back when we saw Briggs round the corner of the apartment building and race inside.

"Holy cow!" Lula said. "He's going back to his apartment."

We ran across the lot, barreled through the door, and took the stairs two at a time. When we got to Briggs' apartment the door was closed and locked.

"We know you're in there," Lula yelled. "You better open this door."

"You can huff and you can puff, but you'll never get through this door," Briggs said.

"The hell we won't," Lula told him. "We could shoot the lock off. And then we're gonna come in there and root you out like a rodent."

No answer.

"Hello?" Lula called.

We listened at the door and heard the computer boot up. Briggs was going back to work.

"Nothing I hate more than a wise-ass dwarf," Lula said, hauling a .45 out of her purse. "Stand back. I'm gonna blast this door open."

Drilling Briggs' door held a lot of appeal, but probably it wasn't practical to shoot up an apartment building for a guy who was only worth seven hundred dollars.

"No shooting," I said. "I'll get the key from the super."

"That isn't gonna do you no good if you're not willing to shoot," Lula said. "He's still gonna have the security chain on."

"I saw Ranger pop a door open with his shoulder."

Lula looked at the door. "I could do that too," she said. "Only I just bought this dress with them little spaghetti straps, and I wouldn't want to have a bruise."

I looked at my watch. "It's almost five, and I'm having dinner with my parents tonight."

"Maybe we should do this some other time."

"We're leaving," I hollered through Briggs' door, "but we'll be back. And you'd better be careful of those handcuffs. They cost me forty dollars."

"We would have been justified to shoot our way in on account of he's in possession of stolen property," Lula said.

"Do you always carry a gun?" I asked Lula.

"Don't everybody?"

"They released Benito Ramirez two days ago."

Lula stumbled on the second step down. "That's not possible."

"Joe told me."

"Piece-of-shit legal system."

"Be careful."

"Hell," Lula said. "He already cut me. You're the one who has to be careful."

We swung through the door and stopped in our tracks.

"Uh-oh," Lula said. "We got company."

It was Bunchy. He was parked behind us in the lot. And he didn't look happy.

"How do you suppose he found us?" Lula asked. "We aren't even in your car."

"He must have followed us from the office."

"I didn't see him. And I was looking."

"I didn't see him either."

"He's good," Lula said. "He might be someone to worry about."

"HOW'S THE POT roast?" my mother wanted to know. "Is it too dry?"

"It's fine," I told her. "Just like always."

"I got the green bean casserole recipe from Rose Molinowski. It's made with mushroom soup and bread crumbs."

"Whenever there's a wake or a christening, Rose always brings this casserole," Grandma said. "It's her signature dish."

My father looked up from his plate. "Signature dish?"

"I got that from the shopper's channel on TV. All the big designers got signature this and that."

My father shook his head and bent lower over his pot roast.

Grandma helped herself to some of the casserole. "How's the manhunt going? You got any good leads on Fred yet?"

"Fred is a dead end. I've talked to his sons and his girlfriend. I've retraced his last steps. I've talked to Mabel. There's nothing. He's disappeared without a trace."

My father muttered something that sounded a lot like "lucky bastard" and continued to eat.

My mother rolled her eyes.

And Grandma spooned in some beans. "We need one of them psychics," Grandma said. "I saw on television where you can call them up, and they know everything. They find dead people all the time. I saw a couple of them on a talk show, and they were saying how they help the police with these serial murder cases. I was watching that show, and I was thinking that if I was a serial murderer I'd chop the bodies up in little pieces so those psychics wouldn't have such an easy job of it. Or maybe I'd drain all the blood out of the body and collect it in a big bucket. Then I'd bury a chicken, and I'd take the victim's blood and make a trail to the chicken. Then the psychic wouldn't know what to make of it when the police dug up a chicken." Grandma helped herself to the gravy boat and poured gravy over her pot roast. "Do you think that'd work?"

Everyone but Grandma paused with forks in midair.

"Well, I wouldn't bury a *live* chicken," Grandma said.

No one had much to say after that, and I felt myself nodding off halfway through my second piece of cake.

"You look all done in," Grandma said. "Guess getting blown up takes it out of you."

"I didn't get much sleep last night."

"Maybe you want to take a nap while your grandmother and I clean up," my mother said. "You can use the guest room."

Ordinarily, I'd excuse myself and go home early, but tonight Bunchy was sitting across the street, two houses down, in the Dodge. So leaving early didn't appeal to me. What appealed to me was to make Bunchy's night as long as possible.

My parents have three bedrooms. My grandma Mazur sleeps in my sister's room, and my room is used as a guest room. Of course, I'm the only guest who ever uses the guest room. All my parents' friends and family live within a five-mile radius and have no reason to stay overnight. I also live within five miles, but I've been known to have the occasional disaster that sends me in search of temporary residence. So my bathrobe hangs in the guest room closet.

"Maybe just a short nap," I said. "I'm really tired."

THE SUN WAS slanting through the break in the curtains when I woke up. I had a moment of disorientation, wondering if I was late for school, and then realized I'd been out of school for a lot of years, and that I'd crawled into bed for a short nap and ended up sleeping through the night.

I rolled out of bed fully dressed and shuffled down to the kitchen. My mother was making vegetable soup, and my grandmother was sitting at the kitchen table reading the paper, scrutinizing the obituaries.

Grandma looked up when I came in. "Weren't you at the garbage company yesterday, checking on Fred?"

I poured myself a cup of coffee and sat across from her. "Yep."

"It says here this woman, Martha Deeter, who was the receptionist at RGC, was shot to death last night. Says they found her in the parking lot of her apartment building." Grandma slid the paper over to me. "Got a picture of her and everything."

I stared goggle-eyed at the picture. It was Martha, all right. With the way she was going at it with her office mate, I'd expected she might have fingerprint marks on her neck. A bullet in the brain never occurred to me.

341

"Says she's being laid out at Stiva's tomorrow night," Grandma said. "We should go on account of it was our garbage company."

The Catholic church held bingo parties only twice a week, so Grandma and her friends enlarged their social life by attending viewings.

"No suspects," I said, reading the article. "The police think it was robbery. Her purse was missing."

THE BROWN DODGE was still parked down the street when I left my parents' house. Bunchy was asleep behind the wheel, his head back, mouth open. I rapped on the window, and he jumped awake.

"Shit," he said, "what time is it?"

"Were you here all night?"

"Sure looks like it."

Looked like it to me, too. He looked even worse than usual. He had dark circles under his eyes, he needed a shave, and his hair looked like it had been styled by a stun gun.

"So, you didn't kill anybody last night?"

Bunchy blinked at me. "Not that I remember. Who bought the farm?"

"Martha Deeter. She worked at RGC Waste Haulers."

"Why would I want to kill her?"

"I don't know. I saw it in the paper this morning and just thought I'd ask."

"Never hurts to ask," Bunchy said.

I LET MYSELF into my apartment and saw the light flashing on my phone machine.

"Hey, Babe," Ranger said, "got a job for you."

The second message was from Benito Ramirez. "Hello, Stephanie," he said. Quiet-voiced. Articulate, as always. "I've been away for a little while . . . as you know." There was a pause and in my mind I could see his eyes. Small for his face and terrifyingly insane. "I came by to see you, but you weren't at home. That's okay. I'll try some other time." He gave a small, girlish giggle and disconnected.

I erased Ranger's message and saved Ramirez's. Probably I should have a restraining order issued. Ordinarily I didn't hold much stock in restraining orders, but in this case, if Ramirez continued to harass me I might be able to get his parole revoked.

I connected with Ranger on his car phone. "What's the job?" I asked.

"Chauffeur. I have a young sheik flying in to Newark at five."

"He carrying drugs? Delivering guns?"

"Negative. He's visiting relatives in Bucks County. Long weekend. Probably he won't even blow himself up."

"What's the catch?"

"No catch. You wear a black suit and white shirt. You meet him at the gate and escort him safely to his destination."

"I guess that sounds okay."

"You'll be driving a Town Car. You can pick it up at the garage on Third and Marshall. Be there at three o'clock and talk to Eddie."

"Anything else?"

"Make sure you're dressed."

"You mean the suit—"

"I mean the gun."

"Oh."

I disconnected and went back to Fred's photos. I spread the color copies out on the table just as I did the first time. Two of the pictures were of the bag all tied up. I was guessing that was how Fred found it. He took a couple pictures, then he opened the bag. The big question was, did he know what was inside before he opened it, or was it a surprise?

I went upstairs to Mrs. Bestler, who had failing eyesight, and borrowed a magnifying glass. I returned to my apartment, took the pages closer to the window, and looked at them with the glass. The glass wasn't much help, but I was almost sure it was a woman. Short dark hair. No jewelry on her right hand. There seemed to be newspapers crumpled into the bag with her. A crime lab might be able to pick something out to help date the photo. The bag with the woman was sitting with other bags. I could count four. They were on asphalt. Garbage stacked outside a business, maybe. A business too small to need a Dumpster. Lots of those around. Or it could be a driveway belonging to a family who made tons of garbage.

Part of a building was visible in the background. Hard to tell what it was. It was out of focus and in shade. A stucco wall was my best guess.

That was all the pictures were going to offer up to me.

I took a shower, scrounged for lunch, and set off to talk to Mabel.

FIVE

I LEFT MY building with more caution than usual, keeping my eyes open for Ramirez. I reached the Buick and was almost disappointed not to have been accosted. On the one hand, it'd be good to get the confrontation over with. On the other hand . . . I didn't want to think about the other hand.

Bunchy wasn't there, either. I had mixed feelings about this, too. Bunchy was a pain in the behind, and I had no idea who he was, but I thought he might be good to have around if Ramirez attacked me. Better Bunchy than Ramirez. I don't know why I felt like that. For all I knew, Bunchy was the butcher.

I chugged out of the lot and drove on autopilot to Mabel's house, trying to prioritize projects. I had to neutralize Ramirez, get to the bottom of the Fred thing, chauffeur some sheik . . . And I felt uncomfortable about the dead garbage lady. Not to mention, I needed shoes for Saturday night. I lined everything up in my mind. The shoes were, hands down, top priority. Okay, so sometimes I wasn't the world's greatest bounty hunter. I wasn't a fabulous cook. I didn't have a boyfriend, much less a husband. And I wasn't a big financial success. I could live with all those failings as long as I knew that once in a while I looked really hot. And Saturday night I was going to look hot. So I needed shoes and a new dress.

Mabel was standing at the door when I drove up. Still on the lookout for Fred, I guess.

"I'm so glad you're here," she said, ushering me into the house. "I don't know what to think."

As if I could help her in that department.

"Sometimes I expect Fred to walk in the door, just like always. And then other times I know he'll never be back. And the thing is . . . I really need a new washer and dryer. In fact, I've needed them for years, but Fred was so cautious about spending money. Maybe I'll just go down to Sears and take a look. It doesn't hurt to look, does it?"

"Looking sounds good to me."

"I knew I could count on you," Mabel said. "Would you like some tea?"

"No thanks on the tea, but I have some more questions. I want you to think about places Fred might go that would have four or five garbage bags sitting outside on garbage day. The bags would be sitting on asphalt. And there might be a light-colored stucco wall behind them."

"This is about those photographs, isn't it? Let me think. Fred had a routine, you know. When he retired two years ago, he took over the errands. In the beginning we did the marketing together, but it was too stressful. So I started staying home and watching my television shows in the afternoon, and Fred took over the errands. He went to the Grand Union every day. And sometimes he'd go to Giovichinni's Meat Market. He didn't go there too often because he thought Giovichinni gypped him on the meat scale. He only went there if he wanted kielbasa. Once in a while he'd splurge on Giovichinni's olive loaf."

"Did he go to Giovichinni's last week?"

"Not that I know of. The only thing different about last week was that he went out in the morning to the garbage company. He didn't usually go out in the morning, but he was really in a state over that missed day."

"Did he ever go out at night?"

"We went to the seniors' club on Thursdays to play cards. And we went to special events sometimes. Like the Christmas party."

We were standing in front of the living room window, talking, when the RGC garbage truck rumbled up the street, bypassed Mabel's house, and stopped next door.

Mabel blinked in disbelief. "They didn't take my garbage," she said. "It's right out there on the curb, and they didn't take it." She threw the door open and trotted out to the sidewalk, but the truck was gone. "How could they do this?" she wailed. "What am I going to do with my garbage?"

I went to the Yellow Pages, found the number for RGC, and dialed the number. Larry Lipinski answered the phone.

"Larry," I said, "this is Stephanie Plum, remember me?"

"Sure," Larry said, "but I'm a little busy right now."

"I read about Martha—"

"Yeah, Martha. What's on your mind?"

"My aunt's garbage. The thing is, Larry, the truck went right by her house just now and didn't pick up her garbage."

There was a big sigh. "That's because she didn't pay her bill. There's no record of payment."

"We went through all that yesterday. You said you'd take care of it."

"Look, lady, I tried, okay? But there's no record of payment, and frankly I'm thinking Martha was right, and you and your aunt are trying to gyp us."

"Listen, Larry!"

Larry disconnected.

"You dumb fuck!" I yelled at the phone.

Aunt Mabel looked shocked.

"Sorry," I said. "I got carried away."

I went down to the cellar, got the canceled RGC check off Fred's desk, and dropped it into my shoulder bag.

"I'll take care of this tomorrow," I said. "I'd do it today, but I don't have time."

Mabel was wringing her hands. "That garbage is going to smell

347

if I leave it sitting out there in the sun," she said. "What will the neighbors think?"

I did some mental head-banging. "No problem. Don't worry about it."

She gave me a tremulous smile.

I said good-bye, marched to the curb, extracted Mabel's nicely tied up plastic garbage bag from her container, and stuffed it into the trunk of my car. Then I drove to RGC, pitched the bag onto the sidewalk in front of their office, and raced away.

Am I a take-charge woman or what?

I drove away thinking about Fred. Suppose Fred saw someone do that? Well, not *exactly* what I just did. Suppose he saw someone take a garbage bag out of the trunk of their car and put it on the curb, alongside someone else's garbage. And suppose for one reason or another he got to wondering what was in the garbage bag?

This made a reasonable picture to me. I could see this happening. What I didn't understand, if in fact any of this occurred the way I imagined, was why Fred didn't report it to the police. Maybe he knew the person dumping the bag. But then why would he take pictures?

Hold on, let's reverse it. Suppose someone saw Fred dump the bag. They went to investigate, found the body and took pictures for evidence, then tried to blackmail Fred. Who would do such a thing? Bunchy. And maybe Fred all of a sudden got spooked and left for points south.

What's wrong with *this* picture? I couldn't see Fred taking a chain saw to some woman. And you'd have to be pretty dumb to blackmail Fred, because Fred didn't have any money.

THE SKIRT TO my black suit hit two inches above my knee. The jacket sat high on my hipbone. My stretchy white jersey tucked into the skirt. I was wearing sheer, barely black pantyhose and black heels. My .38 was in my black leather shoulder bag. And for this special occasion, I'd taken the time to put some bullets in the stupid thing . . . just in case Ranger showed up and gave me a pop quiz.

Bunchy was in the parking lot, parked behind my Buick. "Going to a funeral?"

"I have a job chauffeuring a sheik from Newark. It's going to take me out of town for the rest of the afternoon, and I'm worried about Mabel. Since you like to sit around and do nothing, I thought you might sit around and do nothing across from Mabel's house." Give him something to do, I thought. Keep the guy busy.

"You want me to protect the people I'm squeezing?"

"Yeah."

"It doesn't work that way. And what the hell are you doing going off on a chauffeuring job? You're supposed to be looking for your uncle."

"I need money."

"You need to find Fred."

"Okay, this is the honest-to-God truth . . . I don't know how to find Fred. I run down leads and they don't go anywhere. Maybe it would help if you told me what you were really after."

"I'm after Fred."

"Why?"

"You better get going," Bunchy said. "You're gonna be late."

THE GARAGE AT Third and Marshall didn't have a name. It was probably listed under something in the phone book, but on the outside of the building there was nothing. Just a redbrick building with a paved parking lot, enclosed by chain-link fencing. There were three bays in the side of the building, opening out to the lot. The bay doors were open and men worked on cars in each of the bays. A white stretch limo and two black Town Cars were parked in the lot. I pulled the Buick into a slot next to one of the Town Cars, locked the Buick, and dropped the keys into my shoulder bag.

A guy who looked like Antonio Banderas on an off day sauntered over to me.

"Nice car," he said, eyeing the Buick. "Man, they don't make cars like this anymore." He ran a hand over the back fender. "Cherry. Real cherry."

"Uh-huh." The cherry car got four miles to a gallon and cornered like a refrigerator. Not to mention it was all wrong for my self-image. My self-image called for fast and sleek and black, not bulbous and powder blue. Red would be okay, too. And I needed a sunroof. And a good sound system. And leather seats . . .

"Earth to Babe," Banderas said.

I dragged myself back to the moment. "You know where I can find Eddie?"

"You're looking at him, Cookie. I'm Eddie."

I extended my hand. "Stephanie Plum. Ranger sent me."

"I got a car ready and waiting." He rounded the nearest Town Car, opened the driver's side door, and took a large white envelope from behind the visor. "Here's everything you need. The keys are in the ignition. The car's gassed up."

"I don't need a chauffeur's license to do this, do I?"

He stared at me blank-faced.

"Yeah, right," I said. Probably nothing to worry about anyway. It wasn't easy to get a permit to carry concealed in Mercer County. And I wasn't one of the chosen. If I got stopped by a cop he'd be so overjoyed to be able to arrest me for illegally carrying concealed that he'd no doubt forget to charge me for the driving thing.

I took the envelope and slid behind the wheel. I adjusted the seat and leafed through the papers. Flight information, parking directions, some procedural instructions, name and brief description, and snapshot of Ahmed Fahed. No age was given, but he looked young in the photo.

I eased the Lincoln out of the lot and headed for Route 1. I picked up the turnpike in East Brunswick and glided along in my big, black, climate-controlled car, feeling very professional. Chauffeuring wasn't so bad, I thought. Today a sheik, tomorrow . . . who knows, maybe Tom Cruise. Definitely better than getting some computer nut out of his apartment. And if it wasn't for the fact that

I couldn't stop thinking about that severed right hand and decapitated head, I'd really be enjoying myself.

I took the airport exit and found my way to Arrivals. My passenger was coming in from San Francisco, flying commercial. I parked in the area reserved for limos, crossed the road, entered the terminal, and checked the monitors for gate information.

A half hour later, Fahed strolled through the gate, wearing two-hundred-dollar sneakers and oversize jeans. His T-shirt advertised a microbrewery. His red plaid flannel shirt was wrinkled and unbuttoned, sleeves rolled to the elbow. I'd expected sheik clothes with the head thing and robe. Fortunately for me, he was the only arrogant Arab departing first class, so it wasn't hard to pick him out.

"Ahmed Fahed?" I asked.

His eyebrows raised ever so slightly in acknowledgment.

"I'm your driver."

He looked me over. "Where's your gun?"

"In my shoulder bag."

"My father always orders a bodyguard for me. He's afraid someone will kidnap me."

Now it was my turn to raise an eyebrow.

He shrugged. "We're rich. Rich people get kidnapped."

"Hardly ever in Jersey," I said. "Too much overhead. Hotel rooms and food bills. The payoff's better on extortion."

His gaze dropped to my chest. "You ever do it with a sheik?"

"Excuse me?"

"You could get lucky today."

"Yeah. And you could get shot. How old are you, anyway?"

He tipped his chin up an eighth of an inch. "Nineteen."

My guess would be closer to fifteen, but hey, what do I know about Arabs? "You have luggage?"

"Two bags."

I led the way to baggage, snagged his two pieces, and rolled them out of the building across the pick-up lanes to the parking garage. When I had my charge settled into the backseat, I cruised off into gridlocked traffic.

After a couple minutes of creeping along Fahed was antsy. "What's the problem?"

"Too many cars," I said. "Not enough road."

"Well, do something."

I glanced at him in the rearview mirror. "What did you have in mind?"

"I don't know. Just *do* something. Just *go*."

"This isn't a helicopter. I can't just *go*."

"Okay," he said. "I've got an idea. How about we do this?"

"What?"

"This."

I turned in my seat and looked at him. "What is *this*?"

He wagged his wonkie at me and smiled.

Great. A fifteen-year-old sex fiend, exhibitionist sheik.

"I can make it do tricks," he said.

"Not in *my* car, you can't. Put it back in your pants, or I'll tell your father."

"My father would be proud. Look at me . . . I'm hung like a horse."

I pulled a knife out of my shoulder bag and flipped it open. "I can make you hung like a hamster."

"American whore bitch."

I rolled my eyes.

"This is intolerable," he said. "I hate this traffic. And I hate this car. And I hate sitting here doing nothing."

Fahed wasn't the only one experiencing road rage. Other drivers were coming unglued. Men were swearing to themselves and tugging at ties. Fingers drummed impatiently on steering wheels. Someone behind me leaned on his horn.

"I'll give you one hundred dollars if you let me drive," Fahed said.

"No."

"A thousand."

"No."

"Five thousand."

I glanced at him in the rearview mirror. "No."

"You were tempted," he said, smiling, looking satisfied.

Ugh.

An hour and a half later we managed to reach the New Brunswick interchange.

"I need something to drink," Fahed said. "There's nothing to drink in this car. I'm used to having a stretch with a bar. I want you to find a place to get me a soda."

I wasn't sure if this was limo protocol, but I figured what the hell, it was his nickel. I picked up Route 1 and looked for fast food. Not much of a challenge. The first thing that came up was a McDonald's. It was dinnertime and the drive-through lane looked like the Jersey Turnpike, so I junked the drive-through and parked the car.

"I want a Coke," he said, sitting tight, clearly not interested in standing in line with the rest of New Jersey.

Don't freak out, I told myself. He's used to being waited on. "Anything else?"

"French fries."

Fine. I grabbed my bag and crossed the lot. I swung though the door and chose a line. Two people in front of me. I studied the menu over the counter. One person left in front of me. I hiked my bag higher on my shoulder and looked out the window. I didn't see my car. There was a small twinge of alarm just below my heart. I scanned the lot. No car. I left the line and pushed through the door into the cool air. The car was gone.

Shit!

My first fear was that he'd been kidnapped. I'd been hired as a chauffeur and bodyguard for the sheik, and the sheik's been kidnapped. The fear was short-lived. No one would want this rotten kid. Face it, Stephanie, that little snot took the car.

I had two choices. I could call the police. Or I could call Ranger.

I tried Ranger first. "Bad news," I said. "I sort of lost the sheik."

"Where did you lose him?"

"North Brunswick. He sent me into a McDonald's for a soda, and next thing I knew, he was gone."

"Where are you now?"

"I'm still at the McDonald's." Where else would I be?

"Don't move. I'll get back to you."

The connection was severed. "When?" I asked the dead phone. "When?"

Ten minutes later the phone rang.

"No problem," Ranger said. "Found the sheik."

"How'd you find him?"

"I called the car phone."

"Was he kidnapped?"

"Impatient. Said he got tired of waiting for you."

"That little jerk-off!"

Several people stopped in their tracks and stared.

I lowered my voice and turned, facing the phone. "Sorry, I got carried away," I said to Ranger.

"Understandable, Babe."

"He's got my jacket."

"Bones will get it when he gets the car. You need a ride home?"

"I can call Lula."

"YOU SHOULD HAVE taken me with you," Lula said. "This wouldn't have happened if you hadn't hauled your skinny ass off on your own."

"It seemed like such an easy job. Pick up a kid and drive him somewhere."

"Look at this," Lula said, "we're passing by the mall. I bet some shopping would cheer you right up."

"I *do* need shoes."

"See," Lula said, "there's a reason for everything. God meant for you to shop tonight."

We entered the mall through Macy's and blasted into the shoe department first thing.

"Hold on here!" Lula said. "Look at these shoes!" She'd pulled a pair of black satin shoes off the display. They had pointy toes and four-inch heels and a slim ankle strap. "These are hot shoes," Lula said.

I had to agree. The shoes were hot. I got my size from the salesperson and tried the shoes on.

"Those shoes are *you*," Lula said. "You gotta get those shoes. We'll take these shoes," Lula said to the salesclerk. "Wrap 'em up."

Ten minutes later, Lula was pulling dresses off the rack. "*Yow!*" Lula said. "Hold the phone. Here it is."

The dress she was holding was barely there. It was a shimmery black scrap of miracle fiber with a low-cut neck and a short skirt.

"This is a genuine hard-on dress," Lula said.

I suspected she was right. I looked at the price tag and sucked in some air. "I can't afford this!"

"You gotta at least try it on," Lula said. "Maybe it won't fit so good, and then you'll feel better about not being able to buy it."

It seemed like sound reasoning, so I dragged myself off to the dressing room. I did a fast computation of money left on my credit card and winced. If I caught Randy Briggs and I ate all my meals for the next month at my mother's house and I did my own nails for the wedding, I could *almost* afford the dress.

"Damn skippy," Lula said when I tottered out of the dressing room in the black shoes and black dress. "Holy shit."

I checked myself out in the mirror. It was definitely a "damn skippy, holy shit" outfit. And if I could lose five pounds in the next two days, the dress would fit.

"Okay," I said. "I'll take it."

"We need some french fries to celebrate with," Lula said after I bought the dress. "My treat."

"I can't have french fries. Another ounce and I won't get into the dress."

"French fries are a vegetable," Lula said. "They don't count when it comes to fat. And besides, we'll have to walk all the way down the mall to get to the food court, so we'll get exercise. In fact, probably we'll be so weak from all that walking by the time we get there we'll have to have a piece of crispy fried chicken along with the french fries."

It was dark when we left the mall. I had the button open on my skirt to accommodate the fried chicken and french fries, and I was having a panic attack over my new clothes.

"Look at this," Lula said, sidling up to her Firebird. "Somebody left us a note. It better not be that someone put a ding in my car. I hate when that happens."

I looked over her shoulder to read the note.

"I saw you in the mall," the note said. "You shouldn't tempt men by wearing dresses like that."

"Guess this is for you," Lula said. "On account of I wasn't wearing no dress."

I did a quick scan of the lot. "Unlock the car and let's get out of here," I said to Lula.

"It's just some pervert note," Lula said.

"Yeah, but it was written by someone who knew where our car was parked."

"Could have been someone who saw us when we first got here. Some little runt waiting for his wife to come out of Macy's."

"Or it could have been written by someone who tailed me out of Trenton." And I didn't think that someone was Bunchy. I'd been alert for Bunchy's car. And besides, I was pretty sure Bunchy would watch Mabel, like I asked.

Lula and I looked at each other and shared the same thought . . . Ramirez. We quickly jumped into the Firebird and locked the doors.

"Probably it wasn't him," Lula said. "You would have seen him, don't you think?"

MY NEIGHBORHOOD IS quiet after dark. All the seniors are tucked away in their apartments by then, settled in for the night, watching reruns of *Seinfeld* and *Cop Bloopers*.

Lula dropped me off at the back door to my building at a little after nine, and true to form, not a creature was stirring. We looked for headlights and listened for footfalls and car engines and came up empty.

"I'll wait until you get in the building," Lula said.

"I'll be fine."

"Sure. I know that."

I took the stairs, hoping they'd help out with the chicken and fries. When I'm scared, it's always a toss-up between the elevator and the stairs. I feel more in control on the stairs, but the stairwell feels isolating, and I know when the fire doors are closed, sound doesn't carry. I had a sense of relief when I reached my floor and there was no Ramirez.

I let myself into my apartment and called hello to Rex. I dropped my shopping bags on the kitchen counter, kicked my shoes off, and stripped out of the pantyhose. I did a fast room-by-room check, and no large men turned up there, either. Whew. I returned to the kitchen to listen to my phone messages and shrieked when someone knocked at my door. I squinted out the peephole with my hand over my heart.

Ranger.

"You never knock," I said, opening the door.

"I always knock. You never answer." He handed me my jacket. "The little sheik said you weren't any fun."

"Scratch chauffeuring off the list."

Ranger studied me for a moment. "Do you want me to shoot him?"

"No!" But it was a tempting idea.

He glanced down at the shoes and pantyhose on the floor. "Am I interrupting something?"

"No. I just got home. Lula and I went shopping."

"Recreational therapy?"

"Yeah, but I also needed a new dress." I held the dress up for him to see. "Lula sort of talked me into this. What do you think?"

Ranger's eyes darkened and his mouth tightened into a small

smile. My face got warm and the dress slipped from my fingers and fell to the floor.

Ranger picked the dress up and handed it to me.

"Okay," I said, blowing a strand of hair off my forehead. "Guess I know what you think of the dress."

"If you knew, you wouldn't be standing here," Ranger said. "If you knew, you'd have yourself barricaded in the bedroom with your gun in your hand."

Gulp.

Ranger's attention strayed to the note on the counter. "Someone else shares my opinion of the dress."

"The note was left on the windshield of Lula's Firebird. We found it when we came out of the mall."

"You know who wrote it?"

"I have a couple ideas."

"You want to share them with me?"

"Could just be some guy who saw me at the mall."

"Or?"

"Or it could be Ramirez."

"You have reason to think it's Ramirez?"

"Touching it makes my skin crawl."

SIX

"WORD ON THE street is that Ramirez got religion," Ranger said, relaxed against my kitchen counter, arms crossed over his chest.

"So maybe he doesn't want to rape and mutilate me. Maybe he just wants to save me."

"Either way, you should carry a gun."

When Ranger left I listened to the single message on my phone machine. "Stephanie? This is your mother. Remember you promised to take your grandmother to the funeral parlor tomorrow night. And you can come early and have something to eat with us. I'm going to have a nice leg of lamb."

The lamb sounded good, but I would have preferred the message to have been about Fred. Like, guess what, the funniest thing just happened . . . Fred showed up.

There was another knock on the door, and I looked out the peephole at Bunchy.

"I know you're lookin' out at me," he said. "And I know you're thinking you should go get your gun and your pepper spray and your electronic torture device, so just go get them all because I'm getting tired of standing here."

I opened the door a bit, leaving the security chain in place.

"Give me a break," Bunchy said.

"What do you want?"

"How come the Rambo guy gets in and I don't?"

"I work with him."

"You work with me, too. I just did a surveillance shift for you."

"Anything happen?"

"I'm not telling you until you let me in."

"I don't need to know that bad."

"Yes, you do. You're nosy."

He was right. I was nosy. I slid the chain off and opened the door.

"So what happened?" I asked.

"Nothing happened. The grass grew an eighth of an inch." He got a beer out of the refrigerator. "You know, your aunt is a real boozer. You should get her into AA or something." He noticed the dress on the counter. "Wowy kazowy," he said. "This your dress?"

"I got it to wear to a wedding."

"You need a date? I don't look so bad when I get cleaned up."

"I have a date. I've been sort of seeing this guy—"

"Yeah? What guy?"

"His name's Morelli. Joe Morelli."

"Oh, man, I know him. I can't believe you're going with Morelli. The guy is a loser. Excuse me for saying so, but he porks everyone he meets. You shouldn't have anything to do with him. You could do better."

"How do you know Morelli?"

"We have a professional relationship, being that he's a cop and I'm a bookie."

"I asked him about you, and he said he never heard of you."

Bunchy tipped his head back and laughed. It was the first time I'd ever heard him laugh, and it wasn't bad.

"He might know me by one of my other names," Bunchy said. "Or maybe he just doesn't want to come clean because he knows I might spill the beans about him."

"What would these other names be?"

"They're secret names," he said. "If I told you, then they wouldn't be secret anymore."

"Out!" I said, pointing stiff-armed to the door.

MORELLI CALLED AT nine the next morning. "Just wanted to remind you the wedding is tomorrow," he said. "I'll pick you up at four. And don't forget you have to come in to make a report on the Sloane Street shooting."

"Sure."

"You get any leads on Fred?"

"No. Nothing worth mentioning. Good thing I don't do this for a living."

"Good thing," Morelli said, sounding like he was smiling.

I hung up, and I called my friend Larry at RGC.

"Guess what, Larry?" I said. "I found the check. It was on my uncle's desk. Payment for three months' worth of garbage pickup. And the check has been canceled and everything."

"Fine," Larry said. "Bring the check in, and I'll credit the account."

"How late are you open?"

"Five."

"I'll be there before you close."

I shoveled my gear into my shoulder bag, locked my apartment behind me, and took the stairs to the lobby. I exited the building and crossed the lot to my car. I had the key in hand, ready to unlock my door, when I felt the presence of someone behind me. I turned and found myself toe-to-toe with Benito Ramirez.

"Hello, Stephanie," he said. "Nice to see you again. The champ missed you while he was away. He thought about you a lot."

The champ. Better known as Benito Ramirez, who was too crazy to talk about himself in the first person.

"What do you want?"

He smiled his sick smile. "You know what the champ wants."

"How about you tell me."

"He wants to be your friend. He wants to help you find Jesus."

"If you continue to stalk me, I'll get a restraining order."

The smile stayed on his mouth, but his eyes were cold and hard. Steel orbs floating in empty space. "Can't restrain a man of God, Stephanie."

"Move away from my car."

"Where are you going?" Ramirez asked. "Why don't you go with the champ? The champ'll take you for a ride." He stroked my cheek with the back of his hand. "He'll take you to see Jesus."

I dug down in my shoulder bag and pulled out my gun. "Get away from me."

Ramirez laughed softly and took a step backward. "When it's your time to see God, there'll be no escape."

I unlocked the driver's side door, slid behind the wheel, and drove away with Ramirez still standing in the lot. I stopped for a light two blocks down Hamilton and realized there were tears on my cheeks. Shit. I swiped the tears away and yelled at myself. "You are *not* afraid of Benito Ramirez!"

That was a stupid, empty statement, of course. Ramirez was a monster. Anyone with a grain of sense would be afraid of him. And I was beyond afraid. I was terrified to tears.

BY THE TIME I reached the office I was in pretty decent condition. My hands had stopped shaking, and my nose wasn't running. I still had some nausea, but I didn't think I'd throw up. It seemed like a weakness to be so frightened, and I wasn't crazy about the feeling. Especially since I'd chosen to work in a form of law enforcement. Hard to be effective when you're blubbering in fear. My one point of pride was that I hadn't shown my fear to Ramirez.

Connie stroked vermilion nail polish onto her thumbnail. "You calling the hospitals and the morgue about Fred?"

I placed the check facedown on the copier, closed the lid, and pushed the button. "Every morning."

"What's next?" Lula wanted to know.

"I got a picture of Fred from Mabel. I thought I'd flash it around the strip mall and maybe go door-to-door on the streets behind Grand Union." Hard to believe there wasn't someone out there who saw Fred leave the parking lot.

"Don't sound like a lot of fun to me," Lula said.

I took the copy of the check and dropped it into my shoulder bag. Then I made a folder with Fred's name on it, dropped the original check into the folder, and filed it in the office file cabinet under Shutz. It would have been easier to put it in my desk . . . but I didn't have a desk.

"How about Randy Briggs?" Lula said. "Aren't we gonna visit him today?"

Short of burning the building down, I didn't know how to get Randy Briggs out of his apartment.

Vinnie stuck his head out of his office. "I hear somebody say something about Briggs?"

"Not me. I didn't say nothing," Lula said.

"You have one chickenshit case," Vinnie said to me. "Why haven't you brought this guy in?"

"I'm working on it."

"Yeah, and it's not her fault," Lula said, "on account of he's wily."

"You have until eight o'clock Monday morning," Vinnie said. "Briggs' ass isn't in the slammer by Monday morning, I'm giving the case to somebody else."

"Vinnie, you know a bookie named Bunchy?"

"No. And trust me, I know every bookie on the East Coast." He pulled his head back into his office and slammed the door shut.

"Tear gas," Lula said. "That's the way to get him. We just lob a can of tear gas through his dumb-ass window and then wait for him to come running out, gagging and choking. I know where we can get some, too. I bet we could get some from Ranger."

"No! No tear gas," I said.

"Well, what are you gonna do? You gonna let Vinnie give this to Joyce Barnhardt?"

Joyce Barnhardt! Shit. I'd eat dirt before I'd let Joyce Barnhardt bring in Randy Briggs. Joyce Barnhardt is a mutant human being and my arch enemy. Vinnie hired her on as a part-time bounty hunter a couple months ago in exchange for services I didn't want to think about. She'd tried to steal one of my cases back then, and I had no intention of letting that happen again.

I went to school with Joyce, and all through school she'd lied and snitched and was loosey-goosey with other girls' boyfriends. Not to mention, I'd been married for less than a year when I'd caught Joyce woman-superior on my dining room table with my sweating, cheating ex-husband.

"I'm going to reason with Briggs," I said.

"Oh boy," Lula said. "This is gonna be good. I gotta see this."

"No. I'm going alone. I can do this by myself."

"Sure," Lula said. "I know that. Only it'd be more fun if I was there."

"No! No, no, no."

"Boy, you sure do got an attitude these days," Lula said. "You were better when you were getting some, you know what I mean? I don't know why you gave Morelli the boot anyway. I don't usually like cops, but that man has one fine ass."

I knew what she meant about my attitude. I was feeling damn cranky. I hitched my bag onto my shoulder. "I'll call if I need help."

"Unh," Lula said.

THINGS WERE QUIET at Cloverleaf Apartments. No traffic in the lot. No traffic in the dingy foyer. I took the stairs and knocked on Briggs' door. No answer. I moved out of sight and dialed his number on my cell phone.

"Hello," Briggs said.

"It's Stephanie. *Don't hang up!* I have to talk to you."

"There's nothing to talk about. And I'm busy. I have work to do."

"Look, I know this court thing is inconvenient for you. And I know it's unfair because you were unjustly charged. But it's something you have to do."

"No."

"Then do it for me."

"Why should I do it for you?"

"I'm a nice person. And I'm just trying to do my job. And I need the money to pay for a pair of shoes I just bought. And even more, if I don't bring you in, Vinnie is going to give your case to Joyce Barnhardt. And I hate Joyce Barnhardt."

"Why do you hate Joyce Barnhardt?"

"I caught her screwing my husband, who is now my ex-husband, on my dining-room table. Can you imagine? My dining-room table."

"Jeez," Briggs said. "And she's a bounty hunter, too?"

"Well, she used to do makeovers at Macy's, but now she's working for Vinnie."

"Bummer."

"Yeah. So, how about it? Won't you let me bring you in? It won't be so bad. Honest."

"Are you kidding? I'm not letting a loser like you bring me in. How would it look?"

Click. He hung up.

Loser? Excuse me? Loser? Okay, that does it. No more Ms. Nice Person. No more reasoning. This jerk is going down. *"Open this door!"* I yelled. *"Open this goddamn door!"*

A woman popped her head out from the apartment across the hall. "If you don't stop this racket I'm going to call the police. We don't put up with this kind of goings-on here."

I turned and looked at her.

"Oh, dear," she said and slammed her door shut.

I gave Briggs' door a couple kicks with my foot and hammered on it with my fists. "Are you coming out?"

"Loser," he said through the door. "You're just a stupid loser, and you can't make me do anything I don't want to do."

I hauled my gun out of my shoulder bag and fired one off at the lock. The round glanced off the metal and lodged in the door frame. Christ. Briggs was right. I was a fucking loser. I didn't even know how to shoot off a lock.

I ran downstairs to the Buick and got a tire iron out of the trunk. I ran back upstairs and started whacking away at the door with the tire iron. I made a couple dents but that was about it. Bashing the door in with the tire iron was going to take a while. My forehead was beaded with sweat, and sweat stained the front of my T-shirt. A small crowd of people had collected at the far end of the hall.

"You gotta get the tire iron between the door and the jamb," an old man at the end of the hall said. "You gotta wedge it in."

"Shut up, Harry," a woman said. "Anyone can see she's crazy. Don't encourage her."

"Only trying to be helpful," Harry said.

I followed his advice and wedged the iron between the door and the jamb and leaned into it. A chunk of wood splintered off the jamb and some metal stripping pulled away.

"See?" Harry said. "I told you."

I gouged some more chunks from the doorjamb down by the lock. I was trying to get the tire iron back in when Briggs opened the door a crack and looked out at me.

"What are you, nuts? You can't just destroy someone's door."

"Watch me," I said. I shoved the tire iron at Briggs and put my weight behind it. The security chain popped off its mooring, and the door flew open.

"Stay away from me!" he hollered. "I'm armed."

"What, are you kidding me? You're holding a fork."

"Yes, but it's a meat fork. And it's sharp. I could poke your eye out with this fork."

"Not on your best day, Shorty."

"I hate you," Briggs said. "You're ruining my life."

I could hear sirens in the distance. Swell. Just what I needed . . . the police. Maybe we could call in the fire department, too. And the dogcatcher. And hell, how about a couple newspaper reporters.

"You're not taking me in," Briggs said. "I'm not ready." He lunged at me with his fork. I jumped away, and the fork ripped a hole in my Levi's.

"Hey," I said, "these were almost new pants."

He came at me again, shouting, "I hate you. I hate you." This time I smacked the fork out of his hand, and he stumbled into an end table, knocking the table over, smashing a lamp in the process. "My lamp," he shrieked. "Look what you did to my lamp." He lowered his head and charged at me bull-style. I stepped to the side, and he crashed into a bookcase. Books tumbled out, and knick-knacks shattered on the polished wood floor.

"Stop it," I said. "You're wrecking your apartment. Get a grip on yourself."

"I'll get a grip on you," he snarled, lunging forward, catching me with a body tackle at knee level.

We both went down hard to the floor. I had him by about seventy pounds, but he was in a frenzy and I couldn't pin him. We rolled around, locked together, cursing and breathing heavy. He slithered away from me and ran for the door. I scrambled after him on hands and knees and grabbed him by the foot at the top of the stairs. He yelped and fell forward, and we both went head over heels tumbling down the stairs to the landing, where we tangled again. There was some scratching and hair grabbing and attempted eye-gouging. I had him by the front of his shirt when we lost balance and pitched down the second flight of stairs.

I flopped to a stop in the foyer, flat on my back, gasping for air. Briggs was squashed under me, dazed into inertia. I blinked my eyes to clear my head and two cops swam into focus. They were staring down at me, and they were smiling.

One of the cops was Carl Costanza. I'd gone to school with Carl and we'd stayed friends . . . in a remote sort of way.

"I heard you liked the top," Carl said, "but don't you think this is carrying it a little far?"

Briggs squirmed under my weight. "Get off me. I can't breathe."

"He doesn't deserve to breathe," I said. "He ripped my Levi's."

"Yeah," Carl said, lifting me off Briggs, "that's a capital offense."

I recognized the other cop as Costanza's partner. His name was Eddie Something. Everyone called him Big Dog.

"Jeez," Big Dog said, barely controlling laughter, "what did you do to this poor little guy? Looks like you beat the crap out of him."

Briggs was standing on wobbly legs. His shirt was untucked and he'd lost a shoe. His left eye was starting to bruise and swell, and his nose was bleeding.

"I didn't do anything!" I yelped. "I was trying to take him into custody and he went berserk."

"That's right," Harry said from the top of the landing. "I saw the whole thing. This runty little guy just about ruined himself. And this lady hardly put a hand to him. Except of course when they were wrestling."

Carl looked at the cuff still attached to Briggs' wrist. "Your bracelet?" he asked me.

I nodded.

"You're supposed to cuff both hands."

"Very funny."

"You got papers?"

"Upstairs in my shoulder bag."

We climbed the stairs while Big Dog baby-sat Briggs.

"Holy shit," Costanza said when he saw Briggs' door. "Did you do this?"

"He wouldn't let me in."

"Hey, Big Dog," Costanza yelled. "Lock the little guy in the car and come take a look. You gotta see this."

I gave Costanza the bond documents. "Maybe we could keep this all kind of quiet—"

"Holy shit," Big Dog said when he saw the door.

"Steph did that," Costanza told him proudly.

Big Dog clapped me on the shoulder. "I guess they don't call you the bounty hunter from hell for nothing."

"Everything seems to be in order," Costanza said to me. "Congratulations. You caught yourself a Munchkin."

Big Dog examined the doorjamb. "You know there's a slug in here?"

Costanza looked at me.

"Well, I didn't have a key—"

Costanza put his hands over his ears. "I don't want to hear this."

I limped into Briggs' apartment, found a set of keys on a hook in his kitchen, and used one to lock his door. Then I collected his shoe, which had been left on the landing, gave the shoe and the keys to Briggs, and told Carl I'd follow him in.

When I walked back to the Buick, Bunchy was waiting for me. "Cripes," he said. "You beat the bejeezus out of that little guy. Who the hell was he, the Son of Satan?"

"He's a computer operator who got picked up for carrying concealed. He really isn't such a bad guy."

"Man, I'd hate to see what you do to someone you don't like."

"How did you know where to find me? And why weren't you in my parking lot when I needed you?"

"I picked you up leaving the office. I overslept this morning, so I tried hitting your usual haunts and got lucky. What's new with Fred?"

"I haven't found him."

"You aren't giving up, are you?"

"No, I'm not giving up. Listen, I have to go. I have to get my body receipt."

"Don't drive too fast. There's something wrong with my transmission. It makes this real bad sound when I do over forty."

I watched him walk to his car. I was pretty sure I knew what he was, and he wasn't a bookie. I just didn't know why he was tagging after me.

COSTANZA AND BIG Dog brought Briggs through the back door to the docket lieutenant.

The docket lieutenant looked over his desk at Briggs. "Damn, Stephanie," he said, smiling, "what'd you do to the poor little guy? What, are you on the rag today?"

Juniak was passing through. "You're lucky," he said to Briggs. "Usually she blows people up."

Briggs didn't look like he thought that was funny. "I've been framed," he said.

I got my body receipt for Briggs, and then I went upstairs to Crimes Against Persons and gave my report on the Sloane Street shooting. I called Vinnie and told him I brought Randy Briggs in, so America could rest easier tonight. Then I drove over to RGC with Bunchy close on my bumper.

It was a little after three when I got to Water Street. Clouds had rolled in late in the day, thick and low, the color and consistency of lard. I could feel them pressing on the roof of the Buick, slowing my progress, dulling down the firing of brainy synapses. I cruised on autopilot, my thoughts sliding from Uncle Fred to Joe Morelli to Charlie Chan. Life was good for Charlie Chan. He knew freaking everything.

Two blocks from RGC I snapped out of the stupor, realizing there was something going on in the street ahead. There were cops in front of RGC. Lots of them. The medical examiner's truck was there, too, and this was not a good sign. I parked half a block from RGC and walked the rest of the way, Bunchy trailing after me like a faithful dog. I looked for a familiar face in the crowd. No luck. A small knot of uniformed RGC employees huddled on the fringe. Probably had just come in with the trucks.

"What's going on?" I asked one of the men.

"Somebody got shot."

"Do you know who?"

"Lipinski."

The shock must have shown on my face, because the man said, "Did you know him?"

I shook my head. "No. I was just coming to settle my aunt's bill. How did it happen?"

"Suicide. I was the one who found him," another of the men said. "I brought my truck in early, and I went inside to get my paycheck. And there he was with his brains blown out. He must have put the gun in his mouth. Christ, there was blood and brains all over the place. I wouldn't have thought Lipinski had that much brains."

"Are you sure it was suicide?"

"There was a note, and I read it. Lipinski said he was the one who offed Martha Deeter. Said they'd had a fight over an account, and he shot her. And then he tried to make it look like she was robbed. Said he couldn't live with what he'd done, so he was checkin' out."

Oh boy.

"That's horseshit," Bunchy said. "That smells like a load of horseshit."

I hung around for a while longer. The forensic photographer left. And most of the police left. The RGC men left one by one. And then I left, too, with Bunchy in tow. He'd gotten quiet after his horseshit pronouncement. And very serious.

"Two RGC employees are dead," I said to him. "Why?"

We locked eyes for a moment, and he shook his head and walked away.

I TOOK A fast shower, dried my hair, and dressed in a short denim skirt and red T-shirt. I took a look at my hair and decided it needed some help, so I did the hot roller thing. My hair still didn't look wonderful after the rollers, so I lined my eyes and added extra mascara. Stephanie Plum, master of diversion. If your hair is bad, shorten your skirt and add extra mascara.

Before I left the apartment, I took a minute to go through the Yellow Pages and find a new garbage company for Mabel.

Bunchy was in the lobby when I came down. He was leaning against the wall, and he was still looking serious. Or maybe he just looked tired.

"You look nice," he said to me. "Real nice, but you wear too much makeup."

GRANDMA WAS AT the door when I arrived. "Did you hear about the garbage guy? Blew his brains out. Lavern Stankowski called and said her son, Joey, was working the EMS truck. And he said he never saw anything like it. Said there was brains all over the place. Said the whole back half of the guy's head was stuck to the wall in the garbage office."

Grandma slid her uppers around some. "Lavern said the deceased was being laid out at Stiva's. Imagine the job Stiva's going to have with that one. Probably use up two pounds of putty to fill all the holes. Remember Rita Gunt?"

Rita Gunt was ninety-two when she died. She'd lost a lot of weight in the later years of her life, and her family had asked Stiva to give her a more robust look for her last public appearance. I guess Stiva had done the best he could with what he had to work with, but Rita had gone into the ground looking like Mrs. Potato Head.

"If somebody was going to kill me I wouldn't want it to be with a bullet to the head," Grandma said.

My father was in the living room in his favorite chair. And from the corner of my eye I saw him peek around the edge of his newspaper.

"I want to get poisoned," Grandma said. "That way my hair wouldn't get messed."

"Hmm," my father said thoughtfully.

My mother came out from the kitchen. She smelled like roast lamb and red cabbage, and her face glowed from stove steam. "Any word about Fred?"

"Nothing new," I said.

"I think there's something funny going on with these garbage people," Grandma said. "Somebody's killing the garbage people, and I bet they killed Fred, too."

"Larry Lipinski left a suicide note," I told her.

"It could have been forged," Grandma said. "It could have been a fake to throw everybody off guard."

"I thought it was aliens that took Fred," my father said from behind his paper.

"That would account for a lot of things," Grandma said. "Nothing to say aliens didn't off the garbage people, too."

My mother shot my father a warning glance and went back to the kitchen. "Everyone come to the table before the lamb gets cold," she said. "And I don't want to hear any more talk about aliens and killing."

"It's the change," Grandma whispered to me. "Your mother's been snarfy ever since she started the change."

"I heard that," my mother said. "And I'm *not* snarfy."

"I keep telling her she should take them hormone pills," Grandma said. "I've been thinking about taking them myself. Mary Jo Klick started taking them, and she said there were parts to her that had got all shriveled, and after a week on them hormones she was all plumped up again." Grandma looked down at herself. "I wouldn't mind getting plumped up in some of them parts."

We all went to the table and took our places. Grace was said at Christmas and Easter. Since this wasn't either of those, my father shoveled food onto his plate and dug in, head down, concentrating on the task at hand.

"What do you think happened to Uncle Fred?" I asked, catching his attention between forkfuls of lamb and potato.

He looked up surprised. No one ever asked his opinion. "Mob," he said. "When someone disappears without a trace, it's the mob. They've got ways."

"Why would the mob want to kill Uncle Fred?"

"I don't know," my father said. "All I know is it sounds like the mob."

"We better hurry," Grandma said. "I don't want to be late for the viewing. I want to get a good seat right up front, and there'll probably be a crowd, being that the deceased was shot. You know how some people are nosy about that sort of thing."

There was silence at the table, no one daring to make a comment.

"Well, I guess I might be a little nosy," Grandma finally said.

When we were done I put some lamb and potatoes and vegetables in a disposable aluminum pie plate.

"What's that for?" Grandma wanted to know.

I added a plastic knife and fork. "Stray dog down by the Kerner's."

"He eat with a knife and fork?"

"Don't ask," I said.

SEVEN

STIVA'S FUNERAL HOME was in a big white house on Hamilton. There'd been a fire in the basement, and much of the house was newly rebuilt and refurnished. New green indoor-outdoor carpet on the front porch. New ivory medallion wallpaper throughout. New industrial-strength blue-green carpeting in the lobby and viewing rooms.

I parked the Blue Bomb in the lot and helped Grandma wobble inside on the black patent-leather pumps she always wore to evening viewings.

Constantine Stiva was in the middle of the lobby, directing traffic. Mrs. Balog in slumber room three. Stanley Krienski in slumber room two. And Martha Deeter, who was clearly going to be the big draw, was laid out in room one.

Not long ago I'd had a run-in with Constantine's son, Spiro. The result had been the aforementioned fire and the mysterious disappearance of Spiro. Fortunately, Con was the consummate undertaker, his demeanor always controlled, his smile sympathetic, his voice as smooth as vanilla custard. There was never any ugly mention of the unfortunate incident. After all, I was a potential customer. And with my line of work it might be sooner rather than later. Not to mention Grandma Mazur.

"And who are you visiting tonight?" he asked. "Ah yes, Ms. Deeter is resting in room one."

Resting. Unh.

"Let's get a move on," Grandma said, taking me by the hand and pulling me forward. "Looks like there's already a crowd collecting."

I scanned the faces. Some regulars like Myra Smulinski and Harriet Farver. Some other people who probably worked for RGC and most likely wanted to make sure Martha was really dead. A knot of people dressed in black, staying close to the casket—family members. I didn't see any representatives from Big Business. I was pretty sure my father was wrong about the mob doing in Uncle Fred and the garbage people. Still, it didn't hurt to keep my eyes open. I also didn't see any aliens.

"Will you look at this," Grandma said. "Closed casket. Isn't this a fine howdy-do. I get dressed up and come out to pay my respects, and I don't even get to see anything."

Martha Deeter was shot and autopsied. They'd taken her brain out to get weighed. After she was put back together she probably looked like Frankenstein. I was personally relieved to see a closed casket.

"I'm going to check out the flowers," Grandma said. "See who sent what."

I did another crowd scan and spotted Terry Gilman. *Hello!* Maybe my father was right. It was rumored that Terry Gilman worked for her uncle Vito Grizolli. Vito was a family man who ran a dry cleaning business that laundered a lot more than dirty clothes. What I heard from Connie, who was connected in a nonparticipating sort of way, was that Terry had started out in collections and was moving up the corporate ladder.

"Terry Gilman?" I said with more statement than question, extending my hand.

Terry was slim and blond and had dated Morelli all through high school. None of which endeared her to me. She was wearing an expensive gray silk suit and matching heels. Her manicure was to die for, and the gun she carried in a slim-line shoulder holster was discreetly hidden by the line of her jacket. Only someone who had worn a similar rig would notice Terry's.

"Stephanie Plum," Terry said, "nice to see you again. Were you friends with Martha?"

"No. I'm here with my grandma. She likes to come to scope out the caskets. How about you? Were you friends with Martha?"

"Business associates," Terry said.

That hung in the air for a moment.

"I hear you're working for your uncle Vito."

"Customer relations," Terry said.

Another silence.

I rocked back on my heels. "Funny how Martha and Larry died from gunshots one day apart."

"Tragic."

I lowered my voice and leaned a little closer. "That wasn't your job, was it? I mean, you weren't the one to, uh—"

"Whack them?" Terry said. "No. Sorry to disappoint you. It wasn't me. Anything else you want to know?"

"Well, yeah, actually my uncle Fred is missing."

"I didn't whack him either," Terry said.

"I didn't think so," I said, "but it never hurts to ask."

Terry glanced at her watch. "I've got to give my respects, and then I'm out of here. I have two more viewings tonight. One at Moser and one across town."

"Boy, sounds like Vito's business is booming."

Terry shrugged. "People die."

Uh-huh.

Her eyes focused on something beyond my shoulder, and her interest shifted. "Well, well," she said, "look who's here."

I turned to see who put the purr in Terry's voice and wasn't all that surprised. It was Morelli.

He draped a proprietary arm around my shoulders and smiled at Terry. "How's it going?"

"Can't complain," Terry said.

Morelli cut his eyes to the casket at the end of the room. "You know Martha?"

"Sure," Terry said. "We go way back."

Morelli smiled some more.

"I think I'll go find Grandma," I said.

Morelli tightened his hold on me. "Not yet. I need to talk to you." He nodded at Terry. "Will you excuse us?"

"I need to be moving on anyway," Terry said. She sent Joe a smoochy air kiss and went off in search of the Deeters.

Joe dragged me out to the lobby.

"That was *very* friendly back there," I said, trying hard not to narrow my eyes and grind my teeth.

"We have a lot in common," Morelli said. "We both work in vice."

"Hmm."

"You know, you're kind of cute when you're jealous."

"I'm *not* jealous."

"Liar."

Now my eyes were definitely narrowed, but I was secretly thinking it'd be nice if he'd kiss me. "Did you want to discuss something?"

"Yeah. I want to know what the hell went on today. Did you really beat the shit out of that poor little Briggs guy?"

"No! He fell down the stairs."

"Oh boy," Morelli said.

"He *did*!"

"Honey, I say that all the time, and it's never true."

"There were witnesses."

Morelli was trying to look serious, but I could see the grin twitching at the corners of his mouth. "Costanza said you tried to shoot the lock off, and when that didn't work you took an axe to the door."

"That's totally wrong . . . it was a tire iron."

"Christ," Morelli said. "Is it that time of the month?"

I pressed my lips together.

He tucked a clump of hair behind my ear and trailed a fingertip down my cheek.

"Guess I'll find out tomorrow."

"Oh?"

"A woman's always an easy mark at a wedding," Morelli said.

I thought about the tire iron. It'd be really satisfying to clonk Morelli on the head with it. "Is that why you invited me?"

Morelli grinned.

Yep. He definitely deserved to get smacked with the tire iron. Then after I smacked him I'd kiss him. Run my hand down his chest to his flat hard stomach to his nice hard . . .

Grandma materialized at my elbow. "How nice to see you," she said to Morelli. "Hope this means you're going to start paying attention to my granddaughter again. Things are pretty dull since you got cut out of the scene."

"She broke my heart," Morelli said.

Grandma shook her head. "She don't know much."

Morelli looked pleased.

"Well, I'm ready to go," Grandma said. "Nothing to see here. They've got the lid nailed down. Besides, there's a Jackie Chan movie coming on at nine o'clock, and I don't want to miss it. Eeeya!" she said, making a kung fu–type move. "You could come over to watch it with us," Grandma said to Morelli. "We've got some pie left from dessert, too."

"Sounds good," Morelli said, "but I'm going to have to take a rain check. I'm working tonight. I have to relieve someone on a stakeout."

BUNCHY WAS NOWHERE in sight when we came out of the funeral home. So maybe the way to get rid of him was to feed him. I dropped Grandma off and continued on to my apartment. I circled the parking lot once, looking between cars, making sure Ramirez wasn't waiting for me.

Rex was running on his wheel when I came in. He stopped and twitched his whiskers at me when I flicked the light on.

"Food!" I said to Rex, showing him the brown grocery bag that always accompanied me home from a dinner at my parents. "Lamb leftovers, mashed potatoes, vegetables, a jar of pickled beets, two bananas, a quarter pound sliced ham, half a loaf of bread, and apple pie." I broke off a chunk of pie and dropped it into Rex's food dish, and Rex almost fell off his wheel in excitement.

I would have liked a piece of pie, too, but I thought about the little black dress and had a banana instead. I was still hungry after the banana, so I made myself half a ham sandwich. After the sandwich I picked at the lamb. And finally I gave in and ate the pie. Tomorrow morning I'd get up first thing and go for a run. Maybe. No! Definitely! Okay, I knew how to do this. I'd call Ranger and see if he wanted to run with me. Then he'd be over here first thing tomorrow and make me go out and get some exercise.

"Yo," Ranger said, answering the phone. His voice was husky, and I realized it was late and I'd probably awakened him.

"It's Stephanie. I'm sorry to be calling so late."

He took a slow breath. "No problem. Last time you called me late at night you were naked and chained to your shower curtain rod. I hope this isn't going to be disappointing."

That had happened when we'd first started working together and I barely knew him. He'd broken into my apartment and released me with clinical efficiency. I suspected he'd act differently now. The thought of him coming upon me naked and chained *now* gave me a hot flash.

"Sorry," I said. "You only get one call like that in a lifetime. This call's about exercise. Um, I could use some."

"Now?"

"No! In the morning. I want to go running, and I'm looking for a partner."

"You're not looking for a partner," Ranger said. "You're looking for an enforcer. You hate to run. You must be worried about getting into that black dress. What did you eat just now? Piece of cake? Candy bar?"

"Everything," I said. "I just ate everything."

"You need some self-control, Babe."

Boy, that was the truth. "Are you going to run with me, or what?"

"Only if you're serious about getting into shape."

"I am."

"You're a terrible liar," Ranger said. "But since I don't want to have some fat chick working for me, I'll be there at six."

"I'm not a chick," I yelled. But he'd already hung up.

Damn.

I SET THE alarm for five-thirty, but was awake at five and dressed by five-fifteen. I wasn't all that enthusiastic about running anymore. And I didn't especially care about being on time as a courtesy to Ranger. My fear was that I'd oversleep, and when Ranger broke into my apartment to wake me up, I'd drag him into bed with me.

And then what would I tell Joe? We sort of had an agreement. Except neither of us knew exactly what the agreement meant. In fact, now that I thought about it, maybe we didn't have an agreement at all. Actually, it was more like we were in agreement negotiations.

Besides, I wasn't going to do anything with Ranger because getting involved with Ranger would be the equivalent to sky diving without a parachute. I was temporarily oversexed, but I wasn't any more stupid than usual.

I had a ham sandwich and the rest of the pie for breakfast. I did some stretches. I tweezed my eyebrows. I changed from shorts to sweats. And at six o'clock I was in the lobby, watching Ranger pull into the lot.

"Man," he said, "you must be serious about running. I didn't expect you to actually be *up* at this hour. Last time we ran I had to drag you out of bed."

I was wearing sweats, and I was freezing my butt off, wondering where the hell the sun was. Ranger was wearing a T-shirt with the sleeves cut out, and he didn't look cold at all. He did a couple hamstring stretches, a couple neck rolls, and began jogging in place.

"You ready?" Ranger asked.

A mile later I pulled up and bent at the waist, trying to suck in some air. My shirt was soaked in sweat and my hair was plastered to my head. "Hold it a minute," I said. "I have to throw up. Boy, I'm really out of shape." And maybe I shouldn't have had the ham and pie.

"You aren't going to throw up," Ranger said. "Keep going."

"I can't keep going."

"Do another quarter mile."

I shoved off behind him. "Boy, I'm really out of shape," I said again. Guess running once every three months wasn't enough for maximum fitness.

"Two more minutes," Ranger said. "You can make it."

"I really think I'm going to throw up."

"You're *not* going to throw up," Ranger said. "One more minute."

The sweat was dripping off my chin and running into my eyes, blurring my vision. I wanted to wipe it away, but I couldn't lift my arm that high. "We there yet?"

"Yes. Mile and a quarter," Ranger said. "See, I knew you could do it."

I was unable to speak, so I nodded my head.

Ranger was jogging in place. "Want to keep moving," he said. "You ready to go?"

I bent over and threw up.

"That's not gonna save you," Ranger said.

I gave him a stiff middle finger.

"Shit," Ranger said, looking down at the mess I'd made on the ground. "What's that pink stuff?"

"Ham sandwich."

"Maybe you want to just shoot yourself in the head."

"I like ham."

He jogged a few feet in front of me. "Come on. We'll do another mile."

"I just threw up!"

"Yeah, so?"

"So I'm not running anymore."

"No pain, no gain, Babe."

"I don't like pain," I said. "I'm going home. And I'm walking."

He pushed off. "I'll catch you on the way back."

Look on the bright side, I thought. At least I didn't have to worry about breakfast going straight to my thighs. And throwing up is so attractive that chances were real good I wouldn't have to worry about Ranger having a libido attack over me anytime in the near future.

I was walking one block from Hamilton, in a neighborhood of small single-family houses. Traffic was picking up on Hamilton, but one block over, where I walked, activity was centered in kitchens. Lights were on, coffee was brewing, cereal bowls were being set out. It was Saturday, but Trenton wasn't sleeping in. Kids had to be chauffeured to football and soccer. Laundry had to go to the cleaner. Cars needed washing. And the farmer's market was calling . . . fresh vegetables, eggs, baked goods, and sausages.

The sun was weak in a murky sky, and the air felt cold against my sweat-soaked clothes. I was three blocks from my apartment building, planning my day. Canvass the area around the strip mall, showing Uncle Fred's photo. Get home in time to pour myself into the little black dress. All the while keeping an eye out for Bunchy.

I heard a runner coming up behind me. Ranger, I thought, steeling myself not to get coerced into racing him home.

"Hello, Stephanie," the runner said.

My walking faltered. The runner was Ramirez. He was dressed in sweats and running shoes, but he wasn't sweating. And he wasn't breathing heavy. He was smiling, dancing around me on the balls of his feet, alternately shadowboxing and jogging in place.

"What do you want?" I asked.

"The champ wants to be your friend. The champ can show you things. He can take you places you've never been."

I was torn between wanting Ranger to show up and save me, and not wanting Ranger to see Ramirez at all. I suspected Ranger's solution to my stalking problem might be death. There was a good possibility that Ranger killed people on a regular basis. Only bad guys, of course, so who was I to criticize? Still, I didn't want him killing someone on my behalf. Not even if it was Ramirez. Although, if Ramirez died in his sleep or was accidentally run over by a truck, it wouldn't bother me too much.

"I'm not going anywhere with you, ever," I said. "And if you continue to harass me I'll take steps to make sure it stops."

"It's your destiny to go with the champ," Ramirez said. "You can't escape it. Your friend Lula went with me. Ask her how she liked it, Stephanie. Ask Lula what it's like to be with the champ."

I got a mental picture of Lula left naked and bloodied on my fire escape. Good thing I'd already thrown up because if there was anything in my stomach I'd be ralphing now.

I strode off, walking away from him. You don't debate with a madman. He pitty-patted after me for half a block, and then he laughed softly and called good-bye, and he was gone, jogging off toward Hamilton.

Ranger didn't reach me until I was at my parking lot. His skin was slick with sweat, and his breathing was labored. He'd been running hard, and he looked like he'd enjoyed it.

"Are you okay?" he asked. "Your face is white. I thought you'd have recovered by now."

"Think you're right about ham," I said.

"You want to try this again tomorrow?"

"I don't think I'm cut out to be this healthy."

"You still looking for work?"

I mentally cracked my knuckles. I needed money, but Ranger's jobs weren't turning out so good. "What is it this time?"

Ranger unlocked his car, reached inside, and retrieved a large yellow envelope. "I have a high-bond FTA floating around Trenton. I have someone watching his girlfriend's house and someone watching his apartment. The guy's mother lives in the Burg. I don't think it's worthwhile to put someone on the mother's house twenty-four hours, but you know a lot of people in the Burg, and I thought you might be able to find an informant." He handed the envelope over. "The guy's name is Alphonse Ruzick."

I knew the Ruzicks. They lived on the other side of the Burg, two doors down from Carmine's Bakery, across from the Catholic school. Sandy Polan lived on that block. I'd gone to school with Sandy. She was married to Robert Scarfo now, so I guess she was Sandy Scarfo, but I still thought of her as being Sandy Polan. She had three kids, and the last one looked a lot more like the next-door neighbor than like Robert Scarfo. I peeked inside the envelope. Photo of Alphonse Ruzick, apprehension authorization, bond agreement, and personal information sheet.

"Okay," I said. "I'll see if I can find someone to rat on Alphonse."

I pushed through the glass door to the lobby and did a fast sweep to make sure Ramirez wasn't lying in wait for me. I took the stairs and felt safe when I stepped onto my floor. There was the smell of bacon cooking behind Mrs. Karwatt's door. And the television was blaring in Mr. Wolesky's apartment. A normal morning. Business as usual. Aside from the fact that I'd barfed and been scared half to death by a psychopathic maniac.

I opened my door and found Bunchy on the couch, reading the paper.

"You've got to stop breaking into my apartment," I said. "It's rude."

"I feel conspicuous sitting out in the hall. I figure it doesn't look good for you to have men loitering. What'll people think?"

"Then loiter in your car, in the lot."

"I was cold."

Someone knocked on my door. I went to the door and peeked out. It was my neighbor from across the hall, Mr. Wolesky.

"Did you take my paper again?" he asked.

I got the paper from Bunchy and returned it to Mr. Wolesky.

"Out," I told Bunchy. "Good-bye."

"What are you doing today? Just so I know."

"I'm going to the office, and then I'm putting some posters up at the Grand Union."

"The office, huh? Maybe I'll pass on the office. But you can tell Lula there's gonna be payback for making me lose you the other day."

"You should be happy she didn't use her stun gun."

He stood at the couch with his hands in his pockets. "You want to tell me about the color copies on your table?"

Damn. I hadn't put the prints away. "They're nothing special."

"Body parts in a garbage bag?"

"Do you find them interesting?"

"I don't know who it is, if that's what you're getting at." He moved to the table. "Twenty-four pictures. The whole roll. Two with the bag tied up. That's got me thinking. And they're recent, too."

"How do you know that?"

"There are newspapers stuck in the bag along with the body. I looked at them with your magnifying glass, and you see this one here with the color? I'm pretty sure this is a supplement from Kmart advertising the Mega Monster. I know because my kid made me go get him one the second he saw the ad."

"You have a kid?"

"Why is that such a big shock? He lives with my ex-wife."

"When was the first time the ad ran?"

"I called and checked. It was a week ago Thursday."

The day before Fred disappeared.

"Where'd you get these pictures?" Bunchy asked.

"Fred's desk."

Bunchy shook his head. "Fred was involved in some very bad shit."

I locked and bolted the door after Bunchy left. I showered and dressed in Levi's and a black turtleneck. I tucked the turtleneck in and added a belt. I stuffed Uncle Fred's picture into my shoulder bag and took off to do my pseudo–private investigator thing.

My first stop was at the office to collect my pittance on Briggs.

Lula looked up from the filing when I walked in. "Girl, we've been waiting for you. We heard how you beat the crap out of that Briggs guy. Not that he didn't deserve it, but I think if you was gonna beat the crap out of someone, you could let me in on it. You know how bad I wanted to beat the crap out of that little wiener."

"Yeah," Connie said to me, "you've got some nerve hogging all the brutality."

"I didn't do anything," I said. "He fell down the stairs."

Vinnie opened his office door and stuck his head out. "Jesus Christ," he said. "How many times have I told you not to hit people in the face? You hit them in the body where it doesn't show. Kick them in the nuts. Sucker-punch them in the kidney."

"He fell down the stairs!" I said again.

"Yeah, but you pushed him, right?"

"No!"

"See, that's good," Vinnie said. "Lying is good. Stick with that story. I like it." He stepped back into his office and slammed the door shut.

I gave Connie the body receipt, and Connie wrote me a check.

"I'm off to find a witness," I said.

Lula had her purse in her hand. "I'll go with you. Just in case that Bunchy guy decides to follow you some more. I'll take care of his ass."

I smiled. This should be interesting.

WE STARTED AT the copy store on Route 33. I enlarged Fred's photo and reproduced it onto a hand-printed request for information about Fred's disappearance.

After the copy store, I cruised into the Grand Union lot and was disappointed not to see Bunchy waiting for us. I parked close to the store, and Lula and I took the posters inside.

"Hold on here," Lula said. "They got Coke on sale. This is a real good price for Coke. And they got some good-lookin' lunchmeat in the deli section. What time is it? Is it lunchtime? You mind if I do some food shopping?"

"Hey," I said to Lula, "don't let me slow you down." I tacked a poster onto the bulletin board in the front of the store. Then I took the original photo and started quizzing shoppers while Lula foraged in the bakery aisle.

"Have you seen this man?" I asked.

The reply would be no. Or sometimes, "Yeah, that's Fred Shutz. What a putz."

No one could remember seeing him on the day of the disappearance. And no one had seen him since. And no one especially cared that he was missing.

"How's it going?" Lula asked, wheeling a shopping cart past me, en route to the car.

"Slow. No takers."

"I'm gonna drop these bags off. And then I'm going to look in that little video store at the end."

"Knock yourself out," I said. I showed Fred's photo to a few more people and at noon I broke for lunch. I searched my pockets and the bottom of my bag and came up with enough money to buy a small bag of nutritious, already washed and ready-to-eat baby carrots. For the same amount of money I could also buy a giant Snickers bar. Boy, what a tough decision.

Lula returned from the video store just as I was licking the last of the chocolate off my fingers. "Look at this," Lula said. "They had *Boogie Nights* on sale. I don't care much about the movie. I just like to look at the ending once in a while."

"I'm going door-to-door with Fred's photo," I told her. "Want to help?"

"Sure, you just give me one of them posters, and I'll door-to-door the hell out of you."

We divided the neighborhood in half and decided to work until two o'clock. I was done early, scoring a big zero. One woman said she saw Fred go off with Harrison Ford, but I thought that was unlikely. And another woman said she'd seen a vision of Fred floating across her television screen. I didn't put a lot of stock in that, either.

Since I had some time to kill I went back to the Grand Union to buy pantyhose for the wedding. I stepped into the glass vestibule and noticed an elderly woman was staring at the Fred poster I'd tacked up on the community bulletin board. That's good, I thought. People read these things.

I bought the pantyhose, and as I was leaving I saw the woman was still standing in front of the poster. "Have you seen him?" I asked.

"Are you Stephanie Plum?"

"Yes."

"I thought I recognized you. I remember your picture from when you blew up that funeral home."

"Do you know Fred?"

"Sure, I know Fred. He's in my seniors club. Fred and Mabel. I didn't realize he was missing."

"When did you see him last?"

"I was trying to remember that. I was sitting on the bench outside Grand Union here, waiting for my nephew to come pick me up, on account of I don't drive anymore. And I saw Fred come out of the cleaners."

"That must have been Friday."

"That's what I think, too. I think it was Friday."

"What did Fred do when he came out of the cleaners?"

"He went to his car with the clothes. And it looked like he laid them out real careful on the backseat, although it was hard to tell from here."

"What happened next?"

"A car pulled up alongside Fred and a man got out, and him and Fred talked for a while. And then Fred got in the car with the man and they drove away. I'm pretty sure that's the last time I saw Fred. Except I can't be certain of the day. My nephew would know."

Holy shit. "Did you know the man Fred was talking to?"

"No. He wasn't familiar to me. But I got the feeling Fred knew him. They seemed friendly."

"What did he look like?"

"Goodness. I don't know. He was just a man. Ordinary."

"Caucasian?"

"Yes. And about the same height as Fred. And he was dressed in a suit."

"What color hair? Was his hair long or short?"

"It wasn't like I was paying attention to remember something," she said. "I was just passing time until Carl got here. I suppose his hair was short and maybe brown. I can't actually remember, but if it was unusual, it would have stuck in my mind."

"Would you know him if you saw him again? Would you recognize him from a picture?"

"I don't think I could say for sure. He was a ways away, you know, and I didn't see his face much."

"How about the car he was driving? Do you remember the color?"

She was silent for a moment, her eyes unfocused while she searched for a mental image of the car. "I just wasn't paying attention," she said. "I'm sorry. I can't recall the car. Except that it wasn't a truck or anything. It was a car."

"Did it look like they were arguing?"

"No. They were just talking. And then the man walked around the car and got behind the wheel. And Fred got in the passenger side. And they drove away."

I gave her my card in exchange for her name, address, and phone number. She said she didn't mind if I called to ask more

HIGH FIVE

questions. And she said she'd keep her eyes open and call me if she saw Fred.

I was so psyched I almost didn't see Lula standing two inches from me. "Wow!" I said, bumping into her.

"Earth to Stephanie," Lula said.

"How'd you do?" I asked her.

"Lousy. There's a bunch of dummies living here. Nobody knows nothing."

"I didn't have any luck back there, either," I said. "But I found someone in the store who saw Fred get into a car with another man."

"You shitting me?"

"Swear to God. The woman's name is Irene Tully."

"So who's the man? And where's ol' Fred?" Lula asked.

I didn't know the answers to those questions. Some of the wind went out of my sails when I realized not a whole lot had changed. I had a new puzzle piece, but I still didn't know if Fred was in Fort Lauderdale or the Camden landfill.

We'd been walking back to Lula's Firebird, and I'd been lost in thought. I looked at the Firebird and thought there was something strange about it. It hit me at the same time Lula started shrieking.

"My baby," Lula yelled. "My baby, my baby."

The Firebird was up on blocks. Someone had stolen all four wheels.

"This is just like Fred," she said. "What is this, the Bermuda Triangle?"

We got closer and looked in the car window. Lula's groceries were stuffed onto the front seat, and two of the wheels were in the back. Lula popped the trunk and found her other two wheels.

"What the hell?" she said.

An old brown Dodge rolled to a stop beside us. Bunchy.

Okay, who do we know who can open doors without keys? Who has a score to settle with Lula? And who has returned to the scene of the crime?

"Not bad," I said to Bunchy. "Sort of a sadistic sense of humor . . . but not bad."

391

He smiled at my comment and eyed the car. "You ladies got a problem?"

"Someone took the wheels off my Firebird," Lula said, looking like she'd figured it out, too. "Don't suppose you know who could've done something like this."

"Vandals?"

"Vandals, my ass."

"I have to be getting along now," Bunchy said, smiling ear to ear. "Toodles."

Lula hauled a small cannon out of her shoulder bag and pointed it at Bunchy. "You slime-faced bag of monkey shit."

The smile was gone in a flash, and Bunchy laid rubber out of the lot.

"Good thing I got auto club," Lula said.

An hour later, I was back in my Buick. I was running short on time, but I wanted to talk to Mabel.

I almost zipped right past her house, because the '87 Pontiac station wagon wasn't parked at the curb. In its place was a new silver-gray Nissan Sentra.

"Where's the station wagon?" I asked Mabel when she answered the door.

"Traded it in," she said. "I never did like driving that big old boat." She looked at her new car and smiled. "What do you think? Isn't it zippy-looking?"

"Yeah," I said. "Zippy. I ran into someone today who said she might have seen Fred."

"Oh, dear," Mabel said. "Don't tell me you've found him."

I blinked twice because she hadn't sounded like that would be happy news. "No."

She put her hand to her heart. "Thank goodness. I don't mean to sound uncaring, but you know, I just bought the car, and Fred wouldn't understand about the car."

Okay, now we know where Fred stacks up against a Nissan Sentra. "Anyway, this woman said she might have seen Fred on the day he disappeared. She said she thought she saw Fred talking to a man in a suit. Do you have any idea who the man might be?"

"No. Do you?"

Question number two. "It's very important that I know every-thing Fred did the day before he disappeared."

"It was just like all the other days," Mabel said. "He didn't do anything in the morning. Puttered around the house. Then we ate lunch, and he went out to the store."

"Grand Union?"

"Yes. And he was only gone about an hour. We didn't need much. And then he worked in the yard, cleaning up the last of the leaves. That was all he did."

"Did he go out at night?"

"No . . . wait, yes, he went out with the leaves. If you have too many bags of leaves, you have to pay extra to the garbage company. So whenever Fred had more than his allotted number of bags, he'd wait until it was dark, and then he'd drive one or two bags to Giovichinni's. He said it was the least Giovichinni could do for him being that he always overcharged on his meat."

"When did Fred leave the house Friday morning?"

"Early. Around eight, I guess. When he came home he was complaining because he had to wait for RGC to open."

"And when did he come back to the house?"

"I don't remember exactly. Maybe around eleven. He was home for lunch."

"That's a long time just to go to RGC to complain about a bill."

Mabel looked thoughtful. "I didn't really pay much attention, but I guess you're right."

He didn't go to Winnie's because he was there in the afternoon.

While I was in the neighborhood I cruised over to the Ruzicks'. The bakery was on the corner, and the rest of the houses on the street were duplexes. The Ruzick house was yellow brick with a yellow-brick stoop in front and a front yard that was three feet deep. Mrs. Ruzick kept her windows clean and her porch swept.

There were no cars in front of the house. The backyard was long and narrow, leading to an alley that was one lane wide. The duplexes were divided by double driveways, at the end of which sat single-car garages.

I toyed with the idea of talking to Mrs. Ruzick, but gave it up. She had a reputation for being outspoken and had always been fiercely protective of her two worthless sons. I went to Sandy Polan instead.

"Wow, Stephanie!" Sandy said when she opened the door. "I haven't seen you in a long time. What's up?"

"I need a snitch."

"Let me guess. You're looking for Alphonse Ruzick."

"Have you seen him?"

"No, but he'll be around. He always comes to eat Saturday dinner with Mama. He is *such* a loser."

"Would you mind doing lookout for me? I'd do it myself, but I have to go to a wedding this afternoon."

"Oh my God. You're going to Julie Morelli's wedding! It's true about you and Joe."

"What about me and Joe?"

"I heard you were living with him."

"I had a fire in my apartment, and I rented a room from him for a short time."

Sandy's face scrunched up in disappointment. "You mean you weren't sleeping with him?"

"Well, yeah, I guess I was sleeping with him."

"Oh my God. I knew it! I just knew it! What's he like? Is he excellent? Is he . . . you know, big? He doesn't have a little twinkie, does he? Oh, God, don't tell me if he has a little twinkie."

I looked at my watch. "Gee, look at the time. I have to be going—"

"Oh, you've got to tell me or I'll die!" Sandy said. "I had *such* a crush on him in high school. *Everyone* did. If you tell me, I swear I won't tell another soul."

"Okay, it's not a little twinkie."

Sandy looked at me expectantly.

"That's it," I said.

"Did he tie you up? He always looked like the kind of guy who liked to tie women up."

"No! He didn't tie me up!" I gave her my card. "Listen, if you see Alphonse, give me a call. Try my cell phone number first, and if that doesn't work, try my pager."

EIGHT

I WAS SUPER late when I barreled through the back door to my apartment building. I quickly crossed to the bank of mailboxes on the far side of the lobby, spun the dial on my box, and grabbed my mail. A phone bill, a wad of junk mail, and an envelope from RangeMan Enterprises. My curiosity was stronger than my desire to be punctual, so I tore the RangeMan envelope open on the spot. RangeMan Enterprises is Ricardo Carlos Manoso. Better known as Ranger. Incorporated as RangeMan.

It was a payroll check issued by Ranger's accountant, paying me for the two jobs I screwed up. I had a moment of guilt, but brushed it aside. I didn't have time to feel guilty right now.

I rushed upstairs, hurled myself into the shower, and was out in record time. I went for the big soft curly look to my hair, natural frosted polish on my nails, and an extra sweep of mascara on my lashes. I tugged the little black dress into place, checked myself out in the mirror, and thought I looked pretty darn good.

I transferred a few things to a small black beaded purse, hooked a pair of long, dangly rhinestone earrings into my ears, and slipped my faux-diamond cocktail ring onto my ring finger.

My apartment is on the parking-lot side of the building, and my bedroom window opens to an old-fashioned fire escape. More modern buildings have balconies instead of fire escapes. Those buildings charge twenty-five dollars more a month than mine for rent, so I like my fire escape just fine.

The only problem with the fire escape is that people can climb up as well as down. Now that Ramirez was back on the street, I checked my bedroom window fourteen times a day to make sure it was locked. And when I left the apartment, not only was the window locked, but the curtain was pushed open, so I could immediately see upon entering the room if the window was broken.

I went to the kitchen to say good-bye to Rex. I gave him a green bean from my cache of leftovers and told him not to worry if I came home late. He watched me for a beat and then took the bean to his soup can. "Don't look at me like that," I said to Rex. "I'm *not* going to sleep with him."

I looked down at the black dress with the low scoop neck and slinky little skirt. Who was I kidding? Morelli wouldn't waste any time getting me out of this dress. We'd be lucky if we got to the wedding at all. Is that what I wanted? Shit. I didn't know what I wanted.

I ran back to the bedroom, kicked off the heels, and shimmied out of the black dress. I tried on a tan suit, a red knit dress, an apricot cocktail dress, and a gray silk suit. I ransacked my closet some more and came up with a tea-length rayon dress. It was a soft teal color with a small pink rose print and a skirt that was soft and swirly. It wasn't hot like the little black dress, but it was sexy in an understated romantic way. I changed my pantyhose, junked the earrings, dropped the dress over my head, shoved my feet into low-heeled shoes, and dumped the contents of the black purse into a small tan bag.

I had just buttoned the last button on the dress when the doorbell rang. I grabbed a sweater and hustled to get the door. I threw the door open and didn't see anyone.

"Down here."

It was Randy Briggs.

"Why aren't you in jail?"

"I made bail," he said. "Again. And thanks to you I don't have anyplace to live."

"You want to run that by me again?"

"You wrecked my door, and while I was in jail, thieves came in and ransacked my apartment. Stole everything and set fire to my couch. Now I don't have anyplace to live while they fix my apartment. And when your cousin wrote my bail he said I had to have an address. So here I am."

"Vinnie sent you here?"

"Yeah. Isn't that a kick in the ass? You want to help me with this stuff I've got?"

I stuck my head out the door. Briggs had a couple big suitcases propped against the wall.

"You are *not* living here," I told him. "You must be crazy to think for a single moment that I'd let you live here."

"Listen, Toots, I don't like it any more than you do. And believe me, I'll be out of here as soon as possible." He pushed past me, wheeling one of the suitcases. "Where's my bedroom?"

"You don't have a bedroom," I said. "This is a one-bedroom apartment. And that one bedroom is *mine*."

"Christ," he said, "when was the last time you got laid? You need to relax a little." He had the second suitcase by the handle.

"Halt!" I said, blocking the doorway. "You are *not* living here. You aren't even *visiting* here."

"This is what it says on my bond agreement. Call your rat-faced cousin and ask. You want to violate my bond agreement? You want to come after me again?"

I held my ground.

"It's only for a couple days. They have to put down a new rug and put in a new door. And in the meantime I have a job to do. Which, by the way, thanks to you again, I'm behind schedule."

"I don't have time to stand here and argue. I'm going out, and there's no way I'm leaving you alone in my apartment."

He put his head down and pushed past me. "Don't worry about it. I'm not interested in hocking your silverware. I just want a place

398

to work." He flopped the suitcase on its back, unzipped it, took out a laptop computer, and set it on my coffee table.

Shit.

I dialed Vinnie at home. "What's the deal with Briggs?" I asked.

"He needed a place to stay, and I thought if he stayed with you, you could keep an eye on him."

"Are you nuts?"

"It's only for a couple days until they get a door on his apartment. Which, for your information, I took a lot of grief over. You *destroyed* that door."

"I don't baby-sit FTAs."

"He's harmless. He's just a little guy. And besides, he threatened me with a civil liberties suit. And if he goes through with it, you're not gonna come out looking like roses. You beat the shit out of him."

"I didn't!"

"Look, I gotta go. Just humor him, will you?"

Vinnie disconnected.

Briggs was on the couch, booting up his computer. He was sort of cute with his little legs sticking out. Kind of like a big, cranky doll with a bashed-in face. He had a Band-Aid across his broken nose, and a beauty of a black eye. I didn't think he could win a lawsuit, but I didn't want to put it to the test.

"This comes at a bad time for me," I said to him. "I have a date."

"Yeah, I bet that's a big event in your life. And just between you and me, that dress is a dud."

"I like this dress. It's romantic."

"Men don't like romantic, Sis. Men like sexy. Short and tight. Something you can get your hand up real easy. And I'm not saying *I'm* like that . . . I'm just telling you about men."

I heard the elevator doors open down the hall. Morelli was here. I snatched my sweater and handbag and ran for the door. "Don't touch *anything*," I said. "When I get back I'm going to inspect this apartment, and it better be exactly the way I left it."

"I go to bed early, so be quiet if you get home late. Being that you're wearing that dress, I don't guess I have to worry about you spending the night with this guy."

I met Morelli in the hall. "Hmm," Morelli said when he saw me. "Pretty, but not what I'd expected."

I couldn't say the same for him. He was *exactly* what I'd expected. He was edible. California-cut charcoal silk gabardine suit, French-blue shirt, very cool tie. Black Italian loafers.

"What did you expect?" I asked.

"Higher heels, shorter skirt, more breast."

Damn that Briggs. "I had another outfit," I told him, "but I had to use my little black beaded purse with it, and it was too small to hold my cell phone and pager."

"This is a wedding," Morelli said. "You don't need a cell phone and pager."

"You have a pager clipped to your belt."

"It's this job I'm on. We're close to wrapping it up, and I don't want to miss the takedown. I'm working with a couple Treasury guys who make me look like a Boy Scout."

"Dirty?"

"Crazy."

"I got a break today with Uncle Fred. I found a woman who saw Fred talking to a man in a suit. And then they got in the man's car and drove away."

"You should call Arnie Mott and let him know what you've got," Morelli said. "You don't want to withhold information on a possible kidnapping and murder."

HOLY ASCENSION CHURCH had a small lot that was already filled. Morelli parked a block and a half from the church and blew out a sigh. "I don't know why I agreed to do this. I should have pulled duty."

"Weddings are fun."

"Weddings suck."

"What don't you like about weddings?"

"I have to talk to my relatives."

"Okay, I'll concede you that one. What else?"

"I haven't been to church in a year. The Monsignor's going to assign me to Hell."

"Maybe you'll see Fred there. I don't think he went to church, either."

"And I have to wear a suit and tie. I feel like my uncle Manny."

His uncle Manny was a construction expediter. Manny could expedite the completion of a building project by insuring that no unexplained fires would take place during the construction process.

"You don't look like your uncle Manny," I said. "You look very sexy." I felt the material in his trouser leg. "This is a beautiful suit."

His eyes softened. "Yeah?" His voice pitched low. "Why don't we skip the wedding. We could still go to the reception."

"The reception isn't for another hour. What would we do?"

He slid his arm along the back of my seat and twirled a curl around his finger.

"No!" I said, trying to get some conviction behind it.

"We could do it in the truck. We've never done it in the truck."

Morelli drove a four-wheel drive Toyota pickup. It was pretty nice, but it wasn't going to replace a queen-size bed. And besides, my hair would get mussed. Not to mention I was afraid Bunchy might be watching. "I don't think so," I said.

He brushed his lips across my ear and told me some of the things he wanted to do to me. A rush of heat fluttered through my stomach. Maybe I should reconsider, I thought. I liked all of those things. A lot.

A mile-long car pulled to the curb behind us.

"Damn," Morelli said. "It's my uncle Dominic and aunt Rosa."

"I didn't know you had an uncle Dominic."

"He's from New York State. And he's in retail," Morelli said, opening his door. "Don't ask him too many questions about the business."

Aunt Rosa was out of the car and running toward us. "Joey," she yelled. "Let me look at you. It's been so long. Look, Dominic, it's little Joey."

Dominic ambled up and nodded at Joe. "Long time."

Joe introduced me.

"I heard you had a girl," Rosa said, talking to Joe, beaming at me. "It's about time you settled down. Give your mother more grandchildren."

"One of these days," Joe said.

"You're not getting any younger. Pretty soon it'll be too late."

"It's never too late for a Morelli," Joe said.

Dominic made a move like he was going to smack Joe in the head. "Wise guy," he said. Then he smiled.

THERE ARE ONLY a few places big enough to handle an Italian wedding reception in the Burg. Julie Morelli held hers in the back room of Angio's. The room could hold two hundred and was reaching maximum capacity when Joe and I arrived.

"And when is *your* wedding?" Joe's Aunt Loretta wanted to know, smiling broadly, giving Joe the squinty eye. She shook her finger at him. "When are you going to make an honest woman out of this poor thing? Myra, come here," she called. "Joe's here with his girl."

"This is such a pretty dress," Myra said, examining my roses. "It's so nice to find a modest young woman."

Oh, great. I always wanted to be a modest young woman. "I need a drink," I said to Joe. "Something with cyanide."

I spied Terry Gilman across the room, and she wasn't modest at all. She was wearing a dress that was short and clingy, and shimmery gold. Leaving me to wonder where the gun was hidden. She turned and stared directly at Joe for a couple beats, then she blew him a kiss.

Joe acknowledged her with a noncommittal smile and a nod of

his head. If it had been more I'd have stabbed him with one of the butter knives.

"What's Terry doing here?" I asked Joe.

"Cousin to the groom."

A hush fell over the crowd. For a moment there was total silence, and then talking resumed, first with low murmurings and finally building to a roar.

"What was that silence all about?" I asked Joe.

"Grandma Bella's arrived. That was the sound of terror spreading through the room."

I looked to the entrance and sure enough, there she was . . . Joe's grandma Bella. She was a small woman with white hair and piercing hawklike eyes. She dressed in black and looked like she belonged in Sicily, herding goats, making the lives of her daughters'-in-law a living misery. Some people believed Bella had special powers . . . some thought she was wacko. Even the nonbelievers were reluctant to incur her wrath.

Bella scanned the room and picked me out. "You," she said, pointing a bony finger at me. "You, come here."

"Oh, shit!" I whispered to Joe. "Now what?"

"Just don't let her smell fear, and you'll be fine," Joe said, guiding me through the crowd, his hand at the small of my back.

"I remember this one," Bella said to Joe, referring to me. "This is the one you sleep with now."

"Well, actually . . ." I said.

Joe brushed a kiss across the nape of my neck. "I'm trying."

"I see babies," Bella said. "You will give me more great-grandchildren. I know these things. I have the eye." She patted my stomach. "You're ripe tonight. Tonight would be good."

I looked at Joe.

"Don't worry," he said. "I've got it covered. Besides, there's no such thing as the eye."

"Hah!" Bella said. "I gave Ray Barkolowski the eye, and all his teeth fell out."

Joe grinned down at his grandmother. "Ray Barkolowski had periodontal disease."

Bella shook her head. "Young people," she said. "They believe in nothing." She took my hand and dragged me after her. "Come. You should meet the family."

I looked back at Joe and mouthed "Help!"

"You're on your own," Joe said. "I need a drink. A big one."

"This is Joe's cousin, Louis," Grandma Bella said. "Louis fools around on his wife."

Louis looked like a thirty-year-old loaf of fresh raised white bread. Soft and plump. Scarfing down appetizers. He stood next to a small olive-skinned woman, and from the look she gave him, I assumed they were married.

"Grandma Bella," he said, croaky-voiced, his cheeks mottled in red, mouth stuffed with crab balls. "I would never—"

"Silence," she said. "I know these things. You can't lie to me. I'll put the eye on you."

Louis sucked in some crab and clutched his throat. His face got red, then purple. He flailed his arms.

"He's choking!" I said.

Grandma Bella tapped her finger to her eye and smiled like the wicked witch in *The Wizard of Oz*.

I gave Louis a good hard *thwack* between his shoulder blades, and the crab ball flew out of his mouth.

Grandma Bella leaned close to Louis. "You cheat again, and next time I'll kill you," she said.

She moved off toward a group of women. "One thing you learn about Morelli men," she said to me. "You don't let them get away with a thing."

Joe nudged me from behind and put a drink in my hand. "How's it going?"

"Pretty good. Grandma Bella put the eye on Louis." I took a sip. "Champagne?"

"All out of cyanide," he said.

———

AT EIGHT O'CLOCK the waitresses were clearing the plates off the tables, the band was playing, and all the Italian ladies were on the dance floor, dancing with one another. Kids were running between the tables, squealing and shrieking. The wedding party was at the bar. And the Morelli men were out back, smoking cigars and passing gas.

Morelli had forsaken the cigar ritual and was slouched back in his chair, studying the buttons on my dress. "We could go now," he said. "And no one would notice."

"Your grandma Bella would notice. She keeps looking over here. I think she might be getting ready to do the eye thing again."

"I'm her favorite grandson," Morelli said. "I'm safe from the eye."

"So your grandma Bella doesn't scare you?"

"You're the only one who scares me," Morelli said. "You want to dance?"

"You dance?"

"When I have to."

We were sitting close, with our knees touching. He leaned forward and took my hand and kissed the inside, and I felt my bones heat up and start to liquefy.

I heard the click of stiletto heels approaching and caught a flash of gold in my peripheral vision.

"Am I disturbing something?" Terry Gilman said, all glossy lipstick and carnivorous, perfect white teeth.

"Hello, Terry," Joe said. "What's going on?"

"Frankie Russo's taking the men's room apart. Something about his wife eating potato salad off Hector Santiago's fork."

"And you want me to talk to him?"

"Either that or shoot him. You're the only one with a legal piece. He's racking up a hell of a bill in there."

Morelli gave my hand another kiss. "Don't go anywhere."

They walked off together, and I had a moment of doubt that they might not be going to the men's room. That's dumb, I told myself. Joe isn't like that anymore.

Five minutes later he still hadn't returned, and I was having a hard time controlling my blood pressure. I was distracted by ringing, far off in the distance. I realized with a start that it wasn't far off at all—it was my cell phone, the ringing smothered in my purse.

It was Sandy. "He's here!" she said. "I was just walking the dog, and I looked in the Ruzicks' windows, and there he was, watching television. It was easy to see because the lights are all on, and Mrs. Ruzick never pulls her shades."

I thanked Sandy and dialed Ranger. No answer, so I left a message on his machine. I tried his car phone and cell phone. No answer at those numbers either. I called his pager and left my cell phone number. I tapped my finger on the table for five minutes while I waited for a call back. No call back. No Joe. Little wisps of smoke were starting to escape from my hairline.

The Ruzicks' house was three blocks away. I wanted to go over and keep my eye on things, but I didn't want to walk out on Joe. No problem, I told myself. Just go find him. He's in the men's room. Only he wasn't in the men's room. No one was in the men's room. I asked a few people if they knew where I could find Joe. Nope. No one knew where I could find Joe. Still no call from Ranger.

The steam was coming out my ears now. If this kept up I'd start whistling like a teakettle. Wouldn't that be embarrassing?

Okay, I'll leave him a note, I decided. I had a pen but no paper, so I wrote on a napkin. "Be right back," I wrote. "I have to check on an FTA for Ranger." I propped the napkin up against Joe's drink and left.

I power-walked the three blocks and pulled up across from the Ruzick house. Sure enough, Alphonse was there, big as life, watching television. I could see him crystal clear through the living room window. No one had ever accused Alphonse of being smart. You might say that about me too, because I'd remembered to take my purse, but I'd left my sweater and cell phone at Angio's. And now that I was standing still, I was freezing. No problem, I told myself. Go to Angio's, get your stuff, and come back.

It would have been a good plan, except at that moment Alphonse stood, scratched his belly, hiked up his pants, and walked out of the room. Damn. Now what?

I was across the street from the Ruzicks', crouched between two parked cars. I had good line of sight to the living room and front of the house, but all else was lost to me. I was contemplating this problem when I heard the back door open and close. Shit. He was leaving. He'd probably parked his car in the alley behind the house.

I ran across the street and hugged the shadows on the side of the house. Sure enough, I could see the hulking outline of Alphonse Ruzick making his way to the alley, carrying a bag. He was charged with armed robbery and assault with a deadly weapon. He was forty-six, and he weighed in at 230 pounds, with the bulk of his weight in his gut. He had a little pinhead and a brain to match. And he was getting away. Damn Ranger. Where the hell was he?

Alphonse was halfway down the yard when I yelled. I didn't have a weapon. I didn't have cuffs. I didn't have anything, but I yelled, anyway. It was all I could think to do.

"Stop!" I yelled. "Bail Enforcement Agent! Drop to the ground."

Alphonse didn't even turn to look. He just took off, cutting across yards, rather than going for the alley. He ran for all he was worth, handicapped by his lard butt and beer gut, hanging on to the bag in his right hand. Dogs barked, porch lights flashed, and back doors were thrown open all down the block.

"Call the police," I yelled, chasing after Alphonse, my skirt up around my neck. "Fire, fire. Help. Help."

We reached the end of the block, and I was within an arm's length when he whirled around and hit me with the bag. The impact burst the bag and knocked me off my feet. I was flat on my back, covered in garbage. Alphonse hadn't been leaving at all. He'd been taking the garbage out for his mother.

I scrambled to my feet and charged after Alphonse. He'd rounded the block and was running back to his mother's. He had half a house length on me when he pulled a set of keys from his pocket, pointed at a Ford Explorer parked at the curb, and I heard the alarm system chirp off.

"Stop!" I yelled. "You're under arrest! Stop or I'll shoot!"

It was a stupid thing to say because I didn't have a gun. And even if I had a gun I certainly wouldn't shoot him. Alphonse looked over his shoulder to check me out, and it was enough to uncoordinate the forward momentum of his blubber. The result was that he started to stumble, and I inadvertently plowed into his gelatinous body.

We both went down to the sidewalk, where I hung on for dear life. Alphonse was trying to get to his feet, and I was trying to keep him on the ground. I could hear sirens in the distance and people yelling and running toward us. And I was thinking I just had to wrestle around with him long enough for help to get to me. He was on his knees, and I had a fistful of his shirt in my hand, and he batted me away like I was a bug.

"Dumb cunt," he said, getting to his feet. "You haven't got a gun."

I get called lots of names. That's not one of my favorites. I latched onto his cuff and pulled his feet out from under him. He seemed suspended in air for a fraction of a second, and then he crash-landed with a loud *whump* that shook the ground and hit about 6.7 on the Richter scale.

"I'm gonna kill you," he said, sweating and panting, rolling on top of me, hands to my neck. "I'm gonna fuckin' kill you."

I squirmed under him and sunk my teeth into his shoulder.

"Yow!" he yelled. "Sonovabitch. What are you, a goddamn vampire?"

We rolled around for what seemed like hours, locked onto each other. Him trying to kill me, and me just hanging on like a tick on a dog's back, oblivious to my surroundings and the state of my skirt, afraid if I let go he'd beat me to death. I was exhausted, and I was thinking I was about at the end of the line when I was hit with a splash of ice-cold water.

We both instantly unlocked and flopped onto our backs, sputtering.

"What?" I said. "What?" I blinked my eyes and saw there were lots of people around us. Morelli and Ranger, a couple uniformed cops, and some people from the neighborhood. Plus Mrs. Ruzick was there, holding a big empty pot.

"Works every time," Mrs. Ruzick said. "Except usually I hose down cats. This neighborhood has too many cats."

Ranger grinned down at me. "Good bust, Tiger."

I got to my feet and took stock of myself. No broken bones. No bullet holes. No knife wounds. Ruined manicure. Soaking wet hair and dress. What looked like vegetable soup clinging to my skirt.

Morelli and Ranger were staring at my breasts and smiling at the wet dress that was plastered to my skin.

"So I have nipples," I snapped. "Get over it."

Morelli gave me his jacket. "What's with the vegetable soup on your skirt?"

"He hit me with a bag of garbage."

Morelli and Ranger were smiling again.

"Don't say anything," I told them. "And if you value your lives you'll stop grinning."

"Hey, man," Ranger said, grinning wider than ever. "I'm out of here. I've got to take Bluto for a ride."

"Show's over," Morelli said to the neighbors.

Sandy Polan was there. She gave Joe an appraising once-over, giggled, and left.

"What was that about?" Joe asked me.

I gave him a palms-up. "Go figure."

I traded his jacket for my sweater when we got to his truck. "Out of morbid curiosity, how long were you standing there watching me wrestle with Ruzick?"

"Not long. A minute or two."

"And Ranger?"

"The same."

"You could have jumped in and helped me."

"We were trying. We couldn't get hold of you the way you were tumbling around. Anyway, you looked like you were doing okay."

"How did you know where I was?"

"I talked to Ranger. He called your cell phone."

I looked down at my dress. It was probably wrecked. Good thing I hadn't worn the little black number.

"Where were you? I went to the men's room, and it was empty."

"Frankie needed some air." Morelli stopped for a light and glanced over at me. "Whatever possessed you to go after Alphonse like that? You were unarmed."

Charging after Alphonse wasn't what bothered me. Okay, so it hadn't been the bright thing to do. But it hadn't been as stupid as walking the streets, alone and unarmed, when Ramirez might have been stalking me.

Morelli parked the truck in the lot and walked me up to my apartment. He backed me against my door and kissed me lightly on the lips. "Do I get to come in?"

"I have coffee grounds in my hair." And Randy Briggs in my apartment.

"Yeah," Morelli said. "Makes you smell kind of homey."

"I don't know if I'm up to being romantic tonight."

"We don't have to be romantic," Morelli said. "We could just have some really dirty sex."

I rolled my eyes.

Morelli kissed me again. A good-night kiss this time. "Call me when you want some," he said.

"Some what?" As if I didn't know.

"Some anything."

I let myself into my apartment and tiptoed past Briggs, who was asleep on my couch.

SUNDAY MORNING I woke up to rain. It was coming down in a steady drone on my fire escape, spattering against my window. I opened the curtains and thought, ick. The world was gray. Beyond the parking lot, the world didn't exist at all. I looked at the bed. Very tempting. I could crawl into bed and stay there until the rain stopped, or the world came to an end, or until someone showed up with a bag of doughnuts.

Unfortunately, if I went back to bed I might lie there taking stock of my life. And my life had some problems. The project that was taking most of my time and mental energy wasn't going to get me lunch money. Not that it mattered, I was determined to find Fred, dead or alive. The projects Ranger gave me weren't working out. And the bounty hunter projects were a big goose egg. If I thought about my life long enough I might reach the conclusion I needed to go out and get a real job. Something that required pantyhose every day and a good attitude.

Even worse, I might get to thinking about Morelli, and that I was an idiot not to have invited him to spend the night. Or worse still, I might think about Ranger, and I didn't want to go there *at all!*

And then I remembered why I hadn't invited Morelli into my apartment. Briggs. I closed my eyes. Let it all be a bad dream.

Bam, bam, bam, on my door. "Hey!" Briggs yelled. "You haven't got any coffee. How am I supposed to work without coffee? Do you know what time it is, Sleeping Beauty? What, do you sleep all day? No wonder you can't afford any food in this hellhole."

I got up and got dressed and stomped out to the living room. "Listen, Shorty, who the hell do you think you are, anyway?"

"I'm the guy who's gonna sue your ass. That's who I am."

"Give me a little time, and I could really learn to hate you."

"Jeez, and just when I was thinking you were my soul mate."

I gave him my best eat-dirt-and-die look, zipped myself into my rain jacket, and grabbed my shoulder bag. "How do you like your coffee?"

"Black. Lots of it."

I sprinted through the rain to the Buick and drove to Giovichinni's. The front of the store was redbrick, sandwiched between other businesses. On either side of Giovichinni's the buildings were single story. Giovichinni's was two stories, but the second floor wasn't used for much. Storage and an office. I drove to the end of the block and took the service alley that ran behind the store. The back side of Giovichinni's was redbrick, just like the front. And the back door opened to a small yard. At the end of the yard was a dirt parking area for delivery trucks. Two doors down was a real estate office. The back wall was stuccoed over and painted beige. And the back door opened to a small asphalt parking lot.

So suppose cheapskate Fred drives his leaves to Giovichinni's in the dark of night. He parks the car and turns off his lights. Doesn't want to get caught. He unloads the leaves and hears a car coming. What would he do? Hide. Then maybe he's there hiding, and he sees someone come along and deposit a garbage bag behind the real estate office.

After that I was lost. I had to think about *after that* some more.

Next stop was the 7-Eleven and then home with a large coffee for me and a Big Gulp of coffee for Briggs and a box of chocolate-covered doughnuts . . . because if I had to put up with Briggs, I needed doughnuts.

I shucked my wet jacket and settled down at the dining room table with the coffee and doughnuts and a steno pad, doing my best to ignore the fact that I had a man typing away at my coffee table. I listed out all the things I knew about Fred's disappearance. No doubt now that the photographs played a large role. When I ran out of things to write in the steno pad, I locked myself in my bedroom and watched cartoons on television. This took me to lunchtime. I didn't feel like eating lamb leftovers, so I finished off the box of doughnuts.

"Cripes," Briggs said, "do you always eat like this? Don't you know about the major food groups? No wonder you have to wear those 'romantic' dresses."

I retreated to my bedroom, and while I was retreating I took a nap. I was startled awake by the phone ringing.

"Just wanted to make sure you were going to come take me to the Lipinski viewing tonight," Grandma said.

The Lipinski viewing. Ugh. Trekking out in the rain to see some dead guy wasn't high on my list of desirable things to do. "How about Harriet Schnable?" I suggested. "Maybe Harriet could take you."

"Harriet's car's on the fritz."

"Effie Reeder?"

"Effie died."

"Oh! I didn't know that."

"Almost everybody I know has died," Grandma said. "Bunch of wimps."

"Okay, I'll take you."

"Good. And your mother says you should come for dinner."

I BUZZED THROUGH the living room, but before I could get to the door Briggs was on his feet.

"Hey, where are you going?" he asked.

"Out."

"Out where?"

"My parents' house."

"I bet you're going there for dinner. Man, that's the pits. You're gonna leave me here with nothing to eat, and you're going to your parents' house for dinner."

"There's some cold lamb in the refrigerator."

"I ate that for lunch. Hold on, I'll go with you."

"No! You will *not* go with me."

"What, are you ashamed of me?"

"Yes!"

"WELL, WHO'S THIS little guy?" Grandma asked when I walked in with Briggs.

"This is my . . . friend, Randy."

"Aren't you something," Grandma said. "I never saw a midget up close."

"Little person," Briggs said. "And I never saw anyone as old as you up close, either."

I gave him a smack on the top of his head. "Behave yourself," I said.

"What happened to your face?" Grandma wanted to know.

"Your granddaughter beat me up."

"No kidding?" Grandma said. "She did a pip of a job."

My father was in front of the TV. He turned in his chair and looked at us. "Oh, cripes, now what?" he said.

"This is Randy," I told him.

"He's kinda short, isn't he?"

"He's not a boyfriend."

My father went back to the television. "Thank God for that."

There were five places set at the table. "Who's the fifth person?" I asked.

"Mabel," my mother said. "Your grandmother invited her."

"I thought it would give us a chance to grill her. See if she's holding something out," Grandma said.

"There will be *no grilling*," my mother said to my grandmother. "You invited Mabel over for dinner, and that's what we're going to have . . . a nice dinner."

"Sure," Grandma said, "but it wouldn't hurt to ask her a few questions."

A car door slammed at the front of the house and everyone migrated to the foyer.

"What's that car Mabel's driving?" Grandma asked. "That's not the station wagon."

"Mabel bought a new car," I said. "She thought the old one was too big."

"Good for her," my mother said. "She should be able to make those decisions."

"Yeah," Grandma said. "But she better hope Fred's dead."

"Who's Mabel and Fred?" Briggs asked.

I gave him the condensed explanation.

"Cool," Briggs said. "I'm starting to like this family."

"I brought a coffee cake," Mabel said, handing a box to my mother, closing the door with her other hand. "It's prune. I know Frank likes prune." She craned her neck to the living room. "Hello, Frank," she called.

"Mabel," my father said.

"Nice car," Grandma said to Mabel. "Aren't you afraid Fred'll come back and have a cow?"

"He shouldn't have left," Mabel said. "And anyway, how am I to know he'll come back? I got a new bedroom set, too. It's getting delivered tomorrow. New mattress and everything."

"Maybe you were the one who bumped Fred off," Grandma said. "Maybe you did it for the money."

My mother slammed a bowl of creamed peas down on the table. "*Mother!*" she said.

"It was just a thought," Grandma said to Mabel.

We all took our seats, and my mother set a highball down for Mabel and a beer for my father and brought a kid cushion for Briggs to sit on.

"My grandchildren use these," she said.

Briggs looked over at me.

"My sister Valerie's kids," I said.

"Hah," he said. "So you're a loser in the grandchildren race, too."

"I have a hamster," I told him.

My father forked some roast chicken onto his plate and reached for the mashed potatoes.

Mabel swilled down half her highball.

"What else you gonna buy?" Grandma asked her.

"I might go on a vacation," Mabel said. "I might go to Hawaii. Or I might go on a cruise. I always wanted to go on a cruise. Of course I wouldn't do that for a while. Unless Stephanie finds that man. Then that might speed things up."

"What man?" Grandma wanted to know.

I told her about the woman at the Grand Union.

"Now we're getting somewhere," Grandma said. "This is more like it. All we have to do is find that man." She turned to me. "You have any suspects?"

"No."

"Nobody at all?"

"I'll tell you who I suspect," Mabel said. "I suspect that garbage company. They didn't like Fred."

Grandma waved a chicken leg at her. "That's just what I said the other day. There's something funny going on with that garbage company. We're going to the viewing tonight to look into it." She ate some chicken while she thought. "You met the deceased when you went to the garbage office, didn't you?" she asked me. "What did he look like? He look like the guy who took Fred for a ride?"

"I guess he could fit the description."

"Too bad it's gonna be a closed casket. If it was open we could take the Grand Union woman with us and see if she recognizes Lipinski."

"Hell," my father said, "why don't you just haul Lipinski out and put him in a lineup?"

Grandma looked at my father. "You think we could do that? I imagine he'd be stiff enough."

My mother sucked in some air.

"I don't know if you stay stiff," Mabel said. "I think you might loosen up again."

"How about passing the gravy," my father said. "Could I get some gravy down here?"

Grandma's face lit with inspiration. "There'll be lots of Lipinski's relatives there tonight. Maybe one of them will give us a picture! Then we can show the picture to the Grand Union lady."

I thought this was all a little grim, considering Mabel was at the table, but Mabel seemed unfazed.

"What do you think, Stephanie?" she asked. "Do you think I should go to Hawaii? Or do you think I should take a cruise?"

"Jesus," Briggs said to me, "you turned out pretty good considering your gene pool."

NINE

"WOW, LOOK AT this," Grandma said, peering out at the parking lot. "This place is packed tonight. That's on account of Stiva has a full house. He's got somebody in every room. I was talking to Jean Moon, and she said her cousin Dorothy died yesterday morning, and they couldn't get her into Stiva's. Had to take her to Mosel."

"What's wrong with Mosel?" Briggs asked.

"He don't know nothing about makeup," Grandma said. "Uses too much rouge. I like when the deceased looks nice and natural."

"Yeah, I like that, too," Briggs said. "Nothing worse than an unnatural corpse."

The rain had slowed to a drizzle, but it still wasn't a glorious night to be out, so I dropped Grandma and Briggs off at the door and went in search of a parking place on the street. I found one a block away, and by the time I reached Stiva's front porch my hair was more frizz than curl and my cotton knit sweater had grown two inches.

Larry Lipinski was in room number one, as was befitting a suicidal killer. Family and friends were clustered in a knot around the casket. The rest of the room was filled with the same crowd I'd seen at the Deeter viewing. There were the professional mourners like Grandma Mazur and Sue Ann Schmatz. And there were the garbage people.

Grandma Mazur marched over to me with Briggs running after her. "I already gave my condolences," she said. "And I want to tell you they're a real standoffish group. It's a shame when people like that get to take rooms away from people like Dorothy Moon."

"I guess that means they wouldn't give you a picture."

"Zip," Grandma said. "They gave me zip."

"They gave it to her in a big way, too," Briggs said, smiling. "You should have been there."

"I don't think he's the one, anyway," I said.

"I'm not so sure," Grandma said. "These people look to me like they got something to hide. I think this is a shifty lot."

If I was related to someone who'd confessed to murder, I'd probably be feeling a little uncomfortable, too.

"Don't worry," Grandma said. "I thought this might happen, and I've got a plan."

"Yeah, the plan is we forget about it," I said.

Grandma slid her uppers around while she scanned the crowd. "Emma Getz told me the deceased in room number four is done up real nice. I thought I might take a look."

"Me too," Briggs said. "I don't want to miss anything."

I wasn't interested in how room four was done up, so I volunteered to wait in the lobby. Waiting got old after a couple minutes, so I wandered over to the tea table and helped myself to some cookies. Then the cookies got old, so I went to the ladies' room to check out my hair. Big mistake. Best not to look at my hair. I went back to the cookies and put one in my pocket for Rex.

I was counting the ceiling tiles, wondering what to do next, when the fire alarm went off. Since not that long ago Stiva's almost burned to the ground, no one was wasting any time vacating the premises. People poured from the viewing rooms into the lobby and ran for the door. I didn't see Grandma Mazur, so I struggled through the crowd to viewing room four. The room was empty when I got there, with the exception of Mrs. Kunkle, who was serene in her twelve-thousand-dollar mahogany and solid brass slumber chamber. I ran back to the lobby and was about to check outside for Grandma Mazur when I noticed the door to room one was closed. All the other doors were open, but the Lipinski door was closed.

Sirens whined in the distance, and I had a bad feeling about room one. Stiva was on the other side of the lobby, yelling to his assistant to check the back rooms. He turned and looked at me, and his face went white.

"It wasn't me!" I said. "I swear!"

He followed after the assistant, and the second he was out of sight I ran to room one and tried the door. The knob turned but the door wouldn't open, so I put my weight behind it and gave it a shove. The door flew open, and Briggs fell over backward.

"Shit," he said, "close the door, you big oaf."

"What are you doing?"

"I'm doing lookout for your grandma. What do you think I'm doing?"

At the other end of the room, Grandma had the lid up on Larry Lipinski. She was standing one foot on a folding chair, one foot on the edge of the casket, and she was taking pictures with a disposable camera.

"Grandma!"

"Boy," she said, "this guy don't look so good."

"Get down!"

"I gotta finish this roll out. I hate when there's pictures left over."

I ran down the aisle between the folding chairs. "You can't do this!"

"I can now that I got this chair. I was only getting the side of his face before. And that wasn't working good, on account of there's a lot of his head missing."

"Stop taking pictures this instant and get down!"

"Last picture!" Grandma said, climbing off the chair, dropping the camera into her purse. "I got some beauts."

"Close the lid! Close the lid!"

Crash!

"Didn't realize it was so heavy," Grandma said.

I moved the chair back against the wall. I scrutinized the casket to make sure everything looked okay. And then I took Grandma by the hand. "Let's get out of here."

The door was wrenched open before we got to it, and Stiva gave me a startled look. "What are you doing in here? I thought you were leaving the building."

"I couldn't find Grandma," I said. "And um—"

"She came in here to rescue me," Grandma said, hanging on to me, making her way to the door. "I was paying my respects when the alarm went off, and everybody stampeded out of here. And somebody knocked me over, and I couldn't get up. The midget was in here with me, but it would have taken two of them to do the job. If it wasn't for my granddaughter coming to get me I'd have burned to a cinder."

"Little person!" Randy Briggs said. "How many times do I have to tell you, I'm *not* a midget."

"Well, you sure do look like a midget," Grandma said. She sniffed the air. "Do I smell smoke?"

"No," Stiva said. "It looks like a false alarm. Are you all right?"

"I think so," Grandma said. "And it's a lucky thing, too, because I got fragile bones on account of I'm so old." Grandma glanced over at me. "Imagine that, a false alarm."

Imagine that. Unh. Mental head slap.

There were two fire trucks in the street when we left. Mourners were outside, shivering in the drizzle, kept in place by curiosity and the fact that their coats were inside. A police car was angled at the curb.

"You didn't set that alarm off, did you?" I asked Grandma Mazur.

"Who, me?"

421

———

My MOTHER WAS waiting at the door when we got back to the house. "I heard the sirens," she said. "Are you all right?"

"Sure we're all right," Grandma said. "Can't you see we're all right?"

"Mrs. Ciak got a call from her daughter, who told her there was a fire at Stiva's."

"No fire," Grandma said. "It was one of them false alarms."

My mother's mouth had turned grim.

Grandma shook the rain off her coat and hung it in the closet. "Ordinarily I guess I might feel bad that the fire department had to go out for nothing, but I noticed Bucky Moyer was driving. And you know how Bucky loves to drive that big truck."

Actually this was true about Bucky. In fact, he'd been suspected on more than one occasion for setting off a false alarm himself just so he could take the truck out.

"I have to go," I said. "I have a lot to do tomorrow."

"Wait," my mother said, "let me give you some chicken."

GRANDMA CALLED AT eight. "I got a beauty parlor appointment this morning," she said. "I thought maybe you could give me a ride, and on the way we could drop the you-know-what off."

"The film?"

"Yeah."

"When is your appointment?"

"Nine."

WE STOPPED AT the photo store first. "Do that one-hour thing," Grandma said, handing me the film.

"That costs a fortune."

"I got a coupon," Grandma said. "They give them to us seniors

422

on account of we haven't got a lot of time to waste. We have to wait too long to get our pictures back, and we could be dead."

After I deposited Grandma at the hair salon I drove to the office. Lula was on the Naugahyde couch, drinking coffee, reading her horoscope. Connie was at her desk, eating a bagel. And Vinnie was nowhere in sight.

Lula put the paper down as soon as she spied me walking through the door. "I want to know *all* about it. Everything. I want details."

"Not much to tell," I said. "I chickened out and didn't wear the dress."

"What? Say that again?"

"It's sort of complicated."

"So you're telling me you didn't get any this weekend."

"Yeah."

"Girl, that's a sad-ass state of affairs."

Tell me about it.

"You got any FTAs?" I asked Connie.

"Nothing came in on Saturday. And it's too early for today."

"Where's Vinnie?"

"At the lockup, writing bail on a shoplifter."

I left the office and stood outside, staring at the Buick. "I hate you," I said.

I heard someone laughing softly behind me and turned to find Ranger.

"You always talk to your car like that? Think you need a life, Babe."

"I've got a life. What I need is a new car."

He stared at me for a couple beats, and I was afraid to speculate on what he was thinking. His brown eyes were assessing, and his expression was mildly amused. "What would you be willing to do for a new car?"

"What did you have in mind?"

Again, the soft laugh. "Would it still have to be morally correct?"

"What kind of car are we talking about?"

"Powerful. Sexy."

I had a feeling those words might be included in the job description, too.

A light rain had started to fall. He pulled my jacket hood up and tucked my hair in. His finger traced a line at my temple, our eyes met, and for a terrifying moment I thought he might kiss me. The moment passed, and Ranger pulled back.

"Let me know when you decide," he said.

"Decide?"

He smiled. "About the car."

"Okeydokey."

Unh! I climbed into the Buick and roared off into the mist. I stopped for a light and thunked my head on the steering wheel while I waited for the green. Stupid, stupid, stupid, stupid, I thought while I thunked. Why had I said "okeydokey"? What a dopey thing to say! I did one last thunk and the light turned.

Grandma was getting coated with hairspray when I got to the salon. Her hair was steel gray, and she kept it cut short and curled in rolls that marched in side-by-side rows on her pink skull. "I'm almost done," she said. "Did you get the pictures?"

"Not yet."

She paid for her wash and set, stuffed herself into her coat, and carefully tied the plastic rain bonnet on her head. "That was some viewing last night," she said, being cautious how she walked on the wet pavement. "What a lot of excitement. You weren't even there when Margaret Burger pitched a fit over the guy in room three. You remember how Margaret's husband, Sol, died from a heart attack last year? Well, Margaret said it was all over a problem Sol was having with the cable company. Margaret said they drove Sol to high blood pressure. And she said the guy who did it was the dead guy in room three, John Curly. Margaret said she came to spit on his dead body."

"Margaret Burger came to Stiva's to spit on someone?" Margaret Burger was a sweet white-haired lady.

"That's what she told me, but I didn't actually see her spit. I guess I came in too late. Or maybe after she saw this John Curly person she decided not to do it. He looked even worse than Lipinski."

"How did he die?"

"Hit and run. And from the looks of him he must have got hit by a truck. Boy, I'm telling you these companies are something. Margaret said Sol was arguing over his bill, just like Fred, and this smart-mouth in the office, John Curly, didn't want to hear anything."

I parked in front of One-Hour Photo and got Grandma's pictures.

"These aren't so bad," she said, shuffling through the pack.

I looked over at them. Eeew.

"You think it's real obvious he's dead?" Grandma asked.

"He's in a casket."

"Well, I still think they're pretty good. I think we should see if that Grand Union lady recognizes him."

"Grandma, we can't ring some woman's doorbell and show her pictures of a dead man."

Grandma pawed through her big black patent-leather handbag. "The only other thing I got is the memorial brochure from Stiva. The picture's kind of fuzzy, though."

I took the paper from Grandma and looked at it. It was a photo of Lipinski and his wife. And below it was the Twenty-third Psalm. Lipinski was standing with his arm around a slim woman with short brown hair. It was a snapshot, taken outdoors on a summer day, and they were smiling at each other.

"Kind of funny they used that picture," Grandma said. "I overheard people talking, saying as how Lipinski's wife left him last week. Just up and went. And she didn't show up for the viewing, either. Nobody could find her to tell her about it. Was like she just disappeared off the face of the earth. Just like Fred. Except from what I heard, Laura Lipinski left on purpose. Packed her bags and said she wanted a divorce. Isn't that a shame?"

Now I know there are billions of women out there who are slim with short brown hair. But my mind made the leap anyway to the severed head with the short brown hair. Larry Lipinski was the second RGC employee to die a violent death in the space of a week. And while it seemed like a remote connection, Fred had been in contact with Lipinski. Lipinski's wife was gone. And Lipinski's wife could, in a very vague way, fit the body in the bag.

"Okay," I said, "let's show the pictures to Irene Tully." What the hell. If she freaked out I'd write it off as an average day. I dug her address out of my bag. Apartment 117, Brookside Gardens. Brookside Gardens was an apartment complex about a quarter mile from the strip mall.

"Irene Tully," Grandma said. "The name sounds familiar, but I can't place her."

"She said she knew Fred from the seniors' club."

"I guess that's where I heard of her. There's lots of people in that seniors' club, and I don't go to the meetings all the time. I can only take so much of old people. If I want to see loose skin I can look in the mirror."

I turned into Brookside Gardens and started searching for numbers. There were six buildings arranged around a large parking area. The buildings were two-story brick, done up in colonial modern, which meant the trim was white and the windows were framed by shutters. Each apartment had its own outside entrance.

"Here it is," Grandma said, unbuckling her seat belt. "The one with the Halloween decoration on the door."

We walked up the short sidewalk and rang the bell.

Irene looked out at us. "Yes?"

"We need to ask you about the disappearance of Fred Shutz," Grandma said. "And we got a picture to show you."

"Oh," Irene said. "Is it a picture of Fred?"

"Nope," Grandma said. "It's a picture of the kidnapper."

"Well, actually, we aren't really sure Fred was kidnapped," I said. "What Grandma meant was—"

"Take a look at this," Grandma said, handing Irene one of the photos. "Of course, the suit might be different."

Irene studied the photo. "Why is he in a casket?"

"He's sort of dead now," Grandma said.

Irene shook her head. "This isn't the man."

"Maybe you're just thinking that because his eyes are closed, and he don't look so shifty," Grandma said. "And his nose looks a little smushed. I think he might have fallen on his face after he blew his brains out."

Irene studied the picture. "No. It's definitely not him."

"Bummer," Grandma said. "I was sure he was the one."

"Sorry," Irene said.

"Well, they're still pretty good pictures," Grandma said, when we got back to the car. "They would have been better if I could have got his eyes to open."

I took Grandma home and bummed lunch off my mom. All the while I was looking for Bunchy. Last I saw him was Saturday, and I was beginning to worry. Figure that one out. Me worrying about Bunchy. Stephanie Plum, mother hen.

I left my parents and took Chambers to Hamilton. Bunchy picked me up on Hamilton. I saw him in my rearview mirror, pulled to the curb, and got out to talk to him.

"Where've you been?" I asked. "Take Sunday off?"

"I had some work to catch up on. Bookies gotta work some-times too, you know."

"Yeah, only you're not a bookie."

"We gonna start that again?"

"How'd you find me just now?"

"I was riding around, and I got lucky. How about you? You get lucky?"

"That's none of your damn business!"

His eyes crinkled with laughter. "I was talking about Fred."

"Oh. One step forward, two steps backward," I said. "I get things that seem like leads and then they go nowhere."

"Like what?"

"I found a woman who saw Fred get into a car with another man the day he disappeared. Problem is, she can't describe the man or the car. And then something weird happened at the funeral home, and it feels to me like it might tie in, but I can't find any logical reason why."

"What was the weird thing?"

"There was a woman at one of the viewings who seemed to have a similar problem to the one Fred was having with the garbage company. Only this woman had problems with her cable company."

Bunchy looked interested. "What kind of problems?"

"I don't know exactly. Grandma told me about it. She just said they were similar to Fred's."

"I think we should talk to this woman."

"We? There's no we."

"I thought we were working together. You brought me lamb and everything."

"I felt sorry for you. You were pathetic, sitting out there in your car."

He wagged his finger at me. "I don't think so. I think you're getting to like me."

Like a stray dog. Maybe not that much. But he was right about talking to Margaret Burger. What was the harm? I had no idea where Margaret Burger lived, so I went back to my parents' house and asked Grandma.

"I can show you," she said.

"Not necessary. Just tell me."

"And miss all the action? No way!"

Why not? I had Bunchy tagging along. Maybe I should ask Mrs. Ciak and Mary Lou and my sister, Valerie. I took a deep breath. Sarcasm always made me feel better. "Get in the car," I said to Grandma.

I took Chambers to Liberty and turned onto Rusling.

"It's one of these houses," Grandma said. "I'll know it when I see it. I went to a get-together there once." She looked over her shoulder. "I think someone's following us. I bet it's one of them garbage people."

"It's Bunchy," I said. "I'm sort of working with him."

"No kidding? I didn't realize this had turned into such a big investigation. We've got a whole team here."

I stopped at the house Grandma had described, and we all got out and collected together on the sidewalk. It had stopped raining, and the temperature had risen to pleasant.

"My granddaughter tells me you're working together," Grandma said to Bunchy, looking him over. "Are you a bounty hunter, too?"

"No, ma'am," he said. "I'm a bookie."

"A bookie!" Grandma said. "Isn't that something. I always wanted to meet a bookie."

I knocked on Margaret Burger's door, and before I could introduce myself Grandma stepped forward.

"Hope we aren't disturbing you," Grandma said. "But we're conducting an important investigation. Stephanie and me and Mr. Bunchy."

Bunchy elbowed me. "*Mr.* Bunchy," he said.

"Not at all," Margaret Burger said. "I guess this is about poor Fred."

"We can't find him no-how," Grandma said. "And my granddaughter thought your problem with that cable company sounded real similar. Except, of course, they gave Sol a heart attack instead of making him disappear."

"They were awful people," Margaret said. "We paid our bills on time. We never missed a payment. And then when we had trouble with the cable box, they said they never heard of us. Can you imagine?"

"Just like Fred," Grandma said. "Isn't that right, Stephanie?"

"Uh, yeah, it sounds—"

"So then what?" Bunchy said. "Did Sol complain?"

"He went down there in person and raised a big fuss. And that's when he had his heart attack."

"What a shame," Grandma said. "Sol was only in his seventies, too."

"Do you have any canceled checks from the cable company?" Bunchy asked Margaret. "Something from before you had the problem?"

"I could look in my file," Margaret said. "I keep all my checks for a couple years. But I don't think I have any of the cable checks. After Sol died, that awful cable person, John Curly, came and tried to look like he was being helpful about solving the mix-up. I didn't buy that for a minute. He was just trying to cover his tracks because he messed up the computer records. He even said as much, but it was too late for Sol. He'd already been given the heart attack."

Bunchy looked resigned to what he was hearing. "John Curly took the canceled checks," Bunchy said, more statement than question.

"He said he needed them for his records."

"And he never brought them back?"

"Never. And next thing I know I get a statement from them welcoming me like I was a brand-new customer. I'm telling you, that cable company is a mess."

"Anything else you want to know?" I asked Bunchy.

"No. That's about it."

"How about you, Grandma?"

"I can't think of anything more."

"Well then," I said to Margaret, "I guess there isn't anything else. Thanks for talking to us."

"I hope Fred turns up," Margaret said. "Mabel must be beside herself."

"She's holding up pretty good," Grandma said. "I guess Fred wasn't one of those husbands you really mind losing."

Margaret nodded, like she understood completely what Grandma was saying.

I dropped Grandma off and continued on home to my apartment. Bunchy followed me the whole way and parked behind me.

"Now what?" Bunchy said. "What are you going to do now?"

"I don't know. You have any ideas?"

"I'm thinking there's something going on with the garbage company."

I considered telling him about Laura Lipinski but decided against it.

"Why did you want to see Margaret's canceled checks?" I asked.

"No special reason. Just thought they'd be interesting."

"Uh-huh."

Bunchy rocked back on his heels with his hands in his pockets. "How about the checks from the garbage company? You ever get any of them?"

"Why? You think they'd be interesting, too?"

"Might be. You never know about stuff." His eyes focused on something behind me, and his face changed expression. Wariness, maybe.

I felt a body move so close it was skimming my own, and a warm hand protectively settled at the base of my neck. Without turning I knew it was Ranger.

"This is Bunchy," I said to Ranger, by way of introduction. "Bunchy the bookie."

Ranger didn't move. Bunchy didn't move. And I wasn't moving, held in a kind of suspended animation by Ranger's force field.

Finally Bunchy took a couple steps backward. It was the sort of maneuver a man might make when confronted with a grizzly. "I'll be in touch," Bunchy said, pivoting on his heel, walking to his car.

We watched Bunchy drive out of the lot.

"He's not a bookie," Ranger said, his hand still holding me captive.

I stepped away and turned to face him, putting space between us.

"What was with the intimidation routine you just did?"

Ranger smiled. "You think I intimidated him?"

"Not a whole lot."

"I don't think so, either. He's got a few face-offs behind him."

"Am I right in assuming you didn't like him?"

"Just being cautious. He was carrying and he was lying. And he's a cop."

I already knew all those things. "He's been following me for days. So far he's been harmless."

"What's he after?"

"I don't know. Something to do with Fred. Right now he knows more than I do. So I figure it's worthwhile to play along with him. He's probably a Fed. I think he has a tracking device on my car. Jersey cops can't usually afford to do stuff like that. And I think he must be working with a partner to be able to pick me up, but I haven't spotted the partner yet."

"Does he know you've made him?"

"Yeah, but he doesn't want to talk about it."

"I can help with the tracking problem," Ranger said, handing me a set of keys.

"What's this?"

TEN

"THIS IS TEMPTATION," Ranger said, leaning against a new midnight-black Porsche Boxster.

"Could you be more specific about the temptation? Like, what kind of temptation were you thinking about?"

"Temptation to broaden your horizons."

I had a lot of unease over Ranger's definition of "broad horizons." I suspected his horizons were a teensy bit closer to hell than I might want to travel. For starters, there was the car and the slight possibility that it wasn't entirely legitimate.

"Where do you get these cars?" I asked him. "You seem to have a never-ending supply of new, expensive black cars."

"I have a source."

"This Porsche isn't stolen, is it?"

"Do you care?"

"Of course I care!"

"Then it isn't stolen," Ranger said.

I shook my head. "It's a really cool car. And I appreciate your offer, but I can't afford a car like this."

"You don't know the price yet," Ranger said.

"Is it more than five dollars?"

"The car isn't for sale. It's a company car. You get the car if you continue to work with me. You're ruining my image in that Buick. Everyone who works with me drives black."

"Well, hell," I said, "I wouldn't want to ruin your image."

Ranger just kept looking at me.

"Is this charity?" I asked him.

"Guess again."

"I'm not selling my soul, am I?"

"I'm not in the soul-buying business," Ranger said. "The car's an investment. Part of the working relationship."

"So what do I have to do in this working relationship?"

Ranger uncrossed his arms and pushed off from the car. "Jobs come up. Don't accept any that make you uncomfortable."

"You aren't doing this just to amuse yourself, are you? To see what I'd be willing to do for an expensive car?"

"That would be somewhere in the middle of the list," Ranger said. He looked at his watch. "I have a meeting. Drive the car. Think it over."

He had his Mercedes parked next to the Porsche. He slid behind the wheel and drove away without looking back.

I almost collapsed on the spot. I put a hand to the Porsche to steady myself, and then immediately yanked my hand away, afraid I'd left prints. Dang!

I ran inside and looked around for Randy Briggs. His laptop was on the coffee table, but his jacket was gone. I toyed with the idea of packing all his things into the two suitcases, moving them into the hall, and locking my door, but gave it up as futile.

I cracked open a beer and called Mary Lou. "Help!" I said.

"What help?"

"He gave me a car. And he touched me twice!" I looked at my neck in the hall mirror to see if I was branded where his hand had rested.

"Who? What are you talking about?"

"Ranger!"

"Omigod. He gave you a car?"

"He said it was an investment in our working relationship. What does that mean?"

"What kind of car is it?"

"A new Porsche."

"That's at least oral sex."

"Be serious!" I said.

"Okay, the truth is . . . it's beyond oral sex. It could be, you know, butt stuff."

"I'll return the car."

"Stephanie, this is a Porsche!"

"And I think he's flirting with me, but I'm not sure."

"What does he do?"

"He's gotten sort of physical."

"How physical?"

"Touchy."

"Omigod, what did he touch?"

"My neck."

"Is that all?"

"My hair."

"Hmmm," Mary Lou said. "Was it sexy touching?"

"It felt sexy to me."

"And he gave you a Porsche," Mary Lou said. "A Porsche!"

"It isn't like it's a gift. It's a company car."

"Yeah, right. When do I get to ride in it? You want to go to the mall tonight?"

"I don't know if I should be driving it for personal stuff." In fact, I didn't know if I should be driving it *at all* until I made sure about the butt thing.

"You really think this is a company car?" Mary Lou asked.

"So far as I can see, everyone who works for Ranger drives a new black car."

"A Porsche?"

"Usually an SUV, but maybe a Porsche happened to fall off the back of the truck yesterday." I could hear screaming in the background. "What's happening?"

"The kids are having a conflicting opinion. I suppose I should go mediate."

Mary Lou had started taking parenting classes because she couldn't get the two-year-old to stop eating the dog's food. Now she said things like "the kids are having a conflicting opinion" instead of "the kids are trying to kill each other." I think it sounds much more civilized, but when you come right down to it . . . the kids were trying to kill each other.

I hung up and took the check Fred had written to RGC out of my shoulder bag and studied it. Nothing unusual that I could see. A plain old check.

The phone rang, and I put the check back in my bag.

"Are you alone?" Bunchy asked.

"Yes, I'm alone."

"Something going on between you and that Ranger guy?"

"Yes." I just didn't know what it was.

"We didn't get much chance to talk," Bunchy said. "I was wondering what you were gonna do next."

"Look, why don't you just tell me what it is you want me to do."

"Hey, I'm following *you* around, remember?"

"Okay, I'll play the game. I thought I'd go back to the bank tomorrow and talk to a friend of mine. What do you think of that?"

"Good idea."

It was close to five. Joe would most likely be home now, watching the news on television, fixing himself something to eat, getting ready for *Monday Night Football*. If I invited myself to his house for *Monday Night Football*, I could show him the check and see what he thinks. And I could ask him to check into Laura Lipinski. If things went well, maybe I could also make up for opportunities missed on Saturday night.

I dialed his number.

"Hey," I said. "I thought maybe you wanted company for *Monday Night Football*."

"You don't like football."

"I sort of like football. I like when they all jump on each other. That's pretty interesting. So do you want me to come over?"

"Sorry. I have to work tonight."

"All night?"

There was a moment of silence while Morelli processed the hidden message. "You want me bad," he said.

"I was just being friendly."

"Will you still be feeling friendly tomorrow? I don't think I'll be working tomorrow."

"Order a pizza."

After I hung up I looked guiltily at the hamster cage. "Hey, I'm just being friendly," I said to Rex. "I'm not going to sleep with him."

Rex still didn't come out of his can, but I could see the pine shavings moving. I think he was laughing.

The phone rang around nine.

"I have a job for you tomorrow," Ranger said. "Are you interested?"

"Maybe."

"It's of high moral quality."

"And the legal quality?"

"Could be worse. I need a decoy. I have a deadbeat who needs to be separated from his Jaguar."

"Are you stealing it or repossessing it?"

"Repossessing. All you have to do is sit in a bar and talk to this guy while we load his car onto a flatbed."

"That sounds okay."

"I'll pick you up at six. Wear something that'll hold his attention."

"What bar is this?"

"Mike's Place on Center."

Thirty minutes later, Briggs came home. "So what do you do on Monday nights?" he asked. "You watch football?"

I went to bed at eleven, and two hours later I was still thrashing around, unable to sleep. I had Larry Lipinski's missing wife, Laura, on my mind. The back of her head, severed at the neck, stuffed in a garbage bag. Her husband dead from a self-inflicted gunshot wound. Hacked up his wife. Shot his coworker. I really didn't know if it was Laura Lipinski. What were the chances? Probably not good. Then who was in that bag? The more I thought about it, the more convinced I became that it was Laura Lipinski.

I looked at the clock for the hundredth time.

Laura Lipinski wasn't the only thing keeping me awake. I was having a hormone attack. Damn Morelli. Whispering all those things in my ear. Looking sexy in his Italian suit. Surely Morelli would be home by now. I could call him, I thought, and tell him I was coming to visit. After all, it was his fault I was in this hellish state.

But what if I call, and he *isn't* home, and I get recorded on his caller ID? Major embarrassment. Best not to call. Think of something else, I ordered myself.

Ranger flashed into my mind. No! Not Ranger!

"Damn." I kicked the covers off and went out to the kitchen to get some orange juice. Only there wasn't any orange juice. There wasn't *any* kind of juice, because I never went food shopping. There were still some leftovers from my mother, but no juice.

I really needed juice. And a Snickers bar. If I had juice and a Snickers bar, I probably could forget about sex. In fact, I didn't even need the juice anymore. Just the Snickers bar.

I stuffed myself into a pair of old gray sweats, shoved my feet into unlaced boots, and pulled a jacket over my plaid flannel nightshirt. I grabbed my purse and my keys, and because I was trying not to be stupid, I also grabbed my gun.

"I don't know what the hell you're going after," Briggs said from the couch, "but bring one back for me, too."

I clomped off, out of my apartment, down the hall, into the elevator.

When I got to the lot, as fate would have it, I realized I'd taken the Porsche key. Hah! Who am I to dispute fate? Guess I just had to drive the Porsche.

I started out for the 7-Eleven, but I was there in no time at all, and it seemed a shame not to at least work the kinks out of the car. Especially since I hadn't yet *found* any kinks. I continued on down Hamilton, turned into the Burg, wound around some, left the Burg, and sonovagun, before I knew it, I was in front of Morelli's townhouse. His truck was parked at the curb, and the house was dark. I idled in front of the house for a minute, thinking about Morelli, wishing I was comfy in bed with him. Well, what the hell, I thought, maybe I should ring his doorbell and tell him I was in the neighborhood, so I thought I'd stop by. No harm in that. Just being friendly. I caught a glimpse of myself in the rearview mirror. Eek. Should have done something with my hair. And my legs might need shaving now that I thought about it. Rats.

Okay, maybe it's not such a good idea to visit Morelli right now. Maybe I should go home first and shave and scrounge up some sexy underwear. Or maybe I should just wait until tomorrow. Twenty-four hours, give or take a couple. I wasn't sure I could hold out for twenty-four hours. He was right. I wanted him bad.

Get a grip! I told myself. We're talking about a simple sex act here. This isn't a medical emergency like having a heart attack. This can wait twenty-four hours.

I took a deep breath. Twenty-four hours. I was feeling better. I was in control. I was a rational woman. I put the Porsche into gear and cruised down the street.

Piece of cake. I can last it.

I got to the corner and noticed lights in my rearview mirror.

Not many people out in this neighborhood, at this hour, on a work night. I turned the corner, parked, cut my lights, and watched the car stop in front of Morelli's house. After a couple minutes Morelli got out and walked to his door, and the car began to roll down the street toward me.

I gripped the wheel tight, so the Porsche wouldn't be tempted to go into reverse and zoom back to Morelli's. Less than twenty-four hours, I repeated, and my legs would be smooth as silk and my hair would be clean. But wait a minute! Morelli has a shower and a razor. This is all baloney. There's no need to wait.

I shifted into reverse just as the other car came into the intersection. I caught a glimpse of the driver and felt my heart go dead in my chest. It was Terry Gilman.

Say what? Terry Gilman!

There was an explosion of red behind my eyeballs. Shit. I was such a sap. I hadn't suspected. I'd thought he'd changed. I'd believed he was different from the other Morellis. Here I was worrying over leg hair, when Morelli was out doing God knows what with Terry Gilman. Unh! Major mental smack in the head.

I squinted at the car as it cleared the intersection and motored on. Terry was oblivious to my presence. Probably planning out the rest of her night. Probably going off to whack someone's grandmother.

Well, who cares about Morelli, anyway. Not me. I could care less. There was only one thing I cared about. Chocolate.

I put my foot to the pedal and careened away from the curb. Clear the streets. Stephanie's got a Porsche and needs a Snickers bar.

I reached the 7-Eleven in record time, blasted through the store, and left with a full bag. Hey, Morelli, orgasm this.

I entered my lot at warp speed, screeched to a stop, stomped up the stairs, down the hall, and kicked my door open. "*Shit!*"

Rex stopped running on his wheel and looked at me.

"You heard me," I said. "Shit, shit, shit."

Briggs sat up. "What the hell's going on? I'm trying to get some sleep here."

"Don't push your luck. Don't speak to me."

He squinted at me. "What are you wearing? Is that some new form of birth control?"

I grabbed the hamster cage and bag of candy, carted everything off to my bedroom, and slammed my door shut. I ate the 100 Grand bar first, and then the Kit Kat, and then the Snickers. I was starting to feel sick, but I ate the Baby Ruth and the Almond Joy and the Reese's Peanut Butter Cup.

"Okay, I'm feeling much better now," I said to Rex.

Then I burst into tears.

When I was done crying I told Rex it was only hormones reacting with a prediabetic surge of insulin from eating all those candy bars . . . so he shouldn't worry. I went to bed and immediately fell asleep. Crying is fucking exhausting.

I awoke the next morning with my eyes crusty and puffed from crying and my spirit lower than slug slime. I lay there for about ten minutes wallowing in my misery, thinking of ways to kill myself, deciding on smoking. But then I didn't have any cigarettes, and I wasn't in a mood to traipse back to the 7-Eleven. Anyway, I was working with Ranger now, so probably I could just let nature take its course.

I dragged myself out of bed and into the bathroom where I stared at myself in the mirror. "Get a grip, Stephanie," I said. "You have a Porsche and a SEALs hat, and you're broadening your horizons."

I was afraid after all those candy bars I was also broadening my ass, and I should get some exercise. I was still dressed in my sweats, so I wriggled into a sports bra and laced up my running shoes.

Briggs was already at work at his computer when I came out of my bedroom. "Look who's here . . . Mary Sunshine," he said. "Christ, you look like shit."

"This is nothing," I told him. "Wait until you see what I look like when I'm *done* running."

I returned drenched in sweat and feeling very pleased with myself. Stephanie Plum, woman in charge. Screw Morelli. Screw Terry Gilman. Screw the world.

I had a chicken sandwich for breakfast and took a shower. Just to be mean I put the beer on the top shelf in the refrigerator, told Briggs to have a rotten day, and zoomed off in my Porsche to the Grand Union. Dual-purpose trip. Talk to Leona and Allen and shop for real food. I parked about a half mile away from the store so no one would park next to me and ding my door. I got out and looked at the Porsche. It was perfect. It was a totally kick-ass car. When you had a car like this you didn't mind so much that your boyfriend was boinking a skank.

I did the shopping first, and by the time I was done and had the groceries tucked away in the trunk, the bank was open. Business was slow first thing on a Tuesday morning. No one in the lobby. There were two tellers counting out money. Probably practicing. I didn't see Leona.

Allen Shempsky was in the lobby drinking coffee, talking to a bank guard. He saw me and waved. "How's the Uncle Fred hunt going?" he asked.

"Not that good. I was looking for Leona."

"It's her day off. Maybe I can be of help."

I rooted around in my bag, located the check, and handed it over to Allen. "Anything you can tell me about this?"

He examined it front and back. "It's a canceled check."

"Anything weird about it?"

He looked at it some more. "Not that I can see. What's so special about this check?"

"I don't know. Fred was having billing problems with RGC. He was supposed to bring this check to the office the day he disappeared. I guess he didn't want to take the original, so he left it home on his desk."

"Sorry I can't be more helpful," Shempsky said. "If you want to leave it with me I can ask around. Sometimes different people pick up different things."

I dropped the check back into my bag. "Think I'll hang on to it. I have a feeling people have died because of this check."

"That's serious," Shempsky said.

I walked back to the car feeling spooky and not knowing why. Nothing alarming had happened at the bank. And no one was parked or standing by the Porsche. I checked the lot. No Bunchy. No Ramirez that I could see. Still, there was that uncomfortable feeling. Something forgotten, maybe. Or someone watching. I unlocked the car and looked back at the bank. It was Shempsky I'd sensed. He was standing to the side of the bank building, smoking a cigarette, watching me. Oh man, now I was getting the creeps from Shempsky. I blew out a breath. My imagination was in overdrive. The man was just sneaking a smoke, for Pete's sake.

The only oddity in the act was that Allen Shempsky actually had a bad habit. A bad habit seemed like an excess of personality for Allen Shempsky. Shempsky was a nice guy who never offended anyone and was totally forgettable. He'd been like that for as long as I could remember. When we were in school he was the kid in the back of the room who never got called on. Quiet smile, never a conflicting opinion, always neat and clean. He was like a chameleon whose clothes matched the wall behind him. After knowing Allen all my life, I'd be hard-pressed to name his hair color. Maybe mouse brown. Not that he was rodentlike. He was a reasonably attractive man with an average nose and average teeth and average eyes. He was average height, of average build, and I assumed of average intelligence, although there was no way of knowing for sure.

He'd married Maureen Blum a month after they both graduated from Rider College. He had two young children and a house in Hamilton Township. I'd never driven past his house, but I was willing to bet it was forgettable. Maybe that wasn't so bad. Maybe it was a good thing to be unmemorable. I bet Maureen Blum Shempsky didn't have to worry about being stalked by Benito Ramirez.

Bunchy was waiting when I got back to my apartment building. He was in the lot, sitting in his car, looking grumpy.

"What's with the Porsche?" he wanted to know, coming over.

"It's on loan from Ranger. And if you put a tracking device on it he won't be happy."

"Do you know how much a car like this costs?"

"A lot?"

"Maybe more than you want to pay," Bunchy said.

"I hope that's not the case."

He took one of the grocery bags and followed me upstairs. "You go to the bank like you said?"

"Yep. I talked to Allen Shempsky, but I didn't learn anything new."

"What did you talk to him about?"

"The weather. Politics. Managed health care." I balanced my bag on my hip while I unlocked the door.

"Boy, you're a beaut. You don't trust anybody, do you?"

"I don't trust *you*."

"I wouldn't trust him, either," Briggs said from the living room. "He looks like he's got a social disease."

"Who's that?" Bunchy wanted to know.

"That's Randy," I said.

"Want to see him disappear?"

I looked over at Briggs. It was a tempting offer. "Some other time," I said to Bunchy.

Bunchy unpacked his bag and set everything out on the kitchen counter. "You've got some strange friends."

And they hardly counted at all compared to my relatives. "I'll make you lunch if you tell me who you're working for and why you're interested in Fred," I said.

"No can do. Besides, I think you'll make me lunch anyway."

I made canned tomato soup and grilled cheese sandwiches. I made grilled cheese because that's what I felt like eating. And I made the soup because I like to keep a clean can in reserve for Rex.

Halfway through lunch I looked at Bunchy, and Morelli's words echoed in my ear. I'm working with a couple Treasury guys who make me look like a Boy Scout, he'd said. The Hallelujah Chorus rang out in my head, and I had an epiphany. "Holy cow," I said. "You're working with Morelli."

"I don't work with anyone," Bunchy said. "I work alone."

"That's a load of pig pucky."

This wasn't the first time Morelli had been involved in one of my cases and had kept it from me, but it was the first time he'd sent someone to spy on me. This was a new all-time low for Morelli.

Bunchy sighed and pushed his dish away. "Does this mean I'm not getting dessert?"

I gave him one of the leftover candy bars. "I'm depressed."

"Now what?"

"Morelli is scum."

He looked down at the candy bar. "I told you I work alone."

"Yeah, and you told me you were a bookie."

He glanced up. "You don't know for sure that I'm not."

The phone rang, and I snatched it up before the machine could take over.

"Hey, Cupcake," Morelli said. "What do you want on your pizza tonight?"

"I want nothing. There is no pizza. There is no you, no me, no us, no pizza. And don't ever call me again, you scummy, slimy fungus-ridden dog turd, piece of fly crud." And I slammed the phone down.

Bunchy was laughing. "Let me guess," he said. "That was Morelli."

"And you!" I yelled, pointing my finger, teeth clenched. "You are *no better*."

"I gotta go," Bunchy said, still doing his Mr. Chuckles impersonation.

"So, have you always had a problem with men?" Briggs asked. "Or is this something recent?"

I WAS IN the lobby, waiting for Ranger at six o'clock. I was all showered and perfumed and hair freshly done up to look sexily unkempt. Mike's Place is a sports bar frequented by businessmen. At six o'clock it would be filled with suits catching ESPN and having a drink to unwind before going home, so I chose to look suity, too. I was wearing my Wonderbra, which worked wonders, a white silk shirt unbuttoned clear to the front clasp on the magical bra, and a black silk suit with the skirt rolled at the waist to show a lot of leg. I covered the mess at the waist with a wide fake leopard skin belt, and I stuffed my stocking-clad feet into four-inch fuck-me pumps.

Mr. Morganthal shuffled out of the elevator and winked at me. "Hey, hootchie-mamma," he said. "Want a hot date?" He was ninety-two and lived on the third floor, next to Mrs. Delgado.

"You're too late," I told him. "I've already made plans."

"That's just as well. You'd probably kill me," Mr. Morganthal said.

Ranger pulled up in the Mercedes, and idled at the door. I gave Mr. Morganthal a tweak on the cheek and sashayed out, swinging my hips, wetting my lips. I poured myself into the Mercedes and crossed my legs.

Ranger looked at me and smiled. "I told you to get his attention . . . not start a riot. Maybe you should button one more button."

I batted my eyelashes at him, in fake-flirt, which actually wasn't totally fake. "You don't like it?" I said. Hah! Take that, Morelli. Who needs you!

Ranger reached over and flipped the next two buttons open, exposing me to mid-belly. "That's the way *I* like it," he said, the smile still in place.

Shit! I quickly rebuttoned the buttons. "Wise guy," I said. Okay, so he called my bluff. No reason to panic. Just file it away for future reference. *Not ready for Ranger!*

Mr. Morganthal came out and shook his finger at us.

"I think I just sullied your reputation," Ranger said, putting the car in gear.

"Probably more like you helped me live up to expectations."

We cruised across town and parked half a block from the bar on the opposite side of the street.

Ranger took a photo from behind the sun visor. "This is Ryan Perin. He's a regular here. Comes every day after work. Has two drinks. Goes home. Never parks his car more than half a block away on the street. He knows the dealer's trying to get it back, and he's nervous. Comes out to check on it every few minutes. Your job is to make sure he keeps his eyes on you—not the car. Keep him in the building."

"Why are you taking it here?"

"When he's home the car's in a locked garage, and the regular repo people can't get at it. When he's at work he parks it in a garage with an attendant who takes his Christmas bonus seriously." Ranger made a gun sign with his hand, finger and thumb extended. "For that matter, Perin carries too and isn't slow on the draw. That's why we need to finesse the car. Nobody wants bloodshed."

"What does this guy do for a living?"

"Lawyer. Sending all his money up his nose these days."

A dark green Jaguar rolled past us. There were no spaces open on the street. Just as he got to the end of the block a car pulled out, and the Jag slid in place.

"Wow," I said, "that was lucky."

"No," Ranger said. "That was Tank. We have cars parked all along this street, so Perin has to park down there."

Perin angled out of the car, beeped the alarm on, and headed for Mike's.

I looked at Ranger. "Will the alarm be a problem?"

"None at all."

Perin disappeared into the building.

"Okay," Ranger said. "Go get 'em, Slick. I'll give you a five-minute lead, and then I'll call the truck in." He gave me a buzzer. "If something goes wrong, hit the panic button. I'll come get you when the car's cleared the street."

Perin was dressed in a blue pinstripe. He was in his early forties, with thinning sandy blond hair and an athletic build gone soft. I stepped just to the side of the door and waited while my eyes adjusted to the change in light. There were mostly men in the room, but there were a few women, too. The women were in clusters. The men tended to be alone, eyes turned to the TV. Perin was easy to spot. He was at the far end of the polished mahogany bar. The bartender set a drink in front of him. Something clear on the rocks.

There were chairs open on either side of Perin, but I didn't want to sit down and start a conversation. I didn't want him to feel singled out. If he was nervous the direct approach might be too obvious. So I walked toward him, rummaging in my bag, looking absorbed in finding whatever. And just as I reached his stool I faked a stumble. Not enough to go down to the ground, but enough to knock into him, clutching at his sleeve for support.

"Omigod," I said. "I'm so sorry. This is so embarrassing. I wasn't watching where I was going and . . ." I looked down. "It's these shoes! I'm just not a high-heel person."

"What kind of a person are you?" Perin asked.

I gave him the million-dollar smile. "I think maybe I'm a barefoot person." I slid onto the stool next to him and signaled the bartender. "Boy, I really need a drink. It's been one of those days."

"Tell me about it," he said. "What do you do?"

"I'm a lingerie buyer." Used to be, anyway, before I started bounty-hunting.

His eyes dropped to my cleavage. "No shit?"

I hoped they loaded that car on fast. This guy had a head start on the drinky poos, and was going to be on me like white on rice. I could feel it coming.

"My name's Ryan Perin," he said, extending his hand.

"Stephanie."

He kept hold of my hand. "Stephanie the lingerie buyer. That's very sexy."

Yuk. I hate holding hands with strange men. Damn Ranger and his horizons. "Well, you know . . . it's a job."

"I bet you have a lot of great lingerie."

"Sure. I have everything. You name it, I've got it."

The bartender looked at me expectantly.

"I'll have one of those," I said, pointing to Perin's drink. "And could you hurry?"

"So tell me about your lingerie," Perin said. "You have any garter belts?"

"Oh, yeah. I wear garter belts all the time—red, black, purple."

"How about thong panties?"

"Yeah, thong panties." Every time I feel like flossing my ass.

The alarm went off on his watch.

"What's that?" I asked.

"It's a reminder to check on my car."

Damn! Don't panic. Don't panic. "What's wrong with your car?"

"This isn't such a great neighborhood at this time of night. I had a radio ripped off last week. So once in a while I just look out and make sure no one's messing with anything."

"Don't you have an alarm system?"

"Well, yeah."

"Then you don't have to worry."

"I guess you're right. Still . . ." He looked toward the door. "Maybe I should check just to be safe."

"You're not one of those obsessive-compulsive types, are you?" I asked. "I don't like those types. They're always so uptight. They never want to try anything new like, um . . . group sex."

That got his attention back.

Some spittle collected at the corner of his mouth. "You like group sex?"

"Well, I don't like to do it with too many men, but I have a couple girlfriends . . ." My drink came. I knocked it back and went into a coughing fit. When I stopped coughing, my eyeballs got hot and watery. "What *is* this?"

"Bombay Sapphire."

"I'm not much of a drinker."

Perin slid a hand up my leg to just inside my skirt hem. "Tell me more about the group sex."

Stick a fork in me, I thought. Because I'm done. If Ranger didn't get here soon I was gonna be in big trouble. I was unloading everything I had, and I didn't know where to go from here. I didn't have a whole lot of experience at this sort of thing. And what I knew about group sex was zero. Which was already more than I *wanted* to know. "Thursday is my group sex night," I said. "We do it every Thursday. Unless we can't find a man . . . then we just watch television."

"How about another drink?" Perin asked.

No sooner had he gotten the words out of his mouth than he was off his bar stool, flying through the air. He crash-landed on a table, the table collapsed, and Perin lay still as a stone, spread-eagled on the floor, eyes wide, mouth open, like a big, dead beached fish.

I gasped and turned and was nose-to-nose with Benito Ramirez. "You shouldn't be whoring like this, Stephanie," Ramirez said, soft-voiced and crazy-eyed. "The champ don't like when he sees you with other men. Sees them handling you. You need to save yourself for the champ." He managed a small, sick smile. "The champ's gonna do things to you, Stephanie. Things you've never had done to you before. Did you ask Lula about the things the champ can do?"

"What are you doing here?" I shrieked. I had one eye on Perin, afraid he was going to get to his feet and run for his car. And I had one eye on Ramirez, afraid he was going to draw a knife and carve me up like a Christmas turkey.

"You can't get away from the champ," Ramirez whispered. "The champ sees everything. He sees when you go out for candy bars late at night. What's the matter, Stephanie, having trouble sleeping? The champ could fix that. He knows how to make women sleep."

My stomach clenched, and I broke into an instant cold sweat. I never saw him. He'd been lying in wait for me, following my every move, watching me. And I never saw him. Probably the only reason I was alive was because Ramirez loved the cat-and-mouse game. He loved the smell of another person's fear. Loved to torture, to prolong the pain and terror.

There'd been a black hole in the time continuum when Perin had gone airborne. Everyone in the bar, with the exception of me and Ramirez, had sat frozen in dumbfounded shock. Now everyone in the bar was on their feet.

"What the hell?" the bartender yelled, coming at Ramirez.

Ramirez turned his eyes to the bartender, and the bartender backed off.

"Hey, man," the bartender said. "You gotta take your problems outside."

Perin was standing wobble-legged, glaring at Ramirez. "What are you, nuts? Are you freaking nuts?"

"The champ don't like remarks like that," Ramirez said, his eyes shrinking in his head.

A big, no-neck guy came to Perin's rescue. "Hey, leave the little guy alone," he said to Ramirez.

Ramirez turned on him. "No one tells the champ what to do."

Bam! Ramirez sucker-punched no-neck, and no-neck went down like a house of cards.

Perin pulled his gun and fired one off. The shot went wide of Ramirez, and sent everyone in the bar running for the door. Everyone but Perin and Ramirez and me. The bartender was shouting into the phone for the police to get their asses in gear. And through the open door I caught a glimpse of the flatbed moving down the street with the green Jaguar on board.

"I don't like the police," Ramirez said to the bartender. "You shouldn't have called the police." Ramirez gave me one last look with his nobody's-home eyes and went out the back door.

I hopped off the bar stool. "Nice meeting you," I said to Perin. "I have to go now."

Ranger strolled in, looked around, shook his head, and smiled at me. "You never disappoint," he said.

ELEVEN

RANGER HAD THE Mercedes double-parked outside Mike's Place. I got in, and we took off before Perin made it through the door to the sidewalk.

Ranger glanced over at me. "Are you okay?"

"Never been better."

This brought another appraising look from Ranger.

"Well, maybe I'm a little buzzed," I said. "Think I shouldn't have drunk that whole drink." I leaned closer to Ranger, as he was looking very fine, and I was finding him superior to that rat-fink Morelli.

Ranger downshifted at a light. "Want to tell me about the gun-fire?"

"Perin got one off. It didn't hit anybody, though." I smiled at him. Ranger wasn't nearly so scary when I was tanked on Bombay.

"Perin was shooting at you?"

"Well, no. There was this other guy who sort of didn't like Perin talking to me. And there was an altercation." I touched Ranger's diamond stud earring. "Pretty," I said.

Ranger grinned. "How many drinks did you have?"

"One. But it was a big one. And I'm not much of a drinker."

"Something to remember," Ranger said.

I wasn't sure exactly what he meant by that, but I hoped it had to do with sex and taking advantage of me.

He turned into my lot and rolled to a stop at the door. Major disappointment, because it meant he was dropping me off, as opposed to parking and coming in for a nightcap . . . or something.

"You have a visitor," he said.

"*Moi?*"

"That's Morelli's bike."

I swiveled to look. Sure enough, Morelli's Ducati was parked next to Mr. Feinstein's Cadillac. Damn. I stuck my hand in my shoulder bag and fished around.

"What are you looking for?" Ranger asked.

"My gun."

"Probably it's not a good idea to shoot Morelli," Ranger said. "Cops are real touchy about that sort of thing."

I wrenched myself out of the car, straightened my skirt, and huffed into the building.

Morelli was sitting in the hall when I got upstairs. He was dressed in black jeans, black motorcycle boots, a black T-shirt, and a black leather motorcycle jacket. He had a two-day beard and his hair was long, even by Morelli standards. If I hadn't been mad at him I'd have had my clothes off before I got to my door. Now, I realize I'd just had the same thought about Ranger, but there it was. What can I say? Pretty soon Bunchy and Briggs would be looking good to me.

"Boy, you have a lot of nerve coming here," I said to Morelli, fumbling for my key.

He took his key ring from his pocket and opened my door.

"Since when do you have a key to my apartment?" I asked him.

"Since you gave it to me back when we were friendlier." He looked down at me and amusement softened the set of his mouth. "Have you been drinking?"

"Occupational hazard. I had this job to do for Ranger, and drinking seemed like the right thing to do at the time."

"You want some coffee?"

"No way, that would ruin everything. Anyway, I wouldn't drink your coffee. And you can leave now, thank you."

"I don't think so." Morelli opened the refrigerator, searched around and discovered the bag of Mocha Java I'd bought at Grand Union. He measured out water and coffee and tripped the switch on my coffeemaker. "Let me take a winger here. You're mad at me, right?"

I rolled my eyes so far into the back of my head I saw myself thinking. And while my eyes were all the way back there, I looked for Briggs. Where was the little devil?

"You want to give me a clue?" Morelli said.

"You don't deserve a clue."

"That's probably true, but how about giving me one anyway."

"Terry Gilman."

"Yeah?"

"That's it. That's your entire clue, you creep."

Morelli got two mugs from the over-the-counter cabinet and filled the mugs with coffee. He added milk and handed one of the mugs to me. "I need more to go on than a name."

"No you don't. You know exactly what I'm talking about."

His pager went off, and he did some creative swearing. He looked at the read-out and made a call on my phone. "I have to leave," he said. "I'd like to stay and settle this, but something's come up."

He got to the door and turned and came back. "I almost forgot. Have you seen Ramirez?"

"Yes. And I want to get a restraining order and have his parole revoked."

"His parole has already been revoked. He picked up a hooker on Stark Street last night and almost killed her. Brutalized her and left her for dead in a Dumpster. Somehow she managed to climb out, and two kids found her this morning."

"Is she going to be okay?"

"Looks like it. She's still on critical, but she's holding her own. When did you see him?"

"About a half hour ago."

I told him about the repo and the incident with Ramirez.

I could see emotion bubbling inside Morelli. Frustration, mostly. And some anger. "I don't suppose you'd consider moving back in with me?" he asked. "Just until Ramirez is found."

Be a little crowded what with Terry there, too. "Don't suppose I would," I said.

"How about if I marry you?"

"Now you want to marry me? What happens after they catch Ramirez? We get a divorce?"

"There's no divorce in my family. Grandma Bella wouldn't hear of it. You have to die to get out of a marriage in my family."

"Gosh, that's cheery." And true. I understood some of Joe's attitude about marriage. The Morelli men had a bad track record. They drank too much. They cheated on their wives. They beat their kids. And the misery lasts 'til death do them part. Fortunately for many of the Morelli wives, death visited the Morelli men early. They were shot in bar brawls, killed themselves in DUI car crashes, and exploded their livers. "We'll talk some other time," I said. "You'd better get moving. And don't worry, I'll be careful. I've been keeping my doors and windows locked, and I'm carrying a gun."

"You have a permit to carry concealed?"

"Got it yesterday."

"I didn't hear any of this," Morelli said. He bent his head and kissed me lightly on the lips. "Make sure the gun's loaded."

He was actually a very nice guy. Some of the less desirable Morelli genes had passed him by. He had the Morelli good looks and charm and none of the abusive qualities. The womanizing part was in question.

I smiled and said thanks. Although I'm not sure what I was thanking him for. For being a decent person about the gun, I guess. Or maybe for caring about my safety. At any rate, the smile and the thanks were encouragement enough for Morelli. He pulled me to him and kissed me again, hot and serious this time. Not a kiss I'd easily forget, nor want to end.

When he broke from the kiss, still holding me close, the grin returned. "That's better," he said. "I'll call when I can."

And he was gone.

Damn! I locked the door behind him and thunked myself on the forehead with the heel of my hand. I was such a dope. I'd just kissed Morelli like there was no tomorrow. Not the message I'd wanted to give him at all. What about Terry? What about Bunchy? What about Ranger? Never mind Ranger, I thought. Ranger wasn't part of this problem. Ranger was a different problem.

Briggs stuck his head out from my bathroom doorway. "Is it safe to come out?"

"What are you doing in there?"

"I heard you in the hall and didn't want to screw it up for you. Sounded like you finally had a live one."

"Thanks, but he wasn't all that live."

"So I see."

AT ONE O'CLOCK I was still awake. It was the kiss. I couldn't stop thinking about the kiss, and the way I'd felt when Morelli had taken me in his arms. And then I got to thinking about the way I'd have felt if he'd ripped my clothes off and kissed me in *other* places. And then there was Morelli naked. And Morelli naked and aroused. And Morelli doing something about being naked and aroused. And that's why I couldn't sleep. Again.

At two o'clock I was no closer to sleep. Damn Morelli. I rolled out of bed and padded barefoot into the kitchen. I went through the cupboards and fridge, but I couldn't find exactly the right thing to satisfy my hunger. Morelli was what I wanted, of course, but if I couldn't have Morelli, what I wanted was an Oreo. *Lots* of Oreos. I should have thought to get Oreos when I was at the store.

Grand Union was open twenty-four hours. Tempting, but a bad idea. Ramirez could be out there. Bad enough to worry about him during the day when there are people around and visibility is good. Going out at night seemed foolishly risky.

I went back to bed and instead of thinking about Joe Morelli, I found myself thinking about Ramirez, wondering if he was out there, parked in the lot or on one of the side streets. I knew all the cars that belonged in the lot. If an odd car was there, I'd spot it.

Curiosity had me now. And the excitement of a possible capture. If Ramirez was sitting in my lot, I could have him picked up. I slipped from under the covers and crept to the window. The lot was well-lit. Not a place where a car could be hidden in shadow. I grabbed hold of the curtain and drew it open. I expected to look down at the lot. Instead I looked into the obsidian eyes of Benito Ramirez. He was on my fire escape, leering in at me, his face illuminated in ambient light, his massive body shadowed and threatening against the night sky, his arms outspread, and his hands flat to the window frame.

I jumped back and yelped, and terror filled every part of me. I couldn't breath. I couldn't move. I couldn't think.

"Stephanie," he sang, his voice muffled through the black glass. He laughed softly and sang my name out again. "Stephanieeeee."

I wheeled around and flew out of the room and into the kitchen, where I fumbled in my bag for my gun. I found the gun and ran back to the bedroom, but Ramirez was gone. My window was still closed and locked, the curtains half open. The fire escape was empty. No sign of him in the lot. No strange car that I could see. For a moment I thought I'd imagined the whole thing. And then I saw the paper taped to the outside of my window. There was a hand-printed message on the paper.

God is waiting. Soon it will be your time to see Him.

I ran back to the kitchen to dial police dispatch. My hand was shaking, and my fingers wouldn't go to the right buttons on the phone. I took a calming breath and tried again. Another breath and I was telling the answering officer about Ramirez. I hung up and dialed Morelli. Halfway through the dial I cut the connection. Suppose Terry answered. Stupid thought, I told myself. She'd dropped him off. Don't make more of it than it is. There could be an explanation. And even if Joe wasn't the world's best boyfriend, he was still a damn good cop.

I redialed and waited while the phone rang seven times. Finally Morelli's machine picked up. Morelli wasn't home. Morelli was working. Ninety percent certainty, 10 percent doubt. It was the 10 percent that kept me from calling his cell phone or pager.

I suddenly realized Briggs was standing next to me.

The usual sarcasm was gone from his voice. "I don't think I've ever seen anyone that scared," he said. "You didn't hear anything I was saying to you."

"There was a man on my fire escape."

"Ramirez."

"Yeah. You know who he is?"

"Boxer."

"More than that. He's a very terrible person."

"Let's make some tea," Briggs said. "You don't look too good."

I brought my pillow and quilt into the living room and settled on the couch with Briggs. Every light in my apartment was on, and I had my gun within reach on the coffee table. I sat like that until daylight, dozing occasionally. When the sun was up, I went back to bed and slept until the phone woke me at eleven.

It was Margaret Burger.

"I found a check," she said. "It was misfiled. It's from that time when Sol was arguing with the cable company. I know Mr. Bunchy was interested in seeing it, but I don't know how to get in touch with him."

"I can get it to him," I told her. "I have a few things to do, and then I'll stop around."

"I'll be here all day," Margaret said.

I didn't know what I was going to get out of the check, but I thought it couldn't hurt to take a look. I made fresh coffee and chugged a glass of orange juice. I took a fast shower, dressed in my usual uniform of Levi's and a long-sleeve T-shirt, drank my coffee, ate a Pop-Tart, and called Morelli. Still no answer, but I left a message this time. The message was that Morelli should page me immediately if Ramirez was caught.

I took the pepper spray out of my shoulder bag and clipped it onto the waistband of my Levi's.

Briggs was in the kitchen when I left. "Be careful," he said.

My stomach knotted when I got to the elevator, and again when I stepped out of the lobby, into the lot. I quickly crossed to the car, powered up the Porsche, and watched my rearview mirror as I drove.

It occurred to me that I was no longer looking around every corner for Uncle Fred. Somehow the Uncle Fred search had morphed into a mystery about a butchered woman and dead office workers and an uncooperative garbage company. I told myself it was all the same. That somehow it all tied to Fred's disappearance. But I wasn't completely convinced. It was still possible that Fred was in Fort Lauderdale, and I was spinning my wheels while Bunchy laughed his ass off. Maybe Bunchy was actually Allen Funt in disguise, and I was on funniest bounty hunter bloopers.

Margaret opened the door on the first knock. She had the canceled check ready and waiting for me. I scrutinized it, but didn't see anything out of the ordinary.

"You can take it if you want," Margaret said. "It's no good to me. Maybe that nice Mr. Bunchy would want to see it too."

I dropped the check in my bag and thanked Margaret. I was still spooked from finding Ramirez on my fire escape, so I drove to the office to see if Lula wanted to ride shotgun for the rest of the day.

"I don't know," Lula said. "You aren't doing anything with that Bunchy guy, are you? He has a sick sense of humor."

We'll take my car, I told her. Nothing to worry about.

"I guess that would be okay," Lula said. "I could wear a hat to disguise myself, so no one recognizes me."

"No need," I said. "I have a new car."

Connie looked up from her computer screen. "What kind of car?"

"Black."

"That's better than powder blue," Lula said. "What is it? Another one of them little Jeeps?"

"Nope. It's not a Jeep."

Both Connie and Lula looked at me expectantly. "Well?" Lula said.

"It's . . . a Porsche."

"Say what?" Lula said.

"Porsche."

They were both at the door.

"Damned if it doesn't look like a Porsche," Lula said. "What'd you do, rob a bank?"

"It's a company car."

Lula and Connie did some more of the expectant looking at me with their eyebrows up at the top of their heads.

"Well, you know how I've been working with Ranger . . ."

Lula peered into the car's interior. "You mean like getting that guy to blow hisself up? And like the time you lost the sheik? Hold on here," Lula said. "Are you telling me Ranger gave you this car because you're working with him?"

I cleared my throat and polished a thumbprint off the right-rear quarter panel with the hem of my flannel shirt.

Lula and Connie started smiling.

"Dang," Lula said, punching me in the arm. "You go, girl."

"It's not that kind of work," I said.

The smile on Lula had stretched ear to ear. "I didn't say anything about what kind of work. Connie, did you hear me say anything about this kind of work or that kind of work?"

"I know what you were thinking," I said.

Connie jumped in. "Let's see . . . there's oral sex. And then there's regular sex. And then there's—"

"Getting close now," Lula said.

"All the men who work with Ranger drive black cars," I told them.

"He give them SUVs," Lula said. "He don't give them no Porsche."

I bit into my lower lip. "So you think he wants something?"

"Ranger don't do stuff for nothing," Lula said. "Sooner or later he gets his price. You telling me you don't know the price?"

"Guess I was hoping I was one of the guys, and the car was part of my job."

"I've seen the way he looks at you," Lula said. "And I know he don't look at any of the guys like that. Think what you need is a job description. Not that it would matter if it was me. If I could get my hands on that man's body, I'd buy *him* a Porsche."

We drove to the Grand Union strip mall, and I parked in front of First Trenton.

"What we doing here?" Lula wanted to know.

Good question. The answer was a little vague to me. "I have a couple canceled checks I want to show my cousin. She's a teller here."

"Something special about these checks?"

"Yeah. Only I don't know what." I gave them to Lula. "What do you think?"

"Looks like a couple plain-ass checks to me."

The bank was busy at lunchtime, so we got in line to see Leona. I looked over at Shempsky's office while I waited my turn. The door was open, and I could see Shempsky at his desk, on the phone.

"Hey," Leona said when I got to her window. "What's up?"

"I wanted to ask you about a check." I passed Margaret's check to her. "You see anything unusual here?"

She looked at it front and back. "No."

I gave her Fred's check to RGC. "How about this one?"

"Nope."

"Anything strange about the accounts?"

"Not that I can see." She typed some information into her computer and scanned the screen. "Money comes in and goes out pretty fast on this RGC account. My guess is this is a small liquid account RGC keeps at the local level."

"Why do you say that?"

"RGC is the biggest waste hauler in the area, and I don't see enough transactions here. Besides, I use RGC, and my checks to RGC are canceled through Citibank. When you work at a bank, you notice things like that."

"How about the cable check?"

Leona looked at it again. "Yep. Same thing. My checks are canceled someplace else."

"Is it unusual to assign customers to two different banks?"

She shrugged. "I don't know. I guess not, since both these companies are doing it."

I thanked Leona, and dropped the checks back into my bag. I almost collided with Shempsky when I turned to leave.

"Oops," he said, jumping back. "Didn't mean to bumper-ride you. Just thought I'd come over and see how things are going."

"Things are going okay." I introduced Lula and thought it was to Shempsky's credit that he didn't seem to notice Lula's neon-orange hair or the fact that she'd poured over two hundred pounds of woman into a pair of size-nine tights and topped it off with a Cherry Garcia T-shirt and faux-fur jacket that was trimmed in what looked like pink lion mane.

"What ever happened to that check?" Shempsky asked. "Did you solve your mystery?"

"Not yet, but I'm making progress. I found a similar check from another business. And the curious thing is that both checks were canceled here."

"Why is that curious?"

I decided to fib. I didn't want to involve Leona or Margaret Burger. "The checks *I* write to those companies are canceled elsewhere. Don't you think that's weird?"

Shempsky smiled. "No. Not at all. Businesses often keep small, liquid local accounts, but deposit the bulk of their money somewhere else."

"Heard that before," Lula said.

"Do you have the other check with you?" Shempsky asked. "Would you like me to look at it?"

"No, but thanks for offering."

"Boy," Shempsky said. "You're really tenacious. I'm impressed. I assume you think this all ties in with Fred's disappearance?"

"I think it's possible."

"Where do you go from here?"

"RGC. I still need to get the account straightened out. I was going to do it last Friday, but I got there after Lipinski killed himself."

"Not a good time to take care of business," Shempsky said.

"No."

He gave me a friendly banker smile. "Well, good luck."

"She don't need luck," Lula said. "She's excellent. She always gets her man, you see what I'm saying? She's so good she drives a Porsche. How many bounty hunters you know got a Porsche?"

"It's actually a company car," I told Shempsky.

"It's a great car," he said. "I saw you drive off in it yesterday."

Finally I felt like I was on to something. I had an idea how a lot of stuff might tie together. It was still pretty half-baked, but it was something to think about. I took Klockner to Hamilton and crossed South Broad. I pulled into the industrial area and was relieved at the absence of flashing lights and police cruisers. No human disasters today. The RGC lot was empty of trucks and didn't smell bad. Clearly midday is the preferred time to visit a garbage company.

"They might be a little sensitive in here," I said to Lula.

"I can sensitive your ass off," Lula said. "I just hope they got their wall painted."

The office didn't look freshly painted, but it didn't look bloody either. A man was behind the counter, working at one of the desks. He was somewhere in his forties, brown hair, slim build. He looked up when we approached.

"I'd like to settle an account," I said. "I spoke to Larry about it, but it was never resolved. Are you new here?"

He extended his hand. "Mark Stemper. I'm from the Camden office. I'm filling in temporarily."

"Is that the wall where the brains were splattered?" Lula asked. "It don't look fresh painted. How'd you get it so clean? I never have any luck getting blood off walls like that."

"We had a cleaning crew come in," Stemper said. "I don't know exactly what they used."

"Boy, too bad, because I could use some of that."

He looked at her warily. "You get blood on your walls a lot?"

"Well, not usually on *my* walls."

"About this account," I said.

"Name?"

"Fred Shutz."

He tapped into the computer and shook his head. "Nobody here by that name."

"Exactly." I explained the problem and showed him the canceled check.

"We don't use this bank," he said.

"Maybe you have a second account there."

"Yeah," Lula said, "a local liquid account."

"No. All the offices are the same. Everything goes through Citibank."

"Then how do you explain this check?"

"I don't know how to explain it."

"Were Martha Deeter and Larry Lapinski the only office workers here?"

"In this office, yes."

"When someone mails in their quarterly payment, what happens to it?"

"It goes through here. It's logged into the system and deposited in the Citibank account."

"You've been very helpful," I said. "Thanks."

Lula followed me out. "Personally, I didn't think he was all that helpful. He didn't know nothing."

"He knew it was the wrong bank," I told her.

"I could tell that turns you on."

"I sort of had a brainstorm while I was talking to Allen Shempsky."

"You want to share that brainstorm?"

"Suppose Larry Lipinski didn't enter all the accounts. Suppose he held out ten percent for himself and deposited them someplace else?"

"Skimming," Lula said. "You think he was skimming RGC money. And then Uncle Fred come along and started making a stink. And so Lipinsky had to get rid of Uncle Fred."

"Maybe."

"You're the shit," Lula said. "Girlfriend, you are *smart*."

Lula and I did a high five and then a down low and then she tried to do some elaborate hand thing with me, but I got lost halfway through.

Actually, I thought it was more complicated than Fred getting disposed of because he made some noise over his account. It seemed more likely Fred's disappearance was related to the dismembered woman. And I still thought that woman might be Laura Lipinski. So it did sort of tie in together. I could construct a possible scenario up to the point of Fred seeing Lipinski dump the garbage bag at the real estate office. After that, I was lost.

We were about to get in the car when the side door to the building opened, and Stemper stuck his head out and waved at us. "Hey," he yelled. "Hold up a minute. That check is bothering me. Would you mind letting me make a copy?"

I didn't see where that would do any harm, so Lula and I returned to the office with him and waited while he fiddled with the copier.

"Damn thing never works," he said. "Hold on while I change the paper."

Half an hour later, I got my check back with an apology.

"I'm sorry that took so long," he said. "But maybe it'll be worthwhile. I'll send it to Camden and see what they make of it. I think it's pretty strange. I've never run across anything like this."

465

We got back to the Porsche and sunk into the leather seats.

"I love this car," Lula said. "I feel like the shit in this car."

I knew exactly what she meant. It was a fantasy car. No matter if it was true, when you drove the car you felt prettier, sexier, braver, and smarter. Ranger was on to something with this broader horizon business. When I drove the Porsche I could see myself with broader horizons.

I put the car in gear and headed for the driveway out of the lot. The lot itself was surrounded by a high chain-link fence. Out-of-use trucks parked to the rear in the lot, and office workers and drivers parked in the front. Double gates opened to the street. Probably at night they closed and locked the gates. During the day the gates were open, and it was wide enough for two trucks to pass.

I rolled to a stop at the open gate, looked left and saw the first garbage truck of the day rumble home. It was a colossus of a truck. A green and white behemoth that shook the earth as it thundered closer, its bulk preceded by the stench of rotting everything, its arrival heralded by descending seagulls.

The truck swung wide to enter the lot, and Lula jumped in her seat. "Holy cats, that guy don't see us. He's taking this turn like he owns the road."

I went into reverse, but it was too late. The truck sideswiped the Porsche, shearing fiberglass off half the car. I leaned on the horn, and the truck driver stopped and looked down at us in amazement.

Lula jumped out of the car in full rant, and I followed after her, climbing over the seat because my side was smushed into the monster garbage truck.

"Jeez, lady," the driver said. "I don't know what happened. I didn't see you until you started blowing your horn."

"That don't cut it," Lula yelled. "This here's a Porsche. You know what she had to do to get this Porsche? Well, actually she hasn't done nothing yet, but I think if she gets lucky, she's gonna have to do plenty. This company better be insured." Lula turned to me. "You need to exchange insurance information. That's always the first thing you do. You got your card?"

"I don't know. I guess all that stuff is in the glove compartment," I said.

"I'll get it," Lula told me. "I can't believe this happened to a Porsche. People should be more careful when they see a Porsche on the road." She leaned into the car, rooted around in the glove compartment, and was back in a heartbeat. "This looks like it," she said, handing the card over to me. "And here's your purse. You might need your license."

"Maybe we should get the guy in the office," the driver said. "He fills out the forms for this kind of thing."

I thought that was a good idea. And while we were at it how about if I just slip away unnoticed and get a one-way ticket to Rio. I didn't want to have to explain this to Ranger.

"Yeah, we should get that office guy," Lula said. "Because I might have whiplash or something. I can feel it coming on. Maybe I need to go in and sit down."

I would have rolled my eyes, but I thought I should save my energy in case Lula suddenly got paralyzed from the half-mile-per-hour impact she'd just sustained.

We all went into the building and had just gotten through the door when there was a loud explosion. We stopped in our tracks and looked at each other. There was a moment of stunned immobility, and then we all scrambled to see what had happened.

We burst out the door and faltered when a second explosion went off and flames shot from the Porsche and licked along the undercarriage of the garbage truck.

"Oh shit," the driver said. "Take cover! I've got a full tank of gas."

"Say what?" Lula said.

And then it blew. *Barrrroooom!* Liftoff. The garbage truck jumped off the pavement. Tires and doors flew off like Frisbees, the truck bounced down with a jolt, listed to one side, and rolled over onto the furiously burning Porsche, turning it into a Porsche pancake.

We flattened ourselves against the building while pieces of scrap metal and shreds of rubber rained down around us.

"Uh-oh," Lula said. "All the king's horses and all the king's men aren't gonna put that Porsche back together again."

"I don't get it," the driver said. "It was only a scratch. I hardly scraped against your car. Why would it explode like that?"

"That's what her cars do," Lula said. "They explode. But I gotta tell you this was the best. This here's the first time she exploded a garbage truck. One time her truck got hit with an antitank missile. That wasn't bad either, but it couldn't compare to this."

I hauled the cell phone out of my bag and dialed Morelli.

TWELVE

ONLY ONE FIRE truck was left on the scene, and the remaining firemen were directing the cleanup. A crane had been brought in to move the RGC truck. When they got the truck up and off the Porsche, I'd be able to put the Porsche in my pocket. Connie had picked Lula up and taken her back to work, and most of the returning truck drivers had lost interest and dispersed.

Morelli had arrived seconds after the first fire truck and was now standing threateningly close to me, fist on hip, eyes narrowed, giving me the third degree.

"Tell me again," Morelli said, "why Ranger gave you a Porsche."

"It's a company car. Everyone who works with Ranger drives a black car, and since my car is blue—"

"He gave you a Porsche."

I narrowed my eyes back at him. "Just what is the problem here?"

"I want to know what's going on with you and Ranger is the problem."

"I *told* you. I'm working with him." And I supposed I was flirting with him, but I didn't think it was necessary to report flirting. Anyway, talk about the pot calling the kettle black.

Morelli didn't look satisfied, and he definitely didn't look happy. "I don't suppose you bothered to check the registration number on your Porsche."

"Don't suppose I did." And it was unlikely anyone was going to check it now, being that the Porsche was blown up, and its remnants were only three inches thick.

"You weren't worried that you might be driving a hot car?"

"Ranger wouldn't give me a hot car."

"Ranger would give his mother a hot car," Morelli said. "Where do you think he gets all those cars he gives away? You think he gets them from the car fairy?"

"I'm sure there's an explanation."

"Such as?"

"Such as, I don't know. And anyway there are other things that are more important to me right now. Like why did my car explode?"

"Good question. I think it's unlikely the garbage truck sideswiping you caused the explosion. If you were a normal person I'd be hard-pressed to find an explanation. Since you're who you are . . . my guess is someone planted a bomb."

"Why did it take so long? Why didn't it go off when I started the car?"

"I asked Murphy. He's the demo expert. He thinks it might have been set on a timer, so it would go off when you were on the street, not in the lot."

"So maybe the bomber is someone from the garbage company, and he didn't want the explosion so close to home."

"We looked for Stemper, but he's nowhere."

"Did you check for his car?"

"It's still here."

"Are you kidding me? He's just disappeared?"

Morelli shrugged. "Doesn't mean much. He could have gone out for a drink with a friend. Or he could have gotten fed up with waiting for the lot to get cleared enough to get the cars out and found some other way to go home."

"But you guys are going to look for him, right?"

"Right."

"And he isn't home yet?"

"Not yet."

"I have a theory," I said.

Morelli smiled. "I love this part."

"I think Lipinski was skimming. And maybe Martha Deeter was in on it, or maybe she found out about it, or maybe she was just a pain in the ass. Anyway, I think Lipinski might have been keeping some accounts for himself." I showed Morelli the checks and told him about the banks.

"And you think this other guy who worked for the cable company, John Curly, was skimming, too?"

"There are some similarities."

"And Fred might have disappeared because he was making too much noise?"

"More than that." I told him about the Mega Monster flyer in the garbage bag, and about Laura Lipinski, and finally about Fred and the leaves.

"I'm not liking this picture," Morelli said. "I wish I'd known about these things sooner."

"I just put it together."

"Two steps in front of me. I've been really stupid on this one. Tell me about the fake bookie."

"Bunchy."

"Yeah. Whoever."

I raised an eyebrow. "I figured you two were working together."

"What's Bunchy look like?"

"A fireplug with eyebrows. About my height. Brown hair. Needs a cut. Receding hairline. Looks like a street person. Walks and talks like a cop. Drinks Corona."

"I know him, but I'd be hard-pressed to say I was working with him. He doesn't work *with* anybody."

"I don't suppose you want to share what you know with me?"

"Can't."

Wrong answer. "Okay, let me get this straight," I said. "Some Fed has been following me around for days, camping out on my doorstep, breaking into my apartment, and you think that's okay?"

"No, I don't think it's okay. I think it's grounds for beating the shit out of him. I didn't know he was doing it, and I intend to make sure it stops. I just can't tell you what it's all about right now. What I *can* tell you is that you should back off and let us take it from here. Obviously we're both going down the same road."

"Why should I be the one to back off?"

"Because you're the one who's getting bombed. You notice *my* car exploding?"

"The day isn't over."

Morelli's pager went off. Morelli looked at the read-out and sighed. "I have to go. You want a ride home?"

"Thanks, but I need to stay. I have a call in to Ranger. I'm not sure what he wants to do with the Porsche."

"Some time soon we need to talk about Ranger," Morelli said.

Oh boy. I'll look forward to that conversation.

Morelli skirted the crane and got into the dusty maroon Fairlane that was *his* company car. He cranked the engine over and pulled out of the lot.

My attention swung back to the crane operator. He was maneuvering the boom over the truck. A cable was attached, and the truck was slowly hauled upright, exposing what was left of the Porsche.

I caught a flash of black beyond the crane. It was Ranger's Mercedes.

"Just in time," I said when he strolled over.

He looked down at the flattened, charred piece of scrap metal pressed into the macadam.

"That's the Porsche," I said. "It exploded and caught fire and then the garbage truck fell over on it."

"I especially like the part about the garbage truck."

"I was afraid you might be mad."

"Cars are easy to come by, Babe. People are harder to replace. Are you okay?"

"Yeah. I was lucky. I was just waiting to see what you wanted to do with the Porsche."

"Not much anybody's going to do with that dead soldier," Ranger said. "Think we'll walk away from this one."

"It was a great car."

Ranger took one last look at it. "You might be more the Humvee type," he said, steering me toward the Mercedes.

Streetlights were on when we crossed Broad and the twilight was deepening. Ranger rolled down Roebling and stopped in front of Rossini's. "I have to meet a guy here in a few minutes. Come in and have a drink, and we can have an early dinner when I'm done. This shouldn't take long."

"Is this bounty hunter business?"

"Real estate," Ranger said. "I'm meeting my lawyer. He has papers for me to sign."

"You're buying a house?"

He opened the door for me. "Office building in Boston."

Rossini's is an excellent Burg restaurant. A pleasant mix of cozy but elegant with linen tablecloths and napkins and gourmet food. Several men in suits stood at the small oak bar at the far end of the room. A few of the tables were already occupied, and in a half-hour the room would be filled.

Ranger guided me to the bar and introduced me to his lawyer.

"Stephanie Plum," the lawyer said. "You look familiar."

"I didn't intend to burn down the funeral home," I said. "It was an accident."

He shook his head. "No, that's not it." He smiled. "I've got it. You were married to Dickie Orr. He was briefly with our firm."

"Everything Dickie did was brief," I said. Especially our marriage. The pig.

Twenty minutes later, Ranger had his business concluded, his lawyer finished his drink and left, and we moved to a table. Ranger was black today. Black T-shirt, black cargo pants, black boots, and black Gortex squall jacket. He left his jacket on, and everyone in the room knew why. Ranger wasn't the sort to leave his gun in the glove compartment.

We ordered, and Ranger slouched back in his chair. "You never say much about your marriage."

"You never say much about *anything*."

He smiled. "Low profile."

"Have you ever been married?"

"Long time ago."

I hadn't expected him to say that. "Any kids?"

He stared at me for a full minute before answering. "I have a daughter. She's nine. Lives with her mother in Florida."

"Do you ever see her?"

"When I'm in the area."

Who *was* this man? He owned office buildings in Boston. And he was the father of a nine-year-old. I was having a hard time merging this new knowledge into my mental Ranger-the-gunrunner/bounty-hunter file.

"Tell me about the bomb," Ranger said. "I get the feeling I'm not up to speed on your life."

I told him my theory.

He was still slouched back, but the line of his mouth had tightened. "Bombs aren't good, Babe. They're real messy. Give you a real bad hair day."

"You have any ideas?"

"Yeah, you ever think about taking a vacation?"

I wrinkled my nose. "I can't afford a vacation."

"I'll give you an advance on services performed."

I felt my face flush. "About those services—"

He lowered his voice. "I don't pay for the kind of service you're worried about."

Yeeesh.

I dug into my pasta. "I wouldn't go anyway. I'm not giving up on Uncle Fred. And where would I leave Rex? And Halloween is coming up. I love Halloween. I couldn't miss Halloween."

Halloween is one of my favorite holidays. I love the crisp air and the pumpkins and spooky decorations. I never cared about the candy I collected when I was a kid. I got psyched over the dress-up part. Maybe this says something about my personality, but put me behind a mask, and I'm a happy person. Not one of those ugly, sweaty rubber things that fit over your whole head. I like the kind that just fits around the eyes and makes you look like the Lone Ranger. And face paint is very cool, too.

"Of course, I don't go out trick-or-treating anymore," I said, stabbing a piece of sausage. "I go over to my parents' house now and give out candy. Grandma Mazur and I always get dressed up for when the kids come around. Last year I was Zorro, and Grandma was Lily Munster. I think this year she's going to be a Spice Girl."

"I could see you as Zorro," Ranger said.

Zorro is actually one of my favorite people. Zorro is the shit.

I had tiramisù for dessert because Ranger was paying, and because Rossini's made orgasmic tiramisù. Ranger skipped dessert, of course, not wanting to pollute his body with sugar, not desiring an extra ripple in his washboard stomach. I scarfed up the last smidgens of cake and custard and reached under the tablecloth to discreetly pop the top snap on my jeans.

I'm not a fanatic about weight. Truth is, I don't even own a scale. I judge my weight by the way my jeans fit. And unpleasant as it is to admit, these jeans weren't fitting at all. I needed a better diet. And I needed an exercise program. Tomorrow. Starting tomorrow, no more taking the elevator to the second floor, no more doughnuts for breakfast.

I studied Ranger as he drove me home, details seen in the flash of oncoming headlights and overhead streetlights. He wore no rings. A watch on his left wrist. Wide nylon band. No studs in his ears today. He had a network of fine lines around his eyes. The lines were from sun, not age. My best guess was that Ranger was somewhere between twenty-five and thirty-five. No one knew for sure. And no one knew much of his background. He moved easily through the underbelly of Trenton, speaking the language, walking the walk of the projects and minority neighborhoods. There'd been no trace of that Ranger tonight. Tonight he'd sounded more Wall Street than Stark Street.

The ride back to my building was quiet. Ranger pulled into my lot, and I did a quick scan for creepy people. Finding none, I had my door open before the car came to a complete stop. No sense lingering in the dark, alone with Ranger, tempting fate. I'd made enough of an ass of myself last time when I was half snockered.

"You in a hurry?" Ranger said, looking amused.

"Things to do."

I moved to get out of the car, and he grabbed me by the scruff of my neck. "You're going to be careful," he said.

"Y-y-yes."

"And you're going to carry your gun."

"Yes."

"Loaded."

"Okay, loaded."

He released my neck. "Sweet dreams."

I ran into the building and up the stairs, rushed into my apartment, and dialed Mary Lou.

"I need help with a stakeout tonight," I told Mary Lou. "Can Lenny sit with the kids?"

Lenny is Mary Lou's husband. He's a nice guy, but he hasn't got much upstairs. That's fine with Mary Lou because she's more interested in what's *downstairs*, anyway.

"Who are we staking out?"

"Morelli."

"Oh, honey, you heard!"

"I heard what?"

"Uh-oh. You didn't hear?"

"What? *What?*"

"Terry Gilman."

Argh. Direct shot to the heart. "What about Terry?"

"The rumor is she's been seen with Joe late at night."

Man, you can't get away with anything in the Burg. "I know about the late-night stuff. Anything else?"

"That's it."

"Besides seeing Terry, he's also involved in a project that ties in with Uncle Fred's disappearance, and he won't tell me anything."

"Asshole."

"Yeah. And after I gave him some of the best weeks of my life. Anyway, it seems like he works nights, so I thought I'd see what he was up to."

"You going to pick me up in the Porsche?"

"The Porsche is out of commission. I was hoping you could drive," I said. "I'm afraid Morelli might recognize the Buick."

"No problemo."

"And wear sneakers and something dark."

Last time we went snooping together Mary Lou wore ankle boots with spike heels and gold earrings the size of dinner plates. Not exactly the invisible snooper.

Briggs was standing behind me. "You're going to spy on Morelli? This should be good."

"He's leaving me no choice."

"I bet you five dollars he spots you."

"Deal."

"THERE COULD BE a perfectly good explanation for the Terry thing," I said to Mary Lou.

"Yeah, like he's a prick?"

That's one of the things I like about Mary Lou. She's willing to believe the worst about anyone. Of course it's easy to believe the worst about Morelli. He's never cared a whole lot about public opinion and has never made much of an attempt to improve his rogue reputation. And in the past, his reputation was well deserved.

We were in Mary Lou's Dodge minivan. It smelled like Gummi Bears and grape lollipops and McDonald's cheeseburgers. And when I turned to look out the back window I was confronted with two kiddie car seats that made me feel sort of left out of things. We were idling in front of Morelli's house, staring into his front windows, seeing nothing. The lights were on, but the curtains were drawn. His truck was parked at the curb, so probably he was home, but there was no guarantee. He lived in a rowhouse and that made surveillance difficult because we couldn't creep around the entire house and easily do our Peeping Tom thing.

"We can't see anything like this, " I said. "Let's park on the cross street and go on foot."

Mary Lou had followed my instructions and was dressed in black. Black leather jacket with fringe running down the sleeves, tight black leather slacks—and as a compromise between my suggestion of sneakers and her preferred four-inch heels, she was wearing black cowboy boots.

Morelli's house was halfway down the block, his narrow yard backed up to a one-lane service road, and the side borders of his yard were delineated by bedraggled hedgerows. Morelli hadn't yet discovered gardening.

The sky was overcast. No moon. No streetlights lining the back alley. This was all fine by me. The darker the better. I was wearing a utility belt that held pepper spray, a flashlight, a Smith and Wesson .38, a stun gun, and a cell phone. I'd constantly watched our tail for signs of Ramirez and had seen nothing. That didn't fill me with security, since spotting Ramirez clearly wasn't one of my talents.

We walked the alley and paused when we reached Morelli's yard. Lights were on in the kitchen. Shades were up at the single kitchen window and at the back door. Morelli passed in front of the window, and Mary Lou and I took a step back, further into shadow. He returned and worked at the counter, probably fixing something to eat.

The sound of the phone ringing carried out to us. Morelli answered the phone and paced in the kitchen while he talked.

"Not someone he's happy to hear from," Mary Lou said. "He hasn't cracked a smile."

Morelli hung up and ate a sandwich, still standing at the counter. He washed it down with a Coke. I thought the Coke was a good sign. If he was in for the night he probably would have had a beer. He flipped the light off and left the kitchen.

Now I had a problem. If I chose to watch the wrong half of the house I might miss Morelli leaving. And by the time I ran to the car and took off after him, it could be too late. Mary Lou and I could split up, but that would negate my reason for inviting Mary Lou along. I'd wanted another set of eyes looking for Ramirez.

"Come on," I said, creeping toward the house. "We need to get closer."

I pressed my nose to the windowpane on Morelli's back door. I could see clear to the front, looking through the kitchen and dining room. I could hear the television, but I couldn't see it. And I couldn't see any sign of Morelli.

"Do you see him?" Mary Lou wanted to know.

"No.

She peered through the back door window with me. "Too bad we can't see the front door from here. How will we know if Morelli goes out?"

"He shuts his lights off when he goes out."

Blink. The lights went out, and the sound of the front door opening and shutting carried back to us.

"Shit!" I sprang away from the door and took off for the car.

Mary Lou ran after me, doing pretty good considering the tight pants and cowboy boots and the fact that she had legs several inches shorter than mine.

We piled into the car. Mary Lou rammed the key into the ignition, and the mom car jumped into chase mode. We whipped around the corner and saw Morelli's taillights disappear as he made a right-hand turn two blocks down.

"Perfect," I said. "We don't want to be so close that he sees us."

"Do you think he's going to see Terry?"

"It's possible. Or maybe he's relieving someone on stakeout."

Now that the first rush of emotion was behind me, I found it hard to believe Joe was romantically or sexually involved with Terry. It had nothing to do with Joe the man. It had to do with Joe the cop. Joe wouldn't get himself entangled with the Grizollis.

He'd told me he had something in common with Terry—that they were both in vice. And I suspected that was the connection. I thought it possible that Joe and Terry were working together, although I couldn't imagine in what capacity. And since the Feds were in town, I guessed Vito Grizolli was involved. Maybe Joe and Terry were acting as intermediaries between Vito and the Feds. And Bunchy's interest in the checks might support my skimming theory. Although I didn't know why the government would be interested in skimming.

Joe turned onto Hamilton, drove a quarter mile, and pulled into the 7-Eleven. Mary Lou zipped past him, circled a block, and waited at the side of the road with her lights off. Joe came out of the store carrying a bag and got back into his car.

"Oh, man, I'm dying to know what's in the bag," Mary Lou said. "Do they sell condoms at the 7-Eleven? I never noticed."

"He's got dessert in that bag," I said. "My money's on ice cream. Chocolate."

"And I bet he's taking the ice cream to Terry!"

His engine caught, and he retraced his route down Hamilton.

"He's not going to Terry's," I said. "He's going home."

"What a rip. I thought I was going to see some action."

I didn't actually want to see a whole lot of action. I just wanted to find Uncle Fred and get on with my life. Unfortunately, I wasn't going to learn anything new if Morelli sat in front of his television eating ice cream all night.

Mary Lou dropped a block behind Morelli, keeping him in

sight. He parked in front of his house, and Mary Lou and I parked on the cross street again. We got out of the mom car, skulked back down the alley, and stopped short at the edge of Morelli's yard. The light was on in his kitchen, and Morelli was moving in front of the window.

"What's he doing?" Mary Lou asked. "What's he doing?"

"Getting a spoon. I was right—he went out to buy ice cream."

The light blinked out, and Morelli disappeared. Mary Lou and I scuttled across Morelli's backyard and squinted into his window.

"Do you see him?" Mary Lou asked.

"No. He's disappeared."

"I didn't hear the front door open."

"No, and he's got the television on. He's just out of sight some-where."

Mary Lou crept closer. "Too bad he's got the shades pulled on his front windows."

"I'll try to be more considerate next time," Morelli said, stand-ing inches behind us.

Mary Lou and I yelped and instinctively sprang away, but Morelli had both of us by the back of our jackets.

"Look who we have here," Morelli said. "Lucy and Ethel. Is this the girls' night out?"

"We were looking for my cat," Mary Lou said. "It's been lost, and we thought we saw it run through your yard."

Morelli grinned at Mary Lou. "Nice to see you, Mary Lou. It's been a while."

"The kids keep me busy," Mary Lou said. "Soccer and pre-school and Kenny keeps getting these ear infections—"

"How's Lenny doing?"

"He's great. He's thinking about hiring someone else. His fa-ther's going to retire, you know."

Lenny had graduated from high school and had gone directly into the family business, Stankovik and Sons, Plumbing and Heat-ing. He made a good living at it, but he frequently smelled like stagnant water and metal piping.

"I need to talk to Stephanie," Morelli said.

Mary Lou started backing up. "Hey, don't let me get in the way. I was just leaving. I've got my car parked around the corner."

Morelli opened his back door. "You," he said, releasing my jacket. "Go in the house. I'll be right back. I'm going to walk Mary Lou to her car."

"Not necessary," Mary Lou said, looking nervous, like she was going to run like hell at any moment. "I can find my own way."

"It's dark back here," Morelli said to Mary Lou. "And you've just been contaminated by Calamity Jane. You're not getting out of my sight until you're safely locked in your car."

I did as I was told. I scurried into the house while Morelli walked Mary Lou to her car. And as soon as they cleared his yard I scrolled back through his caller ID. I scribbled the numbers on a pad by the phone, ripped the page off, and stuffed it into my pocket. The last number to come in had an identification block on it. No number available. If I'd known the number hadn't registered I might not have been so fast to jump to Morelli's command.

The ice cream was still sitting on the counter. And it was melting. Probably I should eat it, so it didn't get *totally* melted and have to get thrown away.

I was savoring the last spoonful when Morelli returned. He closed and locked the door behind him and pulled the shades.

I raised my eyebrows.

"Nothing personal," Morelli said, "but you've got bad people following you around. I don't want someone sniping at you through my kitchen window."

"You think it's that serious?"

"Honey, your car was bombed."

I was starting to get used to it. "How did you spot Mary Lou and me?"

"Rule number one, when you've got your nose pressed to someone's window . . . don't talk. Rule number two, when doing surveillance don't use a car with vanity plates that have your best friend's name on them. Rule three, never underestimate nosy neighbors. Mrs. Rupp called and wanted to know why you were standing in the alley, looking into her windows, and she was wondering if she should call the police. I explained it was most likely *my* windows you were looking in and reminded her that *I* was the police, so she needn't bother with another phone call."

"Well, it's all your fault because you won't tell me anything," I said.

"If I told you what was going on, you'd tell Mary Lou, and she'd tell Lenny, and Lenny would tell the guys down at the plumbing supply house, and the next day it'd be in the newspaper."

"Mary Lou doesn't tell Lenny anything," I said.

"What the hell was she wearing? She looked like the friendly neighborhood dominatrix. The only things missing were a whip and a pimp."

"She was making a fashion statement."

Morelli looked down at my utility belt.

"What kind of a statement is this?"

"Fear."

He gave his head a disbelieving shake. "You know what my biggest fear is? I worry that someday you might be the mother of my children."

I wasn't sure if I should be pleased or annoyed, so I changed the subject. "I deserve to know about this investigation," I said. "I'm sitting right in the middle of it." He was just implacably staring at me, so I hit him with the heavy stuff. "And I know about your late-night meetings with Terry. And not only that, but I am *not* going away. And I will continue to harass and follow you until I figure this out." So there.

"I'd tie you up and wrap you in a rug and drive you to the landfill," Morelli said, "but Mary Lou would probably finger me."

"Okay, so how about sex? Maybe we can make a deal?"

Morelli grinned. "You've got my attention."

"Start talking."

"Not so fast. I want to know what I'm going to get for this information."

483

"What do you want?"

"Everything."

"Not working tonight?"

He looked at his watch. "Shit. Yeah, I'm working. In fact I'm late. I need to relieve *Bunchy* on a surveillance watch."

"Who are you watching?"

He stared at me for a moment. "Okay, I'm going to tell you, because I don't want you riding all over Trenton looking for me. But if I find out you leaked this to anyone I swear I'll come get you."

I held my hand up. "Scout's honor. My lips are sealed."

THIRTEEN

MORELLI LEANED BACK against the counter and folded his arms. "Somehow it came to light that there was a discrepancy between how much money Vito Grizolli's cleaning business was taking in and how much was reported for income tax purposes."

"Gee, what a surprise."

"Yeah. Well, the Feds decided they wanted to nail him on it, so they started to do their thing, and it soon became pretty obvious that Vito, in fact, is losing money he has no knowledge of."

"Someone is skimming Vito?"

Morelli started to laugh. "Can you believe it?"

"Man, there's a lot of that going on."

"Enough to make it worthwhile for Treasury to deal with Vito so they can maybe get a bigger fish."

"Like what kind of a bigger fish?"

Morelli shrugged. "Don't know. The two brain surgeons I'm working with think it's some new crime organization."

"What do you think?"

"Until you showed me the checks, I thought it was just some guy with a death wish trying to pay off his mortgage. Now I'm not sure what I think, but a new crime organization feels far out there. I don't see any other signs of a new organization."

"Maybe it's just coincidence."

"I don't think so. There are too many things adding up. Three companies involved so far. Three accounts-receivable clerks have died. Another is missing. Fred is missing. Someone set a bomb to your car."

"How about the bank? Were Vito's missing accounts processed through First Trenton?"

"Yes. It'd be helpful to pull some records, but we'd run the risk of alerting whoever is involved that there's an investigation going on.

"It turns out, RGC had also been flagged for possible tax evasion. The RGC stands for Ruben, Grizolli, and Cotell. I knew Grizolli was part owner, but I didn't know there'd been any irregularities. My Treasury contacts didn't tell me that part."

"You're working as a team, and they didn't tell you about RGC?"

"You don't know these guys. Real hot dogs. And they don't like being coupled with local law enforcement."

I smiled at him.

"Yeah, I know," he said. "Sounds like I'm describing myself. Anyway, Bronfman, the guy you know as Bunchy, was doing surveillance at RGC, looking to see who went in and out. He was sitting in the café across the street the Friday that Fred disappeared. I guess Fred had wanted to get an early start, but he got to RGC before the office opened, so he went across the street for coffee. Bronfman and Fred got to talking and Bronfman realized Fred was one of the nonrecorded accounts. The following Tuesday, Bronfman got to thinking it might be helpful to get a canceled check from Fred, one way or another, went to talk to Fred, and discovered Fred was missing.

"When Mabel told him you were on the case, Bronfman decided he could use you to front for him. You could poke around and ask questions, and it wasn't as likely anyone would run for the hills. Didn't turn out exactly as he'd planned, because he hadn't counted on your ornery, suspicious nature."

"I didn't tell him much."

"No. His efforts got him zero. That's the good part." Morelli locked eyes with me. "Now that you know what's going on, you're going to tell me what you have, though, right?"

"Sure." Maybe.

"Christ," Morelli said.

"Hey, I might tell you something."

"I'm sorry, I didn't have enough pieces to put this together sooner."

"Part my fault," I said.

"Yeah, part your fault. You're not talking to me enough. Part my fault, too."

"What's your role with Treasury?"

"Vito wouldn't talk to them directly. Said he'd only deal with someone he knew. And I guess he feels protected when information goes through a couple of sources. Makes it easier to deny. So Vito talks to Terry, and Terry talks to me, and I talk to Frick and Frack."

"Who are you watching?"

Morelli flipped the kitchen light off. "Vito's accounts-receivable person. Harvey Tipp."

"You better be watching him close. Harvey's life expectancy might not be too good."

MORELLI DROPPED ME off on his way to relieve Bronfman.

"Thanks for the ride," I told Morelli.

He snagged my collar as I turned to leave. "We have an agreement," he said. "And you owe me."

"Now?"

"Later."

"How much later?"

"To be determined," Morelli said. "I just don't want you to forget."

Not much chance of that.

Briggs was working when I got upstairs. "You keep long hours," I said.

"I've got to get this project done. I lost a lot of ground when my apartment got burglarized. I was lucky I had my laptop in the closet in the bedroom, and they missed it. I had most of my work backed up on the laptop, so it wasn't a total disaster."

I WOKE UP at four and couldn't get back to sleep. I lay there for an hour, listening for sounds on my fire escape, planning my escape should someone toss a fire bomb through my bedroom window. Finally I gave up and tiptoed into the kitchen for a snack. I had so many things to worry about I could barely sort through them. Fred was last on the list. Morelli collecting on what was owed was closer to the top.

Briggs padded in after me. "Spooked again?"

"Yeah. Too much on my mind. I can't sleep." I looked down at him. He was wearing Winnie-the-Pooh pajamas. "Nice jammies," I said.

"I have a hard time finding things that fit. When I want to really impress the ladies I wear Spider-Man."

"Is it hard being a little person?"

"Has its ups and downs. I get a lot of perks because people think I'm cute. And I try to take advantage of my minority status."

"I noticed."

"Hey," Briggs said, "you gotta use what God gave you."

"True."

"So, you want to do something? You want to play Monopoly?"

"Okay, but I want to be the shoe."

We were still playing at seven o'clock, when the phone rang.

"I'm in your parking lot," Ranger said. "Do you want to come down, or do you want me to come up?"

"Why are you calling? You always just break in."

488

"I didn't want to take a chance on scaring the hell out of you and getting shot."

"Good thinking. What's the occasion?"

"Wheels, Babe."

I went to the window, pulled the curtain aside, and looked down at Ranger. He was standing alongside a black BMW.

"I'll be right down," I said to Ranger. "Give me a minute to get dressed."

I pulled on a pair of jeans, shoved my feet into ratty sneakers, and covered my flannel nightshirt with an oversized gray sweatshirt. I grabbed my keys and took off for the stairs.

"Looking a little scary, Babe," Ranger said when he saw me.

"A friend of mine suggested this look could be a new concept in birth control."

"It's not *that* scary."

I smoothed an imaginary wrinkle from my sweatshirt and closely examined a speck of lint on my sleeve. I looked up and found Ranger smiling.

"The ball's in your court," Ranger said. "Let me know when you're ready."

"For the car?"

He smiled.

"Are you sure you want to give me another car?"

"This one's equipped with sensors on the undercarriage." He held a small remote. "Push the green button to set the sensors. If there's motion under the car the alarm sounds and the red light on the dash stays lit. Unfortunately, the car doesn't know the difference between a cat, a baseball, and a bomb, so if the light is flashing you have to do some investigating. Not perfect, but better than stepping on the accelerator and being turned into confetti. Probably it's not necessary. It's unlikely someone would try to blow you up twice." He handed the remote over to me and explained the rest of the security system.

"Just like James Bond," I said.

"You have plans for the day?"

"I need to call Morelli and see if the guy who delayed me at RGC, Mark Stemper, turned up. Then I suppose I'll do my rounds. Visit Mabel. Check in at the office. Harass the garbage people." Keep my eyes peeled for Ramirez. Have my head examined.

"Somebody out there's feeling real cranky because you're not dead. You might want to wear your vest."

I watched him drive away, and before I went into the building I armed the car. I finished up the game with Briggs, took a shower, shook my head with the hopes it would style my hair, and applied mascara so people would notice my eyes and not pay too close attention to the rest of me.

I scrambled an egg and ate it with a glass of orange juice and a multivitamin. A healthy breakfast to start the day off right—just in case I lived through the morning.

I decided Ranger might have a good idea about the vest. It made me sort of flat-chested, but then, what didn't? I was wearing jeans and boots and a T-shirt with the vest Velcroed tight to my body. I buttoned a navy flannel shirt over the vest and thought it didn't look too bad.

There were no bomb alert lights flashing when I got to the car, so I slid behind the wheel feeling secure. My parents' house was first on the visitation list. I thought it wouldn't hurt to have a cup of coffee and catch up on the latest rumors.

Grandma appeared at the door the minute I swerved in to the curb. "Boy, that's a pip of a car," she said, watching me angle out and set the security system. "What kind of car is it?"

"It's a BMW."

"We just read in the paper where you had a Porsche, and it got blown up. Your mother's in the bathroom taking an aspirin."

I ran up the porch stairs two at a time. "It was in the paper?"

"Yeah, only they didn't have a picture of you, like usual. They just had a picture of the car. Boy, it looked flat as a pancake."

Great. "Did they say anything else?"

"They called you the Bombshell Bounty Hunter."

Maybe I needed an aspirin too. I dropped my shoulder bag on a kitchen chair and reached for the paper on the table. Oh, God, it was on the front page.

"The paper said the police were pretty sure it was a bomb," Grandma said. "Only after the garbage truck fell on the car I guess they had a hard time figuring out what was what."

My mother came into the kitchen. "Whose car is that parked in front of our house?"

"That's Stephanie's new car," Grandma said. "Isn't it a pip?"

One of my mother's eyebrows raised in question. "Two new cars? Where are these cars coming from?"

"Company cars," I said.

"Oh?"

"Anal sex is *not* involved," I told her.

My mother and grandmother both gasped.

"Sorry," I said. "It just slipped out."

"I thought only homosexual men did anal sex," Grandma said.

"Anybody with an anus can do it," I told her.

"Hmm," she said. "I got one of them."

I poured a cup of coffee and sat at the table. "So what's new?"

Grandma got coffee and sat across from me. "Harriet Mullen had a baby boy. They had to do a C-section on her at the last minute, but everything turned out okay. And Mickey Szajak died. Guess it was about time."

"Are you hearing anything these days about Vito Grizolli?"

"I saw him at the meat market last week, and I thought he'd put on some weight."

"How's he doing financially?"

"I hear he's making big money on that cleaning business. And I saw Vivien driving a new Buick."

Vivien was Vito's wife. She was sixty-five, wore fake eyelashes, and dyed her hair bright red because that's the way Vito liked it. Anyone who voiced a critical opinion got fitted with cement booties and accidentally took a dive into the Delaware River.

"I don't suppose there are any rumors going around about First Trenton."

My mother and grandmother both looked up from their coffee.

"The bank?" my mother asked. "Why do you want to know about the bank?"

"I don't know. Fred had an account there. I was just fishing."

Grandma stared at my chest. "You look different. Are you wearing one of them sports brassieres?" She looked more closely. "Hot dog. I know what it is. You're wearing a bulletproof vest. Ellen, look at this," she said to my mother. "Stephanie's wearing a bulletproof vest. Isn't that something?"

My mother's face had turned white. "Why me?" she said.

NEXT STOP WAS Mabel's house.

Mabel opened the door and smiled. "Stephanie, how nice to see you, dear. Would you like tea?"

"I can't stay," I said. "I just wanted to stop around and see how you were doing."

"Isn't that sweet of you. I'm doing peachy. I think I've decided on a trip to Bermuda."

I picked a brochure off the coffee table. "Singles cruises for seniors?"

"They have some very good rates."

"Anything happen that I should know about? Like, have you heard from Fred?"

"I haven't heard a word from Fred. I suppose he's dead."

Boy, don't get all broken up over it. "It's only been two weeks," I said. "He could still turn up."

Mabel slid a longing look at the brochures. "I suppose that's true."

Ten minutes later I was at the office.

"Hey, girlfriend," Lula said. "Did you see the paper this morning? You got a big spread. And not that I'm bummed or anything, but I didn't even get a mention. And I didn't get a cool name like

Bombshell Bounty Hunter either. Hell, I could bombshell your ass off."

"I know that," I said. "And that's why I was wondering if you wanted to ride along with me again today?"

"I don't know. What kind of car are you driving? You back to driving that Buick?"

"Actually, I have a Beemer."

Lula rushed to the front window and looked out. "Damn skippy. Way to go."

Vinnie stuck his head out of his office doorway. "What's going on?"

"Stephanie got a new car," Lula said. "That's it at the curb."

"Anybody hear about anything funny going on at First Trenton?" I asked. "Anybody shady work there?"

"You should ask the little guy we talked to yesterday," Lula said. "I can't remember his name, but he seemed like a nice guy. You don't think he's shady, do you?"

"Hard to tell who's shady," I said to Lula. Actually, I thought shady would be a step up for Shempsky.

"Where'd you get the car?" Vinnie asked.

"It's a company car. I'm working with Ranger."

Vinnie's face creased into a big, oily smile. "Ranger gave you a car? Hah! What kind of work you doing? Gotta be good to get a car like that."

"Maybe you should ask Ranger," I said.

"Yeah, sure, when I don't want to live anymore."

"Any new FTAs come in?" I asked Connie.

"We got two in yesterday, but they're chump change. I wasn't sure you wanted to be bothered with them. Seems like you've got a lot on your plate right now."

"What's the profile?"

"A shoplifter and a wife beater."

"We'll take the wife beater," Lula said. "We don't allow no wife beaters to just walk away. We like to give the wife beaters personal attention."

I took the file from Connie and sifted through it. Kenyon Lally. Age twenty-eight. Unemployed. Long history of spousal abuse. Two DUI convictions. Living in the projects. No mention of Kenyon shooting any previous bounty hunters.

"Okay," I said, "we'll take this one."

"Oh boy," Lula said. "I'm gonna squash this guy like a roach."

"No. No, no, no, no, no roach squashing. No unnecessary force."

"Sure," Lula said. "I know that. But we could use *necessary* force, right?"

"Necessary force won't be necessary."

"Just don't beat the crap out of him like you did with the computer nerd," Vinnie said. "I keep telling you, kick them in the kidney where it don't show."

"Must be scary being related to him," Lula said, looking over at Vinnie.

Connie filled in my authorization to apprehend and gave the file back to me. I dropped it into my bag and hiked my bag higher on my shoulder. "Later."

"Later," Connie said. "And watch out for garbage trucks."

I beeped the alarm off, and Lula and I got in the Beemer.

"This is cushy," Lula said. "Big woman like me needs a car like this. I sure would like to know where Ranger gets all these cars. See that little silver strip with the numbers on it. That's your registration number. So theoretically this car isn't even stolen."

"Theoretically." Ranger probably had those strips made by the gross. I punched Morelli's number into the car phone and after six rings I got his answering machine. I left a message and tried his pager.

"Not that it's any of my business," Lula said, "but what's going on with you and Morelli? I thought that was over with you two when you moved out."

"It's complicated."

"Your problem is you keep getting involved with men who have lots of potential in bed and no potential at the altar."

"I'm thinking of giving men up altogether," I said. "Celibacy isn't so bad. You don't have to worry about shaving your legs."

The phone rang, and I answered it on the speakerphone.

"What number is this?" Morelli wanted to know.

"It's my new car phone number."

"In the Buick?"

"No. Ranger gave me another car."

Silence.

"What kind of car is it this time?" he finally asked.

"Beemer."

"Has it got a registration number on it?"

"Yes."

"Is it fake?"

I shrugged. "It doesn't look fake."

"That'll go far in court."

"Have you heard anything about Mark Stemper?"

"No. I think he's probably playing rummy with your uncle Fred."

"How about Laura Lipinski?"

"Disappeared off the face of the earth. Left home the Thursday before your uncle disappeared."

Perfect timing to get stuffed into a garbage bag. "Thanks. That's all I wanted. Over and out."

I pulled into the Grand Union parking lot and drove to the end of the mall where the bank was located. I parked at a safe distance from other cars, exited the BMW, and set the alarm.

"You want me to stay with the car in case someone's riding around with a bomb in his backseat looking for a place to put it?" Lula asked.

"Not necessary. Ranger says the car has sensors."

"Ranger give you a car with bomb sensors? The head of the CIA don't even have a car with bomb sensors. I hear they give him a stick with a mirror on the end of it."

"I don't think it's anything space-age. Sounds to me like they're just motion detectors mounted on the undercarriage."

"Boy, I'd like to know where he got the motion detectors. This would probably be a good night to rob the governor's mansion."

I was starting to feel like a regular customer at the bank. I said hello to the guard at the door, and I waved to Leona. I looked for Shempsky, but he wasn't visible, and his office was empty.

"He's out to lunch," the guard said. "Took it earlier than usual today."

No problem. Leona was giving me the *come here!* gesture, anyway.

"I read about you in the paper," she said. "They said your car was bombed!"

"Yeah. And then a garbage truck fell on it."

"It was excellent," Lula said. "It was the shit."

"Boy, nothing fun ever happens to me," Leona said. "I've never had a car bombed or anything."

"But you work at a bank," I told her. "That's pretty cool. And you have kids. Kids are the best." Okay, so I fibbed a little about the kids. I didn't want her to feel bad. I mean we can't all be lucky enough to have a hamster.

"We came to see if you had any suspicious characters working here," Lula said.

Leona looked startled by that. "In the bank?"

"Well, maybe 'suspicious' is the wrong word," I told her. "Is there anyone here who might have connections with people who might not be totally law-abiding?"

Leona rolled her eyes. "Almost everybody. Marion Beddle was a Grizolli before she was married. You know about Vito Grizolli? And then Phil Zuck in mortgages lives next door to Sy Bernstein, the lawyer who was just disbarred for illegal practices. The guard has a brother in Rahway, doing time for burglary. You want me to go on?"

"Let's take this from a different direction. Is there anyone here who looks too successful for his job? You know, has too much money? Or is there anyone here who desperately needs money? Anyone who likes to gamble? Anyone doing expensive drugs?"

"Hmm. That's a harder question. Annie Shuman has a sick kid. Some kind of bone disease. Lots of doctor bills. Couple of people who play the numbers. I'm one of them. Rose White likes to go to Atlantic City and play the slots."

"I don't get what you want to know this for anyway," Lula said to me.

"We know of three companies with extra accounts in this bank. We think there's a possibility those accounts were opened to hold illegal money. So maybe there's a good reason the accounts were opened here."

"Like someone here in the bank is involved," Lula said.

"I see where you're going," Leona said. "You're suggesting we're laundering money. The money comes into those accounts you asked me about and almost immediately goes out."

"I don't know if it's exactly laundering," I said. "Where does the money go?"

"I don't have that information," Leona said. "You'd need a bank officer for that. And probably they wouldn't tell you. I'm sure that would be confidential. You should talk to Shempsky."

We hung around for another fifteen minutes, but Shempsky didn't materialize.

"Maybe we should go get that wife beater," Lula said. "I bet he's sitting in his living room, drinking beer, being a jerk."

I looked at my watch. Noon. Chances were good that Kenyon Lally was just getting up. Unemployed drunks were usually slow risers. Might be a good time to snag him.

"Okay," I said, "we'll take a ride over."

"Gonna fit right in with the BMW," Lula said. "Everybody in the projects gonna think you're a drug dealer."

Oh, great.

"I know about the bomb sensors and all," Lula said after we'd gone about a half mile, "but I still got the heebie-jeebies sitting next to you."

I knew exactly where she was coming from. I felt like that, too. "I could take you back to the office if you're uncomfortable."

"Hell, no. I'm not that freaked out. It just makes you wonder, you know? Anyway, I felt like that when I was a 'ho, too. You never knew when you were gonna get in the car with some maniac."

"It must have been a tough job."

"Most of my customers were repeaters, so that wasn't too bad. The worst part was standing around on the corner. Don't matter if it's hot or cold or raining, you still gotta stand there. Most people think the hard part's being on your back, but the hard part is being on your feet all day and night. I got varicose veins from standing too many hours on my feet. I guess if I'd been a better 'ho I'd have been on my back more and my feet less."

I took Nottingham to Greenwood, turned right off Greenwood, and crossed the railroad tracks. Trenton subsidized housing always reminded me of a POW camp, and in many ways, that's exactly what it was. Although, in all fairness, I have to say they aren't the worst I've ever seen. And they were preferable to living on Stark Street. I suppose the original vision was of garden apartments, but the reality is cement and brick bunkers squatting on hard-packed dirt. If I had to find a single word to describe the neighborhood, I'd have to choose *bleak*.

"We want the next building," Lula said. "Apartment 4B."

I parked around the corner, a block away, so Lally wouldn't see us coming, got out, and studied Lally's photo.

"Nice touch with the vest," Lula said. "It'll come in handy when the Welcome Wagon shows up."

The sky was gray and the wind whipped across yards. A few cars were parked on the street, but there was no activity. No dogs, no kids, no stoop sitters. It looked like a ghost town with Hitler as architect.

Lula and I walked to 4B and rang the bell.

Kenyon Lally answered the door. He was my height and rangy, wearing low-slung jeans and a thermal T-shirt. His hair was uncombed, and his face was unshaven. And he looked like a man who smacked women around.

"Hunh," Lula said when she saw him.

498

"We don't need no Girl Scout cookies," Lally said. And he slammed the door shut.

"I hate when people do that," Lula said.

I rang the bell again, but there was no response.

"Hey!" Lula yelled. "Bail Enforcement Agents. Open this door!"

"Go fuck yourself," Lally yelled back.

"The hell with this bullshit," Lula said. She gave the door a kick with her foot, and the door banged open.

We were both so surprised we just stood there. Neither of us had expected the door to open.

"Government housing," Lula finally said with a shake of her head. "It makes you wonder, don't it?"

"You're gonna pay for that," Lally said.

Lula was standing with her hands in her jacket pockets. "How about you make me? Why don't you come get me, Mr. Tough Guy?"

Lally charged Lula. Lula stuck out her hand, made contact with Lally's chest, and Lally went down like a sack of sand.

"Fastest stun gun in the East," Lula said. "Oops, look at that . . . damn, I accidentally kicked the wife beater."

I cuffed Lally and checked to make sure he was breathing.

"Shoot," Lula said. "I'm so careless, I accidentally kicked him again." She bent over Lally with the stun gun still in her hand. "Want me to make him jump?"

"No!" I said. "No jumping!"

FOURTEEN

AFTER FIFTEEN MINUTES, Lally's eyes were open and his fingers were twitching, but I could see that it might take awhile longer before he was up to walking any kind of distance.

"You should join a gym," Lula told Lally. "And you should lay off the beer. You're out of shape. I only buzzed you once, and look at you. I never saw anybody so pathetic from one measly jolt."

I gave Lula the car keys. "Bring the car over so he doesn't have to walk so far."

"You might never see me again," Lula said.

"Ranger would find you."

"Yeah," Lula said, "that'd be the best part."

Five minutes later, Lula was back.

"It's gone," she said.

"What's gone?"

"The car. The car's gone."

"What do you mean, it's gone?"

"What part of 'gone' don't you understand?" Lula asked.

"You don't mean it's been stolen?"

"Yep. That's just what I mean. The car's been stolen."

My heart did a nosedive. I didn't want to believe what I was

500

hearing. "How could someone steal the car? We didn't hear the alarm go off."

"Must have gone off when we were inside here. It's a distance, and the wind's blowing away from us. Anyway, the brothers know how to take care of that kind of stuff. I'm real surprised, though. I figured you see a nice car in this kind of neighborhood and you think dealer. And messing with a dealer's car don't do a whole lot for your quality of life. Guess these guys were low on their daily quota. I got there just as the flatbed was turning the corner two blocks away. They must have been in the area."

"What am I going to tell Ranger?"

"Tell him the good news is they left him his plates." Lula handed me two license plates. "And guess they didn't want the registration number. They left that, too. Looks like they took it off with an acetylene torch." She dropped a small piece of scorched dashboard with the metal tag still attached into the palm of my hand.

"That's it?"

"Yep. That's what they left at the side of the road for you."

Lally was flopping around on the floor, trying to get to his feet, but his coordination was off and his hands were cuffed behind his back. He was drooling and cussing and slurring his words.

"Fruckin' bish," he said to me. "Fruckin' peesh a shit."

I searched in my bag for the cell phone, found it, and called Vinnie. I explained I had Kenyon Lally in custody, but there was a small problem with my car, and would he please come collect Lally and Lula and me.

"What's the problem?" Vinnie wanted to know.

"It's nothing. It's trivial. Don't worry about it."

"I'm not coming until you tell me. I bet this is something good."

I blew out a sigh. "The car's been stolen."

"That's it?"

"Yeah."

"Jeez, I expected something better . . . like it got hit by a train or sat on by an elephant."

"Are you going to come get us, or what?"

"I'm on my way. Hold your bladder."

We sat down to wait for Vinnie, and my cell phone rang. Lula and I exchanged glances.

"You expecting a call?" Lula asked.

Both of us thinking it might be Ranger.

"Well, answer it," Lally said. "Stoopid fruck."

"It could be Vinnie," Lula said. "He might have found a goat walking down the middle of the road and decided to do a nooner."

I searched through my bag, found the phone, crossed all my fingers and my eyes, and answered.

It was Joe. "We found Mark Stemper," he said.

"And?"

"He doesn't look good."

Damn. "How bad does he look?"

"He looks dead. Shot in the head. Someone tried to make it look like a suicide, but among other things they put the gun in the wrong hand. Stemper was left-handed."

"Oops."

"Yeah. Not very professional."

"Where'd it happen?"

"In an abandoned building a couple blocks from RGC. A watchman found him."

"You ever wonder why Harvey Tipp is still alive?"

"I guess he must pose no threat," Morelli said. "Or maybe he's related to Mr. Big. Or maybe he's not involved. We really have nothing on him, other than the fact that he's the logical person."

"I think it's time you talked to him."

"I think you're right." There was a moment of silence. "One more thing. Are you still driving the BMW?"

"Nope. Not me. Gave up on that puppy."

"What happened to it?"

"Stolen."

I could hear Morelli laughing over the phone.

"It's not funny!" I yelled. "Do you think I should file a police report?"

"I think you should talk to Ranger first. Do you need a ride?"

"No. Vinnie's on his way."

"Later, Hotstuff."

I disconnected and told Lula about Stemper.

"Somebody don't like leaving loose ends," Lula said.

I took a deep breath and dialed Ranger's home phone. No answer. Car phone. No answer. I could try his cell phone, but I didn't want to press my luck, so I left my number on his pager. The condemned woman gets a few extra minutes.

I'd been watching the window, and I saw Vinnie pull up in his Cadillac. I thought it might be satisfying to delay Vinnie for a half hour and see if his car disappeared, but dismissed it as being not practical. I'd only have to call yet another person to come collect us. And even worse, I'd have to spend time with Vinnie.

Lula and I dragged Lally out to the curb and waited while Vinnie popped his door locks.

"Scumbags sit in the backseat," Vinnie said.

"Hunh," Lula said, hand on hip, "who you callin' a scumbag?"

"If the shoe fits," Vinnie said.

"If the shoe fits, you'd have your pervert ass in the backseat," Lula said.

"Why me?" I asked. I realized I sounded like my mother and had a brief panic attack. I liked my mother, but I didn't want to *be* her. I didn't want to ever cook a pot roast. I didn't want to live in a house with three adults and only one bathroom. And I didn't want to marry my father. I wanted to marry Indiana Jones. I figured Indiana Jones was the middle ground between my father and Ranger. Morelli fit in there, too. In fact, Morelli wasn't too far off the Indiana Jones mark. Not that it mattered, since Morelli didn't want to get married.

Vinnie dropped Lula and me at the office and took Lally to the police station on North Clinton.

"Well, that was fun," Lula said. "Too bad about the car. I can't wait to see what you get next."

"I'm getting nothing next. I'm not taking any more cars. From now on, I'm driving the Buick. Nothing ever happens to the Buick."

"Yeah," Lula said, "but that isn't necessarily a good thing."

I dialed First Trenton, asked for Shempsky, and was told he'd gone home early with an upset stomach. I got his home number out of the directory and tried to reach him there. No answer. Just for the hell of it, I ran a fast credit check. Nothing unusual. Mortgage, credit cards all in good standing.

"Why are you checking on Shempsky?" Lula asked. "You think he's involved?"

"I keep thinking about the bomb in the Porsche. Shempsky knew I was driving a Porsche."

"Yeah, but he could have told people. He could have mentioned to someone you were going to the garbage company in your brand-new Porsche."

"True."

"Do you want a ride someplace?" Lula asked.

I shook my head no. "I could use some air and exercise," I said. "I'm going to walk home."

"That's a long walk."

"It's not so long."

I stepped outside and turned my jacket collar up against the wind. The temperature had dropped and the sky was gray. It was midafternoon, but houses had lights on to fight the gloom. Furnaces were running. Cars rolled by on Hamilton, drivers intent on getting somewhere. There were few people on the sidewalks. It was a good day to be indoors, cleaning out closets, making hot chocolate, organizing a fresh start for winter. And it was a good day to be outdoors, scuffing through the few remaining leaves, feeling flushed from the cold air. It was my favorite time of the year. And if it wasn't for the fact that people were dying left and right, and I couldn't find Uncle Fred, and someone wanted to kill me, and Ramirez wanted to send me to Jesus—it would be a *very* good day.

In an hour I was back at my building, in the lobby, and I was feeling fine. My head was clear and my circulation was in top form. The Buick was sitting in the parking lot, looking solid as a rock and just as serene. I had the keys in my pocket, and I was still wondering about Shempsky. Maybe I should ride by and see him, I thought. Surely he'll be home by now.

The elevator doors opened and Mrs. Bestler leaned out. "Going up?"

"No," I said. "I changed my mind. I have more errands to run."

"All ladies' accessories are twenty percent off on the second floor," she said. She pulled her head back and the doors closed.

I recrossed the lot and gingerly unlocked the Buick. Nothing went *boom*, so I slid behind the wheel. I started the car and jumped out. I stood a good distance away and timed ten minutes. Still no explosion. Whew. Big relief. I got back in the car, put it into gear, and drove out of the lot. Shempsky lived in Hamilton Township, off Klockner, behind the high school. Typical suburban development of single-family houses. Two cars, two incomes, two kids per family. It was easy to find his street and his house. It was all clearly marked. His house was a split-entry frame. White with black shutters. Very tidy.

I parked at the curb, walked to the door, and rang the bell. I was about to ring again when a woman answered. She was nicely dressed in a brown sweater, matching slacks, and rubber-soled loafers. Her hair was cut in a short bob. Her makeup was Martha Stewart. And her smile was genuine. She was the perfect match for Allen. I suspected I would immediately forget anything she told me, and a half hour from now I wouldn't recall what she looked like.

"Maureen?" I asked.

"Yes?"

"It's Stephanie Plum . . . we went to school together."

She slapped herself on the forehead. "Of course! I should have remembered. Allen mentioned you the other night. He said you'd stopped by the bank." The smile faded. "I heard about Fred. I'm so sorry."

"You haven't seen him, have you?" Just in case she had him in her basement.

"No!"

"I always ask," I explained, since she looked taken aback.

"And it's a good idea. I might have seen him walking down the street."

"Exactly."

So far, I hadn't seen any sign of Allen. Of course, if he was really sick he might be upstairs in bed. "Is Allen here?" I asked Maureen. "I tried to catch him at the bank, but he'd gone out to lunch, and then I got busy with another matter. I thought maybe he'd be home by now."

"No. He always comes home at five." The smile popped back in place. "Would you like to come in and wait? I could make some herb tea."

The nosy part of me would have liked to snoop through the Shempsky's house. The part of me that wanted to live to see another day thought it wise not to leave the Buick unguarded.

"Thanks, maybe some other time," I said to Maureen. "I need to keep my eye on the Buick."

"Mom," a kid yelled from the kitchen, "Timmy's got an M&M's stuck up his nose."

Maureen shook her head and smiled. "Children," she said. "You know how it is."

"Actually, I have a hamster," I said. "Hard to get an M&M's up his nose."

"I'll be right back," Maureen said. "This will only take a minute."

I stepped into the foyer and looked around while Maureen hustled off to the kitchen. The living room opened off to the right. It was a large, pleasant room done in tones of tan. An upright piano stood against the near wall. Family photos covered the top of the piano. Allen and Maureen and the kids at the beach, at Disney World, at Christmas.

Lots of pictures. Probably one wouldn't be missed if it happened to jump into my purse.

I heard a kid yelp, and Maureen chirped that everything was hunky-dory and the bad M&M's was bye-bye. "I'll be right back," Maureen said. The kitchen television was clicked on, and in the blink of an eye, I snatched the nearest photo, dropped it into my bag, and stepped back into the foyer.

"Sorry about that," Maureen said, returning. "Never a dull moment."

I handed Maureen a business card. "Maybe you could have Allen give me a call when he gets in."

"Sure."

"By the way, what kind of car does Allen drive?"

"A tan Taurus. And then there's the Lotus."

"Allen has a Lotus?"

"It's his toy."

Expensive toy.

It was necessary to pass by the strip mall on my way home, so I did a short detour into the lot and checked out the bank. The lobby was closed, but the drive-through window was open. That didn't do me any good. Allen wasn't going to be doing drive-through duty. I rode around the lot looking for a tan Taurus, but had no luck.

"Allen," I said, "where *are* you?"

And then, since I was in the neighborhood, I thought it wouldn't hurt to stop by and say hello to Irene Tully. And, what the hell, I might as well show her the picture of Allen Shempsky. You never know what could jog a person's memory.

"For goodness' sake," Irene said when she opened the door. "Are you still looking for Fred?" She gave an apprehensive glance to the Buick. "Is your grandmother with you?"

"Grandma's at home. I was hoping you wouldn't mind looking at another picture."

"Is this that dead man again?"

"No. This guy's alive." I gave her the photo of the Shempsky family.

"Isn't this nice," Irene said. "What a lovely family."

"Do you recognize any of these people?"

"Not offhand. I might have seen the man somewhere, but I can't place him."

"Could he have been the man Uncle Fred talked to in the parking lot?"

"I guess it's possible. If it wasn't this man, it was someone very much like him. He was just an ordinary man. I suppose that's why I can't remember him so good. There wasn't anything special to remember. Of course, he wasn't wearing a Mickey Mouse hat and Bermuda shorts."

I retrieved the photo. "Thanks. You've been very helpful."

"Anytime," she said. "You always have such interesting pictures."

I bypassed the street that led to my apartment building and continued down Hamilton to the Burg. I'd been thinking about the bombing, and I had a plan. Since I wasn't going anywhere tonight, I'd lock the Buick up in my parents' garage and bum a ride home from my dad. Not only would it keep the car safe, but it had the added advantage of getting me dinner.

I didn't have to worry about the garage being in use, because my father never put his car in the garage. The garage was used to store jugs of motor oil and old tires. My father had a workbench in there along one wall. He had a vise attached to the workbench, and little jars filled with nails and things lined the back of the workbench. I never saw him work at the workbench, but when he got really fed up with my grandmother, my father would hide in the garage and smoke a cigar.

"Uh-oh," Grandma said when she saw me at the door. "This don't look good. Where's the black car?"

"It got stolen."

"Already? You didn't even have it a whole day."

I went into the kitchen and got the garage keys. "I'm going to put the Buick in the garage overnight," I said to my mother. "Is that okay?"

My mother put her hand to her heart. "My God, you're going to get our garage blown up."

"Nobody's going to blow up the garage." Not unless they were sure I was in it.

"I have a ham," my mother said. "Are you staying for supper?"

"Sure."

I put the Buick in the garage, locked everything up nice and tight, and went into the house to have ham.

"It's gonna be two weeks tomorrow since Fred's been missing," Grandma said at dinner. "I thought for sure he'd have turned up by now—one way or another. Even aliens don't keep people that long. Usually they just probe your insides and let you go."

My father hunkered down over his plate.

"Of course, maybe they started probing Fred and he croaked. What do you think they'd do then? You think they'd just pitch him out? Maybe their spaceship was over Afghanistan when they tossed Fred, and we'll never find him. Good thing he isn't a woman, what with landing in Afghanistan and all. I hear they don't treat women so good over there."

My mother paused with her fork halfway to her mouth, and her eyes darted to the side window. She listened like that for a moment and then resumed eating.

"Nobody's going to bomb the garage," I said to her. "I'm almost sure of it."

"Boy, wouldn't it be something if someone *did* bomb our garage," Grandma said. "That'd be a good story to tell at the beauty parlor."

I was starting to wonder why I hadn't received a call from Ranger. It wasn't like him not to get back to me right away. I set my shoulder bag on my lap and pawed through the clutter, looking for my cell phone.

"What are you looking for?" Grandma asked.

"My cell phone. I've got so much junk in my bag I can never find anything." I started pulling stuff out and setting it on the table. Can of hairspray, hairbrush, zippered makeup pouch, flashlight, mini-binoculars, Ranger's license plates, bottle of nail polish, stun gun . . .

Grandma leaned over the table to take a better look. "What's that thing?"

"Stun gun," I said.

"What's it do?"

"It emits an electrical charge."

My father forked in more ham, focusing his concentration on his plate.

Grandma got out of her seat and came around to examine the stun gun. "What do you do with this?" she wanted to know, picking it up and studying it. "How does it work?"

I was still rooting through my bag. "You press the metal prongs against someone and push the button," I said.

"Stephanie," my mother said, "take that away from your grand-mother before she electrocutes herself."

"Aha!" I said, finding my cell phone. I pulled it out and looked at it. Dead battery. No wonder Ranger hadn't called.

"Look, Frank," my grandmother said to my father, "did you ever see anything like this? Stephanie says you just stick it against someone and push the button . . ."

My mother and I both jumped out of our seats. "No!"

Too late. Grandma had the prongs pressed against my father's arm. *Zzzzzt.*

My father's eyes glazed over, a piece of ham fell out of his mouth, and he crashed to the floor.

"He must have had a heart attack," Grandma said, looking down at my father. "I told him and told him, he uses too much gravy."

"It's the stun gun!" I yelled at her. "That's what happens when you use a stun gun on someone!"

Grandma bent down for a closer look. "Did I kill him?"

My mother was on her knees alongside my grandmother. "Frank?" she shouted. "Can you hear me, Frank?"

I took his pulse. "He's okay," I said. "Grandma just scrambled some brain cells. It's not permanent. He'll be good as new in a couple minutes."

My father opened an eye and farted.

"Oops," Grandma said. "Someone must have stepped on a duck."

We all backed away and fanned the air.

"I have a nice chocolate cake for dessert," my mother said.

I used my parents' phone in the kitchen and left a new message on Ranger's machine. "Sorry about my cell phone. The battery conked out. I'll be home in about a half-hour. I need to talk to you." Then I called Mary Lou and asked her to give me a lift home. I didn't think it was such a good idea to ask my dad to drive so soon after getting zapped. And I didn't want my mom to take me and leave my grandmother and father alone in the house together. And first and foremost, I didn't want to be there when my father went nuts at Grandma Mazur.

"I've been *dying* to hear from you," Mary Lou said when she picked me up. "What happened with Morelli last night?"

"Not a lot. We talked about the case he's working on, and then he took me home."

"That's it?"

"Pretty much."

"No fooling around?"

"Nope."

"So let me get this straight. Last night you were with the two sexiest men in the entire world, and you didn't score with either one of them?"

"There are other things in this life besides scoring with men," I said.

"Like what?"

"I could score with myself."

"You could go blind doing that."

511

"No! I mean, I could feel good about myself. You know, like when you do a job and it turns out excellent. Or when you set a moral standard for yourself and stick to it."

Mary Lou gave me the open-mouth, wrinkled-nose, this-is-a-load-of-bullshit look. "What?"

"Well, okay, so I've never had any of those things happen, but they could!"

"And pigs could fly," Mary Lou said, "but personally, I'd rather have an orgasm."

Mary Lou swung into the lot and stopped short, jerking both of us against the shoulder harness. "Omigod," she said. "Do you see what I think I see?"

Ranger's Mercedes was parked in shadow just beyond the door.

"Damn," Mary Lou said, "if he was waiting for me, I'd need Depends."

Ranger was leaning against the car, arms folded across his chest, not moving. Very foreboding in the dark. Definitely Depends material.

"Thanks for the ride," I said to Mary Lou, my eyes on Ranger, wondering about his mood.

"You going to be okay? He looks so . . . dangerous."

"It's the hair."

"It's more than the hair."

It was the hair, the eyes, the mouth, the body, the gun on his hip . . .

"I'll call you tomorrow," I told Mary Lou. "Don't worry about Ranger. He's not as bad as he looks." Okay, so I fib now and then, but it's always for a good cause. No point Mary Lou spending the night in a state.

Mary Lou gave Ranger one last look and whipped out of the lot. I took a deep breath and ambled over.

"Where's the BMW?" Ranger asked.

I pulled the plates and the piece of dashboard out of my bag and gave them to him. "I sort of had a problem . . ."

His eyebrows raised, and a smile started to twitch at the corners of his mouth. "This is what's left of the car?"

I nodded my head and swallowed. "It got stolen."

The smile widened. "And they left you the plates and registration tag. Nice touch."

I didn't think it was a nice touch. I thought it was very crappy. In fact, I was thinking my *life* was crappy. The bomb, Ramirez, Uncle Fred—and just when I thought I'd succeeded at something and made a capture, someone stole my car. The whole crappy world was thumbing its nose at me. "Life sucks," I said to Ranger. A tear popped out of my eye and slid down my cheek. Damn.

Ranger studied me for a moment, turned, and dropped the plates in his backseat. "It was a car, Babe. It wasn't important."

"It's not just the car. It's *everything*." Another tear squeezed out. "I have all these problems."

He was very close. I could feel the heat from his body. And I could see that his eyes were dilated black in the dark parking lot.

"Here's something else to worry about," he said. And he kissed me—his hand at the nape of my neck and his mouth on mine, soft at first, then serious and demanding. He drew me closer and kissed me again and desire washed over me, hot and liquid and scary.

"Oh boy," I whispered.

"Yeah," he said. "Think about it."

"What I think . . . is that it's a bad idea."

"Of course it's a bad idea," Ranger said. "If it was a good idea I'd have been in your bed a long time ago." He took a notecard from his jacket pocket. "I have a job for you tomorrow. The young sheik is going home and needs a ride to the airport."

"No! No way am I driving that little jerk."

"Look at it this way, Steph. He deserves you."

He had a point. "Okay," I said. "I haven't got anything else to do."

"Instructions are on the card. Tank will bring the car around for you."

And he was gone.

"Omigod," I said. "What did I just do?"

I rushed into the lobby and pushed the elevator button, still talking to myself. "He kissed me and I kissed him," I said. "What was I thinking?" I rolled my eyes. "I was thinking . . . *yes*!"

The elevator door opened and Ramirez stepped out at me. "Hello, Stephanie," he said. "The champ's been waiting for you."

I shrieked and jumped away, but I'd had my mind on Ranger and not Ramirez, and I didn't move fast enough. Ramirez grabbed a handful of hair and yanked me toward the door. "It's time," he said. "Time to see what it's like to be with a real man. And then when the champ is done with you, you'll be ready for God."

I stumbled and went down to one knee, and he dragged me forward. I had my hand in my bag, but I couldn't find my gun or the stun gun. Too much junk. I swung the bag as hard as I could and caught him in the face. He paused, but he didn't go down.

"That wasn't nice, Stephanie," he said. "You're gonna have to pay for that. You're gonna have to get punished before you go to God."

I dug my heels in and screamed as loud as I could.

Two doors opened on the first floor.

"What's going on here?" Mr. Sanders said.

Mrs. Keene stuck her head out. "Yeah, what's the racket?"

"Call the police," I yelled. "Help! Call the police."

"Don't worry, dear," Mrs. Keene said, "I've got my gun." She fired two off and took out an overhead light. "Did I get him?" she asked. "Would you like me to shoot again?"

Mrs. Keene had cataracts and wore glasses as thick as the bottom of a beer glass.

Ramirez had bolted for the door at the first shot.

"You missed him, Mrs. Keene, but that's okay. You scared him off."

"Do you still want us to call the police?"

"I'll take care of it," I told them. "Thanks."

Everyone thought I was a big professional bounty hunter, and I didn't want to ruin that image, so I calmly walked to the stairs. I climbed one step at a time, and I told myself to stay focused. Get yourself into your apartment, I thought. Lock the door, call the police. I should have found my gun and gone into the lot after Ramirez. But the truth is, I was too scared. And if I was being really honest here, I wasn't such a good shot. Better to leave it to the police.

By the time I got to my door, I had my key in my hand. I took a deep breath and got the key in on the first try. The apartment was dark and quiet. Too early for Briggs to be asleep. He must have gone out. Rex was silently running on his wheel. The red light was lit on my answering machine. Two messages. I suspected one was from Ranger, left early afternoon. I flipped the light on, dropped my bag on the kitchen counter, and played the messages.

The first was from Ranger, just as I'd thought, telling me to page him again.

The second was from Morelli. "This is important," he said. "I have to talk to you."

I dialed Morelli at home. "Come on," I said. "Pick up the phone." No answer, so I started working my way down the speed dial. Next on the list was Morelli's car phone. No answer there either. Try his cell phone. I took the phone into my bedroom, but only got as far as the bedroom door.

Allen Shempsky was sitting on my bed. The window behind him was broken. No secret how he got into my bedroom. He was holding a gun. And he looked terrible.

"Hang up," he said. "Or I'll kill you."

FIFTEEN

"WHAT ARE YOU doing?" I asked Shempsky.

"Good question. I thought I knew. I thought I had it all figured out." He shook his head. "It's all gone to heck in a handbasket."

"You look awful." His face was flushed, his eyes were bloodshot and glassy, and his hair was a mess. He was in a suit, but his shirt was hanging out, and his tie was twisted to one side. His slacks and jacket were wrinkled. "Have you been drinking?"

"I feel sick," he said.

"Maybe you should put the gun down."

"Can't. I have to kill you. What *is* it with you anyway? Anyone else would know when to quit. I mean, no one even liked Fred."

"Where is he?"

"Hah! Another good question."

I heard muffled noise coming from my closet.

"It's the dwarf," Shempsky said. "He scared the hell out of me. I thought no one was in here. And all of a sudden this little Munchkin came running in."

I was at the closet in two strides. I opened the door and looked down. Briggs was trussed up like a Christmas goose, his hands tied behind his back with my bathroom clothesline, mailing tape across his mouth. He seemed okay. Very scared and boiling mad.

516

"Shut the door," Shempsky said. "He's quieter if you shut the door. I guess I have to kill him, too, but I've been procrastinating. It's like killing Doc or Sneezy or Grumpy. And I have to tell you I feel real bad about killing Sneezy. I really like Sneezy."

If you've never had a gun pointed at you, you can't imagine the terror. And the regret that life was too short, too unappreciated. "You don't really want to kill Sneezy and me," I said, working hard to keep my voice from shaking.

"Sure I do. Hell, why not. I've killed everybody else." He sniffed and wiped his nose on his jacket sleeve. "I'm getting a cold. Boy, I tell you, when things start going bad . . ." He ran his hand through his hair. "It was such a good idea. Take a few customers and keep them for yourself. Real clean. Except I didn't count on people like Fred stirring things up. We were all making money. Nobody was getting hurt. And then things started to go wrong and people started to panic. First Lipinski and then John Curly."

"So you killed them?"

"What else could I do? It's the only way to really keep someone quiet, you know."

"What about Martha Deeter?"

"Martha Deeter," he said on a sigh. "One of my many regrets is that she's dead, and I can't kill her again. If it wasn't for Martha Deeter . . ." He shook his head. "Excuse my language, but she had a real stick up her ass about the accounts. Everything strictly by the books. Wouldn't budge on the Shutz thing. Even though it was none of her business. She was a stupid receptionist, but she wouldn't keep her nose out of anything. After you left the office she decided she was going to make an example out of you and your aunt. Sent a fax off to the home office suggesting they look into the matter and prosecute you for making fraudulent claims. Can you imagine what that could lead to? Even if they just called to pacify you, it could start an investigation."

"So you killed her?"

"It seemed like the prudent thing to do. Looking back it might have been a little extreme, but like I said before, it's really the only way you can be sure of keeping someone quiet. Human nature, such as it is, is *not* dependable. And you know, I discovered this amazing thing. It's not that hard to kill someone."

"Where did you learn about bombs?"

"The library. Actually, I'd built the bomb for Curly, but by chance I happened to see him crossing the street to get to his car. It was late at night, and he was coming out of a bar. Nobody around. Couldn't believe how lucky I was. So I ran him over a bunch of times. I had to make sure he was dead, you know. Didn't want him to suffer. He wasn't such a bad guy. It was just he was a loose end."

I gave an involuntary shiver.

"Yeah," he said, "it was kind of creepy the first time I ran over him. I tried to pretend it was a bump in the road. So anyway, I had this bomb all ready to go, and then I found out you were going over to RGC again. I called Stemper and gave him some baloney about delaying you for a half hour so the bank could run the check through the system."

"Then you had to kill Stemper."

"Stemper was *your* fault. Stemper'd still be alive if you hadn't been so compulsive about that check. Two dollars," Shempsky said, sniffling. "All these people are dead, and my life is unraveling because of two fucking dollars."

"Seems to me it started with Laura Lipinski."

"You figured that out?" He slumped a little. "She was giving Larry a hard time. He'd made the mistake of telling her about the money, and she wanted it. She was leaving him, and she wanted the money. Said if she didn't get it, she'd go to the police."

"So you killed her?"

"The mistake we made was in getting rid of the body. I'd never done anything like that before, so I figured chop it up, stuff it in a couple garbage bags, leave them spread out over town the night before garbage pickup. First off, let me tell you, it isn't easy to chop up a body. And second, cheapskate Fred was out, trying to save a buck on his leaves, and saw Larry and me with the bag. I mean, what are the chances?"

"I don't get Fred's part in this."

"He saw us dump the bag and didn't think anything of it. I mean he was out there doing the same thing. The next morning Fred goes to RGC, and Martha pisses him off and sends him packing. Fred gets a block away and thinks to himself that he knows Martha's office partner. He thinks about it for another block and realizes he's the guy who dumped the bag. So Fred goes to the real estate office alongside the deli with a camera and starts taking pictures. I guess he was going to wave them in Larry's face, trying to embarrass him enough to give him his money. Only after a couple pictures Fred thinks the bag looks too lumpy and smells pretty bad. And Fred opens the bag."

"Why didn't Fred report this to the police?"

"Why do you think? Money."

"He was going to blackmail you." That's why Fred left the canceled check on his desk. He didn't need it. He had the pictures.

"Fred said he didn't have any retirement account. Worked at the button factory for fifty years and had hardly any retirement account. Said he read where you needed ninety thousand to get into a decent nursing home. That's what he wanted. Ninety thousand."

"What about Mabel? Didn't he want nursing home money for her, too?"

Shempsky shrugged. "He didn't say anything about Mabel."

Cheap bastard.

"Why did you kill Larry?" Not that I actually cared at this point. What I cared about was time. I wanted more of it. I didn't want him to pull the trigger. If it meant I had to talk to him then that's what I was going to do.

"Lipinski got cold feet. He wanted out. Wanted to take his money and run. I tried to talk to him, but he was really freaked out. So I went over to see if I could calm him down."

"You succeeded. You can't get much calmer than dead."

"He wouldn't listen, so what could I do? I thought I did a good job of making it look like a suicide."

"You have a nice life—a nice house, a nice wife and kids, a good job. Why were you skimming?"

"In the beginning it was just fun money. Tipp and me used to play poker with a bunch of guys on Monday nights. And Tipp's wife would never give Tipp any money. So Tipp started skimming. Just a couple accounts for poker money. But then it was so easy. I mean, nobody knew the money was gone. So we enlarged until we had a nice chunk of Vito's accounts. Tipp knew Lipinski and Curly, and he brought them in." Shempsky wiped his nose again. "It wasn't like I was ever going to make money at the bank. I'm in a dead-end job. It's my face, you know. I'm not stupid. I could have been somebody, but nobody pays attention to me.

"God gives everybody a special talent. And you know what my talent is? Nobody remembers me. I have a forgettable face. It took me a bunch of years, but I finally figured out how to use my gift." He gave a crazy little laugh that sent all the hairs on my arm standing at attention. "My talent is that I can rob people blind, kill them on the street, and nobody remembers."

Allen Shempsky was drunk or crazy or both. And at the rate we were going he wouldn't even have to shoot me, because he was scaring me to death. My heart was pounding in my chest, echoing in my ears.

"What will you do now?" I asked him.

"You mean after I kill you? I guess I'll go home. Or maybe I'll just get in my car and drive somewhere. I have lots of money. I don't need to go back to the bank if I don't want to."

Shempsky was sweating, and under the flush on his cheeks his face was pale. "Christ," he said. "I really feel sick." He stood up and pointed the gun at me. "You got any cold medicine?"

"Just aspirin."

"I need more than aspirin. I'd like to sit and talk some more, but I gotta get some cold medicine. I bet I have a fever."

"You don't look good."

"I bet my face is all flushed."

"Yeah, and your eyes are glassy."

There was a scraping sound on the fire escape outside my window, and we both swiveled our heads to look. We saw only darkness beyond the broken pane.

Shempsky turned back to me and cocked the hammer on his revolver. "Now hold still so I kill you with the first bullet. It's better that way. There's a lot less mess. And if I shoot you in the heart, you can have an open casket. I know everybody likes that."

We both took a deep breath—me to die, and Shempsky to aim. And in that instant the air was pierced with a bloodcurdling roar of rage and lunacy. And Ramirez filled the window, his face contorted, his eyes small and evil.

Shempsky instinctively whirled and fired, emptying his gun in Ramirez.

I wasted no time running. I *flew* out of the room, through my living room, and out my front door. I sprinted down the hall, leaped down two flights of stairs, and almost bashed in Mrs. Keene's door.

"Goodness," Mrs. Keene said, "you certainly are having a full night. What now?"

"Your gun! Give me your gun!"

I called the police and went back upstairs with the gun in my hand. My apartment door was wide open. Shempsky was gone. And Briggs was still alive in my closet.

I ripped the tape off. "Are you okay?"

"Shit," he said. "I messed my pants."

THE UNIFORMS CAME first, then the paramedics and finally the homicide detectives and the medical examiner. They had an easy time finding my apartment. Most of them had been there before. Morelli had arrived with the uniforms.

It was now three hours later, and the party was winding down. I'd given my statement, and the only thing left was to get Ramirez into a body bag and haul him off my fire escape. Rex and I had set up camp in the kitchen while the professionals did their thing. Randy Briggs gave his statement and left, deciding his apartment without a door was safer than living with me.

Rex still looked perky, but I was exhausted. I was all out of adrenaline, and I felt like my blood level was a pint low.

Morelli wandered in, and for the first time all night we had a moment alone together. "You should be relieved," he said. "You don't have to worry about Ramirez anymore."

I nodded. "It's a terrible thing to say, but I'm glad he's dead. Any word on Shempsky?"

"Nobody's seen him or his car. He didn't go home."

"I think he's flipped out. And he has the flu. He looked really bad."

"You'd look bad too if you were wanted for multiple murders. We're leaving a uniform here tonight to make sure no one comes in through your window, but it's going to be cold in your bedroom. Probably you want to stay someplace else. My vote's for my house."

"I'd feel safe at your house," I said. "Thanks."

The gurney with the body clattered over the hall floor and rolled out my door. My stomach lurched, and I reached for Morelli. He pulled me to him and wrapped his arms around me. "You'll feel better tomorrow," he said. "You just need some sleep."

"Before I forget. You left a message on my machine that you needed to talk to me."

"We brought Harvey Tipp in for questioning, and he squealed like a pig. I wanted to warn you about Shempsky."

I WOKE UP to the sun streaming in through Morelli's bedroom window, but no Morelli next to me. I had a dim recollection of falling asleep on the ride to his house. And falling asleep again, next to Morelli. I had no recollection of any kind of sexual encounter. I was wearing a T-shirt and underpants. Since the underpants were on me and not on the floor that probably told me something.

I got out of bed and padded barefoot into the bathroom. There was a damp bath towel hanging on the hook on the door. A set of clean towels had been set out for me, neatly stacked on the tub. A note was taped to the mirror over the sink. "Had to leave for work early," the note said. "Make yourself at home." He also confirmed what I'd suspected—that I'd zonked out the minute my head hit the pillow. And since Morelli appreciated response to his lovemaking, he'd passed on last night's opportunity to collect on his debt.

I took a shower and got dressed and went to the kitchen in search of breakfast. Morelli didn't stock Pop-Tarts, so I settled on a peanut butter sandwich. I was halfway through the sandwich when I remembered the chauffeuring job. I'd never gotten around to reading the notecard, and I had no idea when I was supposed to get the sheik. I shuffled through the mess in my shoulder bag and found the card. It said Tank would drop the limo off at nine. I was to pick the sheik up at ten and drive him to Newark Airport. It was almost eight, so I finished my sandwich, stuffed yesterday's clothes into the tote, and called Mary Lou to bum a ride.

"Boy, you really get around," Mary Lou said. "When I dropped you off you were with Ranger. You must have had a busy night."

"You don't know the half of it." I explained to her about the kiss, and Ramirez, and Shempsky, and finally about Morelli.

"I can't imagine being too tired to do it with Morelli," Mary Lou said. "Of course, I've never been attacked by a homicidal rapist, held at gunpoint by a screwy banker, and had a guy killed outside my bedroom window."

Mrs. Bestler was waiting by the elevator when I walked into the lobby. "Going up?" she asked. "Second floor . . . belts, handbags, body bags."

"I'm taking the stairs," I told her. "I need the exercise."

I opened my apartment door and surprised a young cop who was feeding Rex Cheerios.

"He looked hungry," the cop said. "I hope you don't mind."

"Not at all. Feel free to join him for breakfast. Just poke around in the fridge until you find something you like."

The cop smiled. "Thanks. There's a guy here fixing your window. Morelli arranged it. I'm supposed to leave as soon as he's done."

"Sounds good."

I went into the bedroom and collected my chauffeur uniform of black suit and stockings and heels. I changed in the bathroom, added some lipstick and a swipe of mascara, and sprayed my hair. When I came out, the window man was gone, and my window looked sparkly clean. The cop was gone, too.

I grabbed my shoulder bag, said good-bye to Rex, and hustled down to the parking lot.

Tank was waiting for me when I swung through the back door at nine o'clock sharp. He had a map and directions.

"Should take you about a half hour from here," Tank said.

"Does he know I'm driving him?"

Tank's face creased in a wide grin. "We thought it would be a nice surprise."

I took the keys to the Town Car and slid in behind the wheel.

"You're carrying, right?" Tank asked.

"Right."

"And you're okay after last night?"

"How do you know about last night?"

"It's in the paper."

Terrific.

I gave Tank a little finger wave and drove away. I got to Hamilton and turned right. I drove several blocks and turned into the Burg. I had no intention of destroying another black car. I parked at my parents' house and went inside to get the garage keys.

"You made the paper again," Grandma said. "And the phone's been ringing off the hook. Your mother's in the kitchen, ironing."

My mother always irons during times of disaster. Some people drink, some take drugs. My mother irons.

"How's Dad?" I asked.

"He's out at the store."

"No problems left over from the stun gun?"

"Well, he isn't the happiest person I ever saw, but aside from that he's doing okay. Looks like you got another car."

"It's a loaner. I have a job as a chauffeur. I'm going to leave the black car here and take the Buick. I feel safer in the Buick."

My mother came out of the kitchen. "What's this about being a chauffeur?"

"It's nothing," I said. "I'm driving a man to the airport."

"Good," my mother said. "Take your grandmother."

"I can't do that!"

My mother pulled me into the kitchen and lowered her voice. "I don't care if you're driving the Pope, your grandmother is going with you. If she says the wrong thing to your father when he gets home, he'll go after her with a steak knife. So unless you want more bloodshed on your hands, you will fulfill your obligation as a granddaughter and get your grandmother out of this house for a few hours until things calm down. This is all your fault anyway." My mother snapped a shirt onto the ironing board and snatched at the iron. "And what kind of a daughter has shootouts on her fire escape? The phone's been ringing all morning. What am I supposed to say to people? How can I explain these things?"

"Just tell people I was looking for Uncle Fred, and things got complicated."

My mother shook the iron at me. "If that man isn't dead I'm going to kill him myself."

Hmm. Mom appeared to be a little stressed. "Okay," I said, "I guess I can take Grandma with me." Might not be a bad idea anyway. I didn't think the pervert sheik would be so fast to flash his johnson with Grandma on board.

"It's a shame we can't take that nice black car," Grandma said. "It looks more like a chauffeur car."

"I'm not taking any chances," I told her. "I don't want anything to happen to the black car. It's getting locked up nice and safe in the garage."

I loaded Grandma into the Buick, backed it out the driveway, and parked it on the street. Then I carefully eased the Lincoln into the garage and secured the doors.

In exactly thirty-five minutes I was at the address Tank had given me. It was in a neighborhood of expensive houses on two- and three-acre lots. Most houses were behind gated drives, tucked into yards filled with mature trees and professionally landscaped shrubs. I pushed the button on the call box and gave my name. The gates opened, and I drove up to the house.

"I guess this is pretty," Grandma said, "but they aren't gonna get many trick-or-treaters up here. I bet Halloween is a big bust."

I told Grandma to stay put and went to the door.

The door opened, and Ahmed looked out at me and frowned. "You!" he said. "What are you doing here?"

"Surprise," I said. "I'm your driver."

He looked over at the car. "And what's that supposed to be?"

"That's a Buick."

"There's an old lady in it."

"That's my grandmother."

"Forget it. I'm not riding with you. You're incompetent."

I put my arm around him and tugged him to me. "I've been having a difficult couple of days here," I said in confidential tones. "And I'm running a little low on patience. So I'd appreciate it if you'd get into the car without a lot of fuss. Because otherwise, I'm going to shoot you."

"You wouldn't shoot me," he said.

"Try me."

A man stood behind Ahmed. He was holding two suitcases, and he was looking uncomfortable.

"Put them in the trunk," I said to the man.

A woman had come to the door.

"Who's that?" I asked the kid.

"My aunt."

"Wave to her and smile and get in the car."

He sighed and waved. I waved, too. Everybody waved. And then I drove away.

"We would have brought the black car," Grandma said to Ahmed, "only Stephanie's been having real bad luck with cars."

He slouched lower, sulking. "No kidding."

"You don't have to worry with this one, though," Grandma told him. "We had this one locked up in the garage so no one could plant a bomb on it. And knock on wood, it hasn't blown up yet."

I picked up Route 1 and followed it to New Brunswick, where I moved over to the turnpike. I got on the turnpike and headed north, barreling along in the Buick, thankful that my passenger was still fully dressed and Grandma had fallen asleep, mouth open, hanging from her shoulder harness.

"I'm surprised you're still working for this company," Ahmed said. "If I had been your employer I would have fired you."

I ignored him and turned the radio on.

He leaned forward. "Perhaps it's difficult to get a competent person to do a menial job like this."

I glanced at him in the rearview mirror.

"I'll give you five dollars if you'll show me your breasts," he said.

I rolled my eyes and raised the volume on the radio.

He slouched back in his seat. "This is boring," he shouted at me. "And I hate this music."

"Are you thirsty?"

"Yes."

"Would you like to stop for a soda?"

"Yes!"

"Too bad."

I had my cell phone plugged into the cigarette lighter and was surprised to hear it chirp.

It was Briggs. "Where are you?" he asked. "This is your cell phone, right?"

"Yeah. I'm on the Jersey Turnpike, exit ten."

"Are you shitting me? That's great! Wait until you hear this. I've been working all night hacking into Shempsky's files, and I've got something. Late last night he made plane reservations. He's supposed to be flying out of Newark in an hour and a half. He's flying Delta to Miami."

"You *are* the man."

"Hey, don't piss off a little person."

"Call the police. Call Morelli first." I gave him Morelli's numbers. "If you can't get Morelli, call the station. They'll get in touch with the right people in Newark. And I'll watch out for Shempsky on the road."

"I can't tell the police I hacked into the bank!"

"Tell them I got the information and asked you to pass it on."

Fifteen minutes later, I slowed for the tollbooth to exit the turnpike. Grandma was awake, looking for the tan Taurus, and Ahmed was silent in the back, arms sullenly crossed over his chest.

"It's him!" Grandma said. "I see him ahead of us. Look at that tan car that's just leaving the tollbooth all the way to the left."

I paid the toll and glanced at the car. It *did* sort of look like Shempsky, but it was the fourth time Grandma had been sure she'd seen Shempsky in the last five minutes. There were a lot of tan cars on the Jersey Turnpike.

I put my foot to the pedal and roared up behind the car to check it out. The car was a Taurus, and the hair color seemed right, but I couldn't tell much from the back of his head.

"You've got to get to his side," Grandma said.

"If I come up on his side, he'll see me."

Grandma pulled a .44 magnum out of her purse. "Everybody duck, and I'll shoot out his tires."

"No!" I shouted. "No shooting. You shoot one single thing, and I'll tell Mom on you. We aren't even sure it's Allen Shempsky."

"Who's Allen Shempsky?" Ahmed wanted to know. "What's going on?"

I was riding right on the Taurus's rear. It would be safer to put a car or two between us, but I was afraid I'd lose him in traffic.

"My father hired you to protect me," Ahmed said, "not to go off chasing men."

Grandma leaned forward, keeping her eye on the Taurus. "We think this guy killed Fred."

"Who's Fred?"

"My uncle," I told him. "He's married to Mabel."

"Ah, so you're avenging a murder in the family. This is a good thing."

Nothing like a little avenging to bridge the culture gap.

The Taurus took the airport turnoff, and the driver checked his mirror as he merged with traffic, then turned in his seat and took a quick, disbelieving look back. It was Shempsky. And I was made. Not many people in Jersey driving a '53 powder blue and white Buick. Probably wondering how the devil I found him.

"He sees us," I said.

"Ram him," Ahmed said. "Disable his car. Then we'll all rush out and subdue the murdering dog."

"Yeah," Grandma said, "plow this baby right up his behind."

In theory, that sounded like a reasonable idea. In practice, I was afraid it'd result in a twenty-three-car pileup, and headlines that read BOMBSHELL BOUNTY HUNTER CAUSES CATASTROPHE.

Shempsky swerved in front of me, jumping out of his lane. He passed two cars, then swerved back. He was approaching the terminal, and he was panicking, determined to lose me. He changed lanes again and sideswiped a blue van. He overcorrected and crashed into the back of an SUV. Everyone stopped behind the accident. I was four cars back, and I couldn't get closer. No one was moving.

Shempsky was boxed in with his right front fender smashed into his right front wheel. I saw his door open. He was going to bolt. I hurled myself out of the car and hit the pavement running. Ahmed was behind me. And behind him was Grandma.

Shempsky pushed through the curbside check-in, dodging people with kids and bags. I lost him for a moment in the crowded terminal, then picked him out just ahead of me. I ran as fast as I could, not caring who I knocked over. I lunged when I was almost on Shempsky's heels, and I snagged his jacket. Ahmed grabbed Shempsky half a second after me, and the three of us went down. We rolled around a little, but Shempsky didn't put up much of a fight.

Ahmed and I had Shempsky pinned to the ground when Grandma came clattering up on her patent pumps. She had her gun in her hand and both our handbags tucked into the crook of her arm. "You should never leave your purse in the car," she said. "Do you need a gun?"

"No," I told her. "Put the gun away and give me my cuffs."

She searched through my bag, found the cuffs, handed them to me, and I clapped them on Shempsky.

Ahmed and I got to our feet, and we all did a high five with each other. And then we did a down low. And then Ahmed and Grandma did some complicated hand thing that I couldn't get the hang of.

CONSTANTINE STIVA STOOD at the entrance to the viewing room, keeping a close watch on the casket at the far end. Grandma Mazur and Mabel stood at the head of the casket, accepting condolences and making apologies.

"We're real sorry," Grandma Mazur said to Mrs. Patucci. "We had to have a closed casket on account of Fred was in the ground two weeks before we found him and the worms had eaten a lot of his face."

"That's such a shame," Mrs. Patucci said. "It takes something away when you can't see the deceased."

"I feel just like that, too," Grandma said. "But Stiva couldn't do nothing with him, and he wouldn't let us leave the lid up."

Mrs. Patucci turned and looked at Stiva. Stiva gave a small sympathetic nod and smiled.

"That Stiva," Mrs. Patucci said.

"Yeah, and he's watching us like a hawk," Grandma told her.

Allen Shempsky had buried Fred in a shallow grave in a little patch of woods across from the pet cemetery on Klockner Road. He'd claimed he'd shot Fred by accident, but that was hard to believe since the fatal bullet had gone dead center between Fred's eyes.

Fred had been exhumed early Friday morning, the autopsy had been done on Monday, and now it was Wednesday and Fred was having an evening viewing. Mabel seemed to be enjoying herself, and Fred would have been pleased by the crowd he got, so I guess everything turned out okay.

I was at the back of the room, to one side of the door, counting the minutes until I could leave. I was trying to be as inconspicuous as possible, staring down at the carpet, not especially anxious to engage in conversation about Fred or Shempsky.

A pair of motorcycle boots entered my field of vision. They were attached to Levi's-clad legs I knew all too well.

"Hey, Hotstuff," Morelli said. "Having fun?"

"Yeah. I love viewings. The Rangers are playing Pittsburgh, but that can't compare to a viewing. Long time, no see."

"Not since you went into a coma fully dressed in my bedroom."

"I didn't wake up fully dressed."

"You noticed."

I felt my face flush. "I guess you've been busy."

"I had to wrap up the case with Treasury. They wanted Vito in Washington, and Vito wanted me to go with him. I just got back this afternoon."

"I caught Shempsky."

This brought a smile. "I heard. Congratulations."

"I still don't understand why he felt it necessary to kill people. Wasn't he just doing his banker thing by opening accounts for clients?"

"He was supposed to pass the money through to a bank in the Caymans and establish tax-free accounts. The trouble was Shempsky was skimming the skimmers. When Lipinski and Curly panicked and wanted their money, the money wasn't there."

Shempsky hadn't told me that part. "Why didn't Shempsky just replace the money?"

"He'd spent it on venture investments that didn't pay off. I think it was just something that got away from him, and it got worse and worse, until it was so bad it was out of control. There were a couple banking irregularities, too. Shempsky knew it was dirty money."

I felt hot breath on my neck. Morelli looked at the person doing the breathing and gave a grunt of disgust.

It was Bunchy. "Nice collar, Cutie Pie," he said.

His hair was cut and clean and his face was freshly shaved. He was wearing a button-down shirt, crewneck sweater, and tan slacks. If it wasn't for the eyebrows I might not have recognized him.

"What are you doing here?" I said. "I thought the case was over. Don't you go back to Washington now?"

"Not all of Treasury works in Washington. I happen to be a Jersey Treasury guy." He looked around the room. "I thought Lula might be here since you two are such good friends."

I raised an eyebrow. "Lula?"

"Yeah. Well, you know, she looked like she might be fun."

"Listen, just because she used to be a hooker—"

He raised his hands. "Hey, it isn't like that. I just like her, that's all. I think she's okay."

"So call her."

"You think I could? I mean, would she hang up on me because of that tire thing?"

I dug a pen out of my bag and wrote Lula's number on the back of Bunchy's hand. "Take your chances."

"How about me," Morelli said when Bunchy left. "Do I get a number on the back of my hand?"

"You have enough numbers to last you a lifetime."

"You owe me," Morelli said.

A thrill skittered through my stomach. "Yes, but I didn't say *when* I'd pay off."

"The ball's in your court," Morelli said.

I'd heard that before!

Grandma was waving to me from the other end of the room. "Yoo-hoo," she called, "come here a minute."

"I have to go," I said to Morelli.

He took the pen from my bag and wrote his number on the back of *my* hand. "Ciao," he said. And then he left.

"The viewing is almost over," Grandma said. "We're all going over to Mabel's house to see her new bedroom set and have some coffee cake. Do you want to come with us?"

"Thanks, but I think I'll pass. I'll see you tomorrow."

"Thank you for everything," Mabel said to me. "I like this new garbage company you got me much better."

I PARKED THE Buick and took a moment to enjoy the night. The air was crisp and the sky was starless and black. Lights were on in my building. The seniors were watching TV. The bombers and rapists were gone, and this little part of Trenton felt safe again. I walked into the building and went to the bank of mailboxes to collect my mail. A credit card bill, a dental reminder, and an envelope from RangeMan. The RangeMan envelope contained a check for the chauffeuring job. A note was included with the check. It was hand-written from Ranger. "Glad the Lincoln survived, but locking it in a garage is cheating." I remembered his kiss, and I got another one of those skittery thrills.

I ran up the stairs, let myself into my apartment, locked the door behind me, and took stock. My apartment was nice and neat. I'd spent the weekend cleaning. No dishes on the counter. No socks on the floor. Rex had a clean cage, and the pine shavings smelled foresty. It all felt welcoming. And safe. And private. And intimate.

"I should invite someone over," I said to Rex. "After all, the apartment's all cleaned. I mean, how often does that happen, right? And my legs are shaved. And I have this great dress that I've never worn."

Rex gave me a look that told me in no uncertain terms he knew exactly what I was after.

"Okay," I said. "So what's the big deal? I'm an adult. I have adult urges."

I thought about Ranger again, and tried to imagine what he'd be like in bed. And then I thought about Joe. I knew *exactly* what Joe was like.

This was a dilemma.

I got two pieces of paper, wrote Joe's name on one and Ranger's on the other. I dumped the two names into a bowl, closed my eyes, mixed them up, and picked one. Let God decide, I thought.

I read the name and cracked my knuckles. I hoped God knew what he was doing. I showed the paper to Rex, and he looked disapproving, so I covered his cage with a dish towel.

I did the speed-dial thing before I lost my nerve.

"I have this dress I'd like your opinion on," I said when he answered.

A beat went by. "When would you like this opinion?"

"Now."

I SUPPOSE THERE'S a time and place for everything—and this was the time for the slinky black dress. I tugged it over my head and smoothed it out. The fit was perfect. I shook my head to fluff up my hair, and I sprayed some Dolce Vita on my wrist. I slipped my feet into the sexy ankle-strap heels and retouched my lipstick. Bright red. *Yow!*

I lit a candle on the coffee table and another in the bedroom. I dimmed the lights. I heard the elevator doors open down the hall, and my heart jumped in my chest. Get a grip, I told myself. No reason to be nervous. This is the will of God.

Baloney, a voice whispered in my head. You cheated. You peeked when you picked.

Okay, so I cheated. Big deal. The important thing is that I

picked the right man. Maybe he wasn't right forever and ever, but he was right for tonight.

I opened the door on the second knock. Didn't want to seem overly anxious! I stepped back and our eyes met, and he showed no sign of the nervousness I felt. Curiosity, maybe. And desire. And something else—maybe the need to know this was what I wanted.

"Howdy," I said.

He looked amused at that, but not amused enough to smile. He stepped forward into the foyer, closed the door, and locked it. His breathing was slow and deep, his eyes were dark, his expression serious as he studied me.

"Nice dress," he said. "Take it off."

HOT SIX

ACKNOWLEDGMENTS

Thanks to Eileen Hoffman and Larry Martine for suggesting the title for this book.

PROLOGUE

OKAY, SO HERE'S the thing. My mother's worst fear has come true. I'm a nymphomaniac. I lust after a lot of men. Of course, maybe that's because I don't actually actually have sex with *any*. And some of my lustings probably aren't going anywhere. Probably it's unrealistic to think I'll ever get it on with Mike Richter, the goalie for the New York Rangers. Ditto Indiana Jones.

On the other hand, two of the men on my list of desirables actually desire me back. The problem being that they both sort of scare the hell out of me.

My name is Stephanie Plum. I'm a bounty hunter, and I work with both these men. Both are involved in law enforcement. One is a cop. And the other takes a more entrepreneurial approach to deterring crime. Neither is very good at following rules. Both outclass me when it comes to lusting *experience*.

Anyway, there comes a time in a girl's life when she needs to take the bull by the horns (or some other appropriate body part) and take charge of her life. And this is what I just did. I made a phone call, and I invited one of the scary men over for a visit.

Now I'm trying to decide if I should let him in.

My fear is that this could be an experience similar to the time when at age nine I got carried away in a Wonder Woman fantasy, fell off the Kruzaks' garage roof, destroyed Mrs. Kruzak's prize rosebush, ripped my shorts and flowered cotton underpants, and spent the rest of the day not realizing my ass was exposed.

Mental eyeroll. Get a grip! There's no reason to be nervous. This is the will of God. After all, didn't I pick this man's name out of a hat tonight? Well, actually it was a bowl, but still, this is a cosmic meeting. All right, so the truth is, I cheated a little and peeked when I picked. Hell, sometimes fate needs some help. I mean, if I could rely on fate to do the job I wouldn't have had to make the stupid phone call, would I?

Besides, I have some things going for me. I'm prepared for the task ahead. Man-eater dress, short and black. Ankle-strap heels. Glossy red lipstick. Box of condoms hidden in my sweater drawer. Gun fully loaded, on standby in the cookie jar. Stephanie Plum, woman on a mission. Take 'im down, dead or alive.

Just seconds ago, I heard the elevator doors slide open, and I heard footsteps in the hall. The footsteps stopped outside my apartment door, and I knew it was him because my nipples contracted.

He rapped once, and I stood paralyzed, staring at the lock. I opened the door on the second knock and stepped back, and our eyes met. He showed no sign of the nervousness I felt. Curiosity, maybe. And desire. Lots of desire. Desire in *spades*.

"Howdy," I said.

He stepped forward into the foyer, closed the door, and locked it. His breathing was slow and deep, his eyes were dark, his expression serious as he studied me.

"Nice dress," he said. "Take it off."

"Maybe some wine first," I said. Procrastinate! I thought. Get him drunk! Then if it's a disaster he might not remember.

He slowly shook his head. "I don't think so."

"Sandwich?"

"Later. A lot later."

I did some mental knuckle-cracking.

He smiled. "You're cute when you're nervous."

I narrowed my eyes. I hadn't been shooting for cute when I'd set this up and fantasized the evening.

He pulled me in to him, reached behind my back, and slid the zipper down on my dress. The dress dropped from my shoulders and pooled at my feet, leaving me in my slut shoes and Victoria's Secret barely-there string bikinis.

I'm five feet seven inches, and the heels added another four, but he still had an inch on me. He had a lot more muscle, too. His hands skimmed the length of my back, and he looked me over.

"Pretty," he said.

He seen it before, of course. He'd had his head under my skirt when I was seven. He'd relieved me of my virginity when I was eighteen. And, in more recent history, he'd done things to me that I wouldn't soon forget. He was a Trenton cop, and his name was Joe Morelli.

"Remember when we were kids and we used to play choo-choo?" he asked.

"I was always the tunnel, and you were always the train."

He hooked his thumbs into the waistband of my panties and inched them down. "I was a rotten kid," he said.

"True."

"I'm better now."

"Sometimes."

This got me a wolfish smile. "Cupcake, don't you ever doubt it."

And then he kissed me, and my undies floated to the floor.

Oh, boy. *Oh, boy!*

ONE

FIVE MONTHS LATER . . .

Carol Zabo was standing on the outermost guardrail on the bridge spanning the Delaware between Trenton, New Jersey, and Morrisville, Pennsylvania. She was holding a regulation-size yellow fire brick in the palm of her right hand, with about four feet of clothesline stretched between the brick and her ankle. On the side of the bridge in big letters was the slogan "Trenton Makes and the World Takes." And Carol was apparently tired of the world taking whatever it was she was making, because she was getting ready to jump into the Delaware and let the brick do its work.

I was standing about ten feet from Carol, trying to talk her off the guardrail. Cars were rolling past us, some slowing up to gawk, and some cutting in and out of the gawkers, giving Carol the finger because she was disturbing the flow.

"Listen, Carol," I said, "it's eight-thirty in the morning, and it's starting to snow. I'm freezing my ass off. Make up your mind about jumping, because I have to tinkle, and I need a cup of coffee."

Truth is, I didn't for a minute think she'd jump. For one thing, she was wearing a four-hundred-dollar jacket from Wilson Leather. You just don't jump off a bridge in a four-hundred-dollar jacket. It isn't done. The jacket would get ruined. Carol was from

545

the Chambersburg section of Trenton, just like me, and in the Burg you gave the jacket to your sister, then you jumped off the bridge.

"Hey, *you* listen, Stephanie Plum," Carol said, teeth chattering. "Nobody sent you an engraved invitation to this party."

I'd gone to high school with Carol. She'd been a cheerleader, and I'd been a baton twirler. Now she was married to Lubie Zabo and wanted to kill herself. If I was married to Lubie I'd want to kill myself too, but that wasn't Carol's reason for standing on the guardrail, holding a brick on a rope. Carol had shoplifted some crotchless bikinis from the Frederick's of Hollywood store at the mall. It wasn't that Carol couldn't afford the panties, it was that she wanted them to spice up her love life and was too embarrassed to take them to the register. In her haste to make a getaway, she'd rear-ended Brian Simon's plainclothes cop car and had left the scene. Brian had been in the car at the time, and had chased her down and thrown her into the pokey.

My cousin Vinnie, president and sole proprietor of Vincent Plum Bail Bonds, had written Carol's get-out-of-jail ticket. If Carol didn't show up for her court date, Vinnie would forfeit the walking money—unless he could retrieve Carol's body in a timely manner.

This is where I come in. I'm a bond enforcement agent, which is a fancy term for bounty hunter, and I retrieve bodies for Vinnie. Preferably live and unharmed. Vinnie had spotted Carol on his way in to work this morning and had dispatched me to rescue her—or, if rescue wasn't possible, to eyeball the precise spot where she splashed down. Vinnie was worried if he'd be out his bond money if Carol jumped into the river, and the divers and cops with grappling hooks couldn't find her water-logged corpse.

"This is really a bad way to do it," I said to Carol. "You're going to look awful when they find you. Think about it—your hair's gonna be a wreck."

She rolled her eyes up as if she could see on the top of her head. "Shit, I never thought of that," she said. "I just had it high-lighted, too. I got it foiled."

The snow was coming down in big wet blobs. I was wearing hiking boots with thick Vibram soles, but the cold was seeping through to my feet all the same. Carol was more dressy in funky ankle boots, a little black dress, and the excellent jacket. Somehow the brick seemed too casual for the rest of the outfit. And the dress reminded me of a dress I had hanging in my own closet. I'd only worn the dress for a matter of minutes before it had been dropped to the floor and kicked aside . . . the opening statement in an exhaustive night with the man of my dreams. Well, one of the men, anyway. Funny how people see clothes differently. I wore the dress, hoping to get a man in my bed. And Carol chose it to jump off a bridge. Now in my opinion, jumping off a bridge in a dress is a bad decision. If I was going to jump off a bridge I'd wear slacks. Carol was going to look like an idiot with her skirt up around her ears and her pantyhose hanging out. "So what does Lubie think of the highlights?" I asked.

"Lubie likes the highlights," Carol said. "Only he wants me to grow it longer. He says long hair is the style now."

Personally, I wouldn't put a lot of stock in the fashion sense of a man who got his nickname by bragging about his sexual expertise with a grease gun. But hey, that's just me. "So tell me again why you're up here on the guardrail."

"Because I'd rather die than go to jail."

"I told you, you're not going to jail. And if you do, it won't be for very long."

"A day is too long! An hour is too long! They make you take off all your clothes, and then they make you bend over so they can look for smuggled weapons. And you have to go to the bathroom in front of everyone. There's no, you know, privacy. I saw a special on television."

Okay, so now I understood a little bit better. I'd kill myself before I'd do any of those things, too.

"Maybe you won't have to go to jail," I said. "I know Brian Simon. I could talk to him. Maybe I could get him to drop the charges."

Carol's face brightened. "Really? Would you do that for me?"

"Sure. I can't guarantee anything, but I can give it a shot."

"And if he won't drop the charges, I'll still have a chance to kill myself."

"Exactly."

I PACKED CAROL and the brick off in her car, and then I drove over to the 7-Eleven for coffee and a box of glazed chocolate doughnuts. I figured I deserved the doughnuts, since I'd done such a good job of saving Carol's life.

I took the doughnuts and coffee to Vinnie's storefront office on Hamilton Avenue. I didn't want to run the risk of eating all the doughnuts myself. And I was hoping Vinnie would have more work for me. As a bond enforcement agent I only get paid if I bring somebody in. And at the moment I was clean out of wayward bondees.

"Damn, skippy," Lula said from behind the file cabinets. "Here come doughnuts walking through the door."

At five feet five inches, weighing in at a little over two hundred pounds, Lula is something of a doughnut expert. She was in monochromatic mode this week, with hair, skin, and lip gloss all the color of cocoa. The skin color is permanent, but the hair changes weekly.

Lula does filing for Vinnie, and she helps me out when I need backup. Since I'm not the world's best bounty hunter, and Lula isn't the world's best backup, it's more often than not like the amateur-hour version of *The Best of "Cops" Bloopers.*

"Are those chocolate doughnuts?" Lula asked. "Connie and me were just thinking we needed some chocolate doughnuts, weren't we, Connie?"

Connie Rosolli is Vinnie's office manager. She was at her desk, in the middle of the room, examining her mustache in a mirror. "I'm thinking of having more electrolysis," she said. "What do you think?"

"I think it's a good thing," Lula told her, helping herself to a doughnut. "Because you're starting to look like Groucho Marx, again."

I sipped my coffee and fingered through some files Connie had on her desk. "Anything new come in?"

The door to Vinnie's inner office slammed open, and Vinnie stuck his head out. "Fuckin' A, we got something new . . . and it's all yours."

Lula screwed her mouth up to the side. And Connie did a nose wrinkle.

I had a bad feeling in my stomach. Usually I had to beg for jobs and here Vinnie was, having saved something for me. "What's going on?" I asked.

"It's Ranger," Connie said. "He's in the wind. Won't respond to his pager."

"The schmuck didn't show up for his court date yesterday," Vinnie said. "He's FTA."

"FTA" is bounty-hunter-speak for "failure to appear." Usually I'm happy to hear someone has failed to appear, because it means I get to earn money by coaxing them back into the system. In this case, there was no money to be had, because if Ranger didn't want to be found, he wasn't going to be found. End of discussion.

Ranger is a bounty hunter, like me. Only Ranger is *good*. He's close to my age, give or take a few years; he's Cuban-American; and I'm pretty sure he only kills bad guys. Two weeks ago some idiot rookie cop arrested Ranger on carrying concealed without a license. Every other cop in Trenton knows Ranger and knows he carries concealed, and they're perfectly happy to have it that way. But no one told the new guy. So Ranger was busted and scheduled to go before the judge yesterday for a slap on the wrist. In the meantime, Vinnie sprung Ranger with a nice chunk of money, and now Vinnie was feeling lonely, high off the ground, out there on a limb all by himself. First Carol. Now Ranger. Not a good way to start a Tuesday.

"There's something wrong with this picture," I said. It made my heart feel leaden in my chest, because there were people out there who wouldn't mind seeing Ranger disappear forever. And his disappearance would make a very large hole in my life.

"It's not like Ranger to ignore his court date. Or to ignore his pager."

Lula and Connie exchanged glances.

"You know that big fire they had downtown on Sunday?" Connie said. "Turns out the building is owned by Alexander Ramos."

Alexander Ramos deals guns, regulating the flow of black market arms from his summer compound on the Jersey shore and his winter fortress in Athens. Two of his three adult sons live in the United States, one in Santa Barbara, the other in Hunterdon County. The third son lives in Rio. None of this is privileged information. The Ramos family has made the cover of *Newsweek* four times. People have speculated for years that Ranger has ties to Ramos, but the exact nature of those ties has always been unknown. Ranger is a master of keeping things unknown.

"And?" I asked.

"And when they could finally go through the building yesterday they found Ramos's youngest son, Homer, barbecued in a third-floor office. Besides being toasted, he also had a large bullet hole in his head."

"And?"

"And Ranger's wanted for questioning. The police were here just a few minutes ago, looking for him."

"Why do they want Ranger?"

Connie did a palms-up.

"Anyway, he's skipped," Vinnie said, "and you're gonna bring him in."

My voice involuntarily rose an octave. "What, are you crazy? I'm not going after Ranger!"

"That's the beauty of it," Vinnie said. "You don't have to go after him. He'll come to you. He's got a thing for you."

"No! No way. Forget it."

"Fine," Vinnie said, "you don't want the job, I'll put Joyce on it."

Joyce Barnhardt is my archenemy. Ordinarily, I'd eat dirt before I'd give anything up to Joyce. In this case, Joyce could take it. Let her spend her time spinning her wheels, looking for the invisible man.

"So what else have you got?" I asked Connie.

"Two minors and a real stinker." She passed three folders over to me. "Since Ranger isn't available I'm going to have to give the stinker to you."

I flipped the top file open. Morris Munson. Arrested for vehicular manslaughter. "Could be worse," I said. "Could be a homicidal rapist."

"You didn't read down far enough," Connie said. "After this guy ran over the victim, who just happened to be his ex-wife, he beat her with a tire iron, raped her, and tried to set her on fire. He was charged with vehicular manslaughter because according to the M.E. she was already dead when he took the tire iron to her. He had her soaked in gasoline and was trying to get his Bic to work when a blue-and-white happened to drive by."

Little black dots danced in front of my eyes. I sat down hard on the fake-leather couch and put my head between my legs.

"You okay?" Lula asked.

"Probably it's just low blood sugar," I said. Probably it's my *job*.

"It could be worse," Connie said. "It says here he wasn't armed. Just bring your gun along, and I'm sure you'll be fine."

"I can't believe they let him out on bail!"

"Go figure," Connie said. "Guess they didn't have any more room at the inn."

I looked up at Vinnie, who was still standing in the doorway to his private office. "You wrote bail on this maniac?"

"Hey, I'm not a judge. I'm a businessman. He didn't have any priors," Vinnie said. "And he has a good job working at the button factory. Homeowner."

"And now he's gone."

"Didn't show up for his court date," Connie said. "I called the button factory, and they said last they saw him was Wednesday."

"Have they heard from him at all? Did he call in sick?"

"No. Nothing. I called his home number and got his machine."

I glanced at the other two files. Lenny Dale, missing in action, charged with domestic violence. And Walter "Moon Man" Dunphy, wanted for drunk and disorderly and urinating in a public place.

I tucked the three folders into my shoulder bag and stood. "Page me if you hear anything on Ranger."

"Last chance," Vinnie said. "I swear I'll give his file to Joyce."

I took a doughnut from the box, gave the box over to Lula, and left. It was March and the snowstorm was having a hard time working itself up into anything serious. There was some slush on the street, and a layer of ice had accumulated on my windshield and my passenger-side windows. There was a large blurry object behind the window. I squinted through the ice. The blurry object was Joe Morelli.

Most women would have an orgasm on the spot to find Morelli sitting in their car. He had that effect. I'd known Morelli for most of my life, and I almost never had an on-the-spot orgasm, anymore. I needed at least four minutes.

He was wearing boots and jeans and a black fleece jacket. The tails of a red plaid flannel shirt hung under the jacket. Under the flannel shirt he wore a black T-shirt and a .40-caliber Glock. His eyes were the color of aged whiskey and his body was a testament to good Italian genes and hard work at the gym. He had a reputation for living fast, and the reputation was well deserved but dated. Morelli focused his energy on his job now.

I slid behind the wheel, turned the key in the ignition, and cranked up the defroster. I was driving a six-year-old blue Honda Civic that was perfectly good transportation but didn't enhance my fantasy life. Hard to be Xena, Warrior Princess in a six-year-old Civic.

"So," I said to Morelli, "what's up?"

"You going after Ranger?"

"Nope. Not me. No siree. No way."

He raised his eyebrows.

"I'm not magic," I said. Sending me after Ranger would be like sending the chicken out to hunt down the fox.

Morelli was slouched against the door. "I need to talk to him."

"Are you investigating the fire?"

"No. This is something else."

"Something else that's related to the fire? Like the hole in Homer Ramos's head?"

Morelli grinned. "You ask a lot of questions."

"Yeah, but I'm not getting any answers. Why isn't Ranger answering his page? What's his involvement here?"

"He had a late-night meeting with Ramos. They were caught on a lobby security camera. The building is locked up at night, but Ramos had a key. He arrived first, waited ten minutes for Ranger, then opened the door for him. The two of them crossed the lobby and took the elevator to the third floor. Thirty-five minutes later Ranger left alone. And ten minutes after that, the fire alarm went off. Forty-eight hours' worth of tape has been run, and according to the tape no one else was in the building with Ranger and Ramos."

"Ten minutes is a long time. Give him three more to ride the elevator or take the stairs. Why didn't the alarm go off sooner, if Ranger started the fire?"

"No smoke detector in the office where Ramos was found. The door was closed, and the smoke detector was in the hall."

"Ranger isn't stupid. He wouldn't let himself get caught on videotape if he was going to kill someone."

"It was a hidden camera." Morelli eyed my doughnut. "You going to eat that?"

I broke the doughnut in half and gave him a piece. I popped the other into my mouth. "Was an accelerant used?"

"Small amount of lighter fluid."

"You think Ranger did it?"

"Hard to say with Ranger."

"Connie said Ramos was shot."

"Nine millimeter."

"So you think Ranger is hiding from the police?"

"Allen Barnes is the primary on the homicide investigation. Everything he's got so far leads to Ranger. If he brought Ranger in for questioning, he could probably hold him for a while based on priors, like the carrying charge. No matter how you look at it, sitting in a cell isn't in Ranger's best interest right now. And if Barnes has Ranger nailed as his number one suspect, there's a good chance Alexander Ramos has reached the same conclusion. If Ramos thought Ranger blew Homer away, Ramos wouldn't wait for justice to be served by the court."

The doughnut was sitting in a big lump in my throat. "Or maybe Ramos has already gotten to Ranger. . . ."

"That's a possibility, too."

Shit. Ranger is a mercenary with a strong code of ethics that doesn't necessarily always correspond to current popular thinking. He came on board as my mentor when I first started working for Vinnie, and the relationship has evolved to include friendship, which is limited by Ranger's lone-wolf lifestyle and my desire for survival. And, truth is, there's been a growing sexual attraction between us which scares the hell out of me. So my feelings for Ranger were complicated to begin with, and now I added a sense of doom to the list of unwanted emotions.

Morelli's pager beeped. He looked at the readout and sighed. "I have to go. If you run across Ranger, pass my message on to him. We really need to talk."

"It'll cost you."

"Dinner?"

"Fried chicken," I said. "Extra greasy."

I watched him angle out of the car and cross the street. I enjoyed the view until he was out of sight, and then I turned my attention back to the files. I knew Moon Man Dunphy. I'd gone to school with him. No problem there. I just had to go pry him away from his television set.

Lenny Dale lived in an apartment complex on Grand Avenue

and had listed his age as eighty-two. Big groan on this one. There is no good way to apprehend an eighty-two-year-old man. No matter how you cut it, you look and feel like a creep.

Morris Munson's file was left to read, but I didn't want to go there. Best to procrastinate and hope Ranger came forward.

I decided to go after Dale first. He was only about a quarter-mile from Vinnie's office. I needed to make a U-turn on Hamilton, but the car was having none of it. The car was heading for center city and the burned-out building.

Okay, so I'm nosy. I wanted to see the crime scene. And I guess I wanted to have a psychic moment. I wanted to stand in front of the building and have a Ranger revelation.

I crossed the railroad tracks and inched my way along in the morning traffic. The building was at the corner of Adams and Third. It was redbrick and four stories high, probably about fifty years old. I parked on the opposite side of the street, got out of my car, and stared at the fire-blackened windows, some of which were boarded over. Yellow crime-scene tape stretched the width of the building, held in place by sawhorses strategically positioned on the sidewalk to prevent snoops like me from getting too close. Not that I'd let a detail like crime-scene tape stop me from taking a peek.

I crossed the street and ducked under the tape. I tried the double glass door, but found it locked. Inside, the lobby seemed relatively unscathed. Lots of grimy water and smoke-smudged walls, but no visible fire damage.

I turned and looked at the surrounding buildings. Office buildings, stores, a deli-style restaurant on the corner.

Hey, Ranger, are you out there?

Nothing. No psychic moment.

I ran back to the car, locked myself in, and hauled out my cell phone. I dialed Ranger's number and waited through two rings before his answering machine picked up. My message was brief: "Are you okay?"

I disconnected and sat there for a few minutes, feeling breathless and hollow-stomached. I didn't want Ranger to be dead. And I didn't want him to have killed Homer Ramos. Not that I cared a fig about Ramos, but whoever killed him would pay, one way or another.

Finally I put the car in gear and drove away. A half-hour later I was standing in front of Lenny Dale's door, and apparently the Dales were at it again because there was a lot of shouting going on inside the apartment. I shifted foot to foot in the third-floor hall, waiting for a lull in the racket. When it came, I knocked. This led to another shouting match, over who was going to get the door.

I knocked again. The door was flung open, and an old man stuck his head out at me. "Yeah?"

"Lenny Dale?"

"You're looking at him, sis."

He was mostly nose. The rest of his face had shrunk away from that eagle's beak, his bald dome was dotted with liver spots, and his ears were oversized on his mummified head. The woman behind him was gray-haired and doughy, with tree-trunk legs stuffed into Garfield the Cat bedroom slippers.

"What's she want?" the woman yelled. "What's she want?"

"If you'd shut up I'd find out!" he yelled back. "Yammer, yammer, yammer. That's all you do."

"I'll give you yammer, yammer," she said. And she smacked him on top of his shiny skull.

Dale wheeled around and clocked her square on the side of her head.

"Hey!" I said. "Stop that!"

"I'll give you one, too," Dale said, jumping at me, fist raised.

I put my hand out to ward him off, and he stood statue still for a moment, frozen in the raised-fist position. His mouth opened, his eyes rolled into the back of his head, and he fell over stiff as a board and crashed to the floor.

I knelt beside him. "Mr. Dale?"

His wife toed him with Garfield. "Hunh," she said. "Guess he had another one of them heart attacks."

I put my hand to his neck and couldn't find a pulse.

"Oh, jeez," I said.

"Is he dead?"

"Well, I'm no expert . . ."

"He looks dead to me."

"Call 911 and I'll try CPR." Actually I didn't know CPR, but I'd seen it done on television, and I was willing to give it a shot.

"Honey," Mrs. Dale said, "you bring that man back to life and I'll hit you with the meat mallet until your head looks like a veal patty." She bent over her husband. "Anyway, look at him. He's dead as a doorknob. A body couldn't get any deader."

I was afraid she was right. Mr. Dale didn't look good.

An elderly woman came to the open door. "What's happening? Lenny have another one of them heart attacks?" She turned and yelled down the hall. "Roger, call 911. Lenny had another heart attack."

Within seconds the room was filled with neighbors, commenting on Lenny's condition and asking questions. How did it happen? And was it fast? And did Mrs. Dale want a turkey noodle casserole for the wake?

Sure, Mrs. Dale said, a casserole would be nice. And she wondered if Tootie Greenberg could make one of those poppyseed cakes like she did for Moses Schultz.

The EMS unit arrived, looked at Lenny, and agreed with the general consensus. Lenny Dale was as dead as a doorknob.

I quietly slipped out of the apartment and did a fast shuffle to the elevator. It wasn't even noon, and already my day seemed too long and cluttered with dead people. I called Vinnie when I reached the lobby.

"Listen," I said, "I found Dale, but he's dead."

"How long's he been like that?"

"About twenty minutes."

"Were there any witnesses?"

"His wife."

"Shit," Vinnie said, "it was self-defense, right?"

"I didn't kill him!"

"Are you sure?"

"Well, it was a heart attack, and I guess I might have contributed a little. . . ."

"Where is he now?"

"He's in his apartment. The EMS guys are there but there's nothing they can do. He's definitely dead."

"Christ, couldn't you have given him a heart attack after you got him to the police station? This is gonna be a big pain in the ass. You wouldn't believe the paperwork on this kind of thing. I tell you what, see if you can get the EMS boys to drive Dale over to the courthouse."

I felt my mouth drop open.

"Yeah, this'll work," Vinnie said. "Just get one of the guys at the desk to come out and take a look. Then he can give you a body receipt."

"I'm not dragging some poor dead man off to the municipal building!"

"What's the big deal? You think he's in a rush to get embalmed? Tell yourself you're doing something nice for him—you know, like a last ride."

Ugh. I disconnected. Should have kept the whole box of doughnuts for myself. This was shaping up to be an eight-doughnut day. I looked at the little green diode blinking on my cell phone. Come on, Ranger, I thought. Call me.

I left the lobby and took to the road. Moon Man Dunphy was next on my list. The Mooner lives in the Burg, a couple blocks from my parents' house. He shares a row house with two other guys who are just as crazy as Moon Man. Last I heard, he was working nights, restocking at the Shop & Bag. And at this time of the day I suspect he's at home eating Cap'n Crunch, watching reruns of *Star Trek*.

I turned onto Hamilton, passed the office, left-turned into the Burg at St. Francis Hospital and wound my way around to the row houses on Grant. The Burg is a residential chunk of Trenton with one side bordering on Chambersburg Street and the other side stretching to Italy. Tastykakes and olive loaf are staples in the Burg. "Sign language" refers to a stiff middle finger jabbed skyward. Houses are modest. Cars are large. Windows are clean.

I parked in the middle of the block and checked my fact sheet to make sure I had the right number. There were twenty-three attached houses all in a row. Each house sat flush to the sidewalk. Each house was two stories tall. Moon lived in number 45 Grant.

He opened the door wide and looked out at me. He was just under six feet tall, with light brown shoulder-length hair parted in the middle. He was slim and loose-jointed, wearing a black Metallica T-shirt and jeans with holes in the knees. He had a jar of peanut butter in one hand and a spoon in the other. Lunchtime. He stared out at me, looking confused, then the light went on, and he rapped himself on the head with the spoon, leaving a glob of peanut butter stuck in his hair. "Shit, dude! I forgot my court date!"

It was hard not to like Moon, and I found myself smiling in spite of my day. "Yeah, we need to get you bonded out again and rescheduled." And I'd pick him up and chauffeur him to court next time. Stephanie Plum, mother hen.

"How does the Moon do that?"

"You come with me to the station, and I'll walk you through it."

"That sucks seriously, dude. I'm in the middle of a *Rocky and Bullwinkle* retrospective. Can we do this some other time? Hey, I know—why don't you stay for lunch, and we can watch ol' Rocky together?"

I looked at the spoon in his hand. Probably he only had one. "I appreciate the invitation," I said, "but I promised my mom I'd have lunch with her." What is known in life as a little white lie.

"Wow, that's real nice. Having lunch with your mom. Far out."

"So how about if I go have lunch now, and then I come back for you in about an hour?"

"That'd be great. The Moon would really appreciate that, dude."

Mooching lunch from my mom wasn't a bad idea, now that I

thought about it. Besides getting lunch, I'd get whatever gossip was floating around the Burg about the fire.

I left Moon to his retrospective and had my fingers wrapped around the door handle of my car when a black Lincoln pulled alongside me.

The passenger-side window rolled down and a man looked out. "You Stephanie Plum?"

"Yes."

"We'd like to have a little chat with you. Get in."

Yeah, right. I'm going to get into the Mafia staff car with two strange men, one of whom is a Pakistani with a .38 tucked into his Sans-A-Belt pants, partially hidden by the soft roll of his belly, and the other is a guy who looks like Hulk Hogan with a buzz cut. "My mother told me never to ride with strangers."

"We aren't so strange," Hulk said. "We're just your average couple of guys. Isn't that right, Habib?"

"That is just so," Habib said, inclining his head in my direction and smiling, showing a gold tooth. "We are most average in every way."

"What do you want?" I asked.

The guy in the passenger seat gave a big sigh. "You're not gonna get in the car, are you?"

"No."

"Okay, here's the deal. We're looking for a friend of yours. Only maybe he's not a friend anymore. Maybe you're looking for him, too."

"Uh-huh."

"So we thought we could work together. You know, be a team."

"I don't think so."

"Well, then, we're just gonna have to follow you around. We thought we should tell you so you don't get, you know, *alarmed* when you see us tailing you."

"Who are you?"

"That's Habib over there behind the wheel. And I'm Mitchell."

"No. I mean, who *are* you? Who do you work for?" I was pretty sure I already knew the answer, but I thought it was worth asking anyway.

"We'd rather not divulge our employer's name," Mitchell said. "It don't matter to you anyway. What you want to remember is that you don't cut us out of anything, because then we'd be annoyed."

"Yes, and it is not good when we become annoyed," Habib said, wagging his finger. "We are not to be taken lightly. Is that not so?" he asked, looking to Mitchell for approval. "In fact, if you annoy us we will spread your entrails across an entire parking space of my cousin Muhammad's 7-Eleven parking lot."

"What are you, nuts?" Mitchell said. "We don't do no entrails shit. And if we did, it wouldn't be in front of the 7-Eleven. I go there for my Sunday paper."

"Oh," Habib said. "Well, then, we could do something of a sexual nature. We could perform amusing acts of sexual perversion on her . . . many, many times. If she lived in my country she would forever be shamed in the community. She would be an outcast. Of course, since she is a decadent and immoral American she will undoubtedly be accepting of the perverse acts we will inflict upon her. And it is most possible that because *we* will be inflicting the perversions upon her, she will enjoy them immensely. But wait— we could also maim her to make the experience unpleasant in her eyes."

"Hey, I don't mind about the maiming, but watch it with the sexy stuff," Mitchell said to Habib. "I'm a family man. My wife catches wind of anything like that, and I'm toast."

TWO

I THREW MY hands into the air. "What the hell do you want, already?"

"We want your pal Ranger, and we know you're looking for him," Mitchell said.

"I'm not looking for Ranger. Vinnie's giving him to Joyce Barnhardt."

"I don't know Joyce Barnhardt from the Easter Bunny," Mitchell said. "I know you. And I'm telling you, you're looking for Ranger. And when you find him, you're gonna tell us. And if you don't take this to be a serious . . . responsibility, you'll be real sorry."

"Re-spons-i-bility," Habib said. "I like that. Nicely put. I teenk I will remember that."

" 'Think,' " Mitchell said. "It's pronounced 'think.' "

"Teenk."

"Think!"

"That is what I said. Teenk."

"The raghead just came over," Mitchell said to me. "He used to work for our employer in another capacity in Pakistan, but he came over with the last load of goods, and we can't get rid of him. He don't know much yet."

562

"I am not a raghead," Habib shouted. "Do you see a rag on this head? I am in America now, and I do not wear these things. And it is not a nice way that you say this."

"Raghead," Mitchell said.

Habib narrowed his eyes. "Filthy American dog."

"Blubber-belly."

"Son of a camel-walla."

"Go fuck yourself," Mitchell said.

"And may your testicles fall off," Habib responded.

Probably I didn't have to worry about these guys—they'd kill each other before the day was over. "I have to go now," I said. "I'm going to my parents' house for lunch."

"You must not be doing so good," Mitchell said, "you gotta mooch lunch from your parents. We could help with that, you know. You get us what we want, and we could be real generous."

"Even if I wanted to find Ranger, which I don't, I couldn't. Ranger is smoke."

"Yeah, but I hear you got special talents, if you get my drift. Besides, you're a bounty hunter . . . bring 'im back dead or alive. Always get your man."

I opened the door of the Honda and slid behind the wheel. "Tell Alexander Ramos he needs to get someone else to find Ranger."

Mitchell looked like he might hack up a hairball. "We don't work for that little turd. Pardon my French."

This had me sitting up straighter in my seat. "Then who *do* you work for?"

"I told you before. We can't divulge that information."

Jeez.

MY GRANDMOTHER WAS standing in the doorway when I drove up. She lived with my parents now that my grandfather was buying his lotto tickets directly from God. She had steel-gray hair cut short and permed. She ate like a horse and had skin like a soup chicken. Her elbows were sharp as razor wire. She was dressed in white tennis shoes and a magenta polyester warm-up suit, and she was sliding her uppers around in her mouth, which meant she had something on her mind.

"Isn't this nice? We were just setting lunch," she said. "Your mother got some chicken salad and little rolls from Giovicchini's Market."

I cut my eyes to the living room. My dad's chair was empty.

"He's out with the cab," Grandma said. "Whitey Blocher called and said they needed somebody to fill in."

My father is retired from the post office, but he drives a cab part-time, more to get out of the house than to pick up spare change. And driving a cab is often synonymous with playing pinochle at the Elks lodge.

I hung my jacket in the hall closet and took my place at the kitchen table. My parents' house is a narrow duplex. The living room windows look out at the street, the dining room window overlooks the driveway separating their house from the house next door, and the kitchen window and back door open to the yard, which was tidy but bleak at this time of the year.

My grandmother sat across from me. "I'm thinking about changing my hair color," she said. "Rose Kotman dyed her hair red, and she looks pretty good. And now she's got a new boyfriend." She helped herself to a roll and sliced it with the big knife. "I wouldn't mind having a boyfriend."

"Rose Kotman is thirty-five," my mother said.

"Well, I'm almost thirty-five," Grandma said. "Everyone's always saying how I don't look my age."

That was true. She looked about ninety. I loved her a lot, but gravity hadn't been kind.

"There's this man at the seniors club I've got my eye on," Grandma said. "He's a real looker. I bet if I was a redhead he'd give me a tumble."

My mother opened her mouth to say something, thought better of it, and reached for the chicken salad.

I didn't especially want to think about the details of Grandma tumbling, so I jumped right in and got to the business at hand. "Did you hear about the fire downtown?"

Grandma slathered extra mayo on her roll. "You mean that building on the corner of Adams and Third? I saw Esther Moyer at the bakery this morning, and she said her son Bucky drove the hook and ladder to that fire. She said Bucky told her it was a pip of a fire."

"Anything else?"

"Esther said when they went through the building yesterday they found a body on the third floor."

"Did Esther know who it was?"

"Homer Ramos. Esther said he was burned to a crisp. And he'd been shot. Had a big hole in his head. I looked to see if he was being laid out at Stiva's, but there wasn't anything in the paper today. Boy, wouldn't that be something? Guess Stiva couldn't do much with that. He could fill up the bullet hole with mortician's putty like he did for Moogey Bues, but he'd have his work cut out for him with the burned-to-a-crisp part. Course, if you wanted to look on the bright side, I guess the Ramos family could save some money on the funeral being that Homer was already cremated. Probably all they had to do was shovel him into a jar. Except I guess the head was left since they knew it had a hole in it. So probably they couldn't get the head in the jar. Less of course they smashed it with the shovel. I bet you give it a couple good whacks and it'd crumble up pretty good."

My mother clapped her napkin to her mouth.

"You okay?" Grandma asked my mother. "You having another one of them hot flashes?" Grandma leaned in my direction and whispered, "It's the change."

"It's *not* the change," my mother said.

"Do they know who shot Ramos?" I asked Grandma.

"Esther didn't say anything about that."

By one o'clock I was full of chicken salad and my mother's rice pudding. I trotted out of the house to the Civic and spotted

Mitchell and Habib half a block down the street. Mitchell gave me a friendly wave when I looked his way. I got into the car without returning the wave and drove back to Moon Man.

I knocked on the door and Moon looked out at me, just as confused as he had been before. "Oh, yeah," he finally said. And then he did a stoner laugh, giggling and chuffing.

"Empty your pockets," I told him.

He turned his pants pockets inside out, and a bong dropped onto the front stoop. I picked it up and threw it into the house.

"Anything else?" I asked. "Any acid? Any weed?"

"No, dude. How about you?"

I shook my head. His brain probably looked like those clumps of dead coral you buy in the pet store to put in aquariums.

He squinted past me to the Civic. "Is that your car?"

"Yes."

He closed his eyes and put his hands out. "No energy," he said. "I don't feel any energy. This car is all wrong for you." He opened his eyes and ambled across the sidewalk, pulling up his sagging pants. "What's your sign?"

"Libra."

"You see! I knew it! You're air. And this car is earth. You can't drive this car, dude. You're a creative force, and this car's gonna bring you down."

"True," I said, "but this is all I could afford. Get in."

"I have a friend who could get you a suitable car. He's like . . . a car dealer."

"I'll keep it in mind."

Mooner folded himself into the front seat and hauled out his sunglasses. "Better, dude," he said from behind the shades. "Much better."

THE TRENTON COP shop shares a building with the court. It's a blocky redbrick, no-frills structure that gets the job done—a product of the slam-bam-thank-you-ma'am school of municipal architecture.

I parked in the lot and shepherded Moon inside. Technically, I
couldn't bond him out myself, since I'm an enforcement agent and
not a bonding agent. So I got the paperwork started and called Vinnie to come down and complete the process.

"Vinnie's on his way," I told Moon, settling him onto the bench
by the docket lieutenant. "I have some other business in the building, so I'm going to leave you here alone for a couple minutes."

"Hey, that's cool, dude. Don't worry about me. The Mooner
will be fine."

"Don't move from this spot!"

"No problemo."

I went upstairs to Violent Crimes and found Brian Simon at his
desk. He'd only been promoted out of uniform a couple months
earlier and still didn't have the hang of dressing himself. He was
wearing a yellow-and-tan-plaid sports coat, navy suit slacks with
brown penny loafers and red socks, and a tie wide enough to be a
lobster bib.

"Don't they have some kind of dress code here?" I asked. "You
keep dressing like this and we're going to make you go live in Connecticut."

"Maybe you should come over tomorrow morning and help me
pick out my clothes."

"Jeez," I said. "Touchy. Maybe this isn't a good time."

"Good as any," he said. "What's on your mind?"

"Carol Zabo."

"That woman's a nut! She smashed right into me. And then she
left the scene."

"She was nervous."

"You aren't going to lay one of those PMS excuses on me, are
you?"

"Actually, it had to do with her panties."

Simon rolled his eyes. "Oh, crap."

"You see, Carol was coming out of the Frederick's of Hollywood store, and she was flustered because she'd just gotten some sexy panties."

"Is this going to be embarrassing?"

"Do you get embarrassed easily?"

"What's the point to all this, anyway?"

"I was hoping you'd drop the charges."

"No way!"

I sat down in the chair by his desk. "I'd consider it a special favor. Carol's a friend. And I had to talk her off a bridge this morning."

"Over panties?"

"Just like a man," I said, eyes narrowed. "I knew you wouldn't understand."

"Hey, I'm Mr. Sensitivity. I read *The Bridges of Madison County*. Twice."

I gave him a doe-eyed, hopeful look. "So you'll let her off the hook?"

"How far off the hook do I have to let her?"

"She doesn't want to go to jail. She's worried about the out-in-the-open-bathroom part."

He bent forward and thunked his head on the desk. "Why me?"

"You sound like my mother."

"I'll make sure she doesn't go to jail," he said. "But you owe me."

"I'm not going to have to come over and dress you, am I? I'm not that kind of girl."

"Live in fear."

Damn.

I left Simon and went back downstairs. Vinnie was there, but no Moon Man.

"Where is he?" Vinnie wanted to know. "I thought you said he was here at the back door."

"He was! I told him to wait on the bench by the docket lieutenant."

We both looked over at the bench. It was empty.

Andy Diller was working the desk. "Hey, Andy," I said. "Do you know what happened to my skip?"

"Sorry, I wasn't paying attention."

We canvassed the first floor, but Moon didn't turn up.

"I've gotta get back to the office," Vinnie said. "I've got stuff to do."

Talk to his bookie, play with his gun, shake hands with Mr. Stumpy.

We went out the door together and found Moon standing in the parking lot, watching my car burn. There were a bunch of cops with extinguishers working on it, but things didn't look too hopeful. A fire truck rolled down the street, lights flashing, and pulled through the chain-link gate.

"Hey, man," Moon said to me. "Real shame about your car. That's mad crazy, dude."

"What happened?"

"I was sitting there on the bench waiting for you, and I saw Reefer walk by. You know Reefer? Well, anyway, Reefer just got let out of the tank, and his brother was coming to pick him up. And Reefer said why didn't I come out to say hello to his brother. So I walked out with Reefer, and you know Reefer always has good weed, so one thing led to another, and I thought I'd just relax in your car for a minute and have a smoke. I guess a pod must have jumped, because the next thing your seat was on fire. And then it kind of spread from there. It was glorious until these gentlemen hosed it."

Glorious. Unh. I wondered if Moon would think it was glorious if I choked him until he was dead.

"I'd like to stay around and toast some marshmallows," Vinnie said, "but I need to get back to the office."

"Yeah, and I'm missing *Hollywood Squares*," Moon said. "We need to conclude our business, dude."

IT WAS CLOSE to four when I made the final arrangements for the car to get towed away. I'd been able to salvage a tire iron and that was about it. I was outside in the lot, pawing through my shoulder bag for my cell phone, when the black Lincoln pulled up.

"Tough luck with the car," Mitchell said.

"I'm getting used to it. It happens to me a lot."

"We've been watching from a distance, and we figure you need a ride."

"Actually, I just called a friend, and he's going to come pick me up."

"That's a big fat lie," Mitchell said. "You been standing here for an hour and you haven't called anyone. I bet your mother wouldn't like it if she knew you were telling lies."

"Better than me getting into this car with you," I said. "That'd give her a heart attack."

Mitchell nodded. "You got a point." The tinted window slid shut, and the Lincoln rolled out of the lot. I found my phone and called Lula at the office.

"BOY, IF I had a nickel for every car you destroyed I'd be able to retire," Lula said when she picked me up.

"It wasn't my fault."

"Hell, it's *never* your fault. It's one of them karma things. You're a number ten on the Bad-Shit-O-Meter when it comes to cars."

"I don't suppose you've got any news on Ranger?"

"Only that Vinnie gave the file to Joyce."

"Was she happy?"

"Had an orgasm right there in the office. Connie and me had to excuse ourselves so we could go throw up."

Joyce Barnhardt is a fungus. When we were in kindergarten together she used to spit in my milk carton. When we were in high school she started rumors and took secret photos in the girls' locker room. And before the ink had even dried on my marriage certificate I found her bare-assed with my husband (now my ex-husband) on my brand-new dining room table.

Anthrax was too good for Joyce Barnhardt.

"Then a funny thing happened to Joyce's car," Lula said. "While she was in the office talking to Vinnie, someone drove a screwdriver into her tire."

I raised my eyebrows.

"Was an act of God," Lula said, putting her red Firebird in gear and punching on the sound system, which could shake the fillings out of your teeth.

She took North Clinton to Lincoln and then Chambers. When she dropped me in my lot, there was no sign of Mitchell and Habib.

"You looking for someone?" she wanted to know.

"Two guys in a black Lincoln were following me earlier today, hoping I'd find Ranger for them. I don't see them now."

"Lot of people looking for Ranger."

"Do you think he killed Homer Ramos?"

"I could see him killing Ramos, but I can't see him burning down a building. And I can't see him being stupid."

"Like getting caught on a security camera."

"Ranger had to know there were security cameras. That building's owned by Alexander Ramos. And Ramos just don't go around leaving the lid off the cookie jar. He had offices in that building. I know on account of I did a house call there once while I was working at my former profession."

Lula's former profession was being a ho', so I didn't ask for details on the house call.

I left Lula and swung through the double glass doors that led to the small lobby of my apartment building. I live on the second floor, and I had a choice of stairs or elevator. I chose the elevator today, having exhausted myself watching my car burn.

I let myself into my apartment, hung up my shoulder bag and jacket, and peeked in on my hamster, Rex. He was running on his wheel in his glass aquarium, his little feet a pink blur against the red plastic.

"Hey, Rex," I said. "How's things?"

He paused for a moment, whiskers twitching, eyes bright, waiting for food to drop from the sky. I gave him a raisin from the box in the refrigerator and told him about the car. He stuffed the raisin into his cheek and returned to his running. If it was me I'd have eaten the raisin right off and opted for a nap. I don't understand this running-for-fun stuff. The only way I could really get into running would be if I was being chased by a serial mutilator.

I checked my message machine. One message. No words. Just breathing. I hoped it was Ranger's breathing. I listened to it again. The breathing sounded normal. Not pervert breathing. Not head-cold breathing. Could have been telephone-solicitor breathing.

I had a couple hours before the chicken arrived, so I went across the hall and knocked on my neighbor's door.

"What?" Mr. Wolesky yelled, above the roar of his TV.

"I was wondering if I could borrow your paper. I had an unfortunate mishap with my car, and I thought I'd check out the used-car section of the classifieds."

"Again?"

"It wasn't my fault."

He handed me the paper. "If I was you, I'd be looking at army surplus. You should be driving a tank."

I took the paper back to my apartment and read the car ads and the funnies. I was pondering my horoscope when the phone rang.

"Is your grandmother there?" my mother wanted to know.

"No."

"She had some words with your father, and she went stomping up to her room. And then next thing I know she's outside getting into a cab!"

"She probably went to visit one of her friends."

"I tried Betty Szajak and Emma Getz but they haven't seen her."

My doorbell rang and my heart went dead in my chest. I looked out my peephole. It was Grandma Mazur.

"She's here!" I whispered to my mother.

"Thank goodness," my mother said.

"No. Not thank goodness. She has a suitcase!"

"Maybe she needs a vacation from your father."

"She's not living here!"

"Well, of course not . . . but maybe she could just visit with you for a day or two until things calm down."

"No! No, no, no."

The doorbell rang again.

"She's ringing my doorbell," I said to my mother. "What should I do?"

"For goodness' sakes, let her in."

"If I let her in, I'm doomed. It's like inviting a vampire into your house. Once you invite them in, that's it, you're as good as dead!"

"This isn't a vampire. This is your grandmother."

Grandma pounded on the door. "Hello?" she called.

I hung up and opened the door.

"Surprise," Grandma said. "I've come to live with you while I look for an apartment."

"But you live with Mom."

"Not anymore. Your father's a horse's patoot." She dragged her suitcase in and hung her coat on a wall hook. "I'm getting my own place. I'm tired of watching your father's TV shows. So I'm staying here until I find something. I knew you wouldn't mind if I moved in for a while."

"I only have one bedroom."

"I can sleep on the couch. I'm not fussy when it comes to sleeping. I could sleep standing up in a closet if I had to."

"But what about Mom? She'll be lonely. She's used to having you around." Translation: What about me? I'm used to *not* having anybody around.

"I suppose that's true," Grandma said. "But she's just gonna have to make her own life. I can't keep livening that house up. It's too much of a strain. Don't get me wrong, I love your mother, but

573

she can be a real wet blanket. And I haven't got a lot of time to waste. I've probably only got about thirty more years before I start to slow down."

Thirty years would put Grandma well over a hundred—and me at sixty, if I didn't die on the job.

Someone gave a light rap on my door. Morelli was here early. I opened the door, and he got halfway through the foyer before spotting Grandma.

"Grandma Mazur," he said.

"Yep," she answered. "I'm living here now. Just moved in."

The corners of Morelli's mouth twitched up ever so slightly. Jerk.

"Was this a surprise move?" Morelli asked.

I took the bucket of chicken from him. "Grandma got into it with my father."

"Is that chicken?" Grandma asked. "I can smell it all the way over here."

"Plenty for everyone," Morelli told her. "I always get extra."

Grandma pushed past us, into the kitchen. "I'm starved. All this moving gave me an appetite." She looked into the bag. "Are those biscuits, too? And coleslaw?" She grabbed some plates from the cabinet and ran them out to the dining room table. "Boy, this is gonna be fun. I hope you've got beer. I feel like having a beer."

Morelli was still grinning.

For some time now, Morelli and I had been engaged in an off-again-on-again romance. Which is a nice way of saying we occasionally shared a bed. And Morelli wasn't going to think this was so funny when the occasional overnighter turned to no overnighters at all.

"This is going to put a crimp in our plans for the evening," I whispered to Morelli.

"We just need to change the address," he said. "We can go to my house after dinner."

"Forget your house. What would I tell Grandma? 'Sorry, I'm

not sleeping here tonight, because I have to go do the deed with Joe'?"

"Something wrong with that?"

"I can't say that. It would make me feel icky."

"Icky?"

"My stomach would get squishy."

"That's silly. Your grandma Mazur wouldn't mind."

"Yes, but she'd know."

Morelli looked pained. "This is one of those woman things, isn't it?"

Grandma was back in the kitchen, getting glasses. "Where are your napkins?" she asked.

"I don't have any," I told her.

She stared at me blank-faced for a moment, unable to comprehend a house with no napkins.

"There are napkins in the bag with the biscuits," Morelli said.

Grandma peeked into the bag and beamed. "Isn't he something," she said. "He even brings the napkins."

Morelli rocked back on his heels and gave me a look that told me I was a lucky duck. "Always prepared," Morelli said.

I rolled my eyes.

"That's a cop for you," Grandma said. "Always prepared."

I sat across from her and grabbed a piece of chicken. "It's the Boy Scouts who are always prepared," I said. "Cops are always hungry."

"Now that I'm going off on my own I've been thinking I should get a job," Grandma said. "And I've been thinking maybe I'd get a job as a cop. What do you think?" she asked Morelli. "You think I'd make a good cop?"

"I think you'd make a great cop, but the department has an age limit."

Grandma pressed her lips together. "Don't that tear it. I hate those darn age limits. Well, I guess that just leaves being a bounty hunter."

575

I looked to Morelli for help, but he was keeping his eyes glued to his plate.

"You need to be able to drive to be a bounty hunter," I said to Grandma. "You don't have a driver's license."

"I've been planning on getting one of them anyway," she said. "First thing tomorrow I'm signing up for driving school. I've even got a car. Your uncle Sandor left me that Buick and since you aren't using it anymore I guess I'll give it a try. It's a pretty good-looking car."

Shamu with wheels.

When the chicken bucket was empty Grandma pushed back from the table. "Let's get things cleaned up," she said, "and then we can watch a movie. I stopped off at the video store on my way over."

Grandma fell asleep halfway through *The Terminator*, sitting on the couch ramrod straight, head dropped to her chest.

"Probably I should leave," Morelli said. "Let you two girls get things straightened out."

I walked him to the door. "Is there any word on Ranger?"

"Nothing. Not even a rumor."

Sometimes no news was good news. At least he hadn't floated in with the tide.

Morelli pulled me to him and kissed me, and I felt the usual tingle in the usual places. "You know my number," he said. "And I don't give a rat's ass what anyone thinks."

I WOKE UP on my couch with a stiff neck and feeling cranky. Someone was clanking around in my kitchen. Didn't take a rocket scientist to figure out who.

"Isn't this a terrific morning?" Grandma said. "I got pancakes started. And I got the coffee on."

Okay, maybe it wasn't so bad having Grandma here.

She stirred the pancake batter. "I thought we could get going early today, and then maybe you could take me out for a driving lesson."

Thank God my car had burned to a cinder. "I don't have a car right now," I said. "There was an accident."

"Again? What happened this time. Torched? Bombed? Flattened?"

I poured myself a cup of coffee. "Torched. But it wasn't my fault."

"You've got a pip of a life," Grandma said. "Never a dull moment. Fast cars, fast men, fast food. I wouldn't mind having a life like that."

She was right about the fast food.

"You didn't get a paper this morning," Grandma said. "I went and looked in the hall and all your neighbors got papers but you didn't get one."

"I don't have paper delivery," I told her. "If I want a paper I buy one." Or borrow one.

"Breakfast isn't gonna seem right without a paper to read," Grandma said. "I gotta read the funnies and the obits, and this morning I wanted to look for an apartment."

"I'll get you a paper," I said, not wanting to slow down the apartment search.

I was wearing a green plaid flannel nightshirt, which went well with my bloodshot blue eyes. I covered it with a short denim Levi's jacket, stuffed myself into gray sweatpants, shoved my feet into boots, which I left unlaced, clapped a Navy SEALs ball cap onto my rat's nest of shoulder-length curly brown hair, and grabbed my car keys.

"I'll be back in a minute," I yelled from the hall. "I'll just run out to the 7-Eleven."

I punched the button for the elevator. The elevator doors opened and my mind went blank. Ranger was lounging against the far wall, arms crossed over his chest, his eyes dark and assessing, the corners of his mouth hinting at a smile.

"Get in," he said.

He'd abandoned his usual outfit of black rap clothes or GI Joe cammies. He was wearing a brown leather jacket, a cream-colored

Henley, faded jeans, and work boots. His hair, which had always been slicked back in a ponytail, was cut short. He had a two-day beard, making his teeth seem whiter and his Latino complexion seem darker. A wolf in Gap clothing.

"Jeez," I said, feeling a flutter of something I'd rather not admit to in the pit of my stomach. "You look different."

"Just your average guy."

Yeah, right.

He reached forward, grabbed the front of my jacket, and pulled me into the elevator. He pushed the button to close the doors and then hit Stop. "We need to talk."

THREE

RANGER HAD BEEN Special Forces, and he still had the build and the carriage. He was standing close, forcing me to tip my head back ever so slightly to look into his eyes.

"Just get out of bed?" he asked.

I glanced down. "You mean the nightshirt?"

"The nightshirt, the hair . . . the stupor."

"You're the reason for the stupor."

"Yeah," Ranger said. "I get that a lot. I cause stupor in women."

"What happened?"

"I had a meeting with Homer Ramos, and someone killed him when I left."

"The fire?"

"Not me."

"Do you know who killed Ramos?"

Ranger stared at me for a moment. "I have some ideas."

"The police think you did it. They have you on video."

"The police *hope* I did it. Hard to believe they'd actually *think* I did it. I don't have a reputation for being stupid."

"No, but you do have a reputation for . . . um, killing people."

Ranger grinned down at me. "Street talk." He looked at the keys in my hand. "Going somewhere?"

"Grandma's moved in with me for a couple days. She wanted a paper, so I was going to run out to the 7-Eleven."

The grin spread to his eyes. "You haven't got a car, babe."

Damn! "I forgot." I narrowed my eyes at him. "How did you know?"

"It's not in the lot."

Well, duh.

"What happened to it?" he asked.

"It's gone to car heaven."

He pressed the button for the third floor. The doors opened, he hit the hold, stepped out and grabbed the paper lying on the floor in front of 3C.

"That's Mr. Kline's paper," I said.

Ranger handed the paper over to me and pushed the button for the second floor. "You owe Mr. Kline a favor."

"Why did you skip on your court date?"

"Bad timing. I need to find someone, and I can't find him if I'm detained."

"Or dead."

"Yeah," Ranger said, "that, too. I didn't think a scheduled public appearance right now was in my best interest."

"I was approached by two Mob-type guys yesterday. Mitchell and Habib. Their plan is to follow me around until I lead them to you."

"They work for Arturo Stolle."

"Arturo Stolle, the carpet king? What's his connection in this?"

"You don't want to know."

"Like if you told me, you'd have to kill me?"

"If I told you, someone else might want to kill you."

"No love lost between Mitchell and Alexander Ramos."

"None at all." Ranger handed me a card with an address on it. "I want you to do some part-time surveillance for me. Hannibal Ramos. He's the firstborn son and the second in command of the Ramos empire. He lists California as his residence, but he's spending more and more time here in Jersey."

"Is he here now?"

"He's been here for three weeks. Has a condo in a complex off Route 29."

"You don't think he killed his brother, do you?"

"He's not at the top of my list," Ranger said. "I'll have one of my men drop off a car for you."

Ranger loosely employed a small army of men to help with his various enterprises. Most were ex-military and most were even crazier than Ranger.

"No! Not necessary." I have bad luck with cars. Their demise frequently results in police intervention, and Ranger's cars have unexplainable origins.

Ranger stepped back into the elevator. "Don't get too close to Ramos," he said. "He's not a nice guy." The doors closed. And he was gone.

I EMERGED FROM the bathroom, dressed in my usual uniform of jeans and boots and T-shirt, fresh out of the shower, ready to start the day. Grandma was at the dining room table, reading the paper, and Moon was across from her, eating pancakes. "Hey, dude," he said, "your granny fixed me some pancakes. You're, like, so lucky to have your granny living with you. She's totally the bomb, dude."

Grandma smiled. "Isn't he the one," she said.

"I felt real bad about yesterday," Moon said, "so I brought you a car. It's, like, a loaner. Remember I was telling you about this friend of mine who's the *Dealer*? Well, he was ragged when I told him about the fire, and he said it'd be cool if you used one of his cars until you got new wheels."

"This isn't a stolen car, is it?"

"Hey, dude, what do I look like?"

"You look like a guy who'd steal a car."

"Well, yeah, but not *all* the time. This here's a genuine loaner."

I really did need a car. "It would only be for a couple days," I said. "Just until I get my insurance money."

Moon pushed back from his empty plate and dropped a set of keys into my hand. "Knock yourself out. It's a cosmic car, dude. I picked it out myself so it'd complement your aura."

"What kind of car is it?"

"It's a Rollswagen. A silver wind machine."

Uh-huh. "Okay, well, thanks. Can I give you a ride home?"

He ambled out into the hall. "Gonna walk. Need to convene."

"I've got my whole day lined up," Grandma said. "Driving lesson this morning. Then this afternoon Melvina is going to take me around to look at some apartments."

"Can you afford your own apartment?"

"I've got some money put aside from when I sold the house. I was saving it to go into one of them nursing homes in my old age but maybe I'll just use my gun instead."

I grimaced.

"Well, it isn't like I'm gonna eat lead tomorrow," Grandma said. "I've got a whole lot of years left. And besides, I've got it figured out. See, if you put the gun in your mouth, then you blow the back of your head off. That way Stiva don't have to work so hard to make you look good when he lays you out on account of no one sees the back of your head anyway. You just got to be careful not to jiggle the gun so you don't botch the job and take your ear off." She put the paper aside. "I'll stop at the store on the way home and get some pork chops for supper. I gotta go get ready for my driving lesson now."

And I had to go to work. Problem was, I didn't want to do any of the things that were sitting in front of me. I didn't want to snoop on Hannibal Ramos. And I definitely didn't want to meet Morris Munson. I could go back to bed, but that wouldn't get the rent money. And besides, I didn't have a bed anymore. Grandma had the bed.

Okay, might as well take a look at the Munson file. I hauled the paperwork out and thumbed through it. Aside from the beating, the rape, and the attempted cremation Munson didn't seem so bad. No priors. No swastikas carved into his forehead. He'd listed his address as Rockwell Street. I knew Rockwell. It was down by the button factory. Not the best part of town. Not the worst. Mostly small single-family bungalows and row houses. Mostly blue-collar or no-collar.

Rex was asleep in his soup can, and Grandma was in the bathroom, so I left without ceremony. When I got to the lot I searched for a silver wind machine. And sure enough, I found one. And it was a Rollswagen, too. The body of the car was an ancient Volkswagen Beetle, and the front end was vintage Rolls-Royce. It was iridescent silver with celestial blue swirls sweeping the length of it, the swirls dotted with stars.

I closed my eyes and hoped that when I opened them the car would be gone. I counted to three and opened my eyes. The car was still there.

I ran back to the apartment, got a hat and dark glasses, and returned to the car. I slid behind the wheel, slouched low in the seat, and chugged out of the lot. This is *not* compatible with my aura, I told myself. My aura was *not* half Volkswagen Beetle.

Twenty minutes later I was on Rockwell Street, reading numbers, looking for Munson's house. When I found it the house seemed normal enough. One block from the factory. Convenient if you wanted to walk to work. Not so good if you liked scenic. It was a two story row house, very much like Mooner's house. Faced in maroon asbestos shingle.

I parked at the curb and walked the short distance to the door. It wasn't likely Munson would be home; this was Wednesday morning and he was probably in Argentina. I rang the bell and was caught off guard when the door opened and Munson stuck his head out.

"Morris Munson?"

"Yeah?"

"I thought you'd be . . . at work."

"I took a couple weeks off. I've been having some problems. Who are you, anyway?"

"I represent Vincent Plum Bail Bonds. You missed your court date, and we'd like to get you rescheduled."

"Oh. Sure. Go ahead and reschedule me."

"I need to take you downtown to do that."

He looked beyond me to the wind machine. "You don't expect me to go with you in that, do you?"

"Well, yeah."

"I'd feel like an idiot. What would people think?"

"Hey listen, pal, if I can ride in it, you can ride in it."

"You women, you're all alike," he said. "Snap your fingers and expect a man to jump through the hoops."

I had my hand in my shoulder bag, scrounging for my pepper spray.

"Stay here," Munson said. "I'm gonna go get my car. It's parked out back. I don't mind rescheduling, but I'm not riding in that dopey-looking car. I'll come around the block and then follow you into town." Slam. He closed and locked the door.

Damn. I got into the car and turned the key in the ignition, waiting at idle for Munson, wondering if I'd ever see him again. I checked my watch. I'd give him five minutes. Then what? Storm the house? Break the door down and go in guns blazing? I looked in my shoulder bag. No gun. I forgot to bring my gun. Gee, guess that means I have to go home and leave Munson for some other day.

I looked straight ahead and saw a car turn the corner. It was Munson. What a nice surprise, I thought. You see, Stephanie, don't be so quick to judge. Sometimes people turn out just fine. I put the wind machine in gear and watched him come closer. Hold on here, he was speeding up instead of slowing down! I could see his face, pinched in concentration. The maniac was going to ram me! I threw the car into reverse and stomped on the gas pedal. The Rolls jumped back. Not fast enough to avoid the collision, but fast enough to avoid getting totally smashed. My head snapped on impact. No big deal for a woman born and raised in the Burg. We grow up riding bumper cars at the Jersey shore. We know how to take a hit.

Problem was, Munson was banging into me with what looked like a retired cop car, a Crown Victoria. Bigger than the Rollswagen. He came at me again, bouncing me back about fifteen feet, and the wind machine stalled. He scrambled out of his car while I was trying to restart, and ran at me with a tire iron. "You want to see me jump through hoops," he yelled. "I'll show you jump through hoops."

A pattern was emerging here. Ram somebody with your car, beat them with the tire iron. I didn't want to think about what would come after the tire iron. The Rolls engine caught, and I catapulted forward, barely missing him.

He swung the tire iron and caught my back fender. "I hate you!" he yelled. "You women are all alike!"

I went from zero to fifty m.p.h. in half a block and took the corner on two wheels. I didn't look back for a quarter of a mile, and when I did there was no one behind me. I forced myself to ease up on the gas and sucked in some deep breaths. My heart was thumping in my chest, and my hands had the wheel in a white-knuckled death grip. A McDonald's popped up in front of me, and the car automatically turned into the drive-through lane. I ordered a vanilla milkshake and asked the kid in the window if they were hiring.

"Sure," he said, "we're always hiring. You want an application?"

"Do you get held up a lot here?"

"Not a *lot*," he said, passing the application through with the straw. "We get a few crazies, but usually you can buy them off with extra pickles."

I parked in the far corner of the lot and drank my milkshake while I read the application. It might not be so bad, I thought. You probably get free french fries.

I got out and looked at the car. The Rolls-Royce grill was crumpled, and the left rear fender had a big dent in it, and the back light was smashed.

The black Lincoln cruised into the lot and parked alongside me. The window rolled down, and Mitchell smiled at the Rollswagen. "What the hell is that?"

I gave him my PMS look.

"You need a car? We could get you a car. Any kind of car you want," Mitchell said. "You don't need to drive this . . . embarrassment."

"I'm *not* looking for Ranger."

"Sure," Mitchell said, "but maybe he's looking for you. Maybe he needs to get his oil changed, and he figures you're safe. It happens, you know. A man gets these *needs*."

"Do you not have oil changed at a garage in this country?" Habib asked Mitchell.

"Christ," Mitchell said. "Not that kind of oil. I'm talking about the old hide-the-salami thing."

"I do not understand this 'hiding salami,'" Habib said. "What is salami?"

"Fucking vegetarian don't know nothing," Mitchell said. He grabbed himself in the crotch and gave a hike up. "You know—the old salami."

"Ahh," Habib said. "I understand. This man Ranger hides his salami deep in this daughter of a pig."

"Daughter of a pig? Excuse me?" I said.

"Just so," Habib said. "Unclean slut."

I was going to have to start carrying my gun. I really felt like shooting these guys. Nothing serious. Just maybe take out an eye. "I have to go," I said. "I have stuff to do."

"Okay," Mitchell said, "but don't be a stranger. And think about the car offer."

"Hey," I yelled. "How did you find me?" But they were already out of the lot.

I drove around for a while, making sure no one was following me, then headed for Ramos's condo. I caught Route 29 and traveled north toward Ewing Township. Ramos lived in an affluent neighborhood with big old trees and professionally landscaped yards. Tucked away on Fenwood was a small cluster of recently constructed redbrick town houses, with attached two-car garages and brick-walled privacy yards. The houses sat behind well-tended lawns with curving walkways and dormant flower beds. Very taste-ful. Very respectable. Just the place for an international black-market arms dealer.

The wind machine was going to make surveillance tough in this neighborhood. For that matter, any surveillance was going to be tough. A strange car parked too long would be noticed. Ditto a strange woman loitering on the sidewalk.

The drapes were drawn on all Ramos's windows, so it was im-possible to tell if anyone was at home. Ramos was second from the end in a row of five attached houses. Trees peeked from behind the houses. The developer had left a greenbelt between condo sec-tions.

I drove around the neighborhood, getting a feel for it, then cruised past Ramos's house again. No change. I paged Ranger and got a call back five minutes later.

"Just exactly what is it you want me to do?" I asked. "I'm in front of his house, but there's nothing to see, and I can't hang out here much longer. There's no place to hide."

"Go back tonight when it's dark. See if he gets visitors."

"What does he do all day?"

"Different things," Ranger said. "There's a family compound in Deal. When Alexander is in residence, business is conducted at the shore. Before the fire, Hannibal spent most of his time in the building downtown. He had an office on the fourth floor."

"What kind of car does he drive?"

"Dark green Jag."

"Is he married?"

"When he's in Santa Barbara."

"Anything else to tell me?"

"Yeah," Ranger said. "Be careful."

Ranger disconnected, and the phone rang again.

"Is your grandmother with you?" my mother wanted to know.

"No. I'm working."

"Well, where is she? I've been calling your apartment and there's no answer."

"Grandma had a driving lesson this morning."

"Holy Mary, Mother of God."

"And then she's going out with Melvina."

"You're supposed to be keeping an eye on her. What are you thinking? That woman can't drive! She'll kill hundreds of innocent people."

"It's okay. She's with an instructor."

"An instructor. What good is an instructor with your grandmother? And what about her gun? I looked in every nook and cranny, and I can't find that gun."

Grandma has a .45 long-barrel that she keeps hidden from my mother. She got it from her friend Elsie, who picked it up at a yard sale. Probably it was in Grandma's purse. Grandma says it gives the bag some heft, in case she has to beat off a mugger. This might be true, but I think mostly Grandma likes pretending she is Clint Eastwood.

"I don't want her out on the road with a gun!" my mother said.

"Okay," I said, "I'll talk to her. But you know how she is with that gun."

"Why me?" my mother asked. "Why me?"

I didn't know the answer to that question, so I hung up. I parked the car, walked around to the end of the town houses, and picked up a macadam bike path. The path ran through the greenbelt behind Ramos's town house, and gave me a nice view of the second-story windows. Unfortunately, there was nothing to see because the shades were drawn. The brick privacy fence obscured the first-floor windows. And I'd bet dollars to doughnuts the first-floor windows were wide open. No reason to draw the drapes there. No one could look in. Unless, of course, someone rudely climbed the brick wall and sat there like Humpty Dumpty waiting for disaster to strike.

I decided disaster would be slower in coming if Humpty climbed the wall at night when it was dark and no one could see her, so I continued on down the path to the far end of the town houses, cut back to the road, and returned to my car.

———

LULA WAS STANDING in the doorway when I parked in front of the bail bonds office. "Okay, I give up," she said. "What is it?"

"A Rollswagen."

"It's got a few dents in it."

"Morris Munson was feeling cranky."

"He did that? Did you bring him in?"

"I decided to delay that pleasure."

Lula looked like she was giving herself a hernia trying to keep from laughing out loud. "Well, we gotta go get his ass. He got a lotta nerve denting up a Rollswagen. Hey, Connie," she yelled, "you gotta come see this car Stephanie's driving. It's a genuine Rollswagen."

"It's a loaner," I said. "Until I get my insurance check."

"What are those swirly designs on the side?"

"Wind."

"Oh, yeah," Lula said. "I should have known."

A shiny black Jeep Cherokee pulled to the curb behind the wind machine, and Joyce Barnhardt got out. She was dressed in black leather pants, a black leather bustier, which barely contained her C-cup breasts, a black leather jacket, and high-heeled black boots. Her hair was a brilliant red, teased high and curled. Her eyes were ringed by black liner, and her lashes were thick with mascara. She looked like Dominatrix Barbie.

"I hear they put rat hairs in that lash-lengthening mascara," Lula said to Joyce. "Hope you read the ingredients when you bought it."

Joyce looked at the wind machine. "The circus in town? This is one of those clown cars, right?"

"It's a one-of-a-kind Rollswagen," Lula said. "You got a problem with that?"

Joyce smiled. "The only problem I've got is trying to decide how I'm going to spend Ranger's capture money."

"Oh, yeah," Lula said. "You want to waste a lot of time on that one."

"You'll see," Joyce said. "I always get my man."

And dog and goat and vegetable . . . and everybody else's man, too.

"Well, we'd love to stand here talking to you, Joyce," Lula said. "But we got better things to do. We got a big important apprehension to make. We were just on our way to go catch a high-bond motherfucker."

"Are you going in the clown car?" Joyce asked.

"We're going in my Firebird," Lula said. "We always take the Firebird when we got serious ass-kicking lined up."

"I have to see Vinnie," Joyce said. "Someone made a mistake on Ranger's bond application. I checked out the address, and it's a vacant lot."

Lula and I looked at each other and smiled.

"Gee, imagine that," Lula said.

No one knows where Ranger lives. The address on his driver's license is for a men's shelter on Post Street. Not likely for a man who owns office buildings in Boston and checks with his stockbroker daily. Every now and then Lula and I make a halfhearted effort to track him down, but we've never had any success.

"So what do you think?" Lula asked when Joyce disappeared inside the office. "You want to go do some damage on Morris Munson?"

"I don't know. He's kind of crazy."

"Hunh," Lula said. "He don't scare me. I guess I could fix his bony ass. He didn't shoot at you, did he?"

"No."

"Then he isn't as crazy as most of the people on my block."

"Are you sure you want to risk going after him in your Firebird, after what he did to the wind machine?"

"First off, assuming I'd even be able to get my full figure into the wind machine, I think you'd need to take a can opener to it to get me out. And then, being that there's two seats in this little bitty car, and we'd be sitting in them, suppose we'd have to strap Munson to the hood to bring him in. Not that it's such a bad idea, but it'd slow us down some."

Lula walked over to the file cabinets and gave the bottom right-hand drawer a kick. The drawer popped open; Lula extracted a forty-caliber Glock and dropped it into her shoulder bag.

"No shooting!" I said.

"Sure, I know that," Lula said. "This here's car insurance."

BY THE TIME we got to Rockwell Street my stomach was queasy and my heart was tap-dancing in my chest.

"You don't look too good," Lula said.

"I think I'm carsick."

"You never get carsick."

"I do when I'm after some guy who just came at me with a tire iron."

"Don't worry. He do that again, and I'll pop a cap up his ass."

"No! I told you before—no shooting."

"Well, yeah, but this here's *life* insurance."

I tried to give her a stern look, but I sighed instead.

"Which house is his?" Lula wanted to know.

"The one with the green door."

"Hard to tell if anybody's in there."

We drove by the house twice, and then we took the one-lane service road to the rear and stopped at Munson's garage. I got out and looked in the grimy side window. The Crown Victoria was there. Rats.

"This is the plan," I told Lula. "You go to the front door. He's never seen you. He won't be suspicious. Tell him who you are and tell him you want him to go downtown with you. Then he'll sneak out the back door to his car, and I'll catch him off guard and cuff him."

"Sounds okay to me. And if you got a problem, you just holler, and I'll come around back."

Lula cruised away in the Firebird, and I tippytoed up to Munson's back door and flattened myself against the house so he couldn't see me. I shook my pepper spray to make sure it was live and listened for Lula's knock on his door.

The knock came after a few minutes; there was some muffled conversation, and then came the sounds of scuffling at the back door and the lock being retracted. The door opened and Morris Munson stepped out.

"Hold it," I said, kicking the door shut. "Stay exactly where you are. Don't move a muscle or I'll hit you with the pepper spray."

"You! You tricked me!"

I had the pepper spray in my left hand and the cuffs in my right. "Turn around," I said. "Hands over your head, palms flat against the house."

"I hate you!" he shrieked. "You're just like my ex-wife. Sneaky, lying, bossy bitch. You even look like her. Same dopey curly brown hair."

"Dopey hair? Excuse me?"

"I had a good life until that bitch screwed it up. I had a big house and a nice car. I had Surround Sound."

"What happened?"

"She left me. Said I was boring. Boring ol' Morris. So one day she got herself a lawyer, backed a truck up to the patio door, and cleaned me out. Took every fucking stick of furniture, every goddamn piece of china, every freaking spoon." He gestured to the row house. "This is what I'm left with. This piece-of-shit row house and a used Crown Victoria with two years of payments. After fifteen years at the button factory, working my fingers to the bone, I'm eating cereal for supper in this rat trap."

"Jeez."

"Wait a minute," he said. "Let me at least lock the door. This place isn't much, but it's all I've got."

"Okay. Just don't make any sudden moves."

He turned his back to me, locked the door, whirled around, and jostled me. "Oops," he said. "Sorry. I lost my balance."

I stepped away. "What have you got in your hand?"

"It's a cigarette lighter. You've seen a cigarette lighter before, right? You know how it works?" He flicked it, and a flame shot out.

"Drop it!"

He waved it around. "Look how pretty it is. Look at the lighter. Do you know what kind of lighter this is? I bet you can't guess."

"I said, Drop it."

He held it in front of his face. "You're gonna burn. You can't stop it now."

"What are you talking about? *Yikes!*" I was wearing jeans and a white T-shirt, tucked in, and a green-and-black flannel shirt jacket-style over the T-shirt. I looked down and saw that my shirttail was on fire.

"Burn!" he yelled to me. "Burn in hell!"

I dropped the cuffs and the pepper spray and ripped the shirt open. I fumbled out of it, threw it to the ground, and stomped the fire out. When I was done stomping I looked around and Munson was gone. I tried his back door. Locked. There was the sound of an engine catching. I looked to the service road and saw the Crown Victoria speed away.

I picked my shirt up and put it back on. The bottom half on the right side was missing.

Lula was leaning against her car when I turned the corner.

"Where's Munson?" she asked.

"Gone."

She looked at my shirt and raised an eyebrow. "I could have sworn you started out with a whole shirt."

"I don't want to talk about it."

"Looks to me like your shirt's been barbecued. First your car, now your shirt. This could be turning into a record week for you."

"I don't have to do this, you know," I said to Lula. "There are lots of good jobs I could get."

"Such as?"

"The McDonald's on Market is hiring."

"I hear you get free french fries."

I tried Munson's front door. Locked. I looked in the street-level window. Munson had tacked a faded flowered sheet over it, but there was a gap at the side. The room beyond was shabby. Scarred wood floor. A sagging couch covered by a threadbare yellow chenille bedspread. An old television on a cheap metal TV cart. A beechwood coffee table in front of the couch, and even from this distance I could see the veneer peeling off.

"Crazy ol' Munson isn't doing too good," Lula said, looking into the room with me. "I always imagined a homicidal rapist would live better than this."

"He's divorced," I said. "His wife cleaned him out."

"See, let this be a lesson. Always make sure you're the one to back the truck up to the door first."

When we got back to the office Joyce's car was still parked in front.

"Would have thought she'd be gone by now," Lula said. "She must be in there giving Vinnie a nooner."

My upper lip involuntarily curled back across my teeth. It was rumored that Vinnie had once been in love with a duck. And Joyce was said to be fond of large dogs. But somehow, the thought of them together was even more horrible.

To my great relief, Joyce was sitting on the outer office couch when Lula and I swung through the door.

"I knew you two losers wouldn't be out long," Joyce said. "Didn't get him, did you?"

"Steph had an accident with her shirt," Lula said. "So we decided not to pursue our man."

Connie was at her desk painting her nails. "Joyce thinks you know where Ranger lives."

"Sure we do," Lula said. "Only we're not telling Joyce on account of we know how she likes a challenge."

"You better tell me," Joyce said, "or I'll tell Vinnie you're holding back."

"Boy," Lula said, "that's got me thinking twice."

"I don't know where he lives," I said. "No one knows where he lives. But I heard him talking on the phone once, and he was talking to his sister in Staten Island."

"What's her name?"

"Marie."

"Marie Manoso?"

"Don't know. She might be married. She shouldn't be too hard to find, though. She works at the coat factory on Macko Street."

"I'm outta here," Joyce said. "If you think of anything else call me on my car phone. Connie's got the number."

There was silence in the office until we saw Joyce's Jeep pull away and roll down the street.

"She comes in here and I swear I can smell sulfur," Connie said. "It's like having the Antichrist sitting on the couch."

Lula cut her eyes at me. "Ranger really got a sister in Staten Island?"

"Anything's possible." But not probable. In fact, now that I thought about it, the coat factory might not even be on Macko Street.

FOUR

"Uh-oh," Lula said, glancing over my shoulder. "Don't look now, but here comes your granny."

My eyebrows shot up to the top of my head. "*My* granny?"

"Shit," Vinnie said from deep in his inner office. There was the sound of scuffling. The door to his office slammed shut, and the lock clicked into place.

Grandma walked in and looked around. "Boy, this place is a dump," she said. "Just what you'd expect from the Plum side of the family."

"Where's Melvina?" I asked.

"She's next door at the deli, getting some lunch meat. I thought as long as we were in the neighborhood I'd talk to Vinnie about a job."

We all swiveled our heads to Vinnie's closed door.

"What kind of job were you thinking about?" Connie asked.

"Bounty hunter," Grandma said. "I want to make the big bucks. I got a gun and everything."

"Hey Vinnie!" Connie yelled. "You've got a visitor."

The door opened, and Vinnie stuck his head out and gave Connie the evil eye. Then he looked at Grandma. "Edna," he said, trying to force a smile, not having much luck at it.

"Vincent," Grandma said, her smile saccharine.

Vinnie shifted his weight from one foot to the other, wanting to bolt, knowing it was futile. "What can I do for you, Edna? Need to bond someone out?"

"Nothing like that," Grandma said. "I've been thinking about getting a job, and I thought I might like to be a bounty hunter."

"Oh, bad idea," Vinnie said. "Very bad idea."

Grandma bristled. "You don't think I'm too old, do you?"

"No! Jeez, nothing like that. It's your daughter—she'd pitch a fit. I mean, not to say anything bad about Ellen, but she wouldn't like this idea."

"Ellen's a wonderful person," Grandma said, "but she has no imagination. She's like her father, rest his soul." She pressed her lips together. "He was a pain in the behind."

"Tell it like it is," Lula said.

"So what about it?" Grandma said to Vinnie. "Do I get the job?"

"No can do, Edna. Not that I wouldn't want to help you out, but being a bounty hunter takes a lot of special skills."

"I have skills," Grandma said. "I can shoot and cuss and I'm real nosy. And besides, I've got some rights. I've got a right to employment." She gave Vinnie the squinty eye. "I don't see where you got any old people working for you. That don't look like equal opportunity to me. You're discriminating against old people. I've got a mind to get the AARP after you."

"The AARP is the American Association of Retired People," Vinnie said. "The 'R' stands for 'Retired.' They don't care about old people working."

"Okay," Grandma said, "how about this? How about, if you don't give me a job I'll sit on that couch over there until I starve to death."

Lula sucked in a breath. "Whoah, hardball."

"I'll think about it," Vinnie said. "I'm not promising anything, but maybe if the right thing comes in . . ." He ducked back into his office and closed and relocked the door.

"Well, that's a start," Grandma said. "I gotta go now and see how Melvina's doing. We have a big afternoon planned. We have some apartments to look at and then we're going to stop in for Stiva's afternoon viewing. Madeline Krutchman just got laid out, and I hear she looks real good. Dolly did her hair, and she said she gave her a tint to add some color around her face. She said if I like it, she could do it for me too."

"Rock on," Lula said.

Grandma and Lula did one of those complicated handshakes, and Grandma left.

"Anything new on Ranger or Homer Ramos?" I asked Connie.

Connie opened a bottle of top coat for her nails. "Ramos was popped at close range. Some people are saying it smells like an execution."

Connie comes from a family that knows a lot about executions. Jimmy Curtains is her uncle. I don't know his real last name. All I know is if Jimmy is looking for you . . . it's curtains. I grew up hearing stories about Jimmy Curtains like other kids heard stories about Peter Pan. Jimmy Curtains is famous in my neighborhood.

"How about the police? What's their angle today?" I asked.

"They're looking for Ranger, big time."

"As a witness?"

"As far as I can tell, as an anything."

Connie and Lula looked at me.

"Well?" Lula asked.

"Well, what?"

"You know well, what."

"I'm not sure, but I don't think he's dead," I said. "Just a feeling I've got."

"Hah!" Lula said. "I knew it! Were you naked when you got this feeling?"

"No!"

"Too bad," Lula said. "I would have been naked."

"I have to go," I said. "I need to give Mooner the bad news about the wind machine."

———

THE GOOD THING about the Mooner is that he's almost always home. The bad thing is that, while his house is occupied, his head is frequently vacant.

"Oh, wow," he said, answering the door. "Did I forget my court date again?"

"Your court date is two weeks from tomorrow."

"Cool."

"I need to talk to you about the wind machine. It's sort of dented. And it's missing a rear light. But I'll fix it."

"Hey, don't worry about it, dude. These things happen."

"Maybe I should talk to the owner."

"The *Dealer*."

"Yeah, the dealer. Where's he located?"

"He's at the end row house. He's got a garage, dude. Can you dig it? A garage." Since I'd just spent the winter scraping ice off my windshield, I could appreciate Mooner's garage excitement. I thought a garage was a pretty wondrous thing, too.

The end row house was about a quarter-mile away so we drove.

"Do you think he'll be home?" I asked Mooner when we got to the end of the block.

"The Dealer's always home. He's gotta be there to deal."

I rang the bell, and Dougie Kruper opened the door. I went to school with Dougie but hadn't seen him in years. In fact, I'd heard a rumor that he'd moved to Arkansas and died.

"Jeez, Dougie," I said, "I thought you were dead."

"Naw, I just *wished* I was dead. My dad got transferred to Arkansas, so I went with them, but I'm telling you, Arkansas was no place for me. No action, you know what I mean? And if you want to go to the ocean it takes days."

"Are you the dealer?"

"Yessiree. I'm the Dealer. I'm the man. You want something. I got it. We make a deal."

"Bad news, Dougie. The wind machine was in an accident."

"Girl, the wind machine *is* an accident. Seemed like a good idea at the time, but I can't unload it on anyone. Soon as you brought it back I was gonna push it off a bridge. Unless, of course, you want to buy it."

"It doesn't actually suit my purposes. It's too memorable. I need a car that disappears."

"A stealth car. The Dealer might have such a vehicle," Dougie said. "Come around back, and we'll take a look-see."

Around back was wall-to-wall cars. There were cars on the road, and cars in his yard, and a car in his garage.

Dougie led me to a black Ford Escort. "Now this here is a genuine disappearing car."

"How old is it?"

"I don't exactly know, but it's got a few miles on it."

"Isn't the year on the title?"

"This particular car doesn't have a title."

Hmm.

"If you need a car with a title, that would adversely effect the price," Dougie said.

"How adversely?"

"I'm sure we can come to terms. After all, I'm the Dealer."

Dougie Kruper was the big geek of my graduating class. He didn't date, and he didn't do sports, and he didn't eat like a human being. His greatest accomplishment in high school was being able to suck Jell-O into his nose through a straw.

Mooner was walking around laying his hands on the cars, divining karma. "This is it," he said, standing by a small khaki-colored Jeep. "This car has protective qualities."

"You mean like a guardian angel?"

"I mean, like, it has seat belts."

"Does this car come with a title?" I asked Dougie. "Does it run?"

"I'm pretty sure it runs," Dougie said.

———

THIRTY MINUTES LATER I had two new pairs of jeans and a new watch, but no new car. Dougie was also willing to make a deal on a microwave, but I already had one.

It was early in the afternoon, and the weather wasn't terrible, so I walked to my parents' house and borrowed Uncle Sandor's '53 Buick. It was free, and it ran, and it had a title. I told myself it was a very cool car. A classic. Uncle Sandor had bought it new, and it was still in prime condition, which was more than could be said for Uncle Sandor, who was deep in the ground. Powder blue and white with gleaming chrome portholes and a big V-8 engine. I hoped I'd have my insurance money by the time Grandma got her license and needed the Buick. I hoped the insurance money would come through *fast* because I *hated* the car.

When I finally headed home the sun was low in the sky. The lot to my apartment building was filled and the big black Lincoln was parked next to one of the few open spaces. I pulled the Buick into the open space, and the Lincoln's passenger-side window rolled down.

"What's this?" Mitchell asked. "Another car? You wouldn't be trying to confuse us, would you?"

Ah, if only it was that simple. "I've been having some car problems."

"You don't find that Ranger guy soon and you're gonna have other problems that could be fatal."

Probably Mitchell and Habib were very tough guys, but I was having a hard time working up genuine fear. They just didn't seem to be in the same league as psycho Morris Munson.

"What happened to your shirt?" Mitchell asked.

"Someone tried to set me on fire."

He shook his head. "People are nuts. You gotta have eyes in the back of your head today."

From the guy who just threatened me with death.

I entered the lobby, keeping my eyes peeled for Ranger. The elevator doors opened, and I peeked inside. Empty. I didn't know if I was relieved or disappointed. The hall was also empty. No such luck with my apartment. Grandma popped out of the kitchen the instant I opened my front door.

"Right on time," she said. "I've got the pork chops ready to put on the table. And I made macaroni and cheese, too. Only we don't have any vegetables because I figure your mother isn't here so we can eat what we want."

The table in the dining area was set with real dishes and knives and forks and paper napkins folded into triangles.

"Wow," I said. "It's nice of you to make supper like this."

"I could have done an even better job, but you've only got one pot. What happened to that set of Revere Ware you got at your wedding shower?"

"I threw it away when I found Dickie doing . . . you know, with Joyce."

Grandma brought the macaroni and cheese to the table. "I guess I can understand that." She sat down and helped herself to a pork chop. "I gotta get a move on. Melvina and me didn't have time to go to the viewing this afternoon, so we're going tonight. You're welcome to come along."

Next to sticking myself in the eye with a fork, my favorite thing in the world is to go visit dead people. "Thanks, but I have to work tonight. I'm doing surveillance for a friend."

"Too bad," Grandma said. "It's going to be a good viewing."

AFTER GRANDMA LEFT I watched a *Simpsons* rerun, a *Nanny* rerun and a half-hour of ESPN, trying to distract myself from thinking about Ranger. There was a nasty little corner of my mind that harbored doubt of his innocence in the Ramos murder. And the rest of my head was filled with anxiety that he'd get shot or arrested before the real killer was found. And to further complicate things, I'd agreed to do surveillance for him. Ranger was Vinnie's primo bounty hunter, but Ranger also engaged in a variety of entrepreneurial activities, some of which were even legal. I'd worked for Ranger in the past, with varying degrees of success. I'd eventually taken my name off his employment roster, deciding it wasn't in *anyone's* best interest for us to partner up. It seemed like now was the time to make an exception. Although I wasn't sure why he wanted *my* help. I wasn't especially competent. On the other hand, I was loyal and lucky, and I guess I was affordable.

When it was almost dark I changed my clothes. Black spandex running shorts, black T-shirt, running shoes, a black hooded sweatshirt, and, to complete the outfit, a pocket-sized pepper spray. If I got caught snooping I could claim to be out jogging. Every pervert peeper in the state used the same lame M.O., and it worked every time.

I gave Rex a piece of cheese and explained that I'd be home in a couple hours. Out in the parking lot, I looked for a Honda Civic, and then I remembered it had been toasted. Then I looked for the wind machine, but that wasn't right either. And finally, with a disheartened sigh, I picked out the Buick.

Fenwood Street was cozy at night. Lights were on in house windows, and walk lights dotted the pathways leading to the town houses. There was no activity on the street.

Hannibal Ramos still had his drapes drawn, but light peeked from behind the drapes. I drove around the block once and parked the Buick just beyond the bike path I'd walked earlier in the day.

I did some stretches and some jogging in place in case someone was watching me, wondering if I was a suspicious character. I took off at a slow jog and quickly reached the path that ran through the common ground behind the houses. Less ambient light filtered through the trees back here. I took a moment to let my eyes adjust. Each privacy fence had a back door, and I cautiously walked along, counting off doors until I figured I was behind Hannibal's house. His upper story windows were dark, but light spilled over the privacy fence from the ground-level windows in the back of the house.

I tried the door to the fence. Locked. The brick fence was seven feet tall. The brick was smooth, impossible to climb. No handholds or footholds. I looked around for something to stand on.

603

Nothing. I eyeballed the pine growing next to the fence. Slightly misshapen from the fence pressing into some lower branches. The upper branches hanging over the yard. If I could get up in the tree, the branches would give me cover, and I could spy on Hannibal. I grabbed hold of a bottom branch and hoisted myself up. I scrabbled a couple feet higher and was rewarded with a view of Hannibal's backyard. The fence was bordered with flower beds, which were covered with mulch. An irregular stone patio backed up to the patio doors. And the rest of the yard was grass.

Just as I'd suspected, the drapes at the back of the house weren't drawn. A double window looked into the kitchen. The patio doors opened to a dining area. A small piece of another room was visible beyond the dining area. Probably the living room, but it was hard to tell. I didn't see anyone moving around.

I sat there for a while, watching nothing happen. No action in Hannibal's house. No action in either of his neighbors' houses. Very boring. No one on the bike path. No dog walkers. No joggers. Too dark. This is why I love surveillance. Nothing ever happens. Then you have to go to the bathroom and you miss a double homicide.

After an hour my butt was asleep and my legs were feeling twitchy from inactivity. Bag this, I thought. I didn't know what I was supposed to be looking for, anyway.

I turned to climb down, lost my balance, and flopped to the ground. *Wump!* Flat on my back. In Hannibal's backyard.

The patio light flashed on, and Hannibal looked out at me. "What the hell?" he said.

I wiggled my fingers and moved my legs. Everything seemed to be working.

Hannibal stood over me, hands on hips, looking like he wanted an explanation.

"I fell out of the tree," I said. Pretty obvious, since there were pine needles and twigs scattered around me.

Hannibal didn't move a muscle.

I dragged myself to my feet. "I was trying to get my cat to come down. He's been up there since this afternoon."

He looked up at the tree. "Is your cat still there?" Not sounding like he believed a word of it.

"I think he jumped when I fell."

Hannibal Ramos was California tan and couch-potato soft. I'd seen photos of him so I wasn't surprised. What I hadn't expected was the exhaustion in his face. But then, he'd just lost a brother, and that had to be taking a toll. His brown hair was thin and receding. His eyes were assessing behind tortoiseshell glasses. He was wearing gray suit slacks that were badly in need of pressing, and a white dress shirt, open at the collar, also rumpled. Mr. Average Businessman after a hard day at the office. I guessed he was in his early forties and a couple years away from a quadruple bypass.

"And I suppose he ran away?" Ramos said.

"God, I hope not. I'm tired of chasing after him." I am the *best* liar. Sometimes I amaze even myself.

Hannibal opened the door to the fence and gave the bike path a cursory glance. "Bad news. I don't see a cat."

I looked over Hannibal's shoulder. "Here, kitty, kitty," I called. I was feeling pretty stupid now, but there was no place to go with this but forward.

"You know what I think?" Hannibal said. "I think there's no cat. I think you were in that tree spying on me."

I gave him a look of total incredulity. Like . . . oh, duh? "Listen," I said, scooting around him to the door. "I've got to go. I need to find my cat."

"What color is it?"

"Black."

"Good luck."

I looked under a couple bushes en route to the bike path. "Here kitty, kitty."

"Maybe you should give me your name and phone number in case I find him," Hannibal said.

Our eyes locked for a couple beats, and my heart stumbled in my chest.

"No," I told him. "I don't think I want to do that." And then I left, walking in the opposite direction I came.

I exited the bike path and circled the block to get to my car. I crossed the street and stood in the shadows for a few minutes, looking at Hannibal's house, wondering about the man. If I'd seen him on the street I'd have pegged him as an insurance salesman. Or maybe middle management in corporate America. That he was the crown prince of black market arms wouldn't occur to me.

A light blinked on in an upstairs window. The crown prince was probably changing into something more comfortable. Too early for bed, and the lights were still on downstairs. I was about to leave when a car cruised down the street and turned into Hannibal's driveway.

Woman at the wheel. Couldn't see her face. The driver's door opened and a long, stocking-clad leg swung out, followed by a killer body in a dark suit. Short blond hair. Briefcase under her arm.

I copied the license number on the pad I kept in my shoulder bag, got my mini-binoculars out of the glove compartment, and scuttled around to the back of Hannibal's house. Again. Everything was quiet. Hannibal probably felt confident that he'd scared me off. I mean, what idiot would be crazy enough to try to snoop on him twice in one night?

This idiot, that's who.

I went up the tree as quietly as possible. Easier this time. I knew where I was going. I found my perch and got the binoculars out. Unfortunately, there wasn't much to see. Hannibal and his caller were in the front room. I could see a slice of Hannibal's back, but the woman was out of view. After a few minutes there was the distant sound of Hannibal's front door closing and of a car driving off.

Hannibal walked into the kitchen, got a knife from a drawer, and used it to open an envelope. He took a letter out and read it.

Had no reaction. He carefully returned the letter to the envelope and put the envelope on his kitchen counter.

He looked at the kitchen window, seemingly lost in thought. Then he moved to the patio door, slid it open and stared out at the tree. I froze in place, not daring to breathe. He can't see me, I thought. It's dark in the tree. Don't move and he'll go back inside. Wrong, wrong, wrong. His hand came up from his side, a flashlight snapped on, and I was caught.

"Here kitty, kitty," I said, shielding my eyes with my hand to see past the light.

He raised his other arm, and I saw the gun.

"Get down," he said, walking toward me. "Slowly."

Yeah, right. I *flew* from the tree, breaking branches on the way, landing with my feet already running.

Zing. The unmistakable sound of a bullet being fired through a silencer.

I don't ordinarily think of myself as fast, but I moved down that path at the speed of light. I went straight to the car, jumped inside, and roared off.

I checked the mirror several times to make sure I wasn't being followed. Closer to my apartment I drove down Makefield, turned at the corner, cut my lights, and waited. No car in sight. I popped the lights back on and noticed my hands had almost stopped shaking. I decided that was a good sign and headed for home.

When I turned into my parking lot, I caught Morelli in my lights. He was lounging against his 4X4, arms crossed over his chest, feet crossed at the ankles. I locked the Buick and walked over to him. His expression changed from bored calm to grim curiosity.

"Back to driving the Buick?" he asked.

"For a while."

He looked me over head to toe and picked a pine sprig out of my hair. "I'm afraid to ask," he said.

"Surveillance."

"You're all sticky."

"Sap. I was in a pine tree."

He grinned. "I hear they're hiring at the button factory."

"What do you know about Hannibal Ramos?"

"Oh, man, don't tell me you're spying on Ramos. He's a real bad guy."

"He doesn't look bad. He looks ordinary." He had, until he pointed the gun at me.

"Don't underestimate him. He runs the Ramos empire."

"I thought his father did that."

"Hannibal manages the day-to-day business. Rumor has it the old man is sick. He's always been volatile, but a source tells me his behavior is increasingly erratic, and the family has hired baby-sitters to make sure he doesn't just wander away, never to be seen again."

"Alzheimer's?"

Morelli shrugged. "Don't know."

I glanced down and realized my knee was scraped and bleeding.

"You could become an accessory to something ugly by helping Ranger," Morelli said.

"Who, me?"

"Did you tell him to get in touch with me?"

"I didn't get a chance. Besides, if you're leaving messages on his pager, he's getting them. He just doesn't want to answer."

Morelli pulled me flat against him. "You smell like a pine forest."

"Must be the sap."

He put his hands to my waist and kissed me at the base of my neck. "Very sexy."

Morelli thought everything was sexy.

"Why don't you come back to the house with me?" he said. "I'll kiss your skinned knee and make it all better."

Tempting. "What about Grandma?"

"She'll never notice. She's probably sound asleep."

A second-story window opened in the apartment building. My window. And Grandma stuck her head out. "Is that you, Stephanie? And who's that with you? Is that Joe Morelli?"

Joe waved at her. "Hello, Mrs. Mazur."

"What are you standing out there for?" Grandma wanted to know. "Why don't you come in and have some dessert? We stopped at the supermarket on the way home from the viewing, and I bought a layer cake."

"Thanks," Joe said, "but I have to be getting home. I have an early shift tomorrow."

"Wow," I said, "passing up layer cake!"

"I'm not hungry for cake."

My pelvic muscles contracted.

"Well, I'm cutting a piece for myself," Grandma said. "I'm starved. Viewings always make me hungry." The window closed, and Grandma disappeared.

"You're not coming home with me, are you?" Morelli said.

"Do you have cake?"

"I've got something better."

This was true. I knew it for a fact.

The window opened again, and Grandma stuck her head out. "Stephanie, you've got a phone call. Do you want me to tell him to call back later?"

Morelli raised his eyebrows. "Him?"

Both of us thinking, Ranger.

"Who is it?" I asked.

"Some guy named Brian."

"Must be Brian Simon," I said to Morelli. "I had to whine at him to get a deal for Carol Zabo."

"This is about Carol Zabo?"

"God, I hope so." That, or Brian Simon was calling in his marker. "I'll be right there," I yelled to Grandma. "Get his number, and tell him I'll call him back."

"You're breaking my heart," Morelli said.

"Grandma will only be here for a couple more days, and then we can celebrate."

"In a couple days I'll be gnawing my arm off."

"That's pretty serious."

"Don't ever doubt it," Morelli said. He kissed me, and I didn't doubt anything. He had his hand under my shirt, and his tongue deep in my mouth . . . and I heard someone give a wolf whistle.

Mrs. Fine and Mr. Morgenstern were hanging out their windows, whistling, drawn to the shouting between Grandma and me. They both started clapping and making hooting sounds.

Mrs. Benson opened her window. "What's going on?" she wanted to know.

"Sex in the parking lot," Mr. Morgenstern said.

Morelli looked at me speculatively. "It's possible."

I turned and ran for the door and sprinted up the stairs. I cut myself a piece of cake, and then I called Simon.

"What's up?" I said.

"I need a favor."

"I don't do phone sex," I said.

"It's not phone sex. Cripes, what made you think that?"

"I don't know. It just popped out."

"It's about my dog. I have to go out of town for a couple days, and I don't have anybody to take care of my dog. So since you owe me a favor . . ."

"I live in an apartment! I can't have a dog."

"It's only for a couple days. And he's a real good dog."

"What about a kennel?"

"He hates kennels. He won't eat. He gets all depressed."

"What kind of dog is it?"

"It's a little dog."

Damn. "It's only for a couple days?"

"I'll drop him off tomorrow first thing in the morning and pick him up on Sunday."

"I don't know. This isn't a good time. My grandmother is staying with me."

"He loves old ladies. I swear to God. Your grandma will love him."

I looked over at Rex. I'd hate to see him all depressed and not eating, so I guess I could understand how Simon felt about his dog. "Okay," I said. "What time tomorrow?"

"Around eight?"

I OPENED MY eyes and wondered about the time. I was on the couch, it was pitch black out, and I smelled coffee. There was a moment of panicky disorientation. My eyes settled on the chair across from the couch, and I realized someone was sitting in it. A man. Hard to see in the dark. My breathing stopped altogether.

"How'd it go tonight?" he said. "Learn anything worthwhile?"

Ranger. No point asking how he'd gotten in when the windows and doors were closed and locked. Ranger had ways. "What time is it?"

"Three."

"Has it occurred to you that some people sleep at this time of night?"

"It smells like a pine forest in here," Ranger said.

"It's me. I was in the pine tree behind Hannibal's house, and I can't get the sap off. It's all stuck in my hair."

I saw Ranger smile in the darkness. Heard him laugh softly.

I sat up. "Hannibal has a lady friend. She drove up at ten o'clock in a black BMW. She was with Hannibal for about ten minutes, gave him a letter, and left."

"What's she look like?"

"Short blond hair. Slim. Nicely dressed."

"Did you get the license plate?"

"Yeah. I wrote it down. Didn't get a chance to check it out yet."

He sipped his coffee. "Anything else?"

"He sort of saw me."

"Sort of?"

"I fell out of the tree into his backyard."

The smile disappeared. "And?"

"And I told him I was looking for my cat, but I'm not sure he bought it."

"If he knew you better . . ." Ranger said.

"Then the second time he caught me in the tree, he pulled a gun, so I jumped down and ran away."

"Quick thinking."

"Hey," I said, tapping my finger to my head, "no grass growing here."

Ranger was smiling again.

FIVE

"I THOUGHT YOU didn't drink coffee," I said to Ranger. "What about your body being a temple?"

He sipped at the coffee. "It's my disguise. It goes with the haircut."

"Will you let your hair grow back?"

"Probably."

"And then will you stop drinking coffee?"

"You ask a lot of questions," Ranger said.

"Just trying to figure this out."

He was slouched in the chair, one long leg extended, his arms on the arms of the chair, his eyes on me. He set his cup on the coffee table, rose from the chair, and stood over the couch. He bent and kissed me lightly on the lips. "Some things are better left a mystery," he said. And then he moved to the door.

"Hey, wait a minute," I said. "Am I supposed to keep watching Hannibal?"

"Can you watch him without getting shot?"

I gave him a pissy look in the dark.

"I see that," he said.

"Morelli wants to talk to you."

"I'll call him tomorrow, maybe."

613

The front door opened and clicked shut. Ranger was gone. I padded to the door and looked out the peephole. No Ranger anywhere. I slid the security chain in place and went back to the couch. I fluffed up my pillow and crawled under the quilt.

And I thought about the kiss. What was I supposed to make of the kiss? Friendly, I told myself. It had been friendly. No tongue. No groping hands. No gnashing of teeth in uncontrollable passion. A friendly kiss. Only it hadn't felt friendly. It had felt . . . sexy.

Damn!

"WHAT WOULD YOU like for breakfast?" Grandma asked. "How about some nice warm oatmeal?"

Left to my own devices, I'd have eaten the cake. "Sure," I said, "oatmeal would be okay."

I poured a cup of coffee, and there was a knock on the door. I opened the door, and a big orange thing rushed in.

"Holy cow!" I said. "What is it?"

"Golden retriever," Simon said. "Mostly."

"Isn't he big for a golden retriever?"

Simon dragged a fifty-pound bag of dog food into the foyer. "I got him at the pound, and that's what they told me. Golden retriever."

"You said you had a small dog."

"I lied. So sue me."

The dog ran into the kitchen, stuck his nose in Grandma's crotch, and snuffled.

"Dang," Grandma said. "Guess my new perfume really works. I'm gonna have to try it out at the seniors meeting."

Simon pulled Bob away from Grandma and handed me a brown grocery bag. "Here's his stuff. Two dog bowls, some dog treats, a chew toy, a hairbrush and his pooper-scooper."

"Pooper-scooper? Hey, wait a minute—"

"I gotta run," Simon said. "I got a plane to catch."

"What's his name?" I yelled down the hall.

"Bob."

"Isn't this something," Grandma said. "A dog named Bob."

I filled Bob's water bowl and set it on the floor in the kitchen. "He's only staying for a couple days," I said. "Simon will be back for him on Sunday."

Grandma eyeballed the dog food bag. "Awful big bag of food for a couple days."

"Maybe he eats a lot."

"He eats all that in two days and you're not gonna need a pooper-scooper," Grandma said. "You're gonna need a shovel."

I unhooked Bob's leash and hung it on a hall peg. "Well, Bob," I said, "this won't be so bad. I always wanted a golden retriever."

Bob wagged his tail and looked from Grandma to me.

Grandma ladled out oatmeal for the three of us. She and I took our bowls into the dining area, and Bob ate his in the kitchen. When Grandma and I went back to the kitchen, Bob's bowl was empty. The cardboard box that used to hold the cake was also empty.

"Guess Bob's got a sweet tooth," Grandma said.

I shook my finger at him. "That was rude. And besides, you'll get fat."

Bob wagged his tail.

"He might not be too smart," Grandma said.

Smart enough to eat the cake.

Grandma had a driving lesson scheduled for nine o'clock. "I'm probably gonna be gone all day," she said. "So don't worry if you don't see me. After my driving lesson I'm going to the mall with Louise Greeber. And then we're gonna look at some more apartments. If you want, I can stop and get some ground beef this afternoon. I thought a meatloaf might be nice for supper."

Major guilt trip coming on. Grandma was doing all the cooking. "My turn," I told her. "I'll make the meatloaf."

"I didn't know you could cook meatloaf."

"Sure," I said. "I can cook lots of stuff." A big lie. I can cook nothing.

I gave Bob a dog treat, and Grandma and I left together. Halfway down the hall, Grandma stopped. "What's that sound?" she asked.

We both listened. Bob was howling on the other side of my door.

My next-door neighbor, Mrs. Karwatt, stuck her head out. "What's that sound?"

"It's Bob," Grandma said. "He don't like being at home alone."

Ten minutes later I was on the road with Bob riding shotgun, head out the window, ears flapping in the wind.

"Uh-oh," Lula said when we walked in the office. "Who's this?"

"His name's Bob. I'm dog-sitting him."

"Oh yeah? What kind of dog is he?"

"Golden retriever."

"He looks like he been under the blow-dryer too long."

I smoothed some of his hair down. "He had his head out the window."

"That'll do it," Lula said.

I let Bob off the leash and he ran over to Lula and did the crotch thing again.

"Hey," Lula said, "back off, you're getting nose prints all over my new pants." She gave Bob a pat on the head. "He keep this up, and we're gonna have to pimp him out."

I used Connie's phone to call my friend Marilyn Truro at the DMV. "I need to run a plate through," I said. "Do you have time?"

"Are you kidding me? There are forty people standing in line. They see me talking on the phone, and they'll go postal." She spoke more softly. "Is this for a case? Is this for a murderer or something?"

"It might tie in to the Ramos murder."

"Are you shitting me? That is *so* cool."

I gave her the number.

"Hold on," she said. There was some clicking of computer keys, and Marilyn came back on. "The plate belongs to Terry Gilman. Isn't she working for Vito Grizolli?"

I was momentarily speechless. Next to Joyce Barnhardt, I disliked Terry Gilman most. For lack of a better term, she'd *dated* Joe in high school, and I had a feeling she wouldn't mind resuming the relationship. Terry worked for her Uncle Vito Grizolli now, which put a crimp in her Joe designs, since Joe was in the business of stamping out crime, and Vito was in the business of producing it.

"Uh-oh," Lula said. "Did I hear you right? Are you sticking your big fat nose in the Ramos case?"

"Well, I happened to run across—"

Lula's eyes widened. "You're working for Ranger!"

Vinnie popped out of his inner office. "Is that true? Are you working for Ranger?"

"No. It's not true. There's not a shred of truth to it." Well, what the hell—what's *one more lie*?

The front door crashed open and Joyce Barnhardt stomped in.

Lula, Connie, and I all ran to get Bob on the leash.

"You dumb bitch," Joyce yelled at me. "You sent me on a wild goose chase. Ranger doesn't have a sister working at the Macko Coat Factory."

"Maybe she quit," I said.

"Yeah," Lula said, "people quit all the time."

Joyce looked down at Bob. "What's this?"

"It's a dog," I said, shortening his lead.

"Why's his hair standing up like that?"

From the woman who adds five inches to her height with a rat-tail comb.

"Beside the wild goose chase, how're you doin' on the Ranger hunt?" Lula asked. "You track him down yet?"

"Not yet, but I'm getting close."

"I think you're fibbing," Lula said. "I bet you don't have anything."

"And I bet you don't have a waistline," Joyce said.

Lula leaned forward. "Oh yeah? If I throw a stick, will you go fetch it?"

Bob wagged his tail.

"Maybe later," I told him.

Vinnie popped back out of his office. "What's going on out here? I can't hear myself think."

Lula, Connie, and I all exchanged glances and bit down hard on our lower lips.

"Vinnie!" Joyce cooed, pointing her C cups in his direction. "Looking good, Vinnie."

"Yeah, you're not looking so bad yourself," Vinnie said. He looked at Bob. "What's with the dog with the bad hair day?"

"I'm dog-sitting," I told him.

"I hope you're getting paid a lot of money. He's a train wreck."

I fondled Bob's ear. "I think he's cute." In a prehistoric way.

"So what's going on here?" Joyce asked. "You got anything new for me?"

Vinnie thought about it for a moment, looked from Connie to Lula to me, and retreated into his office.

"Nothing new," Connie said.

Joyce narrowed her eyes at Vinnie's closed door. "Chickenshit."

Vinnie opened the door and glared out at her.

"Yeah, you," Joyce said.

Vinnie pulled his head back inside his office, closed the door, and clicked the dead bolt.

"Fungule," Joyce said, with a gesture. She turned on her stiletto heel and swung her ass out the door.

We all rolled our eyes.

"Now what?" Lula wanted to know. "You and Bob got some big day planned?"

"Well, you know . . . a little of this, a little of that."

Vinnie's office door opened again. "How about a little of Morris Munson?" he yelled. "I'm not running a charity here, you know."

"Morris Munson is a nut!" I yelled back. "He tried to set me on fire!"

Vinnie stood, hands on hips. "So what's your point?"

"Fine. Just fine," I said. "I'll go get Morris Munson. So what if he runs me over. So what if he sets me on fire and bashes my head in with a tire iron. It's my job, right? So here I go to do my job."

"That's the spirit," Vinnie said.

"Hold on," Lula said. "I don't want to miss this one. I'll go with you."

She shoved her arms into a jacket and grabbed a purse that was big enough to hold a sawed-off shotgun. "Okay," I said, eyeballing the purse. "What have you got in there?"

"Tech-9."

The urban assault weapon of choice.

"Do you have a license to carry that?"

"Say what?"

"Call me crazy, but I'd feel a lot better if you left your Tech-9 here."

"Boy, you sure know how to ruin a good time," Lula said.

"Leave it with me," Connie told her. "I'll use it for a paper-weight. Give the office some atmosphere."

"Hunh," Lula said.

I opened the office door, and Bob bounded out. He stopped at the Buick and stood there, tail wagging, eyes bright.

"Look at this smart dog," I said to Lula. "He knows my car after only riding in it once."

"What happened to the Rollswagen?"

"I gave it back to the Dealer."

The sun was climbing in the sky, burning off a morning haze, warming Trenton. Bureaucrats and shopkeepers were pouring into center city. School buses were back at the lot, awaiting the end of the school day. Burg housewives were bent over their Hoovers. And my friend Marilyn Truro at the DMV was on her third double decaf latte, wondering if it would help if she added a second nicotine patch to the one she already had on her arm, thinking it would feel really good to be able to choke the next person in line.

Lula and Bob and I kept to our own thoughts as we rolled along Hamilton en route to the button factory. I was going through a mental inventory of equipment. Stun gun: in my left pocket. Pepper spray: in my right pocket. Cuffs: hooked to the back loop on my Levi's. Gun: at home, in the cookie jar. Courage: at home, with the gun.

"I don't know about you," Lula said when we got to Munson's house, "but I'm not planning on going up in smoke today. I vote we bash this guy's door in and stomp on him before he has a chance to light up."

"Sure," I said. Of course, I knew from past experience that neither of us was actually capable of bashing in a door. Still, it sounded good while we were idling at the curb, locked up in the car.

I cruised around back, got out, and looked in Munson's garage window. No car. Gee, too bad. Probably Munson wasn't home.

"No car here," I said to Lula.

"Hunh," Lula said.

We drove around the block, parked, and knocked on Munson's front door. No answer. We looked in his front windows. Nothing.

"He could be hiding under the bed," Lula said. "Maybe we should still bash his door in."

I stepped back and made a sweeping gesture with my hand. "After you."

"Unh-unh," Lula said. "After you."

"No, no . . . I insist."

"The hell you do. *I* insist."

"Okay," I said. "Let's face it. Neither of us is going to bash this door down."

"I could do it if I wanted," Lula said. "Only I don't feel like it right now."

"Yeah, right."

"You think I couldn't do serious damage to this door?"

"That's what I'm suggesting."

"Hunh," Lula said.

The door to the adjoining house opened, and an old woman stuck her head out. "What's going on?"

"We're looking for Morris Munson," I said.

"He isn't home."

"Oh, yeah? How do you know?" Lula said. "How can you be sure he isn't hiding under the bed?"

"I was out back when he drove away. I was letting the dog out, and Munson came with a suitcase. Said he was gonna be gone for a while. As far as I'm concerned, he could be gone forever. He's a wacko. He was arrested for killing his wife, and some idiot judge let him out on bail. Can you imagine?"

"Go figure," Lula said.

The woman looked us over. "I guess you're friends of his."

"Not exactly," I said. "We work for Munson's bail bonds agent." I handed her my business card. "If he returns I'd appreciate a call."

"Sure," the woman said, "but I got a feeling he isn't returning anytime soon."

Bob was waiting patiently in the car, and he got all happy-looking when we opened the doors and slid in.

"Maybe Bob needs breakfast," Lula said.

"Bob already had breakfast."

"Let me put it another way. Maybe Lula needs breakfast."

"You have anything special in mind?"

"I guess I could use one of those Egg McMuffins. And a vanilla shake. And breakfast fries."

I put the Buick in gear and headed for the drive-through.

"How's it going?" the kid at the window said. "You still looking for a job?"

"I'm thinking about it."

We got three of everything and parked on the edge of the lot to eat and regroup. Bob ate his Egg McMuffin and breakfast fries in one chomp. He slurked his milkshake down and looked longingly out the window.

"Think Bob needs to stretch his legs," Lula said.

I opened the door and let him out. "Don't go far."

Bob jumped out and started walking around in circles, occasionally sniffing the pavement.

"What's he doing?" Lula wanted to know. "Why's he walking in circles? Why's he—Uh-oh, this don't look good. Looks to me like Bob's taking a big poop in the middle of the parking lot. Holy cow, look at that! That's a mountain of poop."

Bob returned to the Buick and sat down, wagging his tail, smiling, waiting to be let back in.

I let him in, and Lula and I slumped down low in our seats.

"Do you think anyone saw?" I asked Lula.

"I think *everyone* saw."

"Damn," I said. "I don't have the pooper-scooper with me."

"Pooper-scooper, hell. I wouldn't go near that with a full contamination suit and a front-loader."

"I can't just leave it there."

"Maybe you could run over it," Lula said. "You know . . . flatten it out."

I cranked the engine over, backed up, and pointed the Buick at the pile of poop.

"Better roll the windows up," Lula said.

"Ready?"

Lula braced herself. "Ready."

I stomped on the gas and took aim.

SQUISH!

We rolled the windows down and looked out.

"So what do you think? You think I should make another pass?"

"Wouldn't hurt," Lula said. "And I'd forget about getting a job here."

I WANTED TO do a fast check on Hannibal's town house and I didn't want to get Lula involved in my Ranger business, so I told her a fib about spending the day bonding with Bob, and drove her back to the office. I slid to a stop at the curb and the black Town Car eased up behind me.

Mitchell got out of the Town Car and came to peek in my window. "Still driving this old Buick," he said. "Must be some kind of a personal record for you. And what's with the dog and the big babe, here?"

Lula gave Mitchell the once-over.

"It's okay," I told Lula. "I know him."

"I bet," Lula said. "You want me to shoot him, or something?"

"Maybe later."

"Hunh," Lula said. She heaved herself out of the car and ambled into the office.

"Well?" Mitchell asked.

"Well, nothing."

"That's real disappointing."

"So, you don't like Alexander Ramos?"

"Let's just say we're not on the same team."

"Must be hard for him these days, grieving over his son."

"That son was nothing to grieve over," Mitchell said. "He was a fuckin' loser. Fuckin' cokehead."

"How about Hannibal? Does he do drugs, too?"

"Nah, not Hannibal. Hannibal's a goddamn shark. Alexander should have named that one Jaws."

"Well, I've gotta go now," I said. "Things to do. People to see."

"The raghead and me haven't got a lot to do today, so we thought we'd follow you around."

"You should get a life."

Mitchell smiled.

"And I don't want you following me around," I said.

He smiled some more.

I glanced up at the traffic coming toward us on Hamilton and focused on a blue car. Looked like a Crown Victoria. Looked like Morris Munson behind the wheel!

"Yikes!" I yelled as Munson yanked the car over the white line and aimed it at me.

"Shit!" Mitchell yelped, panicked, dancing in place like a big trained bear.

Munson swerved to avoid Mitchell at the last second, lost control, and crashed into the Town Car. For a moment the cars seemed fused together, and then there was the sound of Munson gunning his engine. The Crown Vic jumped back a couple feet, its front bumper clattered to the ground, and it sped away.

Mitchell and I ran back to the Town Car and looked in at Habib.

"What by everything holy was that?" Habib shouted.

The Town Car's left front quarter panel was crumpled into the wheel, and the hood was buckled. Habib seemed okay, but the Town Car wasn't going anywhere until someone crowbarred the fender away from the wheel. Too bad for them. Lucky break for me. Habib and Mitchell weren't going to be in following mode for a while.

"He was a madman," Habib said. "I saw his eyes. He was a madman. Did you get his license plate number?"

"It happened so fast," Mitchell said. "And cripes, he was coming right at me. I thought he was aiming for me. I thought . . . Jeez, I thought . . ."

"You were frightened like a woman," Habib said.

"Yeah," I said, "like the daughter of a pig."

Now here was a dilemma. I dearly wanted to tell them who was behind the wheel of the car. If they killed Munson, I was off the hook. No more flaming shirttails. No more maniac with a tire iron. Unfortunately, I'd also be sort of responsible for Munson's death, and that didn't feel entirely comfortable. Better to leave him to the court.

"You should report this to the police," I said. "I'd stick around and help out, but you know how it is."

"Yeah," Mitchell said. "Things to do. People to see."

IT WAS ALMOST noon when Bob and I rolled past Hannibal's town house. I parked at the corner and dialed Ranger's number to tell his answering machine I had news. Then I chewed on my lower lip some while I worked up enough nerve to get out of the car and snoop on Hannibal.

Hey, it's no big deal, I told myself. Look at the house. Nice and quiet. He isn't home. Just like yesterday. You go around back, take a peek, and leave. No sweat.

Okay, I can do this. Deep breath. Think positive. I grabbed Bob's leash and headed for the bike path behind the houses. When I got to Hannibal's backyard I stopped and listened. Very quiet. Plus, Bob looked bored. If someone was on the other side of the wall Bob would be excited, right? I studied the wall. Daunting. Especially since I'd gotten shot at the last time I was here.

Hold it, I said to myself. None of that negative thinking. What would Spider-Man do in a situation like this? What would Batman do? What would Bruce Willis do? Bruce would get a running start, plant his sneaker, and scale the wall. I tied Bob's leash to a bush and ran at the wall. I got my size eight Skechers halfway up, slapped my palms onto the top of the wall, and dug in and hung there. I took a deep breath, clenched my teeth and attempted a pull-up . . . but nothing pulled up. Damn. Bruce would have made it to the top. But then, Bruce probably goes to the gym.

I dropped to the ground and cut my eyes to the tree. The tree had a bullet lodged in its trunk. I really didn't want to climb the tree. I did some pacing and knuckle cracking. What about Ranger? I asked myself. You're supposed to be helping him. If the situation was reversed Ranger would climb the tree to take a look.

"Yeah, but I'm not Ranger," I said to Bob.

Bob gave me a long look.

"Okay, fine," I said. "I'll climb the stupid tree."

I went up fast, looked around, saw nothing going on in the house or the yard, and scrambled down. I untied Bob and skulked back to the car, where I settled in and waited for the phone to ring. After a couple minutes, Bob moved to the backseat and got into nap position.

At one o'clock, I was still waiting for Ranger's call back, and I was thinking I needed lunch, when Hannibal's garage door slid open and the green Jag backed out.

Holy cow, the house hadn't been empty!

The door closed; the Jag turned away from me and rolled down the street, toward the freeway. Hard to tell who was behind the wheel but I bet it was Hannibal. I cranked the engine over and raced around the block, picking the Jag up just as it was leaving the subdivision. I stayed as far back as possible without losing sight.

We bypassed the center of town, heading south, and then went east on the interstate. The horses weren't running at Monmouth yet, and Great Adventure was still closed for the season. That pretty much narrowed the field to the house in Deal.

Bob was taking the excitement in stride, sound asleep in the backseat. I wasn't feeling nearly so relaxed. I don't usually tail mobsters. Although technically, Hannibal Ramos wasn't a Mob member. Well, actually I didn't know that for sure, but my understanding was that the Mob was a different fraternal order from the gun cartel.

Hannibal exited Route 195 at the Parkway, drove two exits north, then cut over to Asbury Park, where he left-turned onto Ocean Avenue and followed the road to Deal.

Deal is an oceanside town where gardeners coax grass to grow in the inhospitable salt air, nannies commute in from nearby Long Branch, and property value supersedes all issues of national origin. The houses are large and sometimes behind gated drives. The residents are mostly plastic surgeons and rug merchants. And the only truly memorable event ever to take place in Deal was the gunning down of crime boss Benny "The Roach" Raguchi in the Sea Breeze Motel in 1982.

Hannibal was two cars ahead of me. He slowed and signaled for a right turn into a walled compound with a gated drive. The house sat back on the dune, so the second story and roof were visible from the road and the rest of the property was hidden behind the pink stucco wall. The gate was fancy wrought-iron scrollwork. Alexander Ramos, international arms dealer and all-around macho man, lived in a pink house behind a pink wall. Go figure. Never happen in the Burg. Living in a pink house in the Burg would be right up there with castration.

Probably the pink stucco was very Mediterranean. And probably in the summer, when the awnings were unrolled and the porch furniture was uncovered, and the sun and the heat washed over the Jersey shore, the pink house felt like life itself. In March it looked like it was waiting for the Prozac to kick in. Pale and cold and stolid.

I caught a glimpse of a man exiting the Jag as I cruised past the house. Same build and hair color as Hannibal, so it must be Hannibal. Unless, of course, Hannibal saw me in the tree again, and then saw me watching from the street and had a look-alike next-door neighbor sneak over through the backyards and drive the Jag to Deal, just to throw me off.

"What do you think?" I asked Bob.

Bob opened an eye, gave me a blank stare, and went back to sleep.

That was what I thought, too.

I drove about a quarter-mile down Ocean Avenue, hung a U-turn, and made another pass by the pink house. I parked out of sight, around the corner. I tucked my hair up, under a Metallica ball cap, put on some dark glasses, grabbed Bob's leash, and set off toward the Ramos compound. Deal was a civilized town with pristine cement sidewalks designed with nannies and baby strollers in mind. Also very nice for snoopers masquerading as dog-walkers.

I was a few feet from the gate when a black Town Car rolled up. The gates opened and the Town Car slid through. Two men in front. The back windows were tinted. I fussed with Bob's leash and let him sniff around some. The Town Car stopped at the porticoed house entrance, and the two men in front got out. One went around to get bags from the trunk. The other man opened the door for the passenger in back. The passenger looked to be in his sixties. Medium height. Slim. Dressed in sports coat and slacks. Wavy gray hair. From the way people were dancing attendance I guessed this

was Alexander Ramos. Probably flew in for his son's burial. Hannibal came out to greet the older man. A younger, slimmer version of
Hannibal appeared in the doorway to the house but didn't descend
the stairs. Ulysses, the middle son, I thought.

No one looked especially happy at the reunion. Understandable, I guess, considering the circumstances. Hannibal said something to the older man. The older man stiffened and smacked him
on the side of the head. It wasn't a hard smack. Not something designed to knock a guy out. It was more of a statement. *Fool*.

Still, I reflexively flinched. And even at this distance I could see
Hannibal clamp his teeth together.

SIX

HERE'S THE THING that stuck in my brain all the way home. If you were a father grieving over losing a son, would you greet your firstborn with a smack in the head?

"Hey, what do I know," I said to Bob. "Maybe they're going for Dysfunctional Family of the Year."

And to tell the truth, it's always a comfort to discover a family more dysfunctional than my own. Not that my family is all that dysfunctional, by Jersey standards.

When I got to Hamilton Township I stopped at the Shop Rite, hauled out my cell phone, and dialed my mother

"I'm at the meat counter," I said. "I want to make a meatloaf. What do I need?"

There was silence at the other end, and I could imagine my mother making the sign of the cross, wondering what could possibly have inspired her daughter to want to make a meatloaf, hoping against hope that it was a man.

"A meatloaf," my mother finally said.

"It's for Grandma," I told her. "She needs a meatloaf."

"Of course," my mother said. "What was I thinking?"

I CALLED MY mother again when I got home. "Okay, I'm home," I said. "Now what do I do with this stuff?"

"You mix it together and put it in a loaf pan and bake it at three hundred and fifty degrees for an hour."

"You didn't say anything about a loaf pan when I was at the store!" I wailed.

"You don't have a loaf pan?"

"Well, of course I have a loaf pan. I just meant . . . Never mind."

"Good luck," my mother said.

Bob was sitting in the middle of the kitchen, taking it all in.

"I don't have a loaf pan," I told Bob. "But hey, we're not gonna let a little thing like that stop us, are we?"

I dumped the ground beef into a bowl along with the other essential meatloaf ingredients. I added an egg and watched it slime across the surface. I poked it with a spoon.

"Eeeeyeu," I said to Bob.

Bob wagged his tail. Bob looked like he loved gross stuff.

I mashed at the mess with the spoon, but the egg wouldn't mix in. I took a deep breath and plunged in with both hands. After a couple of minutes of hand squishing, everything was nice and mushy. I shaped it into a snowman. And then I shaped it into Humpty Dumpty. And then I smashed it flat. Smashed flat, it looked a lot like what I'd left in the McDonald's parking lot. Finally I rolled it into two big meatballs.

I'd bought a frozen banana cream pie for dessert, so I slid the pie out of its aluminum plate onto a dinner plate and used the pie plate for the giant meatballs.

"Necessity is the mother of invention," I told Bob.

I put the meatballs in the oven, cut up some potatoes and set them to cooking, and opened a can of creamed corn and dumped it in a bowl so I could heat it up in the microwave at the last minute. Cooking wasn't so bad, I thought. In fact, it was a lot like sex. Sometimes it didn't seem like such a good idea in the beginning, but then after you got into it . . .

I set the table for two, and the phone rang just as I was finishing.

"Yo, babe," Ranger said.

"Yo yourself. I have some news. The car that came to visit Hannibal last night belongs to Terry Gilman. I should have recognized her when she got out of the car, but I only saw her from the back, and I wasn't expecting her."

"Probably carrying condolences from Vito."

"I didn't realize Vito and Ramos were friends."

"Vito and Alexander co-exist."

"Another thing," I said. "This morning I followed Hannibal to the house in Deal." Then I told Ranger about the older man in the Town Car, and the smack in the head, and the appearance of a younger man who I thought was Ulysses Ramos.

"How do you know it was Ulysses?"

"Just a guess. He looked like Hannibal, but slimmer."

There was a moment of silence.

"Do you want me to keep watching the town house?" I asked.

"Do a spot check once in a while. I want to know if anyone's living there."

"Don't you think it's strange that Ramos would smack his son?" I asked.

"I don't know," Ranger said. "In my family we smack each other all the time."

Ranger disconnected, and I stood without moving for several minutes, wondering what I was missing. Ranger never gave much away, but there'd been a moment's pause and a small change of inflection that had me thinking I'd told him something interesting. I reviewed our conversation and everything seemed ordinary. A father and two brothers gathered together at a time of family tragedy. Alexander's reaction to Hannibal's greeting had seemed odd to me, but I got the impression that wasn't what had caught Ranger's attention.

Grandma staggered through the front door. "Boy, have I had a day," she said. "I'm all done in."

"How'd the driving lesson go?"

"Pretty good, I guess. I didn't run anybody over. And I didn't wreck the car. How was your day?"

"About the same."

"Louise and me went to the mall to do some senior citizen power walking but we kept getting sidetracked into the stores. And then after lunch we went looking at apartments. I saw a couple I might settle for, but nothing that really floated my boat. Tomorrow we're gonna look at some condos." Grandma snooped into the potato pot. "Isn't this something. I come home from a hard day of running around and here's dinner all waiting for me. Just like being a man."

"I got a banana cream pie for dessert," I said, "but I had to use the pie plate for the meatloaf."

Grandma peeked at the pie in the refrigerator. "Maybe we should eat it now before it defrosts and loses its shape."

That sounded like a good idea to me, so we all had some pie while the meatloaf was baking.

When I was a little girl I'd never thought of my grandmother as the sort of person to eat her pie first. Her house had always been neat and clean. The furniture was dark wood and the upholstered pieces were comfortable but unmemorable. Meals were traditional Burg meals, ready at noon and at six o'clock. Stuffed cabbage, pot roast, roast chicken, an occasional ham or pork roast. My grandfather wouldn't have had it any other way. He'd worked in a steel mill all his life. He had strong opinions, and he dwarfed the rooms of their row house. Truth is, the top of my grandmother's head comes to the tip of my chin, and my grandfather wasn't much taller. But then I guess stature doesn't have much to do with inches.

Lately I've been wondering who my grandmother would have been if she hadn't married my grandfather. I wonder if she would have eaten her dessert first a lot sooner.

I took the meatballs out of the oven and set them side by side on a plate. Sitting there together they looked like troll gonads.

"Well, will you look at these big boys," Grandma said. "Reminds me of your grandfather, rest his soul."

When we were done eating I took Bob for a walk. Street lights were on, and light poured from the front windows of the houses behind my apartment building. We walked several blocks in comfortable silence. It turns out that's one of the good things about a dog. They don't talk a lot, so you can go along, thinking your own thoughts, making lists.

My list consisted of Catch Morris Munson, Worry about Ranger, and Wonder about Morelli. I didn't exactly know what to do about Morelli. My heart felt like it was in love. My head wasn't so sure. Not that it mattered, because Morelli didn't want to get married. So here I was with my biological clock ticking and nothing around me but indecision.

"I hate this!" I said to Bob.

Bob stopped and looked over his shoulder at me, like, What's the big deal back there? Well, what did Bob know. Someone had whacked off his doodles when he was a puppy. Bob was just left with some extra skin and a distant memory. Bob didn't have a mother waiting for grandchildren. Bob didn't have all this *pressure*!

When I got back to the apartment Grandma was asleep in front of the television. I wrote a note saying I had to go out for a while, pinned the note to Grandma's sweater, and told Bob to behave himself and not eat any of the furniture. Rex was buried under a mound of shavings, sleeping off his piece of pie. All was well in the Stephanie Plum household.

I drove directly to Hannibal's town house. It was eight o'clock, and the place looked like no one was home, but then it always looked like no one was home. I parked two streets over, got out of the car, and walked to the back of the house. No light shining from any of the windows. I climbed the tree and looked down into Hannibal's yard. Totally dark. I dropped out of the tree and retraced my steps on the bike path, thinking this was very spooky. Black trees and bushes. No moon overhead to light the way. Only the occasional streak of light spilling from a window.

Wouldn't want to meet a bad guy out here. Not Munson. Not Hannibal Ramos. Maybe not even Ranger . . . although he was bad in a very intriguing way.

I moved the car to the end of Hannibal's block, where I had better visibility. I pushed the seat back, locked the doors, and watched and waited.

It didn't take long for waiting to get old. To pass the time, I dialed Morelli on my cell phone. "Guess who?" I said.

"Is Grandma gone?"

"No. I'm working, and she's home with Bob."

"Bob?"

"Brian Simon's dog. I'm baby-sitting him while Simon's on vacation."

"Simon's not on vacation. I saw him today."

"What?"

"I can't believe you fell for that vacation scam," Morelli said. "Simon's been trying to pawn that dog off ever since he got him."

"Why didn't you tell me?"

"I didn't know he was gonna give you the dog."

I narrowed my eyes at the phone. "Are you laughing? Is that laughter I hear?"

"No. I swear."

But it *was* laughter. The rat was laughing.

"This is no laughing matter," I said. "What am I going to do with a dog?"

"I thought you always wanted a dog."

"Well, yeah . . . someday. But not *now*! And the dog howls. He doesn't like being left alone."

"Where are you?" Morelli asked.

"It's a secret."

"Christ, you aren't staking out Hannibal's house again, are you?"

"Nope. I'm not doing that."

"I have a cake," he said. "Do you want to come over and have some cake?"

"You're lying. You don't have a cake."

"I could get one."

"I'm not saying I'm staking out Hannibal's house, but if I was, do you think there'd be any value to it?"

"As far as I can tell, Ranger has a handful of people he trusts, and he has those people watching the Ramos family. I've spotted someone at Homer's house in Hunterdon County, and I know there's someone in place in Deal. He's got you sitting over there on Fenwood. I don't know what he expects to find, but my guess is, he knows where he's going. He has information about this crime that we don't have."

"Doesn't look like there's anyone home, here," I said.

"Alexander's in town, so Hannibal has probably moved into the south wing of the Deal house." Morelli let a beat go by. "Probably Ranger's got you sitting there because it's safe. Make you feel like you're doing something, so you don't stumble into a more important surveillance situation. Probably you should give up on it and come over to my house."

"Nice try, but I don't think so."

"It was worth a shot," Morelli said.

We disconnected, and I hunkered in to do my surveillance thing. Probably Morelli was right, and Hannibal was living at the shore. There was only one way to find out: watch and wait. By twelve o'clock Hannibal still hadn't appeared. My feet were cold, and I was sick of sitting in the car. I got out and stretched. A final check of the back, and then I was going home.

I walked the bike path with my pepper spray held in my hand. It was stygian. No lights anywhere. Everyone was in bed. I got to Hannibal's back door and looked up at his windows. Cold, dark glass. I was about to leave when I heard the muffled sound of a toilet flushing. No question which house the sound emanated from. Hannibal's. A chill raced the length of my spine. Someone was living in the dark, in Hannibal's house. I stood dead still, barely breathing, listening with every molecule of my body. There were no more sounds, and no further sign of life in the house. I didn't know what this meant, but I was totally creeped out. I scurried down the path, crossed the grass to the car, and took off.

REX WAS RUNNING on the wheel when I walked in the door, and Bob ran up to me, eyes bright, panting in anticipation of a pat on the head and possible food. I said hello to Rex and gave him a raisin. Then I gave a couple raisins to Bob, making him wag his tail so hard the whole back half of his body whipped side to side.

I set the box of raisins on the counter and went to the bathroom, and when I returned the raisins were gone. Only a slobbery, mangled corner of the box remained.

"You have an eating disorder," I said to Bob. "And take it from someone who knows, compulsive eating isn't the way to go. Before you know it your skin won't fit."

Grandma had set a pillow and blanket out for me in the living room. I kicked my shoes off, crawled under the blanket, and was asleep in seconds.

I woke up feeling tired and disoriented. I looked at my watch. Two o'clock. I squinted into the darkness. "Ranger?"

"What's with the dog?"

"I'm baby-sitting. Guess he's not much of a watchdog."

"He would have opened the door if he could have found the key."

"I know it's not that hard to pick a lock, but how do you get past the security chain?"

"Trade secret."

"I'm in the trade."

Ranger handed me a large envelope. "Check out these pictures and tell me who you recognize."

I sat up, switched the table lamp on, and opened the envelope. I identified Alexander Ramos and Hannibal. There were also photos of Ulysses and Homer Ramos and two first cousins. All four were very much alike; each could have been the man I saw standing in the doorway of the Deal house. Except, of course, Homer, who was dead. There was another woman, photographed with Homer Ramos. She was small and blond and smiling. Homer had his arm around her, and he was smiling back.

"Who's this?" I asked.

"Homer's latest girlfriend. Her name's Cynthia Lotte. She works downtown. Receptionist for someone you know."

"Omigod! Now I recognize her. She works for my ex-husband."

"Yeah," Ranger said. "Small world."

I told Ranger about the town house being dark, with no sign of life, and then the toilet flushing.

"What does that mean?" I asked Ranger.

"It means someone's in the house."

"Hannibal?"

"Hannibal's in Deal."

Ranger snapped the table lamp off and stood. He was wearing a black T-shirt, black Gore-Tex windbreaker, and black cargo pants tucked into black boots, army style. The well-dressed urban commando. I could guarantee that any man facing him in a blind alley would have an empty scrotum, his most prized possessions gone north. And any woman would be licking dry lips and checking to make sure all her buttons were buttoned. He looked down at me, hands in pockets, his face barely visible in the dark room.

"Would you be willing to visit your ex and check out Cynthia Lotte?"

"Sure. Anything else?"

He smiled, and when he answered his voice was soft. "Not with your grandmother in the next room."

Eek.

When Ranger left I slid the security chain in place and flopped back onto the couch, thrashing around, thinking erotic thoughts. No doubt about it. I was a hopeless slut. I looked heavenward, only the ceiling got in the way. "It's all hormones," I said to Whoever might be listening. "It's not my fault. I have too many hormones."

I got up and drank a glass of orange juice. After the orange juice I returned to the couch and thrashed around some more because Grandma was snoring so loud I was afraid she'd suck her tongue down her throat and choke to death.

"ISN'T THIS A pip of a morning!" Grandma said, on her way to the kitchen. "I feel like having some pie!"

I checked my watch. Six-thirty. I dragged myself off the couch and into the bathroom where I stood under the shower for a long time, sullen and bitchy. When I got out of the shower I looked at myself in the mirror over the sink. I had a big zit on my chin. Well, isn't this just great. I have to go see my ex-husband with a zit on my chin. Probably God's punishment for last night's mental lusting.

I thought about the .38 in the cookie jar. I made a fist, thumb up, index finger extended. I put the index finger to my temple and said, "Bang."

I dressed myself up in an outfit like Ranger's. Black T-shirt, black cargo pants, black boots. Big zit on my face. I looked like an idiot. I took the black T-shirt and pants and boots off and stuffed myself into a white T-shirt, topped with a plaid flannel shirt and a pair of Levi's with a small hole in the crotch which I convinced myself no one could see. This was an outfit for someone with a zit.

Grandma was reading the paper when I came out of the bedroom.

"Where'd you get the paper?" I asked.

"Borrowed it from that nice man across the hall. Only he don't know it yet."

Grandma was a fast learner.

"I don't have another driving lesson until tomorrow, so Louise and me are going to look at some condos today. I've been checking out the job situation too, and it looks to me like there's lots of good stuff. There's jobs for cooks and cleaning people and makeup ladies and car salesmen."

"If you could have any job in the world, what would you choose?"

"That's easy. I'd be a movie star."

"You'd make a good one," I said.

"Of course, I'd want to be a leading lady. Some of my parts have started to sag, but my legs are still pretty good."

I looked at Grandma's legs sticking out from under her dress. I guess everything is relative.

Bob was standing at the door with his knees together, so I clipped his leash on him and we headed out. Look at this, I thought, I'm getting exercise first thing in the morning. Probably after two weeks of Bob I'll be so skinny I'll have to buy all new clothes. And the fresh air is good for my pimple, too. Hell, it might even cure it. Maybe the pimple will be *gone* by the time I get back to the apartment.

Bob and I were walking along at a pretty good rate. We rounded the corner and swung into the lot, and there were Habib and Mitchell, waiting for me in a ten-year-old Dodge totally upholstered in chartreuse broadloom. A neon sign on the top of the car advertised Art's Carpet's. It made the wind machine look tasteful.

"Holy cow," I said. "What *is* this?"

"It was all that was available on short notice," Mitchell said. "And I wouldn't make a big deal out of it if I was you, because it's a sensitive topic. And not to change the subject, or anything, but we're getting impatient. We don't want to freak you out, but we're gonna have to do something real mean if you don't deliver your boyfriend pretty soon."

"Is that a threat?"

"Well, yeah, sure," Mitchell said. "It's a threat."

Habib was behind the wheel, wearing a large foam whiplash collar. He gave a small nod of acknowledgment.

"We're professionals," Mitchell said. "You don't want to be fooled by our pleasant demeanor."

"Just so," Habib said.

"Are you going to follow me around today?" I asked.

"That's the plan," Mitchell said. "I hope you're gonna do something interesting. I don't feel like spending the day at the mall lookin' at ladies' shoes. Like we said, our boss is getting antsy."

"Why does your boss want Ranger?"

"Ranger has something that belongs to him, and he'd like to discuss the matter. You could tell him that."

I suspected that discussing the matter might involve a fatal accident. "I'll pass it along if I happen to hear from him."

"You tell him he just gives back what he's got and everyone's gonna be happy. Bygones will be bygones. No hard feelings."

"Uh-huh. Well, I've got to be running along now. I'll see you guys later."

"When you come back to the parking lot I would appreciate your bringing me an aspirin," Habib said. "I am suffering with this neck whiplashing."

"I don't know about you," I said to Bob when we got in the elevator, "but I'm sort of freaked out."

Grandma was reading the comics to Rex when I came in. Bob sidled up to join in the fun, and I took the phone into the living room to call Brian Simon.

Simon answered on the third ring. "'Lo."

"That was a short trip," I said.

"Who's this?"

"It's Stephanie."

"How'd you get my number? I have an unlisted number."

"It's printed on your dog's collar."

"Oh."

"So I imagine now that you're home, you're going to be around to get Bob."

"I'm kind of busy today—"

"No problem. I'll drop him off. Where do you live?"

A moment of silence. "Okay, here's the thing," Simon said. "I don't actually want Bob back."

"He's *your* dog!"

"Not anymore. Possession is nine-tenths of the law. You have the food. You have the pooper-scooper. You have the dog. Listen, he's a nice dog, but I don't have time for him. And he makes my nose run. I think I'm allergic."

"I think you're a *jerk*."

Simon sighed. "You're not the first woman to tell me that."

"I can't keep him here. He howls when I leave."

"Don't I know it. And if you leave him alone he eats the furniture."

"What? What do you mean, he eats the furniture?"

"Forget I said that. I didn't mean to say that. He doesn't actually *eat* the furniture. I mean, chewing isn't really eating. And not that he even chews. Oh, shit," Simon said. "Good luck." And he hung up. I redialed, but he wouldn't answer.

I returned the phone to the kitchen and gave Bob his breakfast bowl of dog crunchies. I poured a cup of coffee and ate a chunk of pie. There was one piece of pie left so I gave it to Bob. "You don't eat furniture, do you?" I asked.

Grandma was hunkered down in front of the television, watching the Weather Channel. "Don't worry about supper tonight," she said. "We can have leftover balls."

I gave her a thumbs-up, but she was concentrating on the weather in Cleveland and didn't see me.

"Well, I guess I'll go out now," I said.

Grandma nodded.

Grandma looked all rested. And I felt all done in. I wasn't getting enough sleep. The late-night visits and the snoring were taking a toll on me. I dragged myself out of the apartment and down the hall. My eyes drooped closed while I waited for the elevator.

"I'm exhausted," I said to Bob. "I need more sleep."

I drove to my parents' house and Bob and I trooped in. My mother was in the kitchen, humming as she put together an apple pie.

"This must be Bob," she said. "Your grandmother told me you had a dog."

Bob ran over to my mother.

"No!" I yelled. "Don't you dare!"

Bob stopped two feet from my mother and looked back at me.

"You know what I'm talking about," I said to Bob.

"What a well-mannered dog," my mother said.

I stole a chunk of apple from the pie. "Did Grandma also tell you she snores, and she's up at the crack of dawn, and she watches the Weather Channel for hours on end?" I poured myself a cup of coffee. "Help," I said to the coffee.

"She's probably taking a couple nips before bed," my mother said. "She always snores after she's belted back a few."

"That can't be it. I don't have any liquor in the house."

"Look in the closet. That's where she usually keeps it. I clean bottles out of her closet all the time."

"You mean she buys it herself and hides it in the closet?"

"It's not *hidden* in the closet. That's just where she keeps it."

"Are you telling me Grandma's an alcoholic?"

"No, of course not. She just tipples a little. She says it helps get her to sleep."

Maybe that was my problem. Maybe I should be tippling. Trouble is, I throw up when I tipple too much. And once I start tippling it's hard to tell when it's too much until it's too late. One tipple always seems to lead to another.

The kitchen heat washed over me and soaked into the flannel shirt, and I felt like the pie, sitting in the oven, steaming. I struggled out of the flannel shirt, put my head down on the table, and fell asleep. I had a dream that it was summer, and I was baking on the beach in Point Pleasant. Hot sand under me, and hot sun above me. And my skin all brown and crispy like pie crust. When I woke up the pie was out of the oven, and the house smelled like heaven. And my mother had ironed my shirt.

"Do you ever eat the dessert first?" I asked my mother.

She looked at me dumbfounded. As if I'd asked whether she ritually sacrificed cats every Wednesday at the stroke of midnight.

"Suppose you were home alone," I said, "and there was a straw-

642

berry shortcake in the refrigerator and a meatloaf in the oven. Which would you eat first?"

My mother thought about it for a minute, her eyes wide. "I can't remember ever eating dinner alone. I can't even imagine it."

I buttoned myself into the shirt and slipped into my denim jacket. "I have to go. I have work to do."

"You could come to dinner tomorrow night," my mother said. "You could bring your grandmother and Joseph. I'm making a pork roast and mashed potatoes."

"Okay, but I don't know about Joe."

I got to the front door and saw that the carpet car was parked behind the Buick.

"Now what?" my mother asked. "Who are those men in that weird car?"

"Habib and Mitchell."

"Why are they parked here?"

"They're following me, but don't worry about it. They're okay."

"What do you mean, 'Don't worry about it'? What kind of thing is that to say to a mother. Of course, I'll worry about it. They look like thugs." My mother pushed past me, walked up to the car, and rapped on the window.

The window slid down and Mitchell looked out at my mother. "How ya doin'?" he asked.

"Why are you following my daughter?"

"Did she tell you we're following her? She shouldn't have done that. We don't like to worry mothers."

"I have a gun in the house, and I'll use it if I have to," my mother said.

"Jeez, lady, you don't have to get your panties all in a bunch," Mitchell said. "What is it with this family? Everybody's always so hostile. We're just following your kid around a little."

"I have your license plate number," my mother said. "If anything happens to my daughter I'll tell the police all about you."

Mitchell pressed the window button and his window slid closed.

"You don't really have a gun, do you?" I asked my mother.

"I just said that to throw a scare into them."

"Hmm. Well, thanks. I'm sure I'll be okay now."

"Your father could pull some strings and get you a good job at the Personal Products plant," my mother said. "Evelyn Nagy's girl is working there, and she gets three weeks' paid vacation."

I tried to visualize Wonder Woman working the line at the Personal Products plant, but the picture wouldn't fine-tune. "I don't know," I said. "I don't think I have a future in Personal Products." I got into Big Blue and waved good-bye to my mother.

She gave Mitchell one last warning glare and returned to her house.

"She's going through the change," I said to Bob. "She gets excited. Nothing to worry about."

SEVEN

I DROVE OVER to the office with Mitchell and Habib tagging along behind.

Lula looked out the storefront window when Bob and I swung through the door. "Looks like those two idiots got a carpet car."

"Yeah. They've been with me since the crack of dawn. They tell me their employer's losing patience with the Ranger hunt."

"He's not the only one," Vinnie said from his inner office. "Joyce is turning up a big fat nothing on Ranger, and I'm feeling an ulcer coming on. Not to mention, I'm in for big bucks with Morris Munson. You better get your ass out there and find that creep."

With any luck Munson was in Tibet by now and I'd *never* find him. "Anything new?" I asked Connie.

"Nothing you want to know about."

"Tell her anyway. This is a good one," Lula said.

"Last night Vinnie bonded out a guy named Douglas Kruper. Kruper sold a car to the fifteen-year-old daughter of one of our illustrious state senators. On the way home from buying the car the kid got picked up for running a light and driving without a license, and the car turned out to be stolen. Now this is the good part. The car is described as a Rollswagen. You happen to know anyone named Douglas Kruper?"

"Also known as the Dealer," I said. "I went to school with him."

"Well, he isn't gonna be doin' any dealing for a while."

"How'd he take to getting arrested?" I asked Vinnie.

"Cried like a baby," Vinnie said. "It was disgusting. He was a disgrace to criminals everywhere."

Just for the heck of it I went to the file cabinet and looked to see if we had anything on Cynthia Lotte. I wasn't too surprised when she didn't show up.

"I have an errand to run downtown," I said. "Is it okay if I leave Bob here? I should be back in about an hour."

"As long as he doesn't come into my private office," Vinnie said.

"Yeah, you wouldn't be talkin' like that if Bob was a female goat," Lula said.

Vinnie slammed his door shut and threw the dead bolt.

I told Bob I'd be back in time for lunch and hustled out to the car. At the nearest ATM I withdrew fifty dollars from my checking; then I drove over to Grant Street. Dougie had two cases of Dolce Vita perfume that had seemed like too much of a luxury when I returned the wind machine but might be marked down now that he had legal problems. Not that I was one to take advantage of someone else's misfortune . . . but, hell, we're talking about Dolce Vita here.

There were three cars parked in front of Dougie's house when I got there. I recognized one as belonging to my friend Eddie Gazzara. Eddie and I grew up together. He's a cop now, and he's married to my cousin Shirley the Whiner. There was a PBA shield on the second car, and the third car was a fifteen-year-old Cadillac that still had its original paint and not a speck of rust anywhere. I didn't want to consider the implications, but it looked a lot like Louise Greeber's car. What was one of Grandma's friends doing here?

Inside, the tiny row house was cluttered with people and merchandise. Dougie shuffled from person to person, looking dazed.

"Everything has to go," he said to me. "I'm shutting down."

The Mooner was there, too. "Hey, it's not fair, dude," he said.

"This individual had a business going on. He's entitled to run a business, right? I mean, where are his rights? Okay, so he sold a stolen car to a kid. Hey, we all make mistakes. Am I right, here?"

"You do the crime, you pay the time," Gazzara said, holding a stack of Levi's. "How much do you want for these, Dougie?"

I pulled Gazzara aside. "I need to talk to you about Ranger."

"Allen Barnes is looking for him big time," Gazzara said.

"Does Barnes have anything on Ranger besides the videotape?"

"I don't know. I'm not in the loop. There's not a lot leaking out on this one. No one wants to make any mistakes with Ranger."

"Is Barnes looking at other suspects?"

"Not that I know of. But then, like I said, I'm not in the loop."

A squad car double-parked on the street and two uniforms came in. "I hear there's a fire sale going on," one of the uniforms said. "Are there any toasters left?"

I picked two bottles of perfume out of the case and gave Dougie a ten. "What are you going to do now?"

"I don't know. I feel real defeated," Dougie said. "Nothing ever works out for me. Some guys just don't have any luck."

"You gotta keep your chin up, dude," Mooner said. "Something else will come along. You gotta be like me. You gotta go with the flow."

"I'm going to jail!" Dougie said. "They're gonna send me to jail!"

"You see what I'm saying?" Mooner said. "Something else always comes along. You go to jail, you don't have to worry about anything. No rent to pay. No food bill to sweat. Free dental plan. And that's worth something, dude. You don't want to stick your nose up at free dental."

We all looked at Mooner for a minute, debating the wisdom of a response.

I walked through the house and peeked out back, but I didn't see Grandma or Louise Greeber. I said good-bye to Gazzara and threaded my way through the crowd to the door.

"Real nice of you to support the Dougster," Moon said as I was leaving. "Damn mellow of you, duder."

"I just wanted some Dolce Vita," I said.

The Cadillac was no longer parked on the street. The carpet car idled at the corner. I sat in the Buick and gave myself a splash of perfume to compensate for the chin zit and the crappy, holey jeans. I decided I needed more than perfume, so I swiped on some extra mascara and teased up my hair. Better to look like a slut with a zit than a dork with a zit.

I drove downtown to my ex-husband's office in the Shuman Building. Richard Orr, attorney-at-law and womanizing asshole. He was a junior partner in a multiname law firm—Rabinowitz, Rabinowitz, Zeller and Asshole. I took the elevator to the second floor and looked for the door with his gold-lettered name. I wasn't a frequent visitor here. It hadn't been a friendly divorce, and Dickie and I don't exchange Christmas cards. Once in a while our professional paths cross.

Cynthia Lotte was sitting at the front desk, looking like an Ann Taylor advertisement in her simple gray suit and white shirt. She looked up in alarm when I pushed through the door, obviously recognizing me from my last visit, when Dickie and I had a small disagreement.

"He isn't in his office," she said.

There *is* a God. "When do you expect him in?"

"Hard to say. He's in court today."

She didn't have a ring on her finger. And she didn't seem grief-stricken. In fact, she seemed downright happy, aside from the fact that Dickie's crazy ex-wife was in her office.

I faked some goggle-eyed interest in the reception area. "This is pretty nice. It must be great to work here."

"Usually."

I took this to mean "almost always, except for now." "I guess this is a good place to work if you're single. Probably you have a chance to meet lots of men."

"Is this going somewhere?"

"Well, I was just thinking about Homer Ramos. You know, wondering if you met him at the office here."

There was a dead silence for several seconds, and I could swear I heard her heart beating. She didn't say anything. And I didn't say anything. I couldn't tell what was going on inside *her* head, but *I* was doing some interior knuckle-cracking. The question about Homer Ramos had actually come out a little more abrupt than I'd planned, and I was feeling sort of uncomfortable. I'm usually only *mentally* rude to people.

Cynthia Lotte gathered herself together and looked me straight in the eye. Her manner was demure and her voice was solicitous. "I don't mean to change the subject, or anything," she said, "but have you tried concealer on that zit?"

I sucked in some air. "Uh, no. I didn't think—"

"You should be careful, because when they get that big and all red and filled with pus they can leave scars."

My fingers flew to my chin before I could stop them. God, she was right. The zit felt *huge*. It was *growing*. Damn! My emergency reaction mode kicked in, and the message it sent to my brain was *Flee! Hide!*

"I should be moving along, anyway," I said, backing away. "Tell Dickie I didn't want anything special. I was in the neighborhood and I thought I'd say hello."

I let myself out, took the stairs, and rushed through the lobby and out the door. I crammed myself into the Buick and yanked at the rearview mirror so I could see my zit.

Gross!

I leaned back in the seat and closed my eyes. Bad enough I had the zit from hell, but Cynthia Lotte had out-ruded me. I'd found out nothing for Ranger. The only thing I knew about Lotte was that she looked good in gray and had pushed my button. One mention of my pimple, and I was out the door.

I looked back at the Shuman Building and wondered if Ramos had done business with Dickie's firm. And what sort of business? It would have made sense for Lotte to have met Ramos that way. Of course, she could also have met him on the street. The Ramos office building was only a block away.

I put the Buick into gear and slowly cruised past the Ramos building. The crime scene tape had been removed, and I could see workmen in the lobby. The service road that ran past the rear door was clogged with repair trucks.

I doubled back through town, stopping at the RadioShack on Third.

"I need some kind of an alarm," I told the kid at the register. "Nothing fancy. Just something that tells me when my front door gets opened. And stop staring at my chin!"

"I wasn't staring at your chin. Honest! I didn't even notice that big zit."

A half-hour later I was on my way to the office to get Bob. Sitting in a little bag, on the seat beside me, was a small motion detector gizmo for my front door. I told myself it was necessary for general security, but truth is, I knew it had one purpose: to alert me whenever Ranger broke in to my apartment. And why did I feel the need for the gizmo? Did it have anything to do with fear? No. Although there were times when Ranger *could* be scary. Did it have to do with distrust? Nope. I trusted Ranger. The fact is, I got the gizmo because just once I wanted to have the advantage. It was driving me nuts that Ranger could get into my apartment without even waking me.

I stopped at Cluck-in-a-Bucket and got a barrel of chicken nuggets for lunch. I figured that was best for Bob. No bones to hork up.

Everyone's eyes got bright when I walked through the door with my barrel of nuggets.

"Bob and me were just thinking about chicken," Lula said. "You must have read our minds."

I took the lid off the barrel, set the lid on the floor, and dumped a bunch of nuggets onto it for Bob. I took a nugget for myself and handed the rest off to Lula and Connie. Then I called my cousin Bunny at the credit bureau.

"What have you got on Cynthia Lotte?" I asked Bunny.

A minute later she was back with the answer. "Not much here," she said. "A recent car loan. Pays her bills on time. No derogatory information. Lives in Ewing." The phone went silent for a couple beats. "What are you looking for?"

"I don't know. She works for Dickie."

"Oh." As if that explained it all.

I got Lotte's address and phone and said adios to Bunny.

The next person I called was Morelli. None of his numbers picked up so I left a message on his pager.

"That's funny," Lula said. "Didn't you put those nuggets on the bucket lid? I can't find that bucket lid anywhere."

We all looked at Bob. He had a small piece of cardboard stuck to his lip.

"Dang," Lula said. "He makes me look like an amateur."

"So, do you notice anything unusual about me?" I asked.

"Only that you got a big zit on your chin. Must be that time of the month, huh?"

"It's stress!" I stuck my head in my shoulder bag and looked for concealer. Flashlight, hairbrush, lipstick, Juicy Fruit gum, stun gun, tissues, hand lotion, pepper spray. No concealer.

"I've got a Band-Aid," Connie said. "You could try to cover it with a Band-Aid."

I stuck the Band-Aid over the pimple.

"That's better," Lula said. "Now it looks like you cut yourself shaving."

Great.

"Before I forget," Connie said, "a call came in about Ranger while you were on the phone with the credit bureau. There's a warrant written for his arrest in connection with the Ramos murder."

"How does the warrant read?" I asked.

"Wanted for questioning."

"That's how it started with O.J.," Lula said. "They just wanted him for questioning. And look how that turned out."

I wanted to check on Hannibal's town house, but I didn't want to drag Mitchell and Habib over with me.

"I need a diversion," I said to Lula. "I need to get rid of those guys in the carpet car."

"Do you mean you want to get *rid* of them? Or do you mean you don't want them following you?"

"I don't want them following me."

"Well, that's easy." She took a .45 out of her desk drawer. "I'll just shoot out a couple tires."

"No! No shooting!"

"You always got all these rules," Lula said.

Vinnie stuck his head out of his office. "How about the burning bag thing?"

We swiveled our heads in his direction.

"Usually you do it as a gag on somebody's front porch," Vinnie said. "You put some dog shit in a bag. Then you put the bag on the sucker's front porch and ring the bell. Then you set the bag on fire and run like hell. When the mark opens the door he sees the bag burning and stomps on it to put it out."

"And?"

"And then he gets dog shit all over his shoe," Vinnie said. "If you did it to these guys and they got dog shit all over their shoes they'd be distracted, and you could drive away."

"Only we haven't got a front porch," Lula said.

"Use your imagination!" Vinnie said. "You put it just behind the car. Then you sneak away and someone from the office here yells out at them that something's burning under their car."

"I kinda like the sound of that," Lula said. "Only thing is, we need some dog poop."

We all turned our attention to Bob.

Connie took a brown paper lunch bag from her bottom drawer. "I've got a bag and you can use the empty chicken bucket as a pooper-scooper."

I snapped the leash on Bob, and Lula and Bob and I went out

the back door and walked around some. Bob tinkled about forty times, but he didn't have any contributions for the bag.

"He don't look motivated," Lula said. "Maybe we should take him over to the park."

The park was only two blocks away, so we walked Bob to the park and stood around waiting for him to answer nature's call. Only nature wasn't calling Bob's name.

"You ever notice how when you don't want dog poop it just seems to be everywhere?" Lula said. "And now when we *want* some . . ." Her eyes opened wide. "Hold the phone. Dog at twelve o'clock. And it's a *big* one."

Sure enough, someone else was walking their dog in the park. The dog was big and black. The old woman at the other end of the leash was small and white. She was wearing low-heeled shoes and a bulky brown tweed coat, and she had her gray hair stuffed into a knit hat. She was holding a plastic bag and a paper towel in her hand. The bag was empty.

"I don't mean to blaspheme or anything," Lula said. "But God sent us this dog."

The dog suddenly stopped walking and hunched over, and Lula and Bob and I took off across the grass. I had Bob on the leash, and Lula was waving the chicken bucket and paper bag, and we were running full tilt when the woman looked up and saw us. The color drained from her face, and she staggered backward.

"I'm old," she said. "I haven't got any money. Go away. Don't hurt me."

"We don't want your money," Lula said. "We want your poop."

The woman choked up on the dog's leash. "You can't have the poop. I have to take the poop home. It's the law."

"The law don't say *you* gotta take it home," Lula said. "It's just *somebody* gotta do it. And we're volunteering."

The big black dog stopped what he was doing and gave Bob an inquisitive sniff. Bob sniffed back, and then he looked at the old woman's crotch.

"Don't even think about it," I said to Bob.

"I don't know if that's right," the woman said. "I never heard of that. I think I'm supposed to take the poop home."

"Okay," Lula said, "we'll pay you for the poop." Lula looked over at me. "Give her a couple bucks for her poop."

I searched my pockets. "I don't have any money on me. I didn't bring my purse."

"I won't take any less than five dollars," the woman said.

"Turns out we don't have any money on us," Lula said.

"Then it's my poop," the woman said.

"The heck it is," Lula said, muscling the old woman out of the way and scooping the poop up in the chicken bucket. "We need this poop."

"Help!" the woman yelled. "They're taking my poop! Stop! Thief!"

"I got it," Lula said. "I got it all." And Lula and Bob and I ran like the wind back to the office with our bucket of poop.

We collected ourselves at the back door to the office. Bob was all happy, dancing around. But Lula and I were gasping for breath.

"Boy, for a while there I was afraid she was gonna catch us," Lula said. "She could run pretty fast for an old lady."

"She wasn't running," I said. "The dog was *dragging* her, trying to get at Bob."

I held the paper bag open, and Lula dumped the poop into it.

"This here's gonna be fun," Lula said. "I can't wait to see those two guys stomping on this bag of shit."

Lula went around front with the bag and a Bic. And Bob and I went into the office through the back door. Habib and Mitchell were parked curbside, in front of the office, directly behind my Buick.

Connie and Vinnie and I peeked out the front window while Lula crept up behind the carpet car. She put the bag on the ground just past the rear bumper. We saw the lighter flame, and Lula jumped away and scuttled off around the corner.

Connie stuck her head out the door. "Hey!" she yelled. "Hey, you guys in the car . . . there's something burning behind you!"

Mitchell rolled the window down. "What?"

"There's something on fire behind your car!"

Mitchell and Habib got out to take a look and we all hustled through the door to join them.

"It's just some trash," Mitchell said to Habib. "Kick it out of the way so it don't damage the car."

"It is flaming," Habib said. "I do not want to touch a flaming bag with my shoe."

"This is what happens when you hire a fucking camel jockey," Mitchell said. "You people have no work ethic."

"This is not true. I work very hard in Pakistan. In my village in Pakistan we have a rug factory, and my job is to beat the unruly children who work there. It is a very good job."

"Wow," Mitchell said. "You beat the little kids who work in the factory?"

"Yes. With a stick. It is a highly skilled position. You must be careful when beating the children not to crush their little fingers or they will not be able to tie the very fine knots."

"That's disgusting," I said.

"Oh no," Habib said. "The children like it, and they make much money for their families." He turned to Mitchell and shook his finger at him. "And I work very hard beating the little children, so you should not say such things about me."

"Sorry," Mitchell said. "Guess I was wrong about you." He gave the bag a kick. The bag broke and some of the debris stuck to his shoe.

"What the hell?" Mitchell shook his foot, and flaming dog shit flew everywhere. A big glob landed on the carpet on the car; there was the hiss of ignition, and flames spread everywhere.

"Holy crap," Mitchell said, grabbing Habib, falling backward over the curb.

The fire popped and crackled, and the interior went conflagration. There was a small explosion when the gas tank caught and the car was engulfed in black smoke and flame.

"Guess they didn't use one of them flame-retardant carpets," Lula said.

Habib and Mitchell were pressed flat to the building, mouths open.

"You could probably go now," Lula said. "I don't think they're gonna follow you."

By the time the fire trucks arrived, the carpet car was mostly carcass, and the fire had settled down to wienie-roast size. My Buick was about ten feet in front of the carpet car, but Big Blue was untouched. The Buick's paint wasn't even blistered. The only noticeable difference was a slightly warmer than usual door handle.

"I've got to go now," I said to Mitchell. "Too bad about your car. And I wouldn't worry about your eyebrows. They're a little singed right now, but they'll probably grow back. I had this happen to me once and everything turned out okay."

"What . . . How . . . ?" Mitchell said.

I loaded Bob into the Buick and eased away from the curb, winding my way around the police cars and fire trucks.

Carl Costanza was in uniform, directing traffic. "Looks like you're on a roll," he said. "This is the second car you've toasted this week."

"It wasn't my fault! It wasn't even my car!"

"I heard someone pulled the old bag-full-of-crapola gag on Arturo Stolle's two stooges."

"No kidding? I don't suppose you know who did it?"

"Funny thing, I was just going to ask if *you* knew who did it."

"I asked you first."

Costanza did a small grimace. "No. I don't know who did it."

"Me either," I said.

"You're a pip," Constanza said. "I can't believe you got suckered into taking Simon's dog."

"I kind of like him."

"Just don't leave him alone in your car."

"You mean because it's against the law?"

"No. Because he ate Simon's front seat. Only thing left was some scraps of foam rubber and a few springs."

"Thanks for sharing that with me."

Costanza grinned. "I thought you'd want to know."

I cruised off, thinking that if Bob ate Big Blue's seat it would probably regenerate. At the risk of sounding like Grandma, I was beginning to wonder about Big Blue. It was as if the darn thing was impervious to damage. It was almost fifty years old and the original paint was in perfect condition. All around it cars got dented and torched and smushed flat as a pancake, but nothing ever happened to Big Blue.

"It's downright creepy," I said to Bob.

Bob had his nose pressed to the window and didn't look like he cared a whole lot.

I was still on Hamilton when my cell phone rang.

"Hey, babe," Ranger said. "What have you got for me?"

"Only basic facts on Lotte. Do you want to know where she lives?"

"Pass."

"She looks good in gray."

"That's going to keep me alive."

"Hmm. Feeling cranky today?"

"Cranky doesn't come close. I have a favor to ask. I need you to take a look at the back of the house in Deal. Everyone else on the team would be suspect, but a woman walking her dog down the beach won't feel threatening to Ramos's security. I want you to catalogue the house. Count off windows and doors."

THERE WAS A public-access beach about a quarter-mile from the Ramos compound. I parked on the road, and Bob and I crossed a short stretch of low dunes. The sky was overcast and the air was cooler than it had been in Trenton. Bob tipped his nose into the wind and looked all perky, and I buttoned my jacket up to my neck and wished I'd brought something warmer to wear. Most of the big, expensive houses that sat on the dunes were shuttered and unoccupied. Frothy gray waves came whooshing in at us. A few seagulls ran around at the water's edge, but that was it. Just me and Bob and the seagulls.

The big pink house came into view, more exposed on the beach side than to the street. Most of the first floor and all of the second story were clearly visible. A porch ran the length of the main structure. Attached to this main structure were two wings. The north wing consisted of first-floor garages and possibly bedrooms over the garages. The south wing was two stories and seemed to be entirely residential.

I continued to plow through the sand, not wanting to seem overly curious as I counted off the windows and doors. Just a woman walking her dog, freezing her ass off. I had binoculars with me but I was afraid to use them. I didn't want to arouse suspicion. It was impossible to tell if I was being observed from a window. Bob raced around me, oblivious to everything but the joy of being outdoors. I walked several houses farther, drew myself a diagram on a piece of paper, turned, and walked back to the public-access ramp where Blue was parked. Mission accomplished.

Bob and I piled into Blue and rumbled down the street, past the Ramos house, one last time. When I paused at the corner, a man in his sixties jumped off the curb at me. He was wearing a running suit and running shoes. And he was waving his hands.

"Stop," he said. "Stop a minute."

I could have sworn it was Alexander Ramos. No, that was ridiculous.

He trotted to the driver's side and rapped on my window. "Have you got any cigarettes?" he asked.

"Gee . . . uh, no."

He shoved a twenty at me. "Drive me to the store for some cigarettes. It'll only take a minute."

Thick accent. Same hawklike features. Same height and build. *Really* looked like Alexander Ramos.

"Do you live around here?" I asked him.

"Yeah, I live in that piece-of-shit pink monstrosity. What's it to you? Are you gonna drive me to the store, or not?"

My God! It *was* Ramos. "I don't usually let strange men in my car."

"Give me a break. I need some cigarettes. Anyway, you got a big dog in the backseat, and you look like you drive strange men around all the time. What'd ya think, I was born yesterday?"

"Not yesterday."

He wrenched the passenger door open and got in the car. "Very funny. I have to flag down a comedian."

"I don't know my way around here. Where do you go for cigarettes?"

"Turn the corner here. There's a store about a half-mile down."

"If it's just a half-mile away why don't you walk?"

"I have my reasons."

"Not supposed to be smoking, huh? Don't want anyone to catch you going to the store?"

"Goddamn doctors. I have to sneak out of my own house just to get a cigarette." He made a dismissive gesture. "I can't stand being in that house, anyway. It's like a mausoleum filled with a bunch of stiffs. Goddamn pink piece of shit."

"If you don't like the house, why do you live in it?"

"Good question. I should sell it. I never liked it, right from the beginning, but I just got married and my wife had to have this house. Everything with her was pink." He reflected for a minute. "What was her name? Trixie? Trudie? Christ, I can't even remember."

"You can't remember your wife's name?"

"I've had a lot of wives. A *lot*. Four. No, wait a minute . . . five."

"Are you married now?"

He shook his head. "I'm done with marriage. Had a prostate operation last year. Used to be, women married me for my balls and my money. Now they'd just marry me for my money." He shook his head. "It's not enough. You've gotta have standards, you know?"

I stopped at the store, and he jumped out of the car. "Don't go away. I'll be right back."

Part of me wanted to flee the scene. That was the cowardly part. And part of me wanted to go *Yippee!* That was the stupid part.

In two minutes he was back in the car, lighting up.

"Hey," I said, "no smoking in the car."

"I'll give you another twenty."

"I don't want the first twenty. And the answer is no. No smoking in the car."

"I hate this country. Nobody knows how to live. Everybody drinks fucking skim milk." He pointed to the cross street. "Turn up there and take Shoreline Avenue."

"Where are we going?"

"I know this bar."

Just what I need, to have Hannibal come out looking for his father and find me buddy-buddy with him in a bar. "I don't think this is such a good idea."

"You gonna let me smoke in the car?"

"No."

"Then we're going to Sal's."

"Okay, I'll drive you to Sal's, but I'm not going in."

"Sure, you're going in."

"But my dog . . ."

"The dog can come, too. I'll buy him a beer and a sandwich."

Sal's was small and dark. The bar stretched the length of the room. Two old men sat at the end of the bar, silently drinking, watching the television. Three empty tables were clustered to the right of the door. Ramos sat at one of the tables.

Without asking, the bartender brought Ramos a bottle of ouzo and two shot glasses. Nothing was said. Ramos drank a shot; then he lit up and dragged the smoke deep into his lungs. "Ahh," he said on the exhale.

Sometimes I envy people who smoke. They always look so

happy when they suck in that first lungful of tar. I can't think of many things that make me that happy. Maybe birthday cake.

Ramos poured himself a second shot and tipped the bottle in my direction.

"No thanks," I said. "I'm driving."

He shook his head. "Sissy country." He knocked the second shot back. "Don't get me wrong. I like some things okay. I like big American cars. And I like American football. And I like American women with big tits."

Oh, boy.

"Do you flag people down a lot?" I asked him.

"Every chance I get."

"Don't you think that's dangerous? Suppose you get picked up by a nut?"

He pulled a .22 out of his pocket. "I'd shoot him." He laid the gun on the table, closed his eyes, and sucked in more smoke. "You live around here?"

"No. I just come down once in a while to walk my dog. He likes to walk on the beach."

"What's with the Band-Aid on your chin?"

"I cut myself shaving."

He dropped a twenty on the table and stood. "Cut yourself shaving. I like that. You're okay. You can take me home now."

I dropped him off a block from his house.

"Come back tomorrow," he said. "Same time. Maybe I'll hire you on as my personal chauffeur."

GRANDMA WAS SETTING the dinner table when Bob and I got home. The Mooner was slouched on the couch, watching TV.

"Hey," he said, "how's it going?"

"Can't complain," I said. "How's it going with you?"

"I don't know, dude. It's just hard to believe there's no more Dealer. I thought the Dealer'd be around forever. I mean, he was doing a service. He was the Dealer." He shook his head. "It rocks my world, dude."

"He needs to have another brewski and chill some more," Grandma said. "And then we'll all have a nice dinner. I always like when there's company for dinner. Especially when it's a man."

I wasn't sure Mooner counted as a man. Mooner was sort of like Peter Pan on pot. Mooner spent a lot of time in never-never land.

Bob ambled out of the kitchen over to Mooner and gave his crotch a big sniff.

"Hey dude," Mooner said, "not on the first date, man."

"I bought myself a car today," Grandma said. "And the Mooner drove it over here for me."

I felt my mouth drop open. "But you already have a car. You have Uncle Sandor's Buick."

"That's true. And don't get me wrong, I think it's a pip of a car. I just decided it didn't fit my new image. I thought I should get something sportier. It was the darnedest thing how it happened. Louise came over to take me driving and she said she heard about how the Dealer was going out of business. And so, of course, we had to hurry over to stock up on Metamucil. And then while we were there I bought a car."

"You bought a car from Dougie?"

"You bet. And it's a beaut."

I cut Mooner the death look, but it was lost on him. Mooner's emotional range didn't go that far beyond mellow.

"Wait'll you see your granny's car," Mooner said. "It's an *excel-lent* car."

"It's a babe car," Grandma said. "I look just like Christie Brink-ley in it."

David Brinkley, I could believe. Christie was a stretch. But hey, if it made Grandma happy then it was fine by me. "What kind of car is it?"

"It's a 'vette," Grandma said. "And it's red."

EIGHT

SO MY GRANDMOTHER has a red Corvette, and I have a blue '53 Buick and a big zit on my chin. Hell, it could be worse, I told myself. The zit could be on my nose.

"Besides," Grandma said, "I know how you like the Buick. I didn't want to take the Buick away from you."

I nodded and tried to smile. "Excuse me," I said. "I'm going to wash my hands for dinner."

I calmly walked to the bathroom, closed and locked the door, looked at myself in the mirror over the sink, and sniffled. A tear leaked out of my left eye. Get a grip, I told myself. It's just a pimple. It'll go away. Yes, but what about the Buick? I asked. The Buick was worrisome. The Buick showed no signs of going away. Another tear leaked out. You're too emotional, I said to the person in the mirror. You're making a big deal over nothing. Probably this is just a temporary hormone imbalance resulting from lack of sleep.

I splashed some water on my face and blew my nose. At least I could sleep easier tonight knowing I had an alarm on the door. I didn't so much mind Ranger visiting at two in the morning . . . it was that I hated him sneaking up on me. What if I was drooling in my sleep, and he was sitting there watching me? What if he was sitting there staring at my pimple?

MOONER LEFT AFTER dinner and Grandma went to bed early after showing me her new car.

Morelli called at five after nine. "Sorry I couldn't get back to you sooner," he said. "It's been one of those days. How about you?"

"I have a pimple."

"I can't compete with that."

"Do you know a woman named Cynthia Lotte? Rumor has it she was Homer Ramos's girlfriend."

"From what I know about Homer, he changed girlfriends like other men change socks."

"Have you ever met his father?"

"I've spoken to him a couple times."

"And your opinion?"

"Typical good ol' boy Greek gun-runner. Haven't seen him lately." There was a pause. "Grandma Mazur still with you?"

"Yep."

Morelli did a big sigh.

"My mom wants to know if you'd like to come to dinner tomorrow. She's making a pork roast."

"Sure," Morelli said. "You're going to be there, right?"

"Me and Grandma and Bob."

"Oh boy," Morelli said.

I hung up, took Bob for a walk around the block, gave Rex a grape, and then watched television for a while. I fell asleep somewhere in the middle of the hockey game and woke up in time to catch the last half of a show on serial killers and forensics. When the show was over I triple-checked the locks on the front door and hung the motion detector from the doorknob. If someone opened the door, the alarm would go off. I sure hoped that didn't happen, because after the show on forensics I felt a little freaked. Ranger staring at my pimple didn't seem like much of a concern compared to someone cutting my tongue out and taking it home for his frozen-tongue collection. Just to play it safe I went into the kitchen and hid all the knives. No sense in making it easy for a madman to sneak in and carve me up with my own steak knife. Then I took my gun out of the cookie jar and tucked it under a couch cushion in case I needed to get at it quickly.

I turned the lights out and crawled under the quilt on my makeshift bed on the couch. Grandma was snoring in the bedroom. The freezer whirred into the defrost cycle in the kitchen. There was the distant sound of a car door slamming shut in the parking lot. All normal sounds, I told myself. Then why was my heart beating with this sickening thud? Because I watched that stupid serial killer show on television, that's why.

Okay, forget the show. Go to sleep. Think about something else.

I closed my eyes. And I thought about Alexander Ramos, who probably wasn't too far down the road from the insane killers who were giving me heart palpitations. What was the deal with Ramos? Here was a man who controlled the flow of clandestine arms worldwide, and he had to flag down a stranger to buy him some cigarettes. The word on the street was that Ramos was sick, but he hadn't seemed senile or crazy when he was with me. A little aggressive, maybe. Not a lot of patience. I guess there are some places where his behavior would have seemed erratic, but this was Jersey, and it looked to me like Ramos fit right in.

I'd been so flustered I'd hardly spoken to him. Now that some time had passed I had a million questions. Not only did I want to talk to him some more, I had a bizarre curiosity to see the inside of his house. When I was a kid my parents took me to Washington to see the White House. We stood in line for an hour, and then we got led through the public rooms. Major rip-off. Who cares about the State Dining Room? I wanted to see the kitchen. I wanted to see the President's bathroom. And now I wanted to see Alexander Ramos's living room rug. I wanted to browse through Hannibal's suite and take a look in the fridge. I mean, they'd all been on the cover of *Newsweek*. So they must be interesting, right?

This led me to thinking about Hannibal, who hadn't looked interesting at all. And about Cynthia Lotte, who didn't look all that interesting either. How about Cynthia Lotte naked with Homer Ramos? Still not interesting. Okay, how about Cynthia Lotte and Batman? That was better. Wait a minute, how about Hannibal Ramos and Batman? *Sick!* I ran into the bathroom and brushed my teeth. I don't think I'm especially homophobic, but I draw the line at Batman.

When I came out of the bathroom someone was fumbling at my front door, making scraping sounds at the lock. The door popped open and the alarm went off. The door caught on the security chain, and when I got to the foyer I could see Mooner looking in at me between door and jamb.

"Hey dude," he said when I shut the alarm off. "How's it going?"

"What are you doing here?"

"I forgot to give your granny the second key to the car. Had it in my pocket. So I brought it over." He dropped the key in my hand. "Boy, that's a cool alarm you've got. I know someone's who got one that plays the theme song to *Bonanza*. Remember *Bonanza*? Man, that was a great show."

"How did you get my door open?"

"I used a pick. I didn't want to bother you so late at night."

"That was thoughtful of you."

"The Mooner always tries to be thoughtful." He gave me the peace sign and ambled off, down the hall.

I closed the door and reset the alarm. Grandma was still snoring in my bedroom, and Bob hadn't budged from his place by the couch. If the serial murderer showed up in this apartment, I was on my own.

I looked in on Rex and explained to him about the alarm. "Nothing to worry about," I said. "I know it's loud but at least you were already up and running." Rex was balanced on his little hamster butt, front legs dangling in front of him, whiskers twitching, parchment thin ears vibrating, black ball-bearing eyes wide open. I

666

dropped a chunk of cracker into his food cup, and he rushed over, shoved it into his cheek pouch, and disappeared into his soup can. Rex knows how to handle a crisis.

I returned to the couch and pulled the quilt up to my chin. No more thoughts about Batman, I told myself. No more peeking under his big rubber codpiece. And no serial killers. And no Joe Morelli since it might be tempting to call him up and beg him to marry me . . . or something.

Then what should I think about? How about Grandma's snoring? It was loud enough to make me hearing-impaired for the rest of my life. I'd put the pillow over my head, but then I might not hear the alarm and the serial killer would come in and cut out my tongue. Oh shit, now I was thinking about the serial killer again!

There was another sound at my door. I tried to see my watch in the dark. It had to be around one A.M. The door clicked open and the alarm sounded. Undoubtedly Ranger. I ran a hand through my hair and checked to be sure the Band-Aid was still in place. I was wearing flannel boxers and a white T-shirt and had a last-minute panic attack that my nipples might be showing through the T-shirt. Rats! I should have thought of this sooner. I hurried to the foyer to silence the alarm but before I reached the door a pair of shears was shoved between the door and the jamb, the shears snipped through the security chain, and the door flew open.

"Hey," I said to Ranger, "that's cheating!"

But it wasn't Ranger who stepped through the open door. It was Morris Munson. He ripped the alarm off the doorknob and stabbed it with the shears. The alarm gave one last squeak and died. Grandma was still snoring. Bob was still sprawled next to the couch. And Rex was standing at attention, doing his grizzly bear impersonation.

"Surprise," Munson said, closing the door, stepping further into the foyer.

My stun gun, pepper spray, bludgeoning flashlight, and nail file were all in my shoulder bag, which was hanging on a hook, out of reach, behind Munson. My gun was somewhere in the couch, but

I really didn't want to use my gun. Guns scare the hell out of me . . . and they kill people. Killing people isn't high on my favorite-things-to-do list.

Probably I should have been happy to see Munson. I mean, I'm supposed to be looking for him, right? And here he is, doing a B & E in my apartment.

"Stop right where you are," I said. "You're in violation of your bond, and you're under arrest."

"You ruined my life," he said. "I did everything for you, and you ruined my life. You took everything. The house, the car, the furniture—"

"That's your ex-wife, you dope! Do I look like your ex-wife?"

"Sort of."

"Not at all!" Especially since his ex-wife was dead, with tire tracks up her back. "How did you find me?"

"I followed you home one day. You're hard to miss in that Buick."

"You don't actually think I'm your wife, do you?"

His mouth pulled back into a loopy grin. "No, but if they think I'm really flipped out I can plead insanity. Poor distraught husband goes berserk. I've laid all the groundwork with you. Now all I have to do is carve you up and set you on fire, and I'm home free."

"You're crazy!"

"See, it's working already."

"Well, you won't have any luck, because I'm a professional trained in self-defense."

"Get real. I asked around about you. You're trained in nothing. You used to sell ladies' underpants until you got fired."

"I wasn't fired. I was laid off."

"Whatever." He opened his hand, palm up, to show me he held a switchblade. He pressed the button, and the blade flicked out. "Now, if you just cooperate it won't be so bad. It isn't as if I want to kill you. I thought I'd just stab you a couple times to make it look good. Maybe cut off a nipple."

"No way!"

"Listen, lady, give me a break, okay? I'm facing a murder charge here."

"This is stupid. This will never work! Have you talked to a lawyer about this?"

"I can't afford a lawyer! My wife freaking cleaned me out."

I was inching my way back toward the couch as we talked. Now that I knew about his plan to cut off a nipple, using the gun didn't seem like such a bad idea.

"Hold still," he said. "You're not going to make me chase you all around the apartment, are you?"

"I just want to sit down. I don't feel so good." And this wasn't so far from the truth. My heart was flopping around in my chest, and the roots of my hair had started to sweat. I plopped down on the couch and dipped my fingers into the space between the cushions. No gun. I ran my hand under the cushion next to me. Still no gun."

"What are you doing?" he wanted to know.

"I'm looking for a cigarette," I said. "I need one last cigarette to steady my nerves."

"Forget it. Time's up." He lunged at me with the knife, I rolled away, and he plunged the knife into the couch cushion.

I let out a shriek and scrambled on my hands and knees, looking for the gun, finding it deep under the middle cushion. Munson came at me again, and I shot him in the foot.

Bob opened one eye.

"Son of a bitch!" Munson yelled, dropping the knife, grabbing his foot. "Son of a bitch!"

I backed away and held him at gunpoint. "You're under arrest."

"I'm shot. I'm shot. I'm gonna die. I'm gonna bleed to death."

We both looked down at his foot. The blood wasn't exactly pouring out. A small spot by the little toe.

"I must have just nicked you," I said.

"Jesus," he said, "what a lousy shot. You were right on top of me. How could you have missed my foot?"

"Want me to try again?"

"It's all ruined now. You ruined it just like always. Every time I have a plan you have to go ruin it. I had it all worked out. I was going to come over here, cut off a nipple and set you on fire. And now it's ruined." He threw his hands into the air in disgust. "Women!" He turned and started limping toward the door.

"Hey," I yelled, "where are you going?"

"I'm leaving. My toe is killing me. And look at my shoe. It has a big rip in it. You think shoes grow on trees? See, this is what I'm talking about. You have no regard for anybody but yourself. You women are all alike. Just take, take, take. Gimme, gimme, gimme."

"Don't worry about the shoe. The state will see to it that you get a new one." Along with a nice orange jumpsuit and ankle chains.

"Forget it. I'm not going back to jail until everyone's convinced I'm insane."

"You've made a believer out of me. And besides, I've got a gun, and I'll shoot you again if I have to."

He held his hands in the air. "Go ahead and shoot."

Not only couldn't I bring myself to shoot an unarmed man, but I was out of bullets. They'd been on my shopping list. Milk, bread, bullets.

I raced past him, snatched my shoulder bag off the wall hook and dumped everything onto the floor, since that was the fastest route to finding my cuffs and pepper spray. Munson and I both dived at the scattered junk, and he won. He snatched the pepper spray off the floor and hopped to the door. "If you come after me I'll spray you," he said.

I watched him do a sort of gallop down the hall, favoring the injured foot. He stopped at the elevator doors and shook the pepper canister at me. "I'll be back," he said. Then he stepped into the elevator and disappeared.

I closed and locked the door. Terrific . . . for what that was worth. I went to the kitchen and searched for something comforting. The cake was gone. The pie was gone. No Mounds bars hid forgotten in the dark recesses of a cupboard. No booze. No Cheez Doodles. The peanut butter jar was empty.

Bob and I tried a couple of olives, but they weren't totally what the situation called for. "They need frosting," I said to Bob.

I scooped up the mess on the foyer floor and dumped it back into my shoulder bag. I put the broken alarm on the counter, turned the lights off, and returned to the couch. I lay there in the dark, and Munson's parting threat kept replaying in my mind. It really didn't matter if he was crazy by design or for real; the bottom line was that I'd come close to being nippleless. Probably I shouldn't go to sleep until I got a bolt put on the door. He'd said he'd be back, and I didn't know if he meant in an hour or a day.

Trouble was, I could hardly keep my eyes open. I tried singing, but I drifted off somewhere in the middle of "Ninety-nine Bottles of Beer on the Wall." Last I remember I was at fifty-seven bottles of beer, and then I was jolted awake with the feeling that I wasn't alone in the room. I lay perfectly still, my heart skipping beats, my lungs in suspended animation. There had been no sound of shoes treading across carpet. No deranged-madman body odor disturbed the air around me. There was just the irrational knowledge that someone was in my space.

And then, without warning, fingertips settled on my wrist, and I was galvanized into action. Adrenaline spiked into my system, and I catapulted myself off the couch into the intruder.

We were both caught by surprise, the two of us crashing into the coffee table, going down to the floor in a tangle of arms and legs. And in an instant I was pinned beneath him, which was not an entirely unpleasant experience once I realized it was Ranger. We were groin to groin, chest to chest, with his hands locked around my wrists. A moment passed while we did nothing but breathe.

"Nice tackle, babe," he said. And then he kissed me. No doubt about the intention this time. Not the sort of kiss you'd give your cousin, for instance. More like the sort of kiss a man would give a woman when he wanted to rip her clothes off and give her a reason to sing the Hallelujah Chorus.

He deepened the kiss and ran his hands under my T-shirt,

splaying them flat on my abdomen. Thank God I still had both of them! A rush of electric heat contracted my nipples.

My bedroom door cracked open and Grandma stuck her head out. "Is everything okay out here?"

Great. *Now* she wakes up!

"Yep. Everything's just fine," I said.

"Is that Ranger on top of you?"

"He was showing me a self-defense move."

"I wouldn't mind knowing some self-defense," Grandma said.

"Well, we were sort of finishing up here."

Ranger rolled off me, onto his back. "If she wasn't your grandmother I'd shoot her."

"Darn," Grandma said, "I always miss the good stuff."

I popped up onto my feet and adjusted my T-shirt. "You didn't miss much. I was just going to make some hot chocolate. Do you want some?"

"Sure," Grandma said. "I'll go get my bathrobe on."

Ranger looked up at me. It was dark in the room, with only a shaft of light coming from the open bedroom door. Still, it was light enough for me to see that his mouth was smiling but his eyes were serious. "Saved by the grandma."

"Do you want hot chocolate?"

He followed me out to the kitchen. "Pass."

I gave him the piece of paper with the house design on it. "Here's the diagram you wanted."

"Anything else you want to tell me?"

He knew about Alexander Ramos. "How do you know?"

"I've been watching the beach house. I saw you pick Ramos up."

I poured milk into two mugs and put them in the microwave. "What's the deal with him? He flagged me down to mooch a cigarette."

Ranger smiled. "You ever try to quit smoking?"

I shook my head.

"Then you wouldn't understand."

"Did you used to smoke?"

"I used to everything." He picked the motion detector off the counter and turned it over in his hand. "I noticed the broken security chain."

"You weren't my only visitor tonight."

"What happened?"

"A failure to appear broke into my apartment. I shot him in the foot, and he left."

"You must not have read the *Bounty Hunter Handbook*. We're supposed to catch the bad guys and drag their ass back to jail."

I mixed the cocoa into the hot milk. "Ramos wants me to return today. He offered me a job as his cigarette smuggler."

"That's not a job you want to accept. Alexander can be impulsive and erratic and paranoid. He's on medication, but he doesn't always take it. Hannibal's hired bodyguards to keep an eye on the old man, but he makes them look like amateurs. Sneaks out on them every chance he gets. There's a power struggle going on between him and Hannibal, and you don't want to get caught in the crossfire."

"Isn't this nice," Grandma said, shuffling into the kitchen, taking her mug of chocolate. "It's much more fun living with you. We never had men visiting in the middle of the night when I lived with your mother."

Ranger returned the alarm to the counter. "I have to go. Enjoy your hot chocolate."

I walked him to the door. "Is there anything else you want me to do? Check your mail? Water your plants?"

"My mail is being forwarded to my lawyer. And I'm watering my own plants."

"So, you feel safe in the Batcave?"

The corners of his mouth curved into the hint of a smile. He leaned forward and kissed me at the base of my neck, just above my T-shirt collar. "Sweet dreams."

Before he left, he said good-night to Grandma, who was still in the kitchen.

"What a nice, polite young man," Grandma said. "And he's got an excellent package."

I went straight to her closet, found the bottle of booze, and dumped some into my cocoa.

THE NEXT MORNING, Grandma and I were both hung over.

"I've gotta stop drinking cocoa so late at night," Grandma said. "I feel like my eyes are going to explode. Maybe I should go get checked for glaucoma."

"Better yet, how about getting checked for the level of hooch in your bloodstream?"

I took a couple aspirin and dragged myself out to the parking lot. Habib and Mitchell were there, sitting waiting in a green minivan with two kiddie seats in the back but no kiddies.

"Nice stakeout car," I said. "Fits right in."

"Don't start," Mitchell said. "I'm not in a good mood."

"It's your wife's car, right?"

He gave me a black look.

"Just to make life easier for you, so you don't get lost, you might as well know I'm going to the office first thing."

"I *hate* that place," Habib said. "It is cursed! It is evil!"

I drove to the office and parked in front. Habib stayed half a block back and kept the motor running.

"Hey, girlfriend," Lula said. "Where's Bob?"

"He's with Grandma. They're sleeping in today."

"Looks like you should have slept in, too. You look awful. If the rest of your face was as black as the circles under your eyes you could move into my neighborhood. 'Course, the good news is what with the dark circles and bloodshot eyes you don't hardly notice that big nasty pimple."

And the *really* good news was that I didn't give a fig about the pimple today. Funny how a little thing like a life-threatening experience can put a pimple into perspective. What I cared about today was nailing Munson. I didn't want to put in another sleepless night, worrying about going up in flames.

"I have a hunch Morris Munson is back at his row house this

674

morning," I told Lula. "I'm going over there, and I'm going to stomp on him."

"I'll go with you," Lula said. "I wouldn't mind stompin' on someone today. In fact, I'm in a real stompin' *mood*."

I took my gun out of my shoulder bag. "I'm sort of out of bullets," I said to Connie. "You have any extras lying around?"

Vinnie stuck his head out of his office. "You're putting bullets in your gun? Did I hear right? What's the occasion?"

"I have bullets in my gun a lot," I said, eyes narrowed, feeling testy. "In fact, just last night I shot someone."

There was a collective gasp.

"Who'd you shoot?" Lula asked.

"Morris Munson. He broke into my apartment."

Vinnie rushed over. "Where is he? Is he dead? You didn't get him in the back, did you? I keep telling everyone—*not in the back*!"

"I didn't shoot him in the back. I shot him in the foot."

"So? Where is he?"

"Omigod," Lula said. "You shot him in the foot with your last bullet, didn't you? You blew off a little piggy and ran out of bullets." She shook her head. "Don't you just hate when that happens?"

Connie returned from the back room with a box of bullets. "You sure you want these?" she asked me. "You don't look too good. I don't know if it's a good idea to give a woman a box of bullets when she's got a pimple."

I put four rounds in my gun, and dropped the box into my shoulder bag. "I'll be fine."

"This here's a woman with a plan," Lula said.

This here was a woman with a hangover who just wanted to get through the day.

Halfway to Munson's house on Rockwell Street I pulled to the curb and threw up. Habib and Mitchell grimaced behind me.

"Must have been some night," Lula said.

"I don't want to think about it." And that was more than just an expression. I *really* didn't want to think about it. I mean, what the hell was this thing going on between me and Ranger? I must be crazy! And I couldn't believe I'd actually sat drinking bourbon and hot chocolate with Grandma. I'm no good at drinking. I get drunk on two bottles of beer. I felt like my brain had been beamed into outer space and my body had been left behind.

I drove another quarter-mile and pulled into the McDonald's drive-through for my never-fail hangover remedy: french fries and a Coke.

"As long as we're here I might as well get a little something, too," Lula said. "Egg McMuffin, breakfast fries, chocolate shake, and a Big Mac," she yelled across me.

I felt myself go green. "That's a snack?"

"Yeah, you're right," she said. "Hold the breakfast fries."

The guy in the drive-through window handed me the bag of food and looked into the Buick's backseat. "Where's your dog?"

"Home."

"Too bad. That was pretty cool last time. Lady, that was a mountain of—"

I stepped on the gas and took off. By the time we got to Munson's house the food was gone, and I felt much better.

"What makes you think this dude's come back here?" Lula asked.

"Just a feeling I have. He needed to bandage his foot and get a new pair of shoes. If it was me, I'd go home to do those things. And it was late at night. Since I was already in my house I'd want to sleep in my own bed."

We couldn't tell anything from the outside of his house. The windows were dark. No sign of life inside. I drove around the block and took the alley to the garage. Lula jumped out and looked in the garage window.

"He's here, all right," she said, climbing back into Big Blue. "At least, his wreck of a car is here."

"Do you have your stun gun and pepper spray?"

"Does a chicken have a pecker? I could invade Bulgaria with the shit I've got in my handbag."

I drove back to the front of the house and dropped Lula off to guard the front door. Then I parked the car two houses down, out of Munson's line of sight, in the alley. Habib and Mitchell parked behind me in the kiddie car, locked their doors, and opened their McDonald's breakfast bags.

I cut through two yards, came up to the back of Munson's house, and carefully looked in his kitchen window. Nothing happening. A box of Band-Aids and a roll of paper towels on the kitchen table. Am I a genius, or what? I stepped back and looked up to the second floor. There was the very faint sound of running water. Munson was taking a shower. Boy, life didn't get much better than this.

I tried the door. Locked. I tried the windows. Locked. I was about to break one when Lula opened the back door.

"Not much of a lock on the front door," she said.

I had to be the only person in the entire world who couldn't pick a lock.

We stood listening in the kitchen. The water was still running overhead. Lula had pepper spray in one hand and her stun gun in the other. I had one hand free and one hand holding cuffs. We crept up the stairs and paused at the top. The row house was small. Two bedrooms and a bath on the second floor. The doors to the bedrooms were open, and the bedrooms were empty. The bathroom door was closed. Lula stood to one side, poised with the spray. I stood to the other side. We both knew exactly how to do this, because we watched the cop shows on television. Munson wasn't known to carry a gun, and it was unlikely he'd be armed in the shower, but it didn't hurt to be careful.

"On the count of three," I mouthed to Lula, my hand on the doorknob. "One, two, three!"

NINE

"WAIT A MINUTE," Lula said, "he's gonna be naked. Maybe we don't want to see this. I've seen a lot of ugly men in my day. I'm not so anxious to see any more."

"I don't care about the naked part," I said. "I care about the part that he won't have a knife or a propane torch."

"Good point."

"Okay, I'm counting again. Get ready. One, two, three!"

I opened the bathroom door, and we both jumped in.

Munson ripped the shower curtain aside. "What the hell?"

"You're under arrest," Lula said. "And we'd appreciate it if you'd get a towel on account of I don't feel like looking at your sad, shriveled privates."

He had his hair full of shampoo, and he had a big bandage on his foot, which he was protecting with a plastic bag held tight at the ankle with an elastic band.

"I'm crazy!" he shrieked. "I'm freaking crazy, and you'll never take me alive!"

"Yeah, whatever," Lula said, handing him a towel. "You want to shut that water off now?"

Munson took the towel and snapped it back at Lula.

"Hey!" Lula said. "Hold on here. You snap that towel at me again, and you're gonna get a snootful of pepper spray."

Munson snapped it again. "Fat, fat, fatty," he sang.

Lula forgot about the pepper spray and lunged for his neck. Munson reached up and turned the shower spray on her and jumped out of the shower. I tried to grab him, but he was wet and slippery with soap, and Lula was flailing around, trying to get away from the water.

"Spray him!" I yelled to Lula. "Electrocute him! Shoot him! Do something!"

Munson knocked the two of us aside and streaked down the stairs. He ran the length of the house and out the back door. I was close behind, and Lula was about ten feet behind me. His foot had to be killing him, but he ran flat out through two yards and then cut off to the alley. I took a flying leap and caught him square in the small of his back. The two of us went down to the ground and rolled around, locked together, swearing and clawing. Munson was trying to scramble away, and I was trying to hang on and cuff him. It would have been easier if he'd had clothes to grab hold of. As it was, I didn't really want to grab what was available.

"Hit him where it hurts!" Lula was yelling. "Hit him where it hurts!"

So I did. A person reaches a point where she just doesn't want to roll around anymore. I hauled back and gave Munson a knee in the gonads.

"Ulk," Munson said, and assumed the fetal position.

Lula and I pried his hands away from Mr. Sad Sack and cuffed him behind his back.

"Wish I had a movie of you wrestlin' with this guy," Lula said. "It reminded me of that joke about the midget at the nudist colony who kept sticking his nose in everyone's business."

Mitchell and Habib had gotten out of their car and were standing a few feet away looking pained.

"I could feel that all the way over here," Mitchell said. "If we get the word that we have to rough you up, I'm wearing a cup."

Lula ran back to the house to get a blanket and lock up. And Habib and Mitchell and I dragged Munson over to the Buick. When Lula got back we wrapped Munson up, tossed him into the backseat and drove him to the police station on North Clinton. We took him to the back entrance, which had a drive-in.

"Just like McDonald's," Lula said. "Except we're dropping off instead of picking up."

I rang the buzzer and identified myself. A moment later Carl Costanza opened the back door and looked over at the Buick. "Now what?" he said.

"I have a body in the backseat. Morris Munson. FTA."

Carl stared into the car window and grinned. "He's naked."

I blew out a sigh. "You aren't going to give me a hard time with this, are you?"

"Hey, Juniak," Costanza yelled, "come take a look at this naked guy. Guess who he belongs to!"

"Okay," Lula said to Munson, "end of the line. You can get out now."

"No," Munson said, "I'm not getting out."

"The hell you aren't," Lula said.

Juniak and two other cops joined Costanza at the door. Everyone was grinning dopey cop grins.

"Sometimes I think this is a really crappy job," one of the cops said. "But then there are other times when you get to see stuff like this, and it makes it all worthwhile. Why's the naked guy got a plastic bag on his foot?"

"I shot him," I said.

Costanza and Juniak exchanged glances. "I don't want to know about it," Costanza said. "I didn't hear anything."

Lula gave Munson her junkyard-dog look. "You don't haul your bony white carcass out of this car, I'm coming back there."

"Fuck you," Munson said. "Fuck your fat ass."

The cops all sucked in a breath and took a step backward.

"That does it," Lula said. "You put me in a bad mood now. You went and wrecked my good disposition. I'm gonna come back there and root you out like the little pencil-dick rodent you are." She heaved herself out of the car and wrenched the back door open.

And Munson jumped out of the car.

I wrapped the blanket around him, and we all shuffled into the police station, except for Lula, who has a phobia about police stations. She backed out of the drive-in, found a space in the lot, and parked.

I cuffed Munson to the bench by the docket lieutenant, handed my paperwork in, and got my body receipt. Next on my list of things to do was visit Brian Simon.

I was on my way to the third floor when Costanza stopped me. "If you're looking for Simon, don't bother. He took off the instant he heard you were here." He gave me the once-over. "I don't want to be insulting, or anything, but you look like hell."

I was dusty from head to foot, the knee was torn out of my Levi's, my hair was in the throes of a *very* bad day, and then there was the pimple.

"You look like you haven't slept in days," Costanza said.

"That's because I haven't."

"I could talk to Morelli."

"It's not Morelli. It's my grandmother. She's moved in with me, and she snores." Not to mention I had the Mooner in my life. And madmen. And Ranger.

"So let me get this straight. You're living with your granny and with Simon's dog?"

"Yeah."

Costanza grinned. "Hey, Juniak," he yelled, "wait'll you hear this." He looked back to me. "No wonder Morelli's been in such a foul mood."

"Tell Simon I was looking for him."

"You can count on it," Costanza said.

I left the police station and drove to the office and went in with

681

Lula so I could bask in my bounty-hunter excellence. Lula and I had captured our man. It was a big capture, too. A homicidal maniac. Well okay, maybe it hadn't been an entirely flawless operation, but hey, we *got* him.

I slapped the body receipt down on Connie's desk. "Are we good, or what?" I said.

Vinnie popped his head out of his office. "Did I just hear news of an apprehension?"

"Morris Munson," Connie said. "Signed, sealed, and delivered."

Vinnie rocked back on his heels, hands in pants pockets, smile stretching the width of his face. "Lovely."

"He didn't even set either of us on fire this time," Lula said. "We were good. We hauled his ass off to the clink."

Connie eyeballed Lula. "Do you know you're all wet?"

"Yeah. Well, we rousted the jerk out of the shower."

Vinnie's eyebrows shot up into his forehead. "Are you telling me you arrested him naked?"

"It wouldn't have been so bad if it wasn't for him running out of the house and down the street," Lula said.

Vinnie shook his head, the smile broader than ever. "I *love* this job."

Connie gave me my fee; I gave Lula her share and went home to change.

Grandma was still there, getting ready for her driving lesson. She was dressed in her purple warm-up suit, platform sneakers, and a long-sleeved T-shirt that had "Eat My Shorts" written across the chest. "I met a man in the elevator today," she said. "And I'm taking him to dinner with us tonight."

"What's his name?"

"Myron Landowsky. He's an old fart, but I figure I have to start somewhere." She took her purse off the counter, tucked it into the crook of her arm, and gave Bob a pat on the head. "Bob's been a good boy today, except for eating that roll of toilet paper. Oh yeah, and I was hoping we could ride over with you and Joseph. Myron don't drive after dark, on account of his night vision is shot."

"No problem."

I made myself a fried-egg sandwich for lunch, changed my jeans, brushed my hair into a half-assed ponytail, and plastered a ton of concealer over my pimple. I gunked up my lashes with mascara and stared at myself in the mirror. Stephanie, Stephanie, Stephanie, I said. What are you doing?

I was working myself up to going back to the shore, that's what I was doing. I was having brain pain that I'd screwed up my opportunity to talk to Alexander Ramos. I'd sat across the table from him like a big doofus yesterday. We were doing surveillance on the Ramos family, and when I got unexpectedly let into the chicken coop I didn't ask the rooster a single question. I was sure Ranger's advice was sound, that I should stay away from Alexander Ramos, but it felt wimpy not to go back and try to take better advantage of the situation.

I grabbed my jacket and clipped the leash onto Bob's collar. I stopped in the kitchen to say good-bye to Rex and to put my gun back into the cookie jar. I didn't think it'd be a good idea to be packing while I chauffeured Alexander Ramos around. It'd be hard to explain the gun if I got patted down by Ramos or his babysitters.

Joyce Barnhardt was parked in my lot when I came down. "Nice pizza face," she said.

I guessed the concealer wasn't totally effective. "You want something?"

"You know what I want."

Joyce wasn't the only idiot loitering in my lot. Mitchell and Habib were parked at the rear. I walked back to them, and Mitchell rolled the driver's-side window down.

"Do you see that woman I was just talking to?" I asked. "That's Joyce Barnhardt. She's the bond enforcement agent Vinnie hired to bring Ranger in. If you want to get Ranger, you need to follow Joyce around."

Both men looked over at Joyce.

"If a woman dressed like that in my village we would throw stones at her until she was dead," Habib said.

"Nice hooters, though," Mitchell said. "Are they real?"

"As far as I know."

"What do you think her chances are of catching Ranger?"

"None."

"What are your chances?"

"None."

"We were told to watch you," Mitchell said. "That's what we're going to do."

"Too bad," Habib said. "I do like to look at the whore, Joyce Barnhardt."

"Are you going to follow me around all afternoon?"

Color crept up Mitchell's neck into his cheeks. "We got some other things to do."

I smiled. "Have to get the car home?"

"Fuckin' car pool," Mitchell said. "My kid's got a soccer game."

I went back to the Buick and loaded Bob into the backseat. At least I didn't have to worry about being followed, thanks to the soccer game. I looked in the rearview mirror just to make sure. No Habib and Mitchell—but Joyce was tailing me. I pulled to the side of the road and stopped, and Joyce stopped a few feet behind me. I got out of the car and walked back to her.

"Knock it off," I said.

"It's a free country."

"Are you going to follow me all day?"

"Probably."

"Suppose I ask you nicely."

"Get real."

I looked at her car. A new black SUV. Then I looked at my car. Big Blue. I walked back to Blue and got in. "Hang on," I said to Bob. Then I threw the car into reverse.

CRASH.

I changed gears and moved forward a few feet. I got out and

surveyed the damage. The SUV bumper was Crumple City and Joyce was fighting with the deployed airbag. The back of the Buick was perfect. Not a scratch. I returned to the Buick and drove away. It's not a good idea to mess with a woman who has a pimple.

IT WAS OVERCAST in Deal, with a mist coming off the ocean. Gray sky, gray ocean, gray sidewalks, big pink house belonging to Alexander Ramos. I rolled past the house, made a U-turn, passed the house a second time, turned, and parked at the corner. I wondered if Ranger was watching. My guess was yes. No vans or trucks were parked on the street. That meant he'd have to be in a house. And the house would have to be unoccupied. Easy to tell the unoccupied beachfront houses. Much more difficult to tell the unoccupied houses on the road. None of those were shuttered.

I checked my watch. Same time, same place. No Ramos. After ten minutes my phone rang.

"Yo," Ranger said.

"Yo, yourself."

"You're not very good at following directions."

"You mean about not taking the cigarette smuggler job? Seemed too good to pass up."

"You're going to be careful, right?"

"Right."

"Our man's having problems getting out of the house. Hang in there."

"How do you know this? Where are you?"

"Get ready. It's show time," Ranger said. And he disconnected.

Alexander Ramos was through the gate and running across the road to my car. He wrenched the passenger door open and dove in. "Go!" he shouted. "Go!"

I took off from the curb and saw two men in suits round the gate and sprint toward us. I floored the Buick, and we roared away.

Ramos didn't look good at all. He was pale and sweating and gasping for air. "Christ," he said, "I didn't think I was going to make it. It's a goddamn freak show in that house. Good thing I looked out the window when I did and saw your car. I was going nuts in there."

"Do you want to go to the store?"

"No. That's the first place they'll look. I can't go to Sal's, either."

I was getting a real bad feeling here. Like, this was one of the days Alexander didn't take his medicine.

"Take me to Asbury Park," he said. "I know a place in Asbury Park."

"Why were those men chasing you?"

"No one was chasing me."

"But I saw them."

"You didn't see anything."

Ten minutes later he pointed with his finger. "Over there. Stop at that bar."

The three of us went into the bar, sat at a table, and went through the same ritual as the last time. The bartender brought a bottle of ouzo to the table without being asked. Ramos slugged two back and then lit up.

"Everyone knows you," I said.

He looked around at the scarred booths that lined one wall and the dark mahogany bar that ran the length of the other. Behind the bar was the usual array of bottles. Behind the bottles was the standard bar mirror. One stool was occupied, at the far end of the room. The man stared down, into his drink. "I've been coming here for a few years," Ramos said. "I come here when I need to get away from the freaks."

"The freaks?"

"My family. I raised three worthless sons who spend money faster than I can make it."

"You're Alexander Ramos, right? I saw your picture in *Newsweek* a while back. I'm sorry about Homer. I read about the fire in the paper."

He poured out another shot. "One less freak to deal with."

I felt the blood drain from my face. It was a chilling statement for a father to make.

He took a long pull on his cigarette, closed his eyes, and savored the moment. "They think the old man don't know what's going on. Well, they're wrong. The old man knows everything. I didn't build this business by being stupid. And I didn't build it by being nice, either, so they better watch their step."

I glanced back at the door. "Are you sure we're safe here?"

"Any time you're with Alexander Ramos, you're safe. Nobody touches Alexander Ramos."

Yeah, right. That's why we're hiding out in a bar in Asbury Park. This was feeling like Bizarro Land.

"I just don't like to be bothered when I smoke," he said. "I don't want to have to look at all the leeches."

"Why don't you get rid of them. Tell them to leave your house?"

He squinted at me through a haze of smoke. "How would it look? They're family." He dropped his cigarette on the floor and stepped on it. "There's only one way to get rid of family."

Oh boy.

"We're done here," he said. "I have to get back before my son runs me into the ground."

"Hannibal?"

"Mr. Big Shot. I should never have sent him to college." He stood and dropped a wad of money onto the table. "How about you? Did you go to college?"

"Yep."

"What are you doing now?"

I was afraid if I told him I was a bounty hunter he'd shoot me. "A little of this and a little of that," I said.

"Big fancy education and you're doing a little of this?"

"You sound like my mother."

"You probably give your mother angina."

That made me smile. He was scary crazy, but I sort of liked

him. He reminded me of my uncle Punky. "Do you know who killed Homer?"

"Homer killed himself."

"I read in the paper that they didn't find a gun, so they ruled out suicide."

"More than one way to kill yourself. My son was stupid and greedy."

"Uh . . . you didn't kill him, did you?"

"I was in Greece when he was shot."

We locked eyes. We both knew that didn't answer the question. Ramos could have ordered his son's execution.

I drove him back to Deal and parked on a side street, a block from the pink house.

"Any time you want to make twenty bucks you just show up on the corner," Ramos said.

I smiled. I hadn't taken any money from him, and probably I wouldn't be back. "Okay," I said, "keep your eyes open for me."

I took off the second he left the car. I didn't want to risk the guys in the suits spotting me. Ten minutes later, my phone rang.

"Short visit," Ranger said.

"He drinks, he smokes, he goes home."

"Did you learn anything?"

"I think he might be crazy."

"That's the consensus."

Sometimes Ranger sounded like he was straight off the street, and sometimes he sounded like a stockbroker. Ricardo Carlos Manoso, Man of Mystery.

"Do you think Ramos might have killed his own son?"

"He's capable of it."

"He said Homer was killed because he was greedy and stupid. You knew Homer. Was he greedy and stupid?"

"Homer was the weakest of the three sons. He'd always take the easy road. But sometimes the easy road got to be a problem."

"How?"

"Homer would drop a hundred thousand gambling and then

look for an easy way to get the money, like hijacking a truck or dealing some drugs. In the process he'd step on Mob toes or have a run-in with the police, and Hannibal would have to bail him out."

Which led me to wonder what Ranger was doing with Homer Ramos the night Ramos was shot. No point in asking.

"Later, babe," Ranger said. And he was gone.

I GOT HOME in time to walk Bob and take a shower. I spent an extra half-hour styling my hair so it was deceptively casual, as if I really didn't care enough to put in a lot of effort but I was so naturally gorgeous I looked outstanding anyway. It seemed like sacrilege to have such sexy hair and such a big ugly pimple, so I squeezed the pimple until it popped. Then what was left was a big bloody hole in my chin. Crap. I stuck a piece of toilet paper over the hole to stop the bleeding while I did my makeup. I put on black stretch pants and a red sweater with a scoop neck. I peeled the toilet paper off my chin and stood back to take a look. The bags under my eyes were considerably reduced and the hole in my chin was already starting to scab over. Not cover model material, but I'd look okay in dim light.

I heard the front door open and close, and Grandma breezed past the bathroom on her way to the bedroom.

"Boy, this driving is something," Grandma said. "I don't know what I was thinking about, going all those years with no license. I had my lesson this afternoon, and then Melvina came over and took me to the mall and let me drive around in circles. I did real good, too. Except for when I stopped too short once, and Melvina got a sprained back."

The doorbell rang and I opened it to find Myron Landowsky wheezing in the hall. Landowsky always reminded me of a box turtle, with his bald liver-spotted head thrust forward, his shoulders hunched, his trousers hiked up to his armpits.

"I'm telling you, if they don't do something about that elevator I'm moving," he said. "I've lived here for twenty-two years but I'll go if I have to. That old lady Bestler gets in there with her walker and then pushes the hold button when she leaves. I've seen her do it a million times. Takes her fifteen minutes just to get out of the elevator, and then she goes off and the hold button's still on hold. And meantime what are we supposed to do on the third floor? I just had to walk all the way down here."

"Would you like a glass of water?"

"You got any liquor?"

"No."

"Never mind, then." He looked around. "I'm here to see your grandmother. We're going out to dinner."

"She's getting ready. She'll be out in a minute."

There was a rap on the door and Morelli walked in. He looked at me. And then he looked at Myron.

"We're double-dating," I said. "This is Grandma's friend, Myron Landowsky."

"Would you excuse us, please?" Morelli said, pulling me into the hall.

"I gotta go sit down, anyway," Landowsky said. "I had to walk all the way down here."

Morelli closed the door, pinned me against the wall, and kissed me. When he was done I looked myself over to make sure I was still dressed.

"Wow," I said.

His lips brushed against my ear. "If you don't get those old people out of your apartment I'm going to self-combust."

I knew just how he felt. I'd self-combusted in the shower that morning, but it didn't help much.

Grandma opened the door and stuck her head out. "For a minute there I thought you left without us."

WE TOOK THE Buick because we couldn't all fit in Morelli's truck. Morelli drove, Bob sat next to him, and I sat by the window. Grandma and Myron sat in the back, discussing antacids.

"Any news on the Ramos murder?" I asked Morelli.

"Nothing new. Barnes is still convinced it's Ranger."

"No other suspects?"

"Enough suspects to fill Shea Stadium. No evidence against any of them."

"What about the family?"

Morelli cut his eyes at me. "What about them?"

"Are they suspects?"

"Along with everyone else in three countries."

My mother was standing at the door when we parked. It seemed strange to see her standing alone. For the past couple years Grandma had always stood beside her. The mother and daughter whose roles had reversed—Grandma gladly relinquishing parental responsibility, my mother grimly accepting the task, struggling to find a place for an old woman who'd suddenly become a strange hybrid of tolerant mother and rebellious daughter. My father, in the living room, not wanting any part of it.

"Isn't that something," Grandma said. "It looks different from this side of the door."

Bob bolted out of the car and charged my mother, driven by the scent of pork roast wafting from the kitchen.

Myron moved slower. "That's some car you've got," he said. "It's a real beaut. They don't make cars like that anymore. Everything's a piece of junk today. Plastic crap. Made by a bunch of foreigners."

My father drifted into the foyer. This was his kind of talk. My father was a second-generation American, and he loved bashing foreigners, relatives excluded. He dropped back a step when he saw Turtle Man was doing the talking.

"This here's Myron," Grandma said by way of introduction. "He's my date tonight."

"Nice house you got here," Myron said. "You can't beat aluminum siding. That's aluminum siding on it, right?"

Bob was running through the house like a crazy dog, high on food smells. He stopped in the foyer and gave my father's butt a good sniffing.

"Get this dog outta here," my father said. "Where'd this dog come from?"

"This here's Bob," my grandmother said. "He's just saying hello. I saw a show on the television about dogs and they said sniffing butts was like shaking hands. I know all about dogs now. And we're real lucky that they whacked off Bob's doodles before he got too old and got into the habit of humping your leg. They said it's real hard to break a dog of that habit."

"I had a rabbit once when I was a kid that was a leg humper," Myron said. "Boy, once he got a hold of you it was the devil to get him off. And that rabbit didn't care who he went to town on. Got the cat in a stranglehold one time and almost killed it."

I could feel Morelli shaking with silent laughter behind me.

"I'm starved," Grandma said. "Let's eat."

We all took our places at the table, except for Bob, who was eating in the kitchen. My father helped himself to a couple slabs of pork and passed the rest to Morelli. We started the mashed potatoes going around. And the green beans, applesauce, pickle jar, basket of dinner rolls, and pickled beets.

"No pickled beets for me," Myron said. "They give me the runs. I don't know what it is, you get old and everything gives you the runs."

Something to look forward to.

"You're lucky you can go," Grandma said. "You're lucky you don't need Metamucil. Now that the Dealer's out of business, drug prices are gonna go sky high. Other stuff's gonna be outta reach too. I bought my car just in time."

My mother and father both looked up from their plates.

"You bought a car?" my mother asked. "Nobody told me."

"It's a pip, too," Grandma said. "It's a red Corvette."

My mother made the sign of the cross. "Dear God," she said.

TEN

"HOW COULD YOU afford a Corvette?" my father asked. "All you get is Social Security."

"I have money from when I sold the house," Grandma said. "And anyway, I made a good deal. Even the Mooner said I got a good deal."

My mother made another cross. "The Mooner," she said with just a touch of hysteria. "You bought a car from the Mooner?"

"Not from the Mooner," Grandma said. "The Mooner don't sell cars. I bought my car from the Dealer."

"Thank goodness," my mother said, hand to her heart. "For a minute there . . . Well, I'm just glad you went to a car dealer."

"Not a *car* dealer," Grandma told her. "I bought my car from the Metamucil dealer. I paid four hundred and fifty bucks for it. That's good, right?"

"Depends," my father said. "Does it have a motor?"

"I didn't look," Grandma said. "Don't all cars have motors?"

Joe looked pained. He didn't want to be the one to rat on my grandmother for possession of stolen property.

"While Louise and I were looking at the cars, there were a couple men in the Dealer's backyard, and they were going on about Homer Ramos," Grandma said. "They said he was a big car distrib-

693

utor. I didn't know the Ramos family sold cars. I thought they just sold guns."

"Homer Ramos sold *stolen* cars," my father said, head bent over his plate. "Everybody knows that."

I turned to Joe. "Is that true?"

Joe shrugged. Noncommittal. Cop face in place. If you knew how to read the signs, this one said "Ongoing Investigation."

"And that's not all," Grandma said. "He cheated on his wife. He was a real skunk. They said his brother is just as bad. He lives out in California, but he keeps a house here so he can see women on the sly. The whole family is rotten, if you ask me."

"He must be pretty rich if he has two houses," Myron said. "I should be so rich. I'd keep a girlfriend, too."

There was a collective pause while we all wondered what Landowsky would do with a girlfriend.

He reached for the potato bowl, but it was empty.

"Here, let me fill that for you," Grandma said. "Ellen always has more keeping warm on the stove."

Grandma took the bowl and trotted off. "Uh-oh," she said, when she stepped into the kitchen.

My mother and I got up simultaneously and went to investigate. Grandma was standing in the middle of the floor, looking at the cake on the table. "The good news is Bob didn't eat the whole cake," Grandma said. "The bad news is he licked the icing off one side."

Without missing a beat, my mother took a butter knife out of the silverware drawer, scooped some icing off the top of the cake, smeared the icing on the side Bob had licked clean, and sprinkled coconut all around the cake.

"Been a long time since we had a coconut cake," Grandma said. "It looks real pretty."

My mother put the cake on top of the refrigerator, out of Bob's reach. "When you were little you used to lick the icing off all the time," she said to me. "We had a lot of coconut cakes."

Morelli gave me raised eyebrows when I got back.

"Don't ask," I said. "And don't eat the outside part of the cake."

THE PARKING LOT was almost full when we got back to my apartment building. The seniors were home, settled down in front of their televisions.

Myron dangled his house keys at Grandma. "How about coming over for a nightcap, sweetie."

"You men are all alike," my grandmother said. "Only thinking about one thing."

"What's that?" Myron asked.

Grandma scrinched her mouth up. "If I have to tell you, then there's no sense going in for a nightcap."

Morelli walked Grandma and me to my apartment. He let Grandma in, then pulled me aside. "You could come home with me," he said.

It was very tempting. And not for any of the reasons Morelli would hope for. I was dead on my feet. And Morelli didn't snore. I might actually be able to *sleep* at his house. I hadn't slept through the night in so long, I couldn't remember what it was like.

He brushed a kiss across my lips. "Grandma wouldn't mind. She's got Bob."

Eight hours, I thought. All I wanted was eight hours of sleep, and I'd be good as new.

His hands slid under my sweater. "It would be a night to remember."

It would be a night without a drooling, knife-wielding pyromaniac. "It would be heaven," I said, not even realizing I was talking out loud.

He was so close I could feel every part of him, pressed against me. And one of those parts was growing. Ordinarily this would have triggered a corresponding reaction in *my* body. But tonight my thoughts were that this was something I could do without. Still, if it was the price I had to pay for a decent night's sleep, then let's get to it.

"Let me just scoot inside and grab a few things," I told Morelli, imagining myself all cozy in his bed, in a toasty flannel nightshirt. "And I have to tell Grandma."

"You aren't going to go inside and close and lock the door and leave me out here, are you?"

"Why would I do that?"

"I don't know. I just have this feeling . . ."

"You should come in here," Grandma called out. "There's a show on the television, and it's all about alligators." She cocked her head. "What's that strange sound? It sounds like a cricket."

"Shit," Morelli said.

Morelli and I knew what the sound was. It was his pager. Morelli was trying hard to ignore it.

I was the one to cave first. "You have to look at it sooner or later," I said.

"I don't have to look at it," he said. "I know what it is, and it isn't going to be good." He checked the readout, grimaced, and headed for the phone in the kitchen. When he came back, holding a paper towel with an address scribbled, I gave him an expectant look.

"I have to go," he said. "But I'll be back."

"When? When will you be back?"

"Wednesday at the latest."

I rolled my eyes. Cop humor.

He gave me a fast kiss, and he was gone.

I pressed the redial button on my phone. A woman answered, and I recognized the voice. Terry Gilman.

"Look at this," Grandma said. "The alligator ate a cow. You don't see that every day."

I took a seat beside her. Fortunately, there wasn't any more cow eating. Although now that I knew Joe was on his way to meet Terry Gilman, death and destruction held some appeal. The fact that this was undoubtedly a business meeting took some of the fun out of getting nuts over it. Still, I could probably have worked myself up into a pretty good frenzy if I just hadn't been so darn tired.

When the alligator show was done, we watched the Shopping Network for a while.

"I'm going to turn in," Grandma finally said. "Gotta get my beauty rest."

The second she left the room I hauled out my pillow and quilt, killed the lights, and flopped onto the couch. I was asleep in an instant, my sleep deep and dreamless. And short-lived. I was dragged awake by Grandma's snoring. I got up to close her door, but it was already closed. I sighed, half in self-pity and half in amazement that she could sleep with all that noise. You'd think she'd wake herself up. Bob didn't seem to notice. He was asleep on the floor at one end of the couch, sprawled on his side.

I crawled under the quilt and willed myself to go back to sleep. I thrashed around some. I put my hands over my ears. I thrashed around some more. The couch was uncomfortable. The quilt was tangled. And Grandma kept snoring. "Arrrrgh," I said. Bob didn't stir.

Grandma was going to have to go, one way or another. I got up and padded out to the kitchen. I looked through the cupboards and refrigerator. Nothing interesting. It was a little after twelve. Not all that late, really. Maybe I should go out and get a candy bar to settle my nerves. Chocolate was calming, right?

I pulled on my jeans and shoes and covered my pajama top with a coat. I snagged my bag from its hook in the foyer and let myself out. It would only take ten minutes to make a candy bar run, and then I'd be home and no doubt I'd clonk right off to sleep.

I stepped into the elevator half-expecting to see Ranger, but Ranger didn't appear. No Ranger in the parking lot, either. I fired up the Buick, drove to the store, and bought a Milky Way and a Snickers. I ate the Snickers immediately, intending to save the Milky Way for bed. But then somehow the Milky Way got eaten right away, too.

I thought about Grandma and the snoring and couldn't get excited about going home, so I drove over to Joe's house. Joe lives just outside the Burg in a row house he'd inherited from his aunt. In the beginning it had felt weird to think of him as a homeowner. But somehow the house had conformed to Joe, and the union had proved comfortable. It was a nice little place on a quiet street. A shotgun-style row house with the kitchen in the rear and bedrooms and bath on the second floor.

The house was dark. No lights shining behind the curtained windows. No truck parked at the curb. No sign of Terry Gilman. Okay, so maybe I was a teensy bit nuts. And maybe the candy bars were just an excuse to come over here. I dialed Joe's number on my cell phone. No answer.

Too bad I didn't have lock-picking skills. I could have let myself in and gone to sleep in Joe's bed. Just like Goldilocks.

I put the Buick in gear and slowly drove the length of the block, not feeling all that tired anymore. What the hell, I thought, as long as I'm out here with nothing to do, why not check up on Hannibal?

I wound my way out of Joe's neighborhood, hit Hamilton, and drove toward the river. I got on Route 29 and in minutes I was cruising past Hannibal's town house. Dark, dark, dark. No lights on here, either. I parked one block up, just around the corner, and walked back to the house. I stood directly in front and looked up at the windows. Did I see the tiniest hint of light in the front room? I crept closer, over the lawn, right into the bushes that hugged the house, and pressed my nose to his window. There was definitely light coming from somewhere in the house. Could have been a night light. Hard to tell where it originated.

I scuttled back to the sidewalk and speed-walked around to the bike path, where I took a moment to let my eyes adjust to the dark. Then I carefully picked my way to Hannibal's yard. I climbed the tree and stared into Hannibal's windows. All the drapes were drawn. But again, there was the hint of a light coming from some-where downstairs. I was thinking the light wasn't significant when it suddenly blinked out.

This got my heart thumping just a little, since I wasn't keen on getting shot at again. In fact, probably it wasn't a good idea to stay in the tree. Probably it would be better to watch from a safer dis-tance . . . like Georgia. I quietly inched down to the ground and was about to tippy-toe away when I heard a lock tumble. Either someone was closing up for the night, or someone was coming out to shoot me. This got me moving.

I was about to turn for the street when I heard a gate creak open. I scrunched myself flat against the fence, deep in shadow. I held my breath and watched the bike path. A lone figure came into view. He closed the gate. He paused for a moment and looked directly at me. I was pretty sure he had come out of Hannibal's yard. And I was pretty sure he couldn't see me. There was a good chunk of distance between us, and he was almost lost in the dark; the ambient light revealed only an outline. He turned on his heel and walked away from me. He passed under a shaft of window light and was briefly illuminated. My breath caught in my throat. It was Ranger. I opened my mouth to call out his name, but he was gone, dissolved into the night. Like an apparition.

I ran to the street and listened for footsteps. I didn't hear them, but there was the sound of an engine catching not far off. A black SUV crossed the intersection, and quiet returned to the neighborhood. I was half afraid that I was losing my mind, that it had all been a hallucination from lack of sleep. I walked back to the car feeling pretty well creeped out and took off for home.

Grandma was still snoring like a lumberjack when I dropped my shoulder bag on the kitchen counter. I said hello to Rex and shuffled to the couch. I didn't bother taking my shoes off. I just crashed onto the couch and pulled the quilt over myself.

The next time I opened my eyes, the Mooner and Dougie were sitting on the coffee table, staring down at me.

"Yow!" I yelled. "What the hell?"

"Hey duder," the Mooner said, "hope we didn't, like, startle you."

"What are you doing here?" I shrieked.

"The dude formerly known as the Dealer needs someone to talk to. He's, like, confused. You know, one minute he's a successful businessman, and then—*wham*—his whole future is ripped out from under him. It just isn't fair, man."

Dougie shook his head. "It isn't fair," he said.

"So we thought you might have some ideas for future employment," Mooner said. "Since you're so successfully employed. You and the Dougster, you're like . . . an entrepreneurial dude and dudette."

"It isn't like I haven't had offers," Dougie said.

"That's right," Mooner said. "The Dougster is in large demand in the pharmaceutical trade. There's always openings for enterprising young men in pharmaceuticals."

"You mean like Metamucil?"

"That too," Mooner said.

As if Dougie wasn't in enough trouble. Selling hijacked Metamucil was one thing. Selling crack was a whole other ball game.

"Probably pharmaceutical sales isn't a good idea," I told them. "It could have an adverse effect on your life expectancy."

Dougie did another nod. "Exactly what I thought. And now that Homer's out of the picture, things are going to get tight."

"Damn shame about Homer," Mooner said. "He was a fine human being. Now *there* was a businessman."

"Homer?" I asked.

"Homer Ramos. Homer and me were like this," Moon said, holding up two fingers side by side. "We were close, dude."

"Are you telling me Homer Ramos was involved in drugs?"

"Well, sure," Mooner said. "Isn't everybody?"

"How did you know Homer Ramos?"

"I didn't actually know him in the physical sense. It was more of a mutual cosmic connection. Like, he was the big drug kahuna, and I'm, you know, like a consumer. It sure was bummer luck that he got his head ventilated. Just when he got that expensive rug, too."

"Rug?"

"I was at Art's Carpets last week, contemplating a rug purchase. And you know how in the beginning you're thinking all the rugs are totally excellent, and then the more you look at them, the more they all start looking the same. And before you know it you're, like, rug hypnotized? And next thing you know, you're taking a break, laying on the floor, chilling? And while I was laying there behind the rugs, I heard Homer come in. He went into the back room, got a rug, and left. And the rug dude, you know, the owner guy, and Homer were talking about how the rug was worth a million dollars, and Homer should be real careful with it. Far out, huh?"

A million-dollar rug! Arturo Stolle had handed a million-dollar rug over to Homer Ramos just before Ramos was killed. And now Stolle was looking for Ranger, the last person to see Ramos alive . . . with the exception of the guy who killed him. And Stolle was thinking Ranger had something that belonged to him. Could this Stolle business be over a rug? Hard to believe. Must be a hell of a rug.

"I'm pretty sure I wasn't, like, hallucinating," Mooner said.

"That would be a strange hallucination," I said.

"Not as strange as the time I thought I'd turned into a giant blob of bubble gum. That was scary, dude. I had these little hands and feet, and everything else was bubble gum. I didn't even have a face. And I was like, all chewed, you know." Mooner gave an involuntary shiver. "It was a bad trip, dude."

The front door opened, and Morelli walked in. He looked at Mooner and Dougie, and then he looked at his watch and raised his eyebrows.

"Hey, man," Mooner said. "Long time no see. How's it going, dude?"

"Can't complain," Morelli said.

Dougie, not being nearly as mellow as Mooner, jumped to his feet at the sight of Morelli and accidentally stepped on Bob. Bob yelped in surprise, sank his teeth into Dougie's pants leg and ripped off a chunk of material.

Grandma Mazur opened the bedroom door and looked out. "What's going on?" she asked. "Am I missing something?"

The Dougster was fidgeting on the balls of his feet, ready to sprint for the door at the earliest opportunity. The Dougster didn't feel comfortable being in the presence of a vice cop. The Dougster was lacking many of the talents necessary for success as a criminal.

Morelli raised his hands in a symbol of surrender. "I give up," he said. He gave me a perfunctory kiss on the lips and turned to leave.

"Hey, wait," I said. "I need to talk to you." I looked at Mooner. "Alone."

"Sure," Mooner said. "No problemo. We appreciate the sage advice on the pharmaceutical issue. Me and the Dougster will have to research other avenues of employment for him."

"I'm going back to bed," Grandma said when Mooner and Dougie left. "This doesn't look too interesting. I liked it better the other night when you were on the floor with the bounty hunter."

Morelli gave me the same kind of look Desi always gave Lucy when she'd just done something incredibly stupid.

"It's a long story," I said.

"I bet."

"You probably don't want to hear the whole, boring story right now," I said.

"I think it sounds like it might be entertaining. Is that how your security chain got destroyed?"

"No, Morris Munson did that."

"Busy night."

I gave a sigh and sank back down onto the couch.

Morelli slouched into a chair across from me. "Well?"

"You know anything about rugs?"

"I know they go on the floor."

I told him Mooner's story about the million-dollar rug.

"Maybe it wasn't the rug that was worth a million dollars," Morelli said. "Maybe there was something inside the rug."

"Such as?"

Morelli just looked at me.

I did some out-loud questioning. "What's small enough to fit in a rug? Drugs?"

"I saw a segment of the security tape from the Ramos fire," Morelli said. "Homer Ramos was carrying a gym bag when he walked past the hidden camera the night he met Ranger. And Ranger was carrying the bag when he left. Word on the street is

702

that Arturo Stolle is missing a load of money and wants to talk to Ranger. What do you think?"

"I think maybe Stolle gives Ramos drugs. Ramos passes the drugs on to be cut and distributed and ends up with a gym bag filled with money, some or all of which might belong to Stolle. Something happens between Ranger and Homer Ramos, and Ranger gets the bag."

"And if that's the way it went down, then probably this was an extracurricular activity for Homer Ramos," Morelli said. "Drugs, extortion, and numbers go to organized crime. Guns go to the Ramos family. Alexander Ramos has always respected that."

Except, in Trenton, it was more like *dis*organized crime. Trenton fell right in the middle of New York and Philadelphia. No one cared a whole lot about Trenton. Mostly Trenton had a bunch of middle-management guys who spent their days running numbers through social clubs. The numbers money helped give stability to the drug trade. And the drugs were distributed by black street gangs that had names like the Corleones. If it wasn't for the *Godfather* movies and PBS specials on crime, probably no one in Trenton would know how to act or what to call themselves.

So now I was getting a better picture of why Alexander Ramos might be disenchanted with his son. The question still being, Was he disenchanted enough to have him killed? And maybe I had a reason for Arturo Stolle to be looking for Ranger.

"All this is speculation," Morelli said. "Just conversation."

"You never share police information with me. Why are you telling me this?"

"This isn't exactly police information. This is loose change rattling around in my head. I've been watching Stolle for a long time without much luck. Maybe this is the break I've been waiting for. I need to talk to Ranger, but I can't get him to call me back. So I'm passing this on to you, and you can feed it to Ranger."

I nodded. "I'll give him the message."

"No details on the phone."

"Understood."

"How'd it go with Gilman?"

Morelli grinned. "Let me guess. Your finger accidentally hit the redial button on the phone."

"All right, I admit it, I'm nosy."

"Crimes R Us is having some organizational problems. I noticed an increase in traffic going in and out of the social clubs, so I expressed some concern to Vito. So Vito sent Terry to assure me the boys weren't stockpiling nuclear arms for World War III."

"I saw Terry on Wednesday. She delivered a letter to Hannibal Ramos."

"Crimes R Us and Guns R Us are attempting to reestablish boundaries. Homer Ramos tore down some fences, and now that he's out of the picture, the fences need to be repaired." Morelli nudged my foot with his. "Well?"

"Well, what?"

"How about it?"

I was so tired my lips were numb, and Morelli wanted to fool around. "Sure," I said. "Just let me rest my eyes for a minute."

I closed my eyes, and when I woke up it was morning. Morelli was nowhere to be seen.

"I'm late," Grandma said, trotting from the bedroom to the kitchen. "I overslept. It's all those interruptions every night. This place is like Grand Central Station. I got my last driving lesson in a half-hour. And then tomorrow I take my test. I was hoping you could take me for it. First thing in the morning."

"Sure. I could do that."

"And then I'm moving out. Nothin' personal, but you live in a loony bin."

"Where will you go?"

"I'm going back with your mother. Your father deserves to have to put up with me, anyway."

It was Sunday, and Grandma always went to church on Sunday morning. "What about church today?"

"No time for church. God's just gonna have to make do without me today. Anyway, your mother will be there representing the family."

My mother always represented the family, because my father never went to church. My father stayed home and waited for the white bakery bag to arrive. For as long as I can remember, every Sunday morning, my mother went to church and stopped at the bakery on the way home. Every Sunday morning my mother bought jelly doughnuts. Nothing but jelly doughnuts. Cookies, coffee cakes, and cannoli were bought on weekdays. Sunday was jelly doughnut day. It was like taking communion. I'm a Catholic by birth, but in my own personal religion, the Trinity will forever be the Father, the Son, and the Holy Jelly Doughnut.

I clipped the leash onto Bob's collar and took him out for a walk. The air was cool, and the sky was blue. Spring felt like it wasn't too far away. I didn't see Habib and Mitchell in the parking lot. Guess they didn't work on Sunday. I didn't see Joyce Barnhardt, either. That was a relief.

Grandma was gone when I got back, and the apartment was blissfully quiet. I fed Bob. I drank a glass of orange juice. And I crawled under the quilt. I woke up at one o'clock, and I thought about my conversation with Morelli the night before. I'd held out on Morelli. I hadn't told him I'd seen Ranger leaving Hannibal's town house. I wondered if Morelli had kept information from me, too. Chances were good that he had. Our professional relationship had a whole other set of rules from our personal relationship. Morelli had set the tone from the very beginning. There were cop things he just didn't share. The personal rules were still evolving. He had his. And I had mine. Once in a while we agreed. A while ago we'd had a short fling at living together, but Morelli wasn't comfortable with commitment, and I wasn't comfortable with confinement. So we separated.

I heated up a can of chicken noodle soup and called Morelli. "Sorry about last night," I said.

"At first I was afraid you'd died."

"I was tired."

"I figured that out."

"Grandma's gone for the day, and I have some work to do. I was wondering if you'd baby-sit Bob for me."

"For how long?" Morelli asked. "A day? A year?"

"A couple hours."

I called Lula next. "I need to do some breaking and entering. Want to come along?"

"Hell, yes. Nothing I like better than illegal entry."

I dropped Bob off and gave Morelli instructions. "Keep your eye on him. He eats everything."

"Maybe we should make him a cop," Morelli said. "What's his liquor capacity?"

Lula was waiting on her stoop when I drove up. She was discreetly dressed in poison green spandex pants and a shocking pink faux-fur jacket. You could stand her on a corner, in a fog, at midnight, and she'd be visible for three miles.

"Nice outfit," I said.

"I wanted to look hot in case I got arrested. You know how they take your picture, and all." She buckled herself in and looked over at me. "You're gonna be sorry you wore that drab-ass shirt. It's not gonna show up. And for that matter, you didn't even mousse your hair. What kind of Jersey hair is that?"

"I'm not planning on getting arrested."

"You never know. Doesn't hurt to take some precaution and add a little extra eyeliner. Who we breaking in on, anyway?"

"Hannibal Ramos."

"Say what? You mean like the brother of the dead Homer Ramos? And the number one son of the Gun King, Alexander Ramos? Are you freakin' nuts?"

"He's probably not home."

"How are you gonna find out?"

"I'm going to ring his doorbell."

"And if he answers?"

"I'll ask him if he's seen my cat."

"Uh-oh," Lula said. "You don't have a cat."

All right, so it was a little lame. It was the best I could come up with. I was betting Hannibal wasn't home. I didn't hear Ranger yodel good-bye to anyone last night. I didn't notice lights on after he left.

"What are you looking for?" Lula asked. "Or do you just want to die young?"

"I'll know it when I see it," I said. At least I hoped so.

The truth is, I didn't want to think too hard about what I was looking for. I was half afraid it'd incriminate Ranger. He'd asked me to watch Hannibal's house, and then he'd gone snooping without me. Made me feel just a tad left out. And it had me a little worried. What had he been looking for in Hannibal's house? For that matter, what was he looking for at the Deal house? I suspected my window- and door-counting expedition had given him information he needed to break in to the building. What on earth could be in there to warrant taking such a risk?

Ranger, the Man of Mystery, was okay when everything was going just fine. But I was involved in something serious here, and I was thinking that the constant mystery surrounding Ranger was getting old. I wanted to know what was going on. And I wanted some assurance that Ranger was on the right side of the law on this one. I mean, who *was* this guy?

LULA AND I stood on the sidewalk and studied Hannibal's house. Drapes still drawn. Very quiet. The houses on either side of Hannibal were quiet, too. Sunday afternoon. Everyone was out at the mall.

"You sure this is the right address?" Lula asked. "This don't look like no big-ass arms-dealer house. I was expecting something like the Taj Mahal. Like where the Donald lives."

"Donald Trump doesn't live in the Taj Mahal."

"He does when he's in Atlantic City. This turkey don't even have no gun turrets. What kind of arms dealer is he, anyway?"

"Low profile."

"Fuckin' A."

I approached the door and rang the bell.

"Low profile or not," Lula said, "if he answers I'm gonna mess my pants."

I tried the handle, but the door was locked.

I looked to Lula. "You can pick a lock, right?"

"Hell, yes. They don't make the lock I can't pick. Only I didn't bring my whatchamacallit."

"Your lock-picking thing?"

"That's it. And anyway, what about the alarm system?"

"I have a feeling the alarm system isn't working." And if it is, we run like hell when we set it off.

We walked back to the sidewalk, around the block, and got on the bike path from one street over, just in case someone was watching. We walked to Hannibal's privacy fence and let ourselves in through the gate, which was now unlocked.

"You been here before?" Lula asked.

"Yep."

"What happened?"

"He shot at me."

"Hunh," Lula said.

I put my hand to the patio door and shoved. The door was unlocked.

"You may as well go first," Lula said. "I know how you like to do that."

I pulled the curtain aside and stepped into Hannibal's house.

"It's dark in here," Lula said. "This guy must be a vampire."

I turned and looked at her.

"Uh-oh," she said. "I just scared myself."

"He's not a vampire. He keeps his drapes drawn so no one can look in. I'll do a preliminary check to make sure the house is empty. And then I'll go room by room and see if anything interesting turns up. I want you down here doing lookout."

ELEVEN

THE FIRST FLOOR was clear. The basement rooms were clear, too. Hannibal had a small utility room down there, and a larger game room with a large-screen television, a billiard table, and a wet bar. It occurred to me that someone could be in the basement, watching television, and the house would appear dark and unlived-in. There were three bedrooms on the second floor. Also empty of human beings. One bedroom was obviously the master bedroom. Another had been converted into an office, with built-in bookshelves and a large leather-topped desk. And the third bedroom was a guest room. It was the guest room that caught my interest. It looked as if someone was living in it. Bed linens rumpled. Men's clothes draped over a chair. Shoes kicked off in a corner of the room.

I rifled the drawers and closet, checking pockets for something that might identify the guest. Nothing to be found. The clothes were expensive. I guessed their owner to be average height and build, under six feet and probably around 180 pounds. I checked the trousers against the trousers in the master bedroom. Hannibal had a larger waist size and his taste was more conservative. Hannibal's bath was attached to the master bedroom. The guest bathroom was off the hall. Neither held any surprises, with the possible exception of condoms in the guest bathroom. The guest had expected to see some action.

I moved to the office, scanning the bookshelves first. Biographies, an atlas, some fiction. I sat at his desk. No Rolodex or address book. There was a notepad and pen. No messages. A laptop computer. I turned it on. Nothing on the desktop. Everything on the hard drive was benign. Hannibal was *very* careful. I turned the computer off and went through his drawers. Again, nothing. Hannibal was neat. His clutter was minimal. I wondered if his suite at the shore was like this, too.

The guy in the guest room wasn't nearly so neat. His desk, wherever it was, would be a mess.

I hadn't found any weapons in the upstairs rooms. Since I knew, firsthand, that Hannibal had at least one gun, this probably meant he had the gun with him. Hannibal didn't seem like the kind of guy to leave his armaments in the cookie jar.

I went to the basement next. Not much to investigate down there.

"This is disappointing," I said to Lula, closing the basement door behind me. "There's nothing here."

"I couldn't find anything on this floor, either," Lula said. "No matchbooks from bars, no guns stuck under the couch cushions. There's some food in the refrigerator. Beer, juice, loaf of bread, and some cold cuts. There's some cans of soda, too. That's about it."

I went to the refrigerator and looked at the wrapper on the cold cuts. They'd been bought at the Shop Rite two days earlier. "This is really creepy," I said to Lula. "Someone's living in this house." And my unspoken thought was that they could be home any minute.

"Yeah, and he don't know much about cold cuts," Lula said. "He got turkey breast and Swiss cheese when he could have got salami and provolone."

We were in the kitchen, looking in the refrigerator and not paying a lot of attention to what was happening in front of the house. There was the sound of a lock clicking open, and Lula and I both stood up straight.

"Uh-oh," Lula said.

The door opened. Cynthia Lotte stepped into the room and squinted at us in the dim light. "What the hell are you doing here?" she asked.

Lula and I were speechless.

"Tell her," Lula said, giving me an elbow. "Tell her what we're doing here."

"Never mind what we're doing here," I said. "What are *you* doing here?"

"None of your business. And anyway, I have a key, so obviously I belong here."

Lula hauled out a Glock. "Well, I got a gun, so I guess that one-ups you."

Cynthia whipped a .45 out of her purse. "I've got a gun, too. We're even."

They both turned to me.

"I've got a gun at home," I said. "I forgot to bring it."

"That doesn't count," Cynthia said.

"It counts for something," Lula said. "It isn't like she don't have a gun at all. And besides, she's wicked when she got the gun. She killed a man, once."

"I remember reading about it. Dickie almost went into cardiac arrest. He thought it reflected badly."

"Dickie's a hemorrhoid," I said.

Cynthia smiled without humor. "All men are hemorrhoids." She looked around the apartment. "I used to come here with Homer when Hannibal was out of town."

That explained the key. And maybe the condoms in the bathroom. "Did Homer keep clothes in the guest room?"

"A couple shirts. Some underwear."

"There are clothes, upstairs, in the guest room. Maybe you could take a look and tell me if they're Homer's."

"First, I want to know what you're doing here."

"A friend of mine is a possible suspect for the fire and shooting. I'm trying to get a fix on what actually happened."

"And you're thinking, what? That Hannibal killed his brother?"

"I don't know. I'm fishing."

Cynthia headed for the stairs. "Let me tell you about Homer. Everyone wanted to kill Homer. Including me. Homer was a lying, cheating worm. His family was always bailing him out. If I was Hannibal, I'd have shot Homer a long time ago, but the Ramos family ties are strong."

We followed her up the stairs to the guest room and waited at the door while she went in and looked around.

"Some of these are definitely Homer's," she said, going through the drawers. "And some I've never seen before now." She kicked at a pair of red silk paisley boxers lying on the floor. "You see these boxers?" She took aim and fired five rounds into the shorts. "These were Homer's."

"Dang," Lula said. "Don't hold back."

"He could be very charming," Cynthia said. "But he had a short attention span when it came to women. I thought he was in love with me. I thought I could change him."

"What happened to make you think otherwise?"

"Two days before he was shot he told me the relationship was over. He said some very unflattering things to me, told me if I gave him any trouble he'd kill me, and then he cleaned out my jewelry box and took my car. He said he needed money."

"Did you report him to the police?"

"No. I believed him when he said he'd kill me." She shoved her gun into her jacket pocket. "Anyway, I got to thinking that Homer might not have had a chance to fence my jewelry . . . that he might have stashed it here."

"I've been through the whole house," I said, "and I didn't see any women's jewelry, but you're welcome to look for yourself."

She shrugged. "It was a long shot. I should have checked sooner."

"Weren't you afraid you'd run into Hannibal?" Lula asked.

"I was counting on Alexander being here for the funeral, and Hannibal being in residence at the shore house."

We all trooped downstairs.

"What about the garage?" Cynthia asked. "Did you look in there? I don't suppose you found my silver Porsche."

"Damn," Lula said, all impressed. "You drive a Porsche?"

"I used to. Homer gave it to me for our six-month anniversary." She sighed. "Like I said, Homer could be very charming."

"Charming" being synonymous with "generous."

Hannibal had a two-car garage that attached to the house. The door to the garage was off the foyer and was locked with a slide bolt. Cynthia opened the door and flicked the light on in the garage. And there it was . . . the silver Porsche.

"My Porsche! My Porsche!" Cynthia yelped. "I never thought I'd see it again." She stopped yelping and wrinkled her nose. "What's that smell?"

Lula and I looked at each other. We knew the smell.

"Uh-oh," Lula said.

Cynthia ran to the car. "I hope he left me the keys. I hope—" She stopped short and looked in the car window. "Someone's sleeping in my car."

Lula and I grimaced.

And Cynthia started screaming. "He's dead! He's dead! He's dead in my Porsche!"

Lula and I approached the car and looked inside.

"Yep. He's dead all right," Lula said. "The giveaway is those three holes in his forehead. You're lucky," she told Cynthia. "Looks like this guy bought it with a twenty-two. If he'd been shot with a forty-five there'd be brains all over the place. A twenty-two goes in and rattles around like PacMan."

It was hard to tell with him slumped over on the seat, but he looked about five ten and maybe fifty pounds overweight. Dark hair, cut short. Mid-forties. Dressed in a knit shirt and sports coat. Diamond pinky ring. Three holes in his head.

"Do you recognize him?" I asked Cynthia.

"No. I never saw him before. This is terrible. How could this happen? There's blood on my upholstery."

"It's not so bad, considering he took three to the head," Lula said. "Just don't use hot water on it. Hot water sets blood."

Cynthia had the door open and was trying to wrestle the dead guy out of the car, but the dead guy wasn't cooperating. "I could use some help, here," Cynthia said. "Someone go around to the other side and push."

"Hey, wait a minute," I said. "This is a crime scene. You should leave everything alone."

"The hell I will," Cynthia said. "This is my car, and I'm driving away with it. I work for a lawyer. I know what happens. They'll impound this car until the world comes to an end. And then his wife'll probably get it." She had the body halfway out, but the legs were stiff and wouldn't unbend.

"We need Siegfried and Roy here," Lula said. "I saw them on television, and they sliced someone in half, and they didn't even make a mess."

Cynthia had the guy by the head, hoping for some leverage. "His foot is stuck around the gear shift," she said. "Someone give his foot a kick."

"Don't look at me," Lula said. "Dead people give me the creeps. I'm not touching no dead person."

Cynthia grabbed his jacket and pulled. "This is impossible. I'm never going to get this idiot out of my car."

"Maybe if you greased him up," Lula said.

"Maybe if you *helped*," Cynthia said. "Go around to the other side and put your foot to his ass while Stephanie helps me pull."

"Long as it's only my foot," Lula said. "Guess I could do that."

Cynthia got the guy's head in a hammerlock, and I grabbed hold of his shirtfront, and Lula pushed him out with one good shove.

We instantly dropped him and stepped back.

"Who do you think killed him?" I asked. Not actually expecting an answer.

"Homer, of course," Cynthia said.

I shook my head. "He hasn't been dead long enough for it to have been Homer."

"Hannibal?"

"Don't think Hannibal would leave a body in his own garage."

"Well, I don't care who killed him," Cynthia said. "I got the Porsche, and I'm going home."

The dead guy was lying in a heap on the floor, legs bent at odd angles, hair mussed, shirt out.

"What about him?" I asked. "We can't just leave him like this. He looks so . . . uncomfortable."

"It's his legs," Lula said. "They froze up in a seated position." She pulled a lawn chair off a stack at the back of the garage and set the chair next to the dead guy. "If we put him in a chair he'll look more natural, like he was waiting for a ride or something."

So we picked him up, set him into the chair, and backed away to take a look. Only, when we backed away, he fell out of the chair. *Smash*, right on his face.

"Good thing he's dead," Lula said, "or that would have hurt like the devil."

We heaved him back into the chair and this time we wrapped a bungee cord around him. His nose was a little smashed and one eye had been jarred closed from the impact when he fell, so one was open and one was closed, but aside from that he looked okay. We backed away again, and he stayed in place.

"I'm outta here," Cynthia said. She rolled all the windows down in the car, hit the garage-door opener, backed out, and took off down the street.

The garage door slid closed, and Lula and I were left with the dead guy.

Lula shifted foot to foot. "Think we should say something over the deceased? I don't like to disrespect the dead."

"I think we should get the hell out of here."

"Amen," Lula said, and she made the sign of the cross.

"I thought you were Baptist."

"Yeah, but we don't got any hand signals for an occasion like this."

We vacated the garage, peeked out the back window to make

715

sure no one was around, and scurried out the patio door. We closed the gate behind us and walked the bike path to the car.

"I don't know about you," Lula said, "but I'm gonna go home and stand in the shower for a couple hours, and then I'm gonna rinse myself off with Clorox."

That sounded like a good plan. Especially since a shower would give me a chance to put off seeing Morelli. I mean, what would I say to him? "Guess what, Joe, I broke into Hannibal Ramos's house today and found a dead guy. Then I destroyed the crime scene, helped a woman remove evidence, and left. So, if you still find me attractive after ten years in jail . . ." Not to mention, this was the second time Ranger had been seen walking away from a homicide.

By the time I got home I had all the makings of a bad mood. I'd gone to Hannibal's town house looking for information. Now I had more information than I really wanted to have, and I didn't know what any of it meant. I paged Ranger and made lunch, which in my distracted state consisted of olives. Again.

I took the phone into the bathroom with me while I showered. I changed clothes, dried my hair, and gave my lashes a couple swipes of mascara. I was contemplating eyeliner when Ranger called.

"I want to know what's going on," I said. "I just found a dead guy in Hannibal's garage."

"And?"

"And I want to know who he is. And I want to know who killed him. And I want to know what you were doing sneaking out of Hannibal's town house last night."

I could feel the force of Ranger's personality at the other end of the line. "You don't need to know any of those things."

"The hell I don't. I just involved myself in a murder."

"You happened on a crime scene. That's different from being involved in a murder. Have you called the police yet?"

"No."

"It would be a good idea to call the police. And you might want to be vague about the breaking-and-entering part."

"I might want to be vague about a lot of things."

"Your call," Ranger said.

"You have a rotten attitude!" I yelled at him over the phone. "I'm fed up with this Mysterious Ranger thing. You have a problem sharing, do you know that? One day you have your hands up my shirt, and next day you're telling me nothing's any of my business. I don't even know where you live."

"If you don't know anything, you can't pass anything on."

"Thanks for the vote of confidence."

"It's the way it is," Ranger said.

"And another thing, Morelli wants you to call him. He's been watching somebody for a long time, and now you're involved with this somebody, and Morelli thinks you could be of some help to him."

"Later," Ranger said. And he hung up.

Fine. If that's the way he wants it, then that's just peachy fine.

I huffed off to the kitchen, got my gun out of the cookie jar, grabbed my shoulder bag, and stomped down the hall, down the stairs, through the lobby to the Buick. Joyce was parked in the lot, in the car with the crumpled bumper. She saw me come out of the building and gave me the finger. I gave it back to her and took off for Morelli's house. Joyce was following one car length behind. Okay by me. She could follow me all she wanted today. As far as I was concerned Ranger was on his own. I was taking myself out of the picture.

MORELLI AND BOB were sitting side by side on the couch, watching ESPN, when I came in. There was an empty Pino's Pizza box on the coffee table, an empty container of ice cream and a couple crushed beer cans.

"Lunch?" I asked.

"Bob was hungry. And don't worry, he didn't get any beer." Morelli patted the seat next to him. "There's room for you, here."

When Morelli was being a cop, his brown eyes were hard and assessing, his face was lean and angular, and the scar that sliced through his right eyebrow gave the correct impression that Morelli had never lived a cautious life. When he was feeling sexy, his brown eyes were molten chocolate, his mouth softened, and the scar gave the mistaken impression that he might need a teensy bit of mothering.

And right now, Morelli was feeling *very* sexy. And I was feeling very *un*sexy. In fact, I was feeling absolutely grumpy. I plopped myself down on the couch and scowled at the empty pizza box, remembering my lunch of olives.

Morelli slid his arm around my shoulders and nuzzled my neck. "Alone at last," he said.

"I have something to tell you."

Morelli went still.

"I sort of happened on a dead guy today."

He slouched back on the couch. "I have a girlfriend who finds dead guys. Why me?"

"You sound like my mother."

"I feel like your mother."

"Well, don't," I snapped. "I don't even like when my *mother* feels like my mother."

"I suppose you want to tell me about this."

"Hey, if you don't want to hear it, that's no problem. I can just call it in to the station."

He sat up straighter. "You haven't called it in? Oh shit, let me guess: you broke into someone's house and stumbled onto a homicide."

"Hannibal's house."

Morelli was on his feet. "*Hannibal's house?*"

"But I didn't break in. His back door was open."

"What the hell were you doing walking into Hannibal's house?" he yelled. "What were you thinking?"

I was on my feet, too, and I was yelling back. "I was doing my job."

"Breaking and entering isn't your job."

"I told you, it wasn't breaking. It was only entering."

"Well, that makes all the difference. Who did you find dead?"

"I don't know. Some guy got whacked in the garage."

Morelli went into the kitchen and dialed dispatch. "I have an anonymous tip here," he said. "Why don't you send someone over to Hannibal Ramos's town house on Fenwood and take a look in the garage. The back door should be open." Morelli hung the phone up and turned to me. "Okay, that's taken care of," he said. "Let's go upstairs."

"Sex, sex, sex," I said. "That's all you ever think about." Although, now that I was rested and had the dead guy off my chest, an orgasm didn't sound like such a bad idea.

Morelli backed me against the wall and leaned into me. "I think about other things besides sex . . . just not lately." He kissed me and put some tongue into it, and the orgasm was sounding better and better.

"Just a quick question about the dead guy," I said. "How long do you think it'll be before they find him?"

"If there's a car in the area, it'll only take five or ten minutes."

Chances were pretty good they'd call Morelli when they took a gander at the guy in the garage. And on my best day, I need more than five minutes. But then probably it would take more than five minutes to get a car to the house, then for the cops to walk to the back and go through to the garage. So, if I didn't waste time taking all my clothes off, and we got right to it, I might be able to do the whole program.

"Why don't we do it here?" I said to Morelli, popping the top snap on his Levi's. "Kitchens are so sexy."

"Hold on," he said. "I'll pull the blinds."

I kicked my shoes off and shucked my jeans. "No time for that."

Morelli gave me a long look. "I'm not complaining, but I can't help feeling this is too good to be true."

"You've heard of fast food? This is fast sex."

I wrapped my hand around him, and he sucked in a quick breath. "How fast do you want this to be?" he asked.

The phone rang.

Damn!

Morelli had one hand on the phone and the other on my wrist.

After a moment on the phone he cut his eyes to me. "It's Costanza. He was in the neighborhood, so he took the call to check on the Ramos house. He says I've got to come over to see for myself. Something about a guy having a bad hair day, waiting for a bus. At least that's what it sounded like, over the laughter."

I gave him a big shrug and a palms-up. Like, well, gosh, I don't know what he's talking about. Just looked like an ordinary ol' dead guy to me.

"Anything you want to tell me about this?" Morelli asked.

"Not without a lawyer present."

We put our clothes back on, gathered our things, and went to the front door. Bob was still sitting on the couch, watching ESPN.

"It's kind of weird," Morelli said, "but I swear it's like he's following the game."

"Maybe we should just let him keep watching."

Morelli locked the door behind us. "Listen, cupcake, you tell anybody I let that dog watch ESPN, and I'll get even." His eyes drifted to my car, and then to the car parked behind me. "Is that Joyce?"

"She's following me."

"Want me to give her a ticket for something?"

I gave Morelli a fast kiss and drove off to the food store with Joyce close on my bumper. I didn't have a lot of money and my Visa was maxed, so I just got the essentials: peanut butter, potato chips, bread, beer, Oreos, milk, and two scratch-off lottery tickets.

Next stop was Home Depot, where I got a bolt for the front door to replace the broken security chain. The plan was to trade a beer for the bolt-installing expertise of my building super and good buddy Dillan Rudick.

After Home Depot I headed back to my apartment. I parked in the lot, locked Big Blue, and waved bye-bye to Joyce. Joyce inserted her thumbnail behind her two front teeth and gave me a genuine Italian gesture.

I stopped off at Dillan's basement apartment and explained my needs. Dillan grabbed his toolbox and we trooped upstairs. He was my age and lived in the bowels of the building, like a mole. He was a really cool guy, but he didn't do much, and as far as I know he didn't have a girlfriend . . . so, as you might expect, he drank a lot of beer. And since he didn't make a lot of money, free beer was always welcome.

I checked my answering machine while Dillan installed my bolt. Five calls for Grandma Mazur, none for me.

Dillan and I were relaxing in front of the television when Grandma came in.

"Boy, did I have a day," Grandma said. "I drove all over, and I almost got the stopping thing figured out." She squinted at Dillan. "And who's this nice young man?"

I introduced Dillan, and then since it was dinnertime I made all of us peanut-butter-and-potato-chip sandwiches. We ate them in front of the television and between Grandma and Dillan, somehow, the six-pack disappeared. Grandma and Dillan were feeling pretty happy, but I was starting to worry about Bob. I was imagining him alone in Morelli's house with nothing to eat but the cardboard pizza box. And the couch. And the bed. And the curtains and rug and Morelli's favorite chair. Then I imagined Morelli shooting Bob, and that wasn't a good picture.

I called Morelli but there was no answer. Rats. I should never have left Bob alone in the house. I had my keys in my hand and was putting my jacket on when Morelli arrived with Bob in tow.

"Going somewhere?" Morelli asked, taking in the keys and jacket.

"I was worried about Bob. I was going to drive over to your house and see if everything was okay."

"I thought maybe you were leaving the country."

I gave him a big fake smile.

Morelli unhooked Bob's leash, said hello to Grandma and Dillan, and dragged me into the kitchen. "I need to talk to you."

I heard a yelp from Dillan and figured Bob was getting acquainted.

"I'm armed," I said to Morelli, "so you better be careful. I have a gun in my purse."

Morelli took the purse and threw it across the room.

Uh-oh.

"That was Junior Macaroni in Hannibal's garage," Morelli said. "He works for Stolle. Very weird to find him in Hannibal's garage. And it gets even weirder."

I did a mental grimace.

"Macaroni was sitting in a lawn chair."

"It was Lula's idea," I said. "Well, okay, so it was mine too, but he looked so uncomfortable lying on the cement floor."

Morelli cracked a grin. "I should arrest you for tampering with a crime scene, but he was such a vicious bastard, and he looked so fucking stupid."

"How do you know I wasn't the killer?"

"Because you carry a thirty-eight and he was shot with a twenty-two. And more than that, you couldn't hit a barn at five paces. The only time you ever shot anyone, there was divine intervention."

True.

"How many people know I sat him in the lawn chair?"

"Nobody knows, but about a hundred have guessed. No one will tell." Morelli looked at his watch. "I have to go. I have a meeting set up for tonight."

"This isn't a meeting with Ranger, is it?"

"No."

"Liar."

Morelli pulled a pair of bracelets out of his jacket pocket, and before I realized what was happening I was cuffed to the refrigerator.

"Excuse me?" I said.

"You were going to follow me. I'll leave the key in your mailbox downstairs."

Is this a relationship, or what?

"I'M READY TO go," Grandma said.

She was dressed in her purple warm-up suit and white tennies.

Her hair was neatly curled, and she was wearing pink lipstick. She had her big black leather purse tucked into the crook of her arm. My fear was that she was packing the long-barrel, and might threaten the DMV guy if he didn't give her a license.

"You don't have your gun in there, do you?" I asked.

"Of course not."

I didn't believe her for a second.

When we got downstairs to the lot, Grandma went to the Buick. "I figure I stand a better chance of getting my license if I'm driving the Buick," she said. "I heard they worry about young chicks in sports cars."

Habib and Mitchell pulled into the lot. They were back in the Lincoln.

"Looks good as new," I said.

Mitchell beamed. "Yeah, they did a great job on it. We just got it this morning. We had to wait for the paint to dry." He looked at Grandma, sitting behind the wheel of the Buick. "What's up for today?"

"I'm taking my grandmother to get her driver's license."

"That's real nice of you," Mitchell said. "You're a good granddaughter, but isn't she kind of old?"

Grandma clamped down on her dentures. "Old?" she yelled. "I'll show you old." I heard her purse click open, and Grandma reached down and came up with the long-barrel. "I'm not too old to shoot you in the eye," she said, leveling the gun.

Mitchell and Habib ducked flat on the seat, out of sight.

I glared at Grandma. "I thought you said you didn't have the gun with you."

"Guess I was wrong."

"Put it away. And you better not threaten anyone at the DMV either, or they'll arrest you."

"Crazy old broad," Mitchell said from low in the Lincoln.

"That's better," Grandma said. "I like being a broad."

TWELVE

I HAD MIXED feelings about Grandma getting her license. On the one hand, I thought it was great that she'd be more independent. On the other hand, I didn't want to be on the road with her. She'd run a red light on the way over, snapped me against my seat belt every time she stopped, and parked in a handicapped spot at the DMV, insisting it went along with joining the AARP.

When Grandma stomped into the waiting room after taking her road test, I immediately knew the streets were safe for a little while longer.

"If that don't tear it," she said. "He didn't pass me on hardly anything."

"You can take the test again," I said.

"Darn right, I can. I'm gonna keep taking it until I pass. I got a God-given right to drive a car." She pressed her lips tight together. "Guess I should have gone to church yesterday."

"Wouldn't have hurt," I said.

"Well, I'm pulling out all the stops next time. I'm lighting a candle. I'm doing the works."

Mitchell and Habib were still following us, but they were about a quarter-mile back. They'd almost plowed into us several times on the way over when Grandma had stopped short, and they weren't taking any chances on the way home.

"Are you still moving out?" I asked Grandma.

"Yep. I already told your mother. And Louise Greeber is coming over this afternoon to help me. So you don't need to worry about a thing. It was nice of you to let me stay. I appreciate it, but I need my shut-eye. I don't know how you get by on so little sleep."

"Well, okay," I said. "I guess your mind is made up." Maybe I'd light a candle, too.

Bob was waiting for us when we walked in.

"Think Bob needs to do you-know-what," Grandma said.

So Bob and I trooped back down to the parking lot. Habib and Mitchell were sitting there, patiently waiting for me to lead them to Ranger, and now Joyce was there, too. I turned around, went back into the building, and exited the front door. Bob and I walked up the street a block and then cut over, back to a residential neighborhood of small single-family houses. Bob did you-know-what about forty or fifty times in the space of five minutes, and we headed home.

A black Mercedes turned the corner two blocks in front of me, and my heart tripped. The Mercedes drew closer, and my heartbeat stayed erratic. There were only two possibilities: drug dealer and Ranger. The car stopped beside me, and Ranger made a slight head movement that meant, "Get in."

I loaded Bob into the backseat and slid in next to Ranger. "There are three people parked in my lot, hoping to get a shot at you," I said. "What are you doing here?"

"I want to talk to you."

It was one thing to have the skill to break into an apartment; it was something else to be able to divine what I was doing at any given moment in the day. "How did you know I was out with Bob? What are you, psychic?"

"Nothing that exotic. I called, and your grandma told me you were walking the dog."

"Gee, that's disappointing. Next thing you'll be telling me you aren't Superman."

Ranger smiled. "You want me to be Superman? Spend the night with me."

"I think I'm flustered," I told him.

"Cute," Ranger said.

"What did you want to talk to me about?"

"I'm terminating your employment."

The fluster disappeared and was replaced with the seed of an ill-defined emotion that settled in the pit of my stomach. "You and Morelli made a deal, didn't you?"

"We have an understanding."

I was being cut out of the program, shoved aside like unnecessary baggage. Or worse, like a liability. I went from hurt disbelief to total fury in three seconds.

"Was this Morelli's idea?"

"It's my idea. Hannibal has seen you. Alexander has seen you. And now half the police in Trenton know you broke into Hannibal's house and found Junior Macaroni in the garage."

"Did you hear that from Morelli?"

"I heard it from *everyone*. My answering machine ran out of space. It's just too dangerous for you to stay on the case. I'm afraid Hannibal will put it together and come after you."

"This is depressing."

"Did you really sit him up in a lawn chair?"

"Yes. And by the way, did you kill him?"

"No. The Porsche wasn't in the garage when I went through the house. And neither was Macaroni."

"How did you get past the alarm system?"

"Same way you did. The alarm wasn't set." He looked at his watch. "I have to go."

I opened the passenger door and turned to leave.

Ranger caught hold of my wrist. "You're not especially good at following instructions, but you're going to listen to me on this, right? You're going to walk away. And you're going to be careful."

I gave a sigh, heaved myself out the door, and extracted Bob from the backseat. "Just make sure you don't let Joyce catch you. That would really ruin my day."

I deposited Bob in the apartment, grabbed my car keys and my shoulder bag, and went back downstairs. I was going somewhere. *Anywhere*. I was too bummed to stay at home. Truth is, I wasn't all that upset about my employment being terminated. I just hated it being terminated for stupidity. I'd fallen out of a tree, for God's sake. And then I'd sat Junior Macaroni in a chair. I mean, how inept can a person get?

I needed food, I thought. Ice cream. And hot fudge. Whipped cream. There was an ice cream parlor at the mall that constructed sundaes for four people. That's what I needed. A mega sundae.

I got into Big Blue, and Mitchell got in with me.

"Excuse me?" I said. "Is this a date?"

"You wish," Mitchell said. "Mr. Stolle wants to talk to you."

"Guess what. I'm not in the mood to talk to Mr. Stolle. I'm not in the mood to talk to *anyone*, you included. So I hope you don't take this personally, but get out of my car."

Mitchell drew his gun. "You should change your mood."

"You'd shoot me?"

"Don't take it personally," Mitchell said.

Art's Carpets is in Hamilton Township, the land of the strip mall. It's on Route 33, not far from Five Points, and is indistinguishable from every other business on that road, save for its glowing chartreuse sign, which can be seen clearly from Rhode Island. The building is a single-story cinder-block with large storefront windows, heralding a year-round sale. I'd been to Art's Carpets many times, along with every other man, woman, and child in New Jersey. I'd never purchased anything, but I'd been tempted. Art's has good prices.

I parked the Buick in front of the store. Habib pulled the Lincoln in alongside the Buick. And Joyce parked beside the Lincoln.

"What does Stolle want?" I asked. "He doesn't want to kill me or anything, does he?"

"Mr. Stolle don't kill people. He hires people to do that stuff. He just wants to talk to you. That's all he told me."

There were a couple women browsing in the store. Looked like mother and daughter. A salesman hovered over them. Mitchell and I walked in together, and Mitchell guided me through the stacks of carpet and displays of broadloom to the office at the back.

Stolle was in his mid-fifties and built solid. He was barrel-chested and had begun to jowl. He was dressed in a flashy sweater and dress slacks. He extended his hand and smiled his best rug-merchant smile.

"I'll be right outside," Mitchell said, and closed the door, leaving me alone with Stolle.

"You're supposed to be a pretty smart girl," Stolle said. "I've heard some things about you."

"Uh-huh."

"So how come you're not having any luck delivering Manoso?"

"I'm not *that* smart. And Ranger's not going to come near me when Habib and Mitchell are around."

Stolle smiled. "To tell you the truth, I never expected you to hand us Manoso. But hell, nothing ventured, nothing gained, right?"

I didn't say anything.

"Unfortunately, since we couldn't do this the easy way, we're going to have to try something else. We're sending a message to your boyfriend. He doesn't want to talk to me? Fine. He wants to be in the wind? That's okay. You know why? Because we got you. When I run out of patience, and I'm just about there, we're gonna hurt you. And Manoso's gonna know he could have prevented it."

All of a sudden I didn't have any air in my lungs. I hadn't thought of this angle. "He's not my boyfriend," I said. "You're over-estimating my importance to him."

"Maybe, but he has a sense of chivalry. Latin temperament, you know." Stolle sat in the chair behind his desk and rocked back. "You should encourage Manoso to talk to us. Mitchell and Habib look like nice guys, but they'll do whatever I tell them. In fact, in

728

the past, they've done some very mean things. You have a dog, don't you?" Stolle leaned forward, hands on desk. "Mitchell's real good at killing dogs. Not that he'd kill *your* dog . . ."

"He's not my dog. I'm baby-sitting."

"I was just giving an example."

"You're wasting your time," I said. "Ranger is a mercenary. You can't get to him through me. We don't have that kind of relationship. Maybe no one has that kind of relationship with him."

Stolle smiled and shrugged. "Like I said before, nothing ventured, nothing gained. It's worth a try, right?"

I looked at him for a beat, giving him my inscrutable Plum glare, and then I turned and left.

Mitchell and Habib and Joyce were idling when I walked out of the store.

I got in the Buick and discreetly felt my crotch to make sure I hadn't wet my pants. I took a deep breath and put my hands on the wheel. Breathe in, breathe out. Breathe in, breathe out. I wanted to put the key in the ignition, but I couldn't get my hands to unclench the wheel. I did some more breathing. I told myself Arturo Stolle was a big bag of wind. But I didn't believe it. What I believed was that Arturo Stolle was a real piece of crapola. And it didn't look like Habib and Mitchell were all that great, either.

Everyone was watching, waiting to see what I'd do next. I didn't want anyone to know I was scared, so I forced myself to release the wheel and start the car. I very carefully backed out of the parking place, put the car in gear, and drove away. I concentrated on my driving, slow and steady.

While I drove I dialed every number I had for Ranger, leaving a terse message: *Call me. Now.* After I ran through Ranger's numbers I called Carol Zabo.

"I need a favor," I said.

"Anything."

"I'm being followed by Joyce Barnhardt—"

"Evil bitch," Carol said.

"And I'm also being followed by two guys in a Lincoln."

"Hmm."

"Not to worry—they've been following me for days, and so far they haven't shot anybody." So far. "Anyway, I need to discourage them from following me, and I have a plan."

I was about five minutes away from Carol. She lived in the Burg, not far from my parents. She and Lubie had bought a house with their wedding money and had immediately set to work building a family. They'd decided to call it quits after two boys. Good thing for the world. Carol's kids were the scourge of the neighborhood. When they grew up they'd probably be cops.

Burg backyards are long and narrow. Many are enclosed in fencing of some sort. Most back up to an alley. All alleys are one lane wide. The alley servicing the houses on Reed Street, between Beal and Cedar, was especially long. I asked Carol to idle at the juncture of Cedar and the Reed Street alley. The plan was that I'd lead Joyce and the Boobie Boys down the alley, and then as soon as I turned onto Cedar, Carol would ease up and block the alley, feigning car trouble.

I got to the Burg and wandered around for another five minutes, giving Carol some extra time to get into position. Then I turned into the Reed Street alley, sucking Joyce and the goons right along with me. I got to Cedar and sure enough, there was Carol. I wheeled around her, she moved forward and stopped, and everyone was trapped. I glanced back to see what was happening and saw Carol and three other women get out of Carol's car. Monica Kajewski, Gail Wojohowitz, and Angie Bono. Every one of them hated Joyce Barnhardt. Rumble in the Burg!

I went straight to Broad and headed for the shore. I wasn't going to sit around and wait for Mitchell to kill Bob to make a point. Bob today . . . me tomorrow.

I rolled into Deal and slowly drove past the Ramos compound. I tried again to reach Ranger by cell phone. No response. I continued to cruise the street. Come on, Ranger. Look out the window, wherever the hell you are. I was a block past the pink house, getting ready to make a U-turn, when the passenger door was yanked open and Alexander Ramos jumped in.

"Hey, cutie," he said. "Just can't stay away, huh?"

Shit! I didn't want him in my car now!

"Good thing I saw you. I was going nuts in there," he said.

"Jesus," I said. "Why don't you get a patch?"

"I don't want a goddamn patch. I want a cigarette. Drive me to the store. And hurry up, I'm dying."

"There are cigarettes in the glove compartment. You left them here last time."

He pulled the pack out and stuck a cigarette in his mouth.

"Not in the car!"

"Christ, this is like being married without the sex. Go to Sal's."

I didn't want to go to Sal's. I wanted to talk to Ranger. "Aren't you afraid you'll be missed at the house? Are you sure it's safe to go to Sal's?"

"Yeah. There's this problem in Trenton, and everybody's busy trying to fix it."

Like, could the problem be a dead guy in Hannibal's garage? "Must be *some* problem," I said. "Maybe you should be helping."

"I already helped. I'm putting the problem on a boat next week. With any luck, the boat will sink."

Okay, now I'm stumped. I don't know how they're going to get the dead guy on a boat. I don't know why they'd *want* to put the dead guy on a boat.

Since I wasn't having any luck getting Ramos out of my car, I drove the short distance to Sal's, and we went inside and took a table. Ramos slugged back a shot and lit up. "I'm going back to Greece next week," he said. "You want to go back with me? We could get married."

"I thought you were through with marriage."

"I changed my mind."

"I'm flattered, but I don't think so."

He shrugged and poured out another shot. "Suit yourself."

"This problem in Trenton—is it business?"

"Business. Personal. It's all the same for me. Let me give you some advice. Don't have kids. And if you want to make a good living, guns are the way to go. That's all my advice."

My cell phone rang.

"What's going on?" Ranger said.

"I can't talk now."

His voice was unusually tight. "Tell me you're not with Ramos."

"I can't tell you that. Why didn't you return my call?"

"I had to turn my phone off for a while. I just got back, and Tank said he saw you pick Ramos up."

"It wasn't my fault! I was down here looking for you."

"Well, you'd better be well hidden, because three cars just left the compound, and my guess is they're looking for Alexander."

I flipped the phone shut and dropped it into my purse. "I have to go," I told Ramos.

"That was your boyfriend, right? He sounds like a real asshole. I could have him taken care of, if you know what I mean."

I flipped a twenty onto the table and grabbed the bottle of booze. "Come on," I said, "we can take this with us."

Ramos looked over my shoulder to the door. "Oh Christ, look who's here."

I was afraid to look.

"It's my baby-sitters," Alexander said. "Can't even wipe my ass without an audience."

I turned and almost passed out with relief that it wasn't Hannibal. They were both in their late forties, dressed in suits. They looked like they ate a lot of pasta, and probably didn't refuse dessert either.

"They need you back at the house," one of the men said.

"I'm with my lady friend," Alexander said.

"Yeah, but maybe you could see her some other time. We still can't find that cargo that's going on the boat."

One of them walked Alexander out the door, and the other stayed behind to talk to me.

"Listen," he said, "it's not nice to take advantage of an old man like this. Don't you have any friends your own age?"

"I'm not taking advantage of him. He jumped into my car."

"I know. He does that sometimes." The guy pulled a money clip out of his pocket and peeled off a hundred. "Here, this is for your inconvenience."

I took a step back. "You've got this all wrong."

"Okay, what'll it take?" He peeled off nine more hundreds, folded them together, and dropped them into my bag. "I don't want to hear nothing more from you. And you gotta promise to leave the old man alone. Understand?"

"Hold on here—"

He swept his jacket aside to show me his gun.

"Now I understand," I said.

He turned and walked out the door and got into the Town Car idling at curbside. The car took off.

"Life can be pretty strange," I said to the bartender. Then I left, too. When I was sufficiently far away from Deal to feel safe, I redialed Ranger and told him about Stolle.

"I want you to go home and lock yourself in your apartment," Ranger said. "I'm going to send Tank to pick you up."

"And then what?"

"Then I'm putting you someplace safe until I can straighten this out."

"I don't think so."

"Don't give me a hard time on this," Ranger said. "I've got enough problems."

"Well, solve your damn problems. And solve them fast!" And I disconnected. Okay, so I lost it. I'd had a stressful day.

MITCHELL AND HABIB were waiting for me when I pulled into my parking lot. I gave them a wave, but I didn't get a wave back. I didn't get a smile. No remarks, either. Not a good sign.

I took the stairs to the second floor and hurried to my door. My stomach was uneasy, and my heart felt fluttery. I stepped into my apartment and felt relief wash over me when Bob bounced over. I locked the door behind me and checked Rex to make sure he was okay, too. I had twelve messages on my machine. One was silence. It felt like Ranger's silence. Ten were for Grandma. The last one was from my mother.

"We're having fried chicken tonight," she said. "Your grandmother thought you might want to come over, since you don't have any food in your house because Bob ate your groceries while your grandmother was cleaning your cupboards. And your grandmother says you might want to walk him when you get home, because he ate two boxes of prunes she'd just bought."

I looked at Bob. His nose was running and his stomach looked like he'd swallowed a beach ball.

"Jeez, Bob," I said, "you don't look too good."

Bob burped and passed gas.

"Maybe we should go for a walk."

Bob started to pant. Drool dripped onto the floor and thunder rumbled in his stomach. He lurched forward and hunched over.

"No!" I shouted. "Not here!" I grabbed his leash and my shoulder bag and dragged him out of the apartment and down the hall. We didn't wait for the elevator. We took the stairs and ran through the lobby. I got him outside and was about to cross the lot when the Lincoln suddenly screeched to a halt in front of us. Mitchell jumped out of the car, shoved me to the ground, and grabbed Bob.

By the time I'd scrambled to my feet, the Lincoln was in motion. I shrieked and ran after it, but the car was already out of the lot, onto St. James Street. Suddenly it stopped short. The doors were thrown open and Habib and Mitchell jumped out.

"Jesus Christ!" Mitchell yelled. "Goddamn! Son of a bitch!"

Habib had his hand to his mouth. "I am going to be sick. Not even in Pakistan have I seen such a thing as this."

Bob leaped out of the car, tail wagging, and ran to me. His stomach looked nice and slim again, and he wasn't drooling and panting. "Feel better now, fella?" I said, scratching behind his ears just the way he liked it. "Good boy. Good Bob!"

Mitchell's eyes were bugged out of his head and his face was purple. "I'm gonna fucking kill that dog. I'm gonna fucking kill him. You know what he did? He did number two in my car. And then he threw up. What are you feeding him? Don't you know nothing about dogs? What kind of a dog watcher are you?"

"He ate Grandma's prunes," I said.

Mitchell had his hands to his head. "No fucking kidding."

I loaded Bob into Big Blue, locked the doors, and drove over the lawn to the street to avoid Habib and Mitchell.

My mother and grandmother were waiting for me, looking through the glass storm door, when I docked the Buick in front of their house.

"We always know when you're coming to visit," Grandma said. "We can hear this car a mile away."

No fucking kidding.

"Where's your jacket?" my mother wanted to know. "Aren't you cold?"

"I didn't have time to take a jacket," I said. "It's a long story. Probably you don't want to hear it."

"I want to hear it," Grandma said. "I bet it's a pip."

"I need to make a phone call first."

"You can do that while I put the food on the table," my mother said. "Everything's done."

I used the kitchen phone to call Morelli. "I have a favor to ask," I said when he answered.

"Good. I love when you're indebted to me."

"I'd like you to take care of Bob for a while."

"You aren't pulling a Simon, are you?"

"No!"

"So what's this about?"

"You know how you have police business that you can't explain to me?"

"Yeah."

"Well, I can't explain this to *you*. At least not in my mother's kitchen."

Grandma bustled into the kitchen. "Is that Joseph on the phone? Tell him we have plenty of fried chicken, but he'll have to get a move on if he wants some."

"He doesn't like fried chicken."

"I love fried chicken," Joe said. "I'll be right over."

"No!"

Too late. He'd already disconnected. "Set an extra plate," I said.

Grandma was at the table and looked confused. "Is this extra plate for Bob or Joe?"

"Joe. Bob's stomach is on the blink."

"No wonder," Grandma said. "What with all those prunes. And then he ate a box of Frosted Flakes and a bag of marshmallows. I was cleaning your cupboards while I waited for Louise to come over, and I went to use the bathroom, and when I got back there was nothing on the counter."

I stroked Bob's head. He was such a dopey dog. Not nearly as smart as Rex. Not even smart enough to pass on the prunes. Still, he had his moments. He had wonderful big brown eyes. And I was a sucker for brown eyes. And he was good company. He never tried to change my radio station, and he never once mentioned my pimple. All right, so I was sort of attached to Bob. In fact, maybe I'd been ready to rip Mitchell's heart out with my bare hands when he dognapped the big guy. I gave Bob a hug. He was good to hug, too. "You're going home with Joe tonight," I told him. "You'll be safe there."

My mother had the fried chicken on the table, along with biscuits and red cabbage and broccoli. No one would touch the broccoli, but my mother put it out anyway, because it was healthy.

Joe let himself in and took his seat, next to me.

"How'd it go today?" Grandma asked Joe. "Catch any murderers?"

"Not today, but I have hopes for tomorrow."

"Really?" I said.

"Well no, not really."

"How'd it go with Ranger?"

Morelli spooned red cabbage onto his plate. "As expected."

"He told me to butt out. Is that what you want me to do, too?"

"Yeah, but I'm smart enough not to tell you to do it. That's like waving a red flag in front of you." He took a piece of chicken. "Did you declare war?"

"Sort of. I refused his offer of a safe house."

"Are you in enough danger to need a safe house?"

"I don't know. It feels extreme."

Morelli slid his hand along the back of my chair. "My house is safe. You could move in with Bob and me. And besides, you do owe me a favor, you know."

"You want to call in the marker already?"

"The sooner, the better."

The phone rang in the kitchen and Grandma went to answer it. "It's for Stephanie," she yelled. "It's Lula."

"I've been trying to get in touch with you all afternoon," Lula said. "You don't answer nothing. You don't have your cell phone working. And you never answer your pager. What's wrong with the pager?"

"I can't afford both the pager and the cell phone, so I chose the cell phone. What's up?"

"They found Cynthia Lotte sitting in that Porsche, and she was dead as a doorknob. I tell you, you wouldn't get me to sit in that car. You sit in that car, and you end up dead."

"When did this happen? How do you know?"

"They found her this afternoon, in the parking garage on Third Street. Connie and me heard it over the police band. And on top of that, I got a skip for you. Vinnie was total postal on account of you were out of touch, and there's no one else to take this skip."

"What about Joyce? What about Frankie Defrances?"

"We can't raise Joyce either. She's not answering her page. And Frankie just had a hernia operation."

"I'll come in to the office first thing in the morning."

"No way. Vinnie says you gotta get this guy tonight, before he flies. Vinnie knows right where he is. He gave me the papers."

"How much is it worth?"

"It's a hundred-thousand-dollar bond. Vinnie's cutting you ten percent."

Be still, my heart. "I'll pick you up in about twenty minutes."

I went back to the table, wrapped two pieces of chicken in my napkin, and dropped the napkin into my shoulder bag. I gave Bob a hug and Morelli a peck on the cheek. "I've got to go," I said. "I have to pick up a skip."

Morelli didn't look happy. "Will I see you later?"

"Probably. Besides paying off on my debt, I need to talk to you about Cynthia Lotte."

"I knew you'd get around to that."

LULA WAS WAITING outside when I got to her house. "I got the papers," she said, "and it don't sound too bad. His name's Elwood Steiger, and he's up on a drug charge. He was trying to make meth in his mother's garage, but the whole neighborhood reeked of the P2P. Guess one of the neighbors called the police. Anyway, his mother put her house up as bond, and now she's afraid ol' Elwood's gonna take a trip to Mexico. He missed his court date on Friday, and Mom found plane tickets in his sock drawer. So she ratted on him to Vinnie."

"Where do we find him?"

"According to his mama, he's one of them *Star Trek* fanatics. And there's some kind of *Star Trek* gig going on tonight. She gave me an address."

I looked at the address and groaned. It was Dougie's house. "I know the guy who lives here," I said. "Dougie Kruper."

Lula slapped her head. "I knew that sounded familiar."

"I don't want anyone to get hurt when we make this apprehension," I said.

"Uh-huh."

"We're not going in there like gangbusters with guns drawn."

"Uh-huh."

"In fact, we're not going to use guns at all."

"I hear you."

I looked at the purse in her lap. "You have a gun in there?"

"Hell, yes."

"You have a gun on your hip?"

"Glock."

"Ankle holster?"

"Only sissies use ankle holsters," Lula said.

"I want you to leave the guns in the car."

"These are Trekkies we're dealing with. They could put the Vulcan death grip on us."

"In the car!" I yelled.

"Boy, no need to get PMS over it." Lula looked out the window. "Looks like a party going on at Dougie's."

There were several cars parked in front, and the house lights were blazing. The front door was open and the Mooner was on the stoop. I parked several houses away, and Lula and I walked back to the Mooner.

"Hey, dude," Moon said when he saw me, "welcome to the Trekarama."

"What's going on?"

"This is the Dougster's new business. Trekarama. We thought of it all ourselves. And the Dougster's the Trekmaster. Is that awesome, dude? This is the business of the new millennium. It's gonna be big, you know? We're gonna like, franchise."

"What the hell's a Trekarama?" Lula asked.

"It's a social club, dude. It's a place of worship. It's a shrine to the men and women who went where no man has gone before."

"Before what?"

The Mooner gazed off into space, transfixed. "Before it all."

"Uh-huh."

"It'll cost you five bucks to get inside," the Mooner said.

I gave him ten, and Lula and I pushed through the crush at the door.

"Never saw so many geeks all in one spot in my life," Lula said. "Except for that Klingon over there by the stairs. He ain't half bad."

We scanned the room, looking for Steiger, trying to identify him from his file photo. Problem was, some of the Trekkies were in costume, dressed like their favorite *Star Trek* characters.

Dougie rushed up to us. "Welcome to Trekarama. There's hors d'oeuvres and beverages over in the corner by the Romulan, and we're gonna start showing the films in about ten minutes. The hors d'oeuvres are real good. They're, uh, liquidation stock."

Translation: hijacked goods that were rotting in storage somewhere because he got closed down.

Lula knocked on Dougie's head with her knuckles. "Hello, anybody home in there. Do we look like a couple dumb-ass Trekkies?"

"Uh, well . . ."

"We're just looking around," I said to Dougie.

"Like tourists?"

"Maybe I'll be a tourist over by that fine Klingon," Lula said.

THIRTEEN

LULA AND I moved deeper into the room, pushing our way through the crowd, looking for Elwood. He was nineteen years old. My height and slim. Sandy blond hair. Second-time offender. I didn't want to freak him out. I wanted to very quietly move him outside and slip the cuffs on him.

"Hey," Lula said, "you see that little dude in the Captain Kirk suit? What do you think?"

I squinted across the room. "Looks like it could be him," I said.

We worked our way over, and I came up beside him. "Steve?" I said. "Steve Miller?"

Captain Kirk blinked at me. "No. Sorry."

"I'm meeting a blind date here," I said. "He told me he'd be dressed as an officer." I extended my hand. "I'm Stephanie Plum."

He shook my hand. "Elwood Steiger."

Bingo.

"Boy, it's really hot in here," I said. "I'm going outside for some air. Want to join me?"

He looked around, nervous, needing to see if he was missing anything. "I don't know. I don't think so. They said they were show-ing the films right away."

Lesson number one: no point in coming on to a Trekkie when

the films are up. So I had a choice. I could force the issue, or I could wait around until he decided to leave. If he stayed to the end and left en masse with everyone else, it could be a problem.

Mooner ambled over. "Wow, nice to see you two getting it on. Elwood here's fallen on some hard times, you know. He was making some great shit, and they shut him down. It was a real blow to all of us."

Elwood's eyes were darting around like his head was a pinball machine. "Are they gonna do the films soon?" he asked. "I just came for the films."

Mooner sipped his drink. "Elwood was making a good living, saving up to go to college, when he lost his business license. Damn shame. Damn shame."

Elwood gave a small smile. "I didn't actually have a business license," he said.

"You're lucky you know Steph, here," Mooner said. "I don't know what Dougie and me'd do without Steph. Lotta bounty hunters would just drag your bony ass back to jail, but Steph here—"

Elwood looked like someone just hit him with a cattle prod. "Bounty hunter!"

"The best there is," Mooner said.

I leaned forward so I could keep my voice low, and still have Elwood hear me. "Maybe it would be best if we went outside where we could talk."

Elwood backed away. "No! I'm not going! Leave me alone."

I moved to cuff him, but he slapped my hand away.

Lula reached out with her stun gun, Elwood ducked behind the Mooner, and the Mooner went down like a house of cards.

"Oops," Lula said, "think I got the wrong little Trekkie."

"You killed him!" Elwood shrieked.

"Time out," Lula said. "Don't you go yellin' in my ear like that."

I caught one of his hands and slapped the bracelet on him.

"You killed him. You shot him," Elwood said.

Lula was hands on hips. "Did you hear a gunshot? I don't think

742

so. I don't even have a gun, because Ms. Antiviolence here made me leave my gun in the car. Good thing, too, or I might shoot you just because you're such an annoying little cockroach."

I was still trying to get the other hand in a cuff, and people were pressing in on us. "What's going on?" they wanted to know. "What are you doing to Captain Kirk?"

"We're haulin' his worthless white ass off to the clink," Lula said. "Step back."

In my peripheral vision I caught something fly by and hit Lula on the side of her head.

"Hey!" Lula said. "What's going on?" She put her hand to her head. "This here's one of them smelly cheese ball hors d'oeuvres. Who's throwing cheese balls?"

"Free Captain Kirk," someone yelled.

"The hell we will," Lula said.

Whap! Lula took it in the forehead with a crab puff.

"Now just a minute," she said.

Whap. Whap. Whap. Egg rolls.

The entire room chanted in unison, "Free Captain Kirk. Free Captain Kirk."

"I'm getting out of here," Lula said. "These people are nuts. They been beamed up one time too many."

I yanked Elwood forward, toward the door, getting nailed with a splotch of hot sauce for the egg rolls, plus a couple cheese balls.

"Get them!" someone yelled. "They're kidnapping Captain Kirk."

Lula and I ducked our heads and fought our way through a barrage of hijacked hors d'oeuvres and ugly threats. We reached the front door and bolted outside, hitting the pavement at a run, half dragging Elwood behind us. We threw him into the backseat, and I put the gas pedal to the floor. Any other car would have rocketed away, but the Buick purposefully eased out of its berth and muscled its way down the street.

"You know, when you think about it, those Trekkies were a

bunch of pussies," Lula said. "If this had happened in my neighborhood, those cheese balls would have had bullets in them."

Elwood was sullen in the backseat, not saying anything. He'd
caught a couple cheese balls and egg rolls by accident, and his Kirk
suit wasn't up to Federation standard anymore.

I dropped Lula off and continued on to the police station.
Jimmy Neeley was at the desk. "Jesus," he said, "what's that smell?"

"Cheese balls," I told him. "And egg roll."

"You look like you've been in a food fight."

"It was the Romulan who started it," I said. "Damn Romulans."

"Yeah," Neeley said, "you can't trust them Romulans."

I got my body receipt and retrieved my cuffs from Captain
Kirk, then I left the police station and walked out into the night air.
The police lot was artificially bright, lit by overhead halogens. Beyond the halogens the sky was dark and starless. A light rain had
started to fall. It would have been a cozy night if I was over at
Morelli's with him and Bob. As it was, I was alone in the rain,
smelling like a big crab puff, feeling a little worried that someone
had terminated Cynthia Lotte and I might be next. The only good
thing about the Lotte murder was that it had temporarily taken my
mind off Arturo Stolle.

I didn't feel totally sexually attractive with my sauce-stained
shirt and cheese-ball hair, so I went home to change before seeing
Morelli. I parked the Buick next to Mr. Weinstein's Cadillac,
locked up, and took a step toward the building before I realized
Ranger was leaning against the car in front of me.

"You need to be more careful, babe," he said. "You should look
around before you get out of your car."

"I was distracted."

"A bullet in the head would distract you permanently."

I made a face and stuck my tongue out.

Ranger smiled. "Trying to get me excited?" He picked a glob of
food out of my hair. "Egg roll?"

"It's been a long night."

"Did you learn anything from Ramos?"

"He said they had a problem in Trenton, which I'm supposing is Junior Macaroni. But then he said he'd fixed it so the problem would go on a boat next week. And with any luck the boat would sink. Then the two goons came in to retrieve him, and they said they couldn't find the cargo. Do you know what any of this means?"

"Yes."

"Do you want to tell me?"

"No."

Christ. "You're a real prick. I'm not working for you anymore."

"Too late. I already fired you."

"I mean *ever*!"

"Where's Bob?"

"With Morelli."

"So all I have to worry about is keeping you safe," Ranger said.

"The sentiment is sweet, but not necessary."

"What, are you kidding me? I told you to drop out and be careful and two hours later you've got Ramos back in your car."

"I was looking for you, and he jumped in the Buick."

"You ever hear about door locks?"

I tipped my nose up, trying to pull off looking indignant. "I'm going inside. And just to make you happy I'll *lock* my door."

"Wrong. You're going with me, and I'm going to *lock* you *up*."

"Are you threatening me?"

"No. I'm flat-out telling you."

"Listen, mister," I said, "this is the twenty-first century. Women aren't property. You just don't go around locking us up. If I want to do something incredibly stupid and put myself in danger, I have the right to do it."

Ranger clapped a bracelet on me. "I don't think so."

"Hey!"

"It'll only be for a couple days."

"I can't believe this! You're actually going to lock me up?"

He reached for my other wrist, and I yanked the cuff out of his hand and jumped away.

"Come here," he said.

I put a car between us. I had his bracelet dangling from my wrist, and in a weird way, which I didn't want to think about, it was sort of erotic. And then in another way, it really pissed me off. I reached into my shoulder bag and came up with my pepper spray. "Come get me," I told him.

He put his hands on the car. "This isn't going well, is it?"

"How did you expect it to go?"

"You're right. I should have known. Nothing is ever simple with you. Men blow themselves up. Cars get flattened by garbage trucks. I've been in full-scale invasions that have been less harrowing than meeting you for coffee." He held the key up for me to see. "Would you like me to take the cuff off?"

"Throw the key over here."

"Uh-unh. You have to come to me."

"No way."

"That pepper spray only works if you get it in my face. Do you think you're good enough to get it in my face?"

"Absolutely."

A junker of a car pulled into the lot. Ranger and I gave it our full attention. Ranger had a gun in his hand, his hand at his side.

The car came to a stop and Mooner and Dougie got out. "Hey, dude," Mooner called to me. "Lucky break finding you here. Me and Dougie need some of your sage advice."

"I have to talk to these guys," I said to Ranger. "Lula and I sort of trashed their house."

"Let me guess, they were serving egg rolls and something yellow."

"Cheese balls. And it wasn't my fault. The Romulan started it."

The corners of his mouth tipped into a small, controlled smile. "I should have guessed it was the Romulan." He holstered his gun. "Go talk to your friends. We'll finish this later."

"The key?"

He smiled and shook his head.

"This is war," I said.

The smile turned grim. "Be careful."

I backed away and moved to the building's back door, Dougie and Mooner following me. I couldn't imagine what they wanted. Restitution for damages? A report on Elwood's future as a drug lord? My opinion of the egg rolls?

I hurried through the lobby and took the stairs. "We can talk in my apartment," I said. "I need to change my shirt."

"Sorry about your shirt, dude. Those Trekkies turned ugly. I'm telling you, they were a mob," Mooner said. "That Federation is in trouble. They're never gonna make a go of it with members like that. They had no regard for Dougie's personal residence."

I opened my apartment door. "Was there much damage?"

Mooner flopped onto the couch. "In the beginning, we thought it was just going to be cheese-ball damage. But then we had trouble with the VCR and had to cut the film portion of the evening short."

"The VCR crapped out right in the middle of 'The Trouble with Tribbles,' and we were lucky to escape with our lives," Dougie said.

"We're, like, afraid to go back there, dude. We were wondering if we could crash here tonight with you and your granny."

"Grandma Mazur moved back to my parents'."

"Too bad. She was happening."

I gave them pillows and blankets.

"Rad bracelet," Mooner said.

I looked at the cuff still locked onto my right wrist. I'd forgotten it was there. I wondered if Ranger was still in the lot. And I wondered if I should have gone with him. I slid the bolt on the door, and then I locked myself in my bedroom, crawled into bed with the cheese gunk still in my hair, and immediately fell asleep.

When I woke up the next morning I realized I'd forgotten about Joe.

Shit.

There was no answer at his house, and I was about to try his pager when the phone rang.

"What the hell's going on?" Joe said. "I just got in to work and heard you got attacked by a Romulan."

"I'm fine. I made an apprehension at a *Star Trek* event, and it sort of got weird."

"Unfortunately, I have some weird news of my own. Your friend Carol Zabo is back on the bridge. It seems she and a whole pack of her friends kidnapped Joyce Barnhardt and left her naked and tied to a tree by the pet cemetery in Hamilton Township."

"Are you kidding me? Carol got arrested for kidnapping Joyce Barnhardt?"

"No. Joyce didn't press charges. It was a real event, though. Half the force went out to turn her loose. Carol got arrested for being too happy in a public place. I think she and the girls were celebrating with wacky tobaccy. She's only looking at a misdemeanor, but nobody can convince her she's not going to jail. We were wondering if you could go out and talk her off the bridge. She's making a mess out of rush hour."

"I'll be right there." This was all my fault. Boy, when things started to go wrong the whole world turned into a toilet.

I'd gone to bed in my clothes, so I didn't have to bother getting dressed. On my way through the living room, I yelled to Mooner and Dougie that I'd be back. By the time I got to the back door of the building I had my pepper spray in hand, just in case Ranger jumped out at me from behind a bush.

There was no Ranger. And there was no Habib or Mitchell either, so I took off for the bridge. Cops were lucky—they had those big red lights when they needed to get somewhere fast. I didn't have any lights, so I just drove on the sidewalk when the traffic clogged up.

There was a steady rain falling. Temperatures were in the forties, and the entire state's population was on the phone checking airfares to Florida. Except, of course, for the people who were on the bridge, gawking at Carol.

I parked behind a blue-and-white and made my way on foot to

the middle of the bridge, where Carol was perched on the railing, holding an umbrella.

"Thanks for taking care of Joyce," I said. "What are you doing on the bridge?"

"I got arrested again."

"You're charged with a misdemeanor. You won't go to jail for it."

Carol climbed off the railing. "I just wanted to make sure." She squinted at me. "What's in your hair? And what's with the hand-cuff? You've been with Morelli, right?"

"Not in a while," I said, wistfully.

We went back to our cars. Carol went home. And I went to the office.

"Oh boy," Lula said when she saw me. "Think we got a good story walking in the door, here. What's with the handcuff?"

"I thought it would look good with the cheese balls in my hair. You know, dress up the outfit."

"I hope it was Morelli," Connie said. "I wouldn't mind being cuffed by Morelli."

"Close," I said. "It was Ranger."

"Uh-oh," Lula said. "Think I just wet my pants."

"It wasn't anything sexual," I said. "It was . . . an accident. And then we lost the key."

Connie fanned herself with a manila folder. "I'm having a hot flash."

I gave Connie the body receipt for Elwood Steiger. All things considered, it had been easy money. No one shot at me or set me on fire.

The front door crashed open and Joyce Barnhardt burst in. "You're gonna pay for that," she said to me. "You're gonna be sorry you messed with me!"

Lula and Connie swiveled their heads to me and gave me the "What?" look.

"Carol Zabo and some friends helped me out by leaving Joyce tied to a tree . . . naked."

"I don't want any shooting in here," Connie said to Joyce.

"Shooting's too easy," Joyce said. "I want something better. I want Ranger." She narrowed her eyes at me. "I know you're cozy with him. Well, you better use that as leverage and deliver him to me. Because if you don't deliver him to me in twenty-four hours I'm pressing kidnapping charges against Carol Zabo." Joyce wheeled around on her high-heeled boots and swished out the door.

"Sheee-it," Lula said. "There's that sulfur smell again."

Connie handed me my check for Elwood. "This is a dilemma."

I took the check and dropped it into my bag. "I have so many dilemmas I can't even remember them all."

OLD MRS. BESTLER was in the elevator, playing elevator operator. "Going up," she said. "Ladies' handbags, lingerie . . ." She leaned on her walker and looked at me. "Oh dear," she said, "the beauty salon's on the second floor."

"Good," I told her. "That's just where I'm going."

My apartment was quiet when I let myself in. The extra blankets were neatly stacked on the couch. A note had been placed on one of the pillows. Only one word had been written on the paper. "Later."

I dragged myself into the bathroom, stripped, and washed my hair, several times. I got dressed in clean clothes, then blasted my hair with the dryer, and pulled it into a ponytail. I called Morelli to see how Bob was doing, and he said Bob was fine and his neighbor was dog-sitting. Then I went down to the basement and got Dillan to hacksaw through the chain on the cuffs, so I didn't have the second bracelet swinging in the breeze.

Then I didn't have anything to do. I didn't have any FTAs to retrieve. I didn't have a dog to walk. I had no one to watch, no houses to break into. I could have gone to a locksmith to have the cuff opened, but I had hopes of getting the key from Ranger. I was going to turn him over to Joyce tonight. Better to deliver Ranger to

Joyce than have to talk Carol off the bridge again. Rescuing Carol from a watery grave was getting old. And it'd be easy to deliver Ranger. All I had to do was arrange a meeting. Tell him I wanted the cuff off, and he'd come to me. Then I'd knock him out with the stun gun and pack him off to Joyce. Of course, after I handed him over I'd have to do something sneaky and rescue him. I certainly wasn't going to have Ranger hauled off to jail.

Since it would appear I didn't have anything on the agenda until tonight, I thought I should clean the hamster cage. And after the hamster cage, maybe I'd do the refrigerator. Hell, I might even get totally carried away and scour the bathroom . . . no, that wasn't likely. I dumped Rex out of his soup can and put him in my big spaghetti pot on the kitchen counter. He sat there, blinking in the sudden light, unhappy to have his sleep interrupted.

"Sorry, little guy," I said. "Gotta clean the ol' hacienda."

Ten minutes later, Rex was back in his cage, frantic because all his buried treasures were now in a big black plastic garbage bag. I gave him a cracked walnut and a raisin. He took the raisin into his new soup can, and that was the last I saw of him.

I looked out my living room window, down into the wet parking lot. Still no sign of Habib and Mitchell. All the cars belonged to tenants. Good deal. It was safe to get rid of my garbage. I shrugged into my jacket, grabbed the bag of hamster bedding, and hustled down the hall.

Mrs. Bestler was still in the elevator. "Oh, you look much better now, dear," she said. "Nothing like spending a relaxing hour at the beauty parlor." The elevator doors opened to the lobby, and I hopped out. "Going up," Mrs. Bestler sang out. "Menswear, third floor." And the doors slid shut.

I crossed the lobby to the rear entrance and paused for a moment to pull my hood up. The rain was steady. Water pooled on the glistening blacktop and beaded on the old folks' freshly waxed cars. I stepped outside, put my head down, and hurried across the lot to the Dumpster.

I pitched the bag inside the bin, turned, and found myself face to face with Habib and Mitchell. They were soaking wet, and they didn't look friendly.

"Where'd you come from?" I asked. "I don't see your car."

"It's parked on the side street," Mitchell said, showing me his gun, "and that's where you're headed. Start walking."

"I don't think so," I said. "If you shoot me, Ranger has no incentive to deal with Stolle."

"Wrong," Mitchell said. "If we *kill* you, Ranger has no incentive."

Good point.

The Dumpster was on the back edge of the lot. I stumbled across a patch of rain-slicked lawn on wobbly legs, too scared to think clearly. Wondering where Ranger was now, when I needed him. Why wasn't he here, insisting on locking me up in a safe house? Now that my hamster's cage was clean, I'd be happy to oblige.

Mitchell was driving the mom-van again. Guess they weren't having a lot of luck cleaning up the Lincoln. And probably I didn't want to choose that as a topic of conversation.

Habib sat beside me in the backseat. He was wearing a raincoat but it looked soaked through. They must have been crouching in the bushes at the edge of the building. He was hatless, and water dripped from his hair, down the back of his neck, and onto his face. He wiped his face with his hand. No one seemed to mind that they were getting the mom-van wet.

"Well," I said, trying to make my voice sound normal. "Now what?"

"Now you do not want to know," Habib said. "You should being quiet now."

Being quiet was bad, since it gave me time to think. And thinking wasn't pleasant. No good was going to come of this ride. I tried to close my emotions down. Fear and regret weren't going to get me anywhere. Didn't want to let my imagination run wild, either. This could just be another meeting with Arturo. No need to go

752

berserk ahead of time. I concentrated on breathing. Nice and steady. Taking in oxygen. I did a mental chant. *Ohhhmm.* I saw someone doing that on television, and she looked like she really got off on it.

Mitchell drove west on Hamilton, toward the river. He crossed Broad and wound around in a part of town that was zoned industrial. The lot he pulled into was next to a three-story brick structure that had been a machine-tool factory but was now sitting unused. A "For Sale" sign had been fixed to the front of the building, but it looked like it had been there for a hundred years.

Mitchell parked the van and got out. He opened my door and waved me out at gunpoint. Habib followed. He unlocked the building's side door, and we all trooped in. It was cold and damp inside. The lighting was dim, coming from open doorways to small offices where the sun filtered through grimy exterior windows. We walked down a short hall and turned into a reception area. The tile was grungy underfoot and the area was bare, with the exception of two metal folding chairs and a small, scarred wood desk. There was a cardboard box on the desk.

"Sit down," Mitchell said to me. "Pick a chair."

He took his coat off and threw it onto the desk. Habib did the same. Their shirts weren't much drier than their coats.

"Okay, here's the plan," Mitchell said. "We're gonna hit you with the stun gun, and then while you're out we're gonna cut off your finger with the shears, here." He picked a pair of bolt cutters out of the cardboard box. "That way we have something to send to Ranger. Then we hang on to you and see what happens. If he wants to trade, we're in business. If he doesn't, I guess we kill you."

There was a loud buzzing in my ears, and I snapped my head to make it go away. "Wait a minute," I said. "I have some questions."

Mitchell sighed. "Women always have questions."

"Perhaps we could cut out her tongue," Habib said. "That sometimes works. We have much luck with that in my village."

I was getting the feeling he'd lied about being Pakistani. Sounded to me like his village was in Hell.

"Mr. Stolle didn't say nothing about a tongue," Mitchell said. "He might want to save that for some future time."

"Where are you going to keep me?" I asked Mitchell.

"Here. We're gonna lock you in the bathroom."

"But what about the bleeding?"

"What about it?"

"I could bleed to death. Then how would you trade me to Ranger?"

They looked at each other. They hadn't thought of that. "This is sort of new for me," Mitchell said. "Usually I just beat the shit out of people or pop them."

"You should have some clean bandages and some antiseptic."

"I guess that makes sense," Mitchell said. He looked at his watch. "We haven't got a lot of time. I need to get the van back to my wife to pick the kids up from school. Don't want them to have to wait around in the rain."

"There is a drugstore on Broad Street," Habib said. "We could be getting these things there."

"Get me some Tylenol, too," I said.

I didn't actually want bandages and Tylenol. What I really wanted was time. That's what you always want when a disaster occurs. You want time to hope it's not true. Time for the disaster to go away. Time to find out it was all a mistake. Time for God to intervene.

"Okay," Mitchell said. "Get into the bathroom, over there."

It was a windowless room, about four feet wide and six feet long. One toilet. One sink. That was it. A padlock had been installed on the outside of the door. It didn't look brand-new, so I assumed I wasn't the first person to be held prisoner here.

I went into the little room, and they closed and locked the door. I put my ear to the jamb.

"You know, I'm getting to hate this job," Mitchell said. "Why can't we ever do this kind of stuff on a nice day? One time I had to clip this guy, Alvin Margucci. It was so fucking cold the gun froze up, and we had to beat him to death with the shovel. And then when we went to dig him a hole we couldn't fucking make a dent in the ground. It was all a big Popsicle."

"That sounds like very hard work," Habib said. "It is better in my country, where it is mostly warmer and the ground is soft. Many times we do not even have to dig because Pakistan can be quite rugged, and we can simply throw the freshly dead into a ravine."

"Yeah, well, you know—we got rivers here, but the stiffs bob up to the surface and then that's not so good."

"Just so," Habib said. "I have experienced that myself."

I thought I heard them leave, heard the door at the end of the hall open and close. I tried the bathroom door. I looked around the room. I did some breathing. I looked around the room some more. I told myself to think. I felt like Pooh Bear, who was a Bear of Little Brain. It was a nasty little room, with a filthy sink and a filthy toilet and dirty linoleum floor. The wall next to the sink was water stained, with a damp spot near the ceiling. Probably a plumbing problem on the floor above. We weren't talking quality construction here. I put my hand to the wall and felt it give. The wallboard was soggy.

I was wearing Caterpillar boots with a hefty lug sole. I put my ass on the sink and gave the wallboard a shot with my Cats, and my foot went clear through to the other side. I started laughing, and then I realized I was crying. No time for hysteria, I told myself. Let's just get the hell out of here.

I clawed at the wall, ripping chunks of board away. I got a good-sized opening made between the studs, and I went to work on the adjoining wall. In a matter of minutes I had both walls destroyed enough to be able to wedge myself between the studs. My nails were broken and my fingers were bleeding, but I was in a small office now with the bathroom behind me. I tried the door. The door was locked. Jesus, I thought, don't tell me I'm going to have to kick my way through this whole fucking building! Wait a minute, fool. The office has a window. I made myself take a breath. I wasn't in top thinking form. I was too panicked. I tried the window, but it wouldn't budge. It had been closed for too long. There'd been numerous paintings over the lock. No furniture in the room. I took my jacket off, wrapped it around my hand, made a fist, and smashed the window. I cleared as much glass away as I could and looked out. It was a long drop, but I could probably do it. I took my boot off and pounded away at the remaining glass in the window, so I wouldn't cut myself any worse than was necessary. I put the shoe back on and swung a leg onto the window ledge.

The window faced front. Please God, don't let Habib and Mitchell drive by when I jump out of the window. I let myself out slowly, back to the street so I could hang by my hands, my toes digging against the brick. When I was fully extended I dropped, landing first on my feet and then falling on my ass. I lay there for a minute, stunned, flat on the sidewalk, rain splattering on my face.

I sucked in some air and got to my feet and started running. I crossed the street and ran through an alley and crossed another street. I had no idea where I was going. I was just putting space between me and the brick building.

FOURTEEN

I STOPPED TO catch my breath, bending at the waist, eyes narrowed against the pain in my lungs. My jeans were torn at the knees, and my knees were scraped from the glass. Both hands were cut. I'd lost my jacket in my rush to escape. It had been wrapped around my hand, and I'd left it behind. I was wearing a T-shirt and a flannel shirt, and I was soaked to the skin. My teeth were chattering from cold and fear. I pressed myself against the side of a building and listened to the rain-muffled sound of cars not far off, on Broad.

I didn't want to go to Broad. I'd feel too exposed. This wasn't a part of town I knew very well. I didn't have too many choices. But I was going to have to go into one of these buildings and get help. There was a gas station–convenience store on the other side of the street. I didn't feel comfortable with that. Too visible. I was next to a building that looked like offices. I slipped in through the front door to a small vestibule. A single elevator sat to the left. A metal fire door leading to stairs was located next to the elevator. The chart on the wall listed the businesses in the building. Five floors of businesses. Didn't recognize any of the tenants. I took the stairs to the first floor and picked a door at random. It opened to a room full of metal shelves, and the shelves were loaded with computers and printers and assorted hardware. A frizzy-haired guy in a T-shirt was working at a table just inside the door. He looked up when I poked my head in.

"What do you do here?" I asked.

"We repair computers."

"I was wondering if I could use your phone to make a local call. My bike slid out from under me in the rain, and I need to call for a ride." Probably the fact that there were men looking to mutilate me was more information than he desired.

He looked me over. "You sure you want to stay with that story?"

"Yeah. I'm sure." When in doubt . . . always lie.

He motioned to the phone at the end of the table. "Help yourself."

I couldn't call my parents. There was no way to explain this to them. And I didn't want to call Joe, because I didn't want him to know how stupid I'd been. I wasn't going to call Ranger, because he'd lock me up, although the idea was gaining in appeal. That left Lula.

"Thanks," I said to the guy, replacing the phone after I'd given Lula the address. "Appreciate it."

He looked sort of horrified at my appearance, so I backed out of the office and went downstairs to wait.

Five minutes later, Lula pulled up in the Firebird. When I got in, she locked the doors and took the gun out of her purse and laid it on the console between us.

"Good call," I said.

"Where are we going?"

I couldn't go home. Habib and Mitchell would eventually look for me there. I could stay with my parents or Joe, but not until I got cleaned up. I was sure Lula would let me stay with her, too, but her apartment was tiny and I didn't want WWIII to start because we were stepping on each other's toes. "Take me to Dougie's house," I said.

"I don't know how you got all those cuts, but you must have got brain damage, too."

I explained it all to Lula. "No one will think to look for me at Dougie's," I said. "Besides, he's got clothes from when he was the Dealer. And he's probably got a car I can use."

"You should page Ranger or Joe," Lula said. "Better one of them than Dougie. They'll keep you safe."

"Can't do that. I have to trade Ranger for Carol tonight."

"Say what?"

"I'm turning Ranger over to Joyce tonight." I punched Joe's office number into Lula's car phone. "I have a huge favor to ask," I said to Morelli.

"Another one?"

"I'm worried someone might break into my apartment, and I can't get home right now. I was wondering if you could get Rex and take him with you."

There was a heavy silence. "How urgent is this?"

"Urgent."

"I hate this," Morelli said.

"And while you're there, maybe you could check the cookie jar and see if my gun is there. And, um, maybe you could also snag my shoulder bag."

"What's going on?"

"Arturo Stolle thinks he can get Ranger to cooperate with him by holding me hostage."

"Are you okay?"

"Peachy fine. It's just that I left the apartment in a hurry."

"I don't suppose you'd want me to pick you up someplace."

"No. Just Rex. I'm with Lula."

"That fills me with confidence."

"I'll try to get over later tonight."

"Try real hard."

Lula came to a stop in front of Dougie's house. The two front windows were boarded over. The shades were drawn in the upstairs windows, but light peeked out from behind. Lula gave me her Glock. "Take this with you. It has a full clip. And call me if you need anything."

"I'll be fine," I said.

"Sure. I know that. I'm gonna wait here until you get in the house and give me the sign to go."

I ran the short distance to Dougie's front door. I'm not sure why. I couldn't have gotten much wetter. I knocked on the door, but no one answered. I imagined Dougie hiding somewhere, afraid a Trekkie had come back to see him.

"Hey, Dougie!" I yelled. "It's Stephanie. Open the door!"

That got results. A shade moved aside and Dougie peeked out. Then the front door was opened.

"Anyone here with you?" I asked.

"Just the Mooner."

I shoved the Glock into the waistband of my jeans and turned and waved to Lula.

"Close and lock the door," I said, stepping into the room.

Dougie was way ahead of me. Not only had he already locked the door, but he was pushing a refrigerator in front of it.

"Do you think that's necessary?" I asked.

"I guess it's overkill," he said. "It's actually been quiet today. It's just that I'm still freaked out from the riot."

"Looks like they broke your windows."

"Only one. The fire department broke the other one when they threw the couch out onto the sidewalk."

I looked at the couch. Half of it was charred. Mooner sat on the uncharred half.

"Hey, dude, you came at the right time," he said. "We just heated up some crab puffs. We're watching an *I Dream of Jeannie* retrospective on Nick at Nite. It's, like, awesome the way Jeannie does that blinking thing."

"Yeah," Dougie said. "We got lots of crab puffs left. We have to eat them before they expire on Friday."

I thought it was strange that neither of them commented on the fact that I was wet and bleeding and had walked in with a Glock in my hand. But then, maybe people showed up here like that all the time. "I was wondering if you had any dry clothes," I said to Dougie. "Did you get rid of all those jeans you were trying to sell?"

"I have a whole bunch in the bedroom upstairs. Mostly small sizes, so maybe you'll find something. And there's shirts up there, too. You can help yourself to whatever you want."

There were some Band-Aids in the medicine chest in the bathroom. I cleaned myself up as well as I could and picked over Dougie's clothes until I found something that fit.

It was midafternoon, and I hadn't had lunch, so I wolfed down some crab puffs. Then I went into the kitchen and called Morelli on his cell phone.

"Where are you?" he asked.

"Why?"

"I want to know, that's why."

Something was wrong. My God, not Rex. "What's wrong? Is it Rex? Is Rex all right?"

"Rex is fine. He's in a squad car with Costanza, on his way to my house. I'm still in your apartment. The door was open when I got here, and the place has been ransacked. I don't think anything's destroyed, but it's a real mess. They dumped everything out of your bag, onto the floor. Your wallet and stun gun and pepper spray are still here. Your gun was still in the cookie jar. Looks to me like these guys were more mad than anything. I think they tore through here and didn't even see Rex's cage."

I had my hand to my heart. Rex was okay. That was all I cared about.

"I'm getting ready to lock up," he said. "Tell me where you are."

"I'm at Dougie's."

"Dougie *Kruper*?"

"We're watching *I Dream of Jeannie*."

"I'll be right there."

"No! I'm perfectly safe. No one would think to look for me here. And I'm helping Dougie clean. Lula and I caused a riot last night, and I feel responsible, and I need to help clean." Liar, liar, pants on fire.

"That sounds reasonable, but I don't believe any of it."

"Listen, I don't interfere with your work, and you can't interfere with mine."

"Yeah, but *I* know what I'm doing."

He had a point. "I'll see you tonight."

"Shit," Morelli said. "I need a drink."

"Check my bedroom closet. Maybe Grandma left a bottle."

I WATCHED *JEANNIE* with Dougie and Mooner for three hours. I ate some more crab puffs. And then I called Ranger. He didn't answer his phone, so I tried his pager. Ten minutes later, I got a call back.

"I want to get this bracelet off," I told him.

"You could go to a locksmith."

"I'm having some additional problems with Stolle."

"And?"

"And I need to talk to you."

"And?"

"I'll be in the lot behind the office at nine o'clock. I'll be in a borrowed car. I don't know what kind, yet."

Ranger disconnected. I guess that meant he'd be there.

Now I had a problem. All I had was a Glock. And Ranger wouldn't be afraid of the Glock. He'd know I wouldn't shoot him.

"I need some stuff," I said to Dougie. "I need handcuffs and a stun gun and some pepper spray."

"I don't have any here," Dougie said, "but I could make a phone call. I know a guy."

Half hour later, there was a knock on the door, and we all pushed the refrigerator out of the way. We opened the door, and my upper lip curled back.

"Lenny Gruber," I said. "Haven't seen you since you repossessed my Miata."

"I've been busy."

"Yeah, I know. So many rotten things to do, and so little time."

"Dude!" Mooner said. "Come on in. Have a crab puff."

Gruber and I went to school together. He was the kind of guy who passed gas in class and then yelled out, "Hey, that stinks! Who cut the cheese?" He was missing a molar, and his pants were never completely zipped.

Gruber helped himself to a crab puff and put an aluminum attaché case on the coffee table. He opened the case and inside was a jumble of tasers, stun guns, defense sprays, cuffs, knives, saps, and brass knuckles. Also a box of condoms and a vibrator. I guess he did a good pimp trade.

I picked out a pair of cuffs, a stun gun, and a small can of pepper spray. "How much?" I asked.

His eyes were locked onto my chest. "For you, a special deal."

"Don't do me any favors," I said.

He gave me a price that was fair.

"Deal," I told him. "But you'll have to wait to get paid. I don't have anything on me."

He grinned, and the missing molar looked like the black hole of Calcutta in his mouth. "We could work something out."

"We'll work *nothing* out. I'll get the money to you tomorrow."

"If I don't get paid until tomorrow the price will have to go up."

"Listen, Gruber, I've had a *very bad day*. Don't push me. I'm a woman on the edge." I hit the "on" button on the stun gun. "Is this thing live? Maybe I should test it on someone."

"Women," Gruber said to Mooner. "Can't live with them. Can't live without them."

"Could you move a little to the left?" Mooner asked. "You're blocking the television, dude, and Jeannie's gonna blink Major Nelson."

I BORROWED A two-year-old Jeep Cherokee from Dougie. It was one of four cars left unsold because their registration and bill of sale had gotten misplaced. I'd found jeans and a T-shirt that sort of fit. And I'd borrowed a lined denim jacket and clean socks from

Mooner. Neither Dougie nor Mooner had a washer or dryer and neither was a cross-dresser, so what I was missing was underwear. I had my cuffs looped over the back of my jeans. The rest of my equipment was stuffed into the jacket's assorted pockets.

I drove to the lot behind Vinnie's office and parked. The rain had stopped and the air felt warm with the promise of spring. It was very dark, no stars or moon showing through the cloud cover. There was room behind the office for four cars to park. So far, mine was the only one there. I was early. Probably not as early as Ranger. He'd undoubtedly seen me arrive and was watching from somewhere to make sure the meeting was safe. Standard operating procedure.

I was watching the alley that led to the small lot when Ranger rapped softly on my window.

"Damn!" I said. "You scared the bejeezus out of me. You shouldn't sneak up on a person like that."

"You should keep your back to the wall, babe." He opened my door. "Take your jacket off."

"I'll be cold."

"Take it off and hand it to me."

"You don't trust me."

He smiled.

I took the jacket off and handed it over.

"Lot of hardware in here," he said.

"The usual."

"Get out of the car."

This wasn't the way it was supposed to happen. I hadn't counted on losing my jacket so soon. "I'd rather you got in. It's warmer in here."

"Get out."

I gave a big sigh and got out.

He put his hand to the small of my back, dipped his fingers below the waistband of my jeans, and removed the cuffs.

"Let's go inside," he said. "I feel safer in there."

"Just out of morbid curiosity, do you know how to get around the alarm, or do you know the security code?"

He opened the back door. "I know the code."

We walked through the short hall to the back room where the guns and office supplies are kept. Ranger opened the door to the front room and ambient light from the street poured in through the plate-glass windows. Standing between the two rooms, he was able to see both doors.

He put my jacket and the cuffs on a file cabinet, out of my reach, and looked down at the hacksawed bracelet on my right wrist. "New design."

"But still annoying."

He took the key out of his pocket, unlocked the cuff, and threw the cuff on top of my jacket. Then he took both my hands in his and turned them palms up. "You're wearing someone else's clothes, you're carrying someone else's gun, your hands are cut, and you're not wearing underwear. What's the deal here?"

I looked down at the outline of breast and protruding nipple, straining against the confines of the T-shirt. "Sometimes I go without underwear."

"You *never* go without underwear."

"How do you know?"

"God-given talent."

He was wearing his usual street clothes—black cargo pants tucked into black boots, a black T-shirt, and a black windbreaker. He took off the windbreaker and wrapped it around me. It was warm from his body heat and smelled very faintly of the ocean.

"Spending a lot of time in Deal?" I asked.

"I should be there now."

"Is someone watching Ramos for you?"

"Tank."

His hands still held the windbreaker, his knuckles resting lightly on my breasts. An act of intimate possession more than of sexual aggression.

"How are you going to do it?" he asked, his voice soft.

"Do what?"

"Capture me. Isn't that what this is about?"

765

That had been the original plan, but he'd taken my toys away. And now the air was feeling hot and thick in my lungs, and I was thinking it wasn't any of my beeswax if Carol took a flying leap off the bridge. I put my hands flat to his abdomen, and he watched me carefully. I suspect he was waiting for me to answer his question, but I had a more pressing problem. I didn't know what to feel first. Should I move my hands up? Or should I move my hands down? I wanted to go down, but that might seem too forward. I didn't want him to think I was easy.

"Steph?"

"Huh?"

I still had my hands on his stomach, and I could feel him laughing. "I can smell something burning, babe. You must be thinking."

It wasn't my brain that was on fire. I felt around a little with my fingertips.

He shook his head. "Don't encourage me. This isn't a good time." He removed my hands from his stomach and took another look at the cuts. "How did this happen?"

I told him about Habib and Mitchell and the factory escape.

"Arturo Stolle deserved Homer Ramos," Ranger said.

"I wouldn't know. No one tells me anything!"

"For years, Stolle's cut of the crime pie has been illegal adoption and immigration. He uses his East Asian contacts to bring young girls into the country for prostitution and to produce high-priced adoption babies. Six months ago, Stolle realized he could use those same contacts to smuggle drugs in with the girls. Problem is, drugs aren't part of Stolle's piece of pie. So Stolle hooked up with Homer Ramos, who is known far and wide as a stupid shit always in need of money, and arranged for Ramos to act as bagman between him and his accounts. Stolle figured the other Mob factions would back off from Alexander Ramos's kid."

"How do you fit into this?"

"Arbitrator. I was acting as a liaison between the factions. Everyone, feds included, would like to avoid a crime war." His pager beeped, and he looked at the readout. "I have to get back to

Deal. Do you have any secret weapons in your arsenal? You want to make any last-ditch efforts at apprehension?"

Ugh. He was so smug! "I hate you," I said.

"No, you don't," Ranger said, kissing me lightly on the lips.

"Why did you agree to meet me?"

Our eyes locked for a moment. And then he cuffed me. Both hands behind my back.

"Shit!" I yelled.

"I'm sorry, but you're a real pain in the ass. I can't do my job when I'm worrying about you. I'm turning you over to Tank. He'll take you to a safe house and baby-sit you until things get resolved."

"You can't do that! Carol will be back on the bridge."

Ranger grimaced. "Carol?"

I told him about Carol and Joyce and how Carol didn't want to get caught on *Candid Camera* and how it was all sort of my fault this time.

Ranger thunked his head on the file cabinet. "Why me?" he said.

"I wouldn't have let Joyce keep you," I told him. "I was going to turn you over to her and then figure out a way to get you back."

"I know I'm going to regret this, but I'm going to set you loose so, God forbid, Carol doesn't jump off the bridge. I'm going to give you until nine o'clock tomorrow morning to work things out with Joyce, and then I'm coming after you. And I want you to promise you won't go near Arturo Stolle or *anyone* named Ramos."

"I promise."

I DROVE ACROSS town to Lula's house. She has a second-floor apartment, facing front, and her lights were still on. I didn't have a phone, so I walked up to her door and rang the bell. A window opened above me, and Lula stuck her head out. "What?"

"It's Stephanie."

She dropped a key down, and I let myself in.

Lula met me at the top of the stairs. "Are you spending the night?"

"No. I need some help. You know how I was going to turn Ranger over to Joyce? Well, it didn't exactly work out."

Lula burst out laughing. "Girl, Ranger is the shit. No one's better than Ranger. Not even you." She took in the T-shirt and jeans. "I don't mean to get too personal, but were you wearing a bra when you started the evening, or is this something recent?"

"I started out this way. Dougie and Mooner don't wear my kind of underwear."

"Too bad," Lula said.

It was a two-room apartment. Bedroom with bath attached, and another room that served as living room and dining room and had a small corner kitchen. Lula had placed a little round table and two ladderback chairs at the edge of the kitchen area. I sat on one of the chairs and took a beer from Lula.

"You want a sandwich?" she asked. "I got bologna."

"A sandwich would be great. Dougie just had crab puffs." I took a long pull on the beer. "So this is the problem: what are we going to do about Joyce? I feel responsible for Carol."

"You can't be responsible for someone else's bad judgment," Lula said. "You didn't tell her to tie Joyce to that tree."

True.

"Still," she said, "it'd feel good to screw Joyce over one more time."

"You have any ideas?"

"How well does Joyce know Ranger?"

"She's seen him a couple times."

"Suppose we slip her someone who looks like Ranger, and then we take back the ringer? I know this guy, Morgan, who could pass. Same dark skin. Same build. Maybe not as fine, but he could come close. Especially if it was real dark, and he didn't open his mouth. He got the name Morgan 'cause he's hung like a horse."

"I'd probably need a couple more beers to think it would work."

Lula looked over at the empty beer bottles sitting on her counter. "I got a head start on you. So I'm real optimistic about this plan." She opened a dog-eared address book and thumbed through it. "I know him from my former profession."

"Customer?"

"Pimp. He's a real asshole, but he owes me a favor. And he'd probably get off on passing as Ranger. He probably got a Ranger outfit in his closet, too."

Five minutes later, Morgan answered his page, and Lula and I had ourselves a fake Ranger.

"Here's the plan," Lula said. "We pick the dude up on the corner of Stark and Belmont in a half hour. Only he hasn't got all night, so we gotta get this thing moving."

I called Joyce and told her I had Ranger, and she should meet us in the lot behind the office. It was the darkest spot I could think of.

I finished my sandwich and beer, and Lula and I packed off in the Cherokee. We got to the corner of Stark and Belmont, and I had to do a double-take to make sure the man standing there wasn't Ranger.

When Morgan got closer, the differences were apparent. The skin tone was the same, but his features were more coarse. There was more age around his mouth and eyes, less intelligence in his expression. "Joyce better not look too close," I said to Lula.

"I told you to have another bottle of beer," Lula said. "Anyway, it's real dark behind the office, and if things go right Joyce'll break down before she gets too far."

We cuffed Morgan's hands in front of him, which is a dumb thing to do, but Joyce wasn't a good enough bounty hunter to know it. Then we gave him the key to the cuffs. The deal was that he'd put the key in his mouth when we got to the lot. He'd refuse to talk to Joyce, playing sullen. We'd arrange for her to get a flat, and when she got out to take a look, Morgan would take the cuffs off and escape into the night.

We got to the alley early, so I could drop Lula. We'd decided she would hide behind the small Dumpster that serviced Vinnie and his neighbor, and when Joyce was busy taking Ranger into custody, Lula would drive a spike into Joyce's tire. Déjà vu. I angled the Cherokee so that Joyce would be forced to park next to the Dumpster. Lula jumped out and hid, and almost immediately lights flashed at the corner.

Joyce pulled her SUV in next to me and got out. I got out, too. Morgan was slumped in the backseat, his head down to his chest.

Joyce squinted into the car. "I can't see him. Put your lights on."

"No way," I said. "And you'd be smart to leave yours off, too. He's got a lot of people looking for him."

"Why's he all slumped over?"

"Drugged."

Joyce nodded. "I was wondering how you were gonna do it."

I made a big deal and some noise over pulling Morgan out of the backseat. He collapsed against me, snatching a cheap feel, and Joyce and I half-dragged him over to her car and stuffed him in.

"One last thing," I said to Joyce, handing her a statement I'd prepared at Lula's. "You need to sign this."

"What is it?"

"It's a document attesting to the fact that you willingly went to the pet cemetery with Carol and asked her to tie you to the tree."

"What are you, nuts? I'm not signing that."

"Then I'm hauling Ranger out of your backseat."

Joyce looked at the SUV and her precious cargo. "What the hell," she said, taking the pen and signing her name. "I got what I wanted."

"You take off first," I said to Joyce, pulling my Glock out of my pocket. "I'll make sure you get out of the alley safely."

"I can't believe you did this," Joyce said. "I didn't think you were such a sneaky little shit."

Honey, you don't know the half of it. "It was for Carol," I said.

I stood there with the Glock drawn and watched Joyce drive away. The instant she turned from the alley to the street, Lula jumped into the car, and we took off.

"I give her about a quarter-mile," Lula said. "I'm the queen of the spike-and-run."

I had a visual on Joyce. There was no traffic, and she was a block ahead of me. Her taillights wobbled and the car slowed.

"Good, good, good," Lula said.

Joyce drove another block at reduced speed.

"She'd like to just drive on that tire," Lula said, "but she's worried about her fancy new SUV."

There was another flash of brake lights, and Joyce pulled to the curb. We were a block behind her with our lights killed, looking parked. Joyce had gotten out and turned toward the back of her car when a van swerved around me and skidded to a stop alongside her. Two men jumped out, guns drawn. One trained his gun on Joyce, and the other grabbed Morgan just as he set foot on the pavement.

"What the hell?" Lula said. "What the fuck?"

It was Habib and Mitchell. They thought they had Ranger.

Morgan got bundled into the mom-van, and the van rocketed off.

Lula and I sat in shocked silence, not sure what to do.

Joyce was yelling and waving her arms. Finally she kicked the flat tire, got into her SUV, and, I assume, made a phone call.

"That worked out pretty good," Lula finally said.

I backed up half a block without lights, turned the corner, and drove away. "Where do you think they picked us up?"

"Must have been at my house," Lula said. "They probably didn't want to make a move when there were two of us. And then they got real lucky when Joyce got that flat."

"They're not going to think they're so lucky when they find out they've got Morgan the Horse."

DOUGIE AND MOONER were playing Monopoly when I got back to Dougie's house. "I thought you worked at Shop & Bag," I said to Mooner. "Why aren't you ever working?"

"I lucked out and got laid off, dude. I'm telling you, this is a great country. Where else could a dude get paid for *not* working?"

I went into the kitchen and dialed Morelli. "I'm at Mooner's house," I told him. "I just had another weird night."

"Yeah, well, it isn't over yet. Your mother's called over here four times in the last hour. You'd better phone home."

"What's wrong?"

"Your grandmother went out on a date, and she isn't back yet, and your mother's losing it."

FIFTEEN

MY MOTHER ANSWERED on the first ring. "It's midnight," she said, "and your grandmother isn't home. She's out with that turtle man."

"Myron Landowsky?"

"They were supposed to go to dinner. That was at five o'clock. Where could they be? I've called his apartment and there's no answer. I've called all the hospitals—"

"Mom, they're adults. They could be doing lots of stuff. When Grandma was living with me I never knew where she was."

"She's running wild!" my mother said. "Do you know what I found in her room? Condoms! What does she want with condoms?"

"Maybe she makes balloon animals out of them."

"Other women have mothers who get sick and go to nursing homes or die in their beds. Not me. I have a mother who wears spandex. What did I do to deserve this?"

"You should go to bed and stop worrying about Grandma."

"I'm not going to bed until that woman comes home. We're going to have a talk. And your father is here, too."

Oh great. There'll be a big scene, and Grandma will be back, living in my apartment.

"Tell Daddy he can go to bed. I'll come over and sit up with you." Anything to keep Grandma from moving back in with me.

I called Joe and told him I *might* be over later, but he shouldn't wait up. Then I reborrowed the Cherokee and drove to my parents' house.

My mother and I were sleeping on the couch when Grandma came in at two o'clock.

"Where were you?" my mother hollered at her. "We were worried sick."

"I had a night of sin," Grandma said. "Boy, that Myron is some kisser. I think he might even have got an erection, except it was hard to tell what with the way he hikes his pants up."

My mother made the sign of the cross, and I looked in my purse for some Rolaids.

"Well, I gotta go to bed," Grandma said. "I'm pooped. And I got another driving test tomorrow."

WHEN I WOKE up I was stretched out on the couch with a quilt over me. The house was filled with the smell of coffee cooking and bacon frying, and my mother was banging pots around in the kitchen.

"Well, at least you're not ironing," I said. When my mother got out the ironing, we knew there was big trouble brewing.

She slammed a lid on the stockpot and looked at me. "Where's your underwear?"

"I got caught in the rain, and I borrowed dry clothes from Dougie Kruper, only he didn't have any underwear. I would have gone home to change, but there are these two guys who want to chop off one of my fingers, and I was afraid they were at my apartment waiting for me."

"Well, thank God," she said. "I was afraid you left your bra in Morelli's car."

"We don't do it in his car. We do it in his bed."

My mother had the big butcher knife in her hand. "I'm going to kill myself."

"You can't fool me," I said, helping myself to coffee. "You'd never kill yourself in the middle of making soup."

Grandma trotted into the kitchen. She was wearing makeup, and her hair was pink.

"Omigod," my mother said. "What next?"

"What do you think of this hair color?" Grandma asked me. "I got one of them rinses at the drugstore. You just shampoo it in."

"It's pink," I said.

"Yeah, that's what I thought, too. It said on the label that it'd be Jezebel Red." She looked at the clock on the wall. "I gotta get a move on. Louise will be here any minute. I got the first appointment for my driving test. Hope you don't mind I asked Louise to take me. I didn't know you were going to be here."

"No sweat," I said. "Knock yourself out."

I made myself some toast and finished my coffee. I heard the toilet flush overhead and knew my father would be down momentarily. My mother looked like she was thinking about ironing.

"Well," I said, jumping up from my seat. "Things to do. Places to go."

"I just washed some grapes. Take some home," my mother said. "And there's ham in the refrigerator for a sandwich."

I DIDN'T SEE Habib or Mitchell when I pulled into my lot, but I had the Glock in hand, just in case. I parked illegally, next to the back entrance, leaving as little space as possible between me and the door, and went directly to my apartment, taking the stairs. When I got there I realized I didn't have a key, and Joe had locked the door when he left.

Because I was the only one in the entire universe who couldn't open my door without a key, I got the spare from my neighbor Mrs. Karwatt.

"Isn't this a nice day?" she asked. "It feels just like spring."

"I guess everything's been pretty quiet here this morning," I said. "No loud noises or strange men out here in the hall?"

"Not that I've noticed." She looked down at my gun. "What a nice Glock. My sister carries a Glock, and she just loves it. I was thinking about trading in my forty-five, but I couldn't bring myself to do it. My dead husband gave it to me for our first anniversary. Rest his soul."

"What a romantic."

"Of course, I could always use a second gun."

I nodded my head in agreement. "You can never have too many guns."

I said good-bye to Mrs. Karwatt and let myself into my apartment. I went room by room, checking closets, looking under the bed and behind the shower curtain to make sure I was alone. Morelli had been right—the apartment was a wreck, but not too many things looked destroyed. My visitors hadn't taken the time to slash upholstery or put their foot into the television screen.

I took a shower and got dressed in clean jeans and a T-shirt. I put some gel in my hair and worked with the big roller brush so I had a lot of loose curls and looked like a cross between Jersey Girl and *Baywatch* Bimbo. I felt dwarfed by the volume of hair, so I added extra mascara to my lashes to balance things out.

I spent some time straightening the apartment, but then I started to get nervous that I was a sitting duck. Not just for Habib and Mitchell, but for Ranger as well. It was past my nine o'clock deadline.

I called Morelli at the office.

"Did your grandmother ever come home?" he asked.

"Yes. And it wasn't pretty. I need to talk to you. How about meeting me for early lunch at Pino's?"

After I hung up with Morelli I called into the office to see if Lula knew anything about Morgan.

"He's fine," Lula said. "But I don't think those guys Habib and Mitchell are gonna get their Christmas bonus."

I called Dougie and told him I was going to keep the Cherokee for a little longer.

"Keep it forever," he said.

By the time I got to Pino's, Morelli was already at a table, working on breadsticks.

"I'll make a deal with you," I said, shrugging out of my denim jacket. "If you tell me what's going on between you and Ranger, I'll let you keep Bob."

"Oh boy," Morelli said. "How can I pass that up?"

"I have an idea about this Ramos business," I said. "But it's pretty far out. I've been thinking about it for three or four days now."

Morelli grinned. "Woman's intuition?"

I smiled, too, because as it's turned out, intuition is the big gun in my arsenal. I can't shoot, I can't run all that fast, and the only karate I know is from Bruce Lee movies. But I have good intuition. Truth is, most of the time I don't know what the hell I'm doing, but if I follow my instincts things usually work out okay. "How was Homer Ramos identified?" I asked Morelli. "Dental records?"

"He was identified by jewelry and circumstance. There were no dental records. They mysteriously disappeared."

"I've been thinking—maybe it wasn't Homer Ramos who got shot. No one in his family seems upset that he's dead. Even if a father thinks his son is rotten to the core, I find it hard to believe there's no emotion at his death. And then I went snooping and discovered someone was living in Hannibal's guest room. Someone the exact size of Homer Ramos. I think Homer was hiding out in Hannibal's town house, and then Macaroni got clipped and Homer ran."

Morelli paused while the waitress brought us our pizza. "This is what we know. Or at least, what we think we know. Homer was the bagman for Stolle's new drug operation. This whole thing sat real bad with the boys in north Jersey and New York, and people started choosing sides."

"Drug war."

"More than that. If a member of the Ramos family was going to deal drugs, then north Jersey was going to deal guns. And nobody was happy about any of this because it meant boundaries would have to be redrawn. Everyone was feeling nervous. So nervous that it became known a contract was out on Homer Ramos.

"What we think but can't prove is that you're right—Homer Ramos isn't dead. Ranger suspected it right from the beginning, and you reinforced the theory when you told him you saw Ulysses in the doorway of the shore house. Ulysses never left Brazil. We think some other poor schnook got toasted in that building, and Homer's squirreled away someplace, waiting to get moved out of the country."

"And you think he's at the shore now."

"It seemed logical, but I don't know anymore. We have no reason to go in and search. Ranger went in but couldn't find anything."

"What about the gym bag? That was filled with Stolle's money, right?"

"We think when word got back to Hannibal that his little brother was about to start a crime wave, he ordered Homer to stop all activity outside the family business and have no further contact with Stolle. Then Hannibal asked Ranger to transport Stolle's money and tell Stolle he was no longer protected by the Ramos name. Problem is, when Stolle opened the suitcase it was filled with newsprint."

"Didn't Ranger check on the contents before he accepted it?"

"The suitcase was locked when it was turned over to Ranger. That was the way Hannibal Ramos had arranged it."

"He set Ranger up?"

"Yeah, but probably only for the fire and execution. I guess he figured Homer had gone too far this time, and promising to be a good boy and stop selling drugs wasn't going to get the contract removed. So Hannibal arranged to have Homer look dead. Ranger makes a good scapegoat because he doesn't belong to anyone. No reason for any retaliation if Ranger's the killer."

"So who has the money? Hannibal?"

"Hannibal set Ranger up to take the fall for the murder, but it's hard to believe he intended to cheat Stolle. He wanted Stolle pacified, not pissed off." Morelli helped himself to another piece of pizza. "I think it sounds like a stunt Homer would pull. He probably switched bags in the car on the way to the office."

Oh boy. "I don't suppose you know what kind of car he was driving?"

"Silver Porsche. Cynthia Lotte's car."

I guess that could explain Cynthia's death.

"What was that face you just made?" Morelli asked.

"It was a guilt grimace. I sort of helped Cynthia steal that car back from Homer."

I told Morelli about Cynthia walking in on Lula and me, and how Cynthia wanted her car back, and how that entailed getting the dead guy out of it. When I was done Morelli just sat there, looking dazed.

"You know, when you're a cop you get to a point where you think you've heard it all," he finally said. "You think there's nothing left that could surprise you. And then *you* come along, and it's a whole new ball game."

I selected another piece of pizza and thought the conversation was probably going to deteriorate now.

"Probably I don't have to point out that you destroyed a crime scene," Morelli said.

Yep. I was right. It was definitely deteriorating.

"And probably I don't have to point out that you withheld evidence in a homicide investigation."

I nodded affirmative.

"Jesus Christ on a crutch, what the hell were you thinking?" he yelled.

Everyone turned and looked at us.

"It wasn't like I could stop her," I said. "So it seemed like the expedient thing to do was to help her."

"You could have left. You could have walked away. You didn't

JANET EVANOVICH

have to *help*! I thought you just picked him up off the cement floor. I didn't know you dragged him out of a car, for crissake!"

People were staring again.

"They're going to find your prints all over that car," Morelli said.

"Lula and I wore gloves." Lucy and Ethel get clever.

"It used to be I didn't want to get married because I didn't want you sitting home worrying about me. Now I don't want to get married because I don't know if I can handle the stress of being married to *you*."

"This would never have happened if you or Ranger had confided in me. First I get asked to help in the investigation, and then I get shoved aside. This is all your fault."

Morelli narrowed his eyes.

"Well, maybe not *all* your fault."

"I have to get back to work," Morelli said, calling for the check. "Promise me you'll go home and stay there. Promise me you'll go home and lock your door and not leave until this gets settled. Alexander is scheduled to fly back to Greece tomorrow. We think that means Homer is leaving tonight, and we think we know how he's going to do it."

"By boat."

"Yeah. There's a container ship sailing out of Newark, headed for Greece. And Homer is a weak link. If we can bring him in on a homicide there's a chance he'll plea-bargain and give us Alexander and Stolle."

"Gee, I kind of like Alexander."

Now Morelli grimaced.

"Okay," I said, "I'll go home and stay there. Yeesh."

I didn't have anything to do that afternoon, anyway. And I couldn't get excited about giving Habib and Mitchell another crack at kidnapping me and chopping off my fingers, one by one. Locking myself into my apartment was actually appealing. I could clean up some more, and watch some junky television, and take a nap.

"I have your shoulder bag at my house," Morelli said. "I didn't think to bring it to work with me. Do you need a key to your apartment?"

I nodded. "Yes."

He took a key off his key ring and gave it to me.

THE LOT TO my building was relatively empty. At this time of day the seniors were either off shopping or making maximum use of the Medicare system, which was fine by me because it got me a good parking space. There were no strange cars in the lot. And as far as I could tell, no one was lurking in the bushes. I parked close to the door and got the Glock out of my jacket pocket. I quickly went into the building and took the stairs. The second-floor hall was empty and quiet. My door was locked. Both good signs. I unlocked my door with the Glock still in hand and stepped into the foyer. The apartment looked just as I'd left it. I closed the door behind me but didn't slide the bolt, in case I had to make a fast exit. Then I went room to room, making sure all was secure.

I went from the living room to the bathroom. And when I was in the bathroom a man stepped out of the bedroom and leveled a gun at me. He was average height and build, slimmer and younger than Hannibal Ramos, but the family resemblance was obvious. He was a good-looking man, but the good looks were ruined by lines of dissolution. A month at Betty Ford wouldn't make a dent in this man's problems.

"Homer Ramos?"

"In the flesh."

We both had guns drawn, standing about ten feet apart.

"Drop the gun," I said.

He gave me a humorless smile. "Make me."

Great. "Drop the gun, or I'm going to shoot you."

"Okay, shoot me. Go ahead."

I looked down at the Glock. It was a semiautomatic, and I

owned a revolver. I had no idea how to shoot a semiautomatic. I knew I was supposed to slide something back. I pushed a button, and the clip fell out onto the carpet.

Homer Ramos burst out laughing.

I threw the Glock at him, hitting him in the forehead, and he fired at me before I had a chance to take off. The bullet grazed my upper arm and lodged in the wall behind me. I cried out and stumbled back, holding tight to the wound.

"That's a warning," he said. "If you try to run I'll shoot you in the back."

"Why are you here? What do you want?"

"I want the money, of course."

"I don't have the money."

"There's no other possibility, sweetie pie. The money was in the car, and before good ol' Cynthia died she told me you were in the town house when she walked in. So you're the only candidate. I've been all through Cynthia's house. And I tortured her sufficiently to be confident she was telling me everything she knew. She originally gave me this bogus story about throwing the bag away, but not even Cynthia would be that stupid. I've been through your apartment and the apartment of your fat friend. And I haven't found the money."

Harpoon to the brain. Habib and Mitchell weren't the ones who'd ransacked my apartment. It was Homer Ramos, looking for his money.

"Now I want you to tell me where you put it," Homer said. "I want you to tell me where you've hidden my money."

My arm stung and a bloodstain was growing on the torn material of my jacket. Little black dots were dancing in front of my eyes. "I need to sit down."

He waved me to the couch. "Over there."

Getting shot, no matter how minor the wound, is not conducive to clear thinking. Somewhere in the muck of gray matter between my ears I knew I should be forming a plan, but damned if I could do it. My mind was scurrying down blank paths in panic. There were tears pooling behind my eyes, and my nose was running.

"Where's my money?" Ramos repeated when I was seated.

"I gave it to Ranger." Even *I* was surprised when this answer popped out. And clearly neither of us believed it.

"You're lying. I'm going to ask you again. And if I think you're lying I'm going to shoot you in the knee."

He was standing with his back to the small hallway that led to my front door. I looked over his shoulder and saw Ranger move into my line of vision.

"Okay, you got me," I said, louder than was necessary, with just a touch of hysteria. "This is what happened. I had no idea there was money in the car. What I saw was this dead guy. And I don't know, call me crazy, maybe I've seen too many Mafia movies, but I thought to myself, Maybe there's another body in the trunk! I mean, I didn't want to miss out on any bodies, you know? So I opened the trunk and there was this gym bag. Well, I've always been nosy, so of course, I had to see inside the bag—"

"I don't give a flying fuck about your life story," Homer said. "I want to know what you did with the freaking money. I've only got twelve hours before my ship sails. You think you could get to the point before then?"

And that was when Ranger yanked Homer Ramos off his feet and pressed the stun gun to his neck. Homer gave a squeak and collapsed onto the floor. Ranger reached down and took Homer's gun. He patted him down for more weapons, didn't find any, and cuffed his hands behind his back.

He kicked Ramos aside and stood over me. "I thought I told you not to hang out with members of the Ramos family. You never listen."

Ranger humor.

I gave him a weak smile. "I think I'm going to throw up."

He put his hand to the back of my neck and pushed my head down between my legs. "Push against my hand," he said.

The bells stopped clanging and my stomach sort of calmed. Ranger pulled me to my feet and took my jacket off.

I wiped my nose on my T-shirt. "How long were you here?" I asked.

"I came in when he shot you."

We both looked at the gash in my arm.

"Flesh wound," Ranger said. "Can't get much sympathy on this one." He steered me into the kitchen and pressed some paper toweling to my arm. "Try to clean it up a little, and I'll go look for a Band-Aid."

"Band-Aid! I've been shot!"

He came back with my first-aid kit, used Band-Aids to hold the wound together, put a gauze patch on it, and wrapped my arm with surgical gauze. He stepped back and grinned at me. "You look kind of white."

"I thought I was going to die. He'd have killed me for sure."

"But he didn't," Ranger said.

"Did you ever think you were going to die?"

"Many times."

"And?"

"And I didn't." He used my phone to dial Morelli. "I'm at Steph's apartment. We've got Homer Ramos bagged and waiting for you. And we could use a blue-and-white. Stephanie caught a bullet in the arm. It just sliced through some flesh, but she should have it looked at."

He slid an arm around me and pulled me to him. I rested my head on his chest, and he nuzzled my hair and kissed me just above the ear. "Are you okay?" he asked.

No way was I okay. I was as unokay as I could get. I was in a state. "Sure," I said. "I'm fine."

I could feel him smile. "Liar."

MORELLI CAUGHT UP with me at the hospital. "Are you okay?"

"Ranger asked me that same question fifteen minutes ago and the answer was no. But I'm feeling better now."

"How's the arm?"

"I don't think it's too bad. I'm waiting to see the doctor."

Morelli took my hand and pressed a kiss to the palm. "I think my heart stopped twice on the way over."

The kiss fluttered in my stomach. "I'm fine. Really."

"I had to see for myself."

"You love me," I said.

His smile tightened, and he gave a small nod. "I love you."

Ranger loved me too, but not quite in the same way. Ranger was at a different place in his life.

The doors to the waiting room crashed open, and Connie and Lula barged in.

"We heard you got shot," Lula said. "What's going on?"

"Omigod, it's true," Connie said. "Look at your arm! How did this happen?"

Morelli stood. "I want to be there when they bring Ramos in. And I think I'm excess baggage now that the troops have arrived. Call me as soon as you're done with the doctor."

I DECIDED TO go from the hospital to my parents' house. Morelli was still busy interrogating Homer Ramos, and I didn't feel like being alone. I had Lula stop at Dougie's first so I could get a flannel shirt to wear over the T-shirt.

Dougie and Mooner were in the living room, watching a new big-screen TV.

"Hey, dude," Mooner said, "check this television out. Is this excellent, or what?"

"I thought you were done with the hijacking."

"That's the astonishing thing," Mooner said. "This is a newly purchased television. We didn't even steal it, dude. I tell you, God works in mysterious ways. One minute we're thinking our future is in the crapper, and then next thing you know, we come into an inheritance."

"Congratulations," I said. "Who died?"

"That's the miracle," Mooner said. "Our inheritance isn't tainted by tragedy. It was given to us, dude. A present. Can you dig it?

"Dougie and me had the good fortune to make a car sale on Sunday, so we took the car to the car wash to get it all spiffed up for the buyer. And while we're there this blonde comes streaking in, in a silver Porsche. And she, like, cleaned this car to within an inch of its life. We were, like, just watching. And then she took this bag out of the trunk and threw it in the garbage. It was a real genuine bag, so Dougie and me asked if she minded if we took it. And she said it was just a disgusting gym bag, and we could freaking do whatever we wanted with it. So we took the bag home and, like, forgot about it until this morning."

"And when you opened it up and looked inside this morning, the bag turned out to be filled with money," I said.

"Wow. How did you know that?"

"Just a guess."

MY MOTHER WAS in the kitchen when I got to the house. She was making *toltott kaposzta,* which is stuffed cabbage. Not my favorite thing in the world. But then my favorite thing in the world is probably pineapple upside-down cake with lots of whipped cream, so I guess it's not a fair comparison.

She stopped working and looked at me. "Is something wrong with your arm? You're holding it funny."

"I got shot, but—"

My mother fainted. *Crash*, onto the floor with the big wooden spoon still in her hand.

Shit.

I soaked a dish towel and put it on her forehead until she came around.

"What happened?" she asked.

"You fainted."

"I never faint. You must be mistaken." She sat up and mopped her face with the wet towel. "Oh yeah, now I remember."

I helped her to a kitchen chair and put the water on for tea.

"How bad is it?" she asked.

"It's just a nick. And the guy's in jail now, so everything's fine."

Except I felt a little nauseated, my heart was skipping a beat once in a while, and I didn't want to go back to my apartment. Otherwise, everything was fine.

I put the cookie jar on the table and gave my mother a cup of tea. I sat opposite her and helped myself to a cookie. Chocolate chip. Very healthy, since she'd put some chopped walnuts in, and walnuts are filled with protein, right?

The front door banged open and closed, and Grandma stormed into the kitchen. "I did it! I passed my driver's test!"

My mother made the sign of the cross and put the wet towel back on her head.

"How come your arm's all puffy under your shirt?" Grandma asked me.

"I'm wearing a bandage. I got shot today."

Grandma's eyes opened wide. "Cool!" She pulled a chair out and joined us at the table. "How did it happen? Who shot you?"

Before I could answer, the phone rang. It was Marge Dembowski reporting that her daughter Debbie, who's a nurse at the hospital, called to say I was shot. Then Julia Kruselli called to say her son, Richard, who's a cop, just gave her the scoop on Homer Ramos.

I moved from the kitchen to the living room and fell asleep in front of the television. Morelli was there when I woke up, the house reeked of stuffed cabbage cooking on the stovetop, and my arm ached.

Morelli had a new jacket for me, one without a bullet hole in it. "Time to go home," he said, gingerly slipping my arm into the jacket.

"I am home."

"I mean *my* home."

Morelli's home. That would be nice. Rex and Bob would be there. Even better, Morelli would be there.

My mother put a big bag on the coffee table in front of us. "There's some stuffed cabbage and a fresh loaf of bread and some cookies."

Morelli took the bag. "I love stuffed cabbage," he said.

My mother looked pleased.

"Do you really like stuffed cabbage?" I asked him when we were in the car.

"I like anything I don't have to cook myself."

"How'd it go with Homer Ramos?"

"Better than our wildest dreams. The man is a worm. He ratted on *everyone*. Alexander Ramos should have killed him at birth. And as a bonus, we picked up Habib and Mitchell and told them they were being charged with kidnapping, and they gave us Arturo Stolle."

"You've had a busy afternoon."

"I've had a very good day. Except for you getting shot."

"Who killed Macaroni?"

"Homer. Stolle sent Macaroni over to get the Porsche. Guess he figured it'd pay off part of the debt. Homer caught him in the car and shot him. Then Homer panicked and ran out of the house."

"Forgetting to put the alarm on?"

Morelli grinned. "Yeah. Homer had gotten into the habit of sampling the wares he carried for Stolle, and he wasn't too with the program. He'd get stoned and go out for munchies and forget to set the alarm. Ranger was able to break in. Macaroni broke in. You broke in. I don't think Hannibal realized the extent of the problem. He thought Homer was sitting tight in the town house."

"But Homer was a wreck."

"Yep. Homer was truly a wreck. After he shot Macaroni, he really freaked. In his drugged-out, deranged state I guess he thought he could hide himself better than Hannibal could, so he went back to the house to get his stash. Only his stash wasn't there."

"And all that time Hannibal had his men out, scouring the state, trying to find Homer."

"Sort of gratifying to know they were scrambling around, looking for the little jerk," Morelli said.

"So what about the stash?" I asked. "Anybody have any idea what happened to the gym bag filled with money?" Anybody besides me, that is.

"One of life's great mysteries," Morelli said. "The prevailing theory is that Homer hid it while in a drug-induced haze and forgot where he put it."

"That sounds logical," I said. "I bet that's it." What the hell, why not let Dougie and Mooner enjoy the money? If it was confiscated it would only go to the federal government, and God only knew what *they*'d do with it.

Morelli parked in front of his row house on Slater Street and helped me out. He opened his front door, and Bob jumped out and smiled at me.

"He's happy to see me," I told Morelli. And the fact that I was holding a bag filled with stuffed cabbage didn't hurt, either. Not that it mattered. Bob gave a terrific welcome.

Morelli had put Rex's aquarium on his kitchen counter. I tapped on the side and there was movement under a pile of bedding. Rex stuck his head out, twitched his whiskers, and blinked his black bead eyes at me.

"Hey, Rex!" I said. "How's it going?"

The whisker twitching stopped for a microsecond, and then Rex retreated under the bedding. It might not seem like much to the casual observer, but in terms of hamsters, that was a terrific welcome, too.

Morelli cracked open a couple beers and set two plates on his small kitchen table. We divided the cabbage rolls between Morelli and Bob and me and dug in. Halfway through my second cabbage roll I noticed Morelli wasn't eating.

"Not hungry?" I asked.

Morelli sent me a tight smile. "I've missed you."

"I've missed you, too."

"How's your arm?"

"It's okay."

He took my hand and kissed my fingertip. "I hope this conversation counts as foreplay, because I'm feeling a real lack of self-control."

Fine by me. I wasn't seeing much value in self-control *at all* at the moment.

He took the fork out of my hand. "How bad do you want those cabbage rolls?"

"I don't even *like* cabbage rolls."

He pulled me out of my chair and kissed me.

The doorbell rang, and we both jumped apart.

"Shit!" Morelli said. "Now what? It's always something! Grand-mothers and murderers and pagers going off. I can't take it any-more." He stormed off to the front of the house and wrenched the door open.

It was his grandma Bella. She was a little lady, dressed in Old Country black. Her white hair was pulled into a knot at the nape of her neck, her face was free of makeup, her thin lips were pressed tight together. Joe's mother stood to the side, larger than Bella, no less scary.

"Well?" Bella said.

Joe looked at her. "Well, what?"

"Aren't you going to invite us in?"

"No."

Bella stiffened. "If you weren't my favorite grandson I'd put the eye on you."

Joe's mother stepped forward. "We can't stay long. We're on our way to Marjorie Soleri's baby shower. We just stopped by with a casserole for you. I know you don't cook."

I came to Joe's side and took the casserole from his mother. "It's nice to see you again, Mrs. Morelli. And nice to see you, too, Grandma Bella. The casserole smells terrific."

"What's going on here?" Bella said. "You two aren't living in sin again, are you?"

"I'm trying," Morelli said. "I'm just not having any luck."

Bella jumped up and smacked Joe on the head. "Shame on you."

"Maybe I should take this into the kitchen," I said, backing away. "And then I should be running along. I wasn't staying long, either. I just dropped in to say hello." Last thing I needed was for Bella to put the eye on *me*.

Joe grabbed me by my good arm. "You're not going anywhere."

Bella squinted at me, and I flinched. I could feel Joe dig in beside me.

"Stephanie's staying here tonight," he said. "Get used to it."

Bella and Mrs. Morelli sucked in a breath and pressed their lips tight together.

Mrs. Morelli tipped her chin up a half-inch and gave Joe a piercing glare. "Are you going to marry this woman?"

"Yeah, for crying out loud, I'm going to marry her," Joe said. "The sooner, the better."

"Married!" Bella said, clasping her hands together. "My Joseph, getting married." She kissed both of us.

"Wait a minute," I said. "You never asked me to marry you. You're the one who doesn't want to get married."

"I changed my mind," Morelli said. "I want to get married. Hell, I want to get married tonight."

"You just want to have sex," I said.

"Are you kidding? I can't even *remember* sex. I don't even know if I can still *do* it."

His pager beeped. "Damn!" Morelli said. He ripped the pager off his belt and threw it across the street.

Grandma Bella looked down at my hand. "Where's the ring?"

We *all* looked at my hand. No ring.

"You don't need a ring to get married," Morelli said.

Grandma Bella gave her head a sad shake. "He don't know much," she said.

"Hold on here. I'm not going to get railroaded into marriage," I told them.

Grandma Bella stiffened. "You don't want to marry my Joseph?"

Joe's mother made the sign of the cross and rolled her eyes.

"Gosh," Joe said to his mother and Bella, "look at the time. I wouldn't want you to miss the shower."

"I know what you're up to," Bella said. "You want to get rid of us."

"That's true," Joe told them. "Stephanie and I have things to talk about."

Bella's eyes rolled back in her head. "I'm having a vision," she said. "I see grandchildren. Three boys and two girls . . ."

"Don't let her scare you," Joe whispered. "I've got an entire box of the best protection money can buy upstairs next to the bed."

I chewed on my lower lip. I'd have felt much more comfortable if she'd said she saw a hamster.

"Okay, we're going now," Bella said. "The visions always make me tired. I'll need to take a nap in the car before the shower."

When they drove off, Joe shut and locked the door. He took the casserole from me and set it out of Bob's reach on the dining room table. He carefully slipped my jacket off my shoulders and let it fall to the floor. Then he unsnapped my jeans, hooked a finger into the waistband, and pulled me to him. "About that proposal, cupcake . . ."